# Contents

**PART THREE**
## These Fragments I Have Shored Against My Ruins

# Death by Water

## Kenzaburo Oe

Translated from the Japanese
by Deborah Boliver Boehm

Atlantic Books
London

First published as *Suishi* in Japan in 2009 by Kodansha.

First published in Great Britain in 2015 by Atlantic Books, an imprint of Atlantic Books Ltd.

This paperback edition published in Great Britain in 2016 by Atlantic Books.

10 9 8 7 6 5 4 3 2 1

A CIP catalogue record for this book is available from the British Library.

Paperback ISBN: 978 0 85789 548 6
E-book ISBN: 978 0 85789 547 9

Printed and bound by CPI Group (UK) Ltd, Croydon, CR0 4YY

Atlantic Books
An Imprint of Atlantic Books Ltd
Ormond House
26–27 Boswell Street
London
WC1N 3JZ
www.atlantic-books.co.uk

# Death by Water

# PART ONE

# The Drowning Novel

# Prologue

# The Joke

## 1

The year I went off to university in Tokyo, something fateful happened when I returned home to Shikoku for one of the last in a series of traditional Buddhist services for my father. (He had died prematurely, nearly a decade earlier.) For the first time in ages our rambling farmhouse was overflowing with assorted friends and relations, and among the guests was an uncle of mine whose eldest daughter had recently been married to a government official, a graduate of Tokyo University's prestigious law school.

"So," this uncle said to me, "you managed to get into that university. Great news, but what's your major?"

When I replied that I was studying literature, he made no attempt to hide his disappointment.

"In that case," he said glumly, "you probably can't expect to find a decent job after you leave school, can you?"

Then my mother, who was usually rather reserved in social situations, came out with a totally unexpected suggestion. Her words threw me into a state of confusion, for until then I had aspired to nothing more ambitious than becoming a French literature scholar.

"Well," she said, "if he can't find a regular job, then he'll most likely become a novelist!" This pronouncement was greeted with stunned silence, but the tension was quickly dispelled by my mother's next remark. "In fact," she went on, "there's more than enough raw material for a novel in the red leather trunk alone!" That made everybody laugh.

All the old families in the region (even if they didn't have an illustrious history or any success in business to boast about) had their own unique legends and traditions, which were passed down from generation to generation. Time and again anecdotes that struck people as funny or strange would resurface as perennially popular in-jokes, though they would have been meaningless to visitors from the outside world. The red leather trunk was a small part of my clan's proprietary strange and funny lore.

My mother's startling words—"Then he'll most likely become a novelist!"—put down deep, spreading roots inside me, and the fact that my close family members had found that notion so amusing simply added to its power.

During the three years that followed I still didn't have a clear idea of what my chosen path would be, but I did try my hand at writing some short stories. To my surprise, one of those early efforts was published in Tokyo University's campus newspaper, and as a result of that success I felt ready to embark on a career as a novelist right out of the gate. In a sense, then, my mother's offhanded quip ended up steering me toward my destiny.

In the tale I'm about to relate, my mother's "joke" will make an encore appearance in a way that is more tragic than comical, but we'll get to that part of the story in due time.

# 2

For the past several years my wife, Chikashi, has been exchanging occasional greetings with my younger sister, Asa, on my behalf. As a rule, my sister would just leave me an occasional message, so it seemed unusual when she called our house in Tokyo one day and asked specifically to speak to me.

"It's been ten years since Mother died," she began, "and in accordance with her will—well, it's really just an assortment of notes she dictated to me, so I don't know whether it would even hold up in court—but anyhow, I promised to hand over the red leather trunk to you this year. If we wait till the actual anniversary of her death on December fifth I'll be busy with other obligations, and when summer rolls around I was thinking that instead of heading to Kita Karuizawa as usual, you might want to come back to Shikoku and pick up the trunk. You haven't forgotten about it, have you? I mean, it's not as if you're too busy to get away; these days you seem to have all but abandoned your fiction and the only thing you're doing, as far as I can tell, is eking out one column a month for a newspaper."

"That's correct," I said, ignoring the sisterly gibe. "And of course I haven't forgotten. Mother was worried that if I got hold of the items she kept in the red leather trunk, I might be able to resume work on the novel about Father's drowning I'd started writing ages ago. That was her reason for instituting a ten-year moratorium—or was the cooling-off period your idea?"

"No, that was Mother, all the way. Her eyesight was failing and it was difficult for her to write, but her mind was still as sharp as ever. I think she figured you probably wouldn't outlive her by ten years, since the men in our family aren't exactly known for their longevity. Anyhow," Asa went on, "when I mentioned I'll be extra busy at the end of the year, it's because I've gotten involved in a drama project with some young people—you may have heard that I've been in touch with Chikashi regarding their use of a number of your early books.

Speaking of which, I've been letting the theater troupe use the Forest House—with Chikashi's permission, of course—and their presence has really breathed new life into the place. Don't worry; they're very conscientious about always leaving everything in perfect order. But anyhow, as I was saying, if you'll be coming down here to take a look at the contents of the red leather trunk, why don't you plan to stick around for a while?"

Ah, the red leather trunk and the drowning novel (that was how I always thought of it). After my telephone conversation with Asa I felt an exhilarating resurgence of my enthusiasm for novel writing. While the sun was still high in the sky I withdrew to my study, which also doubled as a bedroom. I drew the curtains, then stretched out on the narrow bed to contemplate this intriguing new development.

When I was a young writer I had been mocked and criticized by people who said things like "Because he started writing while he was a college student, this novelist lacks the necessary life experience, and he will probably hit a brick wall before too long. Or maybe he's planning to be like other writers of his generation and try to earn his stripes with a dramatic change in direction, such as becoming a war correspondent or some such." Nonetheless, I never wavered. I knew that when the time was ripe I would write a definitive novel about my father. In the meantime, I told myself, I'll be accumulating the necessary skills.

I imagined sometimes that I would begin to write the tale as "I" and would then just go with the flow of the narrative, bobbing along on the currents of memory. But, I fretted secretly, what if the novelist himself ended up being sucked into the whirlpool in a single gulp when he was finished telling his story?

The fact is, even back in the days when I hadn't yet read a single serious work of fiction all the way through, I used to see a pivotal scene from the drowning novel in my dreams, night after night. The basis for the recurrent dream was something I actually experienced when I was ten years old. Then, at twenty, I happened upon the phrase "death by water"—in other words, drowning—in a poem by T. S. Eliot that I first read in the original English (the French translation was given alongside as well). And although I hadn't tried putting my experience down on paper, even as a short story, I felt as if the novel already existed, fully formed, in my head.

So why didn't I go ahead and start to draft the book? Because I realized clearly that I didn't possess the literary finesse to pull it off. But even while I was floundering around, not at all certain that I would be able to survive as a young novelist, I remained essentially optimistic. *Someday,* I vowed, *I will write the drowning novel.*

There were times when I felt it might have been better to tackle that project sooner rather than later, but I always managed to suppress those urges by telling myself the moment still wasn't right. I needed to pay my dues by struggling, and suffering, and striving to overcome all the character-building difficulties I would encounter while writing the other books I was meant to produce first, for practice. If I could escape so easily into writing the drowning novel, then what would be the point of the struggle?

# 3

Nevertheless, I did make a stab at writing the drowning novel, just once, when I was in my midthirties. I had already published *The Silent Cry,* which seemed to prove that I had attained a certain degree of proficiency, and that accomplishment gave me the confidence to dive in at last.

I dashed off a rough prologue and sent it along with a number of related notes to my sixtysomething mother, who was still living in the forests of Shikoku where I grew up. I enclosed a letter saying that in order to continue working on this book, which would focus on my father, I would like to take a look at his papers and whatever else was stored in the red leather trunk (an exotic piece of luggage that had been in our family since before I was born). However, I didn't receive a direct reply from my mother, even though she had been saying all along that the raw materials for the novel in question were in the trunk. Nor did she ever return the rough draft of the prologue or any of the other notes I had sent.

Unable to proceed, I had no choice but to abandon the project. However, in the summer of the following year, fueled by unabated anger at my mother, I published *The Day He Himself Shall Wipe My Tears Away*. The main characters in that novella were grotesquely exaggerated versions of myself and my father, and it also included what some critics perceived as a merciless caricature of my mother (although others lauded the character as a solitary voice of reason).

Not long after, I received a postcard from my sister, Asa, who was still living at home. "Lately Mother has been criticizing you in terms even more scathing than the deliberately spiteful and alienating words you used to describe her at the end of your nasty little book," she wrote. Asa's message concluded by announcing that she and our mother had decided to sever all relations with Kogii (my childhood nickname), effective immediately. I was, she said, disowned.

## 4

Some years before the publication of that novella, my son, Akari, had been born with a defect in his skull, and eventually this ongoing real-life crisis helped to restore my relationship with my mother. Everyone's shared concern about Akari—who, amazingly, survived and overcame his obstacles—seemed to serve as a kind of intermediary buffer. The lines of communication between Chikashi and the Shikoku contingent were reopened, and we all began the long, slow process of easing back into an amicable family relationship.

However, until the day she died at the age of ninety-five, my mother never said a word about the prologue and notes for my drowning novel, or about the red leather trunk. I did hear that she used to reminisce to my sister, saying things like "When Kogii was a young boy here in the village he wasn't very well-adjusted, and because I tried to interfere, his character may have ended up being irreparably damaged," so perhaps she was just determined not to repeat the mistakes she thought she had made in my upbringing. Not only that, but before she passed away she even went to the trouble of planning ten years into the future!

# 5

Setbacks notwithstanding, I never doubted that I would eventually write the drowning novel. If you were to ask whether there were times when I found myself thinking about the stalled project, I would have to acknowledge that there were. (One example that springs to mind is when I was living alone in a foreign country, while another occurred just after I had learned of the death of someone for whom I felt great respect and affection.) But I was never inspired to jot down any new ideas, much less to pick up where I'd left off.

However, after Asa informed me that it was finally time for me to take possession of the red leather trunk, I suddenly found myself unable to think about anything except resuming work on the drowning novel—an undertaking that had been in limbo for what seemed like an eternity. Even amid those feelings of excited anticipation, though, it struck me that on some level I had been gearing up all along to tackle the project again. I was certain everything I needed was in the red leather trunk Asa was about to hand over to me: the materials my mother had preserved for so many years, along with the rough prologue and assorted scribbles I had mailed to her nearly half a century earlier and hadn't laid eyes on since. As for the literary skills I would need in order to complete this challenging book, surely I had acquired the necessary tools during my decades of actively practicing the craft. But that encouraging thought was overlaid with a poignant sense that my life as a novelist might soon be approaching its end.

# 6

At long last I was ready to plunge headfirst into the drowning novel, and in order to do that I needed to pick up the red leather trunk. Then something happened—something very odd and unexpected—that made the idea of a trip to Shikoku seem considerably more appealing.

My house in Tokyo sits on a hill at the far end of the Musashino Plain. If you descend the western slope of the incline, you will see that a large area, originally nothing more than swampland, has been extensively developed around a canal-like waterway. A cycling path was built for the use of the residents of the towering apartment blocks that have gone up one after another, but it is also open to the public.

*One day while I was walking on the path with my disabled son, I happened to run into an entirely unexpected individual . . . .* That line was part of the opening scene of a novel I wrote soon after turning seventy. If I were to write again now that I made a new friend while strolling along the same cycling path, people would probably say with pitying smiles, "Oh, look, the poor old thing is plagiarizing himself—again!" But the simple truth is that for an elderly person like me who lives a somewhat reclusive life, there simply aren't very many locations where chance encounters with the outside world can take place.

It was a morning in early summer. I set out alone for a walk, leaving Akari at home. In recent years my son's physical decline had advanced to the point where any kind of sustained exertion had become an ordeal for him, and he required increasingly large doses of medicine to keep his epileptic seizures under control.

As I was ambling along I heard the sound of light footsteps behind me, beating out an even rhythm on the pavement, and a moment later someone overtook me and swiftly passed on by. I saw then that it was a diminutive young woman; her long black hair had been lightened to a deep brown hue, and she wore it pulled back in a single ponytail. She was dressed in a beige shirt and matching chinos, and there wasn't a single wrinkle in the soft, thin, lustrous fabric of her slacks. They fit her like a glove, and the contours of her lower body were plainly visible. Her thighs appeared to be shapely and sturdy without being excessively muscular, and above them the sinewy curves of her small buttocks undulated lithely as she walked. While I was still observing her retreating figure, the girl quickly left me in the dust and vanished from sight.

As I continued at my usual leisurely pace, I spotted the girl up ahead doing stretches or calisthenics in a small landscaped area equipped with benches, iron bars, and other fitness equipment. She would gently extend one leg in front of her, lower her hips, and hold that stance for several seconds. Then she would change legs and repeat. When the girl had overtaken me earlier I'd caught a glimpse of an attractively round face, but seen now in profile as I passed the little plaza she looked more like a lovely, ivory-skinned demoness—in Japanese mythological terms, a *hannya*. (I once read a theory that Japanese beauties can be divided into two categories: moonfaced, plump-cheeked Otafuku types, named after the bawdy goddess of the underworld, and foxy-looking, angular-featured female demons.)

Meanwhile, the sound of rushing water in the canal had grown louder. This was because the current was stronger along here; also, the framework supporting the steel train bridge—the Odakyu Line passed directly overhead—formed a canopy over the canal and magnified the sound. My eyes were drawn to the surface of the water, where something rather interesting was going on. As I trundled along in a distracted state, staring into the canal, I suddenly collided with a lamppost that had loomed up unnoticed in front of me and I hit my head—hard! (How hard? Well, the resulting hematoma stretched from the right side of my head to the corner of my eye and was still plainly visible four or five days after the accident.)

Just as the world went dark and I was on the verge of toppling over, I was caught from behind in someone's solid yet supple embrace. Two strong arms encircled me, and the next thing I knew I was perched on what seemed to be a sort of spindle-shaped platform. My perch felt strangely warm and alive, though, and I soon deduced that it was a human thigh. I also became aware that my back was resting against a soft female chest. I somehow managed to struggle to my feet, and clinging to the lamppost I had crashed into a moment earlier, I tried to catch my breath. All the while, I could hear myself groaning out loud.

"Sensei, please sit down on my lap again," the girl in the chino pants said in a calm, measured tone and obediently, just like that, this vertiginous old man resumed his previous position. Nevertheless, after a few minutes had passed—it was about the same amount of time it took for Akari to recover from a medium-severe seizure—I once again hoisted my body off the girl's thigh, which had grown noticeably warmer and was now soaked with perspiration.

As I was trying to express my gratitude the girl said politely, "Excuse me for asking, but does this kind of thing happen often?"

"No, not at all."

"That's good, because if it were a frequent occurrence it would be cause for worry."

The girl had the sort of relaxed, easygoing attitude you would expect from someone in her thirties, and she was smiling as she spoke. (I suppose she was a young woman, technically, but she seemed like a girl to me.) Even while I was grimacing with pain, I felt the need to explain the confluence of circumstances that I thought, on brief reflection, had caused my bizarre accident.

"It's rather dark in this particular spot because the Odakyu Line passes overhead," I began, "and also this lamppost has a device in the base to turn it on automatically, so the lower part is quite wide while the upper section is oddly attenuated, and I simply didn't see it. On top of that, my attention was distracted by a sloshing sound in the canal and I was trying to see what was going on. I think the fish have moved to the other shore now—you can still see them splashing around over there—but anyway, four or five splendid-looking male carp were tussling with each other, vying for the favor of one lone female. It must be spawning season for koi. Where I come from you never see such big carp swimming together in a group, and I was momentarily mesmerized by the unusual sight. The next thing I knew, I was about to crash into the pole. In my youth, when my reflexes were sharper, I probably could have made a quick course correction and avoided the collision, but . . ."

"I see," said the girl, barely suppressing a giggle. "Thank you for the explanation. I guess that kind of precision and attention to detail must come in handy in your line of work."

"The most outlandish thing is that the whole time I was trying to piece it all together, I was sitting on the knee of a young woman I've never even met! By the way, please excuse me for not being able to stay on my feet," I added, "but the pain was simply too much to bear. I really can't thank you enough for your assistance."

"It's a good thing the pole didn't smack you in the temple," the girl said. "But it looks as though the blood is still spreading under the skin at the edge of your forehead. You should hurry home and put some ice on it right away."

As I headed toward the bridge over the canal, which was my customary turnaround point, the girl began walking with me, slowing her pace to match mine. That was when it finally dawned on me that this was not some fortuitous chance encounter at all. After the girl had first passed me without a backward glance, she had probably managed to confirm my identity when I passed the small fitness plaza and had followed me from there with the intention of talking to me about something; that's how she happened to be nearby when I collided with the lamppost. She was planning to use the serendipitous rescue as an excuse for continuing our conversation.

"I'm sorry," she was saying now. "I should have introduced myself earlier." Watching my expression, which clearly conveyed, *Well, there were extenuating circumstances—I mean, I banged my head on a pole and had to sit on your lap!* the girl went on: "I'm from Masao Anai's group, the Caveman Group, and I've heard that Masao has been acquainted with you, at least in passing, for many years. Incidentally, our group was given its name by your late brother-in-law, Goro Hanawa. Anyway, when Masao first started the theater company I gather he wrote you a letter, asking for permission to dramatize your early works, and you kindly agreed. After that, his stage version of *The Day He Himself Shall Wipe My Tears Away* had a successful run and won an award, which was a huge career boost for our troupe. So we decided to move the Caveman Group's headquarters to Matsuyama, and now we're busy with a plan to dramatize more of your work. Your sister, Asa, has been unbelievably helpful, and we'll be indebted to her forever. I was lucky enough to appear in the production of *The Day He Himself Shall Wipe My Tears Away*, and on the program where it credits 'Unaiko'? That's me!"

"In that case," I said, "I did hear something about this from Asa, by way of my wife."

"Actually, Sensei, I've been thinking for the longest time that I would like to meet you someday, if I ever had the chance. I needed to come to Tokyo this week on other business, so I decided to seize the moment. When I asked Asa how I should handle it, she said rather than setting up a formal appointment—she explained that you always found that sort of thing bothersome and added that your advancing age was a factor as well—anyway, she suggested that I should try to engineer an 'accidental' encounter, as if by coincidence. She said you often go walking on a nearby cycling path, and she suggested simply lying in wait and ambushing you, as she put it. (She's so funny.) She even called your wife to find out what time you were likely to be here. But then the very first time I ventured out here—and I don't know whether this was good luck, or . . ." Again, she choked back a little burst of laughter before continuing: "I mean, it was rotten luck for *you*, but even so, to be honest, it was really very fortunate for me that you happened to bump into the pole."

My usual exercise course followed a road (paved with a soft, resilient mixture of red and black sand) along the opposite shore, then brought me back to my starting point. The girl followed along, chattering as we walked. There was one rapidly swelling knot between my ear and my eyebrow, and another on my forehead. Both lumps were throbbing and my entire body seemed to be engulfed in a rapidly rising fever, so I assumed the role of passive listener and hardly said a word.

"The truth is," Unaiko began, "I heard from Asa that you're planning to go home this summer after a long absence. I gather you'll be staying in the Forest House, so Asa wanted to give the place a thorough cleaning well in advance. She asked whether the younger members of our troupe—the Caveman Group—might be willing to lend a hand, and of course we happily agreed. But anyway, while we were all working together, we got to hear about the reason for your return. Apparently Asa has been holding on to a certain red leather trunk your mother left in her custody before she passed away, and since this year is the tenth anniversary of your mother's death, that trunk can now be given to you. Also, Asa said you would most likely pick up where you left off on a book you started many years ago, and that you'd be making use of the stuff in that trunk. She spoke of the book as the 'drowning novel,' and I gathered that it begins with an account of what happened one night when the river near your village overflowed its banks.

"Since you'll be coming home in any case, Asa said she thought you would also do some research for your book around the area—location scouting, as the filmmakers say. She also mentioned that since Masao Anai knows all your work by heart and is in the process of writing a play based on some of your books, he could lend a hand with your research, and vice versa. And she suggested that the other members of our troupe might be able to help out, too, not just with cleaning and other chores but with brain-powered tasks as well. Masao is a different story, of course—he's supersmart—but I have to wonder whether the rest of us would be very useful with brainwork." (Even while she was issuing this faux-modest disclaimer, the girl looked as though she had absolute confidence in her own abilities.) "In any case, we were overjoyed at the prospect of getting to work with you and hopefully being able to help. But you've probably heard about this already, from Asa?"

"Yes," I said, "I have spoken with Asa about spending some time in the Forest House, to sort through some things she's been hanging on to for all these years—a prologue I drafted, and some notes, plus some odds and ends having to do with my father. We did discuss the possibility of 'location scouting' for the drowning novel on and around the river. And yes, I have heard her mention the Caveman Group."

The girl looked thoughtful. "Before I left, Masao kept saying things like 'Listen, Unaiko, on the chance you manage to meet up with Mr. Choko in Tokyo, make sure you don't come on too strong. If you do, he may just dig in his heels and refuse to budge.' Masao knows me pretty well, and I guess he was worried I might mess things up by being overly aggressive. But I was only thinking I'd like to have a chance to tell you in person that all of us in the Caveman Group are wishing and hoping your visit will come to pass." And then she added in a burst of candor, "Please forgive me for saying this again, but I can't help feeling what happened at the lamppost was a wonderful stroke of luck, at least for me, because it gave us a chance to talk like this, face-to-face."

We had come to a halt in front of a horizontal steel pipe that served as a barrier to keep vehicles out, at the juncture where the cycling path intersects a busy city street. This was where I would normally start trudging homeward, up the slope. The bumps beside my ear and on my forehead had continued to swell, and as I was pressing on them gingerly with the fingers of one hand, I ventured another explanation.

"This walking course goes along both banks of the canal, and the two sides are joined by a bridge. Needless to say, depending on the person, it could also be used as a running or jogging course. But if you're going to have an accidental encounter, the options are limited: you can bump into another person who's approaching from the front, or you can pass someone, or you can be overtaken from behind. If you had come toward me from the opposite direction and it had been obvious you were targeting me, I would probably have passed by without a word even if you had called out a greeting. On the other hand, when someone creeps up from behind there's even more of a feeling of pressure, and I wouldn't have been likely to respond in a friendly way in that case, either. I agree that my collision with the lamppost must have had some deeper significance because I, too, am glad we've had this chance to talk. Well then, this is where I take my leave. Please tell Asa to give me a call."

At that, I started to walk toward the uphill road that led to my house. But instead of taking the social cue and saying good-bye, the girl asked me a question. She seemed suddenly preoccupied, and a subtle change in her facial expression appeared to reflect some interior reverie.

"This is about something completely different," she said, "but I heard that your old French literature professor at Tokyo University translated an epic novel from the sixteenth century—is that right? And apparently the book contains an episode about a man who uses a crazed bunch of dogs to create some kind of riot in Paris?"

"That's right," I said. "The book you're referring to is *The Life of Gargantua and Pantagruel*, by Rabelais. The first volume of what is, indeed, a monumental novel, is called simply *Pantagruel*. The title character is one of a race of giants, and in one chapter his favorite retainer, Panurge, plays a prank on an aristocratic lady who rejected his attempts to court her. According to the story, Panurge found a female dog in heat and fed her all sorts of delicacies, presumably to enhance her sexual energy. Then he killed the dog and took a certain, um, something out of her insides. He mashed it up, stuffed the resulting pulp into the pocket of his greatcoat, and off he went. He tracked down the snooty Parisian lady and furtively smeared the substance on her dress: on the sleeves, in the folds of the skirt, and so on. Of course, the aroma attracted a huge crowd of male dogs. They all came running and leaped on the lady, and the result was a very unseemly sort of mayhem. I mean, you can imagine what would happen if 'more than 600,014' male dogs—the story gives the exact number—were whipped into a frenzy."

"If the first dog, the one that was killed, was a female, what on earth did the retainer take out of her, um, insides?"

"Well . . . this is a bit awkward. I mean, it isn't the sort of word I feel comfortable introducing into a conversation with a young woman I've only just met." I was truly flustered by the question, but at the same time I was also pleasantly reminded of Professor Musumi's transported expression and exuberant manner of speaking whenever he was illuminating some arcane point for his students. Trying to emulate my late mentor's happily didactic spirit, I did my best to explain, as delicately as possible, one of the footnotes from my late mentor's translation of the famous medieval novel.

"It was the uterus of the female dog," I said. "That organ has been known to scholars since Greek times for its medicinal properties, and I've read that medieval sorcerers also used it as an ingredient in magical love potions."

Without saying another word the girl gave a slight bow, then turned and walked away. I felt curiously refreshed and amused, and I also realized that the request from Unaiko and her colleagues in the Caveman Group had made me much more inclined to act on Asa's invitation to return to Shikoku, after all these years, and explore the contents of the red leather trunk.

# Chapter 1

# Enter the Caveman Group

## 1

Asa picked me up at Matsuyama Airport in her car, and as we drove she shared some local news.

"The young folks from the Caveman Group were delighted to hear you'll be staying at the Forest House for a while," she began. "The head of the theater group, Masao Anai, was especially happy and relieved. Apparently when he found out that Unaiko—who, of course, is a very important part of the group—had made an arbitrary decision to go to Tokyo to talk to you directly, he was worried the whole thing might fall apart.

"On another topic, our local officials have been asking what should be done about the commemorative stone that was erected when you won that prize, since in its current location it would interfere with the building of a new road. I discussed the matter with Chikashi, and then relayed her thoughts to the powers that be. As she said, there's really no need to move the whole thing, and once the stone has been relocated they could go ahead and tear down the pedestal.

First, though, we'll need to salvage the part of the monument that has the words you chose from Mother's writing, along with your own little poem. While I was planning this it occurred to me that you've never even seen the monument in its finished state, so I thought we could go take a look right now—it's down around Okawara, and we should be there in about an hour or so. Do you want to try to catch a few winks on the way?"

Asa then lapsed into silence and concentrated on piloting the car while I dozed fitfully in the passenger seat. Just as she'd said, it was about an hour later when we stopped the car at a place where the riverbank had been made into a park. Asa mentioned that my mother had planted pomegranates and camellias around the monument but they were gone, having been "tidied up" as part of the construction process. Jutting out of the bare ground was a large round stone that appeared to be a fragment of a meteorite. When I gazed up at the stone—it was a pale, vegetal shade of green, like early-spring onions— I saw that it was inscribed with five spare, calligraphic lines of Japanese characters. Some years earlier I had written those lines with a fountain pen, and the words had been enlarged and then expertly engraved on the stone.

*You didn't get Kogii ready to go up into the forest*
*And like the river current, you won't return home.*
*In Tokyo during the dry season*
*I'm remembering everything backward,*
*From old age to earliest childhood.*

"It reads better than I'd expected, considering all the fuss it provoked," I said.

"For some reason the beginning—that is, Mother's two-line poem—just didn't sit well with people from the start," Asa said. "They were complaining it wasn't a proper haiku, yet it wasn't a tanka, either. That couldn't be helped, but the professor who was the adviser for the commemorative-stone committee summoned me to Matsuyama and made no secret of his displeasure. 'What is this supposed to be, anyhow?' he asked. 'A parody of a Misora Hibari song?'

"Needless to say, that got my hackles up. So I told him, in no uncertain terms: 'The line in the Hibari song is *like the flowing of water*, while this is *like the river current*. My mother doesn't plagiarize!' Then I went on to explain that the people around these parts speak of being 'taken by the current' when someone either drowns in the river or else is saved after being carried downstream in a flood. The people borne away by the current—obviously, the drowned, but even those who are rescued from the rushing waters—always seem to end up leaving the village, so the phrase has become a metaphor for going away and not returning, except maybe to visit once in a blue moon. And there's the implied dig about certain people who go off to Tokyo to study and then stay there, almost as if the river *had* carried them away, even though they solemnly promised to return to the village someday . . . well, you know better than anyone that there's nothing obscure about that. I explained those nuances to the adviser, and when I mentioned that I realized the first line of the poem might be difficult for an outsider to understand, he got all arrogant and defensive (I mean, he's a university professor, right?) and informed me that he is the author of several scholarly books about the folklore and history of this area. He never did accept my interpretation, but in the end I made sure the stone was carved with the words you sent, exactly as you wrote them."

Asa took a breath, then continued: "I really have my doubts about whether the professor even understood the first line. I mean, he couldn't be expected to know that in our house your childhood nickname was Kogii, or that you were sharing your life in those days with a supernatural alter ego who was also called Kogii. Only someone who was intimately familiar with your work would be aware of such details. On the other hand, as you're well aware, when we talk about sending someone up into the forest it's usually a metaphor for dying, but it can also refer to holding a memorial service for someone who has passed away. Surely the professor would have discovered that through his research, at least."

"You don't know exactly where Father's body washed up when it was carried downstream from here, do you?" I asked. "You did say that the first memory of your childhood was of the hours just after his body was brought back to our house, but . . ."

"I remember clearly that you told me to check around the futon where our dead father was laid out, to see if a dead child was lying nearby. Twenty-some years later, when I heard you were having a strange recurrent dream, it sounded like a joke at first, but then I realized it could also be the unbearably sad remembrance of something that really did happen. And I couldn't help wondering whether, just maybe, the dream might be rooted in the fact that you ran away from the boat that took our father to his watery grave. But anyhow," Asa continued, "I was walking around and around the dead person, lying on the tatami with a cloth over his face. At one point I stumbled and fell, and when I reached out to brace myself I touched his thick, wet hair with my outstretched hand. I remember that creepy sensation vividly, so I believe you when you say Father drowned after being carried away by the current, even though Mother would never talk about it."

"Do you remember when I commuted for a year to the new postwar high school near here, before our village was incorporated?" I said. "One day during art period, we went to that shoal to do some plein air sketching. The teacher had set up his easel facing a spot on the edge of the sandbank where there was a thick stand of pussy willows, and he was working on an oil painting. As I was wandering aimlessly about, he called me over and said, 'I've heard this spot has been known for years as the place where Mr. Choko washed ashore. Does that have something to do with your family, by any chance?'

"Of course, we were all in deep denial about the circumstances behind Father's drowning, but in the outside world, everyone seemed to know about it. I think that probably goes a long way toward explaining how Mother happened to write the words 'river current' in the little poem on the stone."

Walking along under a canopied row of cherry trees so heavily overgrown that hardly any light fell on the road (I'd heard they were already slated for clear-cutting), we returned to the car. As we drove the twenty-plus minutes to our hometown—the picturesque mountain valley deep in a forest, where we both grew up—Asa spoke about some things she had evidently been mulling over for quite a while.

"Listen, Kogii," she said, "I was very happy when you said you'd be coming to stay for a while in the Forest House. It will be good for you to get some closure with the red leather trunk, after all these years, but at the same time I couldn't help thinking, *Yep, my big brother is definitely getting old*. One thing I've noticed about aging is that it gives rise to a desire to get things settled. And at this stage, it's only natural to start having thoughts about death.

"Needless to say, I'm aging right along with you, and that's why I think about these things. But really, isn't the relevant question what happens between now and then? I mean, even if you've resigned yourself to the inevitability of death, you still have to deal with the intervening time until the day arrives. Death is going to find us all, no matter what, but we still have to take active responsibility for what remains of our lives.

"Take the poem our mother wrote—let's just call it a haiku, shall we? I really think those lines were meant as a message from her to you, to be read when you eventually came home and saw the commemorative stone: *You didn't get Kogii ready to go up into the forest / And like the river current, you won't return home*.

"As a kind of counterpoint, in the three lines you contributed you made it clear you won't be coming back here. You're up there in Tokyo, pondering various things—you were echoing the quote from Eliot about 'an old man in a dry month,' right? And that's fine, but compared with the two lines Mother wrote your response strikes me as much more blasé, which is exactly what I would have expected from you.

"As for our mother, when she wrote those lines she was still seeing you as Kogii, and she was concerned that you weren't doing anything to prepare to send Akari up into the forest, since there's a good chance he won't live as long as you do. But I think part of your reason for wanting to come back down here for a while is a way of taking the first step toward making the necessary preparations to send Akari (and, eventually, yourself) up into the forest—with every bit of metaphorical subtext the phrase carries in local lore."

After her long monologue, Asa drove in silence for several miles, and then stopped on the side of the road. "Just walk up this path—it's really more like a trail for wild animals—and you'll end up at the Forest House. You haven't forgotten the shortcut, have you? We're running late today, so I'm going to let you off here and go straight home. After I've had a little rest I'll come back with some dinner for you. I'll drop off your luggage then, too.

"Oh, and about Unaiko, the young woman you met in Tokyo? She'll be dropping by the Forest House tomorrow with Masao Anai, who as I mentioned is the leader of the theater group. (You probably know he was a pupil of Goro Hanawa's, although 'disciple' might be a better word.) Unaiko said that while you're staying there they would like to talk to you about a number of things—I gather she just hinted at this when you spoke in Tokyo. Tomorrow some of the troupe's younger members will be stopping by to install the commemorative stone, and after that's done Masao and Unaiko are hoping to talk to you about your forthcoming collaboration. They're really looking forward to this, so please be on your best behavior!"

# 2

Early the next morning Asa, who was always very well organized, dispatched a couple of the younger members of the theater group to pick up the stone. The back garden was planted with flowering dogwood and a maple tree of the variety known as Big Sake Cup, which Chikashi had brought from her garden in Tokyo along with a pomegranate tree she'd been given by her mother-in-law (that is, my mother), and these had grown in a way that was beautifully proportional with the intimate scale of the garden. I agreed with Asa that installing the big stone in front of the trees, facing the house, was a perfect plan.

The members of the Caveman Group arrived in a minivan with the name of their theater troupe emblazoned on the side. (Goro Hanawa had evidently written it out for them, and his calligraphy had been professionally enlarged and painted on their car.) As we stood in the front garden—which had simply been carved out of the overhanging rock and spread with gravel—Asa, who had hitched a ride with the group, introduced me to Masao Anai. I remembered having seen him before; he was a man in his forties, very simply dressed, with the look of someone who had been immersed in the theater world for a long time. Next to him, standing up very straight, wearing casual work clothes and a big smile, was the young woman I had met in Tokyo. Asa knew all about our stranger-than-fiction encounter, but she didn't mention it. She simply said, "I'd like you to meet Masao Anai and Unaiko."

After we had exchanged hurried greetings, Masao Anai sent the two apprentices to fetch the poetry stone, wrapped in an old blanket and tied with rope, from the back of the van. Then he led his young helpers to the back garden with their heavy burden, which they carried by balancing it on two sturdy wooden pallets.

Unaiko had remained behind, and as I was thanking her again for coming to my rescue the other day in Tokyo, Asa interrupted. "You know, Chikashi had something to do with Unaiko's adopted name," she announced.

Unaiko nodded. "They say the person who first started calling the leader of our troupe 'the caveman' was Goro Hanawa," she said. "And I heard from Asa that your mother once said that her granddaughter, Maki, looked like a child from medieval times—an *unaiko*—with her unusual *unai*-style hairdo. (I gather it was a bob with bangs and a little ponytail sprouting on top.) And there I was, wearing my hair in a similar style. So I said, half joking, 'Well, maybe I should change my name to Unaiko!' And the younger folks thought it was a great idea, so the name sort of stuck. It was just a bonus that *unai* echoes our leader's surname, Anai."

"I remember hearing that the first time Chikashi brought our children to this valley to meet my mother, our older daughter, Maki, was wearing her hair rather like Unaiko here (though Maki's version was a bit more girlish), and my mother thought it looked wonderful," I said.

"Actually, I was standing right there when Chikashi and Mother were having that conversation," Asa said. "Mother also mentioned an ancient ninth-century song that includes the term *unaiko*, and she even sang a few lines for us! It was lovely—all about summer rain and the cuckoo's song and children running around wearing this same kind of retro-medieval hairstyle. Mother seemed very happy as she was singing those words, but of course she was already in high spirits because her grandchildren had come to visit."

Masao Anai had returned from the garden, so Asa took a minute to fill him in on what he had missed before continuing her story.

"Anyhow," she went on, "for the duration of their visit, everyone was calling little Maki 'Unaiko.' Years later, I told the story to *this* Unaiko, and the rest is history. Well then," she added briskly, "shall we take a peek at how the young people are getting along in the garden?"

But by the time we went into the dining room and peered out at the back garden through the big plate-glass window, the giant stone was already in place and the young workers, who were taking a short break, seemed to be anxiously gauging our reaction. I assured Asa that the placement was flawless, and she flashed an "A-OK" sign. As the young men headed around to the front of the house, she went out to meet them. The rest of us sat gazing at the garden, with everyone's eyes seemingly focused on the poetic inscription carved into the stone.

"Asa explained the significance of 'the river current,'" Masao Anai said. Seeing his face in profile I could understand why Goro, who was always an extraordinarily perspicacious bestower of pet names and sobriquets, had dubbed him "the caveman." While it had obviously started out as a clever play on the first element of Anai's surname (in Japanese, *ana* can mean "cave," "hole," or "cavern"), the nickname was also a reaction to his distinctive physiognomy—especially the way his forehead sloped back from the sharply protuberant ridge of bone above his eyes, giving him an air of wild, primordial ruggedness. That sort of multilayered resonance was typical of Goro's humor, and evidently "the caveman" had also struck Masao as a good name for his troupe.

"Actually," Masao went on, "I've been thinking a lot about the dramatic significance of the way the notional alter ego, Kogii, runs through your novels as a sort of supernatural leitmotif. Reading this poem, I can't help thinking that the idea of being sent up into the forest without making preparations seems like a contradiction of the rules of the mythical world you so often evoke in your work. I mean, his childhood playmate, Kogii, was someone who originally came down from the forest and later flew back up into the woods on his own."

"You're exactly right," I said. "But when this poem mentions Kogii, it's mainly talking about my earliest nickname. My mother uses the childhood name as a sort of verbal spear to ambush my adult self with a serious question about the preparations I've made for my own demise and for that of my son, Akari. So the meaning of her section of this poem is, essentially, that the most important thing I need to do in order to prepare for my own death is to get Akari ready for his trip to the forest, which may well precede mine."

Just then Asa reappeared in the dining room and spoke to Masao Anai. "The young guys are going to take the car and go for a drive around Mount Odami, and they'll return in three hours or so," she announced. "Your theater apprentices are really an impressive group, by the way. Not only were they completely willing to do some heavy lifting, but they also had to deal with the constraints of being at a stranger's house . . . or at least in a stranger's garden."

Masao acknowledged the compliment with a slight bow, then gestured toward his second-in-command. "Unaiko gets all the credit— she's the one who oversees that aspect of their training," he said.

After the young men had departed Asa made some fresh coffee and Unaiko served it. As we were sitting around the table, Asa turned to me. "Masao was saying that during your stay here, his main objective—and that of his entire group—is to be of assistance any way they can, but they are also hoping you'll be willing to help them with the play they're putting together, based on your work," she said. "I'll let him fill you in on the details."

"Ah, well," Anai demurred with a humorous shrug. "Asa makes us sound very noble and altruistic, but the truth is our motivations are purely selfish. Seriously, since we were already hard at work on a plan for a play that incorporated elements from your entire oeuvre, when Asa told us you were going to be spending time here it seemed like a gift from the gods. So one day when we were talking to her about the project, we asked whether there was any chance you might be willing to listen to what we've come up with so far, and she said, 'I gather that while he's down here my brother will try to synthesize all the work he's done till now, so it shouldn't be too hard to coordinate his project with yours.' That arrangement seems to make sense, since we'll both be creating retrospectives of a sort.

"At some point we'd like to ask you to take a look at the treatment for our play-in-progress, but today I'm just going to talk about the general contours of how we're trying to approach your work, if I may.

"We've been extracting individual scenes from your novels and then converting them into dramatic form, one by one. We've barely begun to figure out how to make those vignettes flow as a whole, and since we have this rare opportunity to talk to you in person, we think it would add some depth if we could interview you and incorporate your comments into our play. Once we've accumulated a stash of interviews, we'll find a way to fit them in. In the actual production we'll dress someone up as you (it'll be one of the actors from the Caveman Group, who will play other parts as well), and that person will be interviewed as an ongoing part of the drama. As for the other characters who emerge from the stories you share in the interviews, they'll be portrayed by a rotating cast of actors. That's the method we're planning to use to create a multidimensional narrative.

"I have already created and performed a number of dramatic works based on your novels, but it's my intention to make this current project a kind of summation of everything that's gone before. With that in mind, I'm planning to turn your doppelgänger into the focal point. You might wonder how we're going to portray such a singular character visually, but don't worry—I already have something in mind. Once we start talking, I'm hoping our recorded conversations might be useful for you, too, while you're working on your own project. (We heard from Asa that you'll be sorting through your writings and combining them with some new material.) And if we can somehow help you, even just by providing some perspective on your previous work, it would be very satisfying for us."

When Masao Anai stopped speaking, Asa took the floor and addressed her remarks to me. "I did mention to our friends here that you were planning to try to integrate some of your earlier work with the materials in the trunk and then, I gathered, to combine all those elements in a new book, as a sort of last hurrah," she explained. "You were saying you'd tried to reread your older works but somehow couldn't get through them, and an idea occurred to me. What if you tried revisiting your previous novels as a joint endeavor with these folks? Masao and Unaiko have been approaching the same task in a very bold and innovative way."

I had to admit that I felt intrigued by the prospect of seeing my own books anew through the eyes of Masao Anai and his crew, and it struck me as an excellent way of getting a new perspective on my childhood alter ego, Kogii, who was still (quite literally) haunting my dreams.

"In that case, do you think it would be a good idea to try shaping our interviews to focus mainly on Kogii?" I asked.

"Most definitely," Unaiko said. "And we're ready to start right now!"

Intentionally avoiding her bright, eager eyes, I glanced over at my sister. In our younger days, Asa had often run interference for me by deflecting the overtures of this type of strong-willed, extroverted woman, but she didn't seem to feel any need to do that now, and I trusted her judgment. Unaiko's energetic body language appeared to say, *Come on, let's do this!* and she began to pull an assortment of recording equipment out of a canvas tote bag I had noticed earlier, in passing, and deemed too large to be a woman's purse.

To their credit, Unaiko and Anai didn't rush me into recording mode. Instead, Unaiko carefully laid out the equipment on the dining-room table, piece by piece, while everyone else looked on. This was my first glimpse into the thoughtful, deliberate methodology that would typify my brief collaboration with the Caveman Group. I realized then that I was in capable hands, and any residual reluctance I might have been feeling simply melted away.

# 3

A short while later, with the tape recorder whirring, Masao Anai settled himself in a chair and began to speak. "Even though we hadn't yet obtained your formal permission, Mr. Choko, we went ahead and started brainstorming the conceptual aspects of this new project," he said. "Of course, we did talk things over with Asa, and her attitude was 'I don't foresee any problem with the plan you've described, but be sure to approach my brother with caution.' There's a fund designed to assist the directors of small theater groups, and in order to qualify for one of those grants a group needs to have won some type of prize or award. Even though you haven't seen our performance of the play we based on your book *The Day He Himself Shall Wipe My Tears Away*, I gather you've heard about the gratifying praise that production received?

"Okay, that concludes the shameless self-congratulation portion of our program. Now let's move on to the new project. Our original plan was to follow our success with the dramatization of *Wipe My Tears Away* (as we call it, for short) with a sequel, but as you know better than anyone, in the case of that novel there isn't one. So I got the idea of searching through your complete canon for a recurrent motif linking all your books together.

"The leitmotif I found, of course, is Kogii. Now, I find it interesting that in your books the name 'Kogii' is assigned to a variety of entities. In the beginning, Kogii was your nickname. Later, you ended up sharing the name with your constant companion: the mysterious—dare I say imaginary?—playmate who supposedly lived at your house and who looked exactly like you. (Your body double, in cinematic terms.)

"Kogii never left your side until one day he simply took off, moving effortlessly through the air, and returned to the forest. In other words, this mystical being whose corporeal form was visible only to you had the ability to levitate and float off into the sky, so even though he looked like you, his powers surpassed those of any human child.

"In my formal proposal, I tried to persuade the funding committee to finance this project by explaining how I would portray this entity, who transcends reality, as a tangible flesh-and-blood person. The question was, should I have him appear onstage as a character fully endowed with physical form, or would I simply try to make the audience aware of his presence while he remained invisible? My thought was that in terms of dramatic impact, simpler would be better. I basically lifted all the raw materials for the characterization from your collected works and jotted them down on index cards. By the way, I picked up the index card technique from reading your essays, back in my university days.

"At our practice space in Matsuyama, we've used your descriptions of Kogii as inspiration for the creation of a doll: a sort of three-dimensional cloth figurine. Unaiko made a prototype by sewing together some pieces of fabric and then stuffing the shell. If the doll ends up being part of the final staging, we'll place it as high as possible above the stage, in a place where the audience will still be able to see it. We actually did something similar in another play, so we aren't flying completely blind on this. Anyway, the doll version of Kogii will be looking down at the action and influencing the actors on the stage. Let's call it the 'Kogii effect.'

"The other day I was trying to figure out when Kogii first appeared in your work, and when I remembered that your friend Takamura once mentioned in an interview how much he liked a certain early work of yours, I went through my books and found the story in question."

"Ah," I said. "You're talking about the one where a young composer imagines that his dead baby is floating in the sky, as big as a kangaroo and dressed in a white cotton nightgown. The apparition's name is Aghwee."

"That's the one," Anai said. "The narrator is a student who is working as a part-time personal assistant for the mentally unstable composer, and he thinks the giant creature his employer claims to see in the sky is nothing more than a delusional fantasy. Part of the narrator's job description is to accompany the hallucinating composer on his rambles around Tokyo, and one day they're walking down a narrow street when they happen to encounter a dog walker who is being dragged along by a boisterous pack of Doberman pinschers, all straining to escape their leashes. At any rate, the composer is busy trying to communicate with the giant kangaroo-size baby he sees in the sky—it's the ghost of his brain-damaged child, whom he chose to starve to death shortly after its birth—and the narrator is overcome with panic, fearing he's about to be engulfed in the scrum of dogs. Feeling utterly helpless, he shuts his eyes and tears begin to trickle down his face. Then someone touches his shoulder."

I knew the entire passage by heart. *"On my shoulder was a hand gentle as the essence of all gentleness; it felt like Aghwee touching me,"* I recited.

"That's it!" Masao exclaimed, clapping his hands. "When I reread the story, it occurred to me that what the young narrator perceived as Aghwee's palm touching his shoulder was, in fact, the hand of Kogii. So I wrote a scene in which Kogii, just like the giant ghostly baby floating in the sky above Tokyo, gazes down from a high place at the novelist below—that is, at Kogito Choko. Hang on a sec, let me read you the ending, where the narrator has been hit in the eye and blinded by a stone thrown by a bunch of inexplicably frightened children.

> *"It was then that I sensed a being I knew and missed leave the ground behind me like a kangaroo and soar into the teary blue of a sky that retained its winter brittleness. 'Good-bye, Aghwee,' I heard myself whispering in my heart. And then I knew that my hatred of those frightened children had melted away and*

*that time had filled my sky during those ten years with figures*
*that glowed with an ivory-white light, I suppose not all of them*
*purely innocent. When I was wounded by those children and*
*sacrificed my sight in one eye, so clearly a gratuitous sacrifice, I*
*had been endowed, if for only an instant, with the power to per-*
*ceive a creature that had descended from the heights of my sky."*

Masao Anai's reading of the words I had written so long ago had a powerful impact on me. I felt as though I had just heard, with my own ears, indisputable evidence of his very real talent as a stage director.

"As I've illustrated," Masao said, "we've been talking about making the metaphor of Kogii a focal point. (We can discuss what he represents later on, although it seems fairly obvious.) But there's another approach, which would be to have Unaiko add her own interpretation to the basic premise. The Caveman Group isn't rigidly organized by any means, and I think our flexibility might actually end up having a stimulating effect on the work you're about to undertake as well. The truth is, unlike in the past, university scholars don't seem to be specializing in the work of Kogito Choko these days, so maybe this collaboration of ours will help to revive your waning popularity, even a little."

"Really, Masao?" Asa said sharply. "I mean, I've told you that my brother is inclined to be skittish about this type of situation, and when you say snarky things you're running the risk of making him back away from the entire project. Let's just forge ahead slowly and hope we can all be reciprocally inspired by our creative activities. You were saying that Unaiko might have a different perspective, so how about it, Unaiko? How do you feel about this?"

Unaiko had been listening intently, looking like a little girl with an old-fashioned ponytail who had grown into a woman without changing much at all, but now she wiped the pensive expression off her face and addressed the group. "I have a very active interest in this project," she said, "and I think it will be a meaningful collaboration for Masao and for Mr. Choko as well. Actually, there's something I'd like to ask Mr. Choko privately at some point, if it could be arranged."

"You'd better be careful," Asa warned, but her tone was light. "When you try to get too close to my brother, he tends to run away. Ha ha ha! He really has his work cut out for him, though—he has to wade through all the musty old materials in the red leather trunk. I have my own feelings of ambivalence about the project, so I would be happier if he didn't rush into it."

After making that somewhat inscrutable remark, Asa paused and glanced at her watch. "Okay, then," she said, turning to me. "It's almost time for the youngsters to return from their little jaunt. You're probably going to be relying on them for quite a bit of shuttle service from now on, so why don't you be a sport and invite them to stay for dinner?"

# 4

The following Monday morning at nine o'clock on the dot, the Caveman Group's minivan once again rolled up in front of the Forest House bearing Masao Anai, Unaiko, and the two young troupe members who had helped with the poetry stone. Hoping to avoid the morning rush hour, the little party had left Matsuyama at six A.M., and the predawn departure had evidently taken a toll on the two younger men. They greeted me with faces that seemed to say, *Sorry, we're still half-asleep!* but just a few minutes later, in a spectacular burst of energy, they were hard at work alongside Asa, converting part of the first floor of the house into a small theater.

The two young men were clearly no strangers to manual labor, and the task at hand—setting up the Forest House as a communal workplace and rehearsal space—definitely required physical strength. Asa and Unaiko had hatched this plan earlier, and Asa had managed to quell my initial objections by assuring me the changes would only be temporary. The layout of the Forest House (which Asa had already been allowing the Caveman Group to use for rehearsals) was quite well suited to such activities. The previous day, Asa had done the basic cleaning by herself, and now she was supervising her newly arrived workforce.

The study/bedroom where I worked and slept was on the western end of the second floor, along with a library and one other bedroom. By prior agreement, the entire area had been declared a "no trespassing" zone. As for the ground floor, the northeastern quarter had originally been designed to serve as a parlor or drawing room, but it had never been used. The southern wing included the main entry area where people shed their shoes, a rather cramped foyer, a guest bathroom, and a staircase to the second floor. On the northern side, separated from the narrow foyer by a door, were the dining room and, one step down, the slightly sunken great room. Like the dining room, the large living area featured a massive plate-glass window that looked out on the back garden. Finally, on the west end, there were two guest bedrooms for visiting family members, with a shared bathroom.

"We'll have the guys move the furniture from the great room—the table and chairs, the movable bookshelves, the sofa, and the television set—into the parlor," Unaiko said briskly. "Last year, when it didn't look as if you would be returning to the Forest House any time soon, we took Asa up on her kind offer and started using the entire first floor as a rehearsal space. If we clear out the great room now, the southernmost portion can be used as a stage. And if we move the big table out of the dining room, the area can be used for audience seating as well."

"That sounds fine," I said. "Back in the days when I used to come to the Forest House every year, if I wasn't upstairs reading books or doing some work, I could usually be found stretched out on the sofa on the western side of the great room. I'd be grateful if you could leave that one sofa where it is, but feel free to shuffle everything else around however you wish. Asa has probably told you about this already, but I once used this room as a sort of minitheater myself. I invited a group of professional musicians who had recorded a CD of a little composition of Akari's, and we put on an informal concert. We seated my mother and Asa and a few other guests directly in front of the stage, with the overflow in the dining room. This room has a high ceiling, so the acoustics were quite extraordinary."

"We'll be doing a bunch of different things here, too," Unaiko told me. "Once we've conducted our interviews with you and incorporated the relevant bits into the master script, we'll be staging some rehearsals. We were also talking about the fact that you've never seen the Caveman Group in action, and we were thinking we'd like to put on a compressed version of *Wipe My Tears Away*, specially for you."

With that, Unaiko bounded off to the dining room. She placed both hands on the counter and looked around, then gazed up at the high ceiling with obvious approval.

"As a rule, the Caveman Group's public performances take place on a stage that's on the same level as the audience seating," she said. "We often use a theater-in-the-round arrangement, so if you imagine a ring of spectators on the other side of the glass, peeking in from the garden, you should be able to get a sense of what would be happening onstage in an actual production."

After the two young apprentices had finished emptying the great room of all its movable furnishings, apart from my favorite couch, Unaiko vacuumed the hardwood floor while I busied myself with opening the smaller windows on either side of the big plate-glass window to let in some fresh air. Masao and Asa were standing there shoulder to shoulder, surveying Chikashi's horticultural handiwork in the back garden. There were innumerable rosebushes, both in pots and in the earth, where they had spread to the point of becoming ground cover; the pomegranate tree, with its luxuriant foliage; the flowering dogwood; and some tall Japanese white birches. (For the past few years Chikashi hadn't been able to make the trip down here, so Asa had been tending the garden.)

"These trees look different from the ones in the forest," Masao said. "Up in Matsuyama you sometimes see flowering dogwoods growing along the road, but they aren't nearly as tall or as lush as these. Maybe they're just young, or maybe this is a special spot. But what about these Japanese white birches—isn't it unusual for them to grow so tall?"

"The trees Chikashi brought were some she'd originally transplanted from the summer house in Karuizawa to the house in Tokyo, and she'd been tending them there for twenty-odd years," Asa explained. "She rescued several full-grown trees that had been blown down by the strong winds in those mountains, but the ones she raised here from seedlings are also exceptionally tall for some reason. Chikashi was young and energetic in those days, and she really threw herself into cultivating this garden."

"From the sheer number of potted roses, and the way she seems to have been determined to make the trees grow larger than they normally would, I get the feeling Chikashi might share some character traits with her brother, Goro Hanawa," Masao mused. "A certain tenacity, and an attraction to the unusual . . ."

"Goro never showed any particular interest in trees, though," I said.

"No, but I see Masao's point," Asa said. "I noticed a similarity between Chikashi and Goro in the way she helped Akari with his musical education. There's no such artistic streak in our family. Actually," she added, looking at me, "when you met Goro, while you were both going to school in Matsuyama, weren't you captivated by that aspect of his personality?"

"Well, Goro was definitely a rare human being," I said. "For one thing, because he took an interest in the story of our father's drowning, he was the first person I ever confided in about the recurrent dream, outside of our immediate family."

"Yes," Masao remarked, "I remember Goro used to say things like 'Yes, but Choko has *Kogii!*' So I guess he thought you were pretty special, too, having your own personal guardian angel and all. Anyhow, the bottom line is that the images of both Kogiis—you and your alter ego—are etched into my mind, and that duality is forming the basis for this project we're going to be working on together. Speaking of which, we've decided on the basic layout of the stage, but what we need to get a handle on now is how to present the interviews we'll be doing with you. Needless to say, if you'd like to propose any changes to the staging we would be totally receptive. Now, for starters, can we talk a bit about Kogii?"

Masao Anai's request seemed perfectly natural, and I had no objection. Just as she had done the previous time, Unaiko placed the recording equipment on the divider between the dining room and the great room, then attached a microphone to my collar. Masao dispatched the muscular young apprentices to the drawing room to retrieve a couple of armchairs, which they quickly placed in the center of the impromptu stage. Watching this smoothly orchestrated transition, I felt as if I was being borne along on a wave of competence: a force of nature that was clearly beyond my control.

"Please make yourself comfortable," Masao said to me. "We may use a different approach later on, but for now I'm simply going to stand in front of you and start talking. If I find myself getting tired, I'll grab a chair and sit down. You'll already be sitting, of course, but if you want to stretch your legs at any point please feel free to stand up and walk around. Your wireless microphone will work anywhere in the room.

"The way you're sitting, facing straight ahead—please imagine that you're looking out at the big round stone we moved into the back garden the other day. The poem carved into the stone begins with two lines that we've agreed to call a haiku, strict rules of poetry aside. Let's start with the first line: *You didn't get Kogii ready to go up into the forest*. We know this 'Kogii' is different from the 'Kogii' character who appears in some of your novels, but . . ."

"Since my mother wrote this line, we have to look at the meanings she was ascribing to this particular 'Kogii,'" I said. "The things I'm going to tell you have already been addressed in my books, but when my mother wrote these lines during the last year of her life, she was also using 'Kogii' to mean her grandson, Akari, who was born with an abnormal growth on his head.

"My mother was concerned because she felt that I hadn't made sufficient preparations for dealing with the prospect of Akari's eventual

death. Naturally, her approaching death was very much on her mind
as well. And, of course, she had to be aware that the death of her own
son (that is, me), who had been called 'Kogii' as a child, couldn't be
too far off, either. So I think she mentioned Kogii in this poem as an
oblique way of voicing her fear that I might not be preparing properly for my own inevitable demise—an event euphemistically known
around these parts as 'going up into the forest.' In essence, my mother
was conflating two ideas and using them to level a double-barreled
criticism at me. She was saying that Akari needs a guide to show him
the proper way to go up into the forest, and the responsibility for that
should be mine and mine alone. However, she clearly implies that I
can't even seem to get my own affairs in order, and (in her opinion)
I'm dillydallying around in a state of obliviousness, with my end-of-life
preparations in limbo. This may seem like a lot to read into a short
line but trust me, it's all there.

"The second and last line of my mother's portion of the poem is
*And like the river current, you won't return.* Inspired by my mother's
haiku—and electrified by the feeling that her words were right on
the mark—I wrote my own lines: *In Tokyo during the dry season / I'm
remembering everything backward, / From old age to earliest childhood.*

"Before we move on, there's just one more thing. I'd like to talk
about the nickname 'Kogii' (although I think you may know about this
already, through my novels), which has special significance for me.

"First, obviously, Kogii is derived from my real name: Kogito.
When I was a child, my family used to call me 'Kogii' for short.
Although no one else could see him, I had a constant companion
who was an exact replica of me: same age, same face, same body.
We were as alike as two peas in a pod, as the saying goes. I called
this doppelgänger by my nickname, Kogii, and we lived together in
perfect harmony—right up until the midsummer day when he took
off and wafted up into the forest, leaving me behind. I complained
bitterly to my mother, but she just ignored me. Undaunted, I regaled
her again and again with every detail of exactly how Kogii made his

exit from our house and how abandoned I felt. Asa, among others, has speculated that Kogii's distressing departure (and my endless retelling of it) might have been an underlying cause for my choice of fiction writing as a career.

"Anyway, on that fateful day Kogii was standing on the veranda outside the back parlor, which looked out toward the river. He was wearing an unlined summer kimono of splash-patterned *kasuri* cloth. The long sleeves were draped over the balustrade, and he was staring at the grove of Japanese chestnut trees on the opposite shore. (I still have a vivid memory of that moment, in the form of an imaginary photograph; I'm standing right next to Kogii but I look a bit out of focus, as if someone had moved the camera.)

"And then he climbed up on the railing. I thought he was being playful, because he often used to invent little games. He spread both arms and stood very still, taking a moment to center himself and get his balance. Then he stepped out into space—first with one leg, then the other—and a moment later he flapped his arms and simply wafted away through the air. He cut across Mother's cornfield, passed the stone wall, and floated to a place right above the middle of the river. Then, once again, he spread his arms in their wide kimono sleeves straight out to both sides, and like some great wingless bird he took off on the wind and vanished from my sight. (At that point I was still standing indoors, with the low-hanging eaves partially obstructing my view.) When I stepped onto the veranda and peered up at the sky, I saw Kogii rising ever higher into the forest, twirling upward through the air with a corkscrew motion.

"And just like that, he was gone. From then on I whined incessantly to my mother, telling her how my perfect playmate had abruptly vanished from my life, but she refused to even talk about the other Kogii, as if (it seemed to me) she was unwilling to acknowledge that there had ever been another boy living in her house—a boy who really was as similar to her own son as (I'll say it again) two peas in a pod.

"So life went on, and one day something extraordinary befell me. Several months had passed since Kogii's ascent into the heights of the forest; I remember that the slope on the far side of the river was already crimson with fall foliage. It was a full-moon night, and I seemed to sense something unusual happening beyond the windows. I went out onto the road in front of our house to investigate and there, with his back to me, stood Kogii. Without saying a word, he began to walk away—keeping his feet on the ground this time. He took the narrow, hilly road that wound between the village office and the Shinto shrine, striding along the moonlit path at a rapid pace. I thought I was only a few steps behind him, but the next thing I knew I had ended up deep in the forest, alone. Kogii was nowhere to be seen. For reasons I can't explain, I climbed into the hollow of a giant horse chestnut tree, crouched inside, and spent the night huddled there, either asleep or unconscious. When dawn finally broke, I peeked out into the forest and saw the rain pouring down, drenching the dark red leaves of the trees.

"I must have lost consciousness again. When I regained my senses I was running a fever so high that my entire body seemed to be on fire, and some village firemen were in the act of scooping me out of my hideout in the dry, decaying bowels of the ancient tree. The rescue team wrapped me in a waterproof cloak and carried me away through the rain-scented forest, back to my home in the valley.

"Those heroic firemen deserved all kinds of credit, but as the days went by and my fever abated, I gradually came to realize that my life had been saved by my mother's intuition. I'm not sure when she realized I was missing, but even in the first hours of frantic worry she had crossed over to join me in the realm of imagination, and had figured out that I must have gone into the forest in search of my dearly missed companion.

"In the wee hours of that full-moon night, after I ran out of the house and didn't come back, the rain began to fall and the turbid river thundering through the bottom of the valley turned a murky green, darker than the bamboo grass that grew on the riverbanks. The river was rising, and everyone jumped to the conclusion that the missing child must have fallen in and been carried away on the flood tide.

Which brings us back to the lines that are carved into the round stone: *And like the river current, you won't return home*.

"Now you might think, given the weather conditions and her own experience, that when my mother realized her child was missing and rushed to the fire station, she would have said something like 'Please start your search for my son by looking downriver.' That seems logical, doesn't it? But no—my mother took the opposite tack. She asked the firemen to search for me up in the forest, and even though the torrential rain had flooded the road to the forest, turning it into a muddy river, she insisted that they make their way there, paddling along as if they were in a boat. I'm guessing there must have been a lull in the downpour, and the firemen, who had reluctantly agreed to search the forest, found a small person huddled in the hollow of a giant tree, running a high temperature and clearly very ill. The delirious child tried to fight them off, like some deranged wild boar, but they managed to pick him up and get him safely home. (Incidentally, that particular tree was well known to everyone in the area, and everyone revered it as a sort of naturally created Shinto shrine.)

"It's really rather uncanny, don't you think? I mean, why was my mother so certain I would go up into the forest rather than heading downriver? (It was probably more of a gut feeling on her part, but her instincts still struck me as remarkable.) Some of the adults in our village had a habit of saying cruel, unpleasant things to the local children, and for a long time after my dramatic rescue they used to taunt me with remarks like "Hey, sonny boy, you were so obsessed with finding your imaginary friend that you got lost in the forest and caused a lot of trouble for the firemen. Shame on you!"

# 5

After the first official recording session ended, Masao Anai was in a supremely buoyant mood.

"Today was only supposed to be a run-through to test our system, but we ended up getting a full-fledged interview!" he said. "Of course, you're about to tackle the major task of sorting through the materials in the red leather trunk, but if you could see your way clear to hanging out with us from time to time, just like this, before too long we should be able to create a bundle of interviews that can become a vital part of the play. And while you're working on your own project, perhaps these sessions will provide you with some useful notes, as we say in the theater biz. I think that would be an excellent path, for all of us. We'll come back next week, and in the meantime Unaiko will type up a transcript of today's session. The first thing on the agenda next time will be to have you take a look at those pages.

"I know sometimes, when you give a lecture, you'll polish your notes later on and publish them in a magazine. I usually make a point of reading those articles. But when it comes to our group's approach to making art, smoothing things out too much wouldn't be as enjoyable for the audience, since everything we do is aimed at creating drama. We aren't asking you to remove the irrelevancies and divergences, but we would like you to elaborate a bit more, keeping in mind that we'll be trying to transform your narrative into a physical form onstage."

Unaiko picked up where Anai had left off, speaking in a manner noticeably calmer and more composed than that of her exuberant colleague. "Mr. Choko," she began, "I wanted to talk to you about something I noticed toward the end of the interview. At one point you seemed to be in a bit of a quandary about how to proceed with your story; it seemed as if there were two possible directions, and you were trying to decide which one to choose."

"Yes, that's exactly what was going on," I acknowledged. "You really are exceptionally observant, Unaiko."

"Not really—I've just gotten into the habit of listening very carefully to what people are saying while I'm recording them," Unaiko said modestly.

"You must have noticed that as I was talking, my eyes were fixed on the round stone beyond the big window. I was asking myself, 'Should I start by making a connection between the first line of the poem, about Kogii, and the line about the river current? Or should I take the second fork in this road and go in an entirely different direction?' Obviously, I ended up choosing number one," I said.

"I'd like to hear more about the other option you mentioned," Masao said. "Is that something you've already written about in your novels?"

"Yes, it is," I said. "It's related to the quote you read from one of my books the other day. I was wondering how my mother knew—or intuited—that the firemen ought to look for me in the hollow tree, and as I was trying to express my thoughts I remembered one of the more captivating tidbits of local folklore my mother used to share. She often talked about the 'marvelous forest,' and she said that while there were various ways of seeing the story, she had her own perspective. Her version appears virtually verbatim in my novel *M/T and the Story of the Marvels of the Forest*."

"Hang on a sec, I've got it right here." Masao Anai quickly paged through his large notebook, found the relevant quote, and began to read my mother's words in a theatrical voice.

*"We think now that our individuality is terribly important, but back in the time when we were in the marvelous forest, even though we were individual entities, we were all part of a greater whole. We were perfectly contented with our existences, perpetually awash in feelings of infinite nostalgia. However, at some point, we had to leave the mystical forest and venture into the outside world to be born as human beings. The way I see it, because each and every one of us possesses an individual life, or soul, no sooner do we leave the forest than we are scattered to the four winds. That's my theory, for what it's worth! But as we go about living our own lives, don't we always feel a lingering sense of wistful nostalgia for the earlier time when we were*

*all together, happily unborn yet alive amid the marvels of the forest?"*

Unaiko had evidently talked about the marvels of the forest with Anai, and when he had finished reading my mother's quotation, she added her own comments.

"The obvious assumption would be that the missing child had somehow fallen into the surging river," she said. "But the child had a special sense of direction—not to mention a deep affinity with the forest—and those two things led him to head up (you could even say 'head home') into the marvelous forest. But before he could return to the universal forest-womb for good, his mother led the firemen to the large hollow tree near the entrance to the forest, and he was brought back to the world of the living. If that's what we're talking about, it makes perfect sense."

Masao nodded his enthusiastic agreement, and I got a sense of how completely he relied on Unaiko's artistic instincts. "Yes," he said. "If it unfolds that way, the story of Kogii will be an absolutely perfect motif for our play."

*My sentiments exactly,* I thought.

# Chapter 2

# The Rehearsal

## 1

I was originally thinking that the next step, after I'd settled into my digs in the mountain valley, would be to get my mother's red leather trunk from Asa. However, Asa had mentioned in the presence of the Caveman Group that she would be happier if I took my time investigating the trunk's contents. So the only things she gave me, for starters, were the rough draft of the prologue to my unfinished drowning novel and the auxiliary materials I'd sent to my mother and sister some forty years earlier when they were still living together in our family home. As she was handing over the tote bag containing those papers, Asa said there were some things in the red leather trunk she wanted to have copied, to remember our mother by, before I took that fabled piece of luggage to Tokyo once and for all.

When I peeked into the tote bag there seemed to be far fewer papers than I remembered. Aside from a number of preliminary jottings—*esquisses*, in French—the only remotely novel-like materials were twenty manuscript pages (at most), each with space for four hundred Japanese characters, and a clean copy of the opening lines of a prologue or introduction. I had sent those pages to my mother along with a polite request for access to any resources that might help me develop my embryonic book; I was especially interested in my father's correspondence: both letters he had received and the rough drafts of his replies. In the bag I received from Asa there was also a bundle of letters I had sent from Tokyo over the years, which had evidently been stored in the red leather trunk.

Among those missives was a letter addressed to Asa in which I expressed my anger that not only had my mother ignored the rough draft of my drowning novel, she had also failed to respond to my inquiry regarding my father's correspondence and other research materials.

*I've given up hope on this* [I wrote], *so you may as well burn the manuscript. If our mother is going to willfully deny me access to the materials I need, I'll just have to take a different approach. I will abandon reality and simply write the book as a work of wild imagination, presented as the unhinged ramblings of a young man who is an inmate at a mental institution. And the father in the story will die not by drowning but from a gunshot wound. Because this story will appear to be so far from the truth, Mother won't be able to prevent its publication by claiming I used my father as a model for the central character. However, the essence of what I say about the father (and his ideologies) will, in fact, be true.*

I went ahead and wrote that novella in lieu of the drowning novel I really wanted to write, and it was published in a literary magazine as *The Day He Himself Shall Wipe My Tears Away.* My mother and sister were horrified and very, very angry, and the upshot was that I ended up being "disowned" (the quaint term we settled on to describe our reciprocal estrangement) and barred from returning home for a number of years.

Anyway, in the rough draft of the prologue to the drowning novel
I wrote about something that had happened in 1945—an incident
that, at the time, I had been dreaming about on a regular basis.

There is a place where, under normal conditions, the flow of the
river is diverted around a protruding rock and the killifish congregate in the shallows. On this night, the flooding has turned the
usually quiescent pool into a deep-water cove. That's where the
rowboat is moored, bobbing about on the high, choppy waves.
My father is already on board the little boat, and I am standing
at the base of a stone wall, facing in his direction. I take a step
forward into the dark water and am shocked by how deep it is;
I'm instantaneously submerged in the chilly water, almost up to
my neck. To make matters worse, the skin of my chest is being
pricked, rather painfully, by some aggressive flotsam: either the
spines of grass berries, or some bird lice that have latched onto
my skin. There's no time to scrape off these unwelcome passengers, so I charge through the rushing water, chest first. The
flood tide roars in my ears, loud as thunder.

It's the middle of the night, and the rain has stopped falling.
The full moon shines through a fissure in the clouds, illuminating
my father, who is standing in the stern of the boat dressed in his
civilian wartime uniform with his ramrod-straight back to me and
his head hanging down at a precipitous angle. Beyond him the
moonlight is reflecting off the mountainous wall of water as it
surges downriver. In the plan I've been visualizing for a while now,
I would paddle along through the murky water until I reached
the boat and joined my father on board. But as I'm struggling to
get to the boat, I find myself distracted by something that seems
to need fixing, and I go back to tighten a storm-loosened rope
that is looped around the big rock and tied to one of the wooden
spider lily casks. Just as I finish securing the cask I see that the
boat has been tossed into the raging current, and my father has
apparently lost his footing and fallen down. Then I notice Kogii

standing next to where I last saw my father, looking at me with a
certain ineffable expression on his otherworldly face. It's starting
to feel as though the churning water might wash me away, too,
and I'm clinging for dear life to the spider lily cask. . . .

I'd forgotten how realistically I had described Kogii in the vignette
I dashed off some forty-odd years ago. And when I reviewed the utterly
familiar final image, I recognized anew that whenever I had the dream
(it was essentially the same scenario every time, though there were
small disparities depending upon my state of being on the night in
question) Kogii was always present, and I was always watching him as
he flashed me a look that I could only describe, vaguely, as *a certain
ineffable expression*.

I considered this in the context of the point Masao had made
about the significance of Kogii as an entity who seemed to exist as a
regular person, but who also had a decidedly uncanny (or should I
just say supernatural?) aspect to his nature. I felt certain Masao would
be interested in reading these pages so I asked Asa to make a copy of
the rough draft and give it to him, along with the photocopies she was
having made of the other materials in the red leather trunk—materials
on which I had pinned so many of my artistic hopes.

About a week later Masao, Unaiko, and Asa showed up in the
theater troupe's minivan, driven by a young man whom I hadn't seen
before. Both the driver and his young male colleague in the passenger
seat were wearing such flashy clothes that I was momentarily dazzled,
until Asa introduced the pair and explained that they were dressed
for an important audition. Apparently there was a hall in Uwajima
(a seaside town an hour away) that showcased up-and-coming performers in the hopes of attracting audiences from the main island
of Honshu, who could now travel there by car via a recently opened
bridge. That hall was the destination of the two dapperly turned-out
young men. They were part of the Caveman Group, but also performed
on their own as a comedy duo called Suke & Kaku—always with an
ampersand, they solemnly informed me.

"The work they're doing is very postmodern," Asa explained. "Needless to say, their choice of a retro-sounding name was completely intentional. They borrowed their stage names, Suke & Kaku, from a couple of raffish sidekicks in the popular period drama *Mito Komon*, which has been running on television since these two first opened their eyes as infants."

"Sometimes fans of Suke & Kaku's postmodern skits will come to a public performance by the Caveman Group, and they'll laugh uproariously at all the wrong places," Masao said wryly. "It can be quite unnerving for everyone concerned—not just the actors, but the rest of the audience as well."

I soon learned that Masao and his entire crew had read the transcript of the first interview, and they knew exactly what they wanted me to talk about next: my recurrent "Kogii dream." Once again, Unaiko set up the recording equipment with her trademark swift yet painstaking professionalism.

"Until I reread the fragment recently, I wasn't seeing much significance in the role Kogii played in the dream," I began. "But from what you've said about your dramatization, it has become clear to me that his presence was a pivotal element. When we look at the phrasing of my mother's haiku, where she says, *And like the river current, you won't return home*, a question arises. After thinking obsessively about this matter for a very long time, endlessly refining those lines in her mind, is it possible all she wanted was to have them read and understood by her only son? I recounted my recurrent dream in the opening section of the prologue to my drowning novel, but Kogii was only mentioned briefly at the end. Now, though, I feel I'd like to delve further into the meaning of what Masao has called the 'Kogii effect' through these interviews with you, if only for my own enlightenment.

"At my boyhood home there was a rickety old military rowboat that had been retired from active duty and then delivered to our house by a young army officer, as a gift for my father. We called it, simply, 'the boat.' When the craft was launched into the floodwaters (and we'll never know whether it was an accident) Kogii was at the rear of the boat, standing next to my father with one hand on the tiller. But why do I keep having the dream, even now? Well, when I stopped to think about it I seemed to be remembering Kogii's presence in my father's boat as something that actually occurred, in reality. In other words, it isn't as if I dreamed a total fiction, then conflated the dream with reality, and eventually became convinced that the dream scenario had actually taken place in real life. No, I truly believe the dream was seeded by reality, and not the other way around.

"That night, the plan was for me to shove the boat out into the wide part of the river and then hop on board alongside my father, but I totally botched my life-or-death assignment. Dreams aside, that's what really happened. It isn't some compensatory figment of my imagination, cooked up after my father drowned and his body was delivered to our house. But when I tried to talk about the incident later on, my mother turned a deaf ear, just as she'd done years before when I was grumbling about how Kogii had deserted me and returned to the forest.

"When I was drafting the prologue to my drowning novel, as an adult writer, I revisited that night. I was looking for a way to express what a momentous occurrence my father's drowning was for our family, but in a fit of cowardice I wrote the whole scene as if it were the recollection of a dream. (Though it is true I've had the exact same dream, over and over.)

"If you'll bear with me as I continue with this somewhat convoluted explanation, the event that gave rise to the dream really happened, and all the details I recall are rooted in reality. In the summer of 1945, shortly after our country lost the war, there was an unforgettable night when a storm raged through the forest and the river swelled and roared and overflowed its banks, ultimately rising so high that it engulfed the rocky outcropping above this house. (Incidentally, if you go up there and look down you'll see that the river today, with its splendidly constructed embankment, bears almost no resemblance to the Kame River as it was then.) Anyway, my father launched his little boat into the tumultuous, storm-tossed river, and then he drowned. That was the first big event and it really did occur, although it was always a taboo subject while I was growing up. The only question in my mind was about my father's motivation for setting out on such a perilous night.

"As my mother said in one line of her poem, my father was swept away by the river current, never to return home. In a sense, by drowning he became one with the current. Because of the extreme weather, it wasn't until the following day that my father's drowned body was retrieved from the riverbank and brought home. So, reading between the first and second lines of the poem, I think what my mother was trying to convey to me was this: 'You place a lot of emphasis on the fact that your father went out on the river in the midst of a flood, but his body did come back to us eventually, so it's not as if he was swept away in the extreme sense of *never seen again*.' The line also seems to be saying, 'And what about you, Kogii? Like the river current, you won't return home, either.' Of course, that's a fairly transparent way of chiding me for my selfishness in choosing to live in Tokyo.

"In the first line, too, she's criticizing me by saying, 'If you don't make the necessary preparations for the end of your son's life, and your own, it would be like sending Akari out onto the river in the terrifying, pitch-dark night with no explanation and letting the current sweep him away.' And my lines, which continue the poem, are basically responding: 'Well, since you put it that way, I have to admit it's true.'

"So my part of the poem is meant to be an honest acknowledgment of the current state of affairs. *In Tokyo during the dry season / I'm remembering everything backward / From old age to earliest childhood.*"

"But, Mr. Choko," Masao Anai said, "in your lines, rather than caving in to your mother's pressure, weren't you responding to the rather plaintive voice that permeates her poem by saying in return: 'Hey, maybe I did behave like the river current by going away to Tokyo and not coming back, but before I'm swallowed up in the vortex of the whirlpool I'm going to remember everything that has happened in my life, from my childhood through the present day.' If you did so, then maybe some kind of reversal of the sad state of affairs set forth in the poem might be possible. Otherwise, why would you have made your part of the poem an undisguised echo of those well-known lines by T. S. Eliot?"

I was all talked out for the moment, so I didn't reply to Masao Anai's question. But then Unaiko, without switching off the tape recorder, posed a question of her own: "By the way, what on earth is a 'spider lily cask'? I've never heard that term before."

"Oh, right," I said. "I guess I'd better give you a complete explanation, since it looks as if we're going to be talking a lot about Kogii, and the story of my flood dream is an important part of the saga. As a child I wasn't able to understand my father's world the way I do now, but he must have told me some of these things, and then later on I was able to put them together.

"My father never talked about where he was born and raised, although I suspect that my mother must have known. He and my mother met and married in Tokyo, and from the time the two of them came back together to set up house in her native village—in other words, for the latter half of his life—he seemed to do very little work. (Or at least that's how it appeared to me, as a child.) Anyway, because he was his own boss and had an abundance of free time, young army officers from the regiment at Matsuyama would frequently drop by to visit and drink sake on their days off. What sort of radical things were they discussing at those gatherings? Was my father a leader or a follower? Were they planning some sort of symbolic insurrection? I didn't know for sure, but I was thinking that if I had access to the red leather trunk I would be able to dig up some juicy clues in letters written by the young officers, my father's correspondence with his own mentor, and so on. That was my hope when I came down here.

"In retrospect, I realize that my father probably wasn't as idle as I thought he was. For one thing, he believed there would eventually be food shortages in Japan, and he came up with a rather unusual method for dealing with such a situation. As you know, the Kame River snakes through this mountain valley, and in those days the wide slope on the south bank was entirely covered with forests of chestnut trees. (You can still see a few of those trees today.) My grandfather was in the 'mountain products' business—that is, he would package chestnuts and persimmons and ship them to Osaka, Kobe, Kyoto, and beyond—and at some point he got the idea of encouraging some of the local chestnut-growing households to plant Oriental paperbush plants between rows of chestnut trees.

"The fibrous bark of the paperbush was the basic raw material for paper used in making Japanese currency, so the local harvest from those bushes was sent to the official government printing bureau. First, though, the bushes had to be cut down and the bark stripped off and steamed. After the bark had been dried and separated into bundles, it was temporarily stashed in a warehouse. (Like the paperbush's showy flowers, the processed bark was a brilliant white.) The work was done by farmers, as a group effort, and the women and old people would help by soaking the rough bark in the river, then peeling it off in thin layers.

"My father was something of an amateur inventor, and he designed a machine to strip the bark and had a number of those devices made by a firm that manufactured traditional knives. In order to prepare the bark to be transported by truck, my father would compression-mold it into bricks, to meet government standards. He also invented a good-size packing machine, which he even managed to patent. As far as I know my father had never formally studied engineering, but he clearly enjoyed tinkering with machinery and solving practical problems. I seem to have inherited his penchant for inventive puttering around the house—*bricolage*, as they say in French.

"So how did my father propose to deal with the food shortage he was anticipating? Well, he had observed that every summer the riverside slope I mentioned a moment ago would turn a deep scarlet as the red spider lilies growing wild among the chestnut trees began to bloom. From the autumn of the year before Japan lost the war until the following summer (in other words, until a few months before he drowned), my father became involved in spearheading a public works project—an uncharacteristically social undertaking for a rather private person like him. He began by asking the principal of the local high school whether some students could be assigned to dig up the bulbs of the red spider lilies. He even offered to pay the child laborers a small wage. The high school kids threw themselves into the task with tremendous enthusiasm, and before long the storehouse normally used for chestnuts and persimmons was overflowing with bulbs.

"My father commandeered a portion of my mother's vegetable garden and built a sort of minifactory in our backyard," I went on. "He used bamboo pipes to funnel running water from the nearby river, and he built a mechanism to pulverize the bulbs. This type of amateur-engineering challenge was right in his wheelhouse. He put in some wide stone steps leading down to the river, and then he lined up a large number of barrels on a concrete slab he had installed on the riverbank and secured them with ropes. (It's likely that my father found his pals in the military very useful when it came to getting hold of these materials.)

"The next task was to soak the pulverized spider lily bulbs in water. There was a wide, sandy beach downstream from our house, and that's where my father placed a row of racks covered with straw mats, to use for drying the pulp. After the processed bulbs were dry, the final step in his master plan was to convert them into an edible form.

"Now, even children knew spider lily bulbs were poisonous, but there was a time, long ago, when the bulbs were turned into a flourlike powder and used as an emergency foodstuff in case of famine. People would grind the bulbs, then neutralize the toxicity by adding some medicinal herbs they'd gathered in the forest. Everyone, including my father, knew about this custom; there were even some old botanical illustrations on display in the local historical archives. My mother and grandmother were both locally renowned amateur herbalists, and they knew the forest couldn't possibly provide enough of the medicinal herbs needed to detoxify the poisonous bulbs. Luckily, someone had developed a chemical agent that could be substituted for the elusive herbs, and my father obtained a supply from a friend who worked at a university on Kyushu. The idea was that if he could get the bulb-conversion factory up and running, he would be able to provide an ample quantity of high-quality starch.

"My mother and the other folks from the neighborhood who were helping out in the factory weren't totally convinced the man-made chemical agent would detoxify the bulbs, but nonetheless the work went on. I remember seeing a long row of barrels filled to the brim with pulverized spider lily bulbs at the top of the riverbank. Things seemed to be moving along quite well until the rainy season began."

"That's very interesting," Masao said, but he sounded a trifle impatient. "If we could just get back to the subject at hand, we know the full moon shone through a break in the clouds during a lull in the storm, right around midnight, and that was when your father set off on the flooded river in his little boat and ended up being drowned. Asa has confirmed that timeline as well. But to be honest, I have a feeling the cold, hard truth ends there. Perhaps you really were left behind because you got distracted and didn't manage to climb aboard in time. But the bit about seeing Kogii standing in the boat, staring back at you? I can't help thinking that part of the story was a dream and nothing more. Either way, the dream definitely gives the reality a deeper dimension.

"Needless to say, we aren't trying to make a documentary here," Masao went on, "so I would like to stage the scene not as a dream sequence but as reality, in accordance with your insistence that the ten-year-old boy really did see his doppelgänger, Kogii, against the backdrop of a giant wall of water. But how can we re-create that tableau onstage? I'm hoping we can figure out the logistics as we proceed with these interviews. I'd like very much to conjure up a scene where the Kogii I'm envisioning—who, as we've discussed, is a kind of supernatural being—takes the form of an ordinary child. If we can pull this off, I think it could be fantastic!"

# 2

This was on a Sunday. The original plan had been to stage a rehearsal, right there at the Forest House, of the condensed version of the troupe's prize-winning dramatic adaptation of my novella *The Day He Himself Shall Wipe My Tears Away*, in order to show me the kind of work it was doing. However, two young actors who were slated to participate had gotten a gig (as they called it) to perform elsewhere in the guise of their sketch-comedy personas, Suke & Kaku. As a result, the rehearsal was rescheduled for the following week. I already had a good feeling about the dynamic of the Caveman Group, based on what I had seen so far of Masao Anai's strong but fair leadership style (or rather shared leadership, with Unaiko), and this latest development only strengthened my sense that the group was run as a sort of collegial democracy.

And so it was that a week later, on the following Sunday morning, a caravan of assorted vehicles came bumping down the private road and pulled up in front of the Forest House. Within minutes the young actors were hard at work on the preparations for the rehearsal, under the supervision of Masao and Unaiko.

As for me, I had willingly surrendered the first floor to this energetic group (whose members were so focused on their work that they hadn't even taken the time to greet me one by one) and had retired to my second-floor study. After a while, Masao called to me from the bottom of the stairs. I emerged from my lair to find that Asa, too, had joined the party.

As soon as Asa and I—a command performance audience of two—had seated ourselves with our backs to the partition, Masao strode onto the makeshift stage and began to speak. (The "stage" was furnished with a narrow soldier's bed his young helpers had carried down from the second floor, along with a chair from the dining room.)

To set the scene for his little audience, Masao led off with a general explanation, but the complex timbre of his voice—simultaneously natural, robust, and precise—seemed to offer a glimpse of his particular brand of theater.

"After having read our copy of the prologue of the drowning novel, Unaiko and I were thinking we would like to open the play with a monologue by the person who is visited by the recurrent dream described in the opening passage," Masao began. "A small boat is

moored in a riverside cove, and our narrator's father is standing in the
bobbing boat and facing away from the audience, with the overflowing
river as a dramatic backdrop. In the foreground stands a young boy,
immersed in muddy water up to his chest. He, too, is facing away
from us. Floating high above the boat is the solitary figure of Kogii,
and he's the only one facing the audience. So that'll be the tentative
staging of the opening scene.

"However, the part of the story where the writer sifts through
the contents of the red leather trunk as the entire drowning novel
unfolds before us is just a vague concept. Right now we're in the
process of rereading your complete works, Mr. Choko, with the goal
of making our allusions as powerful as possible, so today we'll only
be presenting a few scenes from our already completed adaptation
of *The Day He Himself Shall Wipe My Tears Away*.

"In the first scene, a ten-year-old boy has tagged along with
his father (known to everyone as Choko Sensei), who is preparing
to charge into battle with a ragtag bunch of army officers—all, we
gather, deserters from the regiment in Matsuyama. The ensuing pan-
tomime unfolds at a snail's pace across the entire stage; the slowness
is unavoidable because Choko Sensei is riding in a 'chariot' made from
a wooden fertilizer box with rough-hewn wheels.

"In actuality, that scene is superimposed over the ongoing narrative of a mentally ill man, reclining on a bed upstage. At the beginning
the role is played by Unaiko, but she is almost completely concealed
by a jumble of sheets and blankets. Seated beside the bed is a large
person in a nurse's uniform, silently listening to the patient's story with
a skeptical look on her face. The role of the nurse is played (in drag)
by Kaku, whom you'll remember as half of the duo of Suke & Kaku.

"The action taking place downstage portrays the recollections
of the patient who is lying in bed reminiscing about the summer of
1945, and the ten-year-old boy is in fact the institutionalized man
himself, twenty-some years earlier. Oh, and, Mr. Choko? Once the
play begins, if the spirit moves you, please feel free to join in and
speak the lines along with the actors. We've tried to bring your novel

to life passage by passage, with maximum fidelity to the original, so chiming in from time to time should come naturally to the author! Seriously, though, audience participation is completely optional. Okay then, here we go."

Only a single pane of glass separated the impromptu stage from the summer garden, where the roses—palest lavender, deepest crimson—were blooming in thick, luxuriant clusters. Inside, a quick switch had been made on the stage, and the person lying in bed was now being played by Suke, while Kaku continued to act the part of the large-boned nurse sitting next to the patient's bed in a metal chair.

Both characters were silent, but the mental patient was evidently remembering his past self as a ten-year-old boy. A hallucinatory vision of the boy, played by Unaiko in a military service cap, entered the foreground of the stage and began to shout in a shrill, piercing voice.

"Mother, Mother, this is terrible—things are really getting out of control! The soldiers have made Father their leader, and they're gonna stage an insurrection! I knew it, I knew it—it's just as I thought. They've gone off the deep end, and they've chosen Father to lead them into battle! We need to check the paper where I wrote down all the people who called Father a spy or a traitor, or said he wanted Japan to lose the war, and then we have to figure out how many names are on that list. It's such a big job, and we're gonna be so busy! Oh, Mother, Mother, this is exactly what I was afraid of, and now it's happening!"

This scene went on and on for a very long time. I seemed to feel my old novel coming back to life inside me, but with an oddly intriguing new twist.

In the next scene, which unfolded across the entire stage, my military-uniform-clad father (who had more or less lost the use of his limbs) was placed in the rough, smelly crate his followers were euphemistically calling a wooden chariot. He was then pushed forward and loaded, crate and all, into a military truck. Simultaneously, the young boy (who had been lurking in the background) emerged from the shadows and spoke—not shrilly and hysterically this time, but in Unaiko's own naturally calm voice.

*"Anyway, in the mountain valley early one morning on a day in August—so early, in fact, that everything was still inky blackness, without even the faintest glimmer of dawn—the soldiers and I loaded Father into a makeshift wooden 'chariot' and, moving as slowly as sleepy turtles, we set off on foot, taking turns pushing the wooden cart. At the mouth of the valley we hoisted the cart, with Father inside, onto a military truck that was waiting there, and, coalesced at long last into a brigade of rebels, the group headed for the provincial capital of Matsuyama by way of the switchback road that wound its torturous way through a mountain pass. And while the army truck, being driven recklessly fast, was screaming along the narrow road, the soldiers in the back kept up a raucous chorus, singing disconnected fragments of a foreign song over and over at maximum volume.*

*"'What does this song mean, anyway?' I inquired, and my father (with his eyes still closed and rivulets of sweat running down his deathly pale, porcelain-smooth, eerily unwrinkled face, and his corpulent body bumping against the boards of the wooden cart) gave an explanation. Of course, after all this time, I'm sure I only remember the barest gist of what he told me: 'It's German. Tränen means "tears," and Tod is "death." They're singing that the emperor himself, with his own hand, will wipe away my tears. In other words, the song is saying the soldiers are waiting and hoping for the day when His Imperial Majesty, with his own fingertips, will gently wipe away their sorrowful tears.'"*

At this point in Anai's staging of the play, one of Bach's solo cantatas suddenly burst forth in the background. (I remembered hearing that same thrilling high-volume sound at an avant-garde performance I'd been invited to attend nearly twenty years earlier, in an intimate little theater space.) The recitation continued, struggling to be heard over the rising wave of music, but the narrator's voice was ultimately swept away on the soaring tide of song.

*Da wischt mir die Tränen mein Heiland selbst ab.*
*Komm, O Tod, du Schlafes Bruder,*
*Komm und führe mich nur fort. . . .*

And as the chorus swelled I felt something beginning to stir in the
deepest recesses of my heart, and I couldn't stop myself from joining in.

# 3

After the play had ended, the young apprentices immediately set to
work clearing away the stage props. When they left the Forest House
it was not quite four o'clock in the afternoon, but the light had already
begun to fade from the jar-shaped valley. The young folks had to get
back to Matsuyama, where they had a job that involved both performing and working backstage at a concert by a singer-songwriter from
Tokyo. Although I myself had never been moved to attend a concert
of that sort, I could imagine what an asset the young members of the
Caveman Group would be to such an event.

Alone in the Forest House as night descended on the valley, I
reflected on what I had just experienced. From the start, the rehearsal
had felt rather dark and dreary. The main characters were a decidedly
gloomy group: the young boy portrayed by Unaiko in costume, shrieking
in a shrill voice (in other words, myself, some sixty-five years earlier);
the reclining patient and the nurse at the back of the stage; and finally
my father, who was in the last stages of bladder cancer, standing in his
wooden "chariot" in a puddle of bloody urine. Not surprisingly, for anyone familiar with the novella, there wasn't a single bright, cheery, attractive face to be found. The staging followed the book closely, including a
scene in which my father—still in his wooden cart—is loaded onto the
bed of a truck whose sides were framed with two-by-fours, then filled
in with corrugated cardboard. The young boy is jammed in beside his
father, while the soldiers line up behind them.

By the end of the impromptu production, there were more than twenty actors onstage: young women and men from the Caveman Group, most of whom I had never laid eyes on. The actors playing the group of soldiers under the renegade officers' command were outfitted with handmade field caps and toy swords, and when they all joined in the rousing chorus of the German war anthem the stage seemed to explode in pyrotechnic splendor.

> *Da wischt mir die Tränen mein Heiland selbst ab.*
> *Komm, O Tod, du Schlafes Bruder,*
> *Komm und führe mich nur fort. . . .*

After the chorus had faded away, the ostensibly male patient (played, at that juncture, by Unaiko), who had been lying on his side in the bed and narrating the scene, stood up. The character's previously nonchalant style of narration suddenly changed radically, and he began to speak in a powerful declamatory voice that dominated the stage.

> "I'll die fighting in the little army my father is leading into this noble insurrection! As I was thinking this, a fighter plane appeared from the direction of the provincial city, coming in low over the pass, and the soldiers began shouting:
> "'Look how recklessly he's flying. He doesn't care what happens anymore!'
> "'We'd better get the planes we need fast, before those bastards crash them!'
> "'We need at least ten airplanes, then we can crash them into the Imperial Palace and go out in a kamikaze blaze of glory!'
> "'Our goal is junshi—suicide in the emperor's name—it's junshi for us all!'
> "'It's junshi for us all'—the hot thorns in those words pierced my small heart, then lodged there and continued to burn. Before long I, too, had begun to sing along with the officers and enlisted men in my high, shrill voice."

After that Unaiko, now playing the role of the young boy, stepped forward to the front of the stage and started to lead the chorus. And as the stirring cantata approached a crescendo even I began to sing along from my seat in the peanut gallery!

"Wow, Kogii—I never expected to hear you singing in such a loud voice, and in German to boot!" Asa exclaimed after the music had died down. "Of course, I don't know whether your pronunciation is any good. Seriously, though, at least you were able to make your voice blend with those of the actors, and they've been practicing the piece for a while. Even after knowing you for all these years, it isn't something I ever expected to see, or hear! I've attended some formal productions by the Caveman Group, and they have always been very well done, but I was never as moved as I am right now."

Asa had returned from her quick run to the train station, and as she delivered this little speech she was standing next to me, staring out at the deepening darkness enveloping the mountain valley. "Unaiko has told me about the meaning of the words of the cantata you were singing," she went on, "and while I can't sympathize with the ideology, that didn't keep me from being moved by the music, and the voices."

"Well," I replied, "in my novella those lines are rendered just as Father explained them to me. *Heiland selbst* means the savior or rescuer himself, which in this case is the emperor, even though obviously there's no way the actual ruler would be involved in this scenario. I remember that the young officers who were always drinking sake at our house used to bellow the German anthem every night at the top of their lungs while listening to the RCA Victor Red Seal recording on the phonograph. When I was starting work on that book, I sang the chorus (which I recalled only vaguely) for Goro, and he knew right away which Bach composition it was.

"Afterward he even went out and tracked down a copy of the LP. One day he brought it by and we proceeded to sing the song together, with Goro stopping from time to time to explain the meaning of the German lyrics, and the words gradually came back to me. That's the

background, but when the actors began to sing and I heard the mag-
nificently loud, theatrical sound, I couldn't help but join the chorus.
I must say, singing along with that ultranationalist anthem has left
me with a strangely ambivalent aftertaste. But this troupe certainly
knows how to put on a play, don't they?"

"You can say that again," Asa said. "There I was, watching the
rehearsal, with half my mind on other things, when suddenly in the
seat next to me my brother began to sing! Sixty-odd years have passed
since your voice changed, but it still sounds kind of screechy, and
when I heard it fervently raised in song, I thought to myself, *Yikes,
this feels like something genuine.*" (Asa used the unflattering word
"screechy" to describe my voice, and that might have been accurate
since I had renewed my acquaintance with the song through the
Dietrich Fischer-Dieskau recording Goro found for me. Still, I was
tempted to say that I would have preferred to hear my singing voice
described as a mellow baritone or even a pleasant countertenor, rather
than a prepubescent screech.)

"I felt as though your singing was coming from a deep well of
emotion," Asa continued, evidently unable to stop marveling at my
unusual behavior. "It seemed, at that moment, as if the intense emotions
of childhood were being rekindled in your heart, so I just sat perfectly
still, letting the sound wash over me. Honestly, I've never heard you
sing with such passion, not even when you were in school. Maybe the
song has been hibernating in your memory—or your soul—all this time,
and was somehow reawakened when you heard it here today.

"But also, I keep going back to the original book this dramatization is based on. I remember *The Day He Himself Shall Wipe My Tears
Away* very well, because it caused so much suffering for Mother and
me. The ultranationalist uprising described in the novella supposedly
takes place on August sixteenth, but in actuality there was never a
single guerrilla uprising, anywhere in Japan, involving soldiers who
were disgruntled about Japan's surrender. As a young novelist, you
were probably afraid of being raked over the coals by the older generation of critics. They tended to be rigorous about matters of historical

verisimilitude, so you found a way around that by portraying the surreal shootout as the delusion of a patient in a mental hospital. The
institutionalized patient—who, as a child, was along for the ride—is
remembering the voices of the soldiers, singing in the truck as they
headed to their doomed insurrection . . . and that's when he begins
to sing the German song.

"However, if you delve deeply enough into your memories, there's
a real-life incident you experienced long before you ever thought of
writing the novella. As you've mentioned, during the four or five days
before Father's death, officers from the Matsuyama regiment kept
stopping by our house to drink sake, and some of them even slept over
in the storehouse next door. At the time, you heard the drunken young
officers singing the song, and it would have stuck in your mind. The
song itself is a Bach cantata, so of course it has nothing whatsoever
to do with the Japanese emperor, but it must have somehow tugged at
your heartstrings, don't you think? And even if you didn't come right
out and say so in the novella, you must have been feeling a visceral
connection to the fervor and excitement of the officers.

"I'm pretty sure you came in here today planning to watch the
rehearsal with a coolly critical eye, but when the rousing chorus began
your face turned bright red and you started to sing along in that high,
squeaky voice. While I was watching you in amazement, I couldn't
help thinking, *This is so intense it's almost scary*. But as I said earlier,
I was feeling deeply moved myself, so the whole thing is rather complicated for me."

I wasn't sure what Asa had found so "scary" and "complicated,"
and I paused for a moment to ponder her choice of words. We were
still sitting there in the gathering dark while outside, Chikashi's tiny
rose garden and the valley beyond it were barely illuminated by the
last remains of daylight. The heavily overcast sky, which had been
threatening to rain since morning, was almost imperceptibly tinted
by traces of a pale, diluted sunset.

After we had shared a contemplative moment, Asa spoke again,
and her concerns became clear. "Now, it's not as if I'm worried that at

this late date my famously liberal brother will be criticized for innocently enjoying the sound of an ultranationalist anthem," she said. "It's just that you're about to embark on what (considering your age) may well turn out to be your final project. I realize your main focus will be on exploring the contents of the red leather trunk, with the help of the Caveman Group, but I can't help wondering what might happen if some echoes of the ultranationalist German song were to show up in the book you ultimately write.

"After the rehearsal Unaiko and I took the young folks to the Japan Rail station in Honmachi, to see them off. Then the two of us—the feisty old lady and Unaiko, the gifted young woman in the prime of life—lingered awhile on the elevated station platform overlooking the picturesque basin of the valley and the mountain range beyond, and we had a very intense conversation. (Incidentally, Unaiko and I have been keeping in touch via email for quite some time, and we agreed to keep the conversation going, like a couple of soul sisters, completely independent of our respective relationships with Masao Anai.)

"As we stood there admiring the view, I confessed to Unaiko that like my brother, who simply couldn't keep from jumping in and singing along with the chorus of young voices earlier today, I, too, was quite stirred by the German song. And I told her the same thing I've been trying to express to you: that the aftermath (to borrow one of your trademark words!) of the Caveman Group's rehearsal has already begun.

"Maybe this afternoon has made me sentimental, but I just want to say how glad I am to have you back in the place where we grew up. And since I now feel certain you're mentally prepared to deal with whatever you may find inside, I'm ready to hand over the red leather trunk at last."

# Chapter 3

# The Red Leather Trunk

## 1

Asa had apparently been listening for the sound of my footsteps. When I arrived at her house near the river, she immediately led me down a hallway to a storage closet. Off to the left, the living-room door stood open and through it I caught a glimpse of a familiar low table with a plate of soft, steamed rice-flour dumplings filled with chestnut jam—which I recognized right away as the handiwork of a long-established sweetshop in the nearby town of Honmachi—already laid out for our tea. Stashed in the closet, next to the discs and the boom box Akari had used for playing CDs during his last visit, was my mother's red leather trunk.

In the eighth year of Showa (that is, 1933), my parents were already married and living in Tokyo, but due to some complications in my father's situation there had been a delay in their plan to return to our village on Shikoku and look after the family interests. My mother decided to go to Shanghai to visit a childhood friend who was married to a Japanese trading-company employee and had just had a baby, and

she ended up staying there for more than a year. Finally my father
went to China to fetch her, and when they returned to Japan my
mother's luggage included the red leather trunk. Even then, the trunk
wasn't new; my mother had bought it at a Japanese-run bookstore
in Shanghai that sold used goods on the side. There was no way of
guessing how old the little suitcase might have been, but after it
came into her possession my mother always took meticulous care
of it. Over time the leather had begun to crack and peel, but the
color was still a deep, rich red. The trunk may have been small, but
it was considerably sturdier than the bags you see young women
toting around nowadays.

"The lock stopped working ages ago," Asa explained. "That's
why it's held together with rope. When Mother died, I took a quick
look at the contents and then put the trunk away, and it hasn't been
opened since. During Mother's lifetime, she used to give it a good
airing once a year. The trunk does have a bit of an antique smell,
though I don't find it unpleasant at all. So, here we are at last. Are
you ready to take a peek?"

"I think I'd rather take the trunk back to the Forest House," I
replied.

"Suit yourself," Asa said. "By the way, Father's papers included
a number of letters from a teacher he especially respected, and they
were always decorated with calligraphy and watercolor paintings.
The notes Father penciled into the margins have faded, but Masao
was saying that if we had color copies made they could end up being
clearer than the originals for reasons I don't really understand. So I
had him go ahead and do that. When the copies are finished, Unaiko
will bring them down from Matsuyama."

# 2

*At last, indeed,* I thought after Asa had dropped me back at the Forest
House. I was finally free to open the red leather trunk and explore

its contents on my own terms. I carried the suitcase upstairs to my study/bedroom, set it down in front of the south-facing window, and untied the rope. The metal fittings that had once attached the lid to the body of the trunk were long gone, and the top slid off with no resistance whatsoever.

There were some large, bulky-looking objects on the bottom, and when I lifted them up the red trunk lurched forward and slammed into my thigh. The heavy things turned out to be three thick books, each bearing the title *The Golden Bough* and the publisher's imprint: Macmillan. When my father was alive, my mother had once remarked that my father's mentor in Kochi was introducing him to books from all over the world, on all sorts of topics. Maybe that was where these had come from. I remembered suddenly that when I was at university I had bought an Iwanami paperback containing an abridged version of *The Golden Bough*, in Japanese translation, but I don't think I ever got around to reading it.

There were no other books in the trunk, so I started off by reading some old journals, an activity that conjured a vivid memory of my mother sitting with her back to me, writing in a small notebook with a metal-nibbed "G pen" she dipped into an inkpot from time to time. On a number of occasions, when there was a temporary lull in the ongoing intrafamilial hostilities and I was on Shikoku for a visit, Asa had secretly borrowed a few of our mother's journals for me to look at (though only after I promised I would never use anything I found in them as fodder for fiction). Our mother apparently knew what Asa was up to, and her silence was a kind of tacit approval. The trunk now contained fifteen volumes of those journals, but I was certain that was only a fraction of the total.

The friend in Shanghai (whom my mother had stayed with for so long that my father had to bring her back) was someone of particular importance to my family. She had grown up as the only child in a mansion on a hill overlooking the village, and she and my mother had been friends for most of their lives. We called her the Shanghai Auntie. The better part of my mother's journal entries consisted of detailed transcriptions of the letters the Shanghai Auntie had sent from China, where she was living after her marriage.

Seeing those old journals again reminded me of my mother's system for keeping me supplied with reading material during the war. Early on I had fallen in love with the children's fantasy novel *The Wonderful Adventures of Nils* and had read it over and over again. My mother used to take some of the thick cotton army socks we received as part of wartime rationing and fashion them into small bags. She would fill the bags with rice and then set out for the nearby cluster of houses, whose occupants were living under perpetual threat of air raids, and she would trade the rice—a precious commodity in those days—for stacks of Iwanami Bunko paperbacks. That was how I came to discover *The Adventures of Huckleberry Finn*, a transformative book that became the cornerstone of my personal Great Wall of Literature.

As for *Nils*, the Swedish classic had been a gift from another childhood friend of my mother's. They had attended the local elementary school together, but then (unlike my mother, who remained in the village) her friend had gone off to an all-girls high school in Matsuyama and later matriculated at a women's university in Tokyo. I learned about this for the first time as an adult, from surreptitiously reading my mother's journals.

When I had originally seen these journals, in my younger days, I had only skimmed the contents, jumping quickly from page to page. Now I was planning to reread them carefully, one by one. After perusing several journals and finding nothing useful, I reached for a newer volume, which was bound in colorfully patterned *chiyogami* paper. To my disappointment, in this journal, too, my mother seemed to be endlessly fixated on wallowing in the feelings of restless nostalgia triggered by the letters she received from the Shanghai Auntie. The entries didn't even touch upon the object of my current quest: information about my father's past, especially the events that transpired in the years leading up to and including 1945. Indeed, it was almost as if my mother had written the journals in such a way as to erase any traces of my father's presence in her daily life.

I realized that I would need to cast a wider net in my subsequent examinations of the red leather trunk, but since I had stayed up until the wee hours of the morning reading my mother's journals, it was after noon the following day when I embarked upon the second phase of my reconnaissance mission.

Because I had laid out the contents of the red leather trunk in roughly organized categories, the various piles had overflowed from the desk onto the bookshelves and even the floor. My father's correspondence, which would ultimately be the main focus of my scrutiny, had not yet returned from the copy shop, so naturally my eye was drawn to the fruits of my mother's secret penchant for journaling. Her private archives included a great many clippings from newspapers and magazines, which had been folded for so many years that they had become brittle and friable. They often disintegrated in my hands when I attempted to smooth out the creases.

I addressed this problem by carefully placing the age-yellowed clippings between random pages of a few of the heavier books from the bottom shelves of the bookcase—for example, the two-volume set of *The Shorter Oxford English Dictionary*. Some of the older clippings were already in shreds, so I patched those relics together with lavish applications of transparent tape. As I went along I quickly skimmed each clipping, then added it to the appropriate pile. The headlines were eclectic, to say the least: LONDON NAVAL-PREPAREDNESS PACT; THE PROBLEM OF INFRINGEMENT ON THE RIGHTS OF THE SUPREME HIGH COMMAND; MAJOR SLUMP IN RAW SILK PRODUCTION; DEBT IN RURAL AGRICULTURAL COMMUNITIES IS NEARLY $42 BILLION. There were articles about other social issues and current events, such as the Musha Incident in Taiwan (or Formosa, as it was known in those days), and all those clippings seemed to be from the year 1930 or thereabouts.

Five years before I was born, my mother was showing a nascent interest in the affairs of the wider world. Evidently the correspondence that began after her cherished friend (the Shanghai Auntie) went off to live in China had been very instructive for my mother. Her education continued when she traveled alone to Shanghai, to visit that friend, and then remained there for much longer than expected. Indeed, if my father hadn't gone to China and bodily dragged my mother home when he did, I would never have been born!

One of the news clippings made reference to a historical event I remembered hearing about from my mother as a bedtime story: a bloody uprising by more than eight hundred aboriginal natives of Formosa, who staged a rebellion armed only with bamboo spears, makeshift cudgels, and wooden poles. In retrospect, it struck me as a strangely sanguinary tale to share with a child, but my mother had presented it factually, as something that really happened a long time ago. Perhaps, I realized now, she had been drawing a parallel with the local farmers' insurrections that were such an important part of our folklore.

Another clipping that caught my eyes was a full-color advertisement for Sapporo beer. The ad, which appeared to have been custom-printed, showed a scantily clad young woman who managed to look both very modern and distinctively Japanese. The image dislodged a recollection from a remote corner of my memory, and I recalled hearing that someone who was a colleague of the founder of the famous beer company was closely connected with the Shanghai Auntie's family, and as a result my mother had happened to make the influential brewer's acquaintance when she was young.

There were also a dozen or so clippings of newspaper articles with more photographs than text, either pertaining to the Shanghai Incident of 1932, or else with headlines like CELEBRATION IN MUKDEN OF THE FOUNDING OF MANCHURIA. One photo showed a quiet procession (too sedate to be called a parade) of bizarrely tall Chinese people. Another clipping bore the stark headline: LINDBERGH BABY FOUND DEAD.

I once read an essay by Maurice Sendak in which he recalled a day in his childhood when he went out for a walk with his parents and happened to pass a newsstand where he glimpsed the horrifying photograph of the kidnapped baby's dead body. (I actually wrote a novel that explored the concept of changelings and was inspired in part by the work of that genius of children's literature.) At the time, I was seized by what I assumed was nothing more than a false or sympathetic memory of the harrowing photo, but I realized now it must have been a genuine recollection of having seen this newspaper clipping at some point during my own childhood.

While I was attempting to put all the clippings in chronological order, guided by the neat pencil notations at the top that gave the newspaper's name and the date (most of which preceded my birth), I began to see a path to getting back on track with the newly resurrected drowning novel. The articles appeared to be wildly disparate, but I thought I discerned a pattern in the way they had been selected. That is to say, I suspected my father's influence must have played a significant role in my mother's evolving interest in political and international affairs, which seemed to be at odds with her own natural inclinations.

So, I decided, I would try to find the relevant accounts either in the letters to my father, or in the drafts of his replies. I would also need to reread my mother's journals, paying close attention to how the entries had changed over the years. With those concrete clues in hand, maybe if I just kept digging—and if I could manage to incorporate the long-held ideas I'd expressed in *The Silent Cry* and had overlaid, in that book, with the area's popular folklore—perhaps I might be able to chronicle my father's life and death as it paralleled and reflected this dark period in Japanese history. The thing is, in his own way my father gave a great deal of thought to the history of the age he lived in, but his rigidly ideological views caused him to plan an action so extreme that it would have been laughable if the outcome hadn't gone beyond mere absurdity to the point of becoming pitiful and, ultimately, fatal.

He set out on the flooded river alone (or with only the other Kogii for company); the boat capsized, and my father was drowned. But surely he didn't die instantly, and while he was being tossed around underwater by the strong current before drawing his last breath, the drowning man (in a scenario that exactly echoed Eliot's poem) must have passed again through the various stages, from youth to adult-hood, of his relatively short life.

Maybe the rapid series of flashbacks would provide a possible structure for my novel: an organic way to recount my father's life story, stage by stage. And when he was finally sucked into the whirlpool, the stirring anthem would be ringing in his ears:

> Da wischt mir die Tränen mein Heiland selbst ab.
> Komm, O Tod, du Schlafes Bruder,
> Komm und führe mich nur fort. . . .

As I was envisioning the scene I found myself singing along in German—sotto voce and, at least to my ears, not screechily at all.

# 3

The next day as I was sitting in my study, surrounded by the con-tents of the red leather trunk, Masao Anai detached himself from the younger members of his troupe (they were hard at work again, moving furniture from place to place) and poked his head through the door.

"I don't mean to put any pressure on you," he said puckishly, "but I can't help wondering whether you've found anything interest-ing so far."

"Your curiosity is only natural," I replied in the same playful tone. "I mean, you have a stake in this, too. But I'm afraid I'm still mired in sorting through the materials and trying to put them in order."

Masao grinned. "The guys and I have been doing hard physi-cal labor since early this morning, while our female counterparts were cooking up some new strategies," he said. "Speaking of which, Unaiko mentioned that she's hoping to be able to steal a few minutes of your time later today. She was originally planning to go back up to Matsuyama and take care of some business after dropping off her colleagues, and then come back here. But apparently when she called the stationery shop to check on the pages we'd left to be copied, she ended up getting into a dispute over the unexpectedly high prices they wanted to charge for color, so it looks as if I'll have to go there myself to straighten out the misunderstanding. I'll take the young ladies with me, but Unaiko will stay behind."

A short while later, I went downstairs and found Unaiko waiting for me in the newly rearranged great room. We sat down in a couple of armchairs and then, wasting no time on the usual formulaic pleasant-ries, she cut right to the chase. "It's about the rehearsal you were kind enough to watch the other day," she said. "I've been wondering what you thought about it, and Asa said I should ask you directly, so here I am! I gather Asa already spoke to you about some of her concerns?"

"Yes, she did," I answered. "But it's not as if she grilled me about my impressions or anything. I mostly just listened to what she had to say."

"I see," Unaiko responded with a vigorous nod of her head. Her samurai-child ponytail bobbed up and down. "Actually, Asa seems to think the best approach might be to start by sharing my own thoughts. She was saying that over the years you've grown accustomed to having people listen to you while you hold forth at great length, so it can be difficult to get you to stop talking long enough for anyone else to get a word in edgewise.

"But seriously, look at Masao Anai—he's totally wrapped up in your novels, to the point where he's in the process of trying to dra-matize your entire canon. At the same time, he's able to view your work with the critical eye of a member of the younger generation. His admiration for your books seems to be tempered by an awareness of their flaws, and I think that's part of his reason for wanting to convert them into theater, using his own methodology.

"When I speak about Masao's 'critical admiration,' the same ambivalence has characterized my own feelings about you, Mr. Choko, but there's a degree of divergence there as well. Like the other day I was immersed in the dramatization of *The Day He Himself Shall Wipe My Tears Away*, but on another level I still felt detached and somewhat skeptical. To be honest, during the rehearsals and afterward, too, those conflicted feelings just kept on getting stronger. In the scene where the soldiers are setting out from the mountain valley, heading toward their doomed insurrection, the child is singing along with the grown-ups. After the song ends, the person who's playing the role of the child in his adult form shrieks the father's Japanese interpretation of those lyrics like a crazy person—which, of course, he is.

> *"The emperor will wipe away my tears with his own hand /*
> *Come quickly, O death, death that is the sibling of sleep / Come*
> *quickly / The emperor himself will wipe away my tears with his*
> *own hand.*

"To tell you the truth, I really don't care for that kind of over-wrought verbiage. In fact, it really creeps me out. And when we were prepping for our first rehearsals, months ago, I asked Masao a bunch of questions. 'Shall we perform this with a critical edge? What about the various characters: the young boy with his high, childish voice; the soldiers, singing the boisterous chorus; and the leader, who's in the throes of terminal cancer and riding in the funky wooden chariot? Should they all project an aura of comical grotesquerie, or should we play it straight?'

"Masao answered my questions with a question of his own: 'Well, what about when you're playing the boy's mother?' I wasn't sure what he was getting at, so I asked, 'Do you mean that I should just put the emphasis on her sarcastically critical words?'

"And then Masao (who tends to be a bit volatile at times) suddenly got angry and went off on a seemingly unrelated tangent. 'Why do I have to be the messenger boy for Choko's infatuation with the whole concept of postwar democracy?' he demanded. He calmed down after a moment, as he always does, and then he went out of his way to help me understand his feelings. He said, 'For Choko, along with a kind of doctrinaire embracing of the postwar strain of anti-ultranationalism, there's also a deeper, darker, more nuanced Japanese sensibility. That's why I've taken such an interest in *The Day*

*He Himself Shall Wipe My Tears Away*, and I have a hunch the same duality will show up in the drowning novel as well, once it's finished.'

"As for me," Unaiko went on, "when we were performing *Wipe My Tears Away* for you the other day, I found myself unexpectedly moved. I could tell from Asa's response that she and I were experiencing similar feelings. If you asked me what I found most affecting I would have to say it was when you suddenly started to sing along with the German song so passionately. It's not as if I was suddenly swept away by a wave of emperor-worshipping nationalism through the medium of Bach's cantata. No, I'm coming from a place of fundamental aversion to that type of thinking, so my activities with the Caveman Group are actually an ongoing way of dealing with my antipathy. (You'll understand this better in a moment, after I tell you my own little story.)

"I was aware that you've taken a strong public stand against the resurgence of ultranationalism, especially through your essays and other writings. Even so, for you to undergo such an intense emotional experience as a child, and to revisit it now through the medium of a stage play . . . that must have had a major impact on you. I know it did on me, because it led me to an interest in you and your work that was different from the feelings I had before—and I think that's also because Masao's dramatization of your book has so much raw power.

"As I mentioned earlier, there's a relevant story I'd like to share with you today, about an experience that made a profound impression on me. It happened at Yasukuni Shrine. Don't get me wrong; I'm not some big authority on the place. It's just . . . when I was seventeen years old my aunt happened to take me along when she went to pray at that famous (and, needless to say, controversial) shrine. That was my first visit and my last. I've never gone back there, but that one experience turned out to be a rather momentous event in my life. I'd like to tell you what happened, if you don't mind."

I gave an encouraging nod.

"My aunt was married to a man who had spent his entire career as a civil servant in the Ministry of Education," Unaiko began. "I don't know whether she was influenced by her husband, or vice versa, but by early middle age they were both right-wing zealots. My aunt's grandfather was a lieutenant colonel in the navy who died in the war, and that's probably why she took me with her to Yasukuni Shrine, seventeen years ago. It wasn't as if she had been invited there for a scheduled ceremony to honor the war dead, though; when we got to the gates we had to stand in a long line with all the other people who had come to pay their respects, or sightsee, or whatever, and we slowly shuffled through the precincts of the shrine like everybody else. After a while we came to the main altar, and my aunt started ringing the bell and clapping her hands to attract the attention of the gods. Then she started praying for the soul of her grandfather, the departed war hero. This ritual went on for an inordinately long time, and I stood next to her, bored out of my teenage mind, staring at the ground. I was startled by the sound of a loud voice, and when I looked up I saw that the area, which had been flooded with people, was rapidly emptying out. Even now, all these years later, the memory of the scene that unfolded before my eyes is totally vivid, as if it had happened this morning.

"The biggest flag I had ever seen was waving wildly right before my eyes; a vast expanse of white cotton with a bloodred rising sun in the center. I recognized it immediately as the Japanese national flag, of course, but it was so abnormally large that I was frightened. The person who was manipulating the gigantic flag, holding the flagpole in front of his body with both hands, was a young man dressed in the black uniform of a student. As he waved it back and forth, the humongous rectangle of white cotton with the bright red sphere in the middle was the only thing I could see. The flag never stopped moving, and I caught a glimpse of a second man behind the flag waver. He was dressed in an old-style military uniform and soldier's cap (the kind they wear in the desert, with hanging flaps to protect the neck from the sun), and he was brandishing a long sword above his head. Both men seemed to be reciting some sort of vow or pledge, but even though they were slowly chanting the same words, over and over, I couldn't figure out what they were saying.

"At that moment I suddenly began to throw up all over the place. My aunt pulled something—maybe a handkerchief—out of the folds of her kimono and tried to cover the lower half of my face, but I just went on endlessly spewing vomit in every direction, with tremendous velocity. My aunt took off the short jacket she was wearing over her kimono and draped it around my upper body, which was covered with the partially digested remains of my breakfast. And then (rather coldly, I thought) she frog-marched me toward the exit. The soldiers must have thought that I'd shown extreme irreverence by being sick on sacred ground, even involuntarily, because they followed close behind us with their long swords drawn. My aunt and I ended up running away from our pursuers at full speed, as if our very lives depended on it. And I know I didn't imagine this melodramatic scene, because my aunt seems to remember it the same way.

"So that's my story about Yasukuni Shrine. We made it home safely, more or less, and I won't go into what happened afterward, but for the past seventeen years I haven't been able to stop thinking about that bizarre and frightening experience.

"After graduating from high school I got an insignificant little job, and then I sort of bounced around from one entry-level position to another. It was a coworker at one of those forgettable jobs who took me to see a stage performance by the Caveman Group, and it came as a total revelation. *Is it really possible to live like this?* I asked myself. I knew I had to try, so I began to study drama in my spare time while continuing to work at my boring day job.

"But even during that busy and exciting period in my life I kept on thinking about the incident at Yasukuni Shrine, which was still festering in my memory like a psychic cancer. The truth is, Mr. Choko, at the time I wasn't very familiar with your work. However, Masao was in the ongoing process of creating plays based on your fiction, and as I began to get drawn into the productions myself, I decided it was time to read your novella *The Day He Himself Shall Wipe My Tears Away*. And that, more than anything, was my first real encounter with the realm you've created in your books.

"I think you have a pretty good idea of what's transpired since then," she went on. "As you know, in his late teens Masao was taken under the creative wing of your late brother-in-law, Goro Hanawa. I gather he also met your wife through that connection. According to Masao, Goro Hanawa used to tell him he ought to familiarize himself with your novel *Adventures in Everyday Life*, because when Goro eventually turned that book into a screenplay, the only actor who could possibly play the part of the picaresque protagonist would be Masao. As you know, the film never got made, but the upshot was that Masao has been constantly reading and rereading your books ever since, while a more typical member of his generation might have dismissed you as an irrelevant fossil from the past. (No offense.) Masao's immersion in your work ended up bearing fruit in the form of his award-winning production of *The Day He Himself Shall Wipe My Tears Away*, and now he's busy trying to create a compressed retrospective of your novels in dramatic form. He even moved our theater troupe's base of operations from Tokyo to Matsuyama, to be closer to the area where so many of your books take place.

"No sooner had we moved down here than Masao started visiting Asa, and he often took me along. Asa was very welcoming, and she totally got what we were doing. She let us hold workshops at the Forest House, and that was when she told us you would be coming to spend some time here. She didn't have a lot of details, but she did say you'd be sorting through a bunch of materials your mother had left behind, as part of the research for a partially written book that might turn out to be the final chapter of your life as a fiction writer.

"When Asa shared the news, Masao was super excited. 'Aha!' he said. 'That must be the long-lost drowning novel!' Asa hadn't mentioned the project by name, but Masao seems to have developed a sort of sixth sense when it comes to you and your work.

"As for me, I couldn't help thinking how great it would be if the author of the original *Wipe My Tears Away* were living nearby. I had this idea that if I could talk to you and hear your thoughts about Yasukuni Shrine and ultranationalism in general, then maybe I would be able to figure out what significance that whole ideological can of worms has for me. Since I'm the type of person who likes to translate thought into action right away, I decided to plead with you directly to join us down here as soon as possible. That's how I came to be lying in wait to ambush you the other day in Tokyo. Of course, due to totally unforeseeable circumstances, my ploy was more successful than I could ever have imagined!"

*Yes,* I thought. *Early one morning on the cycling path beside the canal near my house, I suddenly swooned and started to fall backward, only to be caught from behind by an unseen Good Samaritan. A moment later I found myself in a sitting position, with my entire weight supported by one of this invisible stranger's strong, resilient thighs. I have to confess that I've thought more than once about how odd the tableau would have appeared to a passerby who didn't understand the situation.* I didn't say any of this out loud, though.

"Anyway, for me," Unaiko continued, "putting aside what Masao said about your being totally supportive of the postwar democratic reforms to the point of being doctrinaire, I was slightly concerned about Masao's statement that the Japanese people also have a 'deeper, darker sensibility.' But then when I saw you getting totally carried away and singing along with the German lyrics of the Bach song during the rehearsal of our play . . . well, seeing another side of you was like a revelation, and I started to think about you in a whole different light. And that's why I wanted to share this piece of my past with you today. I'll be grateful for any illumination you can provide."

I didn't feel ready to tackle "that whole ideological can of worms" just then, so I skirted the issue by offering a compliment. "Asa has never been the type to jump into projects with people she barely knows," I said. "Although on the rare occasions when it does happen, she tends to be rather gung ho. To be perfectly candid, I have to say that I'm intrigued by her decision to team up with you."

"Masao was saying that Asa had done her part to support your work by staying behind in the village and looking after your mother," Unaiko said. "Even in our brief acquaintance, I've come to share his feeling that Asa is the kind of person who would go the distance for anyone she cares about."

"That's very true," I said. "But Asa seems totally committed to backing you, even though it isn't exactly clear what direction you're heading in, and as her brother I'm interested in seeing how everything will turn out."

"It's very comforting for me to have Asa here, cheering us on," Unaiko said. "But the thing is, even I don't have a clear idea of where I'm headed. Masao's the one who mentored me, of course, and I'll continue to be involved with his theater projects for the foreseeable future at least, so I expect I'll go on benefiting from Asa's support and kindness as well.

"However, I have a feeling that at some point my path will deviate from Masao's, and I'll strike out on my own. I mean, after all, Masao is the boss of the Caveman Group, and he's a guy as well, right? I think Asa takes a rather sanguine view of the male dynamic. Oh, that reminds me—the other day she said, 'Listen, Unaiko, you really shouldn't expect my brother to do too much, even if the going gets tough. But I want you to know you can always depend on me.' She added that you tend to help people primarily by lending your skills as a writer. (And, I gathered, as an occasional screenwriter? That sounds exciting!) She told me that I need to respect that invisible line and not ask too much of you.

"I totally understand the need for boundaries," Unaiko went on, "but there are some other things I still haven't been able to get a handle on . . . I mean, I do talk to Asa a lot, and I have a sense of what's going on with you just from comments she's made in passing. Even when we first met, Asa used to talk about you all the time. One time she said, 'My brother may come across as an easygoing sort of person, but on another level he has a tendency to brood over his mistakes. He's constantly tormented by regrets and misgivings about the past: deeds not done, roads not taken, and so on. He's been that way for as long as I can remember, going back to childhood. I'm the same way. However, since I've gotten involved with the Caveman Group, and especially as my relationship has grown with the female members of the troupe—and with you especially, Unaiko—I've begun to feel as if I should be able to overcome that undesirable character trait. I've noticed young women nowadays don't appear to have any regrets about anything, or any awareness of the possibility that their present actions might be sowing the seeds for future regrets. That's perfectly natural, of course, since they probably haven't had time to do anything they regret. They seem to feel completely fine about everything: clean and true and pure of heart. Since my eyes have been opened to that approach, I've been trying to adjust my own attitude accordingly.'

"I hope you don't mind my quoting this long monologue, Mr. Choko, but your sister's words made a huge impression on me. Asa went on to say, 'If you can live in such a liberated way, all the more reason for someone like me to try to do the same, even at this late date. I'm not getting any younger, and I may not even have time to properly regret the foolish things I'm doing right now, so I'll just have to follow the lead of my young female role models. Yes, I've made up my mind: from now on, my life will be a regret-free zone!'

"And after that, Asa did something truly touching. She made a solemn promise to stick with me artistically, even if it meant ending up on the opposite side from you, her own brother. As you know, Asa doesn't make a habit of touching the person she's talking to, so the image of her reaching out and putting her little hand on my shoulder as she spoke those words—just like this—is permanently seared into my memory."

## 4

The following day, while I was reshuffling the materials from the red leather trunk that I'd laid out around my study, pausing periodically to speed-read whatever happened to catch my eye, Masao stopped by to drop off the color copies Asa had ordered from the shop in Matsuyama.

"It was terribly kind of you to grant Unaiko a private audience yesterday," he said with exaggerated formality. "To tell you the truth," he went on, lapsing back into his normal speech patterns, "I was sweating it a little bit. Originally I thought that if Unaiko had a bee in her bonnet about our dramatization of *Wipe My Tears Away*—and if she was just going to criticize the play, as she's done in the past, as an orgy of Yasukuni Shrine–worshipping ultranationalism or whatever— then it would have been a waste of time for her to talk to you about it. That's what I was thinking in the beginning. But the other day during the rehearsal, we came to the scene where the young officers and the schoolboy are on their way to the ill-fated insurrection and they spontaneously start singing a song about the *Heiland*—who is on the same exalted level as our emperor—praising him as a savior. To everyone's amazement, you were so moved that you began to sing along with the chorus, and Unaiko told me afterward that when she saw your reaction it made her curious about what you were feeling in that moment. Oh, and another thing she said, after your meeting, was that since you listened so patiently to her story, the fundamental mistrust she used to feel toward you has disappeared (even though I gather you didn't exactly answer her questions). Apparently your attentiveness came as a pleasant surprise because Asa had told us that one thing you and Unaiko have in common is that neither of you is very good at listening to what other people have to say!

"Speaking of listening," Masao continued, "my dramatic method involves incorporating a variety of voices and ways of thinking into every production, and then bringing the collaborative synergy to life onstage. It may seem paradoxical to say this, since I'm supposed to be the director and the man in charge, but Unaiko's artistic input has been increasingly valuable to our group as we develop our own trademark style."

"Considering she was in her late twenties when she joined your group, it's rather remarkable that Unaiko has learned to express her own sensibilities in such a short time," I said.

"Yes, she's truly special in that respect. I'm not sure why, but Unaiko has a powerful ability to influence not only her juniors but also women who are older than she is. It's been only five or six years since Unaiko became a full-fledged member of the Caveman Group, and she has already created her own performance piece, with the help of the younger women in the troupe. It runs for about half an hour, and when they performed it in public it was very well received. The piece is called *Tossing the Dead Dogs*. You may remember having heard the title at some point?"

"I do indeed," I said.

"Of course, this was back when our group was still based in the suburbs of Tokyo," Masao went on. "Our young members used to get up early every morning to do their outdoor exercise routines: walking, running, calisthenics to build core strength, and so on. (I know you've made a habit of going for walks, so you'll understand.) Anyway, this was during the time when the trend of constructing local autonomous townships on the outskirts of Tokyo—what they call 'bed towns'—was just getting off the ground. At the same time, there was a major boom in dog ownership among the residents of these new suburban communities, and some of the young people from our troupe started to clash with the ladies who were out for a leisurely stroll with their dogs. Our members were trying to get in a serious workout on the training course, but the dog-walking ladies were constantly stopping to gossip right in the middle of the track, blocking traffic for the oncoming runners. Naturally, the athletes were annoyed, and they complained about this basic lack of consideration. They didn't take their objections any further than that, but Unaiko, who was there both for her own training and as a group leader, observed the behavior of the women and their dogs with great interest. She had a fantasy about how the problem of the lollygagging ladies with their dogs might be resolved with a judicious show of power, and she turned that high-concept idea into a performance piece. Parts of the dialogue were probably based on things our young colleagues had actually said, but Unaiko gets all the credit for deciding to have the play focus on the dog-walking ladies and their over-the-top reactions to the confrontation. Her portrayal of the escalating hostilities between the entitled ladies with their froufrou dogs and the guys from our theater troupe, as the two factions hurled increasingly scurrilous insults back and forth, was nothing less than masterful. Because of the way the stage was arranged, our actors received a lot of vocal encouragement from a cheering section of ringers we'd planted in the audience. As for the group of women onstage, each clutching her own little boutique dog, their next step was to fling plastic bags full of dog poop in the general direction of our contingent. And then, as things continued to heat up, the women began throwing the dogs themselves at their adversaries, and that was the dramatic climax of the piece. Needless to say, both the 'excrement' and the 'dogs' were stage props: totally fake.

"The title Unaiko gave the piece, *Tossing the Dead Dogs*, is derived from the climactic ending. That title cracks me up—ha ha ha! I still can't help laughing every time I hear it."

At this point, I volunteered a dog-related anecdote of my own. Back in the 1960s, during the time when the popular protests in Europe against the Vietnam War were reaching a crescendo, Günter Grass had published a novel in the form of an on-site report about the youth movement in West Germany. One of the book's most harrowing sections, which I still remembered vividly, told of a young student called Scherbaum who was threatening to burn his pet dachshund alive in public as a consciousness-raising demonstration against the war.

"If a university student had actually done such a thing in Berlin—I mean, presumably it wouldn't have been beyond the realm of possibility—it probably would have created a major uproar," Masao said. "Our group's production of *Tossing the Dead Dogs* provoked quite a bit of protest from dog lovers' groups, too, and as the person in charge of the theater group I was called onto the carpet to defend the piece against the absurd charges that it somehow condoned or even promoted cruelty to dogs. I tried to be circumspect about expressing my personal feelings, but Unaiko and her cohorts weren't nearly so restrained, and they couldn't resist the temptation to speak out. Even after I decided to pull the controversial piece and substitute something less incendiary they were there in the theater, lobbying for their right to freedom of expression. They were so mad at me for knuckling under to outside pressure that I wouldn't have been surprised if they'd hurled some 'feces' and 'dead dogs' at me—I'm sure they must have wanted to! It was a very difficult and stressful time, but fortunately the storm eventually blew over, and we actually ended up receiving some positive publicity as a result."

"Did it ever reach the point where it looked as if the Caveman Group might have to disband?" I asked.

"Oh, no, it never went that far. The male members of the troupe, in particular, found the whole turn of events immensely amusing, and they seemed to get a kick out of all the excitement and notoriety. As for Unaiko, she's someone who lives by the maxim 'Never stop striving.' It's just one of the things that make her so unique, and so powerful."

"My sister, Asa, has some similar traits, and surely that's part of the reason she and Unaiko have hit it off so well," I remarked. "I'm quite certain that whatever Unaiko chooses to do from now on, Asa will try to help in any way she can."

"Unaiko has definitely found a strong ally in Asa," Masao said, "though I can't help thinking that at some point the dynamic duo may try to sway you to their alternative vision of this production. They may very well win the battle in the end—nothing's set in stone. But one thing I'm sure of after talking this over with Unaiko is that I've finally found the key to the retrospective dramatization of your novels I'm working on now.

"As I've mentioned, my plan is to layer scenes from your books with the interviews in which we'll be discussing your work. Even with the supernatural figure of Kogii cropping up throughout the piece as a sort of visual continuo, the focus will still be quite vague and scattered. However, Unaiko has a different idea. She thought we might try superimposing the Kogii theme directly over your progress on the novel you're planning to write about your father."

"Both approaches sound promising," I said noncommittally. "Let's wait and see how things develop, shall we?"

"I hope Unaiko doesn't inadvertently cross any of your invisible lines—or 'friendly barriers,' to use Asa's term," Masao said playfully. "I mean, I have to admit that her willfulness and adventurous spirit haven't caused any major problems for the activities of the Caveman Group—at least not yet. And I'm pleased to report that she hasn't broached the idea of staging an abbreviated performance of *Tossing the Dead Dogs* on the hallowed grounds of Yasukuni Shrine! Seriously, though, assuming you're willing to cooperate, we're all feeling very optimistic about forging ahead with the dramatization of the drowning novel, with Unaiko leading the way.

"But of course," Masao concluded, shooting me a significant look, "we're acutely aware that the whole project hinges on one crucial thing: what you find in the red leather trunk."

# Chapter 4

# Joke Accompli

## 1

The moment Masao Anai handed me the envelopes, I began to feel uneasy. They weren't nearly as bulging as I would have expected, and they were also suspiciously light. All the pages fit into three large square envelopes: both the color copies and the originals, which consisted mostly of folio-size sheets of handmade Japanese *washi* paper decorated with watercolor paintings, illustrations, and calligraphic annotations. (Adding such impromptu embellishments to correspondence was a long-standing tradition among cultured people in Japan.) The photocopies were so precise that they had even captured the attractively blurry places where the ink or paint had run, but I was disappointed because I had been hoping more than anything that the envelope would contain some actual letters, but there wasn't a single one.

I had more than one memory of catching a glimpse of my father in his little study—a cramped, narrow hideaway where he engaged in activities that had nothing to do with running our family business.

He would pick up a large piece of paper covered with pictures and inscriptions, then lift it above his forehead with both hands in the manner of someone giving thanks to the gods, and I noticed that he always seemed to treat the missives from his mentor in Kochi with particular reverence.

"I wonder what sort of stuff is written on those pages," I remember saying to my mother.

"Things that probably couldn't be understood by the likes of you and me!" was her crisp response, but I thought I heard a distinct undertone of awe. Much later, when I'd all but forgotten about having mentioned the pages, my mother finally offered an explanation.

"There were some Chinese characters on those pages that even your father didn't recognize, but he was able to find them in volume one of Morohashi Sensei's kanji dictionary," she said one day out of the blue, adding that once the renowned lexicographer had finished the other twelve volumes of his magnum opus there probably wouldn't be a single character or word you couldn't find in them.

My response was to say, "If every word anyone could think of writing is already listed in the dictionary, then nobody can ever say anything new. Where's the fun in that?"

"When I told Papa what you said, he laughed," she informed me later. "And then he joked, 'Maybe someday our son will write something that can't be found in any dictionaries!'"

As I understood it, all those artistic-looking letters were written on paper my father had made from paperbush bark the government's official money-printing bureau had deemed substandard and returned to us. His decision to use the rejected bark struck me as alarmingly subversive, but my mother just said: "Of course, 'substandard' isn't exactly the verdict we were hoping for, but your father turned it into a positive, saying happily, 'Don't worry, I think I can still make some good paper out of this!'" I got the sense that my mother had been a bit perplexed by my father's cheerful reaction.

Every time my father would send a batch of the paper to his guru in Kochi, whom he held in the highest esteem, the Kochi Sensei (as he was known around our house) would turn those pages into works of art by covering them with paintings and calligraphy. He would then mail them back, often accompanied by letters written on the rougher paper, handcrafted from mulberry or pink mullein, which my father shared with his mentor from time to time along with the sheets he had made from rejected paperbush bark.

Sometimes those letters included little postscripts addressed to my mother. Once when I asked her what they said, she replied coolly, "Oh, he was just thanking me for the gifts of dried matsutake and goby and sweetfish." Her tone seemed to suggest she wasn't the Kochi Sensei's biggest fan, for reasons that (I'm speculating in retrospect here) probably had to do with his far-right political views.

I stuck the big envelopes Masao had given me on a bookshelf, still feeling shocked that they hadn't contained a single copy of the letters my father had received—just copies of the envelopes those letters had arrived in. All my father's replies were missing as well. His usual routine when he received a letter was to scribble a draft of his response, which he then attached with a rubber band to the envelope containing the relevant correspondent's missive. (My mother used to praise him for this efficient filing system.) Those drafts had somehow vanished along the way, along with the letters.

*Oh well,* I thought, making an effort to look on the bright side. *I'll just try to make the best of what I have.* I dragged a chair over to the shelves and continued perusing the contents of the envelopes, one photocopied page at a time. As the afternoon light flooding the mountain valley began to fade, I could feel the enthusiasm I'd felt when I first started working, shortly before noon, ebbing away as well. I struggled to remain hopeful and upbeat, but as the sun sank out of sight at the end of the disappointing day my spirits plummeted at an equally rapid rate.

\* \* \*

## 2

By the time Asa stopped by to deliver my evening meal, the last shreds of optimism had been replaced by full-blown melancholia. One quick glance at my gloomy expression was all it took for my sister to suss out my state of mind, and she observed me closely as I picked up my chopsticks and, without a word, dug into the food she had placed on the table in front of me.

After a while, in a tone of voice that was neutral rather than sympathetic, Asa began to speak. "While Mother still had her eyesight, she used to like to tidy up the clutter in her life from time to time," she said. "And whenever she embarked on that task, I would watch while she attacked our father's archived correspondence with a vengeance. It seemed to be a matter of particular concern to her, and I would think, *At this rate it won't be long until all the letters have been destroyed and there's nothing left but the envelopes* . . ."

"Well, I suppose it was inevitable that Mother's bouts of intensive housekeeping would have a few casualties," I said, trying to sound nonchalant. "I've been thinking a lot about it, and honestly, I really don't feel as though I can complain about the choices she made. I mean, by rights all those things belonged to her, and we knew that she'd gotten appraisals from antiques dealers and used-book stores and had learned they had no value to speak of. It's just that for the longest time I've been wanting to check out the contents of the trunk, and it's become a bit of an obsession, to tell the truth. I was hoping against hope that if I could examine Father's correspondence, journals, and so on (assuming such things even existed), those materials might provide some concrete evidence about the things I've been speculating about for decades—and might even resolve the lingering questions and ambiguities, once and for all."

"Really, though," Asa said, "doesn't it seem likely that Mother knew you wouldn't be able to write the book without some kind of spark to jump-start your imagination? At the end, after she had thrown away the letters, maybe the only reason she kept some of the envelopes was because the senders' names rang a nostalgic bell for her."

"From what I've seen, you're right; this batch of papers doesn't contain a single document that could be used to jump-start my imagination, as you put it," I said. "I've already accepted that, reluctantly, and I'm even finding it rather odd that I still haven't managed to give up daydreaming about Father after all these years. I've indulged in conjecture about what might have been going on while Father was alive, up through the events I chronicled in my partial draft of the drowning novel. (The truth is, there have been times when I've wondered whether what happened in the middle of that stormy night might just be a figment of my imagination.) As you know, I put some of the wilder scenarios into *The Day He Himself Shall Wipe My Tears Away*. I think for Mother, choosing to burn the letters was her way of smashing my wishful imaginings to bits, as if she were saying, *See? Your ridiculous theories about your father being a hero really don't have a leg to stand on*. And now I've finally been forced to give up for the simple reason that I don't have a single clue or scrap of evidence to support my position. If this had been a court case, it would have been a decisive victory for our mother."

"Well," Asa said, "from my point of view the strange thing is that it's taken you so long to reach this realization. Better late than never, I suppose. The fact is, I've completely ignored the red leather trunk during the ten years since Mother's death because I was dreading the Pandora's box effect opening the trunk might have on you, and I didn't want to do anything to cause you pain. However, while Mother was still alive I did have a few chances to read bits and pieces of the papers stored in the trunk. There were times when she would suddenly open the trunk and fish something out, as if she were possessed by some ancient memory, and I was always standing nearby, peeking over her shoulder. That's how I knew she had started burning the papers to ashes on an old compost heap behind the house. She never told me what she was tossing into the flames, or why, but if I showed the slightest concern she would say something like 'Oh, this is just some rubbish I don't need to hang on to anymore.' I thought it was perfectly reasonable that Mother would continue those periodic purges as she embarked on the second half of her very long life. And it was clear those weren't spur-of-the-moment decisions by any means; she was obviously determined to tidy up the past, a few chapters at a time.

"In your work to date, you've portrayed Father as a grotesquely exaggerated character, almost a cartoon—sometimes ludicrous, sometimes tragic, sometimes a bit heroic—but really, your take on him has been all over the map. In other words, for you, there was no clarity so there could be no absolution or closure, either. I think while Mother may have appeared to be systematically destroying your dreams, she was also trying to be true to her late husband, in her own way. I suspect that she burned a lot of papers after I moved out of her house. Maybe she was upset by the content of Father's correspondence with some of his more eccentric cohorts, or perhaps she was just trying to protect her dead husband against any more of what she perceived as the defamatory caricaturing in *Wipe My Tears Away*.

"For me, right now, seeing you laid so low really does make me feel sorry for you, but at the same time it also confirms my belief that Mother did the right thing. The ten years since she passed away should have served as a sort of cooling-off period, and by now you ought to be able to deal with these things in a rational, levelheaded manner. Even if you're in low spirits, you know what they say about people in our age group: 'For an older person, there's a thin line between reasonably copacetic and downright depressed.' So I'm sure you'll get over this disappointment before too long.

"When I gave Unaiko and her colleagues the partial manuscript of your drowning novel," Asa went on, "I kept the index cards that were in the same bundle, and I've been reading them. As you probably remember, they contain little sketches or vignettes about incidents you witnessed, such as when the young officers came to our place for a get-together, or when the enlisted men (who were even younger) took you out in the boat and showed you how to operate the tiller. In the notes, you seem to have somehow conflated those memories with a vague recollection of what happened on the night of the massive flood. The section where you describe how Father's boat gets swept away by the current seems to be written more or less realistically, and it's entertaining the way those events are layered with your patented flights of fancy about seeing your doppelgänger and so on. But somehow it didn't ring true, and I couldn't help thinking how much Mother would have hated that sort of ungrounded narrative.

"Look, as long as we're being candid, I'll admit that I thought it was pretty willful of Mother to take such a radical approach to 'tidying up' the contents of the red leather trunk. But I honestly don't believe she did it with malice aforethought, for the express purpose of destroying your plan to someday finish writing the drowning novel. If that had been her intention, she could have just told me to take the trunk and chuck it into the river at high tide, and that would have been the end of the story.

"Listen, I'm about to say something shamelessly sentimental, but I believe Mother really did love you. And as for the drowning novel you were always so preoccupied with, I think she ended up feeling that you should be free to complete it according to your own artistic vision. She wanted you to realize your perception of our father was mistaken, and she thought you should keep that in mind while you were writing the book. For her, those feelings were probably tantamount to love—which would mean she also loved our poor, misguided father as well. His life wasn't exactly short on folly, but the thing Mother found the most foolish of all was the way he allowed himself to be led down the garden path of political extremism by his so-called mentor. Because of that connection, when the war finally came to an end our father got tangled up in the stupid, futile plot with the officers from Matsuyama. So it's only natural that Mother would decide the most prudent course of action would be to eliminate the hard evidence pertaining to that particular bit of madness by throwing out any incriminating correspondence. Don't you agree? It's also possible that Mother burned those letters, over time, because she felt sorry for Papa for having been such a gullible fool. I mean, there were still lots of empty envelopes, right? When I was doing my summer housecleaning one year, I read one of those letters—just one. It was very friendly and congenial, with the writer teasing our father (whom he addressed as 'older brother') about being a member of the 'elite mountain battalion' and so on. Even if a plan for some sort of uprising to protest the end of the war really did exist, I suspect Papa might have been the only person who believed in it, and I can't help feeling as if the only thing the plan produced was his dead body, drowned in the river.

"To Mother's way of thinking (which seems quite reasonable to me), there was no point in your chronicling the ill-fated scheme in a book, but despite those strong feelings she at least hung on to the envelopes. As for me, I felt honor bound to take care of the red leather trunk and what was left of its contents, in accordance with Mother's final wishes."

"You're right," I said. "I've been nursing my own illusions and fantasies about our father for a very long time, and all this information you're sharing now is news to me."

"You know, during the three years after you published *The Silent Cry* you were writing constantly," Asa said. "You made clean copies of the pages you'd drafted of the drowning novel and sent them to Mother along with the index cards we've been talking about. She wrote to me in Kyoto, where I was living at the time, saying basically: *Please come home as soon as possible and help me read this stuff. I can't make head or tail of it on my own!*

"So I rushed home on the train that same night. When I wondered out loud why you would send our mother fragments of a book you had barely started writing, she said astutely you probably couldn't proceed any further without the materials in the red leather trunk, and you must be hoping she would grant you access to the trove. I said to Mother, 'I think you'd better refuse,' and she replied that after reading the pages you'd sent, she had reached the same conclusion. Then when I wrote to let you know what we'd decided, you accepted our verdict so meekly I could hardly believe it. You even said that since your hopes of gaining access to the red leather trunk had been dashed, we should go ahead and burn the partial manuscript you had sent. That made Mother really happy, but as for burning your work, she said, 'I will do no such thing—that would be a terrible waste! I'll just stick those pages in the red leather trunk. They'll be the first new additions in twenty years, at least.' The only other time I can ever remember seeing her so cheerful was when Akari, in spite of his disabilities, managed to compose an amazing piece of music called 'The Marvels of the Forest,' and he sent her a recording of it.

"But anyhow, about a year later, you published *The Day He Himself Shall Wipe My Tears Away*. Mother was too shocked to put together a coherent sentence, but when I relayed her strong objections to the novella your response was to say that anyone who read the book would surely realize it was meant to be a work of fiction—and as I, Asa, should know better than anyone, you had written it without recourse to the materials in the red leather trunk. You followed up with an explanatory letter, admitting you'd turned Papa into a total caricature and pointing out that the book was equally merciless toward the character of the son, who represented you. 'Self-critical to the point of exaggeration' was how you put it, as I recall.

"As for the mother's calm, critical observations, she was clearly being presented as the lone voice of sanity, but that cold comfort didn't mitigate her extreme loathing for your book. Mother and I both had the distinct feeling that this glib, self-critical writer, who came across as a full-fledged Tokyoite, wasn't the same person we used to call Kogii. We simply didn't recognize you anymore. At any rate, that's how we came to be estranged from you for such a long time. Mother suffered terribly when it happened, and for years afterward as well."

When I didn't respond, my younger sister began to cry. Her face was deeply flushed, and I was reminded that our mother used to cry in the same open, red-faced way, making no attempt to hide her vulnerability behind her hand. Asa paused for a long moment, then spoke through her tears.

"Kogii, the part of your drowning novel I returned to you after all this time—forty years!—begins by recounting a recurrent dream of yours, isn't that right? As you wrote in those pages, the big question seems to be whether your dream is based on something you actually experienced, or whether you first dreamed about the scene you described, then came to believe it had actually happened and, later on, began to dream about it again in a new and different form. And, as you wrote in the early draft, you really weren't sure where reality or memory ended and dreams began. Ever since I first read your account, after rushing home from Kyoto on the overnight train, I've always somehow thought you were only pretending not to know the answer to those questions. I mean, seriously, is there any doubt about what happened that night? I remember vividly how you sent me into the back parlor to see our father after they brought his body home. He was lying on a futon, and I reached out and touched his wet hair. I think the reason you keep saying you're unsure whether the scene on the river was a dream or reality—and the reason you've been so obsessed with wanting to finish your drowning novel—is that you feel you should have been with Father when he rashly set out on the raging river in his little boat and ended up losing his life, and the guilt about what you see as a personal failure has haunted you ever since. As I recall, he had told you to come with him and steer the boat, but you took your own sweet time getting there and Papa, who was never a very patient man, got tired of waiting and took off without you. (Or maybe the boat just got tossed into the waves; we'll never know for sure.)

"Mother swore me to silence about what I'm about to tell you, but here goes. That night, she walked over to the cornfield and stood on the stone wall looking down on the river, so she saw what happened. And she said to me, on more than one occasion, 'I'm terribly glad Kogii didn't go with his father after all.' I guess she felt it would have been cruel to tell you she was watching, and that was why she never mentioned it to you. She must have realized that knowing there was a witness would have deprived you of your only refuge: pretending to be unable to distinguish between dream and reality."

"I'm absolutely stunned," I said. "I had no idea. Mother really thought it was a good thing I blew my assignment and literally missed the boat? The light from the full moon would have been shining through some breaks in the cloud cover, so if she was watching from above she must have witnessed my moment of shame. I mean, Father had put his trust in me—he even took the trouble to teach me how to use the tiller to steer the boat—and then when he needed my help the most I just stood there, totally useless, with the muddy water swirling around my chest, and watched the storm surf carry him away."

"Anyhow," Asa said, "Mother said that after Father's boat was swept away you came slowly dog-paddling back to shore, and her heart was filled with indescribable joy. And now—were you thinking that if you could pick up where you left off with your drowning novel, you would somehow be able to make posthumous amends to our father and restore the good name of the little boy who swam sadly back to shore, feeling like a failure? And were you hoping you might be able to obtain some sort of magical absolution just by sorting through the materials in the red leather trunk?"

Though no longer red, Asa's face was still contorted by emotion, and the tears continued to course down the deep furrows that ran from her cheeks to her mouth. I just sat there in a daze, feeling utterly annihilated. After some time had passed, my sister once again lifted her eyes and spoke to me. She'd stopped crying, but the expression on her face was markedly somber and subdued. She had evidently been wrestling with a difficult decision, but she now appeared to have made up her mind.

"Since I've already betrayed Mother's trust by telling you something I promised not to share, I may as well go ahead and spill the rest of the beans," she said. "Three years before she died, Mother recorded her account of what happened on that night when Father went out on the stormy river and lost his life. I have the cassette, and I want you to listen to it. You're aware, of course, that after Mother's eyesight began to fail and she wasn't able to write letters, she started to use the tape recorder—which until then she had only been using to listen to Akari's musical compositions—to create verbal thank-you notes, and she would send those tapes to people in lieu of letters. In fact, you even lifted her comments about the marvels of the forest from one of those tapes, and quoted them in a novel, as I recall.

"I was the one who oversaw the making of the tapes—who else, right?—but when Mother first said, 'You know, I think I'd like to talk about that night,' I didn't fully understand her motives, and I couldn't help thinking this material might just end up being something else for you to use in your books. I could tell it was important to her, though, so I did what I could to help. There were a number of Mother's recordings stored in the red leather trunk, but I recently took that one out and set it aside.

"Okay then, I'm going to head home," Asa said, getting to her feet. "Unaiko is staying at my house tonight, so I'll send the tape over with her instead of bringing it myself. She has lots of expertise in using the sound system she set up earlier, but that isn't the only reason I want her to be here. Given what's on the tape, I really think it would be better if you weren't alone when you listened to it."

# 3

The minivan pulled into the front garden, and Unaiko stepped out. She was dressed, as usual, in casual work clothes. "I come bearing gifts from Asa," she announced as she walked into the house and deposited a lumpy bundle, wrapped in a large *furoshiki* cloth, on the dining table.

The care package contained an unglazed vessel filled with some high-end *shochu*—fifty-proof distilled liquor some people describe as Japan's answer to vodka, though I think it has an earthier flavor—that Asa had apparently received as a posthumous bequest from some connoisseur, along with three attractive ceramic sake cups. To this largesse Asa had added several Bizen ware dishes containing an assortment of her culinary creations, tightly covered with plastic wrap. In recent years

I had been trying to keep my distance from strong drink, but I seemed to have a primordial muscle memory of how to handle the bottle.

While I was studying the label, Unaiko was busy setting up the playback equipment. "Would you like to listen to the tape while you're eating dinner?" she asked as she tweaked an assortment of knobs and dials.

I nodded. "Asa was saying she wouldn't normally have included an alcoholic beverage with the meal, but she had you bring this bottle of *shochu* because she thought I might need a drink after I'd finished listening to the tape. I'd like to do it while I'm still sober, though," I said.

While Unaiko stationed herself at the board that controlled sound and lighting, I dragged one of the dining-room chairs to the south end of the great room (which resembled a small theater, with all the equipment). For a moment I let my gaze wander outside to the garden, where a sconce affixed to the wall was casting a pale glow on the Japanese birches.

My mother's recorded voice, sounding weaker than I remembered, began to emanate from the industrial-size speakers. At first the voice was little more than a whisper, and even after Unaiko adjusted the volume, rewound the tape to the beginning, and started again, it still sounded very faint. After a moment, I realized my mother was addressing her narrative to her two children: Asa and me.

> "Papa had made up his mind to set out on the flooded river in his rowboat, so while he was taking a nap that afternoon we added some things we thought he might need—a change of clothes, a towel, and so on—to the items he had already packed in the red leather trunk. These included a bunch of papers and documents, placed on top of a narrow rubber inner tube that had been removed from a bicycle tire. As you know, Papa made a hobby of dismantling and overhauling old, decrepit bicycles, all by himself. Normally, Kogii's only job was to add a squirt of oil here and there, so he was very excited when Papa told him to take the inner

*tube out of the tire. (Bicycle pumps were in short supply during
the war, so he had to use his mouth to inflate it, like blowing up
a balloon.) There used to be a bicycle store on the road beside
the river, but at some point it stopped selling bikes and was only
doing repairs—and even those were hit or miss because the shop
didn't carry any new parts. Since the bike-repair shop couldn't
do anything much beyond reattaching a loose chain or mending
a puncture with gum arabic, once the tube had been removed
from a bicycle tire there was no way to get a replacement. So until
things started to get back to normal after the war, Kogii would
pack old bicycle tires full of straw and ride around like that. We
always knew when he was on his way home 'cause we could hear
the rickety sound of his makeshift bike, with its jerry-built gears
and straw-filled tires, from miles away!*

*"Anyhow, after the inner tubes had been removed from the
tires and blown up nice and plump, what were they used for?
Flotation buoys, of course. In theory, if you blew one up and put
it in the red leather trunk, then even if the boat ended up sinking it would have been possible to stay above water by hanging on
to the trunk because the inner tube would keep it afloat. If worst
came to worst, at least the trunk would eventually find its way to
shore. As for the other things your father had packed in the trunk,
I didn't see anything besides a bunch of letters and papers. Some
of those letters talked in detail about who had originally suggested
the insurrection to your father and his cronies, and told them how
they should go about preparing for it. Because the plan was being
hatched here in the forest, where no one can ever keep a secret,
the conspirators had no choice but to stay in touch by mail. If they
had tried using the telephone the village switchboard operator
would have been able to eavesdrop on their conversation. That's
why there were so many letters, and your father was trying to take
them all with him, every last one. His plan, apparently, was to
pack up his correspondence and then ride the rowboat down the
flooded river to a spot where the water was wider and the current*

wasn't so strong; in other words, someplace where the fields and rice paddies were completely submerged in water from the flooding. He must have figured that if he could get that far, he would be able to scramble onto the shore and ditch the boat, and then he could make his escape by following the train tracks, thus managing to outrun the people who (he thought) were going to be pursuing him. If he had managed to make a clean getaway by following this plan, I have no idea what his next step would have been. The only thing we know for sure is that your father had made up his mind to run away that very night.

"As for why he chose to go by boat, the explanation is obvious. Everyone around here knew him by sight, so he was likely to be spotted by suspicious eyes no matter which road he took out of town. That's why he decided to ride the river to a place beyond the neighboring town and start his overland journey from there. If the weather had been better his plan might have worked, but the boat snagged on a sandbar downriver and capsized in the high waves, and he drowned. Even so, I can't help thinking he had been making surprisingly good progress till then!

"The fact that Papa felt the need to fill the red leather trunk with all the papers pertaining to the insurrection seems to indicate that he thought those materials were too important (or too incriminating) to leave behind. It's as if he felt it would be disastrous for any outsiders to see what he had been plotting, but yet he also put a flotation device in the trunk so the papers would eventually find their way back to us. At least that's what I believed for many years after he drowned. But why on earth would he set up an outcome in which his folly would be exposed? And wasn't he worried about having his subversive correspondence fall into the wrong hands? Those are just some of the unknowables that make my head spin, even now. Of course, the trunk was found downstream and taken to the police, quite a while after the war ended. They evidently had bigger fish to fry, and the trunk was returned to us without comment.

"Recently, though, I've come to believe there may be a
much simpler explanation for the flotation device. Papa obviously wasn't thinking straight, and maybe he just wanted to
make the trunk buoyant so he could use it as a life preserver in
case the boat capsized. It's likely that he didn't even consider the
possibility he might perish, while the trunk survived.

"It does seem as though my husband honestly believed the
guerrilla bombing of the Imperial Palace was going to take place.
Even though the officers used to come to our house and get drunk
and talk big about staging some kind of violent uprising, in the
beginning those discussions seemed rather abstract. But they gradually became more focused, and I believe when Papa somehow
reached the conclusion that the officers were seriously planning to
carry out their radical scheme, he became frightened.

"We know how the story ends: Papa launched his boat on
the flooded river and ended up drowning. But did he ever seriously believe he would be able to survive the churned-up current in the wobbly little rowboat? It seems to me, in retrospect,
that he was concentrating on the immediate goal of making his
escape from the valley, and he didn't take the time to think about
the next step. I think it was shamefully irresponsible, given the
haphazardness of his plan, that he would even think about taking his young son along on that wild, doomed flight. And when
I watched from above as Kogii came paddling back to shore
through the muddy, turbulent water, it truly was one of the hap-
piest moments of my life!

"Anyhow, the one thing we know for sure is that Papa participated in plotting a guerrilla uprising along with a bunch of
disgruntled soldiers, and even though it turned out to be nothing
more than an idle fantasy, he was afraid he might be forced to go
through with it. That's why he felt the need to flee like a thief in
the night in the midst of the biggest storm of the year.

"Kogii always seemed to idolize his father, and if I had
given him access to the red leather trunk when he first asked

*(before I began to weed out the contents), I was afraid it would have broken his heart to learn the truth about his father. Also, of course, I didn't relish the idea of having our family's dirty laundry aired in public. I couldn't explain my reasons without disclosing the secret, and as a result we were estranged for years.*

*"Kogii's reaction was to write* The Day He Himself Shall Wipe My Tears Away, *which was apparently designed to punish and embarrass me. That dreadful novella portrayed Papa's conduct in a way that made him look ludicrous and pathetic, while I came across as a sarcastic, hypercritical harpy. Even so, it was clear to me that Kogii was still hoping to write his drowning novel someday, to celebrate the father he always thought of as brave and heroic."*

I gave the high sign to Unaiko, who had been standing next to the recording equipment all this time, keeping a watchful eye on me. Then I told her I wanted to listen to the rest of the tape alone, at my leisure, adding by way of explanation that I felt like trying the liquor Asa had sent with the tape. Dexterously, Unaiko rewound the cassette to the beginning, so I would only need to press the play button.

I took the bottle and filled a large sake cup for myself, then pointed at another cup and looked inquiringly at Unaiko, who was in the process of pulling plastic water bottles out of the cloth-wrapped bundle and lining them up on the table. She declined, saying she would be leaving shortly to drive herself home. I quickly drained my cup, then refilled it.

Unaiko must have noticed how distressed I was by the contents of the tape; her body language seemed to suggest that she would be willing to take on the role of sympathetic listener, but I didn't feel like talking things out with her (or anyone else) at that particular moment. She watched me thoughtfully as I continued to drink alone, in silence, and after a while she spoke.

"The story you've been trying to write about your father, who died more than sixty years ago—well, Asa was saying that your mother thought it was meant to be a novel of redemption, and she seems to have been right. I understand now why your mother was so opposed to the project.

"Before you came to the Forest House this summer, Asa kindly offered to let us use it. We did a major cleaning, since the house had been empty for quite a while, and then Masao Anai and I and some of the younger members of the troupe used it as both a training center and a place to stay. It was supposed to be for only a week, but the younger folks had obligations in Matsuyama, so I would often stay down here alone. Asa thought I might be lonely, and she would sometimes come over in the evenings to keep me company.

"I tried never to ask Asa any direct questions, but as the time approached for you to come down here and take possession of the red leather trunk (which, I gathered, had quite a bit of history), I got the distinct feeling that while she was looking forward to your arrival, at the same time she was also quite worried. Masao tends to be very perceptive about such things, and he said that he had a feeling it might turn out there was nothing packed away in the red leather trunk after all—or, at least, nothing that would provide you with the impetus (and the materials) you would need to finish your novel. That was worrying me, too, and one night as I sat here talking with Asa till the wee hours I inadvertently voiced my concerns. 'Listen,' I said, 'if our worst fears are realized and the materials Mr. Choko is hoping to find aren't in the trunk, maybe it would be a good idea to let him know as soon as he arrives.'

"I knew I had probably overstepped my boundaries, and I wasn't surprised that Asa seemed a bit offended at first. When Masao is directing a play, he'll sometimes say something like 'You know, I'm deliberately restraining myself from getting angry at you guys,' in order to keep the younger actors from 'shrinking' (that's the term he uses). And I kind of got the feeling Asa was doing the same: reining in her annoyance. But after a rather tense couple of minutes I kind of sensed that she was saying to herself, *Oh well, what the heck, I may as well go ahead and tell Unaiko about all the things I've been losing sleep over.* She went back to her house beside the river to get her pajamas and other necessities, and after she returned we laid out our bedding side by side on the floor, crawled under the covers, and proceeded to talk the night away.

"The gist of what she told me is that the red leather trunk was recovered by the police a fair distance downstream from where they found your drowned father's body and was subsequently delivered to your house. The trunk was initially put away unopened, but as the years went by, your mother started to sort through and dispose of the papers, and through that process she gradually came to have a clearer understanding of what her husband had been involved in.

"You probably know all of this already, but I'm going to repeat everything Asa told me, on the chance some of it might be helpful. In the beginning, apparently, your father just seemed to enjoy sharing drinks and conversation with the young officers from the regiment in Matsuyama who showed up one day bearing a letter of introduction from the Kochi Sensei, and soon became regular visitors to your house. Your dad would serve the visitors sake, along with various delicacies, such as sweetfish caught with nets during the months when their bodies have the most oil, then roasted, dried, and put aside to eat when those fish were out of season. I gathered that freshwater crabs and eels, plucked from the river by the village children, were another favorite delicacy. Your father even went so far as to serve meat, or jerky, from secretly slaughtered cows hung up to cure in natural caves in the mountains. You've written that the bloody tail of the cow would be delivered, wrapped in newspaper, and your father would then proceed to cook it, but according to your mother's version of the same story, the guests were simply served the customary cuts of beef. In any case, the officers would dig into those lavish spreads, with their distinctively regional flavors, and your father would mostly sit quietly and listen as the animated conversation—lubricated by large quantities of locally brewed sake your family had somehow managed to obtain—swirled around him. That's how it was, at first. "Gradually, those discussions began to take on an air of urgency, and the officers started talking about the necessity of doing something radical to change what they perceived as the disastrous course of Japanese history since the Meiji Restoration. From that point on, the local girls who had been working those banquets were no longer allowed in the house, and your mother had to do all the serving herself, unassisted.

"Apparently, according to what your mother told Asa about those get-togethers, at first your father's role consisted mainly of making sure the sake was kept warm, but the way he listened to the officers' conversations gradually became more attentive and more intense. Before long, he evidently allowed himself to be drawn into the intrigue, and he began to take an active part in the discussions about the insurgency the young officers were planning.

"And then they learned that a kamikaze aircraft base had recently been established on Kyushu, not too far away, and they got the delusional idea of stealing some of those planes, which were laden with bombs and filled with enough gas for their one-way missions. From then on, when one of the top secret planning sessions was in progress, your mother was only allowed to come into the main house to deliver trays of food. It was around that time, for reasons your mother didn't understand, that your father got into the habit of burning the midnight oil in his cramped little study while he pored over an assortment of big, heavy books written in English. If those books were somehow significant, doesn't it seem likely they would have been stashed in the red leather trunk, along with the letters?"

"You're right," I replied. "I discovered this only the other day, but the trunk did contain several volumes of Frazer's classic work *The Golden Bough*. It was a kind of fad with my father's generation to read (or at least carry around) the Japanese translation of the abridged version of those books, in the Iwanami paperback edition."

"Why that particular book, I wonder?" Unaiko asked.

"I don't have the foggiest idea," I said, shaking my head.

"So your father drowned, and time passed," Unaiko went on. "You became a published novelist, and it was when you declared your intention of having your next book focus on your father's life and death that your mother started to get worried. She refused to give you access to the background materials you needed, and you ultimately decided to put the entire project on ice, even though the first chapter was already written. When you told your mother you wouldn't be needing the materials from the red leather trunk after all, she was tremendously relieved. But then you wrote *The Day He Himself Shall Wipe My Tears Away*, and from what Asa told me, its publication changed everything. In that fever dream of a novella you portrayed your father as a grotesque figure riding in a funky wooden chariot who leads his ragtag disciples into Matsuyama to rob a bank in order to get money to finance his little band of insurgents, but ends up being fatally shot by the police. Your mother was appalled by what she saw as your betrayal of your family, and apparently she kept repeating over and over that your book was an affront to the memory of your drowned father, and saying things like 'Who does Kogii think he is, anyhow—and what makes him think he has a right to publish this kind of garbage?'

"I have to say that Asa's facial expression as she was telling me all this was something an actress of my generation would find difficult, if not impossible, to emulate. I don't know whether to call it pain, or anguish, or grief, but it was clearly welling up from a very deep place. And this evening, too, when Asa was looking for the tape I just played for you, I noticed she was wearing the same expression. Oh dear, I'm afraid I've said more than I should have, again . . ."

"Please don't worry about it," I said. "I'm going to listen to my mother's tape now, and I'll make a point of imagining that Asa is sitting here beside me, wearing exactly the facial expression you've described. Well then, to top off the evening's festivities, won't you join me in a little drink?"

I was trying to be charming and persuasive, but my voice sounded pitiful in my own ears. I poured the *shochu* (which really was exceptionally good) into the large sake cup sitting on the table in front of Unaiko, but she stood up without even taking a token sip.

"Needless to say, Asa has been concerned about the effect listening to this tape might have on you. Masao's been worrying, too.

Anyway, please don't overdo it with the booze tonight." And with that, she vanished into the night.

Once I started drinking I had a bad habit (or perhaps it was a character flaw) of throwing back shot after shot, and as I wandered over to the chair in front of the speakers, I did pause for a moment to quaff the cup I had filled for Unaiko. However, I refrained from replenishing my own, and I left the bottle of liquor on the table.

## 4

The next morning I woke up early, after a rare night during which I didn't have even the tiniest sliver of a dream. When I rolled out of bed and headed downstairs to get a drink of water—it was around six o'clock—I saw Masao Anai loitering in the back garden just outside the dining room. He was alone, and his bowed head was haloed by the gilded light streaming through the leaves of the pomegranate tree. There was something tentative and uncertain about the way he was perching atop the large, round poetry stone, as if he wasn't sure he ought to be there.

I went into the dining room and sat at the table in a position that allowed me to keep a diagonal eye on Masao, who was off to one side. Everything was as I'd left it the night before. I picked up the plastic carafe, poured water into one of the large sake cups (which was still faintly redolent of Japan's answer to vodka), and emptied it in a single gulp. I repeated the sequence several times until my morning-after thirst was quenched.

Beyond the big picture window, Masao raised his head and appeared to notice that I was up and about. He didn't make any of the usual gestures of greeting, but a moment later he vanished around the west side of the house. I heard jingling as he unlocked the kitchen door, evidently using a bunch of keys entrusted to the theater group, and let himself in. After settling into the chair across from me, Masao sloshed some water into a cup he'd carried from the kitchen and drank it. Then he poured himself another draught and partially refilled my cup as well, after first hefting the plastic pitcher and thoughtfully calculating how much water remained so we would both get an equal amount.

"If the novel you came here hoping to finish ends up going down the drain, will that also spell doom for the drama project we were hoping to work on in tandem with your own writing and research?" he asked.

"I haven't really had a chance to think that far ahead," I said, "but it's true my plan to stay down here and make a new start on my long-dormant novel, using the materials I'd expected to find in my mother's trunk, has hit a brick wall."

"So does that mean your current sojourn will be canceled as well? (I think you mentioned this was probably going to be your last visit, in any case.) To be honest, having your stay at the Forest House cut short would be a very regrettable development from our point of view, but wouldn't it also be a major blow to the final stage of Kogito Choko's career? Asa is very concerned about how you're handling this setback, emotionally. I received a phone call from her early this morning while it was still dark, and she was talking about what a monumental letdown this must have been for you, and saying you'd mentioned that as you've grown older you seem to wake up every morning at the crack of dawn with your mind awash in pessimistic thoughts. She was worried about your being alone at a time like this, and—of course, I realize I'm not her brother's keeper, so to speak, but here I am anyway, barging in on you uninvited at this ungodly hour."

I didn't reply. After a moment, I became aware of a kind of subliminal ringing in my ears. In the small forest that bordered the back garden and marked the perimeter of my mother's property, there were still some ancient stands of broadleaf trees that hadn't merged with the mixed groves of cedars and Japanese cypresses surrounding them. When I gazed up at the luxuriant foliage of those trees, their green leaves luminous in the early-morning sunshine, the sight was almost transcendentally dazzling.

During the past ten years or so, every time I had come back to the Forest House the uncanny quietude of the forest had always made me aware of the residual clamor in my ears, and I could almost feel myself being reunited with the mystical sound of the forest: that beautifully musical hush. Now, once again, I seemed to hear the living forest's melodic vibrations amid the radiance of all that grand and glorious greenness. I was suddenly oblivious to the existence of Masao Anai, and I had an illusion that I (in my present guise of feeble, useless old man) was hearing my mother's line of poetry—*You didn't get Kogii ready to go up into the forest*—overlaid with the subtle music that seemed to be emanating from the same forest.

While I was in this trancelike state Masao had returned to his seat in the garden, under the pomegranate tree. He had an unusually large notebook open on his lap, but he didn't appear to be looking at it. (I had seen the same tableau, featuring Unaiko and her own oversize notebook, any number of times.)

I went outside and joined him under the tree. "What's that you've got there? Is it some kind of director's notebook?" I asked.

"Not exactly," Masao said. "I've read quite a few books written by the leaders of the New Drama movement in Japan—you know, adherents of the Stanislavski method—but my notes aren't nearly so methodical or technique oriented. I jot things down as they occur to me; sometimes I'll look at my notes later and I won't even remember when I wrote them, or why. The funny thing is, the tidbits from various sources that I either transcribe or photocopy and paste onto these pages are often more useful than my original ideas. Maybe that's because all my dramatic creations are basically just eclectic collages of quotations and allusions."

My eyes were irresistibly drawn to the notebook lying open on Masao's knees, and while he made no move to show those pages to me, he didn't try to hide them, either. There were blocks of prose and neat lines of poetry, some written in roman letters, others in Japanese, and everything was annotated with red-ink underlinings and marginal notes in pencil. The pages were intricate and artistic-looking, and I got the feeling I was being allowed to glimpse another side of Masao Anai, the dynamic and innovative director.

"These are some excerpts from the manuscript of the drowning novel that you shared with us," Masao said. "They don't have to do with the dream scene, though. I was interested in the quotes from T. S. Eliot, both in the original and in Motohiro Fukase's translation, which I know you've been studying since you were young. What surprised me was that the epigraph for the entire book, at least in the draft we saw, was in French—even though it was a quote from Eliot, who of course wrote in English.

"What I find most interesting are the subtle variations among the three versions: the English, the French, and the Japanese. (Of course, you primarily used Fukase's version, but you also seem to have incorporated elements of the well-known translation by Junzaburo Nishiwaki.)

"Anyway, what I'm saying is that I make notes about such details as I go along. For example, take the Eliot line *He passed the stages of his age and youth / Entering the whirlpool*. In the Fukase translation, it becomes *He passed through the stages of age and youth*, while Nishiwaki renders the line considerably more loosely as *One after another, he recalled the days of his youth and the days of his dotage*.

"The whole time I was reading your manuscript, the Eliot lines kept running through my head: *A current under sea / Picked his bones in whispers. As he rose and fell / He passed the stages of his age and youth / Entering the whirlpool*. And I couldn't help wondering how you would have gone about portraying the way your father's life flashed before his eyes while he was drowning."

"Oh, you mean in the drowning novel?" I asked absently. Masao's recitation of the Eliot lines had momentarily transported me back in time.

"Yes, I gather the idea was to reprise the various stages of your father's life, but I can't help thinking it would have been difficult for you to pull that off, as a writer who was still quite young and inexperienced."

"You've read the scrap of prose I call the drowning novel, so you know I had drafted the story only to the point where my father sets out in his little boat, heading right into the towering waves, with Kogii—my supernatural alter ego—manning the tiller in place of me. Fast-forward forty years or so, and here I am, or was, trying to pick up where I left off and finish the book. You seem to be asking how I was planning to proceed. Well, you're right that creating the retrospective scene where my father's entire past flashes before his eyes would have been a major challenge, but at any age. When I was younger, I lacked the necessary life experience, and now I—the narrator of that passage—have become an old writer myself and I can't very well be projecting my own history onto my father, who died relatively young.

"At the time, I wanted to try to answer the question: *As my father was drowning in the vortex of the raging river, how did he pass the last moments of his life? What was going through his mind just before he died?* The other day when I was looking over the index cards I'd included in the packet with the pages I had written, decades ago, I saw that I'd started by composing a straightforward chronicle, including things I had heard from my grandmother and mother when I was a young child: local legends and folklore, bits of our family history, and so on. But how did my father fit into those accounts? Where did he come from, and what was his story before he met my mother? My only clues were a few vague memories of overheard conversations, but as a young writer I had the option of letting my imagination fill in the blanks. But what should I, the writer, have my drowning father remember—and in what sequence? At first I took an oblique approach to the problem, doing things like rereading 'The Snows of Kilimanjaro.' Before I embarked on the actual writing, I needed to find a way to incorporate bits of history and folklore into the narrative, one by one, without fretting about realism or verisimilitude. At the same time, I was trying to layer brief vignettes throughout the story.

"I wrestled endlessly with questions of technique. How should I have the drowning man remember his five decades of life, until the night it ended abruptly on a storm-tossed river? Should I begin with miscellaneous occurrences from his late adulthood? Or should I go all the way back to the beginning of my father's life during the Sino-Japanese War in Manchuria, and use a combination of imagination and hearsay to create episodes from his infancy and youth?

"While I was simultaneously ruminating about such matters and mulling over the stories I'd heard, a few at a time, mostly from my grandmother, it occurred to me that it would be ideal if I could somehow find a way to establish certain biographical details. At one point I used Asa as a go-between to ask my mother how she and my father met, and also about the time, early in their marriage, when she went to China to visit her childhood friend, the Shanghai Auntie. My mother kept extending her stay, so my father finally followed her to China for the sole purpose of bringing her back, and I've thought more than once that if he hadn't made that trip, I would never have been born. Anyway, even at that early date there were already signs that a rift was developing between my mother and me, and as you know the conflict eventually escalated and turned ugly. Now everything seems to have come to naught, so I guess this is the end of the road for the drowning novel. I remember, in those early days, the prospect of someday getting to sift through the contents of the red leather trunk seemed like some wild, impossible dream, and that's exactly what it turned out to be."

"I see," Masao said. He sounded more peeved than sympathetic. "I suppose this is also the end of my current project as well. Oh well—easy come, easy go. After all, until your recent attempt to resurrect this book it had been lying dormant for nearly forty years, right?"

"Yes, that's true," I said. "But when I gave another listen to the tape Unaiko brought over last night, I realized what a fool I had been to think my mother would blithely help me write a novel about something that would have hit so close to home for her. Really, I must have been delusional, or at least absurdly optimistic, to assume she would eventually give her approval and hand over the red leather trunk so I could get back to work. Asa knew the truth all along, but until now I guess she didn't see any reason to destroy my illusions about our father's heroism. In the end, I was no match for my mother and sister.

When those two females pooled their resources, they were really a force to be reckoned with."

"That reminds me of something I said to Asa and Unaiko," Masao said. "This was before you came to stay at the Forest House, and I was only reacting to what I'd heard about the various complications. Anyway, I remember saying, 'I can't help wondering whether it was Mr. Choko's desire to write a revisionist version of history—creating an alternative reality in which his father was some sort of fallen hero—that doomed the project to failure from the start.'

"Of course, it's water under the bridge now—no pun intended, and I don't want you to think I'm taking this lightly at all. What I mean is, even though your drowning novel is never going to be finished I still think your younger self's idea of telling your father's story through the prism of T. S. Eliot's 'Death by Water' poem is a beautiful thing. For me, it would have been very illuminating to see how you went about transmuting that into prose. Just in terms of methodology—a term you often used when you were in your forties, much to the amusement (or horror) of some of your lit-crit colleagues—I think it could have been quite a tour de force."

"It's true that when I was younger a lot of critics used to make fun of me for daring to discuss my writing in terms of methodology—and they were already down on me for my chosen method of transmuting my private life into fiction," I said. "But the 'I novel' method was the reason I was staking my hopes on the red leather trunk, then and now. The year I started college in Tokyo also happened to be the tenth anniversary of my father's death, and when I came home to attend the traditional Buddhist service my mother jokingly predicted that I might someday become a novelist and write a book based on the materials in the red leather trunk. But now it's looking as though the joke was on me, in more ways than one.

"Of course, my sister seems to have known that all along. Speaking of Asa, there are still a few drops left in the bottle she sent over last night. How about it, Masao—won't you join me in a little hair of the dog?"

# Chapter 5

# The Big Vertigo

## 1

There was no word from Asa for several days, so we hadn't yet talked about our mother's cassette-tape bombshell. Unaiko (who was staying at Asa's house) had informed me that she would be bringing over my meals while my sister tended to her own affairs, which she had apparently been neglecting since my arrival. As for me, I had definitely made up my mind to decamp from the Forest House. I thought this might be the last time I ever came down here for an extended stay, so I needed to spend a large chunk of time tidying up my own effects and getting ready to vacate the premises.

One day I asked Unaiko to tell Asa I was planning to leave for Tokyo at the beginning of the following week. Upon hearing that news, Asa called to ask whether she could stop by to discuss some practical matters.

"I phoned Chikashi a while ago," Asa declared with her trademark directness as she strode through the front door of the Forest House not long afterward. "She was perfectly calm, as usual, and she said that when she heard about the failure of your quest to find the materials you needed to complete your drowning novel—which was, of course, your primary purpose in coming to Shikoku—she figured you would probably pack up and return home. I'm only mentioning how cool she sounded because I'd been concerned that your decision to abandon a major literary project might create some cash-flow problems for your family, but Chikashi put my mind at ease by addressing the issue on her own.

"She told me that while the income from both foreign-rights and paperback sales of your books had definitely tapered off, you were continuing to write a series of essays for one of the big newspapers, and whenever you went to deliver lectures at small venues outside of Tokyo there was a magazine that paid to publish your lecture texts after you'd polished them a bit. She said this is how it's always been for writers of pure, noncommercial literature, especially in the latter phases of their careers. I know I've mentioned this before, but you really hit the jackpot when you persuaded Chikashi to become your wife. She truly is a magnificent human being.

"On another topic, I wanted to talk about the tape recording I sent over for you to listen to. Since I already knew what was on Mother's tape I naturally felt a bit guilty (or at least conflicted) about passing it on to you. That's why I included some strong liquor to dull the pain. I thought it would be all right, just this once, even though you haven't been drinking much lately. I was worried about the impact the tape might have on your emotional state, but when I quizzed Masao after he'd seen you the next morning he said you appeared to be bright-eyed, bushy-tailed, and none the worse for wear. Even so, I couldn't stop thinking that maybe I shouldn't have given you a bottle, especially after you've made such a valiant—and successful—effort to overcome your fondness for the hard stuff. When I walked in today I was afraid I might find the kitchen strewn with empty bottles of the cheap Scotch you can buy everywhere these days, even at our local supermarket here in the boonies, but when I peeked in there just now the only bottle in sight was the one I sent you the other night, so that was a relief.

"Anyhow, for your supper tonight I'll be sending Unaiko over with some dishes I prepared, along with some more of the *shochu* from the other night—properly chilled this time. I was thinking it might be nice for you and Unaiko to share the bottle and keep each other company. Since your writing project has fizzled out, I imagine the work you've been doing till now with the Caveman Group will probably be a lost cause as well. It's natural that Unaiko would want to talk to you about various things and also, in terms of improving your mood, I figured hanging out with her would probably be a lot more fun than sitting around with your sister—am I right?"

# 2

When Unaiko showed up for our farewell dinner, she was wearing a stylish summer outfit: a pale blouse in a floral print and a full, flouncy skirt. During the recent rehearsal, Unaiko's rather drab, functional attire had made her look more like a stagehand than an actress, but seeing her now in a casual situation, she seemed much more youthful than usual—girlish, even. Asa had prepared several tasty dishes using ham, sausage, and various types of edible wild plants she'd picked herself in the nearby mountains and then stir-fried. Unaiko dug into the meal with gusto and matched me drink for drink as well. Perhaps to reassure me, she mentioned that she had a tendency to become intoxicated rather quickly, so she had sensibly arranged for Masao to drive her home at the end of the evening.

Once again, Unaiko was in a very talkative mood. And while I should theoretically have still been mired in the depression that had been dogging me for several days, I soon found myself cheerfully joining in the conversation.

Unaiko started off with the usual anodyne small talk, but before long she segued into speaking candidly about what was on her mind.

"I imagine you'd prefer not to dwell on things that are over and done with, but there's one image from your recurrent dream that I just can't stop thinking about," she said. "It's the scene where your father sets out on the river in his small boat and is borne away by the current. In the dream, you can see what your father's wearing because the moon breaks through the storm clouds and illuminates the scene below, right?"

"Yes," I said. "The visibility was perfect."

"And all the times you've had the dream, over the years, did the details change at all?"

"Not in any significant way," I replied. "The dream is nearly identical every single time. It's almost like watching a video. That may be why I have a persistent feeling the boat-launching scene is something I actually witnessed in reality."

"Getting back to your father's clothing," Unaiko said, "what exactly was he wearing in the dream? (Let's put the reality aside for a moment, even though I gather there was quite a bit of overlap.) Asa was saying that he was dressed in the type of uniform civilians wore during wartime, but can you tell me what it would have looked like style-wise? When we staged the dramatic adaptation of *The Day He Himself Shall Wipe My Tears Away*, we just put his character in the same type of uniform a retired serviceman would have worn."

"The uniforms for civilians were khaki colored," I explained. "During the war, everyone was required to wear them. In the dream, my father was dressed in that uniform, complete with a matching military-style hat, and the red leather trunk was by his side."

"Your mother mentioned on the tape that at first your father was only listening to what his visitors were saying, as an interested observer, but as the conspiratorial plotting gathered steam he ended up being drawn in ever deeper," Unaiko said. "And the reason he tried to run away on that stormy night was because he was afraid the ill-advised guerrilla action was about to take place. To me, your father's behavior seems perfectly natural. In your dream, at least, he comes across as a reasonably sane human being, unlike the grotesque, pathetic father figure portrayed in *Wipe My Tears Away*. Isn't that correct?"

"That's exactly right," I said. "I may have gotten carried away the other day and started singing along with the German song, but that doesn't change my feeling about the novella I wrote. It was an embarrassingly immature piece of work. In retrospect, I think the only well-written thing in the entire book is the way the mother criticized the foolhardiness of the activities her husband and son were involved in."

Unaiko, who was evidently already feeling quite tipsy, gazed at me with a face that looked, as always, far younger than her years. "But, Mr. Choko," she said, "didn't you want to portray your father in the drowning novel as a man who set out on that flooded river while he was in full possession of his faculties?"

"Yes, I did, absolutely. And while I went on clinging to my childish naive conviction that my father was embarking on a hero's journey, I also wanted to chronicle his ill-fated boat trip as part of a sequence of events that was supposed to culminate in some kind of paramilitary insurrection. My recurrent dream reflected the idealized perspective of the young boy who believed wholeheartedly that his father was on his way to commit a doomed act of heroism when he drowned. While my father was being tossed around by the current on the river bottom he would have flashed back over his entire life, the way people do when they're drowning, and that was the story my novel was going to tell."

Unaiko nodded and took another sip of *shochu*. "In *Wipe My Tears Away* the mother is skeptical all along, but the father is portrayed as someone who's absolutely essential to the radical action the young officers are planning," she said. "Clearly, the young boy regards his father as a kind of hero."

"I wrote that book after I'd promised my mother that I would abandon my drowning novel," I said. "I think my feelings of resentment are clearly evident in the surrealistic novella I ended up writing instead."

"Even so, for me, the mother is the character who seems the most genuinely human at the conclusion of the story," Unaiko mused. "She was the only one who dared to disagree when her son kept insisting his father had died a heroic death. Was she meant to come across as the only person who was rational about the whole situation?"

"No, when I wrote the novella I really wasn't trying to imply that any one person had remained compos mentis while everyone else had completely lost their minds. All the characters in the book—the cancer-ridden father in his fertilizer-box chariot, the young boy wearing a fake military cap, the army officers belting out the German song at the top of their lungs—are supposed to be given equal weight."

"Well, I know I'm not very sophisticated intellectually," Unaiko said self-deprecatingly, "but I still can't help wondering whether there was some underlying significance behind your decision. You came down here intending to work on your drowning novel; we all know how that turned out, but if you had actually managed to finish it, isn't there a chance the book's outcome would have been similar to that of *The Day He Himself Shall Wipe My Tears Away*? No matter how many anecdotes you tell in the voice of the drowned narrator, that talking corpse is always going to be sucked into the whirlpool, right? I mean, for your purposes, there's no other way for the story to end.

"The other night as you were listening to your mother's tape, you finally realized that your father ran away because he was terrified about what might happen if he didn't. And while he was attempting to flee into the storm, his little boat capsized and he drowned. Personally, I've been thinking that if you ever do write the drowning novel, instead of having a tragic anticlimax, it might be more interesting to fictionalize the narrative so your father somehow makes it to shore, eluding the dragnet of his police pursuers, and really does manage to carry out some kind of guerrilla action along with his wild-eyed partners in crime.

"Of course, even I know that no such event ever took place in 1945, during the days that followed Japan's surrender. My thought, plot-wise, was that having an actual dramatic occurrence would be a refreshing change from your usual type of ambiguous, anticlimactic ending. Anyway, everything is moot now, since it looks as though you aren't going to write the drowning novel after all. And really, isn't that the ultimate anticlimax, in a way?"

Unaiko had a point, but I didn't say anything in response. After an expectant moment, she continued: "Asa felt awful when she saw how downhearted you were about not finding the information you needed to complete your book. It was almost as if she thought she owed you an apology for handing over the trunk in the first place, since she already knew how that whole operation was going to turn out. But I guess she realized that it was what it was, as they say, and there was nothing she could do about it.

"I think Asa was simply trying to force her seventysomething brother—who had created a falsely heroic image of his drowned father, and who was still having recurrent dreams about something that happened one night when he was ten years old—to face reality. What I'm trying to say is, I think she was just trying to bring you back to your senses, for your own good."

Unaiko held her glass up for a refill and I silently obliged. "I helped Asa restore your mother's tape to a listenable state, so naturally I feel a measure of responsibility as well," she went on. "From what I've heard, your father was far from being an active or essential participant in the insurgency scheme. It sounds to me as though he was nothing more than a country bumpkin who became so alarmed about what his sketchy cohorts were planning that he felt compelled to run away as fast as his little boat would carry him."

So how did I respond to this crescendo of confrontation from my clearly intoxicated companion? Did I get angry and make a scene, like an ill-behaved old man? No, I was the perfect picture of serenity, sitting there surrounded by the vibrant sounds of the forest while my mood oscillated wildly between an irrepressible urge to laugh and a descent into infinite melancholy. I felt oddly salubrious, and I didn't even feel the need to refill my own cup.

Toward the end of the evening Masao Anai joined us, and I got the impression that he was accustomed to playing designated driver when Unaiko had been out drinking. The curious thing was that when my outspoken dinner companion finally vanished into the night, leaving me in peace, I was genuinely sorry to see her go.

# 3

The next day Masao Anai came by to deliver a late breakfast, explaining that Unaiko was still in bed recovering from a hangover. While I was eating, Masao gazed out at the back garden, staring intently at the round stone engraved with the linked poems my mother and I had written. After a moment he started talking, saying Unaiko had asked him, as her emissary, to raise a question she had neglected to broach the night before.

Some time ago, Masao told me, he had run into a college friend who was now teaching Japanese at a local high school, and they had renewed their acquaintance. As a result of subsequent discussions, the Caveman Group initiated a visiting-artist program wherein the theater troupe would choose works of modern literature, turn them into dramatic readings, and then go around giving interactive performances at junior high schools and high schools in the area. They had been working on a new program as part of an integrated learning curriculum for the upcoming school semester, and that was what Unaiko had wanted to discuss with me.

"Each forty-five-minute performance would be divided into two segments, or rounds," Masao told me. "The first would present the story as a condensed dramatic reading, while the second segment would incorporate the students' questions. The idea is that a lively debate would inevitably ensue, adding a dramatic aspect of its own.

"We've already done a number of presentations based on this model: Miyazawa's *Night of the Milky Way Railway*, Tsubota's *Children in the Wind* and *The Four Seasons of Childhood*, Akutagawa's *Kappa*, and so on. This year we've had a request to do Soseki's *Kokoro*, and we're in the preliminary preparation stage of that project. One of our main actors will handle the role of Sensei, including his conversations and his suicide note, while another will be in charge of the external dialogues and internal monologues voiced by the narrator (whom we know only as 'I'), and our younger members will be cast in the

auxiliary roles. Right now we're busy converting our condensed version of the book into a script for the dramatic reading, and an aspect
of the process has been worrying Unaiko from the start."

Masao Anai flipped open his vade mecum: the giant notebook he
never seemed to be without. He was also carrying a pocket-size Iwanami edition of Soseki's *Collected Works*, and he opened that as well.

"Near the end of the novel," Masao said, "we've hit a snag in
the section about the death of Emperor Meiji. I'll read it aloud, if
that's okay.

> "Then, at the height of the summer, Emperor Meiji passed away.
> I felt as though the spirit of the Meiji Era that began with the
> Emperor had ended with him as well. I was overcome with the
> feeling that I and the rest of my generation, who had grown up in
> that era, were now left behind to live as anachronisms. I shared
> this epiphany with my wife, but she just laughed and refused to
> take me seriously. Then she said a curious thing, albeit in jest:
> 'Well then, maybe you should go ahead and commit *junshi*, and
> follow the emperor to the grave.'

"Needless to say, the wife was referring to the fact that General
Nogi had chosen to follow the emperor in death by committing suicide
himself. As we've been mapping out the section featuring Sensei's long
suicide note—which basically relates his life story—Unaiko has been
reading the lines, and then I repeat them for emphasis. At some point
Unaiko started to fret, and she asked me this question, but I wasn't
able to give her a clear answer. That's why she was going to request
a second opinion from you last night, and now I've been tasked with
following up. So here's the question: If it was true that what Soseki
calls 'the spirit of the Meiji Era' flowed through Emperor Meiji's entire
reign, then would every single person who lived during the era have
been imbued with that spirit? This may seem like a rather simplistic
question, but we haven't been able to come up with a satisfactory
answer on our own, so we wanted to ask you. For me, and for Unaiko

as well, it seems to resonate with the type of transformation you've written about in the trilogy that began with *The Changeling*. Soseki's character Sensei feels isolated from his era, and he has already decided to go on living as if he were dead. But even someone like that . . . I mean, could he really have escaped the influence of his own time—in other words, the spirit of Meiji?"

"That's an excellent question," I said. "As it happens, when I was young I often used to wonder about the exact same thing, but at the time I wasn't really able to formulate a proper response. However, when you ask me now, the answer springs to mind with surprising clarity. It may sound paradoxical, but I think it is precisely the people who are trying to live in a way that's detached from their own eras, and from their contemporaries as well, who end up being most influenced by the spirit of the time they were born into. In my novels, I usually portray characters who exist in very private worlds, but even so, my ultimate goal is to somehow express the spirit of the era I'm writing about. I'm not claiming there's any special merit in my approach—and, as you've so kindly pointed out, my readership has nearly dried up as a result. This may seem like a stretch, but if I should die I can't help thinking that it would almost be as if I were committing *junshi* myself: following my own era (and the principles I've fought for) into death. I'm speaking metaphorically, of course."

"So are you thinking of your demise abstractly, as something that will take place in the distant future?" Masao asked lightly. "Or are you ready to predict a specific date, based on some psychic premonition?"

"Is that another of Unaiko's questions, or did you come up with it just now?" I said, parrying Masao's facetious inquiry with one of my own.

"Moving right along," Masao said, changing the subject, "it looks as though you're nearly finished with your packing, so what do you have planned for today? Asa was telling me that you'd been thinking about scouting locations for your book, before you decided to abandon it. I've already done quite a bit of research on the topic, so how would it be if we took a stroll down to the Kame River? The thing is, these days you're more of a stranger around here than I am, so if you should come face-to-face with any of the local citizens, I think the surprise would probably be mutual! Even so, the other party would most likely know who you are, and if you were to ignore them when they spoke to you it could be kind of awkward. Here's my plan: when someone calls out to you, I'll respond to the greeting with the usual pleasantries, and you can just nod in their direction. Shall we stage a quick rehearsal? No? Okay, never mind. I'm sure it'll be fine." Clearly, Masao Anai had given serious thought to our proposed outing.

"Well then, Mr. Choko," he continued, "how would you feel about going for a swim around Myoto Rock, where you once came close to drowning as a child after you'd stuck your head in a fissure in the rock to look at a school of dace and weren't able to pull it out? Before you arrived from Tokyo, Suke & Kaku—you know, our resident comedy duo—said they wanted to check out the site of that famous story, so they went and dived off the rock. When they came back, they reported having seen quite a few of those little silver fish still swimming around!"

Masao and I went our separate ways for a few minutes while we changed into our swim trunks, worn under T-shirts and knee-length shorts. Then we met up again and set off walking down the slope into the river valley. The school term had started early because of a break in the farmers' busy season, and there were no children to be seen on the road that snaked along beside the river or on the other road between the rows of houses lining the embankment above. No adults rushed to greet us, either. If I were to run into any old acquaintances from the area, they would most likely be in their sixties or seventies, if not older, but down in the valley on that sunny morning it appeared as if all the humans had simply vanished.

Masao and I took a rustic flight of stairs down to the banks of the river. There wasn't a soul to be seen in the vicinity of Myoto Rock, which was normally the most popular swimming hole in the area. The famous rock was a pyramid-shaped boulder, and the part above the waterline was a good three meters high. There had once been a similarly shaped rock next to it, but some years ago, when building materials were scarce, that half of the "couple" had been dynamited and ground up to make cement for the construction of a now-abandoned bridge. In local lore, the sundered rocks were seen as a metaphor for marital separation, and by felicitous coincidence there were a great many widows living along the river (my own mother included). A deep pool had been created where the remaining rock blocked the flow of the current, and the natural cove was a popular destination. This was the same cove where I had watched the flooded river carry my father and his boat away on the night of the big storm.

Masao and I shed our tops and shorts and waded into the water until it reached our hips, then turned toward the rock. As the current bore us upstream, I gazed at the forest on the opposite bank. The towering trees were taller than I remembered, and the branches appeared to be healthy, mature, and nicely filled out. Overall, the landscape looked much healthier than it had in the years immediately following the end of the war when the forest surrounding the valley was in a sadly weakened state, probably due to neglect. Since then the forest had gradually recovered its vitality, in what struck me as inverse proportion to the mass exodus of young people.

When the water level reached our chests Masao and I began to swim, both using the overhand freestyle stroke known as the Australian crawl. My eyes were protected by the same goggles I had been using for years whenever I swam in the heavily chlorinated public pools in Tokyo. When we reached the big rock we latched on to the submerged part of the monolith, caught our breath, and rested for a while, just as I had done so many times during my childhood.

Masao looked at me with reddened eyes (he wasn't wearing goggles) and said teasingly: "You've written about teaching yourself to swim using instruction books written in French and English, and after seeing your stroke, I totally believe in the veracity of the story."

"Yes, that method did help me refine my own naturally elegant style," I replied, echoing his tongue-in-cheek tone.

"On the right side, if you go about a meter along the rock and then look underwater, you'll see a large crack in the base," Masao said, serious now. "You remember that, of course. Suke was saying that the crack is wide enough for a child's head to fit through it quite easily. We know what happened the last time you tried, but how about today? Are you game to give it another go?"

"Sure," I said. "Why not?" I began to creep slowly across the rock face, battling the current all the way. When I had tried to pull off the same maneuver as a child, I seemed to recall losing my grip and being swept away by the overwhelming force of the water crashing against the bifurcated rock. On this day, however, I was able to use a vigorous scissors kick to hold my own, and it occurred to me that I was now confronting the challenges of Nature with grown-up skills— notwithstanding the physical weakening that was a palpable reminder of the passage of years. When I reached the well-remembered spot, I dove underwater and tried to wedge myself between the two slabs of rock. My feet and body slipped through easily enough, but my adult-size head was simply too large. I did, at least, catch a glimpse of the shimmering water in the brightly lit grotto beyond the fissure. *Mission unaccomplished,* I thought as I allowed the dynamic swirl of the water to buffet my body for a moment. Then I planted my feet firmly on the river bottom, turned around, and returned to where Masao was waiting.

"Hey," he greeted me, in his overly familiar, slightly sardonic way. "It was a foregone conclusion that your head wasn't going to fit through the crack in the rock. But if you lower your expectations and just try to peer directly through the crack into the grotto, I can almost guarantee success."

Focusing my efforts on that more modest goal, I made my way back to the crack in the rock. Peering through my prescription goggles (custom-made to remedy my severe myopia), I saw a nostalgic sight: in the shady grotto illuminated by pale blue-green light, dozens upon dozens of dace were futilely struggling to swim upstream against the current. The glossy black eyes on the sides of those lustrous silvery-blue heads seemed to rotate briefly in my direction, as if the fish were peripherally aware of my presence.

I stayed there, watching, until I ran out of breath. Then I pushed off from the edge of the rock I'd been holding on to, thrust my face above the water, filled my lungs with a deep draught of fresh air, and simply let my body drift, borne along by the kinetic current. After floating passively for a while, I swam back to the spot beside the rock where Masao had stationed himself.

Right away, he began talking. "In the first edition of *The Child with the Melancholy Face*, you wrote about seeing hundreds of those tiny fish here when you were ten years old," he said. "You stuck your head through the underwater crack and you saw your child-self, Kogii, reflected in the eyes of the fish. And then as you were trying to get a better look you got your head wedged between the rocks, and if your mother hadn't come to the rescue you would almost certainly have drowned. The fish you found so fascinating that day probably numbered only in the dozens, as opposed to hundreds. I was talking to some people who used to fish this river in the old days, and they said the dace population around Myoto Rock hasn't really fluctuated much over the years. What I'm trying to say is you were probably looking at pretty much the same scene today as the one that made such an impression on you more than sixty years ago. There were only a few dozen fish today, right?"

"I didn't really get a clear sense of how many there were," I said. "The first time, when I got my head stuck between the rocks and was fading fast, I remember feeling as if I was somehow going to be magically transformed into a dace. And if that had happened, I thought, then *I*-as-fish would be looking back at the human me."

"Wait, that doesn't make sense. If you had drowned on that day, then the *you* who was peeping at the school of fish would no longer exist in this dimension at all."

"You're right," I said dreamily. "I'm the old man who wasn't able to become one of those fish (however many there may have been) swimming eternally in the bluish-green light of the grotto beyond the crack in the rocks."

"Speaking of drowning," Masao said. "You mentioned that you had never been able to imagine what it was like for your father—who was twenty years younger than you are now, at least—when he set out on the overflowing river, propelled by the powerful current, and was carried far downstream, where his lifeless body ended up rising and falling on the riverbed."

"True," I said. "And I can't help thinking my father's drowned body must have been moving exactly like one of those fish." My eyes were suddenly wet in a way that had nothing to do with swimming in the river.

Masao paid no attention to my momentary lapse into grief. "Unaiko got mad at me when I told her I was planning to drag your old bones down here," he remarked, speaking in a rather disrespectful manner. Along with the contrast between my elderly shoulders and his strong brown torso (we were both submerged in the river up to our sternums), his cocky tone seemed like a brutally explicit reminder of the difference in our ages. "She was worried you might catch a cold, or worse, from being in the water for such a long time."

Masao turned around and looked downstream, where two concrete bridges—one old, one new—were suspended side by side. Atop the older of the two bridges (long since retired from active duty because it couldn't handle the increased traffic) two women were wildly windmilling their arms in greeting. I immediately recognized one of them as Unaiko.

"Shall we head back now?" Masao said.

He and I let go of the rock we'd been clinging to, and after allowing the current to gently push us into place we commenced swimming, using the usual crawl stroke. Evidently showing off for the women—who continued to wave energetically in our direction and whom he could see every time he raised his head to take a breath—Masao made a visible effort to open up a lead on me. I wasn't going to let that happen if I could help it, so I redoubled my own efforts.

In my childhood, we used to make our way home by riding the vigorous current that rippled out from the deep water next to Myoto Rock and then climbing up the cliff next to the road along the river, but Masao kept heading diagonally toward the shore until the water became so shallow that we had to stop swimming. By the time we both stood up on the sandy gravel of the river bottom, with the water barely covering our knees, we must have swum at least 150 meters. I didn't think about it until afterward, but I was no longer in shape for serious competitive swimming and the long burst of intense exertion clearly took a toll on my body.

We made our way onto the riverbank where we had left our things, and as we were drying off with the towels we'd brought, I couldn't help feeling apprehensive about the prospect of having Unaiko observe my legs, which were quivering with exhaustion. But when I glanced at the bridge after Masao and I had finished throwing on our clothes, I saw that she and her companion had been engulfed in a gaggle of junior high students on their way home from school, and the two older women were focused on dealing with their clamorous admirers. There was no way I was going to climb up to the bridge in my bedraggled state with an audience of teenage girls, so I stood at the mouth of the river with Masao, chatting desultorily.

"In the autumn of last year," he said, "there were masses of glorious red flowers on the slope below what's left of the chestnut groves, and it occurred to me that they must be the red spider lilies you've written about."

"Right, that's where they harvest the bulbs of the red spider lilies—if anyone's even doing those old-fashioned jobs these days. When those long-stemmed flowers are in full, extravagant bloom, with their delicate stamens and pistils bursting forth from inside the curvaceous outer petals of the bright red flowers, they almost look like fireworks. The entire slope becomes a sea of scarlet, and it's really something to behold."

"Oh, I know," Masao agreed. "I was thinking last fall that if someone with entrepreneurial inclinations came across a field of these flowers they would naturally see the business possibilities and think, *Ka-ching!* I mean, there's always a market for cut flowers. And then it occurred to me that when the young soldiers who were here during the war saw this slope in full bloom they might have thought it was on fire, like a great wave of flames blanketing the entire hillside."

I really didn't feel like getting into a discussion of the young officers—a subject to which Masao appeared to have given a great deal of thought. When I didn't respond, he started talking about Unaiko's throng of admirers.

"Unaiko has tons of fans around here," he said. "Not only those girls you see on the bridge, but high school girls from the neighboring towns as well. Her master plan is to use the kids as conduits to reach their parents; that's why she's making such an effort to cultivate friendly relations with the young students. She's thinking way beyond the theatrical aspect and is hoping to exploit these relationships for a higher purpose: to advance some of the social issues she cares about."

I nodded, but I had something else on my mind. "Our swim seems to have taken rather a lot out of me," I said. "Would you mind bringing the car around to the foot of the bridge? I mean, assuming Unaiko and her friend came down in the car."

For the first time, Masao seemed to notice that I was in a state of complete exhaustion. However, it turned out Unaiko, too, had come on foot, so I wearily showed Masao an old shortcut back to the Forest House, by way of an iron ladder located a short ways upstream.

# 4

I turned in unusually early that night and awakened abruptly long before dawn. Even during the last stages of slumber, I was already in the throes of a panic that was distinctly physical as opposed to psychosomatic. Then something bizarre appeared in my darkly dreaming mind: a sort of emblem of entropy, a shapeless shape and formless form whose entire raison d'être seemed to be to disintegrate and crumble into nothingness. The force of the breakdown came as a massive shock to my system, but the part of my brain that should have registered the blow was strangely silent. Still vaguely dream-dazed and half asleep, I switched on the bedside lamp.

A startling sight met my newly opened eyes. A rough-edged, angular black disk, something like a dinged-up flying saucer, appeared to be lodged in the juncture where the bookcase met the sloping ceiling. The disk began to rotate sharply to the right, gaining power and momentum as it moved, and then it suddenly seemed to collapse with a thud. (I knew I was imagining the sound effects, but that didn't make the sensation any less vivid.)

Instinctively, I closed my eyes. *I've never experienced anything like this before, but I know what's happening,* I thought. *I'm being attacked by a monstrous dizzy spell.* When I opened my eyes again, the same thing happened: I saw the whirling-disk apparition, and then it tipped over to the right and dissolved roughly into nothingness.

This time, I kept my eyes open. It dawned on me that the entire time I had been asleep, I'd been seeing the disk (which was, I thought later, half metaphor and half hallucination) on a continuous loop, repeatedly tipping over and shattering into pieces. And now the phantom disk had somehow slipped behind the spines of the books on the shelf, and the books appeared to be falling over as if mowed down by machine-gun fire. With a supreme effort I extended my limp, inert right arm (really, it felt almost boneless) and switched off the lamp, plunging the room into darkness again. Even with the light off, I had a visceral sense that the unstable black disk was incessantly somersaulting around me, but imagining the disintegrative spinning was slightly more bearable than opening my eyes and actually seeming to *see* it. Clearly, the force that had ambushed me as I lay sleeping (or perhaps the ambush had only begun when I was swimming upstream toward a painful awakening) wasn't abating at all. On the contrary, it was gathering strength and becoming ever more intense.

Without opening my eyes, I raised my upper body and tried to sit up, but since my torso was every bit as weak and floppy as my wet-noodle arms, the episode made me feel as if my upper body, too, was twirling around, and I immediately toppled over. As my faculties gradually returned, it struck me that this was the most extreme loss of equilibrium I had ever experienced by far. And in the midst of the epiphany—which was only possible because while my body (including my eyes) was overcome by wooziness, my brain was still functioning normally—I found myself thinking that this was surely just the beginning. As the affliction progressed, wouldn't the next stage be epic, excruciating headaches? Also, with vertigo of this magnitude, wasn't it likely that I would soon be assailed by violent spasms of nausea? Quickly, before either of those symptoms manifested, there was something I needed to attend to.

I opened my eyes. The disorienting tilt-a-whirl sensation caused me to quickly squeeze them shut again, but I was still able to get my bearings in relation to the contours of the room. Based on that brief reconnaissance I knew my first move should be to slide my body out of the bed and onto the floor, while keeping my eyes closed. However, when I tried to execute that simple maneuver it didn't go too well.

I eventually managed to turn over onto my stomach, and from there I was finally able to tumble from the bed onto the floor. After lying inert for a moment I made my shaky way into the hall, creeping along on my weakened extremities. The dreaded headache hadn't yet made its appearance, and as long as I kept my eyes closed I could think quite lucidly. (However, the moment I opened them my consciousness would immediately shatter into a million vertiginous fragments.) Keeping my eyes tightly shut, I slowly made my way down the hall toward the bathroom, crawling blindly along on all fours while I theorized about what might be happening. *Something must be going haywire inside my brain,* I speculated. *Maybe some sort of aneurysm, or a stroke?*

A number of my contemporaries had been stricken with this type of disorder out of the blue, and some had simply dropped dead on the spot. As for the ones who went on living, in many cases their mental acuity was adversely affected, and they were never the same again. If that happened to me it would be curtains for my work as a

writer, and my life would effectively be over. I didn't know whether
I was about to suffer irreversible brain damage or die outright, but
either way I would be finished as a novelist. Therefore, I concluded,
I needed to tidy up all the loose ends of my work before the onset
of the potentially fatal headache that, I felt certain, was waiting in
the wings.

I thought first of my journalism projects. I wanted to have someone discard the entire lot—both the pieces I had just started drafting
and the manuscripts that were further along. If I could leave behind
a note containing those instructions, surely someone would carry out
my wishes (although at the moment, nobody's name sprang to mind).
It occurred to me that in the empty space between the end of the bed
and the south-facing window there was an armchair where I liked to
sit and work, using a clipboard equipped with a supply of manuscript
paper. In my present state there was no way I could have written a
coherent last will and testament, or even held a fountain pen, but
there were several fat, already sharpened pencils nearby—Lyra-brand
colored pencils, made in Germany, in a deep sky blue—and I thought
I could grab one of those and scribble something reasonably legible
without having to open my eyes.

But what, exactly, was I going to tell my unnamed literary execu-
tor to dispose of? I couldn't think of a thing, and it wasn't because the
seizure had scrambled my brain; on the contrary, I felt as though my
mind was functioning with complete clarity. The reason nothing came
to mind was that I really didn't have any work in progress to speak of.

A complex wave of emotions—a kind of wretched, self-mocking
contempt for my current state of being, coupled with a feeling of relief
that I wouldn't be leaving any important assignments uncompleted—
washed over me. The existential bottom line seemed to be that the
*I* who was here right now was already as good as dead. And if I was
already dead, it was only natural that I wouldn't experience the slightest fear of dying.

A moment later, though, I was hit by an avalanche of a different
kind of apprehension: the concern that, as my mother had pointed

out, I hadn't done anything to prepare Akari for his own journey to the Other Side. If I had dared to look down at the poetry stone in the back garden I would surely have been plunged into depression by the realization that on the cusp of old age I had neglected my parental duties, my work was in shambles, and my life was essentially devoid of meaning.

Even so, against my better judgment, I opened my eyes. And before the diabolical disk came crashing down around me again, I imagined myself reading the first lines of the poem carved into the big round stone:

*You didn't get Kogii ready to go up into the forest*
*And like the river current, you won't return home.*

# 5

Three days after the terrifying dizzy spell, I was back at home in Seijo. As it happened, there was an excellent physician nearby (he had become a family friend and had helped us countless times), and he was optimistic about my prognosis. After listening carefully to my description of the extreme vertigo I had experienced just before leaving Shikoku, he said it would most likely be a transitory thing, and that cheered me up considerably. The doctor recommended waiting awhile before going to the hospital for a complete examination, and in the meantime I was dutifully taking the medications he'd prescribed.

I spent a week or so lounging around the house in recovery mode. One morning when I was asleep in my second-floor bedroom I was awakened by the sound of the telephone ringing downstairs in the living room. I had heard from Chikashi that a side effect of Akari's continuing depression was that he had stopped answering the phone. Since returning from Shikoku I'd been having trouble falling asleep at night, so I had been getting up after the rest of the family had already finished lunch, but when I glanced at the clock on the wall it showed half past nine. I got out of bed, and as I was making my groggy way down the stairs the phone stopped ringing.

Akari was perched on the edge of a dining-room chair, leaning backward with both feet propped on a second chair while he stared at the five-line composition paper he was holding on his knees. He was the very picture of a middle-aged man in the throes of deep depression. Even so, he appeared to be engrossed in erasing one section of his composition, and he didn't look up when I entered the room.

Just then the phone began to ring again. As I had expected, it was Chikashi calling from the post office. Apparently a special delivery package had arrived very late the previous night, and the postman, assuming we would all be asleep, had thoughtfully decided to leave a note rather than disturb us with the doorbell. The next morning when Chikashi called the local post office, a clerk had read the sender's name and address to her and had suggested that if the package was important the quickest option would be to pick it up in person. She was at the post office now, waiting in line, but the place was mobbed and the queue was longer than usual.

Also, Chikashi went on, Akari had an appointment for a routine physical, but she wasn't feeling well enough to take him to the university hospital herself and hoped I wouldn't mind going in her stead. By the time I had managed to make myself somewhat presentable (Akari was already dressed and was still working on his composition), Chikashi was back. She handed me my package as she got out of the cab, and then Akari and I piled in and headed for the hospital.

We made it there barely in time for our eleven o'clock appointment, but as it turned out there was a notice posted near the receptionist's window saying that the doctor we needed to see was running at least an hour behind schedule. The delay didn't bother me at all. Chikashi had chosen this particular specialist because he was well known for his expertise in treating patients who had been born with brain damage, and we understood that he would sometimes be called away on unforeseen emergencies. When I presented Akari's patient

ID card to the nurse on duty, she told me to go ahead and get his blood work done.

As I was looking through the file containing our insurance information and other documents, I saw that an appointment for blood tests was scheduled for two days later, so I suspected that the nurse had thoughtfully found a way to make use of the fallow time we were going to spend waiting for the doctor. The blood tests took only a few moments to complete, but they left Akari in a foul mood. He had a phobia about having blood drawn and hadn't been expecting to undergo that ordeal on this visit.

After securing a couple of seats in the waiting area, I finally set about opening my exotic-looking package. The sender was a cherished friend, a distinguished American woman whom I had known for decades (I'll call her Jean S.). The enclosed note explained that she had finally gotten around to sorting through the mementos left behind by a mutual friend of ours, the late university professor, author, and comparative culture scholar Edward W. Said. During the process, Jean wrote, she had come across something she thought I might like to see, so she was sending it along. The item in question was still in its original, stiff paper file folder, and Jean had simply wrapped up the folder and popped it in the mail. The folder contained a trio of custom-bound booklets: the musical scores for three of Beethoven's piano sonatas, printed on the finest grade of thick cotton paper.

Jean S. was the person who had first brought Edward W. Said and me together, many years ago. The two of them were old friends, and her posh apartment on a high floor in one of the most desirable neighborhoods in Manhattan even boasted an "Edward W. Said Room" decorated with motifs inspired by antique Islamic books. By chance, I was in New York City at the time of Said's discharge from the hospital after a stay there (the first of many) to treat the leukemia that would eventually kill him; Jean threw a party to celebrate, and I was invited. Every year since we had met, Said and Jean had made a custom of telephoning me late at night on New Year's Eve (which was already New Year's Day, postmeridian, in Japan) from wherever they happened to be enjoying dinner together along with their respective families.

Shortly after my brother-in-law, the film director Goro Hanawa, committed suicide, Jean S. happened to be throwing another of her famous parties. Edward W. Said was there, and he entertained the guests by playing the piano—something he did exceedingly well. When Jean shared the news about Goro, Said apparently sat down and wrote a condolence note on the back of the score of the Beethoven piece he had just finished playing. Later, Jean made a clean copy of the draft on plain paper, carefully transcribing Said's longhand scrawl for added legibility, and faxed it to me in Tokyo (I've never made the transition to email). After Said died, Jean told me that if the original note ever turned up again, she would send it to me.

For the first time that day Akari was showing an active interest in what I was doing, and he cast an expert eye on the sheet music as it emerged from the wrappings. "Those are the three sonatas dedicated to Haydn," he announced. I knew from a long letter Jean S. had sent earlier that Said had been playing the second of those sonatas at her party. Looking through the score, I quickly located his distinctive penciled annotations, and then I stuck the slim booklets back in their folder.

I shepherded Akari to the nearest restroom, which was down on the first floor. Then, in the interest of efficiency, I quickly washed his hands and mine as well. This was another departure from the normal routine—he usually performed such simple functions by himself— and it clearly intensified his already disgruntled mood. On the way back upstairs we stopped in at the hospital gift shop, where I bought a plastic pouch containing two sharpened pencils: HB and B (medium soft and slightly softer, respectively).

When we returned to the seats where we'd left our things, I handed Akari the B pencil (the softer of the two) along with the sheet music for the sonatas. As he held out his hands to receive these

unexpected gifts, my son's formerly downcast face was transmogri-
fied by joy.

Whenever Akari was reading sheet music he would always draw
light circles around certain bars or measures with a pencil, exerting
barely any force. For reasons unknown to me, he would also write
an assortment of glyphlike symbols in the margins. I had already
ascertained that the sheet music (which was, in effect, a posthumous
bequest from my dear friend Edward W. Said) was printed on exceptionally thick, sturdy paper. My long-range plan was to transcribe
any notations Akari might make on those pages onto the ordinary
music-store sheet music for the same sonatas, which I knew we had
at home. I figured if I wielded the eraser with particular care, no visible marks would remain on the originals.

Akari began reading the sheet music, holding one booklet at
arm's length in front of his chest, and I caught a whiff of the same
intoxicating aroma of vintage ink and paper that suffused the innumerable volumes of European special editions in my library. Before
long my son was completely immersed in the scores, and I hesitated
to disturb him.

In a low voice, I ventured a question: "Is it interesting?"

"Yes, very interesting!"

"I'm glad. Could I take a quick peek at the sheet music for the
second sonata?"

"Oh, that part is really interesting!" Akari replied, tapping his
finger on the relevant section with an emphatic staccato rhythm.

"My friend Jean mentioned in an earlier letter that Edward Said
played the first theme humorously, while the second one sounded sad
and mournful," I said. "At the time, I said to you, 'Please choose your
favorite CD of this piece from your collection.' Do you remember?"

"Yes! And I put on the Friedrich Gulda recording," Akari said
eagerly. "He played it the same way, too."

"You're right," I agreed. "It was just the same, and with the volume
muted as well. Could you please circle the relevant sections to show

me where those passages are? Then when we get home I'll listen to the CD again, using your annotated score for reference."

A huge grin spread across Akari's face, and it occurred to me that this was the first time I had seen my son looking so happy since my return to Tokyo. He turned his attention back to the sheet music, and I felt a sense of relief as I watched him intently following the tempo of the written notes, while the imagined music welled up inside him. Then I remembered that as we were rushing out of the house earlier I had grabbed the first volume of *The Golden Bough* and brought it along. (I'd been randomly paging through those books since finding them in the red leather trunk.) I fished the book out of my bag and began to read.

Akari, meanwhile, had finished examining the second of the three booklets of sheet music and was now going through it again, starting with the first movement. I was sitting next to my son, of course, and the seat on his other side was occupied by a woman who looked as if she might be a schoolteacher. The sheet music was so large that it protruded into her space; I felt awkward and apologetic about the encroachment, but the woman didn't seem to mind. On the contrary, she appeared to be intrigued by Akari's fervent concentration.

By the time we were finally summoned to see the doctor, after waiting for a good three hours, Akari had placed the sheet music on his knees and was staring blankly at it, wearily cradling his head in his hands. It took me longer than expected to fit the booklets back into their envelope, and Akari, who was watching me anxiously out of the corner of his eye, became agitated and marched off to the exam room by himself.

At that point, the woman in the neighboring chair spoke. "Why don't you just leave those things with me?" she suggested. "It doesn't look as if my name will be called any time soon."

After our session with the doctor, Akari and I returned to our seats in the waiting room. The woman handed me the envelope containing the sheet music, and Akari resumed his intensive perusal of the scores. Leaving him there, I ambled over to the cashier's window and took my place at the end of the line. After I'd settled the bill and was returning to the seating area, I saw Akari handing something to the woman as she got to her feet (she had apparently been called in for her own appointment at last).

Our paths crossed in the middle of the room, and the woman laughingly brandished a fat ballpoint pen in my face. "This is really handy—it has two different colors!" she said. "The ink is easier to see, too, so Akari didn't need to squint so much."

It took an epic effort of will to control the borderline-violent feelings welling up inside me. I rushed back to where Akari was sitting with one booklet of sheet music open on his lap. He had drawn a heavy, dark circle around the passage we had discussed earlier, and in the blank space at the top of the page he had written "K. 550" in gigantic, indelible letters!

Akari glanced at me, beaming happily, but when he saw the grim expression on my face his smile was quickly extinguished. He stammered in a weak voice, "I-I don't like to write with pale, thin letters, so . . ." The sentence trailed off, unfinished.

"You're an idiot!" I shouted.

Akari's face crumpled into a roiling mass of strong emotions. After a brief, frozen moment he raised both arms above his head and began to flap them violently against his ears, like flightless wings. There was only one way to interpret this behavior: clearly, he was trying to injure himself. It had been quite a while since I had seen Akari act out like this, but on the rare occasions when I had scolded him in the past, he had invariably reacted with sullen defiance accompanied by an attempt to punish himself physically, as he was doing now.

While the people around us stared openly—I couldn't really blame them; at the very least, this behavior wasn't the sort of thing you expect to see from a large man in his forties—I yanked Akari to his feet. I grabbed the sheet music booklets, which had fallen to the floor, and marched my distraught son downstairs and out of the building.

I couldn't have imagined then how vast the repercussions of my thoughtless and intemperate speech would be, but I was already thinking, over and over again, *YOU'RE the bloody idiot.*

## 6

As we were riding home in the taxi, Akari kept his face turned away from me, and his body language conveyed a single unambiguous message: *I reject you completely.* He wasn't rubbing his forehead against the window, as he sometimes did when he was upset; he simply sat and stared at the passing cityscape while keeping his back unnaturally straight.

When Chikashi opened the gate to let us in, Akari practically knocked her over in his headlong rush to get to his room. I put the envelope containing the three scores on the dining table and sat down on the nearest chair. Chikashi, with her finely tuned mother's intuition, had immediately sensed something unusual about Akari's behavior, and after sitting with me in silence for a few moments she got up and went into his bedroom.

Being careful not to look at the pages that had been permanently defaced with two different colors of ballpoint ink, I took the three scores out of the envelope and laid them on the table. Then I began to read the tiny words written in pencil on the back cover of the second score. I recognized those scribbles immediately as the words Jean S. had copied over in fountain pen and faxed to me. That fax had been pinned to the wall in front of my desk for the past several years.

What Said had written on the back of the Beethoven score, in English, was his supportive outpouring of sympathy upon learning that my longtime friend and brother-in-law, the film director Goro Hanawa, had committed suicide by jumping off a building in Tokyo. I had translated the note into Japanese and had later quoted it at the memorial service held in Tokyo for Edward W. Said himself after he finally succumbed to leukemia in 2003. (By that time, I had long since committed those eloquent condolences to memory, in both languages.)

*I've just heard from Jean about the difficulties you've been hav-
ing, and therefore thought I'd write and express my solidarity and
affection. You are a very strong man and a sensitive one, so the
coping will occur, I am sure.*

Chikashi returned to the table. The desecrated sheet music lay
spread out in front of me, but I wasn't looking at it. With her eyes
fixed on the three scores, Chikashi began to speak.

"Akari is very concerned about having inadvertently damaged the
sheet music for the Beethoven piano sonata," she said, "but he also told
me that you called him an idiot? Nothing like that has ever happened
before, not even once, and to be honest I'm in a state of shock. In the
past, you've always gone to the opposite extreme. Surely you remember
the time when you actually came to blows with someone who said those
same cruel words to Akari when we were on the train coming home from
Kita-Karuizawa, and you ended up being forced to get off the Takasaki?
Then when the railway police decided the incident was too serious for
them to handle, you were dragged to the municipal police station, and
we all went there together. I told Akari that his father would never say
such a thing to him, but he won't listen. He just keeps repeating, 'Papa
said to me, *"You're an idiot."*'

"Akari knows he did something wrong," Chikashi continued,
"but he seems to want to explain the reason behind his actions. He
says he was only writing some notes about Beethoven's second piano
sonata, which I gather you had asked for, in ballpoint pen."

"It's true," I interrupted. "I did call Akari an idiot." (I was feeling immeasurably sad and sorry, of course, but I still wasn't able to
subdue the anger churning inside me, so I took refuge in self-serving
rationalization.) "The thing is, the draft of the condolence message
Edward Said wrote at Jean's house right after Goro died was on the
back of the sheet music for the second sonata. So you can see why
that particular score is so precious to me."

After I had shown Chikashi the cover of the booklet in question,
I opened it to the defiled page—again, with my eyes averted because

it would have been too painful to look at it directly. Chikashi took the opened score and went into Akari's room. I could hear the conversation: Chikashi asking the same questions over and over in a gentle, restrained voice and then, after a long pause, Akari's replies, in which he seemed somehow to be resisting his own resistance.

I went into the kitchen to get a drink of water, but soon changed my mind. Instead, I poured a mixture of dark beer and lager (one full bottle of each) into a giant goblet, then drained the entire glass in a single gulp and let out a deep sigh that somehow morphed into a loud belch. As I was about to return to the dining room, I saw Akari coming in through the other door, propelled from behind by Chikashi. Ignoring me completely, he took a CD off the shelf and handed it to his mother.

In the meantime, I had made a hasty U-turn and was in the kitchen refilling my goblet (this time only with regular beer) when I heard the sounds of a piano recording. As I stood there listening to the first strains of Gulda's performance (he was playing the first movement of the second of the three sonatas Beethoven wrote and dedicated to Haydn in 1795), I was jolted once again by the thought that this was probably the same way Edward Said would have performed this composition.

The music ended, and a few seconds later the air was filled with the sound of Mozart's Symphony no. 40 in G Minor, K. 550. I couldn't tell who was wielding the baton, but the melody was an unmistakable echo of the theme of the passage we had heard a few minutes earlier. I downed my second glass of beer and went into the dining room, where Akari was in the process of carefully replacing the two CDs in their clear plastic cases.

"Akari keeps saying he was trying to use the sheet music he was looking at in the waiting room to show you what these two compositions have in common," Chikashi said. "So he was shocked when you responded by screaming, 'You're an idiot!'"

I glanced reluctantly at the page of sheet music, hideously defaced by two colors of ballpoint pen, which Chikashi had laid out again on the dining-room table. No one spoke for several minutes, but there seemed to be some kind of crucial decision floating in the air. Then Akari, who appeared to have been waiting for me to make some sort of conciliatory gesture, gave up and shambled off to his room. I couldn't help thinking, not for the first time, that his distinctive gait bore a startling resemblance to the way Goro Hanawa used to walk.

This all happened on a Saturday. A week passed, during which I hardly saw my son at all. I spent most of my time in my upstairs lair—a book-filled study equipped with a narrow bed—while Akari remained sequestered in his room. (This wasn't a dramatic change from his usual behavior; he always spent a great deal of time in his bedroom, where he could listen to classical music programs on the FM radio next to his bed. When he got bored with the radio, he kept several of his favorite CDs cued up in his personal boom box and he enjoyed letting them play over and over on an endless loop.) In order to avoid running into Akari at breakfast or lunch I would creep downstairs in midmorning and eat a solitary brunch, then trudge back upstairs.

One day during this bleak period Chikashi brought me the mail as usual, along with a cup of coffee. While I was glancing over the letters she tidied up my bed and sat down on the newly smooth covers. Then she began to talk about the extra-large elephant in the room— a topic that hadn't been touched upon since the tense, emotionally fraught session in the dining room.

"Akari says that when you were at the hospital the other day, you asked him to show you the musical similarities between the Beethoven piano sonata and the Mozart symphony," she said slowly. "Evidently he was in the process of marking the pertinent passages in pencil when the lady who was sitting next to him lent him a ballpoint pen. Naturally, it's hard for Akari to understand the subtle distinction whereby it's perfectly fine to use pencil but switching to pen causes his father to have a major meltdown and call him names in public. Akari just happened to accept the seemingly innocuous loan of a pen. Really, wasn't that his only mistake? He does seem to understand now that he shouldn't have defaced the pristine sheet music, even though the damage he did was unintentional. But because of the extreme way you reacted, shouting, 'You're an idiot'—which, as you know, is the single most hurtful thing you could possibly say to him—he doesn't feel inclined to return to the amicable relations the two of you enjoyed before this happened. For your part, you're apparently unwilling to make the first move toward a peaceful settlement, so things seem to be at an impasse.

"I talked to Maki on the phone this morning, and I have to say that the way she criticized your behavior gave me chills. 'Papa doesn't have the courage to make his peace with Akari,' she said. 'I mean, he called Akari an idiot, for God's sake. I'm sure Papa is wallowing in his own private darkness now, wondering if there's any way to erase the egregious incident from Akari's memory, weighing various options before ultimately deciding there's nothing to be done. And that's why Papa won't even try to make his peace with Akari; he figures it's hopeless, and he's simply given up.' And then she went on to say that for the past year or so, every time she has come to visit us here in Seijo she's been noticing a gradual change in Akari, but she thinks you have probably overlooked it. She said, 'Papa and Akari have been practically inseparable for more than forty years, and it seems to me that Papa's oppressive (some might even say tyrannical) attitude toward Akari has become more and more set in stone. I know it probably has something to do with Papa's advancing age; I understand the reasons, and I'm not unsympathetic, but I'm afraid that if this situation continues to fester it could go way beyond the level of terrible insults like "You're an idiot." I mean, I think matters could easily escalate to the point of physical violence or permanent estrangement.'

"Maki was quite worked up, and she said some pretty extreme things. 'I'm afraid Papa could end up like King Lear,' she told me, 'wandering lost in the wilderness without even a Fool to accompany him. And if he went on wandering alone until he started to lose his mind, then maybe he would decide to resolve things himself, in the most drastic way, before he did anything that might cause a public scandal. And if he did decide to do away with himself, God knows there's plenty of deserted wasteland around here where he could do the deed . . .'

"Maki was very angry about your calling her big brother an idiot," Chikashi continued, "and I'm sure that's why she said those things. But putting her concerns aside for now, there are some issues I've been worried about myself, and I'd like to discuss them with you. It goes without saying that both you and I are growing older, but have you given any serious thought to the fact that Akari is aging rapidly as well, especially on the physical level? As you know, you added a daily walk to your normal sedentary routine of sitting around the house reading and writing after the doctor said you should take Akari out walking as part of a fitness regimen. It went on for a long time, and then when Akari started having more and more epileptic seizures during your daily walks together, you got into the habit of walking for an hour early in the morning by yourself. You simply gave up taking Akari along. But I think we both understand that the worsening of his epilepsy wasn't the real reason you gave up walking with Akari. Rather, it was because the degenerative aging process was making it too difficult for him to continue with those outings.

"And then there's the dental situation. As you know, more than half of Akari's teeth are already bad. I know the doctor talked to you about the results of the most recent set of blood tests, and while I only skimmed the written report, there seemed to be very few items on the list that weren't marked 'Requires Medical Care.' His sleep apnea hasn't improved, either, even though we've done our best to get his weight down. The reason he takes so many catnaps during the day is to compensate for all the sleep he loses at night.

"Back in the days when Akari was still going to work at the support center for disabled people, the head of the institute showed me a disheartening statistical chart of average life expectancy based on all the people who had ever been enrolled there. You were with me that day, remember? Anyway, he explained that after a certain point children with disabilities begin to age more rapidly than their parents, and when I tried to talk to you about it later, your only reply was silence.

Now, though, I realize that what the doctor said is absolutely true, and the problem is we're aging at a worrisomely rapid rate as well.

"On another topic, I don't think I fully understood how heartsick you were about having to abandon work on the drowning novel. On reflection, I think this is the first time you not only didn't finish a book you'd started, but simply stopped writing altogether. (You did take a short break once, early on, but it actually involved this very same book in its earliest incarnation.) Little by little, though, I'm starting to grasp the impact this disappointment has had on you, just from seeing how low your spirits have been since you returned from your fruitless trip to Shikoku. I don't know when I've seen you as miserable as you are now, and it's also obvious that Akari has been in seriously low spirits. You know how sometimes you'll be sitting in the living room reading a book while he's in the dining room studying a musical score? (That is, when you aren't both holed up in your rooms.) Well, the scenario appears outwardly unchanged, apart from the fact that you aren't speaking to each other. But for quite a while I've felt as if there were two giant mounds of depression permanently camped out in the house, and I couldn't help worrying about what might happen if those two volatile lumps of unhappiness were to collide. And now what I think has happened is that they finally did crash into each other.

"Since Akari was born, you have never once said anything even remotely like 'You're an idiot' to him. Akari clearly understands the meaning of the heartless phrase you blurted out, and when I think about it I can understand why, as Maki mentioned, you're unable to summon the courage to patch things up with your son. I know you're sincerely sorry about hurting Akari, but some combination of the stubbornness of age and a deep-seated personality trait is keeping you from saying the simple words that might restore harmony to our little family.

"This morning I was wide-awake from a very early hour, and I couldn't stop turning this horrible situation over and over in my mind. Apparently Akari, too, had awakened while it was still dark outside; I had a feeling something wasn't right, and when I went into his room, thinking he might be having a seizure, I found him crying his eyes out. I don't know whether you've noticed, but he hasn't made any attempt to listen to music on his own since the episode at the hospital, even when he's alone in his room. That hasn't happened since he was a baby."

I was truly cornered. And I know this is unspeakably childish, but at that moment I was actively hoping to be ambushed by another attack of vertigo, just to free me from Chikashi's relentless and entirely justified criticism. But alas, no dizzy spell rode to the rescue and I didn't have the acting chops to fake one, so I had no choice but to sit quietly while my wife's quiet censure rained down on me.

Very late that evening, as I was lying on the bed in my study still feeling as though my heart had been put through a meat grinder, I heard the strains of the second of the three sonatas Beethoven wrote and dedicated to Haydn (Op. 2 no. 2 in A Major, to be precise) wafting up through my pillow. Someone was playing the CD downstairs in the living room, with the volume unusually loud. I didn't move, but when I heard the next piece—Mozart's Symphony K. 550—being played full blast, I couldn't control myself any longer, and I went charging down the stairs. Akari was crouched on the floor in front of the stereo.

"It's after midnight, so why don't you do this tomorrow instead?" I said mildly. Akari didn't even glance in my direction, and I was suddenly galvanized by anger. When I went over and squatted beside him in an attempt to get his attention, he responded by boldly turning the volume up even louder. He continued to stare straight ahead, refusing to acknowledge my presence, and I could see the back of his neck flushing a deep crimson. Chikashi emerged from her bedroom and stood in the doorway, shooting me an inquiring look, but after she saw the expression on my face she retreated without speaking.

When the piece had ended, Akari carefully put the compact disc away and stood up. When he met my eyes at last I said flatly, "You know what? You really are an idiot."

I went upstairs, and after spending a long time staring into the depths of a darkness that wasn't nearly as black as my mood, I switched on the bedside lamp. For the first time since returning to Tokyo, I groped around on the nearby bookshelf and grabbed the first paperback that came to hand. As I began to read a random page, the rectangle of tiny, tightly packed Japanese characters and the border of white space surrounding the dense block of type suddenly began to blur and whirl before my eyes.

(Incidentally, that reminds me of a gathering I once attended where I got into an animated discussion with an anthropologist, an architect, and several other friends about the fact that in English those borders are called margins, while scribbled comments and annotations in the blank spaces are known as marginalia—although our discussion was primarily focused on the more abstract idea of the intrinsically marginal nature of culture. Another dear friend, the composer Takamura, seemed to be lost in his own thoughts. I assumed he was only half listening to our conversation, so I was surprised when not long afterward he published an exquisite composition titled *Marginalia*. Now that I think about it, those days when all my brilliant friends were still alive were probably the most creative and stimulating time of my entire life.)

Anyway, as I was saying, my hands and wrists, which were holding the book out in front of me, suddenly collapsed and crashed into the bookshelf while the visible world began to spin so violently that my normally straight line of vision seemed to be tilted at a wildly exaggerated angle, as if I were on some out-of-control carnival ride.

That was the beginning of the second coming of the bouts of extreme dizziness that would become a chronic condition throughout my later years: an alarming series of breakdowns everyone in my family (except Akari) ended up calling "the Big Vertigo."

# PART TWO

# Women Ascendant

# Chapter 6

# Tossing the Dead Dogs

## 1

After the Big Vertigo struck again, I developed some singular new habits. Once a dizzy spell had abated, I would tumble precipitously into a sleep of total, unrelenting darkness. If what followed the initial episode had been the sleep of death, I mused, then I must now be existing in a state beyond life. And yet my consciousness was still functioning, so according to the principle of *Cogito, ergo sum*, I was still present and alive in reality.

What, exactly, was my state of being? There were times when my eyes would pop open in the dark—it could have already been morning, but the curtains were drawn against the light—and I didn't have the slightest idea who I was, or where. In my ears I would hear a nostalgic, songlike poem repeated over and over, and those lines seemed to offer a clue to my peculiar existential state: *A current under sea / Picked his bones in whispers. As he rose and fell / He passed the stages of his age and youth / Entering the whirlpool.* Yes, I would think, taking the sequence a step further. Buffeted by the deep-water current, he keeps rising and falling, floating and sinking, seconds away from being dragged into the maelstrom of the whirlpool.

I am *I*, and yet I'm something more, because I feel that I am *he* as well: in other words, I am my father. My father, who drowned in what I realize now was the prime of his life; my father, who died when he was twenty years younger than I was when the Big Vertigo ambushed me for the first time. That realization would often be followed by another half-conscious epiphany: *I loved my father!* I would usually wake up again then (more completely this time), awash in dueling emotions: an almost sheepish feeling of relief doing battle with soul-deep despair.

Another new behavior pattern had to do with the way I emerged from sleep. There were times when I would lie awake until the wee hours, assailed by an anxious premonition that another attack was on its way, and I would finally resort to taking the medicine prescribed for such emergencies, which (as a side effect) would cause me to wake up far too early the next morning. However, if I just lay quietly in bed, I often managed to fall into a completely natural sleep, and I would roll out of bed sometime before noon feeling abundantly well rested.

Those prescription meds were potent, so I tried not to take them too often. The side effects weren't entirely negative, though. When I first resurfaced after a medicated sleep, long before dawn, I would be engulfed in what I thought of as hypermemory: wave upon wave of extraordinarily intense recollections. After I opened my eyes for the second time, usually just before noon, I would jot down some quick notes—rough and rudimentary, like an artist's initial pencil sketches— about the memories that had washed over me. I couldn't help wondering whether those remembrances might be connected somehow with the powerful force that ushered in the dizzy spells, and I had an unshakable feeling that the advent of those seizures must have some larger significance. Surely the Big Vertigo's cataclysmic appearance in my life couldn't be completely random and devoid of meaning?

I fell prey to another odd notion as well: a strong certainty that the serial attacks of vertigo (which were so much more powerful than anything I had ever experienced) must eventually, inevitably, result in permanent damage to my mental faculties. I wasn't merely terrified by this bleak prospect; I also felt that—especially if my days of mental acuity were numbered—I ought to pay extra-close attention to the surges of remembrance, which were clearly trying to tell me something before it was too late. For the past fifty years, at least, I had started my daily work ritual by making notes on index cards about whatever had emerged during my dreams and the interstitial sessions of hazy, half-waking contemplation. Those jottings would often provide useful clues for my current writing, so I couldn't very well let the waves of memory slide by unrecorded.

But I had made a firm decision to abandon the drowning novel, and I had also made up my mind that I would never write long-form fiction again. I simply didn't feel I had another book in me. So why was I still compulsively transcribing those resurgent memories? There's really no way to explain it except by saying that for me, scribbling on index cards was like a chronic disease, and there didn't appear to be a cure.

## 2

During the bouts of hypermemory, I kept remembering the day the war ended.

Many writers of my generation have described the weather as cloudy and overcast, but in the forests of Shikoku it was a perfect blue-sky day. Just before noon, the local children were herded into a line. Then we followed our teachers up the hill behind the national school to the mansion of the village headman (in effect, the mayor), which stood on an elevated bluff overlooking the valley. Because no children were allowed inside, we congregated next to a hedge that surrounded the property. There had been some cloud cover in the early morning, but the sky had gradually cleared; the forest was glittering in the sunlight and the entire area was alive with the sound of cicadas. Even with all the ambient noise, we could still hear what was going on inside the mansion.

First there was a loud commotion among the adult males and then, after the headman had given a little speech to calm them down, the sound of the women's quiet weeping rose to a wail. A moment later two of the teachers from our school appeared, ducking through the small wicket gate next to the main entrance. They told us the emperor's broadcast had ended and ordered us to head back to the valley. As we were marching along in formation, with the road hot beneath our bare feet, we were informed by some of the older kids that Japan had lost the war, and then we split up and went our separate ways. When I passed my house I noticed that the tall, slatted-wood storm windows were closed, and I got the sense that my mother was probably doing some kind of handwork in the rear parlor. (After my father died, those windows would remain unopened for many years.) I took the narrow footpath through the fields next to my house and headed toward Myoto Rock.

Down by the river, there was a spot where the women from the hamlet on the north shore did their washing. Above it was a round outcropping of rock with pussy willows growing out of a fissure in the ledge. In the shadow of the boulder, along the riverbank, there was a triangular patch of water that formed a natural wallow. I used to wade along with the current, then throw myself down and settle into the little grotto until I was completely submerged. Using my legs for leverage, I would force my small body into the interior, with the rock jutting out over me like a protective roof.

This secluded part of the river was protected from the current, so there was a permanent accumulation of dissolved clay on the bottom. When I stretched out, my entire body would be enveloped in the soft, smooth, slippery mud. If I was lying flat, my presence couldn't be detected by the women who were squatting at the water's edge not far away, washing dishes or doing laundry. Once I had mastered the art of squeezing into that secret grotto without being seen, I would

head there alone on a regular basis to luxuriate in the freedom of
simply lying in the mud for hour upon blissful hour.

Whenever I was in early-morning remembrance mode the memory of this cozy hiding place would come flooding back, overlaid by a
later but uncannily parallel memory that made it even more potent.
As an adult, I had read a novel in which a French writer retold the
Robinson Crusoe story, with a particular focus on the character of
Friday. Crusoe, stranded on a desert island and exhausted by a daily
life of endless toil and perpetual danger, had a hideaway not unlike
mine where he could revel in submerging his weary body in a grotto
of soft, wet clay. Every time I read the scene, I felt completely swept
away—not only in my heart but somatically as well, on the deepest
level. And now the memory of that book was permanently superimposed over the recollections of my muddy retreat.

When I reached the bank of the river on that day in August
1945, I took off my sweat-soaked clothes and laid them on a rock by
the alfresco laundry spot. Wearing nothing but a skimpy Etchu-style
loincloth, I immersed myself in the placid water of my hidden grotto.
I lay there faceup, letting my body sink until the water started to fill
my ears. I stayed that way for a long time, lost in reverie. After a while
I stuck one arm out of the water and discovered that the afternoon
air had turned chilly. I raised my torso and fixed my gaze on Myoto
Rock, which reared above the glimmering flow of the river.

Suddenly, I knew what I had to do. Leaving the wallow, I swam
toward the place where the river waves were crashing violently against
the enormous rock, and as I approached the monolithic landmark I
gave myself up to the current. It carried me along and deposited me
on one side of Myoto Rock. Muscle memory took over then, and I
knew exactly how to move. Using my arms and legs, I propelled myself
forward, with the swirling current tickling my chest. When I reached
my destination, I stuck my head through the underwater fissure in the
giant rock. On the other side of the crack, diagonal rays of sunlight
slanted down, illuminating the dark blue pool. In that space I could

see dozens of silvery dace, brimming with latent power, suspended in the water in quiescent repose.

At this point, as remembrance merges with fantasy, I seem to see the naked body of a large man in the murky depths below the school of dace. There on the river bottom the corpse sways gently, nudged by the current. It's my father, of course. And I—that is, my retrospectively imagined child-self—am trying to imitate the way the dead body moves.

Back in the present moment, I reached for an index card and my fountain pen. *I love my father desperately,* I wrote in Japanese. But even in my deeply moved state I felt compelled to add a little orthographic embellishment, so a moment later I spelled out the phonetically Japanized version of the English word "desperately" in the margin: *de-su-pe-ree-to-rii.*

# 3

*Dear Kogii,*

*I received a very thoughtful letter from Chikashi. "Thoughtful" really is the only way to describe it, in every sense of the word. Not a single line was wasted on futile optimism or pointless pessimism; she simply gave a straightforward account of your current condition. However, since it's entirely possible that my interpretation of what she said may have been colored in part by wishful thinking, I'm writing to ask if you would be so kind as to corroborate my conclusions.*

*1. The Big Vertigo wasn't some freakish occurrence that happened once while you were visiting down here on Shikoku and never again. There have been three more episodes since you returned to Tokyo.*

*2. You've been taking it easy on order from your family doctor, but you haven't followed up by going to a university hospital for an MRI and so on. Both your wife and daughter have encouraged you to do so, but you haven't been receptive to their suggestions. Because the dizzy spell that knocked you for a loop on Shikoku took you completely by surprise, perhaps you're afraid the results of the examination might be even more of a shock—anyhow, that's our theory. If the tests show some irreparable abnormality in your brain, you probably wouldn't be able to do your literary work, and we would all have to accept that you would never be the same.*

*When Professor Musumi refused to be screened for lung cancer even though he was aware that something was very wrong inside his chest, you took on the task—at his wife's request—of trying to convince your longtime mentor to submit to treatment. He refused, with fatal consequences, and now it looks as though you're borrowing the same excuses he gave you virtually verbatim. Chikashi is prepared to respect your choices, and I agree completely. No matter what happens I really feel as if your homecoming trip to our little valley in the mountains made you realize something important about everyone in our family, including yourself. If I'm mistaken, I hope we can laugh it off the way we've done with so many of your preconceived notions and misperceptions.*

*3. Whatever the diagnosis turns out to be, if you would simply take a break and get some rest, then you should be able to get back to your usual regimen of work—within your new limitations, of course—just as Professor Musumi did toward the end. However, if you remain mired in the denial stage and if your prose starts to show any degree of mental decline, it would be a very serious matter. To make sure that doesn't happen, Chikashi has been thinking about creating a system whereby any manuscripts you produce from here on would be vetted by some of the editors you've been working with for years, before publication. And if they find significant problems, then we would have your publishers announce that Mr. Choko will be retiring from writing, effective immediately.*

4. *At the moment, even though you're feeling rather low, I gather your life isn't too different from when you were in good health, and while you've stopped work on the drowning novel, you're still continuing to crank out a newspaper essay every month. I assume that your reading habits are pretty much the same as always, except that you're being careful not to spend too much time reading books in foreign languages because constantly stopping to look things up in dictionaries can be a strain.*

Another reason I'm writing this letter is to figure out the best way for us to stay in touch now that the Big Vertigo is part of the equation. (Needless to say, if an emergency should arise Chikashi would telephone me at home.)

There isn't much news to report on my end, aside from Masao and Unaiko's theatrical activities. Ever since you returned to Tokyo they've been nice enough to keep me in the loop much more than before, and Unaiko, in particular, seems to have really opened up lately. She's been confiding in me in a much deeper way, and I have a feeling our talks will raise some matters I'll need to discuss with you at some point.

However, since Chikashi mentioned that there's no guarantee you'll always be able to answer every letter I write, and since you've been jotting things down on index cards at a great rate—though not as part of any particular writing project—she kindly offered to make copies of any relevant notes (with your approval, of course) and send them to us down here. Unaiko and I will view those dispatches as your replies to our queries. As you know, I've already received the first batch of photocopied notes from Chikashi, and Unaiko and I have been perusing them with great interest—a task Unaiko approached with the same verve and intensity you'll remember from your own interactions with her. During the process, one thing that jumped out at her was where you confess your feelings of love to the point of desperation (or words to that effect) for our father.

Unaiko said that while you were staying at the Forest House, she shared the story of what happened to her at Yasukuni Shrine. I gather she was hoping to get some reciprocal feedback from you, as a liberal peacenik who also happened to have idolized his right-wing-fanatic father, and who got carried away to the point of singing along with a German military anthem himself. Anyhow, she was apparently left with the sense that you had been less than forthcoming about your own emotions.

Unaiko wants to use the theater to express her feelings about ultranationalism, militarism, gender politics, and so on—feelings that seem to stem from some sort of long-ago personal trauma. I think it was because she feels so strongly about those issues that she took the rather extreme step of criticizing you for declaring your sudden, unexpected surges of love for our poor, misguided father.

That reminds me—the drowning novel may be totally kaput as far as you're concerned, but the young people who have been hanging out at the Forest House seem to be clinging to some hope that you will tell the story eventually. They seem to be saying, in effect, "Hey, Choko, don't think we're going to let you off the hook so easily!"

Now I'd like to give you an update about what Unaiko is working on these days. Out of the entire group, Masao Anai was hit the hardest by your decision to abandon the drowning novel. Unlike me, he tends to take setbacks very much to heart.

When he first heard that you were coming back to Shikoku to finish writing the book, Masao was running around exclaiming, "At last! At last!" I've never seen him so excited, and even Unaiko stopped for a minute to laugh. Of course, we're all aware that Masao is obsessed with the idea of dramatizing all your novels, so his childlike delight seemed entirely natural—as did his subsequent disappointment when the plan fell through.

Unaiko, on the other hand, is choosing to put a positive spin on things by focusing on the fact that you've finally been

*liberated from the drowning novel and can now move on. This
seems a bit counterintuitive to me, but she seems to think that
by being critical of you and your work she will somehow be
able to entice you into further collaboration. (Reverse psychol-
ogy, maybe?) In any event, I gather you've already heard about
the Caveman Group's program for teaching drama in secondary
schools all over the prefecture, so you know that its current project is an adaptation of Natsume Soseki's classic novel* Kokoro.
*Unaiko and Masao lost no time in drafting a script, and they've
already presented it at several schools. The early version was very
well received, and the troupe has been inundated with requests
and invitations from a number of additional schools.*

*But Unaiko isn't someone who rests on her laurels after a
handful of favorable reviews and just repeats the same performance over and over. No, she's been busy tape-recording the
students' impressions of this special style of teaching and then
giving careful consideration to their comments. For the dramatic
reading of* Kokoro, *Unaiko is trying to make the piece evolve
organically, one step at a time. And now, with Masao's help, she's
attempting to distill the result of her preliminary labors into a
finished work of art (or, more precisely, into a perpetually evolving work of art). All along, she's been continually polishing the
style and technique that emerged from the dog-tossing piece, and
she's been using the same lapidary process to enliven her drama
classes as well. She has gotten the students at various schools to
throw a great many symbolic "dogs." At the moment, she's busy
compiling those responses, including a fair number of critical
remarks, and synthesizing them into a revised script for the play.*

*The plan is for Unaiko and her colleagues to give a
major public performance of* Kokoro, *showcasing their unique
interactive approach, at the middle school's cylinder-shaped
auditorium, which will be converted into a theater for the occasion. (That rather daring structure has gotten a lot of criticism
because it was very costly to build, and the middle school's*

*dwindling enrollment didn't seem to warrant the investment.)
They're thinking that if the building could be given a catchy
name like "theater in the round" and turned into an active cultural venue, it might revitalize the village. That's why everyone is
excited about this new idea.*

*But what does this have to do with you, up there in Tokyo?
Well, I took the liberty of offering to ask whether you'd be willing
to help Unaiko create the script for the upcoming play, which
is something you could do without actually being here. (As you
know, there was some tentative discussion about the possibility of
your delivering a related lecture, but it isn't going to happen, for
obvious reasons.) At any rate, I'll be very grateful if you would do
this favor for me   or rather, for us.*

*You know, here in this tiny village I've been typecast for
many years as the younger sister of an illustrious author and activ-
ist who has always been a lightning rod for all sorts of criticism.
As a result of dealing with that sort of thing on a regular basis, I've
had no choice but to evolve into a political animal myself!*

# 4

I was already familiar with the *Tossing the Dead Dogs* project, but
when I'm asked to commit to something I can't help wanting to know
exactly what is involved. That's just the way I am. I was aware that
the young members of the Caveman Group were working on turning
*Kokoro* into a dramatic reading aimed at students, and I was happy
to help, but I still had some questions.

For one thing, when it came time to actually mount a performance, I couldn't see how they were going to turn Soseki's subtle,
understated novel into an interactive dramatic free-for-all. In Unaiko's approach to drama, the spontaneous exchanges that can occur
between the audience and the actors onstage become a major aspect
of the production.

Granted, the so-called dead dogs that are her trademark props are just stuffed toys, but how would throwing them back and forth be integrated into a play about friendship, betrayal, existential malaise, and suicide? And in this instance (as opposed to the earlier performance piece, which was literally about dogs), what was the significance of the canine "corpses" supposed to be?

I tried to imagine various scenarios but I finally gave up and had Chikashi telephone Unaiko, on my behalf, to ask for additional details about how the Caveman Group was planning to pull this off. Unaiko replied (via Chikashi) that the practice script she was currently using was derived from recordings of comments by the students she had met through her dramatic presentations at various schools. Unaiko then proceeded to read some of the raw, unedited lines to Chikashi over the phone, saying she hoped I would share my thoughts about them.

Chikashi, who appeared to be enjoying her go-between role immensely, wrote those lines down and then showed them to me. She also filled me in on the origin story of the dog-tossing trope, including some details I hadn't heard before.

It had begun accidentally, during the Caveman Group's revival of a play dating back to the New Drama movement that had blossomed in Japan before the war. During the scene in question, a young wife played by Unaiko was sitting on a chair in a Western-style parlor holding a pet dog (represented by a stuffed animal) on her lap. The audience began heckling Unaiko's character for some reason and, spurred on by the jeers and catcalls, she pretended to strangle the dog—acting up a storm and making the "murder" look very realistic. She tossed the "carcass" into the rowdy audience, whereupon the "dead dog" was immediately heaved back onto the stage.

Apparently it was a seminal moment in the evolution of Unaiko's dramatic method, as she realized that while in reality most of the audience members were positively disposed toward her and her colleagues, in the context of the play those same spectators were clearly getting a tremendous kick out of razzing the actors on the stage. (As an aside, Chikashi mentioned having read somewhere about a psychiatric method called drama therapy, in which throwing stuffed animals is used to help patients work through various issues. Unaiko, it seemed, had serendipitously stumbled upon the same cathartic technique.)

The first, unscripted melee created a great deal of buzz, so in the next performance the bit with the stuffed dog was repeated, only this time with conscious intent. The dramatists added the confrontational give-and-take with the audience to the original script, and a rather staid prewar play was reinvented as *Tossing the Dead Dogs*. The interactive element turned out to be extremely popular, and it soon became the Caveman Group's dramatic calling card.

The technique had grown ever more sophisticated, to the point where the stage directions now called for surreptitiously planting a number of shills or decoys throughout the audience—people whose sole purpose was to raise a choreographed ruckus while pretending to be ordinary members of the crowd. There were also quite a few fans who happily paid their own way and came to the show armed with stuffed animals, so there was no way of knowing how many "dead dogs" might fly back and forth on a given night. Over time, the art form evolved to the point where most (though not all) of the performances tended to end abruptly right at the apex of the dog-flinging pandemonium.

Unaiko told Chikashi that she was wondering, a bit nervously, what would happen during the upcoming presentation of the Caveman Group's dramatization of *Kokoro*. Based on her prior experience, Unaiko sketched out her vision of how the evening might go, with the caveat that since audience participation was always a wild card, there was really no way to predict the outcome. Her innovative stagecraft could turn out to be a brilliant success or an unmitigated disaster; they would just have to wait and see.

Unaiko explained that the audience would be made up of students from junior high and high schools all over the prefecture, along with teachers and family members, and the event would take place in the circular auditorium, which had been converted for the occasion into a "theater in the round" (technically, a theater in a semicircle).

The performance would begin with a straightforward dramatic reading. When that came to an end, the official thespians would congregate at stage left and the stealth participants (who had until then been sitting unobtrusively in the audience) would line up on the opposite side. These imposters would start directing questions and critical comments at the actors; the responses would quickly become heated, and the civil discussion would degenerate into a raucous argument. Up until then, everything would have been scripted in advance and the actors would be reciting lines they had already rehearsed. But when the ringers began quarreling with the actors, the audience members would soon realize that such interaction was not only allowed but encouraged, and would presumably follow suit. Then, if everything went according to plan, the scene would escalate into a near riot, with "dead dogs" being hurled back and forth with wild abandon.

# 5

*Dear Kogii,*

*I'm happy to report that Unaiko's play was a complete triumph! (As you know, it was performed at our local theater in the round on the last Saturday in September, as her first dramatic project targeted at an audience of junior high and high school students.) I hope you will share this letter with Chikashi, as I think you'll both find it very entertaining.*

*I must confess that I'm writing partly to coax you, brother dear, into lending your long-distance assistance to Unaiko and me once more as we tackle a new challenge. I'll save some energy for making that pitch, but first I want to tell you about Unaiko's theatrical tour de force.*

*Picture this: you walk into a round building and see an empty stage in the shape of a half circle, with the other half of the sphere filled with curved tiers of seating. No curtain*

*separates the stage from the spectators, and the audience mem-
bers look down at a darkened stage that almost appears to be a
hole or abyss in the center of the room. It's still daylight outside,
and while several high windows and domed skylights provide a
small amount of natural light, inside the theater it's quite dim.*

*Only one thing is visible at first: Unaiko's slender form,
standing motionless at the center of the stage. As the lights come
up, we see that she is costumed and made up to look like the
very model of a veteran teacher of Japanese language and literature at the high school level. (Incidentally, for the past three
years Unaiko has been going around to junior high schools as a
visiting instructor of drama, so she's known and loved by hundreds of students, and the audience is packed with her fans.)*

*Unaiko is holding a small hardcover edition of Natsume
Soseki's Kokoro, in the familiar binding we associate with his
collected works. The basic premise of the play is that Unaiko is
delivering a lecture to the teenage students who are onstage and in
the audience. Needless to say, both the words she addresses to this
imaginary class and the way the second half of the play unfolds
were shaped (and enriched) by our earlier discussions with you.*

*"The first time I read this book, I was just about the same
age most of you are now," she begins. "On that occasion, and
subsequent readings as well, I wielded my red and blue pencils
freely, underlining certain things and drawing circles around
others. (These days I guess you would probably be using high-
lighters or marking pens, right?) Anyway, I read this book over
and over. However, from the very beginning I had doubts and
questions, and I'm going to start by talking about them.*

*"As preparation for this lecture, I gave you two homework
assignments. One was a questionnaire asking you to list some
of the words in this novel that strike you as significant. The
second assignment was this: I asked all of you to read Kokoro
by yourselves, just as I did many years ago. The story starts out
as the narrator, a young man we know only as 'I,' enters into an*

*unusual friendship with an older man whom he always refers to,*
*respectfully, as Sensei.*

"However, the Sensei character commits suicide, leaving
behind nothing but a long note of explanation and farewell.
The young narrator, in a state of shock, reads the note through
to the end—and as we all know, that's more or less the structure
of the entire book. We're going to begin by reading the part of
the suicide note where Sensei is remembering the time when
he initially opened up to the young narrator. The reader will be
an actor from our theater troupe; he'll be out here in a moment
with the text. This time, his only job will be to read the one
passage, but in our actual play a number of other actors will
appear in a variety of roles. Some of them will remain onstage,
while others will make a brief appearance and then vanish into
the wings, but either way, there's no need to applaud every time a
new character appears. All right—here we go!"

**Sensei:** *Sometimes, you used to look at me with a dissatisfied ex-*
*pression, and you even tried pressuring me to unfurl my past before*
*you, like a picture scroll. That was the first time I really respected*
*you, in my heart of hearts. I was moved by your determination,*
*however audacious or unseemly it might have been, to try to grasp*
*the essence of my being. At the time I was still alive. I didn't want*
*to die. That is why I refused to grant your request, choosing instead*
*to postpone the revelations until some future date. That time has*
*come, and I am about to cut open my heart and drench your face*
*with my blood. And I will be satisfied if, when my heart stops beat-*
*ing, a new life is lodged in your breast.*

After the actor finishes reading this vivid passage, Unaiko
continues with her scripted lecture. "As I said in the beginning, when I first read this passage I was about the same age as
you students are now. This will probably sound simplistic, but
when the Sensei character agrees to allow the young man to start

*addressing him by that respectful term, he starts to seem like*
*a sympathetic protagonist, so I thought this novel might be an*
*attempt to teach my generation a thing or two about life.*

"However, that turned out not to be the case at all. While
*there is a fair amount of direct dialogue between the two main*
*characters, for the most part Sensei doesn't really teach the*
*young narrator anything. For example, the young man asks,*
*'Is there really guilt in loving?' and Sensei simply replies, 'Yes,*
*surely.' He does offer his young friend some practical advice*
*about steps he could take to be sure of receiving his rightful*
*share of the family property when the time comes, but that's*
*about it. As we learn later, both of these topics—love and*
*inheriting one's fair share of worldly goods—created significant*
*problems for Sensei and shaped his life.*

"Then when I reached the point of reading the long
*note Sensei left behind, I realized that this book was probably*
*just written to express the author's own thoughts through the*
*medium of Sensei's letter. Sensei lived out his life in self-imposed*
*seclusion, closed off from society, and I felt that he wrote the*
*long suicide note knowing it was his one shot at sharing his*
*story. You may ask, what was the basic message of the note Sensei*
*left behind when he took his own life? As we will see, that note*
*includes the lines* I'd like you to remember something. This
is the way I have lived my life. *So for Sensei, writing a sort of*
*regretful retrospective was apparently his only means of talking*
*about his own conduct after decades of silence.*

"But what was that conduct exactly? Well, when he was
*twenty years old, Sensei was swindled out of his inheritance by*
*an unprincipled uncle. After that, he turned into a wary, guarded*
*person who rarely opened up to another human being. When he*
*was at university, Sensei did have one friend (identified only as 'K')*
*to whom he had been so close that they had chosen to live in the*
*same lodging house, and when Sensei learned that K was in love*
*with the daughter of their landlady, Sensei went ahead and got*

*engaged to the girl himself, without saying a word to his friend. K
was so heartbroken by this betrayal that he committed suicide, and
Sensei happened upon the bloody scene not long afterward. I'm
going to read an abridged version to you now."*

**Sensei:** *I stood up and went as far as the doorway. From there, I
glanced quickly around his room, which was dimly lit by a single
lamp. As soon as I realized what I was seeing, I stood rooted to the
spot, unable to move, staring in horror through eyes that seemed
to be made of glass. But the initial shock was like a sudden gust
of wind, and it only lasted for a moment. "Oh no," I thought.
"This can't be happening." It was then that the great, luminous
shadow—almost like a black light—that would irrevocably darken
my life, forever, spread out before my mind's eye. My whole body
began to tremble.*

As you know, Kogii, I'll always be the first to acknowledge
that Unaiko is enormously talented and endowed with a cutting-
edge sensibility, but the truth is she wasn't generally thought of
as an outstanding performer. When I watched her putting on
a small production like Tossing the Dead Dogs, it struck me
that the way it started out so light and comical, then suddenly
morphed into a display of unbridled aggression, was typical of
her unique dramatic style.

However, when Unaiko stood onstage and read the agonized recollections that Sensei forces himself to recount, I saw
something amazing. Apart from the stage lights, the theater was
lit only by the natural light leaking in through the high windows (they were just open a crack) and the domed skylights in
the ceiling. As Unaiko read those powerful lines, I seemed to
see a flash of black light slashing across the stage. That's how
moved I was.

A later section in Kokoro talks about how even after his
friend died Sensei went ahead and married the girl they had

both been courting, without ever telling her what had driven their friend to suicide. But Sensei never stopped blaming himself, and he was so crippled by guilt that he was never able to venture out into society and work for a living. When Unaiko was reading that section, a short while later, I could have sworn I saw the black light again.

I even asked Masao about it after the play. I said, "Even though Unaiko is doing the directing this time around, you're acting in the play and also somehow managing to handle the light board. (And I know that in the scene where the 'dead dogs' are being thrown, the lighting plays a very important role because it's used to ramp up the excitement level.) So I was wondering whether what appeared to be a flash of black light cutting across the stage was an effect you deliberately engineered?" Masao laughed, the way he does, so I knew it must have been my imagination. Anyhow, here's the excerpt that made me see the black light of despair for the second time:

**Sensei:** *From then on, a nameless fear would assail me from time to time. At first, it seemed to come over me without warning from the shadows surrounding me, and I would gasp at its unexpectedness. Later, however, when the experience had become more familiar to me, my heart would readily succumb —or perhaps respond—to it; and I would begin to wonder if this fear had not always been in some hidden corner of my heart, ever since I was born.*

Unaiko's powerful dramatic reading made an indelible impression on me, and I'm now convinced that in addition to all her other talents she is a genuinely gifted actress. Of course, since she was standing on the stage in the guise of a schoolteacher, she had to offer some short explanations as she went along, but I guess the most effective way of showing how Sensei came to terms with his guilt and found a way to continue living was to have him recite a relevant quotation from the book.

**Sensei:** *Although I had resolved to live as if I were dead, my heart would at times respond to the activity of the outside world, and would almost seem to dance with pent-up energy. But as soon as I tried to break through the cloud that surrounded me, a mysterious and terrifying force would descend upon me from I know not where, and the malign power would grip my heart so tightly that I could not move.*

Unaiko, as Sensei, delivers those lines, then immediately switches back to schoolteacher mode and addresses the high school students. Under these circumstances, she explains, we can see that a life in which Sensei would venture out into society and hold down a normal job probably wouldn't have been a realistic possibility. So, Unaiko goes on (I'm paraphrasing here), Sensei muddled along, living in quiet seclusion with his wife and supporting them both on what was left of his inheritance (a lifestyle that, as the vital and adventuresome Meiji Era neared its end, would have struck people as rather unusual). Then, after a chance meeting at the seashore, a young university student inserts himself into Sensei's low-key, reclusive existence and a bond begins to develop between them. (This explanatory interlude was a truly masterful performance on Unaiko's part, by the way.) Next Unaiko goes back to the suicide note, which (she explains) shows how Sensei finally reached the conclusion that ending his own life was the only option that made sense anymore.

Now, I was very familiar with the staging of Tossing the Dead Dogs, but this was my first encounter with one of these literature-based productions, and to tell you the truth I was taken completely by surprise when the air was suddenly filled with "dead dogs" being flung in the general direction of Unaiko's feet to show the audience members' disagreement with what she was saying. (They could easily have targeted her torso, but I guess they were just trying to make a symbolic point, not injure their idol!) Unaiko's only response to the kids who had *bombarded her with stuffed animals was to calmly continue the dramatic reading.*

**Sensei:** *You may wonder why I have chosen to take such a radical way out. But you see, the strange and terrible force that gripped my heart whenever I tried to find an escape in life seemed at last only to leave me free to find escape in death. If I wished to move at all, then I could move only towards my own end.*

And then Unaiko read aloud the line she had mentioned a while before, as if she wanted to engrave it onto our hearts.

**Sensei:** *I'd like you to remember something. This is the way I have lived my life.*

After a short pause for effect, Unaiko spoke again. "Class, your responses to the questionnaire were excellent," she announced, to the obvious delight of the authentic students in the audience. "Everything you listed jibes perfectly with the terms the author uses again and again as leitmotifs."

She went on to explain that among the repeated words, kokoro, *meaning* "heart" *or* "the heart of things," was used most often (forty-two times), followed by the related term kokoro-mochi (*translatable as* "feelings, mood, or frame of mind"), which popped up twelve times. Not far behind was kakugo ("readiness, resolution, resignation") with seven appearances. Unaiko pointed out that while all these concepts played an important role in the story, an external event caused Sensei to decide the time had finally come to end his guilt-ridden life. After this explanation, she resumed the dramatic reading in a voice that vibrated with emotion.

**Sensei:** *Then, during the height of the summer, Emperor Meiji passed away. I felt as though the spirit of the Meiji Era that began*

*with the emperor had ended with him as well. I was overcome with*
*the feeling that I and the rest of my generation, who had grown up*
*in that era, were now left behind to live as anachronisms. I shared*
*this epiphany with my wife, but she just laughed and refused to*
*take me seriously. Then she said a curious thing, albeit in jest:*
*"Well then, maybe you should just go ahead and commit* junshi,
*and follow the emperor to the grave." I had almost forgotten that*
*there was such a word as* junshi, *but now I turned to my wife and*
*said: "If I did commit* junshi, *it would be out of loyalty to the spirit*
*of the Meiji Era."*

At that point the first half of the play ended and the lights
came up for intermission. This letter is already far too long, so
I'll save the rest of the story to share in the next installment.

# 6

*Dear Kogii,*

*The second act of the play began with the covering of the five*
*domed skylights by means of a clever mechanical device. Those*
*of us in the audience couldn't see Unaiko standing on the stage,*
*but the dramatic reading recommenced in the darkness and once*
*again Soseki's term "black light" flashed across my mind.*

**Sensei:** *"Hey!" I called. There was no answer. I called out again,*
*"Hey, K! What's the matter?" K's body did not move at all. I stood*
*up and went as far as the doorway. From there, I glanced quickly*
*around his room, which was dimly lit by a single lamp. As soon as*
*I realized what I was seeing, I stood rooted to the spot, unable to*
*move, staring in horror through eyes that seemed to be made of glass.*
*But the initial shock was like a sudden gust of wind, and it only*
*lasted for a moment. "Oh no," I thought. "This can't be happening."*

*It was then that the great, luminous shadow—almost like a black light—that would irrevocably darken my life, forever, spread out before my mind's eye. My whole body began to tremble.*

When this reading ended, the stage was illuminated by slanting shafts of directional lighting. Because there were motes of dust visibly rising from the entire stage, the angle of the rays was very conspicuous, and they looked to me like a visual echo of the black light I had imagined earlier. The angular rays illuminated two large antique screens that were being pushed forward from the back. The screens bore livid traces of red, obviously made by a thick brush dipped in crimson paint. While this bit of stagecraft didn't exactly match Soseki's description, it was clearly meant to represent the projectile bloodstains Sensei saw when he happened upon the scene of his friend's suicide.

An instant later the shafts of light from above were extinguished and a bunch of high school kids (including some young members of the Caveman Group who were impersonating students) rushed down from the audience onto the stage and dragged the screens off into a dark corner. All the young people who performed the task were boys, but they were soon joined by a number of female students. Then Unaiko, still in character as a high school teacher, separated herself from the crowd of students and stood downstage alone. She began to speak, addressing her remarks to the students who were sharing the stage with her.

"I know I mentioned this earlier, but when I read *Kokoro* for the first time, I initially thought that it was going to be an educational book. However, I was disappointed to find that there were almost no exchanges between the student (the 'I' character) and Sensei that could be described as edifying. However, when I reread the book recently, with a clear agenda in mind, it struck me that it is an educational book after all. In the long letter Sensei leaves behind, he actually asks outright what sort of lessons the young man ought to be learning from

Sensei's experiences. As we've already heard, at one point he
says: I'd like you to remember something. This is the way I
have lived my life. The logical next step, in educational terms,
would seem to be a statement phrased in the future tense, don't
you think? Maybe something along the lines of 'And this is the
way I shall die.'

   "And now I would like to ask all of you, individually, to put
yourselves in the place of the young narrator and think accordingly. Speaking from the point of view of that character, do you
feel you've learned anything useful from reading this letter from
Sensei, which was in effect a message from beyond the grave?"

   The students who were standing on the stage proceeded
to answer one by one, and I'll paraphrase some of their replies
here from memory. (I got the sense that these lines were derived
from the off-the-cuff comments Unaiko had collected from the
students during her visiting lectures, but the teenagers spoke the
words perfectly, and the lines sounded completely natural.) As
you'll see, the students' remarks were interspersed with questions
and comments from the adults who were onstage with them.

   "I don't think I learned a single thing."

   "I think I might have learned something."

   "Oh? What kind of thing did you learn?"

   "Well, a person I respect decides to end his own life, but
before doing so he shares his darkest secrets with me—secrets
that have already driven him to kill himself by the time I read
his letter. So after the person has made this stunning confession and then killed himself, leaving me behind, there must be
something to be learned from what he's shared with me. As the
narrator, I would feel as if this is the first time a life lesson has
been so vividly seared into my heart, and I wouldn't be likely to
forget it any time soon."

   "But what's the practical meaning of this unforgettable lesson? You shouldn't betray your friend and drive him to suicide?
Really, who doesn't know that already? It's just common sense. I

*think the situation depicted in this novel is personal and unique,
rather than universal."*

*"All right, fair point. Let's say there's a girl you aren't
particularly interested in, but when your friend ends up falling
for her you're surprised to discover that you're upset about losing
someone you didn't even realize you wanted. When you confess
your newfound interest the girl is very receptive, but your friend
is so shattered by this development that he kills himself. Do you
think such a thing would happen in real life? I mean, seriously,
are you guys really so intense at this age? Let's suppose that
scenario did take place, and the woman in question agreed to
marry you. If you never got your act together, don't you think she
would eventually leave you? And before that happened, would
you really hatch a plan to express the spirit of the modern age by
committing ritual suicide?"*

*The high school students—both the fifteen or so who were
onstage and the larger group still sitting in the audience—
responded to this fusillade of questions by roaring with laughter. Amid the merriment there was only one person who stood
by in disgruntled silence, glowering at the young woman who
had subjected him to those queries. That glum-looking person
wasn't a student at all, but rather a member of the comedy duo
Suke & Kaku (whom you may remember meeting at the Forest
House). Beside him on the stage was the other half of the duo,
laughing at his partner's discomfiture. The woman who had
been questioning Suke or Kaku—in the dim light, I couldn't
tell who was who—wasn't a student, either; it was actually
Ricchan, the Caveman Group's music director. (She has been
a friend and mentor to Unaiko ever since Unaiko joined the
troupe, and now she's a friend of mine as well. Despite her
seniority, she's a very low-key, unassuming person, the kind
you can always count on in a pinch.) Anyhow, Ricchan—in a
costume and hairstyle that made her look much younger—was
doing such a convincing job of playing the part of a schoolgirl*

*that I couldn't help myself. I just had to shout, "Ricchan, you
look so cute!"*

After a moment, Unaiko came forward and joined the
conversation. *"Even if it seems a bit ludicrous to describe our
modern condition as the 'spirit of the Heisei Era,' the famous
spirit of Meiji mentioned in Kokoro really is important, so let's
discuss it a bit more later on,"* she said. *"First, though, I'd like
to ask everyone who believes that the book's narrator (the never-
named 'I') didn't learn anything of value from Sensei's suicide
note to assemble on the right side of the stage. Everybody else:
left side, please.*

*"All right, now I have a question for the group on the right.
Am I correct in thinking that you don't believe Sensei was an
educator in any real sense of the word, even though he basically
staked his life on sharing the lessons you dismiss as useless? If
that's the case, why do you think he made a point of writing a
long, confessional letter? Was it just an empty act on his part?"*

The person who responded to Unaiko's question was either
Suke or Kaku; it was still too dark for me to tell the two men
apart.

*"To me, at least, it doesn't seem to have been an empty act,"*
he said. *"Sensei felt he was living his life as if he were already
dead and perpetually beset by the strange, terrible force he talks
about so eloquently. After all those years of living with his guilt,
maybe he had reached a point where dying seemed to him to be
the most natural course of action."*

*"Point taken,"* Unaiko said. *"But if—as some of you
believe—Sensei wasn't acting as a teacher, shall we talk about
what you think he was trying to accomplish with the letter he
left behind for his young friend?"*

At that point, Masao Anai, who had been sitting in the
audience, stood up and signaled his desire to speak. I think the
gesture might have been a bit of spontaneous ad-libbing on
Masao's part, but I'm not completely sure. Watching this new

tactic of dividing the participants into two camps and then revitalizing the discussion by introducing a third line of thought, I got the feeling it was all part of the continuing evolution of the technique they'd used in Tossing the Dead Dogs.

"I'm probably closer to your fathers' generation than to yours, and I definitely have a lot more years under my belt than you do," Masao began. "I'm a playwright and a director, and just as the author Kogito Choko, who originally hails from this part of the country, expresses himself through novels, I use the theater as my vehicle for self-expression. I'm constantly thinking about the phenomenon of expression, day in and day out, so if you don't mind I'd like to talk a bit about the suicide note written by the Sensei character in Kokoro.

"As you know from reading the book, Sensei is hoping his death will kindle a new spark of life in the breast of the young man who is reading his posthumous letter. I was very moved when I read this for the first time as a young man, and I asked myself, 'Do people really say this sort of thing when they're about to die?' Obviously, I was identifying with the narrator and projecting my own thoughts and feelings onto him. And I couldn't help wondering: 'How would I feel if someone on the threshold of death was kind enough to write down something like this just for me?'

"But the thing is, as the years have gone by I've suffered a sort of sea change, and I've noticed that when I reread Kokoro these days I'm not as receptive as I used to be. I find myself asking questions like: 'Is Sensei giving any thought at all to the effect his words, and his death, will have on this young man who looks up to him and considers him a friend?' I really don't think he is; it doesn't seem to me as if Sensei is ever thinking about anyone except himself. And what's with the sudden suicide drama, anyway? Until then, Sensei had been quietly living out his years, systematically shutting himself off from society—as we say today, he was holed up like a hermit. By his own admission *he was never much of a writer, and this suicide note is his one and only attempt at self-expression. In other words, the only reason he picked up brush and paper was to write his final communiqué.*

"Even so, you have to wonder how he could have believed that reading his suicidal confession would cause a new life to be sparked in the heart of the young. *This passage has been read aloud already, but for me, the highlight of the farewell note is* I'd like you to remember something. This is the way I have lived my life.

"You see, this is how Sensei expresses himself: by basically oversharing with someone who isn't even part of his inner circle. *To be honest, the more I thought about this behavior, the less I liked it. I'm sure some of you must have had the same reaction. Or maybe not?"*

At this point, Masao Anai (who had struck a dramatic pose at the end of his monologue) began to be pelted from all sides with "dead dogs." As the toys rained down on him Masao picked up the stuffed animals that had bounced off his body and landed at his feet. He made a great show of examining them carefully, one by one. Then, clutching a double armload of dogs, he docilely resumed his seat, bowing to the audience around him as if to acknowledge his defeat.

Once again, the audience burst into laughter. Masao's deliberately bombastic tone had captured the students' attention, and his pretense of having been both intrigued and humbled by the onslaught of "dead dogs," too, was a skillful way of neutralizing the tension by making them laugh. They were still chuckling when Unaiko, evidently deciding it was time to intervene, strode down to the front of the stage. Projecting the kind of unruffled dignity you'd expect from an experienced teacher, she attempted to calm the antic, exuberant crowd.

"Let me ask you something, class," she said. "When you hear people being so critical of the things Sensei wrote, don't any *of you feel like firing back with 'Yes, but Sensei was on the verge of taking his own life, so maybe it isn't fair to hold him to normal standards of behavior'? Let's explore that question together, shall we?"*

While she was speaking, Unaiko gestured to Ricchan and the comic duo Suke & Kaku to step out from the two groups of high school students onstage. (Those three were convincingly dressed as students, but by then it must have been clear to the audience that they were grown-up actors pretending to be teenagers.)

"A short while ago, one of you suggested that it was a perfectly natural thing for Sensei to have committed suicide at this point in his life," Unaiko said. "Would you please explain your thinking based on what's in the suicide note? And then, for balance, we'll need to ask the person who was expressing the opposing view to elaborate a bit more. You'll do that for us, won't you? Then, after we've given a fair hearing to both sides of the argument, I'd like to invite everyone to summon all your strength and throw your 'dead dogs' at the faction you don't agree with!"

In response to Unaiko's request, Suke began to read aloud from the opened copy of Kokoro he was holding. (Suke's & Kaku's faces were helpfully illuminated by the stage lighting now, so I was finally able to tell them apart.)

**Sensei:** *You may wonder why I have chosen to take such a radical way out. But you see, the strange and terrible force that gripped my heart whenever I tried to find an escape in life seemed at last only to leave me free to find escape in death. If I wished to move at all, then I could move only towards my own end.*

"This is the sort of thing I had in mind," Suke said. "Sensei felt that after Emperor Meiji died of natural causes and General Nogi committed suicide to follow his master in death, this

unusual set of circumstances had created an opportunity for him
to end his own life as well. How is that not natural?"

"Well, okay, but how do you connect the dots between that
opportunity and the so-called spirit of Meiji?" inquired Ricchan,
still in character as a high school girl. "We know Sensei betrayed
his friend, K, so horribly that K couldn't bear to go on living, and
Sensei was haunted by that misdeed for the rest of his life, right?
Yet the awareness, however painful, never drove him to commit
suicide himself. When he declares, There was nothing I could
do, so I decided to go on living as if I were dead, wasn't he just
granting himself a temporary stay of execution? I mean, it seems
as if he decided arbitrarily that the reprieve he'd granted himself
had finally run out, and he made up his mind the time had come
for him to die. And because the spirit of Meiji had effectively
perished along with the emperor who gave the era its name, you
could say Sensei was simply following that spirit into the valley
of death, right? But why does the spirit of Meiji suddenly become
a factor at this point? If we're going to talk about naturalness,
is it natural for this phrase to crop up at such a late stage in the
story? I mean, until now, both before and after Sensei's betrayal
of his friend, Sensei never really talked about the spirit of Meiji,
did he? So why in the world does he suddenly drag that concept
into the conversation? Wouldn't it have been more natural if
he'd simply declared that he had lost the will to go on living as
if he were already dead and had decided to put an end to his
lifelong misery? And what is the spirit of Meiji, anyway? Is it
somehow related to the strange and terrible force Sensei invokes,
or is it that force's polar opposite, or what?

"Hang on a minute," Ricchan said, stopping herself mid-
rant. "I'm getting carried away and losing sight of the point I
want to make. Okay, here's what I don't understand. Are we supposed to believe that all the people who lived through the period
of nation building that started with the Meiji Restoration—
including Sensei—shared some sort of ideological or spiritual

*common ground? I see this book as the story of one damaged individual who withdrew from the world because he couldn't forgive himself for a youthful error in judgment that had unforeseeably tragic consequences. How do you make a connection between one gloomy, introverted person and the bright, shiny 'spirit of Meiji' as embodied in all the people who were cheerful, eager, hardworking members of society during that time?"*

*"The reason you don't understand is because you're a woman!" Kaku screamed, storming to the front of the stage. In baseball terms, this rashly chauvinistic (and completely nonsensical) declaration was the wild pitch that lost the game for Suke & Kaku. Within seconds the two comedians were under siege and the air was filled with a flurry of soft-toy dogs aimed directly at them.*

*The female students who were standing nearby naturally allied themselves with their own gender in the face of such blatant sexism, and they immediately got in on the act by scooping up the "dead dogs" that had landed on the stage around them. However, the girls didn't heave those missives at Suke & Kaku; instead, they used the stuffed animals to pummel the two actors about their heads and faces, like the aggressors in a particularly violent pillow fight.*

*An instant later everyone onstage joined the fracas, snatching up the incoming plush toys and slinging them back into the audience with all their might, while continuing to express their opinions in loud voices. It wasn't long before the scripted play had given way to a festively anarchic fracas. But just as the chaos was reaching its peak the lights were dimmed, transforming the movements of the throng onstage into a sort of shadow play (yet another demonstration of the show's high production values). At the same time those people's voices grew gradually fainter, until finally all that could be heard was a passionate, heartfelt whispering, and then the action in the shadow play slowed to a halt as well.*

*Since a theater in the round doesn't have a curtain, the illusion of a curtain coming down was created by plunging the stage into total darkness. When the lights came up again, the female high school students, led by Ricchan, were standing there looking very pleased with themselves, while the male scholars on the other side, captained by Suke & Kaku, were crouching down on the stage so that they appeared to be virtually buried under a massive pile of "dead dogs." This sight evoked an enthusiastic surge of applause and widespread calls for an encore. Once again the stage went dark, and this time when the lights came on Suke & Kaku stood up and loomed over the scrum with stuffed animals dropping around them—a sight greeted by a mixture of applause, laughter, and catcalls. The alternating blackouts and encores went on and on, and almost as an afterthought, innumerable toy dogs continued to be hurled back and forth.*

*All in all it was a truly extraordinary evening, and everyone agreed that the dog-tossing version of Kokoro was a spectacular success!*

# Chapter 7

# The Aftermath Continues

## 1

*Dear Kogii,*

*I've already told you about the phenomenal success of Unaiko's play. When I saw her later, I broached an idea that had come to me during the performance and was gratified to find that she shared my enthusiasm.*

*I'm writing to you about this now because my little epiphany has a direct connection to the Forest House, and I'm hoping very much that you will give this plan your blessing. If my introduction seems excessive, it's probably because I'm a trifle nervous; I've never before asked you for such a large favor, and I may never do so again. Nonetheless, I feel as though I'm putting you on the spot, and that really isn't my style. As you read this letter, please keep in mind that I was fully conscious of what I was doing and felt very awkward about it.*

*What originally started me thinking about this in the
first place was your decision to abandon the drowning novel.
In all honesty, I should say "your decision to do me the favor of
abandoning the project." I won't pretend I was sorry about that
outcome. That's because when you decided to give up trying to
write about our father through the prism of his death, I felt as
if I had fulfilled Mother's final wish, since the possibility you
might someday publish that book was something she was very
concerned about for a long time. During the ten years since she
passed away, I have to confess that I behaved rather duplici-
tously, although I did have my reasons. The truth is, I knew the
materials you needed in order to complete your drowning novel
had long since been destroyed, but I needed to hear from your
own lips that you had decided to abandon the project based
on what you found—or, more precisely, failed to find—in the
trunk.*

*Anyhow, since the drowning novel has finally been flushed
away once and for all (yes, I realize that may not be the most
tasteful choice of words), I can finally escape from our mother's
long shadow and start to walk alone, on my own. Even as I was
becoming aware of that exhilarating possibility, I realized I'd
already started to march in step with Unaiko, so to speak.*

*As you know, I was deeply impressed and inspired by her
recent performance, and when I announced that from now
on I'd like to pour my energy and resources into helping with
her creative projects, her response was very quick and totally
positive. Unaiko did take some time to discuss the matter with
Ricchan, but she got back to me almost immediately, saying they
both agreed it was time for a change, and rather than continuing to work for Masao Anai (or some other man), they would
rather team up with a woman like me. Then the three of us had
a lovely group hug and laughed about feeling as if we had just
graduated from—or perhaps to?—an all-girls school. What I'd*

*like to say to you now is that until recently the unresolved issue
of Mother's red leather trunk was always taking up valuable
space in my brain, but from here on out I'm going to be single-
mindedly devoting myself to the perpetually evolving* Tossing the
Dead Dogs *project. I'm going to live every day with the aim of
supporting Unaiko and her creative work in any way I can. As
it happens, this decision of mine coincides with an exciting new
stage in Unaiko's career, and I'm delighted to have the chance to
commit my time and abilities, such as they are, to helping her
realize her unique artistic vision.*

*So I guess this is my personal declaration of independence!
I know with absolute certainty that I need to free myself from
Mother's influence, and from yours as well, before I can join
Unaiko in this adventure. If you were to ask what else I've done
in my life that felt as challenging as this, I would have to say it
was making the movie about a local folk heroine, even though
(as you know)* Meisuke's Mother Marches Off to War *was
never distributed because of contractual problems. But now that
I think about it, on that project, too, I was always toiling in your
shadow—and Mother's, too. I mean, you wrote the screenplay,
and of course you were the reason we were able to attract an
international movie star like Sakura Ogi Magarshack.*

*For our current undertaking, though, I'm absolutely deter-
mined not to be dependent on you in any way. So Unaiko and
I are thinking that (if you approve) we would like to enter into
a formal contractual agreement with you, as the original author
of the screenplay, before we do any more work on turning it into
a stage play. Realistically, we wouldn't be able to get our new
enterprise off the ground without your cooperation, but once it
gets rolling Unaiko and I should be able to bring her innovative
ideas to fruition on our own, as an independent partnership.*

*Unaiko is considerably younger than I am, but she's car-
rying some heavy emotional baggage—things in her past that*

*are far more severe than anything I've experienced in my own
comparatively sheltered life. I'm talking about seriously dark and
damaging violations, the kind you wouldn't wish on your worst
enemy. As a teenager Unaiko had some truly harrowing experiences, and right now she's plotting a crucial battle of her own
that's directly connected with a traumatic chapter in her life. I
wouldn't call it a vendetta or a quest for revenge; it's more like
an attempt to obtain a long-overdue measure of justice.*

*Our dear friend Ricchan, who is a supercapable manager
and administrator in addition to being very creative in her own
right, will be accompanying Unaiko and me on our journey.
Since the time has come for me to emerge from the shadows,
I'm excited to be joining forces with Unaiko as we go forth to
fight our battles together: mine rather small, hers potentially
epic.*

*I guess this next bit is what movie people call the backstory,
but at any rate I think the idea for the giant favor I'm leading up
to first began germinating when you mentioned that there will
come a time, perhaps quite soon, when you'll no longer be able
to return to the forest, and you asked me to give some thought
to how we ought to handle the business aspect of the equation.
I started thinking now might be the perfect time to make some
changes, so I went down to the town hall and had a chat with
one of the clerks.*

*When we built the Forest House, Mother's idea was that
the land should be in my name, while the house would belong
to you. Since Unaiko is planning to strike out on her own and
establish her own theater group based on the "tossing the dead
dogs" model, I've been thinking about what a boon it would be
for her to have the use of the Forest House on a more permanent
basis. I'm not proposing that you should deed the house over
to me—I suspect I'll eventually need to move somewhere less
remote myself. Nor am I suggesting that the property be passed
down to my son.*

*What I'm saying is that I would be very grateful if you would formally bequeath the Forest House to Unaiko. (Naturally I would do the same with my claim to the land it sits on.) In addition, I'd like to ask you to continue paying the property taxes and to subsidize the conversion of the downstairs into a proper rehearsal space—a project that, as you know, is already under way. I know it's a lot to ask, but would you please consider doing these things, perhaps as a way of compensating me for having looked after the Forest House all these years? Of course, if you should ever want to come to see any of Unaiko's new productions, or if you ever feel like taking an active part in those projects (and, to be honest, we're going to be counting on your assistance on the artistic side), or if you simply decide to pay us a visit, you will always be more than welcome to set up camp on the second floor for as long as you like.*

*As for the timing of this new chapter of Unaiko's career, something has happened that makes her going solo necessary, and maybe even inevitable. After the success of her recent show—the dog-tossing play built around some of the concepts set forth in Kokoro—she started getting even more flak than usual from the right-wing factions around these parts. At this stage the criticism is still only verbal, but if it should escalate into actual interference she'll have no choice but to fight back. Because the leader of the Caveman Group, Masao Anai, tries to be apolitical in both his private life and his art, Unaiko needs to make it clear to the public that she is leaving the group and going her own way. Since Unaiko will almost certainly need to borrow some start-up capital from the bank, the question of what she has in the way of assets or property—things that could serve as collateral for a loan—will be crucial. That's why I'm asking you to give careful consideration to my request, at your very earliest convenience.*

# 2

*Dear Kogii,*

*I'm absolutely thrilled that you agreed to my big request! How can I ever thank you enough? Since my previous letter ended up being a shameless plea for assistance, I'd like to try to make up for that by telling you about what's been going on, theater-wise, since the beginning of the year, following last fall's boffo performance at the theater in the round.*

*After the resounding success of the Kokoro play, Unaiko immediately got to work on a revised version targeted at a more adult audience. She staged the play at a small venue in Matsuyama where avant-garde theater groups from Tokyo appear from time to time, and it was another smash hit. I was particularly impressed by the way Unaiko took some of the critiques of the earlier version of the play, which was tailored to appeal to students, and cleverly found a way to incorporate those responses into her revised script.*

*Until now, I've mostly been sending you brief descriptions and on-the-scene reports, but I'd like to give you a broader sense of what's taking place in the theater during one of Unaiko's plays. (Although I think it would be difficult for an accomplished journalist, much less an amateur like me, to write an account that does justice to the entire panorama; I mean, there are so many different things going on at the same time while the performance unfolds.) I would also like to try to evoke the distinctive atmosphere of freshness, openness, and unpredictability Unaiko brings to all her productions.*

*As I've mentioned before, lively, unscripted arguments and discussions often erupt spontaneously among the actors onstage and the animated interplay spills over into the audience as well, drawing the spectators into the action. Meanwhile, Unaiko is making a continuous effort to monitor everything that's going on. (It's truly phenomenal the way she's able to focus on several conversations simultaneously; I can't help being reminded of Prince Shotoku, with his legendary facility for listening to individual requests or complaints from ten citizens at once!) At any rate, she'll usually beckon two or three interesting-looking participants from the audience to join her at the front of the stage. Then some of the established performers from the troupe will take the new arrivals under their wings and offer vocal support for whatever opinions the newcomers might be expressing.*

*Of course, this sort of interactive approach   blurring the usually clear demarcation between performers and audience—is at the heart of Unaiko's theatrical modus operandi. However, she runs a tight ship, and when a side discussion that seemed to be heading in an interesting direction begins to lose steam, the people in that group will soon find themselves the targets of a dismissive hail of stuffed animals.*

*On opening night at the cozy little theater in Matsuyama, one of the first audience members to be invited onstage by Unaiko was an acquaintance of mine, a high school teacher from Honcho. (He also came to see the initial* Kokoro *performance last fall.) The teacher started by pointing out that at the beginning of the play an actor was speaking as Sensei himself, in the first person. However, when it came time to quote from Sensei's suicide note, the monologue was voiced in the third person. The teacher's complaint was that because the Sensei character didn't actively participate in the discussion, it simply wasn't as effective or entertaining as when that pivotal character was speaking as himself.*

*My acquaintance was immediately heckled by people saying things like "Wasn't that as it should be, since Sensei had already committed suicide?" He didn't back down, though. "So what if Sensei had already killed himself?" he retorted. "Why couldn't he be sent onstage as someone who's dead, like the ghost in* Hamlet? *I mean, it's a play, right?" He even offered a concrete suggestion: "I noticed a wheelchair out in the lobby," he said. "Couldn't you seat an actor representing Sensei in the wheelchair, with his head and face covered by a cloth to let us know he was supposed to be dead? Then when someone asked him a question, he could reply in his own voice! That would be some gripping theater. Personally, I'd like to call the deceased Sensei back to this dimension from wherever he is now and ask him some tough questions, and based on conversations I've had here tonight I don't think I'm the only one who feels this way." I'm not quoting verbatim, of course, but that's the gist of what the teacher said.*

*And voilà—no sooner said than done! Seriously, I was amazed. It took Unaiko only a few minutes to implement the teacher's suggestions, and in the interlude I could feel the audience's growing excitement about this bit of improvised stagecraft. While we watched, the wheelchair was carried onstage, and after Suke & Kaku had thrown a white cloth over Unaiko's head they seated her in the chair and pushed it into the center of the stage. From then on the high school teacher—whose request had set this impromptu scenario in motion—had no choice but to address his questions to the "corpse."*

*"Sensei," he said, "I'd like to ask about your final letter, or suicide note, which I've read many times along with my students. The thing is, when it comes to making statements about this nation of ours in a public high school in the twenty-first century, an educator has to be extremely circumspect. About six months ago, when this same play was staged in our little town for an audience that included both students and regular citizens—and I'd appreciate it if you would make a point of remembering that I used the word 'citizens' rather than 'townspeople'—anyhow, while a number of students and citizens did participate in the performance, I decided to keep my comments to myself. Today, before I say anything, I'd like to emphasize the fact that I'm here*

*on my own, as a theatergoer. I am not speaking as I would in the classroom.*

*"In case you might wonder to whom the disclaimer is addressed, the answer is: to the members of the school board in the town where I teach. They have made a special trip up here to Matsuyama this evening just to see this play. Because the previous performance at our local junior high gave rise to some very public controversy, I imagine the board members wanted to see for themselves what all the fuss was about. Take a good look at these people; I think you'll agree that they aren't the sort who would normally come to an experimental performance in a small theater like this.*

*"I'd like to begin by talking about what happened when this play was performed in the town where we live. The original plan was to combine the play with a lecture by Kogito Choko, the novelist who was one of the first students to enter the new postwar junior high in our village. However, because Mr. Choko was sidelined with an attack of vertigo—which was completely understandable, since whenever we try to read his convoluted sentences I think we all start to feel a bit dizzy, too [laughter]— anyhow, the planning committee decided to go ahead and present the play as a stand-alone event.*

*"From the perspective of the school board that outcome may actually have been preferable, politically speaking. Why? Because as a writer, Kogito Choko has shown a deep emotional attachment to the archaic version of the Fundamental Law of Education. Back in the prewar era there were students who were unable to advance to the next educational level because of family finances, and that's why a new junior high was built in the village. Mr. Choko was one of the students who benefited. The school was created according to the postwar principles embodied in the New Constitution and the revised—some might say watered-down—version of the Fundamental Law of Education. At the time laws were being modified left and right, and*

*Mr. Choko suggested that everyone ought to make the original
Fundamental Law of Education into pamphlets, to carry around
in our breast pockets. He even had a bunch of those booklets
printed at his own expense, but apparently they didn't sell too
well—you know, not like novels. Or maybe I should say they sold
about as well as Mr. Choko's own novels. [Laughter.] I was one
of the people who actually purchased some of those booklets, so
if you don't mind I'd like to read an excerpt from the one I just
happen to have in my pocket."*

*At this point, the teacher began to read aloud, but the
passage he'd chosen ventured so deeply into the intricacies of
educational politics that the audience around me started to
fidget in obvious boredom and impatience. He must have sensed
this because he stopped reading and said, a bit sheepishly, "Anyhow, the bottom line is that we have to tread carefully whenever
we talk about the topic of education. Why, tonight alone three
people have already thrown 'dead dogs' at me, so I'll move on to
my main point before I get hit again.*

*"It has to do with the note Sensei left behind, in which he
wrote:* Then, during the height of the summer, Emperor Meiji
passed away. I felt as though the spirit of the Meiji Era that
began with the emperor had ended with him as well. I was
overcome with the feeling that I and the rest of my generation, who had grown up in that era, were now left behind to
live as anachronisms. I shared this epiphany with my wife,
but she just laughed and refused to take me seriously. Then
she said a curious thing, albeit in jest: 'Well then, maybe
you should just go ahead and commit *junshi,* and follow the
emperor to the grave.'"

*After he finished reading, the teacher addressed the shrouded
figure in the wheelchair. "Sensei, when you said that to your wife
she laughed at you and didn't seem to take you seriously at all.
She even teased you, saying, ' Maybe you should just go ahead
and commit* junshi.' *On this point, I have to say I really—I don't*

mean to give you a hard time about this, but it just struck me as extremely odd. And that's why I would like to go back in time and ask for some clarification. You talk about how strongly you and your contemporaries were influenced by the spirit of the Meiji Era, but is that true? Your friend was driven to commit suicide as a direct result of your betrayal, yet that betrayal sprang from your own character and the choices you made, so you couldn't really blame your behavior on the sensibilities of the Meiji Era, could you? And as a result of your youthful error, isn't it true that you ended up more or less dropping out of society for personal reasons and then living for many years as if you were already dead, as you put it? In any case, I don't believe your private motivations were shaped by the spirit of the era—although I wouldn't presume to say you were entirely removed from the influence of the society and the era you were living in, either.

"No, I think what moved you to behave as you did was your own secret heart. You speak repeatedly of a strange and terrible force. But didn't the force originate in your soul, or in your gut, rather than somewhere external? Even so, your conviction that the spirit of Meiji was alive in your psyche doesn't seem far-fetched to me at all; I just don't believe it was the primary motivation for anything you did.

"Then there's the matter of your long-suffering wife. She may appear to be a rather unworldly and submissive person, but the fact is she's still a full-fledged member of the sibylline tribe known as womankind. Think about her life for a moment: spending every day and night with a man who doesn't go to work and stays cooped up at home, a man who is immobilized by a mysterious force he can't talk about, even to his spouse. When a man like that blurts out something grandiose and melodramatic about killing himself, wouldn't his wife simply laugh it off? I think she would. And when she says, 'Well then, maybe you should just go ahead and commit junshi'—I mean, isn't it possible she wasn't joking at all? Maybe she was just fed up."

*Kogii, at this point, without thinking, I spontaneously stood up and started clapping. And I wasn't the only one—at least a third of the spectators in the theater applauded too, and some even jumped up and waved their arms in the air. That was the kind of passionate response the teacher's speech evoked.*

*However, in the very back of the theater (it was completely sold out for once) there were three or four men dressed in trench coats. They started swinging "dead dogs" in circles above their heads with an ominous whistling sound, evidently as a way of declaring their objections to what the high school teacher had said. (I don't know; maybe they felt throwing the dogs right away would somehow diminish the impact of their protest?) I won't say those men were members of the school board, but they were most likely from the same camp, ideologically speaking. I can say with certainty that they were people who had heard about what happened at the junior high school last fall and had come to see for themselves. To save time, I'll compress their remarks and bundle the speakers into one, under the generic name "Citizen."*

*"Are you questioning Sensei's feeling that the Meiji Era began and ended with Emperor Meiji? I mean, Sensei stated clearly that he and his contemporaries were profoundly influenced by the essence of Meiji, didn't he? So it rings true that he really did commit* junshi *out of solidarity with the spirit of his age. Are you trying to disparage this noble death?"*

*And with that, the citizens hurled their "dead dogs" in the direction of the high school teacher. However, most of the people in the audience (including a great many young people) apparently sided with the teacher's point of view, because they responded by sending a hailstorm of stuffed animals in the direction of the citizens—an attack that had both numbers and energy on its side. In the midst of the jubilant chaos, Unaiko, who had been sitting motionless in the wheelchair, still in character as the late Sensei, suddenly leaped to her feet. She tore off the white cloth covering her head, revealing a corpselike*

*face made up to appear, quite literally, deathly pale. A hush
fell over the small theater as Unaiko began to speak, displaying
her superb talent for recitation. Using the same voice she had
employed when she was pretending to be Sensei, she started to
talk about the character in the third person.*

*"I've been playing the role of Sensei, but I still don't under-
stand what's in the 'secret heart' of this character whose costume
I'm wearing right now. I'm not sure whether he even understood
himself. For me, this quote says it all."*

**Sensei:** *I read in the newspaper the words General Nogi had
written before killing himself. I learned that ever since the Seinan
War, when he lost his banner to the enemy, he had been wanting
to redeem his honor through death. I found myself automatically
counting the years that the general had lived, always with death
at the back of his mind. The Seinan War, as you know, took place
in the tenth year of Meiji, so he must have spent thirty-five years
waiting for the proper time to die. I asked myself: "When did he
suffer greater agony—during those thirty-five years, or at the moment when the sword entered his bowels?"*

*It was two or three days later that I decided at last to commit
suicide. Perhaps you will not understand clearly why I am about
to die, any more than I can fully understand why General Nogi
killed himself. You and I belong to different eras, and so we think
differently. There is nothing we can do to bridge the gap between
us. Of course, it might be more accurate to say that we are different
simply because we are two separate human beings. At any rate, I
have done my best in the above narrative to make you understand
the strange person that is myself.*

*After delivering this long quote, Unaiko addressed the
crowd directly, in her own words. "Look, I think for Sensei . . . as
this quote says, he was perpetually obsessed with the question of
the human heart—of the individual, by the individual, for the*

*individual—and after having done his best to make his young*
*friend understand this, he took his own life. But how can it be*
*seen as a sacrifice on the altar of the spirit of Meiji? I keep going*
*back to the idea that Sensei ultimately committed suicide as a*
*kind of belated atonement, which is to say he did it for himself.*
*If you agree, please feel free to throw as many 'dead dogs' as you*
*like at those citizens in the audience who take a different view.*
*Go ahead, everybody—knock yourselves out!"*

# 3

*Dear Kogii,*

*Until now I've mostly been writing to you about artistic projects*
*and practical matters, but this letter is going to be much more*
*personal. Of course, you probably have a pretty good idea of*
*what I'm talking about. As you can imagine, the news I've just*
*heard from Chikashi came as a tremendous shock, especially*
*since it doesn't involve one family crisis, but two.*

*Not only is your relationship with Akari at its lowest point*
*ever, but Chikashi has recently been diagnosed with a serious*
*illness. Fortunately, it sounds as though the doctors are optimis-*
*tic about her prospects for recovery, which seems like a welcome*
*ray of hope. As someone who worked as a nurse for many years,*
*I know that while doctors sometimes withhold information and*
*say only what they think a patient wants to hear, they wouldn't*
*resort to that type of sugarcoated subterfuge for someone as*
*strong-minded as Chikashi.*

*Needless to say, you're already fully aware of these very*
*grave situations, and I must say I was surprised that you didn't*
*tell me what was going on with Akari. Instead, Chikashi, who*
*is probably tired of watching you mope around, took the initia-*
*tive and sent me a calm, rational account, which struck me as a*

*perfectly appropriate thing to do. I can't help remembering that you agreed to keep me abreast of any new developments after your return to Tokyo, and the deal was that instead of writing letters you would write things down on cards and someone would send me copies. You've been quite good about reporting on your recuperation from the Big Vertigo, but you didn't say a single word about what happened between you and Akari.*

*Look, I know you're upset because your relationship with Akari seems to be in an unprecedentedly precarious state, and it's only natural for you to feel ashamed since it was your own behavior that created this mess. But we had a deal, and I was disappointed when Chikashi told me you've been writing detailed entries about this situation on the index cards you use instead of a diary, but you apparently instructed Maki (who has been transcribing selected notes on a computer and sending them via email) not to share them with me.*

*Speaking of Chikashi, how do you propose to deal with her illness? Because of the way you've been behaving recently, I don't feel I can rely on you. I gather that Maki will be going over to your house and attending to the household chores, but Chikashi wrote that she would like to ask me, as an experienced nurse, to come up to Tokyo and lend a hand during her stay at the hospital as well as later, when she is recuperating at home. It goes without saying that I'll be more than willing to do anything I can to help.*

*However, your strained relations with Akari are almost as concerning to me as Chikashi's battle against cancer. To begin with, I gather you're expecting Maki to handle the household matters and the administrative aspects of your professional work, and she can't very well attend to Akari's needs, too, while Chikashi is sidelined. Also, if Maki starts to feel stressed about having too many things to deal with, her chronic depression could flare up again.*

*As I was trying to figure out the best way to address the troubling issues raised in Chikashi's letter, I received a typically*

*thoughtful call about those very matters from Chikashi herself.
She waited until I had finished mumbling my greetings and
expressions of sympathy, and then she got right down to business.
She didn't sound like a patient at all; her way of speaking about
her illness was completely pragmatic and unemotional. I know
your family doctor has already briefed you on Chikashi's medical
situation, so I won't repeat those details here.*

*Because Chikashi is the kind of person she is, before
she called me she already knew exactly what she wanted. She
confirmed that she wanted me to come to Tokyo and lend a
hand in my capacity as a nurse, and she also said she'd like to
send you and Akari down to Shikoku to spend some time in the
forest. She had thought through all the details—that's just her
style—and I was happy that she felt she could depend on me. I
was immediately on board with both facets of the plan, and I've
already spoken with Unaiko and Ricchan about looking after
you and Akari while you're at the Forest House, once I've moved
up to Tokyo to act as Chikashi's private nurse. (That's just my
style.)*

*Here's the thing, Kogii: Chikashi mentioned that Akari
hasn't been listening to music for the past six months or so. That
news was almost as shocking to me as her cancer diagnosis,
because music has been the most important thing in Akari's life
for as long as I can remember. Really, I haven't felt so blindsided
by anything since Goro committed suicide.*

*I think anyone who knows you could have predicted that
you would be monumentally depressed after deciding to scrap
your drowning novel, and the Big Vertigo may have affected your
behavior as well. Even so, there's no excuse for treating Akari
the way you did. If Mother were still around, I can almost hear
her saying something like "That's downright disgraceful!" Medical explanations aside, you are a hundred percent responsible
for everything you said to Akari and for the effect those horrible
words have had on him. But I also know that apart from Akari,*

*you're the one who has been hurt the most by this, and I can't help feeling very sad for you both. To be honest, though, I can't get over what you did. I mean, how could you have behaved so heartlessly?*

*Chikashi talked about that situation, too, in her trademark cool, calm, and collected manner. She only got emotional about one thing, when she confided in me that she was very worried about what might happen from now on between you and Akari. When I heard that, I just kind of blurted out the first thing that came to mind.*

*"Chikashi," I said, "in a situation like this, all you can do is bide your time. I mean, um, it's like the period a while back when Akari stopped working on his compositions . . ." (Now every time I think about my glib, meaningless words, I get so mad at myself that I have to get up and pace around like a caged animal. And again, I just feel so terribly sad about everything that's going on.)*

*I could tell Chikashi was disturbed by my comment, but she replied coolly and calmly as usual: "In that situation, Akari stopped composing of his own free will, and when he started again it was also by his own choice. In both cases, he was in control of his own destiny. I'll admit that when I thought he might never write another composition I felt utterly devastated, but the decision was Akari's and I had no choice but to accept it. Also, during that time Akari was still listening to music, both on CDs and on the radio.*

*"But the way things are at present, some truly terrible words have been spoken, and they can never be forgotten or unsaid. It seems as though Akari has decided that he no longer wants anything to do with this family and with Papa in particular. We've never experienced a crisis even remotely like this, and the strangest thing of all, for me, is to be living in a house that isn't constantly filled with music."*

*Since I don't always learn from my mistakes, this was my ill-considered response: "How would it be if you tried playing*

CDs of Mozart and Bach and so on at low volume, when my
brother is away from the house?"

"But why should Akari need to behave in such a fur-
tive manner? Or are you saying that I should just put on some
random CDs and force the issue?" Chikashi asked sternly. I
pictured her normally serene face with the brow furrowed in an
expression of disapproval, and it gave me a chill. To my relief,
she continued in a neutral, reflective tone, almost as if she was
talking to herself. "I appreciate the suggestion, but music has
always been Akari's domain, and I'm afraid having me fill our
silent house with my own choices could make the situation even
more uncomfortable than it already is."

Unfortunately, after having had my clumsy faux pas
redeemed by Chikashi's generosity of spirit—she is always so
extraordinarily gracious, even in the midst of her own travails—I
ended up saying something that I fear was even more irritating.

"You mentioned that there's never before been such a serious rift between Akari and my brother, but hasn't Kogii tried to
repair the damage?" I asked. "In the past, if things had ever gotten to this point, it seems to me that everyone would have gone
all out to get the situation back to normal. I mean, if you read
Rouse Up O Young Men of the New Age! . . ." I trailed off.

Chikashi responded to my question in a tone I'd never
heard from her before. Until then she had been referring to you
as "Papa," and hearing her suddenly switch to calling you "that
man" made my blood run cold. The things she said were so rigorous and unforgiving that I must have somehow rearranged the
words in my mind afterward as a defense mechanism. However, I
haven't been able to forget the underlying message.

In essence, this is what she said: "That man's way of extending a conciliatory hand to Akari is shallow and superficial; I won't
go so far as to say it's disingenuous, but even if such an approach
has occasionally been effective in the past, hasn't that man's
oppression of Akari been part of the problem all along? True, that

man *has some little tricks that have been useful for patching up minor rifts in the past, but if he tries to deploy them now, when his relationship with Akari has reached a complete impasse—well, the truth is it won't work, and I don't even want him to try. He sits around drinking and stewing about the situation, and does impulsive things like rushing out to buy new CDs he thinks might interest Akari and bringing them home as a peace offering. I really wish he would refrain from doing that sort of thing as well. As you know, music has been the single most important element in Akari's life practically forever. The basic principle of listening to music of his own free will must be preserved no matter what. And in order to make sure his freedom to listen to music is protected, his freedom not to listen to music must be respected as well. To borrow one of that man's favorite phrases—doesn't it come down to fundamental human rights? If he somehow decided to force Akari to listen to music against his will, as yet another form of oppression, it could do irrevocable damage to Akari, psychologically. It's even possible that Akari might express his opposition by violently lashing out at that man in an unprecedented way.*

"By the way, what I said just now? I actually borrowed some of the phrasing from Maki, but the things she said echoed what I had been thinking on my own. If things go on like this Maki might end up taking Akari away to live at her house, and I'm not sure I could oppose such a plan, in good conscience."

At this point Chikashi seemed to sense that my hands were trembling uncontrollably on the other end of the line, and she stopped referring to you as "that man," which I had found extremely distressing.

"I've been going around saying that our house in Seijo is inhabited by two giant lumps of depression, and when I think of those two being alone together in their current state, it really frightens me," she went on. "So before I check in to the hospital, I'd like to send them away to a place where they might have a better chance of figuring out how to live together with at least a *modicum of peace and harmony. And for Papa, being on Shikoku surrounded by his beloved forest would be very restorative, don't you agree? I'm afraid setting things up would involve imposing on you even more—I mean, I'm already asking you to come to Tokyo and nurse me through my recovery—but if you don't mind, that's how I'd like to handle it."*

Chikashi's courteous words at the end of our conversation made me feel better about the critical things she had said about you, but after I hung up the phone the sound of her fierce soliloquy was still ringing in my ears. I couldn't bear to stay at home alone so I headed over to the Forest House, hoping to talk to Unaiko. However, she wasn't there—apparently she and Ricchan were both taking care of some business matters—and the house was closed up tight. Since I hadn't brought my key, I went around to the back garden, sat down in front of the poetry stone, and looked at the lines Mother wrote: You didn't get Kogii ready to go up into the forest / And like the river current, you won't return home.

*Kogii, what you're doing now is even worse than that, isn't it? There's no point in raking you over the coals, but we both know you're in a far more dire situation now than when you wrote your part of that poem:* In Tokyo during the dry season / I'm remembering everything backward, / From old age to earliest childhood.

*I hope you'll listen carefully to whatever Chikashi and Maki have to say, and please, please don't even think about doing anything rash. When I mention the need for caution, I'm talking about two aspects of your current situation. First, now that the ill-fated drowning novel has come to naught, I'm afraid the resulting disappointment may have severed the only work-related bond connecting you to this world. Then, on the personal side of the equation, there's the deplorable situation with Akari. The two of you have been practically joined at the hip for all these years, and that link seems to have been sundered as well. At this point, I'm worried that you may be asking yourself whether you have any ties to this life anymore. So I just want to ask you to be very careful not to fall into the kind of tediously nihilistic, self-destructive state of mind old people are especially vulnerable to, because we both know where it can lead.*

*Needless to say, I won't be expecting an actual letter in reply to this. However, I will be looking forward to receiving Maki's copies of any notes you might scribble on your ubiquitous index cards.*

# 4

Some notes from my index cards:

> ➤ Basically, I think the way Akari has made it through life until now—it's hard for me to believe, but he is already forty-five years old—is by creating a world where the interconnected activities of listening to classical music and creating his own brief yet beguiling compositions have formed a stable foundation for his daily existence . . . that is, until the recent catastrophic turn of events.

> ➤ Akari has four successful CDs of original music to his credit, and his uncle Goro even made a film based on my novels about our home life, both of which (the life and the books) revolved around Akari. When Akari was taking music lessons from an expert in the field, he never shirked his studies. This process was interrupted when he took an extended break from composing, but after a couple of years he resumed his study of music theory with the same diligence. Every day the communal living area of our house was filled with the sound of recorded music, played at low volume: Bach, Mozart, Beethoven, Schubert, Chopin, and even some Messiaen and Piazzolla thrown into the mix from time to time. For years, the music Akari played was the sound track of our lives.

➤ And now all that sublime classical music has completely vanished from our home. Oh, Akari still checks the program listings in the weekly FM radio guide, and he hasn't abandoned his daily self-set task of correcting any misprints in the composers' names or titles of works in the programming details at the back of the monthly music magazines. There has been no change in his customary routine of constantly reorganizing his shelves of CDs in accordance with the complex taxonomic principles he seems to keep in his head. However, during the past six months there hasn't been a single moment when Akari enlivened the space we share with the sounds of classical music. As Chikashi put it, with her usual succinctness, our son has turned into a musical recluse. He listens to music only late at night when he is alone in his room, using headphones connected to his radio, as if he wants to keep it all to himself.

➤ So what is at the root of this sadness and silence and turmoil? The words I rashly spoke to Akari in an unpardonable fit of anger: "You're an idiot." That short, simple declarative sentence . . . the epitome of unreflective cruelty.

➤ Many years ago, in a grove of Erman's birches in North Karuizawa, I was carrying Akari piggyback when he uttered the first words of his young life in response to hearing the call of a bird on a nearby lake. "It's a water rail," he said clearly. (He had already learned to recognize and mimic the songs of a variety of wild birds from a recording we had at home.)

➤ From that point on Akari's vocabulary grew at a rapid rate, and within three or four years he was able to understand the discriminatory slurs and insults the outside world flung his way. I remember one time when Maki came home from middle school and immediately ran into the kitchen to tell Chikashi about how she had gone to pick Akari up after his special education class and had found him being taunted by a menacing group of older male students. Akari, meanwhile, was in the living room listening to music, and when I peeked in I saw him with both hands clamped over his ears and his elbows sticking out at right angles, obviously trying to filter the unpleasant "noise pollution" of what his sister was saying while still continuing to listen to his beloved music.

➤ And now Akari has evidently reclassified his own father from trusted protector to source of discordant noise and pain: someone who would hurl the most hurtful word imaginable at his own son more than once. This situation has already been festering for half a year, and it could easily continue for another six months—perhaps even a year or two. The truth is, at times even those rather bleak estimates seem wildly optimistic. There is a distinct possibility that Akari and I could go on sharing a living space in which the sound of music is never heard for the next ten or fifteen years, or more.

## 5

*Dear Kogii,*

*Maki is always very accommodating and easy to deal with, and she kindly took your reflections on the rift between you and Akari, transcribed their index cards on her computer, and emailed them to me. I don't know whether she was trying to balance the mournful tone of your contributions, but she also included some letters Chikashi wrote to you. I'm sure you read them at the time and wrote proper replies, but because Maki sent me the originals of those letters (rather than photocopies) you no longer have them at hand, so I'll fax them back to you just in case you might want to take another look. Here's the first one, which I found very interesting:*

*I recently remembered a day, many years ago, when you read a letter from one of your young readers and then went into your study without*

*a word and stretched out on your army cot. The memory was triggered
the other afternoon when I noticed a book you had been reading next
to the chaise longue. (You had gone off to get a haircut while I was
getting ready to head for the hospital alone to check myself in, as we'd
agreed.) The book had a handmade dust cover, and when I opened it
and took a peek at the title page, I saw that it was Soseki's* Kokoro.

*Anyway, the young reader—this was when you were quite
young yourself, so that person was probably only ten years your junior at most—was responding to a short essay of yours that appeared
in one of those little publishing-company advertising brochures
they give away at bookstores and university co-ops. The title was a
quote from* Kokoro: I'd like you to remember something. This is
the way I have lived my life. *Apparently after reading the essay (or,
at least, after glancing at the title) the student scrawled some rude
remarks—things like "Who do you think you're talking to, anyway?
Why should I waste my time remembering how you've lived your
life? As if I cared!"—on a page torn out of a school notebook and
mailed it to you. The student's comments struck me as oddly reasonable and I inadvertently burst out laughing, which just made you
more depressed. (I could tell, even though you didn't say anything.)*

*Getting back to the present, before I left for the hospital I
wandered around the rooms on the second floor of our house. As I
was looking at the shelves in the library where all your books are
lined up, I remembered the indignant reaction of the young reader
(now presumably grown old) to your* Kokoro *quotation and it made
me giggle again, even though it isn't a particularly pleasant memory.
In any event, my little tour of your bookshelves gave me an idea,
and I'd like to ask for a favor. Would you please copy out the parts
of your novels where you quote things Akari has said and send them
to me? I thought maybe I could ask Maki to make those excerpts
into a miniature book, using a nice, clean-looking Mincho typeface
on her computer (which she insists is already outmoded). Then she
could finish them by hand.*

*I have to say, I'm feeling very optimistic about our chances of weathering the current storm. In the past, whenever we've had to deal with a crisis of any magnitude I have always felt we would make it through somehow, and we've done just that, every single time. Upon reflection, everyone in our family, including Akari (aside from the disabilities he was born with), has been blessed with fundamentally healthy bodies. Do you remember the famous aphorism Musumi Sensei translated so precisely from the Latin,* Mens sana in corpore sano, *adding his own observation that a sound mind can easily coexist with an unhealthy body, and vice versa? That's probably true, but—no, I'm going to resist the temptation to point out that we're both growing old and before long our crises will be at an end. I would rather be positive and borrow a phrase of Céline's that you once translated, aeons ago: "Let's keep our chins up and be of good cheer!"*

*The truth is, when I glanced over those books in the library I couldn't help thinking (like the young reader) that being told to "please remember all this" was, indeed, a rather tall order. Of course, I stopped reading your novels somewhere around the middle of* Letters to a Nostalgic Time—*though I did continue reading your essays, since I illustrated the bulk of them. But anyway . . . you know how Soseki writes that Sensei found himself automatically tallying the years on his fingers? Well, when I did that just now I realized it's been twenty years since I decided to stop reading your fiction. And even now, to be honest, I don't feel any desire to use my downtime in the hospital to catch up on your books.*

*That's why I'd like to ask you to go through your work and extract the passages where you quote things Akari has said. I remember you once told me in all seriousness that you write down Akari's comments verbatim, without embellishment, because you can't very well hand over the rough draft and ask him whether he wants to make any corrections.*

# 6

*Dear Kogii,*

*Maki sent me a copy of the charming little* My Own Words
*book she put together after you went through your novels
and picked out a number of the quotes attributed to Akari.
(Of course, his remarks would have been easy to spot because
they were always in bold type—or in italics, in the English
translations.)*

*Unaiko was completely enchanted with the compilation,
from the very first page, and she's been running around quoting
from it ever since. However, Maki enclosed a note saying that
she didn't necessarily agree with the way you chose the excerpts,
although I gather she hasn't shared those thoughts with you
directly.*

*Chikashi once told me that Maki was very outgoing and
vivacious as a young child but her personality suddenly changed
when she was halfway through middle school, and she became
much more subdued and withdrawn. Also, she started having
bouts of extreme melancholy and she would just say whatever
she was thinking, without any of the customary filters. I remember the conventional wisdom in the nursing community at the
time was that many antidepressants contained an ingredient that
could cause an abnormal degree of aggressiveness in patients. In
any event, I know Maki is taking antidepressants now, and I'm
telling you this because I think it may be relevant to what's going
on between the two of you.*

*In her note, Maki expressed the opinion that there have
been many other times when you were very controlling toward
Akari. (She used the word "oppression," which seems to keep
popping up.) She reminded me of a time you described in your
autobiographical novel* Rouse Up O Young Men of the New

Age! *when you went over to Europe, during the rise of the grass-roots antinuclear protest movement there, to participate in the making of a television documentary. You ended up staying quite a bit longer than expected, and Akari became convinced you were dead. "Is that right? Is he coming back on Sunday? Even if he is, right now he's dead! Papa is really dead!"*

*Of course you know this story better than anyone. Anyhow, in the book Akari started talking back to his mother, who was very much alive. He kept responding to her questions in a belligerent way, and when the father finally did get home he gave Akari a good scolding, and that triggered a rift between them. However, not long afterward, when the father was laid up with an acute attack of gout, Akari addressed his dad—whose ailment had temporarily transformed him into the weakest member of the family—through the intermediary of the father's badly swollen feet. As a result, amicable relations were restored, both in the book and in real life, but as Maki points out there are some significant differences between that situation and what's going on now. On second thought, I'm just going to copy the rest of what she said instead of trying to paraphrase:*

*If Mama is hoping to orchestrate some kind of peaceful accord, like what happened before, and if Papa created this little book of Akari's quotations in the hopes that it will miraculously smooth things over, then they're both being way too optimistic. If Papa really thinks the same approach will work this time, when the damage is so much more severe, it only shows that his oppressive attitude toward Akari hasn't changed a bit. At least that's how it seems to me. And isn't this exactly what Mama has been talking about all along as well?*

*Those were Maki's main points, but she ended her note by raising an interesting question: "Don't you think everyone's getting a kick out of the My Own Words booklet just because of the unique way Akari uses language?"*

Since Chikashi went into the hospital earlier than expected
and I wasn't able to adjust my own departure date to accommodate the change, I've been talking to Maki on the phone quite
frequently these days about various practical matters. During
one of those conversations I mentioned offhandedly that I would
be interested in hearing an explanation of the rationale behind
the harsh things she's been saying about you lately and her unforgiving attitude toward you in general. I had heard from Chikashi
about how rough things were at your house, but I didn't really
understand what was going on.

Maki was completely candid. She told me, "Papa flung some
unspeakably cruel words at Akari, not once but twice. The first
incident was bad enough, but there's no way he can forgive himself for letting it happen again. Papa knows this is an intolerable
situation, and I'm sure he's been trying to figure out how to make
it better, but suppose Papa and Akari don't manage to work things
out this time and they just go on living completely separate lives.
Would that really be so bad? Akari could come live with me. I've
been talking to Mama about that solution, too."

That seems to be where Maki stands right now. As I see it,
we might be able to make allowances for the first incident by saying that when Akari innocently defaced the flawless Beethoven
score—a memento of your friendship with Edward W. Said—
you were so upset that you simply lost control of yourself. However, the second lapse is a different story. I mean, you had already
gone to bed, but you got up and made a special trip downstairs
to confront Akari, and then you called him that shocking name
again. True, it was the middle of the night and you were probably under the influence of your usual nightcap. Even so, there's
no excuse for such appalling behavior, and I was literally speechless when I heard about it.

I don't want to end on an unpleasant topic, so let's get back
to the delightful little book Maki assembled. As I said earlier,
Akari's quotations made a deep impression on Unaiko. She and

Ricchan have both been working very hard to get everything ready for when you and Akari arrive, but even though Unaiko already knows you fairly well she told me she's been feeling nervous about meeting Akari, so she gave the little booklet an extra-careful reading. I gather she has also been trying to formulate a strategy that could lead to an eventual reconciliation between you and Akari. Apparently she found a glimmer of hope in the passage where your foot was inflamed and swollen from gout, and Akari's response was so sweetly solicitous. She thinks that scene has great dramatic potential, too, although she was saying they would need to find a way to make a stuffed-toy likeness of your gouty foot!

This is Unaiko's take on the scene, which she analyzed with her usual intensity: the head of the household, who is the family's authority figure, is angry at Akari, who, in turn, is going through a rebellious stage. Even so, he wants to make peace with his father, but he doesn't have the courage to address his conciliatory gestures to the more central parts of his father's anatomy—especially the angry face, which he finds frightening. However, the red, swollen, gout-ridden feet that are causing the father so much suffering are peripheral and therefore, somehow, easier to approach. Also, those feet seem to be staging a mutiny of their own against the more entitled and politically powerful parts of the body, so Akari feels he can engage with those extremities and speak to them directly with affection and concern. "Foot, are you all right? Good foot, nice foot! Gout, are you all right? Nice foot! Nice foot!" Unaiko found that section very moving. Of course, she sees everything from a theatrical perspective, and she said Akari's touching speech to his father's feet is an unusually deep expression of his own complicated feelings, the likes of which she's never seen on any stage.

My recent letters to you must have seemed like an endless barrage of criticism, I know, so I'd like to end by reminding you of another nice passage in the same novel, where it's clear that

*Akari is worrying more about his father than about himself. Since you didn't choose to include those lines in your compilation, I'm planning to write them in the miniature book Maki sent me. I'll include them here as well, on the chance they might make you feel better.*

*"Can't you sleep, Papa? I wonder if you'll be able to sleep when I'm not here. I expect you to cheer up and sleep!"*

*Well then, I'll be looking forward to seeing you when our paths cross at Haneda Airport. I'm glad we were able to arrange it so I'll be flying into Tokyo right around the time you and Akari are taking off for Shikoku!*

# Chapter 8

# Gishi-Gishi/Mr. Rhubarb

1

As the day of Chikashi's surgery approached I headed back to my original home turf, the rustic valley deep in the forests of Shikoku, this time with Akari in tow. Asa was by my wife's side at the hospital; both Chikashi and our daughter, Maki, acknowledged that no one was better qualified to see Chikashi through the surgery and the subsequent recovery period than my sister, who had spent more than half her life working as a nurse.

Maki, meanwhile, would be at our house in the Seijo district of Tokyo, holding down the domestic fort and dealing with incoming correspondence regarding copyrights, writing commissions, and miscellaneous business matters. Akari's preference would naturally have been to stay home and keep Maki company. However, Chikashi (who couldn't stop worrying about the precarious state of my relationship with Akari) believed the two of us might find it healing to spend some time together on Shikoku, and she almost seemed more concerned with advancing the plan than with her own impending surgery. Maki somehow managed to convince her brother that this was the best option, and while Akari must surely have sensed the underlying motivation, he agreed.

As for me, I didn't feel particularly sanguine about the chances our stay on Shikoku would result in a return to familial harmony, but I did understand that it would be less stressful for Chikashi not to have a couple of depressive lumps moping around the house, or the hospital. She had said all along that since I tended to be a worrywart, I should leave dealing with her illness to the female warriors in the family. I agreed to this hands-off approach, and the only medical information I had received was that a uterine tumor, benignly dormant for many years, had somehow become malignant and needed to be removed as soon as possible.

As things stood, I wasn't being allowed to share in Akari's music, which had long been both the most essential element in his life and his primary mode of communication within the family. Whenever my thoughts strayed to that torturous subject, I couldn't help feeling a sense of utter desolation and spiritual bankruptcy. As we set off for Shikoku, Akari was in an understandably sour mood; after all, I had given him every reason to carry a major chip on his shoulder. He wasn't speaking to me, and as far as I could see there was nothing I could do about that.

Our flight had been scheduled so that we would depart from Haneda Airport not long after Asa had flown in, so Maki was able to see Akari and me off while also meeting her arriving aunt. The exceedingly strained relations between me and both my children had made the taxi ride to the airport more than a little awkward, but naturally the ever-indomitable Asa had come equipped with a plan to drag me back into the land of the living.

"Kogii," she said after we had exchanged cursory greetings, "I've arranged for someone to come by and keep you company at the Forest House from time to time. You'll never guess who it is: Daio!" She then launched into a lengthy etymological explanation about the evolution of that person's name and history, presumably for Maki and Akari's benefit.

"So when he was repatriated to Japan as an unidentified orphan, the immigration officials gave him a made-up name: Ichiro Daio," Asa concluded. "Our mother felt sorry for him, and because one of the medicinal herbs she used to gather—a type of wild rhubarb called *daio*—was known locally as *gishi-gishi*, she bestowed that playful nickname on him and it stuck. Of course, nobody calls him Gishi-Gishi anymore, and his first name somehow lost the long 'o' over the years. Kogii, I haven't felt the time was right to tell you about Daio's return, what with the whole drowning-novel debacle and all. When he first resurfaced, ages ago, Mother actually forbade me to share the news with you. But since you've now abandoned your novel for good, I don't think I need to worry about Mother's wishes anymore. Really, though, isn't it like a nostalgic blast from the past to hear Daio's name? I saw him at the memorial service on the tenth anniversary of Mother's death, and when we started chatting I could tell he was thinking fondly about years gone by. He specifically mentioned that he was hoping to have a chance to see you again someday."

Apart from this announcement, which she tossed off in a casual, matter-of-fact manner, Asa spent most of our shared time at the airport chatting with Akari. The unexpected mention of Daio reminded me that whenever my mother had addressed him as Gishi-Gishi—a nickname that could be translated, loosely, as "Mr. Rhubarb"—she always pronounced those words with an oddly singsong lilt, as if she were speaking Chinese. However, my attention at the airport and during the plane trip was entirely focused on my upcoming sojourn on Shikoku with Akari, so Asa's news didn't really register.

On the flight to Matsuyama, Akari seemed to be feeling some degree of pain or discomfort in his knees and lower back, but he didn't complain. I sat next to him, alternately dozing and waking, and after a while I began to think my aging ears had somehow misheard what Asa had said. It hardly seemed likely that Daio (who had been dead for several years, as far as I knew) would be coming to visit me at the Forest House.

A day or so after I returned from my first guest-teaching stint in Berlin, I had received a large wooden crate along with a letter notifying me of Daio's death, ostensibly sent by the few remaining disciples who were still living with him at his old paramilitary training camp. After offering the customary flowery greetings, the letter explained that with the demise of their leader the training camp was being disbanded and sold off piece by piece. It then went on to explain that the crate contained a gigantic freshwater turtle, which Daio had supposedly caught, just before his death, in a mountain stream at the lower end of the camp. The turtle was a remarkable specimen: a good fourteen centimeters tall and brimming with youthful strength and vigor. I interpreted the turtle's sudden appearance as a personal challenge and, feeling rather like a jet-lagged gladiator, I immediately charged into battle. It took me from midnight until the break of dawn to subdue that formidable foe, and by the time I finally triumphed the kitchen was completely covered with blood and I was soaked in gore from head to foot.

Akari and I hailed a taxi outside Matsuyama Airport, then sat back in silence as the driver followed the road along the Kame River all the way to the Forest House. Upon our arrival we learned that Unaiko and Ricchan, having completed the preparations for our stay, had returned to Matsuyama, where the theater group had its offices. In their stead a young female member of the drama troupe, whom I had met briefly the last time I was at the Forest House, had prepared our evening meal and was waiting to greet us. Akari and I ate dinner without exchanging a word. After the girl from the Caveman Group had shown Akari around the premises—he had been there before, but it always took some time for him to get acclimated to any change of living situation—she gave us the keys to the house and took off. Akari climbed the stairs to the room she had pointed out as his, which was next to my combination study/bedroom.

I went into the great room on the ground floor, which was clearly in the process of being converted from a rehearsal area back into a living space. After opening my luggage and making a halfhearted stab at unpacking, I poured myself a little nightcap and drank it down. As I climbed the stairs, I couldn't hear any sounds emanating from Akari's room. Feeling an overwhelming sense of loneliness, I crawled into my bed, which smelled of sunlight. When I got up again a moment later to check whether the night-light in the bathroom was on, I saw that Akari's pill organizer and a used drinking glass—clear evidence he hadn't forgotten to take his bedtime medicine—had been left out in plain sight, where I would be sure to notice them.

The next morning I was awakened by the ringing of the telephone. When I ran downstairs to answer it (Akari was evidently still asleep), an unmistakably familiar voice on the other end said, "Hello, this is Daio." Despite Asa's warning, I was startled. Daio must have picked up on my reaction, because he immediately launched into an apologetic explanation about the circumstances surrounding his spurious "death."

When the training camp was breaking up, he told me, his mischievous disciples apparently decided that it would be amusing to play an elaborate prank on Kogito Choko, and the resulting jape was somehow connected with a "pre-death wake" they had staged in Daio's honor before the members of the group went their separate ways.

"I'm already in the neighborhood, down by the river," Daio went on. "I'll wander around here for half an hour or so before heading to the Forest House. I've been there once before, when Asa invited me to a meeting of the drama group, so I know the way. She gave me a key as well." "Thank you for calling," I said. "If you had just appeared at the door with no advance notice, I might have thought I was seeing a ghost. On the other hand, my list of friends and acquaintances includes more and more dead people these days, so it might have seemed perfectly natural . . ."

"Asa said I should drop by as soon as possible after you arrived," Daio said. "By the way, I gather you went through quite an ordeal with the turtle my disciples sent you as a joke. For quite some time now, reading has been my only pleasure; I read all your books as soon as they come out, so I know you wrote about that epic struggle in *The Changeling*. Speaking of turtles, there's a much easier way to kill them, you know. You just put the creature on the cutting board, belly up, and when it sticks out its neck and starts thrashing around, trying to turn over, bam! You chop off its head, easy as pie. But hey—I guess even an erudite person like you has a few gaps in his knowledge!"

Half an hour later I came downstairs again and found Daio waiting in the great room. On the south side of the spacious room, between some professional lighting equipment and a pair of giant speakers, there were an oblong table and two chairs.

Daio was perched on one of those chairs, and I noticed that my opened trunk had been neatly placed on the floor of the makeshift stage in front of the large plate-glass window overlooking the back garden. I left the luggage strewn around the room when I went to bed, and Daio had apparently tidied it up without being asked. The sofa had been cleared off, too, evidently for Akari and me to use when we came downstairs. I couldn't help thinking, *This must be how it feels to have a butler, or a valet*: a luxurious perk I had only read about in British novels.

Daio got up from his chair and gestured for me to take a seat on the couch. Then he shot a glance toward the stairs, clearly hoping to see Akari on his way down. I recalled that in the seemingly solemn letter his prankish training-camp disciples sent me they had used the term "one-legged and one-eyed" (which is often employed, both in period fiction and anime, to describe swordsmen with mythical powers) in reference to their leader. Just as I remembered, Daio was missing an arm, and one of his sleeves was neatly pinned up in the usual way.

"Hello, Kogito. It's been a while," he said, openly giving me the once-over. "I can't help thinking that if your father had lived to enjoy his old age, he would have looked a lot like you do now—aside from your bad posture, of course. Your father always thought you would grow up to be an interesting chap, and you seem to have turned out just as he hoped."

"Actually, I think the term he used was 'joker,' rather than 'interesting chap,'" I said lightly.

"No, but seriously, you really are an interesting guy," Daio insisted. "And that isn't the same as being a joker, or a jester, or whatever. As a child you were always searching for obscure characters in your father's dictionary—you were kind of like an insect collector, only with kanji. I remember one time when your father was happily expounding on the meaning of some word or other and you interrupted, saying, 'That's not what it says in the dictionary!' Then you added, a bit more kindly, that the print was extremely tiny and it was a rather complicated character, so your father had probably just misread it. And when he fished out his magnifying glass and examined the word in question, sure enough: you were right."

It was actually a rather proud memory for me. At the time my father was only fifty years old, but because of a combination of wartime privations and the remoteness of our mountain village he was malnourished, and he probably had the eyesight of a much older man. As a result he would occasionally misread something, especially when the print was very small. I was obsessed with finding unusual kanji, so I used to spend hours poring over the index of my father's big dictionary. That's why I was able to suss out his mistakes on more than one occasion. I even made a point of memorizing potentially problematic characters, and whenever I came across one that I thought my father might be likely to misread at some point, I would be filled with youthful excitement.

Perhaps the most memorable example involved Shinobu Origuchi's explanatory comments regarding his most famous novel, *The Book of the Dead*. Those remarks took the form of an essay titled "The Motif of the Mountain-Crossing Buddha," which was published several years later. The passage in question was a description of how, in olden days, pilgrims used to flock to Shitennoji (the Temple of the Four Heavenly Kings) to watch the sun set over the western gate—a view popularly considered to be a preview of the heavenly paradise known as the Pure Land. Some of the most fervent believers would actually seek to take a shortcut to the Pure Land by drowning themselves in the Inland Sea or whatever body of water happened to be nearby.

When my father read this passage, he mistook 淼淼 (a duplicated-kanji compound meaning "an endless expanse of water," entirely composed of 水, the character for water) for a similar-looking compound: 森森, which consists of repetitions of 木, the character for "tree," and is used to describe tall trees growing densely in a forest.

One day while my father was hard at work at our family business, inspecting the bundles of dried, bleached-out paperbush bark for any untidy scraps that might have adhered to them (he did this by turning the large bundles with a specially designed cargo hook), he started talking to my mother about the Origuchi book he had been reading. She was sitting next to him, busy with her own tasks.

"'A dense forest of ocean waves' is a rather intriguing turn of phrase," he remarked. "Around here they say when someone passes away, that person's spirit rises through the air and returns to the forest, isn't that right? To the people who descend into the depths of the forest from the heights of the sky, the leaves of the trees might appear to resemble waves in the sea. So there really could be a thick forest of waves, figuratively speaking."

My father was referring to the local belief that when people from our area die their souls return to the upper tier of the forest above the valley. In our family, the belief was fostered not by my father (who originally came from another part of the country) but by my grandmother and my mother, both of whom used to volunteer at the local shrine. My father tended to be quite taciturn and it was unusual for him to start a conversation in such a way, so it must have made my mother very happy.

I happened to be standing nearby, and their exchange made me prick up my ears. Because of my obsessive penchant for perusing the index of the kanji dictionary I was familiar with both of the characters in question, and when I ran to check the Origuchi book my hunch that my father had misread the compound was confirmed.

"The kanji in the quotation is written with the character for water, arranged in a sort of pyramid," I announced triumphantly when I returned. "The one you mistook for it is constructed in the same way, only with the character for tree. The first one is used to talk about floods and so on, and also to describe a scene where a body of water stretches as far as the eye can see."

My father put on the silver-framed reading glasses he always kept nearby and then, wearing an expression so serious that it almost made him look like a different person, he went into his small study in the interior of the house, presumably to double-check what I had said. Later, he apparently shared his pride and amusement over the incident with my mother and also, as I was learning just now, with Daio.

While I listened to Daio on that morning in early spring, an image floated across my mind: my father, not out on some vast ocean but rather spinning around on the river bottom during the big flood, on the verge of being inexorably drawn into the whirlpool. My father, who at that moment must have been experiencing the sensations of venturing deep into the forest and, simultaneously, being sucked into a watery vortex. My father, who (for all I knew) might even have believed in some paradisiacal world beyond—a realm that could somehow, magically, be reached by drowning.

"Choko Sensei was studying the ways in which society and the nation as a whole were moving forward," Daio was saying. "He used to tell us about some of the things he learned from his correspondence with supposedly illustrious people, but when we asked whether those people were recognized experts in the field of politics or economics it always emerged that, in fact, they were not. But you yourself gravitated toward the study of literature, and we've all heard the story of how you became interested in the subject because of the books your mother brought home for you when you were a child, during the war."

While Daio and I were enjoying a desultory chat, Unaiko (who had driven down from Matsuyama) was busy in the kitchen fixing breakfast for us. When she came into the great room bearing coffee, she was dressed more or less as usual in Chinese-style trousers and a loose shirt that was almost like a jacket. However, I also got a clear sense of something Asa had spoken of in one of her letters: Unaiko did, indeed, project a kind of heightened aura, as if the major success of her theater-in-the-round play had somehow peeled away part of a protective carapace while also giving her self-confidence a visible boost.

Unaiko needed to consult with me about some practical matters, such as what time Akari should be awakened and when was the latest he could take his morning medicine—Maki had provided a list of all the meds and their dosages—but she conducted even that quotidian exchange in a lively, energized way. Evidently she had already had some preliminary discussions about division of labor with Daio.

"I'll go upstairs and get Akari out of bed myself," I said. "I don't foresee any particular problems during the morning hours, at least."

At this point Unaiko produced a fax from Maki that gave detailed instructions about Akari's breakfast menus, complete with illustrations in the margins, and began to study it carefully.

The night before I had checked to make sure Akari was asleep and breathing normally before going to bed myself, but I hadn't waited until he made his nightly midsleep trip to the bathroom. Before my disastrous outburst in the clinic's waiting room, I had made a ritual of getting up whenever I heard Akari making his way to the toilet; I would go into his room and tidy the sheets and quilts, then wait for him to return so I could tuck him in again. Since that dark day, though, I hadn't once performed my familiar middle-of-the-night task—which I had always thought of as something I would be doing forever.

Now, as I opened the door and entered the room (which was still dark because of the drawn curtains, and redolent of Akari's body odor), I felt reluctant to turn on the light. After a moment I got a sense that something was stirring in the bed and then, finally, I flipped the switch. Akari was lying stretched out on the bed, wrapped in a cotton quilt and staring at the ceiling.

"You and I are going to be staying here at the Forest House for a little while," I said, by way of orientation. "Mama and Maki aren't here, so can you get dressed by yourself? A friend of Auntie Asa's named Unaiko is making breakfast for us. If you've already used the toilet, let's go downstairs. You can brush your teeth in the guest washroom there, all right?"

"I understand," came the uninflected reply.

As Akari began to climb out of bed, I noticed that his movements were slower and clumsier than usual, and there seemed to be a hitch in his basic locomotion. I started to offer to help him to his feet, but then I lost my nerve. Instead, I walked over to the window next to the bed and pulled open the drapes. The trees hadn't yet begun to bud, and the front garden looked barren and deserted. The river shoreline beyond the wooded valley was shrouded in clouds, and the slope above it had a bleak, desolate aspect. I was standing with my back to Akari, but I got the feeling that he was dressing himself with unusual alacrity.

My son and I descended the staircase in single file, keeping several steps between us. Unaiko was waiting at the bottom, and she led Akari to the washroom. When he didn't take any notice of the visitor in the great room, Daio withheld his own greeting as well, but I could see him studying the hesitation in Akari's gait.

While I was upstairs Daio had apparently been looking at a monochromatic woodblock print on the wall next to the sofa in the great room, which was the only decoration.

"What's the story behind this piece of art?" he asked. "This dog looks really ferocious, as if with the proper training it could be taught to kill people."

"Ah, you're wondering about the print?" I said. "Well, I originally brought it down on my previous trip with the intention of hanging it in the space where I thought I would be working on a novel about my father, before and after his death. (That project is now defunct, as you may have heard.) When I went back to Tokyo I simply forgot to take it with me."

"Maybe leaving it behind was just another symbol of your decision to give up on your drowning novel," Daio said. "Asa was saying that it almost seemed as if the project was doomed from the start."

Unaiko had returned from escorting Akari to the downstairs restroom and now she, too, was gazing at the woodblock print on the wall. "Maybe I'm being obtuse," she said, "but I don't see any great significance in your having forgotten to take this picture back to Tokyo. On the other hand, it's certainly true that you did make a special point of grabbing this one particular work of art and lugging it all the way down here."

I responded with an account of the print's provenance. "I really don't think this dog has the sort of evil mojo Daio seems to be ascribing to it," I said. "On the other hand, I won't pretend it's a tranquil and pastoral image, either. As you can see, the date is written in pencil under the author's signature. This piece was created in 1945, the year my father died, by a printmaker in Mexico, but I didn't acquire it until the seventies. It's actually a rather interesting story. At the time, just after the war, the government was oppressing some newspaper companies in Mexico City, and the reporters for those papers staged a major strike. They solicited support from every sphere of culture and the arts, and the printmakers helped raise money by selling work from their private collections. From what I heard, this print was one of them. I bought it at a gallery several decades later, when I was teaching in Mexico City.

"For those reporters, having their freedom of expression thwarted was exactly the same as if their newspapers had been physically trampled into the ground, and this print could be interpreted as a symbolic depiction of the dilemma they faced. In the foreground, the angry-looking dog that's facing in our direction, just beginning to bark, is shown in extreme close-up. But is the dog meant to symbolize the newspaper reporters who were resisting the government's interference, or does it represent the oppressive wielders of authority? I talked about this with some of the cultural movers and shakers who took me to the exhibition where I bought this print, and their opinions were divided between those two interpretations. But the truth is, I just bought this piece, in all innocence, because I liked it. At the end of my term at El Colegio de México (the national graduate school), I received a half year's pay as a single lump-sum payment, and I used it to buy the print. It's signed by the artist: Siqueiros."

"Oh, you mean *the* Siqueiros?" Unaiko asked. She looked genuinely surprised and impressed. "I had no idea. I've seen photos of his big public murals in art books. The funny thing is, I've been thinking all along that whoever created this little print must be quite an exceptional artist. Asa was even saying the other day that we should try to make some stuffed dogs with this same kind of visual impact!"

"That reminds me, when you were in tech for your dog-tossing play at the theater in the round, Asa mentioned something about wanting to hang this in the auditorium lobby," I said.

"Yes, she was saying that the only complaint she had about the production was that there were some people in the audience who thought the stuffed dogs were *cute*," Unaiko said, wrinkling her nose. "She wanted to hang this fierce picture in the lobby to dispel that impression. Next time we do a show, would you please let us borrow it? And, if you didn't mind, it would be great if we could photograph this print and put the image on T-shirts for our entire crew to wear, like a uniform."

"Please put me on the list for one of those shirts, too!" Daio said brightly. I had noticed earlier that he was rather stylishly dressed (especially for someone his age) in a beige corduroy jacket worn over a shirt of heavy brown cotton, and it occurred to me that his fashion sense appeared to have evolved considerably during the years since I'd seen him last.

We all trooped into the dining room, where Unaiko had laid out a meal of eggs, toast, and coffee. Daio had eaten breakfast before he came, so he only wanted coffee. Holding his cup, he stood behind Akari's chair. "Akari, your back's hurting, isn't it?" he asked. "Especially here at the very base, on this side?"

"Yes, it hurts a lot," Akari replied in a voice unusually full of emotion. "It's been hurting all the time, for a while now."

"Please just go on eating," Daio said. "I'm going to try touching your back in a few places but it won't hurt, I promise."

As he spoke those reassuring words Daio knelt next to Akari's chair and began to apply light pressure in the vicinity of Akari's lower back, using his right hand. (Since he didn't have a left arm, Daio had to lean his upper body against the back of the chair for leverage.)

"How about here, Akari? It probably felt sore when you were lying in bed, am I right?"

"Yes, very sore," Akari said.

"I'm not actually going to touch this spot, but I want to ask you about the bottom of your spine—your backbone," Daio said. "Did you by any chance fall and land on your backside?"

"Once when I was having a seizure I fell down in the entryway at home," Akari replied. "It started feeling bad after that."

"Akari, I know your back hurts, so I haven't been touching the area around that bone. But now Uncle Daio is going to touch the sore place, just for a second. All right?" As Daio continued poking around, Akari's torso, which was rigid with tension, gave an involuntary start.

"Oh, I'm sorry," Daio said. "You're a very stoic person, aren't you, Akari? I mean, you're very patient and brave. You have had some discomfort when you were in bed at night, but you never mentioned it to anyone?"

"No, I didn't tell anybody," Akari replied, looking up at Daio.

Daio turned to me. "Kogito, after my training camp closed, one of my former disciples got some medical training and then came back and opened an osteopathy office in Honmachi. Some years later, the man's son-in-law went to a university med school, and when he returned after graduation he converted the osteopathy offices into a regular medical clinic. We ought to take Akari there and get some X-rays, for starters. I think we'll find that one side of the lowest thoracic vertebra in his spinal column has somehow gotten crushed. I have to say it again: Akari is being exceptionally patient and brave about this."

Akari had gone back to staring down at his plate, but it was apparent that he had already come to trust the much older man (slightly built but with perfectly erect, military-style posture) who was kneeling beside his chair. Daio appeared extremely flushed: his entire face was suffused with blood, from his shriveled, walnut-colored cheeks all the way to the base of his neck, evidently from pride about his amateur diagnosis.

Perhaps because I didn't immediately concur with Daio's suggestion, Unaiko shot me a critical look, then said, "The X-rays should probably be done as soon as possible. Ricchan is using our car this morning, so could you please take Akari to the clinic you mentioned in your car, Daio? I'll ride along, if that's okay."

# 2

After their visit to the local clinic, Akari and Daio returned to the Forest House. The X-rays had confirmed Daio's intuitive diagnosis: Akari's lowermost thoracic vertebra had been crushed and he had muscular damage in his back as well. When I called to tell Asa, she gave me the name of a specialist at the Red Cross Hospital in Matsuyama who would be able to make a plaster cast. (At the time I was still feeling flustered by this new development and I mistakenly said that it was the thirteenth vertebra, but Asa was quick to inform me that the human anatomy contains no such bone.)

After lunch Akari and Daio headed out again, this time to Matsuyama. I saw them off (noting again that my son had placed his entire trust in the older man), then went upstairs and lay motionless on my bed, unable to summon enough energy even to read a book. I couldn't stop thinking about Akari's back trouble, which was unlike anything we'd dealt with before. I had felt uneasy about his evident discomfort while we were seated on the airplane, but why hadn't I followed up right away? I thought, too, about the state of mind that had caused Akari to choose suffering in silence over sharing his pain with his father.

I heard the sound of someone loitering at the bottom of the stairs, and when I went down to check I found Unaiko standing in the entry hall.

"Ricchan's back, and when I told her I was concerned about how dejected you seemed to be, she reminded me that Asa had told us about a place out in the boonies called the Saya," she said. "We've been meaning to go there for some recon, since the location will have some bearing on our next public performance, and she suggested you might be willing to give us a guided tour."

I returned to my room to change into the proper gear for traipsing through a forest, and when I went downstairs again I found Unaiko waiting for me in the elevated driver's seat of the Caveman Group's van, looking fresh and crisp after her own change of clothes. I climbed into the passenger seat.

"Even though Ricchan and I haven't talked to Akari very much so far, he's been very good about doing whatever we ask," she said. "But he seems so sad and disheartened, and he doesn't appear to do anything on his own initiative. Is that just the way he is these days? Asa told us that Akari always used to listen to music and study scores, while also working on his own compositions, so I guess we were expecting something different."

I knew I would eventually have to explain what had transpired between Akari and me, but that prospect made me feel even gloomier than before. I suspected Unaiko wasn't the type of person who would wait patiently for me to share the full story on my own timetable, but as it turned out she had already heard most of the details from my sister.

"I hope you don't mind, but Asa told me pretty much everything she heard from Chikashi," Unaiko said. "She mentioned that nowadays when you and Akari are together in the same place, he doesn't listen to music at all. Apparently after the Big Vertigo struck you didn't go out, aside from visits to the hospital for tests and so on, and you just puttered around the house day and night. As a result, there was never a time when Akari could relax by himself and enjoy listening to music, especially since the doctor had advised against prolonged use of headphones. I don't know whether you expressly forbade Akari to listen to music, but apparently that was the impression he got."

"Yes, Chikashi said I was probably sending that message unconsciously. There was just a little misunderstanding about the volume on the CD player," I said, radically understating the problem.

"Well, it seems as if Akari has been feeling as though he did something bad and made you angry, and he hasn't been able to forgive himself."

"No, as I understand it, he simply decided not to share music with his father anymore, in any form."

"Akari has a lot of pride, doesn't he?" Unaiko asked.

"When families have offspring with cognitive disabilities, it's very common to go on treating them like children long after they've reached maturity, and that has certainly been true in my own household at times," I admitted. "Akari is a full-fledged adult now—he's forty-five years old—but you're definitely right about my son's having an inordinate amount of pride."

"Well, here's an idea," Unaiko offered. "You might not even be willing to consider something like this but I wanted to ask, at least. Actually, it's about the van. In order to get the best use out of it, we converted it into a sort of studio on wheels. It's furnished with high-end recording equipment, and we've already used it to record some radio dramas.

"So I was thinking that from time to time either Ricchan or I could take Akari out for a drive, maybe up into the mountains. We could park the van somewhere and then we could stay in the front seat doing paperwork or whatever while he would be in the back, listening to music with complete freedom. Does that sound like a workable plan?"

"If you're able to persuade Akari to go for a drive, more power to you," I said. "I would have no objections at all."

"Well, as you know, Akari didn't hesitate to go up to Matsuyama today with Daio at the wheel," Unaiko pointed out. She sounded relieved. "That's what made us think the system I just outlined might work. So I'll wait for an opportune moment, and then I'll try inviting Akari for a musical drive."

We continued heading east on the national highway that runs along the Kame River, and then we took a secondary road through the bamboo grove where the farmers who took part in the famous insurrection cut bamboo stalks to make into spears. We emerged from the grove onto a smooth, well-maintained byway that led to a number of hamlets, then forked again. This time we headed north, following a serpentine lane into the wooded slope above the valley. Finally a meadow shaped like the sheath of a sword—the area's local nickname, "Saya," carries that meaning, among others—came into sight. At that point the road narrowed considerably, becoming no wider than a walking trail through the forest, so the only way to get to the Saya was on foot.

We left the van in a clearing and I led the way, since I had been there many times in the past. Scrambling down the slope, Unaiko and I entered a grove of broadleaf trees with dark, lush foliage and then climbed back up, following a slender path to a clearing drenched in sunlight. This was the lower end of the Saya. We were standing in a long, grassy, open space that had been carved out of the forest by a renegade meteor, with a little follow-up assistance from local residents. (It was perfectly suited for flower-viewing parties during cherry blossom season, but as yet there was no sign the buds had begun to swell.) We gazed at the gentle slope stretching above us to the north.

"Do you see the black rock just above the midway point?" I asked. "It's part of a meteor that fell to earth, creating a clearing and this scabbard-shaped depression. I think what actually happened is that the meteor landed right in the middle of the virgin forest and the area below it, the Saya, was collateral damage—or should I say collateral construction? In feudal times, the young samurai supposedly turned this place into a makeshift racetrack or riding course, and used it to train for the tumultuous period of internecine strife that began during the last days of the Tokugawa Era. That's another tidbit of the rich lore about this place."

"I've heard that they leveled the flat area beyond the big black rock and then moved the timberline so it would seem to begin naturally right above there," Unaiko said. "Asa told me about the time she and her colleagues put on a play here, as part of the film project; apparently they turned the whole lower part into audience seating, with as many as five hundred local women crowded in, going crazy over what was happening onstage—and then the scene was filmed. Asa was saying it was a once-in-a-lifetime event, bringing those local people together to participate in something so glorious and so inspiring."

"Yes," I said. "Asa was responsible for the cinematography aspect of the film, and her part of the project went perfectly. The problems began after primary shooting had wrapped. When the film reached the final editing stage, both in Japan and America, the NHK faction of the production team raised some objections, claiming the subject matter of the film had deviated from what was agreed upon in the contract. Meanwhile, on the American side, the woman who had been pouring her own money into the project—an internationally known actress and family friend whom Asa had managed to turn into an enthusiastic participant—anyway, she took the opposite position and refused to budge. As a result of the impasse, the production ground to a halt and everyone involved found themselves in limbo. The project ultimately ended up going broke, and it wasn't clear who owned the rights. Asa ran around trying to create a nonprofit organization down here to keep the project alive, and that was how she started networking with the local theater community, including you and your colleagues at the Caveman Group. So for Asa, at least, I guess that abortive enterprise wasn't completely meaningless."

"But didn't the movie win a prize at some Czech and Canadian film festivals, even though it never went wide?" Unaiko inquired. "Asa mentioned something about a whole slew of difficulties, but she was reluctant to go into detail because several issues are still being contested in court. What I'm getting at is that Ricchan and I have been thinking about what to do for our next big drama project, and we've become very interested in the movie and the local history it was based on. However, we haven't even been able to get our hands on a copy of the screenplay because everything related to the film is tied up in litigation. And since the project was an international collaboration, trying to make sense of the contract is a huge hassle. Asa told us she gave her only copy of the script to the attorney, and he still has it today. We've been wanting to talk to you about this for ages, Mr. Choko, but Asa kept telling us to bide our time and wait for the right moment."

I had been sent a final version of the screenplay, with certain portions translated into English alongside the Japanese, but I kept that information to myself. Unaiko didn't pursue the matter any further; she just stood there with her perfect posture, gazing up at the trees. But her face wore an expression of renewed determination, and as I looked at her slim profile I felt certain I hadn't heard the last about her desire to get her hands on a copy of the script.

# 3

Ever since the Caveman Group had turned the Forest House into a rural outpost of its headquarters in Matsuyama, one large room on the west end of the ground floor was used by Unaiko and Ricchan as a combination studio and sleeping space. After Akari and I moved in the two women had continued to work and sleep in that room, but their style seemed to be somewhat cramped by our presence. Perhaps that was why they sometimes drove over to Asa's empty house by the river and spent the night there.

When the troupe members were in rehearsal mode, whether they were running lines or choosing musical cues, I could sense that everyone was being careful not to let any extraneous sounds drift upstairs where they might disturb Akari and me. Sometimes I would even hear the voices of the young actors wafting in on the breeze from the forest road above the house, where they apparently felt they could practice their art with fewer inhibitions.

Daio turned up every other day or so, and it soon became clear that he had taken it upon himself to do most of the yard work and whatever else might be needed in the way of general maintenance.

On the evenings when I fixed dinner myself, he would run me down to the supermarket in Honmachi in his vintage Mercedes-Benz sedan to buy the necessary groceries. If I happened to be downstairs in the great room while Akari was out on a music-appreciation outing, Daio would often engage me in conversation, although I could sense he was trying to keep our exchanges relatively short out of consideration for me. Before long, I began paying Daio the going rate for hourly labor around those parts. (Admittedly, it hadn't occurred to me to do so until Asa made the suggestion in one of her responses to the informal "Forest House reports" Unaiko emailed to her every week.)

Starting with the first trip to Matsuyama, when Daio took Akari to get fitted for a plaster cast, the number of tasks I was able to delegate to Daio seemed to be increasing on a daily basis, which was a great weight off my mind. He even took on the duty of bringing us our own mail from the post office, along with any packages the postman left at Asa's unoccupied house.

From what I gathered, one of Unaiko's weekly reports to Asa mentioned her concerns about the fact that I didn't appear to be living a very dynamic life at the Forest House, to put it mildly. Not long afterward, I received a worried-sounding fax from Asa. Unaiko had apparently written that while she knew I was taking a break from writing after the disastrous demise of the drowning novel, I didn't even seem to be reading with my usual concentration (at least not when I was downstairs, where she could observe my behavior). Unaiko added that I was evidently in extremely low spirits and basically seemed to be sitting around in a daze, passively watching the hours slip by. In her fax, Asa asked whether the doctor had told me to cut back on my reading in the aftermath of the Big Vertigo. Or, she speculated, maybe I was trying to keep my intellectual endeavors to a minimum, in the hopes of reducing the frequency of those chronic dizzy spells.

I wrote back that shortly before Akari and I moved down here I had pulled a number of books I might want to read off some bookshelves in our house in Tokyo and had left them on the floor, but I hadn't had time to pack them up and send them to Shikoku. Asa responded by promising that the next time she was able to get away from the hospital she would go to our house in Seijo and complete the task. After a few days, three large cardboard boxes full of books were delivered to the door by courier.

As twofold evidence of my somber, senescent state of mind, not only did I procrastinate unpacking the cartons Asa had sent, but I also overlooked the fact that there was a smaller box from a different sender sitting on top of them. I noticed the extra one only when I finally got around to tackling the stack a day or two later; its brown-paper wrappings so closely resembled those of the others that it had simply blended in. The small, sturdy box had been carefully packed, and the return address was the Caveman Group's office in Matsuyama.

When I opened the box I found a masterfully crafted picture frame wrapped in brown paper, along with a taped-on card signed by all the members of the Caveman Group. The card read simply, *For Mr. Choko: We're glad you came back to the forest!* When I tore away the wrapping I saw a full-length photograph of a voluptuous young woman standing, completely naked, in front of a painted backdrop depicting a large city at night. After I had spent several minutes gazing at the portrait, I suddenly recognized the woman's resolute, triumphant-looking profile. It was, unmistakably, Unaiko!

In order to get the shot, I mused, the photographer must have been directly in front of the stage, with an assistant crouching down on one side and aiming a handheld light to illuminate the subject at the proper angle. The woman in the photograph was wearing black high heels and she looked as if she might be getting ready to step off the edge of the stage, with the bulk of her weight supported on the left side of her body. Although the muscles were overlaid with a layer of soft fat, the firm solidity of her thighs was clearly apparent, as was the luxuriant thicket of hair covering her gently rounded pubic area. As for her breasts, they were so perfect that they reminded me of the impossibly idealized portrayals of the female form in comic books and graphic novels. Evidently the senders wanted me to feast my eyes on this photograph and I was doing just that, so I was startled when I heard Unaiko's voice behind me, from the stairs.

"Before the photograph was sent to you, my colleagues in the Caveman Group hung it on the wall of our headquarters for a day," she said. "It seemed to be common knowledge that you have what they called a 'pubic-hair fetish,' so I guess they thought it would be a witty gift. Anyway, this photograph was taken five years ago during a public performance, without my knowledge. I don't think the motivation behind their sending it to you now was anything more sinister than a desire to tease Old Man Choko a little bit, but I wouldn't want you to think of me as belonging to a group that would joke around about someone's, um, private predilections. Backstory aside, though, I gather you've taken a liking to the picture?"

"Yes, I like it very much," I said. After a moment I added, "Since this was a gift to me, I think I'd better keep it in my study, just to be safe." Akari had been a step or two behind Unaiko when she came down from the second floor, and he had passed by on his way to the restroom. I was hoping he hadn't seen the framed photograph I was holding, since it was the kind of thing he always found upsetting, but when he stormed into the washroom, slamming the door behind him, I knew he must have caught a glimpse of the photo and formed an impression of the subject matter, if not the subject.

Even before we had fallen into the current deplorable state of affairs, it had been clear that Akari felt particularly ill at ease whenever I was conversing with visitors on topics with the slightest hint of a sexual connotation, even though he probably didn't understand what was being discussed with any degree of clarity. Unaiko had evidently intuited the reason behind Akari's door-slamming discomfiture, because she redirected our playful conversation about the photograph into a more serious channel.

"From this angle I appear to be standing on the stage stark-naked, like a fool, but there's actually a military formation downstage from me, waving an assortment of flags," she explained. "The naked woman is meant to be confronting that group, although there's some doubt as to whether it poses any actual threat, and she is seen by the audience for only a split second before the stage is plunged into total darkness. Masao is a big proponent of deliberate ambiguity in his theater work, so while the naked woman was supposed to be standing there openly and proudly, the original plan was for her torso to be covered by a nude-colored tank top that came down to the tops of her thighs. I was actually the one who insisted full-frontal nudity was the only honest way to go. The next day we gave my 'little striptease' (as Masao insisted on calling it) a trial run at the first performance, to see how it would play onstage, and someone who was there returned the next night and took a surreptitious photo, and then sold it to a photography magazine. That photo created quite a sensation, and it's one of the reasons the Caveman Group got a reputation for doing outrageous things, even before we started throwing 'dead dogs' around. Masao was so incensed that he threatened legal action, but the other party had proof the photo had been taken legitimately at a public performance, so that was the end of it.

"Getting back to the gift, I can't help speculating about the motivation. I know that certain members of our troupe decided to send you this photo on the pretext of indulging your supposed pubic-hair fetish, but I can't help wondering whether they might also have had a hidden agenda. I think this bizarre gesture might have been rooted in their apprehensions about our next big public-performance project—you know, the one Ricchan and I have been trying to put together, with Asa's help. I know there's a faction in the Caveman Group that isn't completely thrilled with what I've been doing, and these members also voiced concern that my projects could end up overshadowing their own work. As I'm sure you're aware, even in a theater group that appears to be made up of forward-looking artists there can still be a strong undertone of sexist discrimination directed toward 'uppity females,' especially in the more rural parts of this country."

# 4

Later that morning, toward the end of the breakfast hour, Daio stopped by to relay an important message: Akari's custom-made plaster cast had been delivered to the clinic in Honmachi.

"The cast is removable, so it will need to be taken off every night at bedtime and put back on first thing in the morning. Once you get the hang of it, Akari, you should be able to handle both those tasks by yourself," Daio explained. "During the early stages, though, would you be able to take on that responsibility, Kogito? If so, I'd like to take you and Akari down to the clinic to get some pointers about how to deal with the cast."

"I've been getting Akari's bed ready every evening for the past forty-some years, except when I've been away from home, so I don't think dealing with a cast will be excessively challenging," I said drily.

"I'm making my bed all by myself now," Akari muttered, looking down at his plate.

"Yesterday evening I was sticking special tape on the most painful places for you, isn't that right, Akari?" I said. "I was being very careful not to touch your crushed vertebra, but . . ."

"It never hurt when Unaiko and Ricchan did it, either," Akari retorted.

"Then would you rather have those two help you with the cast during the early stages, while you're getting used to it?" I asked, unable to keep the despondency out of my voice. "If they have time, of course."

"We were planning to ride along to the clinic in any case—that is, either Ricchan or me," Unaiko said. "Since all we're doing right now is outlining our next big production, we would be happy to help Akari in any way we can. Akari, would you like me to drive you today?"

"That sounds great!" Akari exclaimed.

"Thanks, Unaiko. I'll leave it to you then," Daio said. He, too, kept his face averted so he wouldn't have to meet my eyes.

After Akari and Unaiko had set off in the van I went back to work unpacking the rest of the books Asa had sent. Daio sat on the sofa, reaching out from time to time to pick up a book and leaf idly through it. After a moment, I began to reminisce aloud.

"As you mentioned the other day, when Goro and I were still in high school, during the Occupation, we paid a visit to your training camp and we brought along an American officer who was a language expert," I said. "His name was Peter, and your students hatched a plan to use him as a conduit to get their hands on some automatic pistols, rifles, and so on that the Americans had scrapped after the Korean War. Goro and I somehow got dragged into it, and we ended up overreacting just a bit."

"Yes, I remember," Daio said, and chuckled. "You put all the lurid details into one of your recent novels. Someone told me about the book, and when I read it I thought, *Ah, so this is what was going on in Kogito's head that weekend.*

"As you say, Peter sold us some old army-surplus guns, which we thought we could turn around and sell to a scrap-iron dealer to raise a few bucks. However, when you wrote about that transaction in your novel, you added an imaginary scene in which Peter's own pistol is forcibly confiscated by the guys from my training camp. You left it ambiguous, as you tend to do, but the implication was that Peter might have met with foul play at the hands of my followers. One of the local policemen happened to read the book and he came snooping around the camp, asking questions. This was a long time ago, of course. The truth was, we had kept a few of the surplus guns to use for target practice and that kind of thing, but everything was perfectly innocent and above board, and no harm came to Peter at all."

"Yes, I realize that now," I said. "But at the time, based on what Goro and I saw and heard at the training camp that weekend, we seriously believed you and your disciples were planning to attack the American military base on the outskirts of Matsuyama the night the peace treaty went into effect: September 8, 1951. When the date rolled around we were glued to the radio till well past midnight, expecting to hear some breaking news about your exploits."

"Oh, right." Daio smiled sheepishly. "You mentioned in your book that you even took a photo to commemorate the occasion. It seems as though we inadvertently set you boys up for a big disappointment, and I'm sorry about that," he added, but he didn't sound very contrite.

"Of course, we knew those discarded guns wouldn't be of any use in actual combat," I said. "After all, they were old and rusty and obsolete. We figured you were just using them as props for playing war games, but we really did believe your group was planning to stage some kind of suicidal attack on the American MPs who were guarding the gate of the army base. If you and your subordinates had actually followed through on that plan you would have been shot dead in the blink of an eye—although it would have gone down in history as the only uprising ever staged during the tenure of the occupying forces."

"Well, the guerrilla warfare didn't take place, and to be candid there was really never any chance it was going to," Daio said. "The truth is, we did have one serious goal, although it was probably more of a wild hope. Since you obviously believed our goal was to get ourselves killed and go out in a blaze of glory, we thought you might be moved to drop by the training camp again on the day in question to try to intervene. If you had, I was hoping we would be able to persuade you—as the son and heir of Choko Sensei—to become our leader going forward.

"Going back a few years to when Japan lost the war, the most upsetting thing was that all the army officers and sailors who had seemed to be so gung ho about our earlier plan suddenly began acting as if they had just been released from an evil spell or something," Daio went on. "They started acting as though everything we had talked about was a big joke and pretending they had never been serious about it at all. Choko Sensei was the only one who was fully committed to our ideologies, to the point where he felt compelled to flee the village, but of course he was swept away by the flooded river and ended up drowning before he could make his escape. Your father cared enough about our beliefs to stake his life on them, so we, as his survivors, were trying to preserve those principles through our work at the training camp after the war was over. Even today, I can't help thinking about how inspiring it would have been if we could have had Choko Sensei's son as our leader, to look up to. But yes, it's true that even though we did have some abstract discussions about staging a kamikaze attack as a sort of posthumous tribute to your father's devotion to the cause, when that day arrived my young disciples and I sat around laughing about that over-the-top scenario, and everyone agreed it had been a ridiculously unrealistic idea all along.

"Then many years later, when I read your novel, I was surprised to discover how seriously you and Goro had taken the whole thing. I mean, you two were so worried about the possibility of getting into trouble for your part in the illegal gun exchange that you actually went so far as to take a commemorative photo in case you ended up going to jail."

Daio paused for a moment before adding, with a wry smile, "It's really kind of funny, when you think about it!"

# Chapter 9

# Late Work

## 1

Several days later I plunked myself down on the great-room sofa, which had been jammed into a corner to create more space for rehearsals, and continued unpacking the books Asa had sent down from Tokyo. (I had already devoted three full days to this task.) I spent a few moments leafing through each volume before moving on to the next. When I had finished perusing one stack I put that batch back into its cardboard box, extracted a new pile of books, and began the process anew.

Normally I would have been prospecting for some riveting research topic to throw myself into as the first step toward beginning a new novel, but that wasn't the case now. These were mostly books I had stashed on the top shelf of a certain bookcase at my house in Tokyo with the idea of eventually getting around to rereading them. In my upstairs study/bedroom there I kept my indispensable collection—many years in the making—of books by an assortment of authors, poets, and thinkers (including the collected works of my mentor, Professor Musumi) and a number of those were in the boxes as well. Finally, there were numerous unexplored volumes that I'd been planning to read someday at my leisure. Since I had abandoned the drowning novel and didn't have a clue what else I might tackle as part of a late-work plan, the inchoate someday was suddenly at hand.

In the past whenever I had decided to seize the moment and begin rereading a certain book, before long I would toss it aside and move on to the next volume on the shelf. You might think such a scat-tershot approach would be an unsatisfying way to pass the time, but it wasn't uncommon for me to look up from the pages and discover that two or three hours had passed in a pleasant blur. This was similar to the process I always went through when I was casting around for subject matter for my next book, but I already knew I wouldn't be tackling another novel-length fiction project any time soon, if ever. At least, I thought, I could use this fallow time to catch up on my reading—and my rereading as well.

On this day, Unaiko and Akari had driven away in the Caveman Group's van for an outing that would combine listening to music with exercise. (Those jaunts were now an almost daily occurrence.)

Not long after they set off, I received a phone call from Unaiko. There was a good deal of background noise and I couldn't quite make out what she was saying, but she was clearly upset. When I realized that she was trying to tell me something about Akari, I jumped up from the sofa in alarm. The crackling static on the line kept getting louder and louder, and then the phone abruptly went dead. I replaced the handset in its cradle, then stood anxiously next to the phone and waited. Ten endless minutes later, it finally rang again. This time Asa was on the other end, calling from Tokyo. She sounded perfectly calm—almost too calm, as if she was making a conscious effort to convey that impression.

"Akari had a seizure," she said. "He and Unaiko were up at the Saya, doing one of their fitness walks, and apparently it happened when they stopped to rest. Unaiko called me in a state of panic, saying she had tried to reach you but it was a bad connection to start with, and then the call was dropped. Luckily she was able to get through to Tamakichi's mobile phone, and he called me in Tokyo. As it happened he's already in the neighborhood, doing some forestry work not far from your house—planting saplings and whatnot. Anyhow, you need to head over to the Saya as soon as possible, so Tamakichi will swing by shortly to get you. He said it would help if you could be waiting for him at the top of the driveway."

As I rushed around getting ready to leave, I couldn't stop worrying about Akari's seizure. There was a chance he might have fallen and hit his head on one of the rocks scattered around the Saya, I thought. For some reason that image reminded me of the strength and resiliency of Unaiko's thighs the day we first met on the cycling path near my house in Tokyo, when she caught me from behind and saved me from toppling over.

In any event, I managed to find Akari's prepacked emergency bag (which I had forgotten to give to Unaiko to take along on their outing), and as I emerged from the house my nephew Tamakichi was already sitting in the driveway in a pickup truck. Without getting out of the cab, he stretched one suntanned arm across the passenger seat and opened the door for me. No sooner had I climbed in than he put his foot on the gas pedal and sped away.

"I'm sorry you had to drive all the way down here," I said. "I know I was supposed to be waiting for you up by the forest road, but when you start getting older everything seems to move in slow motion."

"No worries," Tamakichi replied. "I called Unaiko back, and she said that Akari was already up and about. I gathered they were just heading to the river to get him cleaned up."

This news came as a great relief, but then I noticed that instead of taking the forest road through the valley, Tamakichi was heading uphill. "Is this the right way?" I asked.

"If you take the forest road to the Saya, you have to park the car and walk quite a ways," Tamakichi explained. "I'm planning to take a detour, so we'll be approaching from the top."

I was forced to admit (although only to myself) that there were some gaps in my knowledge of the local topography these days. "Your mother was saying that when she was making her movie, your knowledge of the entire forest area made location scouting and filming much easier," I said. "I gather you're serious about making a career of forestry work?"

Tamakichi nodded. "I am," he said. "You had the same inclination when you were a child, didn't you, Uncle Kogito? You mentioned it in a couple of your books. Anyhow, long before we started working on the movie, the local village board had been doing a lot of maintenance work on the Saya and the surrounding area. Then when filming began there was a 'no men allowed' rule in effect, so my male colleagues and I were relegated to doing cleanup and postproduction work. I've never even seen the finished movie."

"Didn't you at least get to watch the daily rushes on video, to see how your carefully tended forest came across on film?"

"No, not really," Tamakichi replied. "We asked the NHK office in Matsuyama whether that would be possible, and when nothing came of our request we tried contacting the main office of the American production company. They said we would need to submit a request in English, and at that point we just gave up. However, it was really something to have so many local women gathered in one place, and it turned into a kind of giant party or festival. Everyone agreed that the Gathering, as it came to be known, was the biggest women-only event since the famous insurrection. Now whenever people get together at the Saya to celebrate the fall colors or the cherry blossoms someone will always yell, 'Hurray for the Gathering!' and that's the signal for everyone to take a drink."

"'The Gathering,' eh? I'll drink to that!" I said with feeling.

The forest road we were traveling on passed through a rather sparsely wooded area of broadleaf trees, but soon after crossing a gentle mountain ridge we came upon a lofty wall of cypress and cryptomeria trees, nearly as old as I was, that completely covered the long hill sloping down to the northeast. As we drove along the tree-shadowed road I was reminded of a day in my childhood when all the students at the new postwar middle school I attended were rounded up to participate in a mandatory horticultural project: planting tiny saplings to create the very trees we were looking at now.

By and by we arrived at the uppermost border of the Saya, and Tamakichi stopped the truck. Below us I could see a large rock that looked like an old-fashioned boat, if a boat had somehow become embedded in a grassy meadow. My eyes were drawn to a small stream at the bottom of the hill. On the edge of the little brook I spied some signs of human life: Akari was lying on the faded brown grass and Unaiko was sitting next to him, hugging her knees. Tamakichi and I went charging down the slope, heading straight for that spot.

Akari and Unaiko must surely have noticed our approach, but they didn't react in any visible way. Unaiko, especially, looked completely shell-shocked and tuckered out. As we drew closer we could hear a CD playing—it was Schubert's piano quintet, the *Trout*—but then I saw Akari reaching toward the sound system, and the music stopped in mid-trill.

Unaiko spoke first. "I'm so sorry for causing such a ruckus," she apologized. "It seemed like a much more serious attack than the kind Asa had told me to expect and I panicked, thinking it might be a new problem. I mean, Akari's entire body was in the throes of major convulsions."

"Akari, the seizure's over now, right?" I asked gently. Akari didn't reply, but his body language seemed to be saying, *You can see perfectly well that it is.*

"It happened a few minutes after we got here," Unaiko said. "We parked the car as usual, and right after we'd started walking, we came upon a puddle left over from last night's rainstorm. We weren't able to cross it by holding hands, and Akari was a bit nervous about that. We did somehow manage to get across, one at a time, but a moment later he took a tumble. I thought at first he was lying there for fun, laughing in relief, but then I realized that wasn't the case." (It was a natural mistake; the expression Akari wore when he was being stoic about pain could easily be mistaken for mirth.) "Anyway, he got up again, and we kept on walking. The seizure happened just as we reached the Saya, and I'm afraid I kind of lost it."

"In a situation like this, the best remedy for Akari is to lie down and get some rest," I said. "Akari, do you want to use the restroom before we head back to the Forest House?"

When Akari didn't reply, Unaiko picked up on the fact that my son was once again giving me the cold shoulder, and she jumped into the chilly void.

"Asa told me to watch out for the loose bowels that often accompany this type of episode," she said. "We've already dealt with that issue, but Akari was upset because he didn't have a change of trousers or underwear."

As I handed the emergency bag to Unaiko, I noticed that the lower part of Akari's body was covered by a large shawl, which I recognized as Unaiko's. Her jacket was draped on top for good measure.

"If the road to the valley is too muddy to drive on, my truck is up the hill, and we can go back in that," Tamakichi offered. "I'd be glad to carry Akari to where it's parked."

"No, I want to go home in Unaiko's van," Akari declared.

"You might fall again," I pointed out.

"I'll carry him on my back, so that won't happen," Tamakichi said.

"Okay then," I said to Akari. "Since the worst is over, there's no big hurry to get back. Let's rest here for a while longer before we go."

"Tamakichi, thank you so much for coming to the rescue," Unaiko said. "I got your cell-phone number from your mom, and . . . I hate to impose on you even more, but is there any chance of getting a guided tour as long as you're here? You seem to know a lot about forestry, and I'd love to hear about the trees around the Saya."

"That's the easiest request I've had all day!" Tamakichi said happily.

"Oh, and also, I heard that during the filming you were responsible for turning the big, flat rock into a stage, so I'm assuming you must have had a chance to read the screenplay?" Unaiko asked rhetorically. "It would be great if I could pick your brain about that, too."

Tamakichi looked somewhat taken aback by this additional request—or perhaps he was just feeling shy in the presence of an attractive woman—but he nodded, and he and Unaiko set off toward the Saya. Akari had changed into clean clothes behind a nearby tree and was once again reclining on the grass, so I lay down nearby (being careful not to intrude on his space) using the indispensable emergency bag as a pillow.

Gazing upward, I saw that the branches of the trees encircling the Saya were aglow with fresh new leaves of yellowish green, dull red, and every shade in between. I couldn't be certain from a distance, but there might have been some subtle buds beginning to form as well. Even the mountain cherries looked as though they might be on the brink of bursting into a pale canopy of blossoms over the next few days. Beyond the cherry orchard was a dense backdrop of evergreen trees. They were younger than the tall trees we had seen on the mountain ridge on our way here, but the varieties were the same: the Japanese iterations of cypress and cedar (also known as cryptomeria).

As I was swiveling my head around, I noticed that the bag beneath it felt somehow higher and bulkier than it should have. When I sat up and peered inside, I saw that Akari's soiled trousers had been stuffed into a trash sack and that bundle (along with a summer blanket I'd added to the emergency kit as I was leaving the house) was taking up a great deal of space. I took out the blanket and went over to where Akari was lying down, then spread it over him from neck to toes. He didn't move a muscle in response and he kept both palms in place, completely covering his large face.

As I was walking back to my own space, a line of poetry floated through my mind: *You didn't get Kogii ready.* . . .

I could see now, more clearly than ever, that "Kogii" was meant to signify Akari. I saw, too, that I was the person—right here, right now—whose job it would be to send him into the forest when the time came. But how was I supposed to go about laying the groundwork for that inevitable process? I hadn't even begun to make my own preparations for the next step; how on earth was I supposed to facilitate the transition for someone else? I didn't have a clue. In essence I was still a powerless child, just as I was in the days when everyone called me Kogii. And what about the other long-departed Kogii—the elusive doppelgänger who abandoned me and wafted up into the forest, where the trees meet the sky? If he could look down and see me in my current state of confused fragility, he would probably find it hard to keep from laughing out loud.

By and by another thought drifted across my mind. In a few minutes Unaiko and Tamakichi (who was, of course, doing whatever he could to be of use to her as a stand-in for his absent mother) would be returning from their tour of the Saya, chummier than ever. At some point those two would probably induct Akari into their inner circle as well. And then wasn't it conceivable that the three of them would somehow get together and conspire to do whatever was necessary to get me (yes, me) ready for my own final journey up into the forest? In that case, perhaps they would help me find a way to conduct myself appropriately during the transition and to move on to the next stage with a measure of ease.

Then I was struck by an even more radical thought: maybe what I had been perceiving as reality all along was nothing but a dream, or an illusion! I thought about everything I had labored so hard to accomplish after moving to Tokyo: all the endless striving, studying, thinking, and writing. Putting aside the question of whether I had accomplished anything worthwhile, what if those eventful years and those supposed achievements were nothing more than figments of my imagination? Suppose that in reality I never even left this village and had been living here all along, from birth until now: my seventy-fourth year. If that were true, I would no doubt be casually getting ready to die a perfectly ordinary death, in the traditional way the old people in this mountain valley surely know by heart, or in their bones. Indeed (I mused, half dreaming) at this very moment Unaiko and Tamakichi could be standing in the shadow of the great meteoric boulder at the top of the slope, talking about how they could help to facilitate my preparations for moving on to the next great adventure . . .

"Mr. Choko?" My eyes snapped open and I saw Unaiko hovering over me, looking down with a solicitous expression. "If you go on snoozing out here in the open air, you're going to catch a cold! I mean, I certainly understand how you could be so worn out that you'd need a big nap, after the stress I put you through with the hysterical phone call and all."

The newly returned twosome soon shifted their attention from me to Akari. Being very careful not to hurt Akari's back, Tamakichi pulled his cousin to his feet and lifted him into a piggyback position. Tamakichi was a bit shorter than I was, but he was exceptionally strong and muscular from the physical labor of forestry work, and after getting Akari's considerably larger body snugly ensconced on his back, he loped easily off toward the parking area where Unaiko had left the van. She and I followed a moment later, each carrying some components of the Caveman Group's professional-quality (but still portable, barely) sound system.

"Tamakichi was telling me about the women Asa brought together at the Saya and how excited they were about being a part of the movie," Unaiko said as we tramped along. Her weariness appeared to have abated and she sounded even more energized than usual. "When I remarked that supervising such a large group must have been a challenging task, Tamakichi said his mother had told him that the women around here seemed to feel as if they, too, were taking part in an insurrection of sorts, and she was able to coax them into letting those feelings out for the first time in a long while. I'm sure there was probably more to it, but *Meisuke's Mother Marches Off to War* seems to have been an unforgettable experience for everyone who took part in the project."

By the time we got to Unaiko's van, Tamakichi had already set Akari down and was about to head up to the place above the Saya where he had left his truck. Unaiko thanked my nephew again and again for his help, and then we said our good-byes.

# 2

That afternoon there was a phone call from Maki. Apparently Asa (who was spending all her time at the hospital with Chikashi) was concerned about Akari's recent episode and had asked Maki to call and find out how things were going. I suggested that Maki ask Akari directly, and I carried the cordless handset into his room. After what seemed to be a long, leisurely conversation, Akari brought the phone back to me. Maki was still on the other line, and she proceeded to tell me about her chat with her brother.

First, she had told Akari how worried she had been when she heard that he'd had a major seizure deep in the forest, when Papa wasn't on hand to help. Akari's response was to paraphrase a quotation from the *My Own Words* booklet. (He, too, had received a copy from Maki, and since he wasn't currently engaged in reading musical scores he was probably applying his customary concentration to perusing the little book instead.)

"'Cause I'm gonna die! Ahhh! I can't hear my heart beating, even a little bit! I really think I'm dying! My heart isn't making any sound at all!"

Maki knew that those mock histrionics were Akari's idea of a joke, but even so, she responded to his concerns point by point in complete seriousness.

"No, Akari, you aren't going to die," she said. "The seizure is over now, isn't it? I guess when you collapsed in the forest, you could probably hear your heart pounding very loudly, right? But don't worry, it doesn't mean you're going to die. And there isn't any danger when your heart is beating so quietly that you can't hear it, either."

Akari had responded with a calmer and more positive remark, which was also an echo of something from *My Own Words*: "The seizure really hurt a lot, but I hung in there!"

Although Akari was ostensibly talking about his seizure, Maki thought there was a distinct undertone of apprehension about his mother's illness as well. After assuring Akari that there was no need to worry since his seizure was safely in the past, she added that Mama had come through her surgery very well and was already on the road to recovery.

But when Maki said that, Akari suddenly began to shout something that sounded like a parody or at least a paraphrase of some of the quotations in *My Own Words*: "No, no, Mama is already dead! Oh, wait, you say she'll be coming home in two or three weeks? Okay, that's good, but even if she comes home then, right now she's dead! Mama is really dead!"

Maki thought that was Akari's oblique way of showing his true feelings. "Before Mama went into the hospital, she asked you to write down Akari's quotes from your novels, including the parts where he was somehow conflating his father's long absence with the idea of death, right?" she said. "It seemed kind of weird that Mama would make such a request at a time when she was dealing with a health crisis of her own, but I think she was just trying to imagine how Akari might respond to the death of one of his parents. Mama knows most of Akari's quotes by heart, so I'd like to hear her play a game with Akari sometime when they talk on the phone. It could be a sort of call and response. Maybe Akari could say, 'Mama was in a very bad way, but she pulled through!' and Mama could respond by saying, 'Thank you very much—with your support I'll keep hanging in there and doing my best!'"

Late that night, I got a call from Asa. She had finished her duties at the hospital and was about to take an Odakyu Line train back to my house in Tokyo, where she was staying.

"Today I asked Chikashi whether she might want me to arrange for Unaiko and Ricchan to look after Akari while you made a trip up here to visit her in the hospital," she began. "But Chikashi said that after all your years together, and all the joy and sadness you've shared, she was afraid it would be too hard on you to see your aged wife in such a weakened state, and rather than being able to comfort her, she was worried you might fall into depression or even start blubbering—we laughed at that—and she would need to prop *you* up instead! (By the way, I was very impressed by her efforts to be sprightly and humorous, making a literary allusion to the famous parable about a devoted old Chinese couple and so on.)

"Seriously, though, I think Chikashi has a valid point. I know that when her brother, Goro, jumped off a building and she had to go to the police station to identify his badly damaged body, she was able to look at it without flinching or turning away. But later, when you went to the wake at Goro's house down in Yugawara and his widow wanted you to view the body, Chikashi said she thought it would be better if you didn't, even though by then Goro's face had been restored to its usual handsome state. She understands better than anyone that you tend to be squeamish about such things.

"On top of that, Chikashi said, 'In my husband's current mood I don't think the kind of visit you're suggesting is even in the realm of possibility. Ever since he stopped working on the drowning novel he's been floundering around, and he totally lost control and called his mentally disabled son an idiot—not once, but twice. I know he was annoyed and upset about something on both occasions, but there is simply no excuse for that kind of behavior. No one is angrier at him than Maki, and I've been afraid that the tension between those two might come to a head at some point. That's partly why I rec- ommended that my husband and son go down to Shikoku together, on the assumption that Papa was serious about wanting to take the initiative in patching things up. Not so much for Akari, but for *that man*, I think reaching some kind of détente with his estranged son should be the first priority right now.' Anyhow, that's what Chikashi said. I have to admit I cringed when she referred to you as 'that man' again—it just sounds so cold—but on the positive side, she did call you 'Papa' once or twice as well.

"Kogii, one thing that fills me with hope is knowing Unaiko and Ricchan will be at the Forest House with you and Akari most of the time. As you know, I truly believe Unaiko is a genius. I'm not saying she's a towering intellectual or anything, but even if you take her out of the theatrical milieu where she shines so brightly, she's still a genius.

Her special gift is the way she tries to think everything through on her own, in a completely original way, and I'm sure she'll bring the same approach to bear on the situation between you and Akari. No matter what happens, I'm confident she'll be a good influence on you. Because she has such a strong sense of certainty about her own beliefs I think she'll be a reliable touchstone, much as a straightedge helps a carpenter keep things properly lined up."

# 3

Ever since the occurrence at the Saya, the bond between Akari and Unaiko seemed to have grown noticeably stronger— and, of course, Ricchan was also a member of their cozy little in-group. The activities that Akari had previously been pursuing in either the dining room or the great room, depending on the theater group's schedule, were now taking place in the downstairs room Unaiko and Ricchan shared: poring over the classical music program guides in the weekly FM radio magazine and elsewhere, listening to music on the radio, playing CDs, and so on. In that room, which also doubled as the young women's sleeping quarters, Akari could be absolutely certain his father would never come bumbling in; that was part of an unspoken agreement among the residents of the house. Clearly, Akari was making good on his implicitly declared intention to never again share a single note of music with me.

Some of Akari's medications were on the verge of running out and he happened to be nearby, listening, when I was talking to Maki on the phone one day about the logistics of refilling those prescriptions. The next morning when Maki called back, Akari piped up to say that if someone from the Forest House was going to Tokyo to get his medicine, he would like to ask them to bring down some of his CDs when they returned. As it turned out, shortly after Akari made the request it became necessary for Unaiko and Ricchan to head to Tokyo on business of their own, so no one had to make a special trip to fetch his prescriptions and CDs.

The news about what Unaiko had done in Matsuyama and at the theater in the round had been spreading by way of the national grapevine. Evidently some prominent theater people had taken notice and were offering her the opportunity to apply her talents to the much larger stages of Tokyo. There were some producers and directors (their names were familiar even to me) who were always on the lookout for innovative and ambitious dramatic work, and they had contacted Unaiko to invite her to meet with them. Asa, of course, was already in Tokyo to help Chikashi through her surgery and recuperation, and it went without saying that Unaiko and Ricchan wanted to share this development with her. I knew that Ricchan—the person most familiar with the sad state of my current relationship with Akari—was also hoping to ask Chikashi, in person, for some information regarding Akari's daily routines. I was resigned to the fact that any such line of inquiry would inevitably make me look bad and would culminate in more criticism of my behavior from my outspoken wife.

# 4

*Dear Kogii,*

*At the moment, Unaiko is being lionized by her new cronies in the theater world, and she has been spending every day (and night!) running around Tokyo doing all sorts of exciting and constructive things: seeing plays, visiting rehearsals, going to parties, and so on. She'll be staying here for a while longer but Ricchan will be back at the Forest House very soon, and she should be able to bring you up to speed on all the details of Chikashi's condition.*

*The way things are going, it looks as if Unaiko's trademark dramatic style may end up being incorporated into a major production at a big theater in Tokyo. Ricchan is actively involved, of course, and she has been doing a lot of work behind the scenes to help advance Unaiko's career. For me, having a chance to chat*

*at length with Ricchan during this time has been very fruitful,
and she also found time to talk to Maki and Chikashi about
managing Akari's health situation. It's a great relief to me to
know someone so conscientious is looking after you and Akari
while you're down on Shikoku.*

*On the days when Maki took over for me at the hospital
and I went back to your house in Seijo to get some rest, Unaiko
and Ricchan would always be there waiting up for me, no matter how late the hour, and the three of us would help ourselves to
the contents of your liquor cabinet and talk until the wee hours.
I suspect the discussions we had about a certain Kogito Choko
may have broken some new ground, and I'll reconstruct one of
the conversations here, just for fun.*

*Unaiko started things off, holding forth about you and your
work in general terms. (I'll skip over that part, since it's nothing
you haven't heard before.) After a while Ricchan joined in and
then—uncharacteristically for her—she took the lead. In keeping
with the basic precepts of the dog-tossing method, there was a tape
recorder rolling the entire time, even on an informal occasion like
this, so I'm able to give a verbatim account of what was said.*

*"The truth is," Ricchan began, "ten years ago I hardly
knew anything about Mr. Choko's work. During the time when
I was still bouncing around Tokyo doing various sound-related
jobs, I booked a one-off assignment for a performance by an
up-and-coming theater group. That night I happened to meet
one of the group's volunteer actresses, who was still working an
outside job of her own, and I was captivated by her charisma.
Needless to say, I'm talking about Unaiko. Before long we were
both invited to join the troupe, and working with the Caveman
Group became our full-time jobs. Of course, Masao Anai was
the group's leader. At some point he fixed on the idea of turning Kogito Choko's novels into stage plays, and that became the
guiding principle behind his work. So I ended up being in contact with Mr. Choko's books on a regular basis, but they never*

*really drew me in, personally. Unaiko felt the same way. By the time we were born, of course, Mr. Choko's best years as a writer were already behind him. I figure kids like us would probably start exploring Japanese literature on our own (that is, outside of school) when we were eighteen or nineteen, maybe later, and even then we would mostly stick with writers of our own generation, so it would never have occurred to us to read Mr. Choko's work—at least not voluntarily.*

"When I first met Masao and the rest of the group, they were focusing on books by contemporary novelists. They didn't seem to think Mr. Choko fell into that category, although at the same time they saw something interesting in the slightly retro, nostalgic feeling that infuses so much of his work—what you might call a divergence from the now. Still, it wasn't until several years later that Unaiko really immersed herself in Mr. Choko's work. It happened when we were doing the adaptation *of* The Day He Himself Shall Wipe My Tears Away, *and as we all know, she was exceedingly critical of that book. But now look at her; she's turned into a full-on Choko freak, even more fanatical than Masao Anai! When I stop to think about it, I realize I'm always a few steps behind Unaiko in everything we do, but at any rate, I've finally started reading and appreciating Mr. Choko's work, too."*

"It was pretty much the same for me, only I was trying to catch up with Masao," Unaiko acknowledged. "I guess I'm what they call a late adopter."

Kogii, I was surprised to hear that Unaiko and Ricchan had only recently become acquainted with your work. I told them about an article I'd seen in a theater magazine—you know, "meet the new drama groups" sort of thing—in which a certain critic wrote that while Masao Anai had begun adapting your works into theater pieces early in his career, the group only started having major success with those plays after Unaiko joined the creative team.

Ricchan nodded and said, "I think that's true, but while Unaiko's dramatic method may differ from Masao's style as a director, it's absolutely consistent within those differences, if that makes sense."

"It makes perfect sense to me," Unaiko said with a smile. "Ricchan's on a roll tonight, so I'll let her explain how I ended up getting converted."

"Actually, as I understand it, the thing that transformed Unaiko into a card-carrying Choko devotee wasn't reading his novels per se," Ricchan said. "One day she happened to come across something Mr. Choko had written regarding Edward W. Said's definition of 'late style,' and that catalyzed her conversion. She made a photocopy of the page and pinned it above her desk at work, and then she said to me, all excited, 'This quote from Said is so amazing!' Said's basic premise seems to be that when a true artist starts getting on in years, the sort of philosophical mellowness that comes with age can also backfire, and may sometimes even end up having catastrophic consequences."

"Yes," Unaiko interrupted excitedly. "Professor Said was riffing on the statement by Adorno that in the history of art, 'late works are the catastrophes,' and Said added that work created late in life is not always as serene and transcendent as you might expect. It's been a while since I looked at those quotes, but as I recall Said was talking about Beethoven."

"To me," Ricchan went on, "it seems as if it would be beneficial for an aging author to weather that kind of stormy situation alone, and if such adversity ended up being the crucible in which his later work was forged, well, wouldn't it be a good thing? I mean, isn't the freedom to charge blindly ahead into the uncharted realm of one's own late work one of the perks of being old? Even so, I couldn't help feeling it just wasn't right, somehow, for a thirtysomething woman like Unaiko to be sitting sit around hoping that an older person would go galloping headlong into catastrophe! But since Mr. Choko has abandoned

*the drowning novel, and he and Akari are living at the Forest
House, it's making me very happy to see how easy it seems to be
for Unaiko to hang out with both of them, and vice versa. And
when Akari had his seizure and I saw how flustered Unaiko was,
I couldn't help thinking,* Wow, she's really changed a lot. That
is to say, I feel as though she's become more human and more
compassionate than when we first met.*"

"*When you say something like that it really makes me
realize how selfishly I must have behaved toward you, Ricchan,*"
Unaiko said solemnly, with a self-effacing modesty that was very
different from her usual confident, assertive personality.

"No, no, not at all!" Ricchan protested. "*I've always
depended on you for everything, Unaiko, and I have every intention of continuing to do so going forward. I really can't imagine
living any other way.*" She was unmistakably sincere but I sensed
an undertone of affectionate teasing beneath her words.

Somehow, hearing Unaiko apologize for her past behavior confirmed my sense that joining forces with her, and with
Ricchan, for my own late work (so to speak) had been the right
decision, without a doubt. At the same time I got the heartening
feeling that Unaiko was no longer just the ambitious, talented
girl-genius dramatist, but was also—and this was more important to me and, clearly, to Ricchan as well—developing into a
more complete and empathetic human being.

As our conversation continued, I posed this question:
"Unaiko, this is something I was planning to ask Masao, but
I'd like to hear your thoughts, too. Up until now, the Caveman
Group has derived a large measure of its inspiration from my
brother's fiction, and while you were waiting for him to finish his
own late work, the so-called drowning novel, you were planning
to combine the saga of his work on the book with the story about
how our father went out one night and drowned in the river.
I know you even recorded some interviews with my brother, to
use as a resource. What I was wondering is, how were you and

Masao proposing to put the Caveman Group's distinctive theatrical stamp on the novel if it had come to fruition? Or maybe I should ask how you were planning to fit the book into the dog-tossing mold that's been so successful for you?"

"Well, we were looking at those initial recording sessions as preliminaries, like a dry run," Unaiko replied. "We were just trying to get a handle on the general parameters of Mr. Choko's drowning novel so we could start figuring out how to go about dramatizing it. Really, everything was pretty nebulous at that point.

"The idea was that Masao and I would sort of lurk around the Forest House and observe Mr. Choko while he was in the process of writing, and he seemed to be amenable to that. Of course, you of all people were already well aware of the arrangement, Asa. We were also hoping to be able to create a kind of synergy between Masao's usual style and my own dog-tossing approach. (In both cases, we would have been counting on Mr. Choko's active participation.) Then we would have tried to combine the two elements into a cohesive dramatic piece. The thing is, for me—and I think the same was true for Masao—the only concrete ideas I had were about the first and last scenes.

"The first scene was going to be something we'd heard about from Mr. Choko: a scenario from the recurrent dream he's been having for the past sixty years or so. It's night, and against the backdrop of a flood-swollen river we see your father, illuminated by the moon and looking away from us, sitting in a small rowboat. Meanwhile, a sort of Greek chorus of actors is onstage, chanting the story of a young boy who is struggling to reach the boat with the cold, muddy water lapping against his chest. Suspended high above the stage, the young boy's supernatural alter ego, Kogii, is gazing down on the action.

"Not surprisingly, the idea for the other scene also came from something Mr. Choko told us. It was going to evoke the last image in the drowning novel, and the idea would have been to have the book's final words read aloud, verbatim, by me and the other actors *onstage. Those words would have suggested the thoughts that were going through the father's mind just as he was about to drown. Then all the reciters would have been sucked into the whirlpool themselves, while the Kogii doll looked on from above.*

*"When we talk about it like this, though, it isn't clear how the book would have been constructed, or how the story would have unfolded scene by scene. To be honest, I get the feeling the only thing floating around in Mr. Choko's head might have been those T. S. Eliot lines about the Phoenician sailor drowning in the whirlpool."*

*Unaiko lapsed into a thoughtful silence, and I found myself remembering the lines she mentioned. I imagine the same thing must be happening to you, Kogii, while you're reading this fax:*

> *A current under sea*
> *Picked his bones in whispers. As he rose and fell*
> *He passed the stages of his age and youth*
> *Entering the whirlpool.*

# 5

*Dear Kogii,*

*The day after the late-night conversation I described in my previous fax, Ricchan came to the hospital to say her good-byes to Chikashi, and that allowed me to grab a few winks in a nearby chair. While I was napping Chikashi apparently started talking to Ricchan about your late work, and Ricchan gave me a blow-by-blow account of their conversation after I woke up. I'll transcribe it here from memory:*

*Apparently the first thing Chikashi said to Ricchan was this: "Choko went down to the forests of Shikoku to write his drowning novel, but he ended up abandoning it instead. He's*

been living the writer's life for a long time now, but he quit
rather easily on what was supposed to be the crowning work
of his career. Even if the project is out of the picture for good,
Choko will probably live for quite a few more years, so the question is, how can he move ahead with his late work? When my
brother, Goro, died in such a horrible way, a lot of his colleagues
in the movie business were saying his best work was behind him
and his career was probably over anyway, but I believe if he had
gone on living he would have produced some new films that
were every bit as good as his previous work.

"My husband never seemed to have much to say about
Goro's films, one way or another, but there's a recording of a seminar Choko gave while he was teaching at the Free University in
Berlin. I've listened to it so many times that I know it almost by
heart, but I'll just paraphrase the highlights.

"Apparently in Goro's later years he didn't tend to take
his interviews with Japanese journalists very seriously, but he
responded differently when he was talking to the passionate
cinema buffs he encountered in his travels overseas. In the
seminar, my husband said he had read a number of newspaper
articles about Goro in English and French, but since he doesn't
know much German, he asked some of his university students in
Berlin to find similar articles in German publications and then
put together essay-style reports about them in English. Based on
that research, he concluded that Goro would have gone on to
make a number of films in the future, if he had lived. I remember that my husband concluded his little speech by saying, 'So
why would Goro have decided to commit suicide in the prime of
life? I really have no idea.'

"My husband tends to torment himself and keep his worries bottled up inside," Chikashi went on, "but lately I know he's
been trying to rebuild his relationship with Akari in his own
slow, silent way. And even though he's feeling rather discouraged
about his writing these days, I believe my husband is an optimist

*at heart and I think it's very likely that he (like Goro, if he had
lived) will eventually find his way to the late work he's meant to
do, whatever it might turn out to be. If someone were to theorize
that Kogito felt more relief than disappointment about the failure of the drowning novel, well, I would have to disagree."*

Kogii, I hope you'll take Chikashi's words, which were
spoken not long after she had been through a serious operation,
as her way of trying to cheer you on from afar.

I also want to share something else I heard. Ricchan has
been a huge help to Maki—in fact, apart from the days when
Ricchan needed to go somewhere with Unaiko, she has spent
all her time in Tokyo making herself useful around the house in
Seijo—and even though she and Maki have low-key, easygoing
personalities, they both share the trait of being willing to voice
hard truths when they feel the need. They've come to trust each
other, and that's probably why Maki felt comfortable saying this
to Ricchan:

"My mother realized that sending my father and Akari
off to Shikoku together under the current circumstances could
create problems for you, but she did it anyway. I think it was
because she wasn't confident she would survive the surgery, and
she felt uneasy about having my father and brother around during a time like that. Before she went into the hospital she tidied
up a lot of loose ends, and after she was admitted she wouldn't
let either one of them come to visit her. I think sending them to
stay on Shikoku was her way of forcing them to find a way to go
on living together after she was gone, and she was hoping their
time down there would help.

"When I went to the airport to see my father and Akari off
to Shikoku—and also to meet my aunt Asa, who had just flown
in—I got the sense that Akari knew what was going on with our
mother and was aware of what the worst-case outcome could
be. He seemed so lost and depressed that I impulsively blurted
out, 'Mama is going to come home from the hospital around

*the beginning of May,' even though I knew as I was saying those words that they could undermine my mother's intentions.*

*"Akari's response was typical of his peculiar sense of humor—in fact, it was a playful variation on one of his quotes from the little book I put together. He said, 'Oh, is that so? Mama's coming home at the beginning of May? Well, even if she comes home then, right now she's dead. Mama is really dead!'"*

*Kogii, I can't help thinking about one of the terms you're so fond of: "rebirth." Isn't that the essence of what Akari is talking about here and in* My Own Words *as well?*

# Chapter 10

# A Memory . . .
# or the Coda to a Dream

## 1

When Unaiko was offered a four-week job as guest director at a large theater—a far cry from the small-scale venues where she had been mounting her own productions—she naturally jumped at the opportunity. There was nothing more for Ricchan to do, so she left Tokyo as soon as she had finished attending to some personal business of her own.

Ricchan's first task after returning to the Forest House had been to rearrange the room she shared with Unaiko to create a designated space for Akari. He immediately settled into his downstairs pied-à-terre and busied himself with organizing the CDs Ricchan had brought back from Tokyo for him. After spending half a day lining up the discs according to his own method of classification he began listening to one track from each CD, starting with a Piazzolla piece for guitar, until he'd worked his way through the entire stack.

Meanwhile, Ricchan came upstairs to clean my study/bedroom. While she worked, she told me about her farewell conversation with Chikashi at the hospital, although of course (as Ricchan knew) Asa had already given me a partial recap. While she was bundling some sheets, pillowcases, and pajamas to be laundered, Ricchan caught sight of the photograph of Unaiko's heroic onstage pose, which I had tucked away on the bookshelf with my big dictionaries, and she quietly moved it to a more conspicuous place. Then she mentioned having noticed that Chikashi had only one photo of her late brother, Goro, on display in her hospital room—and even that was just a book cover rather than a framed photo.

"It's been ten years since Goro died," I said, "and some books are finally coming out now that aren't completely tainted by the tabloid newspaper scandal everyone was obsessed with immediately after his death. The photo was probably taken by a young photographer friend of Goro's, whom we'd heard about but never met. Chikashi said it was an unusually relaxed-looking photo of Goro, and she added that for someone who was in the film business, he was surprisingly self-conscious about being photographed."

Ricchan nodded. "I mentioned to Chikashi that I couldn't help noticing there weren't any photos of Akari, or of you, Mr. Choko. I was really just making small talk, with no particular agenda, but she seemed to be thinking carefully about how to reply. Finally she said there was one photo of Akari she particularly liked—a black-and-white portrait that was on the cover of a magazine after sales of his second CD took off—but it was too large to bring to the hospital. She also mentioned that something she's noticed about photographs of young people with brain damage (and she seemed a bit hesitant about saying this) is that most of the photos somehow seemed to emphasize those disabilities. She thinks it has as much to do with the photographers as with the subjects. But in the magazine photo, she said, Akari looks completely natural and relaxed. Then she went on to add, 'As for a photograph of my husband, there's one Goro took when they were both in high school, but it's the polar opposite of a candid shot. It was posed within an inch of its life, but it's still oddly unforgettable.'

"When I said I would very much like to see the photograph, Chikashi told me it was published in *The Changeling*, as an illustration amid the pages where you talk about what was going on at that time in your life. So while Maki and I were at your house, sorting through Akari's CDs and choosing a few for me to bring here, I helped myself to a copy. I haven't had time to read it yet, and I haven't looked at the photo, either."

# 2

While she was in Tokyo, Ricchan went to the university hospital to pick up some of Akari's prescriptions, and she asked the pharmacists for advice about the major seizure Akari had experienced in the forest. They told her increasing the dosages of any of his meds wasn't an option and cautioned that special care should be taken to ensure he was getting enough exercise. As soon as she got back to the Forest House, Ricchan instituted a more rigorous fitness program based on walking and calisthenics interspersed with rest periods. She added a water flask to Akari's portable kit (this was a new addition), and on her first morning back they set out together.

Not long afterward, Daio dropped by. After touching on several innocuous household matters, the conversation soon progressed to a more volatile topic: Unaiko and Ricchan's latest dog-tossing project.

"Since my training camp went bust I haven't really gotten together with any of my former disciples, but a number of them have become quite influential, both in the local prefectural government and elsewhere," Daio began. "One way or another, I hear things, and they're apparently keeping tabs on me as well. The other day I happened to run into a man who's in touch with some of those guys; he's in the shipping and transport business, so I guess he gets around quite a bit.

"Anyhow, this person was expressing concern about Unaiko's theatrical work and also about my own involvement with her group. He kept harping on the open-discussion format in the latter part of the plays—which, as you've surely heard, was the talk of the countryside around here (and not always in a good way!) after the performance at the junior high school. He was saying the faction that opposed whatever opinion she was espousing always seemed to be on the losing side of the dog-tossing battles, and he was complaining because he felt the other side (which was, in his opinion, making a fair point) inevitably ended up being 'covered in dead dogs,' as he put it. He believes Unaiko's plays are biased, and he seemed to be blaming you, Kogito, at least in part. He said you didn't come back here for the longest time, but as soon as you arrived, earlier this month, there was a sudden spike in what he called 'subversive activity' at the Forest House. (Apparently his spies are everywhere.) Suffice it to say he and his right-wing cronies have never been your biggest fans—and as you know better than anyone, that's putting it mildly—and now they've gotten themselves all worked up with righteous indignation about Unaiko and her avant-garde approach to drama. This isn't over, by a long shot."

We talked for a few more minutes about local politics, and then I said, "On another topic, when I decided to abandon my drowning novel, Asa told me you were happy about my decision because of your deep loyalty to my mother. She also said that since the red leather trunk is out of the picture and won't be causing any problems in the future, you were hoping to renew our acquaintance. I gather that's why we're having the pleasure of seeing you around again on a regular basis, after all these years.

"In any event, it so happens that you're the person I want most to talk to right now. As you know, I've been thinking a lot about my father lately. You've suggested in passing that he had a stronger interest in the realms of literature and folklore than in politics as such, and what you've told me about the way his reading preferences also tended to skew in those directions strikes me as a very strong clue. After I went through the contents of the red leather trunk and found those three volumes of Frazer's *The Golden Bough*—in the original English, no less!—I lugged those books back to Tokyo and started to read my way through them, a few pages at a time. However, because of some, uh, family issues, I put the project on hold.

"Since arriving here I've gotten back into the mood to read all three volumes in their entirety, but first I wanted to ask you a question. Do you have any idea why my father would have given those books—and those books alone—such preferential treatment, even going to the trouble of packing them in the trunk when he set out on his getaway run?"

Daio stared at me with such intensity that after a second I had to look away. I focused instead on the garden behind him, where the trees had just begun to put forth the fresh new foliage of spring: the reddish shoots of the pomegranate, the yellow-green leaflings of the Konara oak. I remembered that during my previous reunion with Daio, back when Goro and I were both attending high school in Matsuyama, Daio had sometimes had this same coruscating light in his eyes. Finally he spoke, and his manner threw those old memories into even sharper relief for me.

"You're wondering about those books," he said. "I don't read English, but I do have some ideas about why your father might have been so interested in them. I'd like very much to talk to you about that but first I need to gather my thoughts, and I'm not quite there yet. Would you mind waiting a bit longer?"

# 3

With both Unaiko and Asa away in Tokyo, Ricchan was working even harder than usual. In the beginning I didn't have a clear sense of how the members of the Caveman Group were managing to get by financially, although I was aware that the younger members always seemed to be juggling a variety of part-time jobs. When it came to the weekly expenses for Akari and me, Asa mentioned up front that I needed to contribute such-and-such a sum, so I was regularly depositing the prescribed amount, along with a bit extra, in an empty biscuit tin that was a permanent fixture on the dining-room table. However, when I lifted the lid at the beginning of every week to replenish the cash, I always found an assortment of receipts along with leftover funds in the form of coins and paper currency.

Since Ricchan was helping us in many different ways I asked whether I could at least pay her something comparable to the hourly wages Daio had agreed to accept, but she refused even to discuss the matter, saying simply, "Let's wait till Asa gets back."

I felt uneasy about the existing arrangement because Ricchan didn't merely keep up with household chores and prepare all our meals; she also looked after Akari on a daily basis. On top of that, while Unaiko was away doing her guest-artist stint at a big theater in Tokyo, Ricchan was attending to a variety of managerial duties, both for the Caveman Group and for Unaiko's next big dramatic project. (Ricchan tended to be somewhat closemouthed, but I did manage to learn Unaiko had been cast as a last-minute replacement for a well-known actress, which had delayed her return to Shikoku.) No doubt about it: Ricchan was an exceptionally diligent worker and a woman of many talents. As for Daio, he cheerfully lent a hand around the house and also took care of any outdoor-maintenance tasks Ricchan suggested.

No matter how busy she was with her other obligations, Ricchan was always remarkably conscientious about Akari's rehabilitation program, and every day—unless it happened to be raining—she would drive him to the Saya and assist him in his quest to strengthen the muscles surrounding the injured thoracic vertebra, while being careful not to inflict further damage. During these workout sessions Akari was free to play his chosen music, cranked up as loud as he pleased, and he must have found those freewheeling interludes a welcome release from the oppressive tension of sharing a house with me in our current state of estrangement.

Ricchan's days were filled to overflowing, but she was so adept at multitasking that she somehow found time to go out in the field on a regular basis and collect oral histories from some of the people who lived along the riverside and on the slope below the Saya. Although Ricchan didn't talk much about this, I gathered from Daio that this research was part of the groundwork for the next dog-tossing project: a major theatrical presentation that Unaiko, Asa, and Ricchan would be collaborating on in the near future.

Evidently Ricchan was trying to interview people who had been involved in the filming of Asa's ill-starred movie about our local heroine, Meisuke's mother. (No one ever used her given name, nor had I ever heard a single mention of Meisuke's father.) Daio seemed certain that Unaiko and Ricchan's next project was going to be an attempt to dramatize a famous guerrilla insurrection that took place after the Meiji Restoration, using Unaiko's distinctive method of interactive theater. And, he added excitedly, they were hoping to use the screenplay I'd written for Asa's film, *Meisuke's Mother Marches Off to War* (which was based on actual history mixed in with some well-known local lore), as a source of guidance and inspiration—if they could ever get their hands on a copy of it.

When Ricchan learned that Daio had already spilled the beans about this nascent plan, she decided to tell me why it had been kept under wraps. There were two reasons for the cloak of secrecy, and she explained them fully, albeit with her usual verbal economy. Reason number one: Asa was all in favor of having her brother (i.e., me) take a helpful role in the new project, and she had promised to nudge me gently in that direction. However, given the distressing complexity of my current situation (quite aside from the lingering repercussions from the Big Vertigo, I was having to cope with my wife's serious illness as well as with some monumental difficulties in my relationship with my son) Asa had suggested that it might be more considerate to wait awhile before depositing anything new on my plate, so to speak.

Ricchan went on to say that Unaiko had her heart set on putting together a play shaped by some mysterious theme derived from her personal history—a motif that apparently echoed the story of the insurrection on some level. Ricchan, by way of preliminary preparations, had been visiting the Honmachi library to look for archival materials pertaining to the uprising, while also gathering anecdotal evidence by talking to local women who had actually participated in the filming of the movie.

After that disclosure there was no further need to keep me in the dark, and Ricchan's fieldwork became a frequent topic of conversation around the dining-room table at the Forest House. One evening Akari, who had clearly been pondering something throughout the meal, left the table and trudged up the stairs to his room with an air of determination. A few moments later, he came back down clutching what appeared to be a large, custom-bound portfolio covered in blue cloth. (Back in Tokyo, Maki had sorted through her brother's effects and had mailed him a number of things, apparently including this portfolio.)

Still hugging the large blue folder, Akari announced: "Okay, this is it. The sheet music for the Beethoven piano sonata is in here, too." It was obvious that while he didn't want to hand the blue binder over to me directly, this was his oblique way of prodding me to explain the contents to Ricchan. "Mrs. Sakura Ogi Magarshack gave it to me," he added.

"Oh, I know," I said, as recollection kicked in. "It's the copy of the final shooting script Sakura gave you to commemorate the completion of the film, when she returned the Beethoven sheet music you loaned her while they were recording the sound track."

While I was speaking Akari had presented the blue portfolio to Ricchan, but when she opened the cloth cover the sheet music inside (just as Akari had said) fell to the floor. Akari bent over to pick up the pages with an easy alacrity, and it was evident that his muscle-building physical therapy was already yielding results in the form of flexibility and diminished discomfort. After shuffling the sheet music into the proper order, he handed it back to Ricchan.

"All the people I've interviewed who were working as extras in the scenes filmed up at the Saya have talked about the way the sound of this music rang out over the meadows," Ricchan said. "I told you

about the women who were talking about that, right? Hearing Sakura
Ogi Magarshack perform her battle-cry recitative with this music
playing in the background seems to have made a deeper impression
on them than almost anything else about the filming."

"Sakura had the idea of using this Beethoven sonata in the movie,
even though it reminded her of some painful memories from her childhood," I said. "She knew the title of the piece, but it was Akari who
helped her to find a recording of the specific performance she had in
mind. Sakura was very impressed, as I recall. Akari also figured out
the precise length of all the passages that would need to be included
in the sound track, and he made those notations on his own copy of
the sheet music before he passed it along to the NHK orchestra."

Ricchan looked thoughtfully at Akari, who was holding the score
open to the relevant pages. Then she said, "Akari, do you by any
chance have a CD of the performance you chose?"

"You bet I do!" Akari exclaimed enthusiastically. "You're the one
who brought it down from Tokyo for me, Ricchan!" With that, he
ran upstairs again, his face alight with an animation I hadn't seen in
recent memory.

Meanwhile, Ricchan and I set about plugging in the sophisticated sound system set up in the great room for use in rehearsals.
The speakers were on either side of the raised, brick-floored area that
served as a makeshift stage, and in order to maximize the acoustics
Ricchan opened the curtains at the south end of the room. During
our sojourn at the Forest House, Akari and I had been getting by
with just the light from the plate-glass window on the north end.
When the young people needed to use the space for rehearsal, we
would go upstairs to wait it out. They would open the curtains while
the room was in use and then close them again before returning the
living area to us.

I knew from previous visits that beyond the window, as spring-
time marched along, you could see the maples, with their wine-colored
buds gradually shading into the palest green; the tall, lush-leafed
white birches; two kinds of flowering persimmons—one with edible

fruit, the other strictly ornamental; and, finally, the late-blooming dogwoods (both red and white). This spring, however, we had kept the curtains perpetually closed on the south-side garden, so we had missed the seasonal parade of loveliness. The realization struck me as a poignant reminder of the stifling, hermetic existence Akari and I had been mired in since arriving here.

Akari returned with the CD, and as the opulent sound of Beethoven filled every atom of the cavernous space, he was clearly transported into some private realm of sublimity. (Both the composition—the Piano Sonata no. 32 in C Minor, op. 111—and the performance, by Friedrich Gulda, were among his particular favorites.) When the recording reached the second movement, which was the section of the piece used in the film, Akari lifted his head from the score and gave Ricchan a meaningful glance as if to say, *This is it*.

Ricchan was sitting with the screenplay for *Meisuke's Mother Marches Off to War* open on her knees, and she caught Akari's eye and solemnly bobbed her head, to show she had gotten the message.

# 4

The next morning, before Akari had emerged from his bedroom and joined us at the breakfast table, Ricchan informed me that she had already called Asa and Unaiko to share the exciting news about the unexpected appearance of the screenplay.

"Asa responded cautiously, as usual. She was happy that I've finally gotten a chance to read your version of the story of Meisuke's mother, but she reminded me that we'd agreed not to pressure you into getting involved with our project on any particular timetable. She also suggested that I ought to take your screenplay with several grains of salt because your interpretation of the saga 'reeks of male chauvinism,' as she put it. She said I should tread very carefully going forward.

"Unaiko was really happy to hear that a copy of the screenplay had turned up, and she seems to be eager to forge ahead and express her own concerns through the medium of our upcoming collaboration. As you know, I've been asking people from around here to talk about their experiences as extras in the film about Meisuke's mother, and since I'm passing everything on to Unaiko bit by bit and then taking notes on her comments, I've been learning a lot about her method of putting together a dramatic piece. Of course, I hope our wavelengths will eventually become synchronized to the point where I'll be able to intuit things without even having to ask.

"Regarding the recitative that features so prominently in your screenplay, I asked a number of locals to try to recite it from memory, and I was able to record quite a few different versions. (I gather you can still hear parts of the battle chant—you know, where Meisuke's mother is rallying her troops before they march off to stage the uprising—at Bon Odori celebrations around these parts.) I'd almost like to say that every person's rendition was different—both the words and the melody. When I saw the version in the screenplay I said to myself, 'Ah, this must be written in the slightly old-fashioned style Mr. Choko's mother and grandmother used when they were reciting this.' I had to read this part over and over to Unaiko on the phone, but I'm afraid my rendition sounded kind of singsongy. Wait, I'll show you." Whereupon Ricchan began to recite, in her trained-musician's voice:

> *Women warriors, let us go*
> *Off to face our latest foe.*
> *Into battle we will soar*
> *Strong and brave forevermore.*
> *All together, here we go*
> *We shall vanquish every foe!*

"In the screenplay," Ricchan went on without waiting for me to react, "you used a form of the chant that had apparently been around for a long time, and the chorus section was also in an archaic literary style. I asked Asa whether that was the way you would have heard the recitative from your mother and grandmother when you were a little boy, and she said that, on the contrary, she thought the chant in the screenplay was the result of your applying your novelist's skills to rewriting it over and over. During the time Unaiko and I have been recording the local women's memories, in all their disparity, I've been entering those accounts into the computer, and it did occur to me that if I kept revising and polishing during the process, we would eventually arrive at a kind of literary style of our own. I was quite excited, but when I mentioned it to Unaiko, she said that since there's a specific theme she wants to express through this play, she wants to see our play's language evolve naturally."

"She's absolutely right that the theme should shape the literary style," I said. "It really ought to work that way with any writing project, and I think a distinctive style can be the most compelling part of the whole."

"When I told Unaiko that Akari had unexpectedly shared his copy of the screenplay, the first thing she wanted to know was how Meisuke's mother's remarks were presented," Ricchan said. "She was wondering about one scene in particular. It takes place just after the second uprising, which was led by the teenage reincarnation of the original Meisuke. His mother (who was, of course, the mother of the first Meisuke as well) and her troops have broken camp in Okawara, and the mother and her eight-year-old son are on the way back to their village when they are surrounded by a group of young hooligans—unemployed former samurai who are filled with free-floating resentment and looking for trouble. These brutes trap young Meisuke II in a hole and stone him to death, and then a bunch of them gang-rape his mother.

"After the ruffians are gone Meisuke's mother, who is injured and unable to walk, is carried home to the village by her supporters on a stretcher made from an old wooden shutter. The procession stops at a sake brewery, and while the proprietor is making a show of giving them some water to drink, it's obvious he is consumed with prurient curiosity. So how does Meisuke's mother respond to his oblique inquiries in the script? When I posed the question to some of the women who participated in the making of the movie, most of them remembered her saying something like 'If you're so curious about how it was, kind sir, maybe you should try being raped yourself sometime!'"

I didn't respond, and Ricchan seemed to cast a mildly critical glance in my direction before she went on speaking. "So anyway, when Unaiko posed that question I had a major epiphany, and I understood for the first time why she was creating this new play and what its theme was going to be as well," she said. "I made up my mind then that no matter what happened I would do everything I could, without compromise, to help Unaiko find the language to get her message across."

Once again, I sat there in unresponsive silence, not sure what to make of this cryptic disclosure. After a beat or two I said, "I gather you're planning to begin by performing this piece at the junior high's theater in the round. In that case, many of the women you've been interviewing will most likely be in attendance, so it's probably safe to assume they'll be drawn into the interactive dialogue and the hurling of soft toys that are an integral part of the dog-tossing approach to theater."

"Absolutely!" Ricchan chirped. "In fact, every time I go out to do these interviews I've been promising to invite them all to the premiere when the time comes. I tell everyone I meet that I really hope they'll come with their arms full of handcrafted 'dead dogs' they've created themselves at home!"

# 5

Daio and I were standing side by side in the Saya, up to our ankles in fresh green grass, leaning back against the big meteoric boulder while our conversation meandered aimlessly along.

"This is something I heard from Asa," Daio said, abruptly switching gears from unfocused small talk, "but I gather you still have a very clear memory of the scene that night when your father set out on the stormy, flooded river."

"Actually, the account I shared with Asa and Unaiko—the version I was planning to use as the prologue of my drowning novel—is different from the memory of what I actually saw that night," I said. "For a very long time, I kept having a recurrent dream that was almost always exactly the same in every detail, and the prologue was based on my dream. At this point I honestly don't know whether my memories have been retroactively shaped by the endless repetitions of that dream, or whether the dream reflects my actual experience."

Daio nodded thoughtfully. "Well, if it hadn't been a dream, your supernatural alter ego wouldn't have been standing on the boat next to your father," he said. "I remember hearing that you used to insist there was another child who was an exact duplicate of you living in your house. That was the same Kogii from the dream, right? The story of Kogii was well known around the village, and I heard people mention it more than once after I returned from China. It was one of the things that made me begin to realize what an unusual person you were, from a very young age. As for your dream, I've heard about it quite a few times from various sources, but it still knocks me for a loop every time someone mentions offhandedly that Choko Sensei set out on the river with your double standing next to him.

"That's because I was there, watching, and I have a very clear memory of seeing you! You probably didn't even notice me, did you? As you'll recall, the officers and I used to visit your father, and in the old stone storehouse where we talked and ate and slept, there was a big room with a floor that was half dirt and half wooden planks. It was where your father kept his vintage Takara-brand barber's chair, which everyone understood was for his private use only. That night, I had spread a futon in the interior part of the room and had just settled down to try to get some sleep. Right about then you came in from outside, alone. There was one light burning—a single bulb with an air-raid shade, which illuminated the path to the staircase leading to the second floor. I started to get up because I assumed you had been sent to tell me that your father wanted me to do some task or other, but then I saw that you appeared to have something on your mind. You left your sandals in the entryway and crossed the dirt-floored room to the staircase without ever raising your head, so I just pretended to be asleep. I felt a lot of contempt for myself at that moment, and I remember thinking, *What good am I to anyone, anyhow, with only one arm?*

"In the big room upstairs there were three young conscripts from the flight-training school along with a couple of young officers who basically made a cottage industry out of ordering me around, and they had all presumably gone to sleep. After a few minutes you came back downstairs, carrying something wrapped in a raincoat. As soon as you went outside again, I got up and tiptoed up the stairs to check whether the officers were awake.

"The thing you were carrying wasn't very large, but it had sharp corners, so I naturally assumed it must be the red leather trunk. Earlier in the day, sometime around noon, the officers had been worrying that maybe your father wasn't planning to come over to the outbuilding where we were bunking. They decided that they needed to get their hands on the red leather trunk as a way of finding out whether your father might be plotting some extreme course of action on his own, so they sent me to the main house to fetch it. By early evening the serious partying was well under way, but the only ones who were drinking heavily were the officers and the young navy pilots. The night before there had been a big strategy meeting and, as the officers put it later, they had a breakdown in their talks with your father. He withdrew to the house and didn't show his face in our quarters the next day, so when I came back with the red leather trunk the officers pulled off the raincoat it was wrapped in and everyone crowded around eagerly to see what was inside. But the thing is, the contents turned out to be a complete disappointment, to the point where the officers were actually laughing and saying rude things like 'Hey, there's just a bunch of boring crap in here!'

"I didn't say anything, but since they were rifling through Sensei's private property I kept an eye on them the entire time from a corner of the room. One thing I remember clearly was the three heavy books—I wouldn't have been able to read the titles from a distance, especially since they were written in English, but years later, when I was helping your mother with her annual spring cleaning, I saw those books again. That was when it hit me that they must be the same ones we had carried back from a visit to the Kochi Sensei's house, when I trekked down there once with your father. And this time, when your mother wasn't looking, I copied down the title on a scrap of paper. It was *The Golden Bough*, and there were three big, thick volumes.

"Getting back to the fateful day in 1945, apart from those books the trunk mainly contained an assortment of papers and letters, tied in neat bundles. The army officers examined the envelopes and their contents, one by one, and then returned most of them to the trunk. There was an oblong hibachi in the room that was being used for warming sake or heating stewpots, and some of the letters ended up getting tossed onto the coals and going up in flames. As for the rest of the stuff from the trunk—well, your family was in the paper business so there probably would have been an oilcloth, or something of the sort, lying around. But anyhow, the officers wrapped the remaining materials in water-repellent paper and put them back in the trunk, and then they rewrapped the trunk in one of the raincoats we used to wear when we went into the mountains to work. So that was the red leather trunk you came to pick up late that night."

"You know, it's strange, but I have no memory of the part of the evening you've just described," I mused. "I don't remember going to get the trunk late that night at all, although I do recall having a small role in packing it earlier in the day. The thing I do recollect with what feels like absolute certainty is the scene that took place a while later.

"Picture this, if you will. My father has already boarded the little boat. I'm in the water nearby, and I have just handed him the red leather trunk. Looking back toward the shore, I notice one of the ropes that keeps the wooden barrels securely moored—you know, the barrels we used for the spider lily bulbs—is about to be torn loose by the current, so I plow through the chilly water with the muddy waves lapping against my chest, intending to tie a better knot. That's what happens in the dream, too, so it's possible my memories may have gradually modified themselves to match the dream. At any rate, the mooring rope for the boat was tied to the same metal ring, which was embedded in a stretch of poured concrete along the shoreline. But isn't it possible that I'm going back because my father has asked me to untie the mooring line so the boat can cast off? Come to think of it, I realize that must be what happened. It wasn't about the barrels at all. And then—I don't know whether I didn't have time to return to the boat, or maybe I turned around and saw it being catapulted into the middle of the river by the force of the waves, but in any case it was gone. And that's the story of what happened that night, in a nutshell."

"Good heavens, Kogito. All these years you've been reliving that night over and over in your dreams, torturing yourself with guilt, and while we're talking you suddenly realize that you didn't get sidetracked by some trivial issue with a wooden barrel and literally miss the boat? Now, this is pure conjecture, but it seems to me that if your father was ready to take off he wouldn't have needed to send you back to shore to untie the mooring rope. He could have cut it with the short sword he used for trimming the paperbush bark and so on, which was always hanging from his belt. He set out on the boat trip with no plans to return home, right? So he wouldn't have needed to use the rope again to tie up the boat, since he would have simply abandoned it when he got to his first destination, downriver. You know, Kogito, the more I think about it the more convinced I am that your father consciously intended to leave you behind, and sending you to cut the mooring rope could have been his way of saving your life!

"And then, of course, Choko Sensei ended up drowning in the river. It was only a few days earlier that you had precociously pointed out that your father was mistaking one complex kanji for a similar-looking one—you know, when he misread the water-related 淼淼 for the woodsy 森森? This may be a stretch, but given the way things turned out, doesn't it strike you that your father's misreading may actually have been oddly apt and even prescient on a deeper level?

What I mean is that in his last moments of existence Sensei wasn't really being borne along to the end of the river, where it becomes one with the vast and endless sea. I'm sure you can see where I'm going with this: I'm talking about the belief around these parts that when people die, their spirits go up into the forest and settle at the base of one particular, foreordained tree. In other words, while your father may have taken his last breath on the water, I think he was really on his way back to the forest!

"Of course, I wasn't born here, so there's probably no spirit tree in the forest with my name on it. Even so, when it comes time for me to die, I'd like to believe my soul could go to a place in some cosmic forest and find refuge and salvation there. By the way, Asa mentioned that the poem you collaborated on with your mother wasn't exactly well received, but I really like it a lot. Of course, Akari was born and raised in Tokyo, but I think that if you're very careful to make the proper preparations well in advance, when Akari's time comes his spirit should be able to go up into the forest and find its way to its own designated tree."

Although Daio wasn't originally from Shikoku, he had remained in the area after closing the training camp, and he had clearly absorbed a great deal of local lore. He was highly intelligent and often surprisingly articulate, and I imagined that he had probably always had a genuine love of learning. Admittedly, I did question his choice of my father as a role model when there must have been more sensible options available, but that was ancient history. Daio and I had been barefoot while we were talking, to give our feet a break. Now we put our shoes back on, and as we strolled the length and breadth of that grassy meadow my companion shared his fascination with the Saya. There was a local legend (or perhaps it was more of a rumor) that if you dug deep enough it was still possible to unearth prehistoric stone axes made by our distant ancestors. Daio was intrigued by this possibility, and he had apparently spent a fair amount of time poking around in the soil in this general vicinity. On this day, after a brief impromptu dig with a twig he'd found, he proudly brought me a large chunk of dirt-encrusted rock that could conceivably have once been the head of a stone ax.

As we started to head downhill from the Saya we could see Akari and Ricchan finishing their calisthenics beside the river, where the willow trees bursting into fresh new foliage looked like a massive cloud of green smoke. Daio and I were midway down the steep slope when we noticed a couple of men striding toward Akari and Ricchan from the opposite direction.

By this time Akari was half sitting, half reclining on a portable air mattress (a position that showed how much his back pain had abated), with Ricchan next to him. As we watched from afar the two men squatted nearby and began speaking intently to Ricchan and Akari. Suddenly, Akari clapped his hands over his ears. I knew that gesture well; it was his way of expressing disapproval or revulsion when (for example) some giddy comedian on a TV talk show would launch into an off-color joke. Seeing this, I quickened my pace and scrambled down the slope as fast as I could go.

As I approached, the two men (who appeared to be in their forties) stopped talking and shifted their torsos so that they were facing my direction in a tense, watchful-looking stance that I interpreted as "ready to rumble." When I arrived, panting, Ricchan stood up. Sliding her bare feet into a pair of canvas walking shoes, she explained what was going on.

"These men here were asking whether we knew the hidden meaning behind the Saya's name," she said, "but then without waiting for an answer they went ahead and told us the term they had in mind. Akari doesn't like hearing that sort of thing, and that's why he has his hands over his ears."

As I explained earlier, the word *saya*, meaning a sheath for a sword, has long been the local nickname for the spot where a meteor landed in the midst of the forest and left a long, narrow indentation in the ground. However, *saya* also happens to be a crude colloquialism for the female sex organs—more precisely, the vagina. Daio was a few seconds behind me, and when the two men saw him charging in their direction they finally went on their way, laughing loudly and slapping each other on the back as if they had just shared some grand, uproarious adventure. From time to time they looked over their shoulders at us with faces that were red from an excess of sophomoric mirth.

"Well, those two ran away with their tails between their legs," Daio said jocularly. "And no wonder, since Kogito was armed with a stone ax. Ha ha."

"They were so persistent, I really didn't know what to do," Ricchan said.

At this, Akari finally removed his hands from his ears. "Don't worry, Ricchan," he said in a voice that was filled with emotion. And then he added, to my surprise, "If they come back, Papa will beat them up for us!"

I immediately recognized that phrasing as an echo of one of the more poignant quotes from *My Own Words*. It had been a very long time since I'd heard my son say anything so positive about me, and my heart swelled with a cautious infusion of hope.

# Chapter 11

# But Why *The Golden Bough*?

## 1

Since the first stirrings of my rapprochement with Akari (which, while still a work in progress, seemed to have taken a definite step in the right direction), our daily life had undergone a transformation. The sound system from Unaiko and Ricchan's room was moved into the dining room, and Akari would often stretch out diagonally on the floor and listen to music or work on his compositions. Ricchan never took a single day off from their rehab sessions at the Saya, and even though she was busy with the usual plethora of activities, she never dropped the ball where Akari's well-being was concerned.

I had set up my own base camp on the sofa that had been banished to the southwest corner of the great room to create more space for rehearsals, with my assorted work supplies—books, papers, and index cards—in (and on) a small filing cabinet next to the couch. As I soon realized, our current living arrangement was not so different from the one we'd had at home in Tokyo, except that in this house Akari and I would both retreat to the second floor when a rehearsal began.

Ricchan spent a fair amount of time staying on top of bookkeeping and other office tasks on the computer she shared with Unaiko, but after Akari started listening to music in the dining room she would often sit at the dining-room table with her head bent over the production notes from the filming of *Meisuke's Mother Marches Off to War*.

Daio continued to be a regular visitor, and in the spirit of sociability he and I would often join Ricchan at the table. Akari kept the volume on his music fairly low, and it never seemed to have an adverse effect on Ricchan's concentration. By the same token Daio's and my speaking voices, which had to be raised slightly to be heard over the music, didn't seem to be an impediment to Akari's listening pleasure. Noticing this, I was reminded of something Maki had once observed. When Akari was in listening-to-music mode, she said, his brain seemed to be in a separate realm than when he was speaking or hearing words.

As for my own brain, it was still completely devoid of ideas for a late-work book. I realized in retrospect that I had foolishly put all my creative eggs into the drowning-novel basket and hadn't bothered to formulate a backup plan. Because I wasn't working on anything in particular, I didn't have to cleave to the kind of focused bibliographical list that normally accompanied my novel-writing process, so for once I was free to explore whatever caught my fancy on a given day. My current reading habits were shaped by a conscious continuo of self-restraint born of my fear that the Big Vertigo might pay me another unwelcome visit, so rather than poring over books in my study/bedroom it seemed to make more sense for me to wander downstairs, stretch out on the sofa, and browse through books at a leisurely pace.

It was while I was in this relaxed mode that some reading material I had requested from an editor friend in Tokyo—*The Golden Bough: A Study in Magic and Religion*, by James George Frazer—was delivered. My friend had kindly sent all twelve volumes of the Elibron Classics facsimile, published in 2005, of Macmillan's 1920–1923 edition. Part of the reason I had wanted to get my hands on a complete set was so I could ascertain where the three volumes from the red leather

trunk fit into the whole. I was also making frequent reference to the
Japanese translations of several volumes of *The Golden Bough*'s third
edition. A certain publisher was in the process of issuing a translation
of the entire set, and I had been receiving a complimentary copy of
each volume as it came out (there was never any card, but I suspected
that the gift had been arranged by a cultural anthropologist friend of
mine), so I'd had those sent down here, too.

After my skirmishes with the Big Vertigo, instead of reading with
maximum concentration for long stretches of time I fell into the habit
of keeping a few books on the desk next to my bed and desultorily
flipping through the pages whenever the mood struck me. But now
that my conversations with Daio had led me to the Frazer books, my
page-turning sessions had taken on a new intensity and focus. I was
no longer merely browsing; I was on an active quest.

In keeping with this new resolve, I began to work my way through
the three volumes of *The Golden Bough* I'd found in the red leather
trunk, systematically parsing all the underlinings and marginal notes:
the visible evidence of my father's struggle, given his limited proficiency in English, to read these difficult books. (When I was paging
through the books for the first time, back in Tokyo, I hadn't paid
any attention to these marks.) I didn't find anything that would warrant being called marginalia, but there were a number of faint markings in hard-leaded colored pencil (primarily red and blue)—marks
I suspected had been made in pencil rather than ink so they could
eventually be erased.

Because the books had gotten wet in the river, many of the pages
were stuck together and it was difficult to separate them without
causing the old, brittle paper to tear or even disintegrate. Nonetheless, I could clearly see that some of the subtitles or subheadings had
been lightly circled in colored pencil. At some point I realized the
three books must have been a loan (if they had been a gift, the set
would surely have been complete), but because my father had died
unexpectedly they were never returned. It seemed safe to deduce
that the barely legible notations had been made by the books' original

owner, perhaps as a way of letting my father know which segments that person considered especially significant.

If my assumption was correct (and I was confident it was), then the assiduous wielder of those colored pencils must have been the mentor whose name I had heard my father invoke in reverent tones on numerous occasions. *Eureka,* I thought. *That's it!* These books had undoubtedly come from the so-called Kochi Sensei, who lived on the other side of Shikoku's Sanmyaku mountain range: the same person my father had once gone to visit in search of knowledge, dragging Daio along with him. The pair had walked for many kilometers, following a route to the town of Kochi that followed the river and eventually fed into a road made famous in the mid-1860s by the Kochi-born samurai Ryoma Sakamoto. (As every Japanese schoolchild knows, Sakamoto traversed that roadway when he deserted his feudal clan to embark on a life of idealistic anti-shogunate political activism inspired by the democratic principles of the United States—a life cut short in 1867 when he was murdered by assassins at a lodging house in Kyoto.)

I began to probe in earnest, exploring the books in sequential order as I thought my father would have done. My goal was to replicate his experience as he attempted to read Frazer's work in its original form, armed with nothing but a small, dog-eared copy of *The Concise English-Japanese Dictionary* (which I remembered having seen around the house), after his faithful disciple, Daio, had toted those heavy volumes home following their visit to the Kochi Sensei.

And what about the annotations? I was curious to see whether the Kochi Sensei had confined his explanations to the subheadings, or had commented on the text line by line. To my surprise, after a cursory flip through the pages (pausing only to peruse the headings and passages marked with red and blue pencil), it became clear why the Kochi Sensei had chosen these particular volumes as a means of furthering my father's education. There was no doubt about it; the Kochi Sensei was using *The Golden Bough*'s anthropological and folkloric principles as a metaphor for politics!

I was on the third day of skimming the entire *Golden Bough* when Ricchan ventured into the great room to bring me a cup of coffee. She set the ceramic mug on the filing cabinet near the sofa and said, "I guess whenever you feel like working on this project, you have to make several trips to lug all the books down from the study. That must be good exercise!"

"These are the books I found in the red leather trunk during my previous visit," I explained. "I've been trying to figure out why my father was reading them, and how, and I think I'm close to finding some answers."

"I'm aware that *The Golden Bough* has been translated into Japanese, but I've never read it," Ricchan said. "If you're at a good stopping point, would you mind giving me a crash course? Hang on, I'll just go grab my own coffee."

I gathered the relevant materials and laid them out on the L-shaped sofa between the end where I was sitting and the perpendicular segment where Ricchan took a seat when she returned from the kitchen, mug in hand.

"*The Golden Bough* is a scholarly work about folklore," I began, "but it also provides practical insight into interpersonal dynamics, particularly as they pertain to the realm of politics. My father was using these books as a means for furthering his own political education, but he seems to have had a penchant for the literary aspects as well, and I've been intrigued by the discovery that he apparently enjoyed the text on an artistic level, too. Ricchan, you've probably heard Daio referring to my father as 'Choko Sensei,' and I'm guessing it might have struck you as odd. 'Sensei' is a vestigial title, left over from the time when my father was running an ultranationalistic training camp and Daio was one of his disciples. But recently, as Daio and I have been talking, something rather surprising has emerged. He told me that my father sometimes liked to ramble about political matters, tossing around hard-line terms such as nation-state, Greater East Asia Co-Prosperity Sphere, and so on. However, according to Daio, below the blustery ultranationalistic surface my father's true nature, even at the age of fifty, was still that of a literature-besotted youth.

"When I first started examining *The Golden Bough*, trying to see it through my father's eyes, I noticed that in all three volumes someone had circled some of Frazer's marginal notes, which are rather like summaries of the passages or subsections in question, in colored pencil. Look, here's one right here. These confident markings appear to have been made by an experienced teacher, but what I didn't notice at first was that there are also some more tentative notations, evidently added by a reader who hadn't done much of this sort of thing before—underlining, question marks, exclamation points, and so on. As I continued reading, I realized that this second set of markings must have been made by my father. As Daio said, it's obvious my father was captivated by the literary—or should I say poetic?—attributes of the book. But it's equally clear that his mentor was trying to use *The Golden Bough* as a tool for teaching my father about politics. My father was obediently going along with the plan, but it appears to me as though he was trying to read it from a more artistic perspective as well. This has been a revelation for me; for the first time since I was born, I feel as if I'm seeing my father for who he really was. (At the time he was reading this book, of course, he was nearly twenty-five years younger than I am now.)

"The epigraph of the first volume is a quotation from a poem by Thomas Babington Macaulay. Here, take a look. I've laid out both the English and the Japanese translations, and as you can see the English style is quite archaic."

*From the still glassy lake that sleeps*
*Beneath Aricia's trees—*
*Those trees in whose dim shadow*
*The ghastly priest doth reign,*
*The priest who slew the slayer,*
*And shall himself be slain. . . .*

"I think the translation is reasonably true to the original," I continued after Ricchan had finished studying both versions of the poem. "I mean, this is one of those epic poems where everything is on the surface, so what you see is what you get. What's intcresting is that Frazer more or less echoes the same content—only in prose, of course—in various parts of his book. His style can be a bit flowery in places, but it's mostly lucid and straightforward, and sometimes it's absolutely gorgeous. I think my father managed to grasp that beauty, even through the laborious process of reading the text one word at a time with frequent recourse to *The Concise* (as we used to affectionately call the little English-Japanese dictionary). Seeing the evidence of his painstaking quest has almost made me feel pity, or at least sympathy, for my father: that fifty-year-old man who was on the cusp of a premature death by drowning."

# 2

Next, I moved on to telling Ricchan about the sections that my father himself had circled, with particular emphasis on the concept of the "dying God."

"The 'King of the Wood,' who's mentioned in an early sentence, is so widely known that you could safely call him a major character in cultural history," I explained. "In the Alban Hills of Italy, deep in the woods around Lake Nemi—which is basically a volcanic crater filled with water—there is a huge oak tree. A dark-visaged king, sword at his waist, is stationed nearby to protect the sacred tree. (Of course, you could also say that the king is protecting himself.) One after another, vigorous young men come to challenge the king to a sword fight. Once a challenger has vanquished the current monarch, that individual will become the new king. As the term 'dying God' suggests, in this mythology gods are not immortal; on the contrary, it is their destiny to die. When a king grows old and feeble, he and his realm will inevitably fall into ruin and be replaced. (Of course, the physical life force has long been associated with fertility cults and crop cycles in many cultures, including our own.)

"So how did the citizens cope with the impending crisis? Well, the people made a conscious effort to prevent the king from dying a natural death—that is, from illness or old age. While the old king still had some energy left, they would send a parade of candidates to attempt to kill him, until someone finally succeeded. And with the ascension of a new king the world, too, would experience a rebirth of sorts: a renewal of fertility. That's the basic premise. Anyone can see that the myth of the Forest King of Nemi is one of the underlying themes of the entire *Golden Bough*, from beginning to end. The archetypal myth about the new king who kills his aged predecessor, thus engendering a renascence of fertility in the world, was already firmly established in the folkloric canon when Frazer arrived at the party, so to speak. However, Frazer expanded on the theme at great length, and I think the person who loaned my father these books made the marks to indicate that my father ought to jump ahead and read the pages about the way the old king was killed, and the earth regained its power and vitality as a result. It's clear from the marginal annotations that my father was under the influence of a mentor who was exceedingly intense about the teaching of political science."

While I was speaking to Ricchan, Daio ambled into the great room and I saw Akari (who was lying on the floor nearby) raise one hand in greeting. Daio had been out in the south-side garden, doing his usual landscaping chores, and he had apparently been listening to our conversation through a partially open sliding glass door.

"Holy cow, Kogito," he said. "I think the last time I heard you talking so passionately about anything was while you were still in high school, the weekend you brought Goro to the training camp. Please continue your discussion—don't mind me!"

"All right," I replied. "I'm going to get back to Frazer's book, but I'll keep in mind that you're listening too now, Daio. Anyway, I think I've figured out the overarching point that the Kochi Sensei was trying to make with all his little notes in the margins. As I told Ricchan, I've also realized that while my father was dutifully reading *The Golden Bough* in order to glean the lessons in political theory his own mentor was trying to impart, he was also reading it on another, more personal level and appreciating the beauty of the prose as a work of literary art. That's something you've mentioned as well, Daio. However, his guru's notes were clearly focused on posing the question: *What should the old king's followers be doing, in a political sense?*

"If you'll bear with me, I'd like to read this excerpt from the Frazer book aloud: *But no amount of care and precaution will prevent the man-god from growing old and feeble and at last dying. His worshippers have to lay their account with this sad necessity and to meet it as best they can. The danger is a formidable one; for if the course of nature is dependent on the man-god's life, what catastrophes may not be expected from the gradual enfeeblement of his powers and their final extinction in death? There is only one way of averting these dangers. The man-god must be killed as soon as he shows symptoms that his powers are beginning to fail, and his soul must be transferred to a vigorous successor before it has been seriously impaired by the threatened decay. The advantages of thus putting the man-god to death instead of allowing him to die of old age and disease are, to the savage, obvious enough."*

After I had finished reading, Akari walked silently past us on his way to the restroom. (He had been lying on the floor for a long time, and getting to his feet obviously caused some lower-back pain.) A moment later we heard a loud noise as the door banged shut behind him.

"Akari really hates it when they interrupt his music programs with a breaking-news bulletin, especially when it has to do with murder or any other kind of violent crime," Ricchan said. "I don't think our discussion about the state-sanctioned killing of kings sat well with him. That's why he slammed the door."

I turned to Daio. "By the way," I said, "I've finally come to understand why my mother and sister were so terrified I might some-day finish the drowning novel. I think they were afraid I would tell the world that the Kochi Sensei was using *The Golden Bough* to convince my father and his cohorts to kill the living god: that is, Emperor Hirohito."

When Daio didn't respond, I went on, "The thing is, Daio, the events of that night—the feverish atmosphere of the meeting at the storehouse, and the way the officers seemed to suddenly be ostracizing my father—struck me as completely mystifying at the time. I still find them baffling, even now. What I'd like to know, and I'm hoping you'll be able to tell me, is whether my father and the young officers really understood each other. I mean, suddenly their ties are severed, and my father rushes out alone and drowns. Surely those occurrences must have had some effect on you, as a young man who looked up to my father?"

The sunlight from the back garden seemed to have turned Daio's close-cropped white hair into a kind of golden aureole. He stood there for a moment with his head held high, thinking, while I waited for an answer. Evidently something about this tableau rubbed Ricchan the wrong way because she snapped, "Hey, how long do you guys expect Akari to stay barricaded in the restroom in self-defense? I mean, he was down here trying to relax, and then he was forced to put up with your talk about death and murder and drowning, just a few feet away! It's almost time for one of his favorite FM radio programs, *Classics Special*, so maybe you two could give him a little space. Please?"

Then she added in a softer tone, "This afternoon we'll be going to the Saya again, and you're both welcome to tag along. If you could just do us the favor of not hanging around too close to where Akari's listening to his music, you can continue your gruesome discussion at the top of your lungs, if that's what you want to do!"

# 3

After leaving the van in a large open space (a designated turnaround for forestry trucks), we set out on foot along the pathway, thickly bordered by trees and bushes, that crossed over the mountain stream.

Daio led the way, with a thin exercise mat and a blanket draped over his one arm, and the rest of us followed in single file. Ricchan was the very model of a perfect caregiver. Carrying a large Boston bag, she stepped carefully in her canvas walking shoes while her body language seemed to be saying, *If Akari should lose his balance and start to fall, I'm ready to jump into the shrubbery and hold him up.*

The path dead-ended at the lower part of the Saya. We stopped there and Daio spread out the exercise mat on a flat, narrow strip of grassland next to the stream. Ricchan, meanwhile, was extracting the components of the portable sound system and an assortment of CDs from the ubiquitous Boston bag. After Akari had taken a seat on the mat and started to remove his shoes, Daio and I took our leave and headed toward the upper reaches of the Saya.

"I remember the war was still going on when I was given the second floor of the paperbush warehouse down by the river as a place to stay," Daio said as we climbed the hill, side by side. "I settled in nicely, but I didn't set foot in the 'Saya zone'—that is, this area right here—until quite a bit later."

"The Saya has had an important place in local history for centuries," I replied, "but it was never one of the spots local people would share with a visitor from the outside world."

"I remember one time I was invited to go fishing with the man I've mentioned, whose son-in-law became a doctor," Daio said. "It was sweetfish season, as I recall. Anyhow, he told me the triangular delta where your father's body washed ashore is considered a 'special spot,' and he said that even after all these years children still won't go in the water there. When you think about the ancient landmarks in an area like this, each with its own story, it kind of makes sense that a relatively new site could have taken on 'special' overtones as well.

"Kogito, I know you've been having a recurrent dream about what you saw the night of the big flood, when your father took off in his little boat. Asa said you kept insisting that you felt as though you had really seen your father sinking to the bottom of the deep river, and I can't help thinking the image might have been something you dreamed.

Why? Because I was the one who spotted Choko Sensei's dead body lying on the riverbed in shallow water, and you were nowhere in sight. Asa said you were always saying that Kogii (who was already in the boat) and you were the only ones who saw what happened that night, but she knew for a fact that your mother was standing on top of the promontory, watching the whole scene unfold. And I know there was at least one other witness, because that witness was me.

"After I saw Choko Sensei take off in his little boat, I ran back to tell the army officers. After a great deal of discussion, some of us decided to go out looking for your father as soon as it began to get light. I remember the sky was just beginning to show some faint signs of dawn when we jumped on bicycles and set off down the road along the river. At the top of the sandbar down by Honmachi, we ran into someone who had happened to see a boat flipping over by the light of the moon, so we figured we should start by searching the area along the sandbar. We split up, and as I've mentioned before, I was the one who found Choko Sensei's body lying in some shallow water.

"That's how it happened, but afterward your mother tried to make sure you never got a chance to talk to anyone who had been involved in pulling your father's body out of the water; I guess she wanted to protect you from hearing the awful details. You left home when you were fifteen, and from then on you didn't really hang out much with anyone from here, did you? And even during the five years between your father's death and your departure for Tokyo, you were kind of a loner. I've run into some people who knew you in those days, and they said that whenever they saw you at the new middle school you always seemed to be sitting alone in an empty classroom between classes and at lunchtime, reading a book. Asa was really your only link to this area, and thanks to your mother, you and your sister were estranged for many years. I'm not sure, but I think you may be the only person raised around here who ever uprooted himself so completely—roots, trunk, branches, leaves, and all, as the saying goes.

"But even after everything that's happened since you moved away, I think at heart you're still a boy from the forest. I mean, the things you write draw heavily on the stories your mother and grandmother told you growing up, and no matter how much you embellish them with imagination, for me, your books always seem to smell like the truth. That reminds me of something I used to say to your mother during her later years—of course, by then you had long since become a Tokyoite and rarely visited, even though she had finally relented and granted you the freedom to visit whenever you pleased (just as long as you didn't show up too often).

"Anyhow, I remember one time I said to her, 'Kogito's novels are pure fantasy, aren't they? It's amazing to me that he can exercise his imagination to such a degree and make things up out of whole cloth. When you come right down to it, I guess it's a simple matter of talent.'

"And then—maybe it was because she thought I was using some highfalutin-sounding words or something—your mother cut me down to size, snapping, 'That isn't fantasy; it's just imagination.' Then she went on to say, 'My husband used to read the books of Kunio Yanagida, and he told me that according to Yanagida there is a clear difference between fantasy and imagination, because imagination has some basis in reality. So what Kogii's doing is writing mostly about real things, which he augments by using his imagination. He has a very good memory for the tales his grandmother and I used to tell him, and because he used folklore as a sort of launching pad for his imaginings, when we read his early books there wasn't a single thing to make us think, *Gee, this right here is some really far-fetched fantasy*.'

"That's what your mother said to me. Her comments made me angry, and I countered by saying, 'Yeah, but what about the really crazy book, *The Day He Himself Shall Wipe My Tears Away*, where Choko Sensei is portrayed as a grotesque caricature who has bladder cancer, and he gets loaded into a makeshift wooden chariot and goes off to rob a bank?' And your mother came back with, 'Oh, *that* wasn't imagination, or fantasy. That was outright delusion!' Ha ha ha!"

While Daio was delivering this animated monologue, we had been making steady progress up the grassy hill and were now standing at the heart of the Saya: the scabbard-shaped indentation in the meadow.

"Sorry," Daio continued after he had finished laughing, "I got kind of carried away reminiscing about the fun I used to have talking with your mother. Now that we've come to a place where we don't have to worry about being overheard, we should probably get back to the serious matters we were discussing earlier, don't you think? Because I keep coming up against a vexing problem, and every time I try to work it out on my own, I seem to end up getting sidetracked or else giving up entirely. If I could only get this matter resolved, there might turn out to be some connection with the recurrent dream that's been plaguing you for all these years.

"As I mentioned, Asa told me about the dream and I know you've even put it down on paper. From my perspective, I don't believe it should be dismissed as 'just a dream.' Now, I'm no expert—this is something I happened to read in a book about dream interpretation, aimed at amateurs like me—but apparently when a child tries to tell its mother something and she refuses to listen, the things the child wanted to express can be turned inward and incorporated into dreams, which eventually merge seamlessly with memories. And then, according to the book, the child can grow up to be someone like you who's haunted by recurrent dreams. I would never presume to psychoanalyze you, but based on what I've heard I can't help feeling that your genuine memories (even if you don't actively remember them when you're awake) have somehow been filtered through those dreams.

"You told this story in one of your newspaper columns, but apparently a cultural anthropologist friend of yours was doing fieldwork somewhere in Indonesia—I believe it was on Flores Island—when he made an interesting discovery in a remote settlement up in the mountains. The people of the tribe had created a giant replica of an airplane from twigs and bits of wood and enshrined it in a clearing in the forest. In your essay you said that when you first heard about this, your heart skipped a beat, and when I read that line I thought, *I'll bet Kogito was remembering a dream he had when he was a child.*"

"It's certainly true I was captivated by a drawing of the primitive replica of a plane I saw in some field notes made by that anthropologist friend of mine—he was an accomplished artist as well, and his sketches would have put a professional to shame—and you're right in thinking it reminded me uncannily of one of my childhood dreams," I said. "And now I'm feeling shaken up all over again, because this place you've brought me to, the Saya, is the spot where the dream in question took place. In my dream it was above here to the north, beyond the big meteoric boulder, that I came across the tail of a wrecked aircraft. The plane's body was nearby, facing downward. It wasn't made of wood, though; it appeared to have been cobbled together from spare machine parts. But really, Daio, your powers of deductive reasoning are quite extraordinary!"

"Really? I don't know—maybe your mother's analytical approach to things somehow rubbed off on me! No, but seriously, like she said, imagination (as opposed to pure fantasy) usually has some basis in fact.

"In this case, during the days before your father's death there was a series of meetings combined with a nonstop drinking party, and even though you were just a child you must have overheard quite a bit of the discussion. I'm not sure about this, but my guess is that you would have been feeling dismayed and confused by what you heard. On the day before your father took off alone, I remember seeing you lurking in the corridor behind the big tatami-matted room upstairs during one of those meetings with a worried look on your face. And I thought, *All this conspiratorial talk must sound pretty scary to a kid*, but it wasn't my place to shoo you away. And then after your father died you must have locked those memories away somewhere deep in your unconscious and then convinced yourself that the things you overheard were just part of a dream. I think the time has come for me to blow the lid off some of those secrets, so I'm going to tell you what actually happened.

"The plan was to sneak onto the military airfield at Yoshidahama and steal a fully loaded kamikaze plane, then fly east from there. The pilots were supposed to land the stolen plane in the Saya, right here in the middle of the forest, and somehow hide it until it was needed.

That risky maneuver was the main point of contention during those meetings you were eavesdropping on."

"Yes, I wrote about it in *The Day He Himself Shall Wipe My Tears Away*, only I framed it as the fantastical imaginings of a young man who was in the process of losing his mind," I said.

"Hey, I read that little book!" Daio exclaimed. "It was right after your mother summoned me and basically held my feet to the fire, demanding to know whether I'd ever told you about the meeting or whether you, as a ten-year-old child, had been listening through the walls. Again, I'm no psychiatrist, but it seems as if a disturbing memory that had been buried or suppressed for many years found its way to the surface through your dreams—probably helped along by the fact that a novelist's mind moves in strange and mysterious ways. Anyhow, when your mother showed me the passage in *The Day He Himself Shall Wipe My Tears Away*, I told her in no uncertain terms: 'I see what you're getting at, but I don't see any cause for concern. Your deepest fear seems to be that Kogito understood what was going on in his father's meetings with the military officers, and that at some point he might write a much bigger novel than this one and you would all end up in complete disgrace, like the family of Kotoku Sensei after the High Treason Incident, but I'm sure it will never happen. Even for me, and I was quite a bit older, the things I heard at some of those meetings seemed like total gibberish. They made no sense to me, and I'm sure they would have been even more incomprehensible to a child.'

"As it turned out, I was right. You never did write the big exposé your mother was so afraid of. And since you've completely given up on the drowning novel, your practical-minded sister, Asa, can finally breathe a sigh of relief, and I think that's a very good thing.

"However, the truth is that I'm still left with a few nagging doubts. We aren't talking about your conscious mind now but rather the unconscious, right? Either way, I doubt if you really understood the words you were hearing when you eavesdropped on those meetings, but somehow your dreaming mind was able to figure everything out, and the significance of what you'd overheard became clear in your dreams. Doesn't that seem like a plausible explanation? On some level you knew there was a plan to steal a military plane and hide it at the Saya for future use, to bomb the Imperial Palace. And as you realized in your dream, the radical plan was the reason your father behaved so erratically during his last hours on earth. But the plan never came to fruition, and your unconscious mind invented the next scene."

"Even so, the image of a warplane hidden on the grassy area of the Saya had no basis in reality," I said. "I don't know whether you'd call it fantasy, or the surreal inventiveness of the dreaming mind . . ."

"What do you mean, 'fantasy'? The image was definitely grounded in fact, or at least in possibility. As I already told you, the issue of 'borrowing' the aircraft was a major sticking point in the endless discussions between your father and the military guys who were at your house. At that final meeting, they were talking about how Japan's defeat in the war appeared to be much more imminent than they had been led to believe, and the discussion got very heated because your father kept insisting they ought to rush ahead with his favorite scheme, which involved a suicide attack on the Imperial Palace from the air. As I've mentioned, there were some new faces at the meeting: several young trainee pilots who were attending the Imperial Navy course in the village. They had been brought along by the usual army-officer participants, and they all went up to the Saya to dig out turpentine from the roots of the pine trees—needless to say, turpentine oil has dozens of uses, and like almost everything else it was in short supply during the war. Anyhow, I guess seeing the layout of the Saya gave the young pilots some ideas of their own, because after they returned to the house they were saying the best approach would be to 'liberate' a kamikaze plane at the airfield, make sure it was loaded with bombs, and then hide it somewhere around the Saya. You must remember that, at least; it was a major point of discussion."

"Well, it's not as if everything that went on at those drinking parties and meetings was clearly delineated in my dream, much less in my memory," I said, shaking my head. "Even today, I'm still puzzled by many of the things I overheard. For example, the lines from *The Golden*

*Bough* I read aloud a while ago were definitely circled in colored pencil by the Kochi Sensei, but I can't help wondering why he placed so
much emphasis on 'killing the living God' as a way of bringing rebirth
and prosperity to a country. Did he really think those precepts could be
applied directly to postwar realpolitik? I honestly don't know. I mean,
incendiary marginalia aside, there's no actual proof my father (or his
teacher) was reading *The Golden Bough* pragmatically, with the idea
that its ancient mythologies could be translated into action to help steer
this country's imperial system through the postwar morass of chaos and
disintegration. I know the others saw you as a kind of loyal retainer
whose main job was to warm the sake and keep everyone's cups filled,
but it's clear you were paying close attention to everything that went on
in those meetings. So what I'd like to ask you now, Daio, is whether the
group had a definite plan, in the form of a military strategy, to rescue
this country from its postwar predicament, and if so, whether my father
was the primary author of the plan."

"Yes, most definitely," Daio replied without hesitation. "At that
point the strategy sessions had become deadly serious, and given
the extent of your eavesdropping I'm surprised you even need to ask
about your father's role. He was the one who came up with the idea
of bombing the Imperial Palace, but the others took the idea and ran
with it, and some of the young military guys started talking about
blowing up the big meteoric rock at the Saya to create a landing strip
for the plane they were planning to steal. When he heard that, Choko
Sensei got very upset and started shouting things like 'What's this
nonsense about bombing the big rock? Do you really think I'm going
to let a bunch of outsiders come in and deface the Saya? That spot
isn't some flash-in-the-pan landmark from the Meiji Era or something.
It's been an important local site since olden times, and you can't just
waltz in and start blowing things up to build a temporary airstrip!' You
must have heard that tirade, right?"

"Yes, I did," I said. "To be honest, when I heard my father shouting I literally began to tremble. A moment later one of the officers
came out into the hall where I was standing, still shaking like a leaf,

and he said, 'Listen, kiddo, we're going to be talking about some important things from now on, so you'd better run along to the main house.' So I did.

"It was much later when my father returned, and while I was aware that he and my mother were talking in low voices, I was in my bedroom so I couldn't make out what they were saying. In retrospect I realize they were probably discussing my father's decision to run away in his little boat. As a mere child, I couldn't very well ask what was going on, but it was obvious the next day that my mother was helping my father get ready for a trip. At one point my father asked me to extract the tube from an old bicycle tire and blow it full of air, but that was nothing unusual. All day, from morning to evening, my chest seemed to be constricted with a vague feeling of anxiety, but I didn't know why. During that time the military guys were still quietly holed up in the outbuilding next door. The scene I remember so vividly—my father's departure on the stormy river—happened very late at night, long after my usual bedtime. I'm not sure what time it was, but . . ."

"So you didn't really understand what you overheard outside the meeting room!" Daio interjected. "I always used to wonder how much you knew. I even suspected you might be feigning ignorance, but now I realize that wasn't the case. Rather, I think your memories have been quarantined or frozen somewhere deep in your unconscious because the things you heard (the army officers clashing with your father about the Saya and so on) were just too confusing for your childish mind to deal with.

"Sorry, I don't mean to monopolize the conversation, but I want to explain my theory. First, under the guidance of his teacher in Kochi, your father read *The Golden Bough*, with special emphasis on the part about the tradition of killing the old king to protect the country from succumbing to decay and debilitation, and that gave him the idea of bombing the Imperial Palace. He was able to get the army officers on board with this rather extreme plan, at least at first, and they started to get excited about it (to say the least) during the two-day drinking party masquerading as a policy meeting. But I really don't think that discussion would have made sense to you, not only because you were an innocent child, but also because your formal education was based on the nationalistic, emperor-worshipping model. Actually, the thing that made the lightbulb go on in my head was seeing Unaiko's 'dog-tossing' dramatization of *Kokoro*. That really got me thinking. The Sensei character in *Kokoro* talks about the 'spirit of the age' or 'the spirit of the Meiji Era,' right? In any case, during the performance someone from the audience asked whether a person like Sensei, who had turned his back both on his own era and on society in general, could really be said to have been influenced by the spirit of his age to the point where he ended up taking his own life when the era came to an end. As you know, that sparked a major ruckus, with stuffed dogs flying through the air in all directions.

"Anyhow, that somehow made me think about you, Kogito. Your early education had a militaristic slant, so the 'spirit of the age' you grew up in demanded total allegiance to an emperor who was believed to be a god incarnate. (I don't believe a valid comparison can be drawn between those sentiments and the so-called spirit of Meiji Soseki wrote about, but that's another discussion for another day.)

"Fifteen years or so ago, you turned down the emperor's highest cultural award because of your unwavering belief in the principles of postwar democracy, and as a result my young disciples at the training camp (who were still totally committed to emperor worship) decided you were their archenemy. I think that was probably the motivation behind the practical joke they played, sending you a giant live turtle and telling you I was dead, but they could have just done it for mischief, pure and simple. As for me, I think if you're going to talk about Kogito Choko in terms of the spirit of an age, there are two distinct facets. The first half of the Showa Era you grew up in—in other words, until 1945—revolved around a godlike emperor, while the second half, after the war, was shaped by democratic principles. I think your personal trajectory reflects that as well.

"So we have a ten-year-old boy who was born in the first half of the era and who is, in effect, a poster child for that period in history.

This boy happens to overhear his father—whom he holds in great esteem—talking about a scheme in which some navy men, trained in piloting military aircraft, would stage a suicide attack to kill the living god—that is, the emperor. Does it really seem likely that a boy whose schooling was rooted in emperor-worshipping nationalism would be able to process such a radical idea? No, I think what young Kogito heard was so shocking that his conscious mind simply suppressed it. And the only thing the eavesdropping kid retained, indelibly lodged in his unconscious, was the image of the young pilots at the Saya practicing their takeoffs and landings—a fantasy scene he had only heard described through a wall. And there you have it: the source of your Saya dream. Of course, the additional details and embellishments were provided by your famously fertile imagination, which would later bear fruit in the form of novels, but mark my words: your imaginings were firmly based on things that were discussed in the meeting you were surreptitiously listening in on!"

Daio paused for a moment in triumph and then went on: "And so I've come to the conclusion that for you, as the unofficial representative of the spirit of the prewar half of the Showa Era, it was simply impossible to wrap your head around what you heard your father saying. On the one hand, your father was an outsider who had married into the village and had embraced many of the local traditions, and I think those stories had a deeper hold on his psyche than the ultranationalist dogma he was spouting to the young officers. The land around the Saya was considered by local folks to be the heart of the forest, so there was no way your father was going to let a bunch of young whippersnappers come charging in and tramp all over the ancient site, digging up the roots of the pine trees with pickaxes and trowels to get at the valuable turpentine, then adding insult to injury by proposing to raze that hallowed ground for use as an airstrip. That was the father you knew and looked up to. But on the other hand, from what you'd overheard it also sounded as if your father was the instigator of a crazy plan to kill the living god!

"I honestly believe your father was probably opposed to such radical tactics, in his heart, but maybe he had just reached a point where he felt the need for a grand symbolic act. So when it became clear that Japan was going to lose the war, he and his cohorts probably discussed a scenario wherein, if the emperor abdicated his throne, they would commit premeditated ritual suicide—you know, *junshi*. The truth is, Kogito, by the time your father reached the stage of talking about dispatching a kamikaze bomber to target the center of Tokyo, where the palace is, I think he had already resolved to end his own life, one way or another. I didn't have the courage to tell you this before, but I never thought Choko Sensei was the type of man who would live a long, uneventful life and die a peaceful death in his own bed. To be honest, I don't believe his drowning was an accident at all."

# 4

There we stood, Daio and I, leaning against the big meteoric rock. The sun was sinking in the west, and the new growth on the trees around the Saya was shrouded in a rosy-hued haze. As I gazed at the forest I was picturing a faraway scene in Frazer's ancient Forest of Nemi, where there wouldn't yet have been any sign of the multifarious foliage we associate with modern-day Italy—no bay laurels, no olives, no oleanders, no citrus trees—and only the beeches and oaks would be growing in abundance. I thought with pleasure of the charmingly archaic language Frazer used to describe those trees: *the beechwoods and oakwoods, with their deciduous foliage.* . . .

Daio, meanwhile, was pointing toward the bottom of the hill. "Hey, look, Ricchan's waving at us," he observed. "Akari's standing up as well, putting his cast back on by himself. I'm glad we were able to have this long chat, Kogito; I've been wanting to tell you some of these things for the longest time. When I heard from your mother that you were going away to college in Tokyo, I thought, *Well then, I'd better study really hard and make sure I become the kind of person who can carry on an intelligent conversation with Kogito when he comes back*, so I started taking correspondence courses right away, after you left. The tuition wasn't terribly expensive, but the students were also required to go up to Tokyo once a year for some classroom time, and your mother helped me with the fees. Of course, after the war ended I wanted to keep the training camp going as a tribute to your father's memory—after all, I was his number one disciple. As a result I was never able to live a normal life, and your mother was kind enough to sympathize with my situation."

Daio and I quickly traversed the grassy downhill slope below the Saya, which was now completely in the shade. When we reached the sandy shore of the river, Daio used his one sturdy arm to grab a large bag that Ricchan had just finished packing and hoisted it onto his shoulder. Akari, who had clearly benefited from his rehab exercises, picked up the Boston bag and started to walk toward the van, with Ricchan by his side to lend support if needed. I brought up the rear of our little procession, trudging along in silence and carrying nothing except the immeasurable weight of the things Daio had just told me.

Daio had no reason to share in my wordless reverie, and after a few moments he spoke. "Kogito, it occurred to me that more than half a century has passed since Choko Sensei died prematurely, at the age of fifty. Most of the people who knew your father are gone as well, including your mother—who was larger than life in her own right—but she died without ever having said anything regarding her husband, as far as I know. I mean, seriously, not a single word! Asa told me how disappointed you were when you finally got to open the red leather trunk, which should theoretically have contained the papers and correspondence your father left behind, and didn't find anything you could use. But on the bright side, as an indirect result of your discovery of the three volumes of *The Golden Bough*, I got to talk to you about some serious matters that have been weighing on my mind for years.

"I know I usually start blathering every time I meet up with you, while you seem to mostly listen in silence, and I'm always left with the feeling that I don't really know what's going on in your head. Actually, that's been the case ever since you were a high school sophomore, when you brought Goro Hanawa to visit us at the training camp. Even after the intense conversation you and I just had, I still have no idea what you're thinking, or feeling. Even so, it looks to me as though we're both remembering the events of the night your father drowned, over and over again . . . and of course you keep reliving it in your dreams as well.

"Oh, that reminds me. I know your mother told Asa that she thought your father had become frightened by what he'd gotten himself into, and that was why he tried to run away. (I gather you've listened to the recording she made?) Obviously, that isn't how I see it, and I was there. I guess you've been processing everything in your own silent, inscrutable way, but I have finally come to the conclusion that no matter how much we speculate about your father's motivations, no one will ever know for sure why he behaved as he did on that night. Maybe it's one of those riddles that can never be solved.

"Well, here I am rambling on again, but I remembered just now that the officers were saying some rather rude things behind Choko Sensei's back during those highly charged days before he died. And a word that cropped up more than once during those surreptitious conversations was *mononoke* (you know, in the sense of a supernatural spirit that possesses a living person). I wasn't familiar with the word at the time, but when I encountered it later I remember thinking, *Ah, so that's what those officers were whispering about.*

"Actually, on reflection, I used to hear that word in the officers' private conversations even during the earlier time when they were getting along relatively well with your father. In the beginning, your father rarely participated in the officers' discussions. But then he suddenly got very gung ho and vocal about everything, and he even went so far as to make the trek to the Kochi Sensei's house to talk things over with him.

"I remember what one of the officers said: 'As someone who was born and raised deep in this forest'—your father had deliberately given them that impression—'Old Man Choko gets all fired up about things to a degree that seems alarming to guys like us who were raised in cities and towns. It's almost as if he's been possessed by a spirit or a demon or a fox or something.' The officer added that a person like your father could get totally carried away by his ideas and turn into a loose cannon. During that meeting your father and the officers had a difference of opinion about their plan, and they reached an impasse. By the next morning everybody knew he was planning to run away in his little rowboat, but while he was making the preparations for his departure none of the military guys made any effort to stop him. It wasn't much past noon when they got into party mode and started drinking themselves silly, and they ordered me to fetch the red leather trunk. As I mentioned before, they somehow knew your father was planning to take it with him when he fled, and they obviously wanted to censor the contents and remove anything that might have incriminated them. Then around midnight you came over to the storehouse to retrieve the trunk.

"After your father left, I got a very clear sense that the military guys were all thinking that if your father rushed off in a panic and ended up drowning in the flooded river, it would be good riddance from their point of view, as long as he didn't leave any evidence behind to implicate them. That's why they didn't try to stop him from going. They even made a point of warning me, as a very junior member of the group, not to do anything to dissuade Choko Sensei from his rash plan, so I just had to watch him go. After I assured them he really had taken off in his rowboat, it seemed to set their minds at ease. They even went with me to look for Sensei's remains once it got light, since no one really expected him to survive his trip down the flooded river in the flimsy little boat.

"I'll never forget what one of the officers said to one of his young cohorts right about then. He was talking about your father's plan to steal a kamikaze bomber from the Yoshidahama airfield (an idea everyone had pretended to be enthusiastic about when it first came up) and he said, 'Of course, to us, the plan seemed like a big joke all along!' And then they both gave kind of a weak, mean-spirited laugh—I guess you'd call it a snigger. I still can't forgive those two officers, although I suppose both of them are probably long since dead and gone.

"Only . . . I don't mean to go on and on about this, but I can't get it out of my mind. I really think the two of us—you still having the same dream after all these years, and me still obsessed with trying to figure out the truth about that night—are the only people left in the world who can even spare a thought for Choko Sensei anymore!"

At this point, I remembered a question I had been wanting to ask. "Daio, you seem to have very lucid memories about the night of the big flood and the following morning, but what about the red leather trunk I took to my father when he was already on board the boat? Do you know how much time elapsed before that trunk was finally returned to my mother?"

"Oh, the trunk," Daio said. "Yeah, apparently it floated downstream and finally washed ashore a few kilometers past the spot where the boat capsized. It was retrieved by some fishermen and taken to the police station, and eventually (it could have been weeks, or months) the cops went to your house and returned it to your mother. As for the letters and papers that were inside, those had already been sifted through and censored by the officers. Whether the war had ended in victory or defeat for Japan, there was nothing left in the trunk to raise a warning flag for anyone on any side. No incriminating evidence at all—the officers made sure of that. Of course during that time of crisis, with the Occupation and whatnot, those local policemen certainly didn't have time to be poring over an English-language edition of *The Golden Bough* looking for evidence of subversive activities! Until recently the only people who had seen inside the trunk in recent memory were your mother and your sister, as far as I know. And even though the trunk had been more or less sanitized by the officers, I guess those two strong women decided to keep the remaining contents out of your hands to avoid any possible negative repercussions from the drowning novel you wanted to write. In retrospect, maybe they were being overly cautious, but I guess they felt it was important to try to protect the family name from any hint of scandal."

Daio paused for a moment, then continued. "Choko Sensei was—
and still is—the most important teacher I've ever had, but to be honest, I hold your mother in even higher esteem. In my personal ranking
system, she's at the very top, above your father. From the time you were
a child, I always believed you were no ordinary person. But since we're
ranking things, I'm sure you know your mother always thought Asa was
a more balanced human being than you are, in a practical sense, and I
think she died happy, knowing that Asa would outlive us all.

"I remember your mother used to say that in the House of Choko,
the women never fail to outshine the men. Apparently it's been true
going back to your grandmother's time. Or if you wanted to go even
further, maybe you could include Meisuke's mother. Your mother
always said she might have been a distant relative of yours!"

# PART THREE

# These Fragments I Have Shored Against My Ruins

# Chapter 12

# All About Kogii

## 1

Very early one morning I heard the sound of something stirring outside, behind the Forest House. After lying awake, listening, for the better part of an hour, I finally got out of bed and ventured downstairs.

Masao Anai was standing in the back garden, gazing intently at the large, round poetry stone, and it occurred to me that this was the first time I'd seen him during my current sojourn in the forest. Masao raised his head and looked at me calmly, but his expression seemed to bear a tinge of disappointment. (My phrasing may be a trifle disingenuous, since I had been directly responsible for dashing his hopes.) At the same time, I discerned a kind of pellucid freshness in his gaze, as if he might be ready to let bygones be bygones and begin anew. When I caught Masao's eye, through the window, I got the sense that he was picking up a similarly positive vibration from me.

I glanced at the small clock on the kitchen counter and saw that it was only five A.M. Then I set to work brewing four cups of fresh coffee in the coffeemaker Maki had recently sent down from the house in Tokyo; the amount was based on my expectation of visiting with Masao for the time it took to drink two large cups apiece. Ricchan was asleep in the west wing of the house, while Akari was in his room upstairs, and I knew no one else was likely to be up and about for another couple of hours, at least.

When Masao came inside, I caught a strong whiff of tobacco. He didn't make any move to light up another cigarette, and I surmised that he had been lingering in front of the poetry stone for the primary purpose of having one last smoke before entering the house. Typically for him, Masao didn't bother to break the ice with anything resembling the customary "long time no see" greetings. Instead, he resumed our conversation where we had left off, jumping right back into a topic he had evidently been continuing to think about during the intervening months.

"Lately Unaiko and Ricchan have been spending a lot of time here, pouring all their energy into the new project, so I've been holding down the fort at our headquarters in Matsuyama by myself," he began. "I've kept busy taking inventory and getting organized, and in the process I reviewed all the works of yours that we've converted into stage plays so far."

"Asa was saying how sorry she was your plan for dramatizing the drowning novel in conjunction with my own work on that book came to naught because of what happened on my part," I said by way of indirect apology.

"Well, this has turned out to be the end of an era for us, so it's given me a good chance to reflect and gain some perspective," Masao said graciously. "Until now, converting Kogito Choko's fiction into stage plays has been the mainstay of our work, which has caused some theater critics to suggest facetiously that the Caveman Group ought to change its name to something like 'the People Who Live in the Cave of Kogito Choko.' You know, the usual sarcasm and cheap plays on words.

"If your drowning novel had been completed, we were planning to find a way of combining it with whatever we had cooked up along the way to create a kind of contrapuntal synergy, to put it in musical terms. Capping off our 'Choko phase' with a big finale would have been a great way to thumb our noses at those cynical critics. Unaiko was approaching the project from a different angle, as usual, and some of the younger guys were talking about staging what they called 'a living wake for Kogito Choko' and using that as a selling point. I only heard the rough outlines, but I gathered it would have been a sort of retrospective.

"Anyway, as you may recall, the opening scene we had sketched out, before the whole project went to hell in a handbasket, depicted the launching of your father's little rowboat onto the flooded river. That scene was inspired by your recurrent dream, so if the critics had wanted to make rude remarks about the Caveman Group's dependence on the works of Kogito Choko . . . well, they might have had a valid point. It's all moot now, of course, and today I'm more interested in discussing your uncanny alter ego, Kogii, who was in the boat with your father. As you know, we were going to give the vision physical form by making a Kogii doll and suspending it in the air above the stage, and even now, I still find myself wondering how that might have turned out. That's actually what moved me to drop by this morning to talk to you.

"This may sound like a simplistic question," Masao wound up, "but in the final analysis, what exactly *was* Kogii to you, anyway? Do you by any chance feel like kicking that question around for a while?"

"Sure, why not?" I said. "After all, you and your colleagues in the Caveman Group are the first people who have ever been willing to believe Kogii might actually have existed! When I was a child, no one else supported me the way you do. If I happened to mention matter-of-factly that Kogii was 'right over there, right now,' all I ever got in return was a giant dose of ridicule and teasing. I mean, some people pretended to believe, but I think they were just having fun at my expense. In the poem etched into the stone out back, when my mother mentions Kogii she appears to be referring to my childhood nickname. However, I believe she's also talking in a subtle but unmistakable way about Akari. That's evident, at least to me, from the way she says, *You didn't get Kogii ready. . . .* Going up into the forest is obviously a metaphor for dying, and I'm certain she was chiding me for not having done enough to prepare Akari for death, in case he doesn't outlive me.

"But when I talked about the recurrent dream, you folks came up with the idea of having Kogii appear early on as a sort of mannequin hovering over the boat as it takes off down the flooded river. I took that as a heartening sign, since it seemed to indicate that you weren't dismissing Kogii as a phantom or something I hallucinated."

"I guess it's just what you might call my director's habit, but I created a kind of questionnaire about Kogii," Masao said. "Of course, when we learned that the drowning novel was out of the picture we had to stop working on our dramatization of the story, so these notes don't have any practical application at this point. Even so, would you mind answering a few questions, just to resolve this gestalt for me?"

Before I'd had a chance to nod my assent, the ever-confident Masao had already opened the jumbo-size notebook balanced on his knees.

# 2

**Masao:** Mr. Choko, you've mentioned that the existence of your alter ego, Kogii, wasn't acknowledged by the people around you, but in the course of her research Ricchan has run into a number of people who have said they remember hearing that you had a constant companion who was called 'Kogii,' like you, although no one ever actually saw the other child. One of those people was a classmate of yours who has become a leader of the farmers in the region, and another one—also a classmate, unsurprisingly—is a member of the family who owns the medical clinic in town. However, there wasn't anybody who could say when Kogii first appeared, or how you and he met. It wasn't her fault, of course, but Ricchan seems to feel that not having been able to interview your mother about a number of things—the uprising, and Kogii, and so on—has left some lamentable gaps in her research.

As I mentioned during our first conversation, we had won a prize and were embarking on the next stage of our group's artistic evolution when I turned my attention to Kogii. I reread all your essays, hoping to find his first appearance. I mean, surely the initial encounter with a mystical being would be one of the major treasures in a child's box of memories, right? I thought the evidence I was searching for must be hidden away somewhere in your published work, but I kept striking out. When it came to Kogii's departure there was an abundance of detailed accounts, yet I couldn't find a single description of how or when he first arrived on the scene. Ultimately, I concluded that by the time you became conscious of yourself as an entity living in this world, Kogii must already have been by your side.

We know Kogii couldn't be seen by anyone but you. However, you always behaved as if you had a constant companion who was exactly like you—an identical twin, for all intents and purposes. I heard about it from your sister, Asa. She also told me that Kogii was your one and only playmate, so apparently you didn't even interact with your only sister very often. She said she would often see you engaged in conversation, chattering at the invisible Kogii and then seeming to strain your ears to hear his reply, and she figured your friend must be telling you secrets about what went on in the realm of the forest. She thought the whole concept of Kogii must somehow have been overlaid with (or even inspired by) the folktales you children had heard from your mother and grandmother: the mythology of the forest that has shaped so many of your novels. You've written about a scenario in which kids go into the woods to play hide-and-seek, and both the hiders and the seekers became lost children who are still wandering deep in the forest to this day. Evidently Asa was intrigued by that dark fable, and she pestered your mother to tell her more, but your mom claimed not to know anything about it. Then when Asa suggested you might have invented the story on your own, your mother said that she didn't think you would be able to make up such a sophisticated tale from scratch, so it was probably something you had heard from your grandmother. Then she went on to say that maybe when you were having all those intense conversations with a companion no one else could see, your pal was telling you stories. But then your mother added that, joking aside, it seemed likely you'd heard the story about the lost children from someone who had intimate knowledge of the forest. So what I'm wondering is, would it be accurate to say that Kogii's main reason for existing was to keep you informed about whatever might be going on in the forest?

**Kogito:** Yes, that's correct.

**Masao:** Okay, good. So this brings us to the day when Kogii goes off and leaves you behind. You're standing on the wraparound verandah outside the back parlor of your house by the river. Kogii is beside you, as usual, but then he suddenly leaps onto the balustrade. By the time you realize what's happening, Kogii has taken off, spreading his arms like wings and floating through the air until he's just above the midpoint of the river. From there he wafts high up into the forest and vanishes from sight. And that was how you came to lose your beloved doppelgänger.

**Kogito:** Yes, that's exactly what happened. There's really no way around it: Kogii simply went away and left me in the lurch.

**Masao:** However, Kogii did come down from the forest on one other occasion. It was a full-moon night and you were lying awake, unable to sleep, when you heard what sounded like some sort of signal. When you went out the front door of your house, Kogii was standing there illuminated by the moon. Without saying a word he began walking away, heading up the road into the forest, with you following close behind as the rain began to fall. The next thing you knew, Kogii was nowhere to be seen and you were caught in a torrential downpour.

Now, what strikes me as important about the events of that moonlit night is the fact that even though we have never heard that Kogii came from such-and-such a place, it seems clear that on this evening he came down from the forest. Oh, and there's another thing: the internal conflicts you had as a child. When Kogii climbed up on the railing and floated across the river, if you'd had the courage to follow him right then—walking through the air to the center of the river, and then spreading your own arms as if they were wings—maybe you would have been able to ascend into the forest, too. But you were a coward, so you missed your big opportunity. Later, while you were brooding in your dark little bedroom, sick at heart and awash in vain regrets, Kogii came down from the forest and gave you another chance. That's what you were thinking when you went eagerly traipsing after him, isn't it?

**Kogito:** That's exactly right.

**Masao:** However, after you'd followed Kogii into the forest, he disappeared and you ended up getting stranded by a huge rainstorm. The firemen said that the reason you stayed there overnight was because the forest road had turned into a river. (I can't help feeling that there was some special significance to their choice of words, given the way your father died.) Anyway, they refused to go and rescue you. You sought shelter in the hollow of a Castanopsis tree, and before long you began to run a high fever. If you had spent another night exposed to the elements, you would almost certainly have died. It seems possible that both times Kogii invited you to follow him, he was acting as an intermediary for the Other Side, trying to lead you to an early grave. I mean, when he took off in the air above the river—if you had tried to emulate his flying motion, like some wingless Icarus, you could easily have hit your head on a rock on the bottom of the river and died.

So on both of those occasions you managed to stay alive, but the second time you lost your best friend, Kogii, forever. While you were recovering from your illness and your condition was still touch and go, you felt very alone and frightened. Your mother felt sorry for you, and that was when she told you the story of Meisuke's mother, including the reassuring line about how there's no need to worry, because even if you were to die, she would just give birth to you again. Isn't that what happened?

**Kogito:** Yes, that's the gist of it, except that as I recall my mother spoke those words in the local dialect.

**Masao:** Anyway, if you had remained in that hollow tree for much longer you would probably have crossed over to the Other Side, with Kogii as your spirit guide, and the two of you could have been together forever. To me, it seems perfectly reasonable that you would have felt some ambivalence or even regret about the way things turned out—that is, about being rescued. In one of the books you wrote for children, I think the scene where you and your mother talk about mortality and rebirth is really a beautiful thing.

**Kogito:** . . . [silence]

**Masao:** And then when you were ten years old, you watched your father take off down the flooded river in his little boat. You weren't with him, even though that was supposedly the plan when you set out from your house. Instead, next to your father, in the place where you thought you yourself should have been standing, you saw your alter ego, Kogii. And for the past sixty-some years you've been dreaming and redreaming the same scene, over and over again. The third time's the charm, as they say, and isn't it a fact that even now you're still thinking, *If only I had gone with my father . . . ?*

**Kogito:** Yes, that sounds about right.

**Masao:** So for me, at least, it seems as if you were hoping to use the drowning novel to rewrite history and reverse the outcome of the scene. I think you were imagining that even if it was only in a book, you might be able to invent a scene in which you and Kogii were working together to help your father. The author of the drowning novel is also the "I" who appears throughout the story, and if you tried to tell me that type of narrative device would be impossible to depict onstage, my response would be, "Well then, I'll just create a third-person hero and dramatize the scene that way!" There are all sorts of other possibilities, too, but the problem is you've abandoned the project. I know you said giving up was your only option after the contents of the red leather trunk turned out to be useless, but I can't help wondering whether you might simply have lost the courage to even try to create the authentic type of late work E. W. Said talks about in *On Late Style*, as a final endeavor in the life of an artist. You know: thrillingly catastrophic work that manages to overturn and surpass all the creations that went before?

**Kogito:** You may very well be right about that, too.

# 3

Unaiko's time in Tokyo as an assistant director—and, unexpectedly, as a lead actress—had finally come to an end. After checking in at the Caveman Group's headquarters in Matsuyama she hopped in the company van, with Masao Anai at the wheel, and headed down to the Forest House. It was obvious at a glance that Unaiko's four weeks of working on a play at a major theater in Tokyo had been an emotional roller coaster, and even now that she was back in familiar surroundings she seemed still to be on the wild ride, with its exaggerated highs and lows. The moment she walked through the door the words started tumbling out, and she went on talking nonstop while we were assembling in the great room.

"The play we were doing was inspired by the *Heike Monogatari*," Unaiko enthused, naming one of the most famous narratives in classical Japanese literature. "However, it took a very popular approach, focusing on the heroic Kiyomori and also incorporating material from *The Poetic Memoirs of Lady Daibu*, which came later. As for the role I ended up playing—I kept thinking you might find this interesting and amusing, Mr. Choko—it was, quite literally, weird. In the script, the only description of my part was the single word 'medium.' The director told me a character like that appears in volume three of the *Heike Monogatari*, and he described *yorimashi* (meaning a medium or channeler) as a sort of spiritual nickname. But because that was the only background he provided, I didn't have any kind of concrete understanding of the character. The guy who was playing the role of Kiyomori is also quite well known as a highbrow intellectual who frequently pops up on TV as a talking head, so I asked him for advice, but he just said, 'Why don't you look it up in the dictionary?' That seemed rather cold at the time, but it actually turned out to be a helpful suggestion. I called and asked Ricchan to check the big dictionary you keep on the filing cabinet in your study, and she made a copy of the pertinent page and sent it to me."

Unaiko reached into her handbag for a giant notebook—a virtual duplicate of Masao's omnipresent vade mecum—and extracted two photocopied sheets from between the pages. One depicted the front cover of my *Iwanami Dictionary of Archaic Japanese*, while the other was a replica of the page that included a definition of *yorimashi*.

Unaiko passed the page to me, and I proceeded to read the definition aloud. "*Usually when a soothsayer—it could be a mountain ascetic, or an esoteric Buddhist priest—offers a summoning prayer to invoke a certain deity or spirit, that entity will take possession of a medium. The medium is frequently a child with paranormal gifts who has been brought in to serve as the mouthpiece for the divine message or revelation from the god or spirit. That type of channeler is called a* yorimashi."

After I had finished reading, I continued in my own words. "Suppose, for example, that a highborn lady is suffering in childbirth. Based on the assumption that the problem is caused by an evil spirit or spirits, an attempt will be made to pacify it, or them. In order to appease a supernatural spirit, it first has to be summoned and provided with a voice through some sort of medium. In the exorcistic prayer chants mountain ascetics use for that purpose, the person who serves as a mediumistic mouthpiece is called a *yorimashi*. The young empress Kenreimon, who as you mentioned later became the tragic Lady Daibu, was the daughter of Kiyomori, of the Taira clan. The characters onstage represent some of the most powerful people of the era."

"That's totally true," Unaiko said. "And the angry spirits that possessed me, as the medium, were nothing to sneeze at, either: cosmic heavy hitters, so to speak. As you probably know, there's a whole slew of different terms for the disembodied entities I was channeling: departed souls, hungry ghosts, angry spirits, or whatever you want to call them."

"Sometimes the spirit of someone who's still alive will appear through a medium as well," I said. "For example, the irate spirit of a priest named Shunkan who eventually died in exile on Kikaigashima— Devil's Island—after having been banished there by Kiyomori."

"That's right!" Unaiko agreed. "Anyway, there are tons of spirits floating in the ether, and since we were on a tight budget I had to take on the job of portraying the different specters by myself. The basic concept was to create a classical version of our dog-tossing plays, so I did a fair amount of over-the-top ranting and raving along the way! The author of the play kindly took a liking to the idiosyncratic spin I put on it in rehearsals, and he even went to the trouble of writing a bunch of extra lines to clarify the lineage of the spirits, but it still took some fancy footwork for me to play all those different parts. When the author and director created the role—by which I mean those roles, plural—they were apparently visualizing the medium as a woman, but I managed to persuade them to let me portray the character as a young boy."

"I think that was incredibly perceptive of you," I said. "In one of my more arcane dictionaries, I noticed that the word *yorimashi* has etymological and mythological connotations of 'a dead child.' The kanji in question means 'dead' or 'cadaver,' and if you write it in its primitive pictographic form, it looks like this," I explained as I drew a shape that resembled a turkey's wishbone, or an extremely abstract human form, on the nearest scrap of paper.

"Oh, that's adorable!" Unaiko exclaimed. "Actually, when I was brainstorming the role I used a certain someone as my model, and it was—"

"Kogii!" Masao jumped in, excitedly finishing Unaiko's sentence for her. "Or rather, the Kogii doll that was hanging over our rehearsal space."

"Exactly!" Unaiko exclaimed. "The Kogii doll was my inspiration, so at least the time we spent groping around for a way to dramatize the drowning novel wasn't entirely in vain."

"Since Unaiko's still pretty amped from her experience on the big stage of Tokyo, this seems like as good a time as any to take a look at her artistic plans from here on out," Masao said. "By the way," he went on, "we're very grateful for your generous financial sponsorship of Unaiko's first solo flight—venturing out of the nest of the Caveman Group—and, of course, we greatly appreciate Chikashi's and Asa's support, too, especially the way they exercised their powers of persuasion on you! The Caveman Group has been on a temporary hiatus ever since our collaboration came to a halt, but I think this unforeseen confluence of circumstances has created a crucial make-or-break opportunity for Unaiko: a chance to try her wings in a big way. You've probably heard from Ricchan that they already have a solid plan in place, and it's looking as if the first offering of Unaiko's new group will be a stage-play version of the movie *Meisuke's Mother Marches Off to War*—filtered through her trademark 'dog-tossing' template, of course. Even while she was madly running around in Tokyo, Unaiko has been thinking about this nonstop, and Ricchan has been doing her part down here by conducting background interviews and so on.

"When Unaiko asked Asa for advice on how to involve you in the project, Asa said that rather than standing at the crossroads of crisis and opportunity, as the saying goes, you were smack-dab in the middle of a crisis phase, and she thought it would be better not to pester you about anything just yet. She said she would be more than willing to provide guidance for the project, and she added that she would be happy to try to bring you into the fold after she returned. Anyway, Ricchan has been chronicling the progress on this end in a daily journal, and it struck me that it might be a good idea for everyone who is involved in this project—or at least the people who'll be coming to the Forest House to work on it—to read Ricchan's notes. I'd especially like for you to take a look at them, Mr. Choko, and I would be grateful if you could do it now, as a favor to all of us."

# 4

*I've been given the assignment of keeping a daybook, and I'm writing these entries in full awareness of the fact that they will eventually be read by Mr. Choko, who is old enough to be my father (at least). However, I'm also writing with the intention of making these notes available to any members of our troupe who might find their way into the rehearsal area of the Forest House. Since (unlike a diary) these pages are not for my eyes only, I will inevitably exercise a certain degree of self-censorship, but I would still like to try to write as freely and spontaneously as possible. I'm resigned to the fact that some readers may feel baffled by the inclusion of certain personal matters, and I may very well express some controversial views, but there's nothing I can do about that. Needless to say, I hope all the readers will feel free to note their complaints or dissenting opinions right in the margins of these pages.*

*I'd like to start by talking about Unaiko. While she was working in Tokyo we kept in close touch by telephone, and one day I told her about how, out of the blue, Akari had shown me his copy of the final-draft screenplay for the film about Meisuke's mother. With her usual focus, Unaiko immediately wanted to know how a certain pivotal scene had been put together. The scene in question shows the injured folk heroine being carried back to the village on an old storm shutter repurposed as a makeshift stretcher, and trying to figure out how to dramatize the final scene onstage has turned out to be a thorny problem. At present we're trying to juggle the shooting script for the film along with Mr. Choko's own notes from when he first agreed to get involved with that project and the rough draft he hammered out in the form of a novel before even starting the screenplay. Using those materials as a jumping-off point, I've been trying to create a new script in our own dramatic style. I've been agonizing over the best way to tell the story, and the pieces are just beginning to fall into place.*

*In the movie, as a narrative device to move the action along, the spirit of the late Meisuke's mother appears and chants in a melodic, singsongy way, while the story of the second uprising unfolds on the screen. However, the movie wasn't one-dimensional by any means, and it utilized a large variety of techniques and a number of different locations. For instance, in the scenes featuring the spirit or ghost of Meisuke's mother, the musical base is a revival of the kind of old-style samisen accompaniment we associate with Kabuki. That seems to jibe with the first-person accounts I've heard from people who participated in the filming, mostly as extras. Mr. Choko's grandmother and mother started things off, right after Japan lost the war, by mounting a stage production at the local playhouse. Much later, when Sakura became involved, the play was reenacted on a specially constructed stage at the Saya, and the performance was informally recorded on film, just for reference. The next step was to create a feature film that would be a full-fledged period drama. The basic story, in every version, is about the cruel oppression of the farmers in this area by the local feudal clan. A charismatic young farmer named Meisuke leads the first uprising in response to that tyrannical treatment, and it is a success. After the victory, however, Meisuke is captured by the losing faction and imprisoned in the clan-operated*

*jail, where he becomes desperately ill. In an important scene,
Meisuke's mother (who is still young and attractive) visits her
son in jail. As she is leaving, she bids farewell to her ailing
son in a deeply affectionate way, speaking the famous lines:
"There's no need to worry—even if you die, I'll just give birth to
you again."*

*The next scene features a reprise of the recitative by
Meisuke's mother's ghost or spirit, in which she tells us how, a
decade and a half after the first uprising, the local farmers once
again find themselves in exceedingly dire straits. On that occasion
as well, those brave souls aren't willing to knuckle under without a fight. At this point in the filmscript, the spirit of Meisuke's
mother stands up from the platform where she has been chanting,
suddenly transformed back into a real, live person. A moment later
she is joined by Meisuke II, the young boy who is widely believed
to be the reincarnation of her late son, Meisuke (the hero of the
first uprising). There are a number of female farmers surrounding
Meisuke's mother, wailing and shaking their bodies in an apparent display of sympathy. Now they line up along the proscenium,
and as they drop to their knees and gaze at their leader, Meisuke's
mother begins the famous battle cry:*

*Women warriors, let us go
Off to face our latest foe.
Into battle we will soar
Strong and brave forevermore.
All together, here we go
We shall vanquish every foe!*

*The women join in, singing along, and they begin to dance
as well. Hoisting their primitive armaments—bamboo spears,
pointed sticks, and the like—the village women shuffle around
until they're in a perfectly regimented formation. Then the group
goes marching off to battle, led by Meisuke II and his mother.*

*The screenplay doesn't show what happens to Meisuke's
mother and her son following the successful uprising. (According to legend, they were set upon by a gang of masterless samurai
who raped Meisuke's mother after they had thrown her young
son into a hole in the ground and stoned him to death.) Instead,
in the filmed version, we're back on the platform at the Saya,
and the ghost of Meisuke's mother is sitting there relating the
tale of the victorious uprising. She tells us that the country is
in the throes of a major reconstruction, and the adversary who
was vanquished in the second uprising wasn't the despotic clan,
but rather some troops sent from Tokyo by the administrator in
charge of the area. While the triumphant insurrectionists were
raising a flag of victory over their base camp at Okawara, the
government administrator committed suicide in shame and the
interlopers slunk away with their tails between their legs.*

*As the majestic voice of Meisuke's mother seems to take
flight, the camera is borne along with it, pulling up into a crane-
shot panorama of the stunning scenery of the Saya and beyond.
The entire mountain is ablaze with colorful autumn leaves. We
see Meisuke's mother leading a horse with Meisuke II riding
astride, and we watch as they ascend a steep, narrow path into
the forest, occasionally emerging from behind the trees and then
vanishing once more, but we never see the depraved samurai
who are lying in wait to ambush them. After a moment the
theme music—one of Beethoven's piano sonatas—kicks in, and
then over the music we hear the voice of a woman wailing "Aah,
aah" in agony and anguish. The background music grows ever
louder, and then the words "THE END" appear on the screen.*

I gave Unaiko a quick synopsis of this sequence over the
phone. Then later, after I'd sent her a copy of the shooting script,
she read the whole thing from beginning to end, and this is what
she said to me during our next phone convo:

"When Sakura's wailing voice suddenly rends the air in
the final scene, I found it intensely sad. I also think, without a

doubt, that her heartfelt cry represents the misery and suffering of all the women who have been raped on an unbroken continuum from the time of Meisuke's mother until today. I mean, you have to keep in mind that the film was made to give expression to Sakura's own traumatic memories of being sexually abused as a young girl. So why do I feel compelled to turn it into another 'dog-tossing' play? I think it's because I identify so strongly with this story on a personal level, and I want to dramatize its terrible, timeless realities openly and honestly, with my own body, rather than merely suggesting the hideous acts of violence by the faraway sound of someone keening offstage."

While Unaiko was speaking, I just listened in silence. I felt somehow as if she had abandoned me as a collaborator and was going off by herself to explore some private, uncharted realm. For some reason I thought about how, after the uprising had been won, Meisuke's mother and her son split off from their female followers and headed into the forest, on their way back to the village. Since the feudal structure had been abolished, a great many young samurai had banded together in gangs of freelance thugs, and they were hiding out between the former castle town and a high mountain pass, lying in wait to cause whatever violent mischief they could. At that moment I felt as disenfranchised as those young outlaws, but Unaiko didn't seem to notice.

"Look, I can see that it would have been inappropriate to show a graphic rape as the ending of a movie with this kind of soft, elegiac tone," she continued. "But even so, the denouement of the tragedy, in the original stage version produced here after the war, was the scene where Meisuke's mother sat onstage and told that dreadful story as a recitative, right? I'm sure you've heard about how, after the war ended, Mr. Choko's mother and grandmother made a nice pile of money by selling their stock of paperbush bark on the black market. (The bark was no longer being used to make paper currency, but it was still in demand for making paper, which was one of many scarce commodities

*in those postwar days.) Anyway, they used some of their profits
to stage a play at the little playhouse in the valley, and apparently every time the battle cry was invoked the audience went
nuts and joined in, and the interactive chanting seems to have
enabled the postwar women from around here to feel a visceral
connection with their ancestors who had taken part in the uprising some eighty years earlier. Of course, this was during a period
when all the menfolk were struggling to come to terms with the
mortifying fact that Japan had lost the war.*

*"In the same spirit, let's hope it will cheer Mr. Choko up
to work with us as we try to dramatize the connection between
ourselves, as modern-day women, and the brave women who carried out the uprising," Unaiko said before we hung up. "I'd love
it if we could give one last chance at creative fulfillment to the
aging author who's still tormenting himself after all these years,
asleep and awake, because he wasn't able to save his father from
drowning!"*

# 5

Clearly, Ricchan's journal entries had been composed in the conscious
knowledge that they would eventually be read by Unaiko and by me.
Even so, I found them quite illuminating. One day I took Unaiko aside
to talk about this, and she happened to mention that she was trying
to respect Asa's request not to pressure me into becoming involved
in a new undertaking until I was ready. By then, though, I didn't see
any way (or, really, any reason) to refuse.

When the young troupe members heard I was on board with
Unaiko's project, they were gratifyingly happy. What struck me as
remarkable was that they (Suke & Kaku, in particular) didn't want
me to simply take the original screenplay and adapt it into a stage
play. Using Ricchan's fieldwork as a jumping-off point, they wanted
to see Unaiko's personal vision brought to life, thus transforming the

filmscript into an entirely new play. The rehearsal space had over-flowed from the great room into the dining room as well, and that area became the main forum for discussing the project.

My initial participation consisted primarily of recalling details from my own script for the long-ago movie—scenes that hadn't made the final cut. Ironically, the desire to share those very details with the world had been a large part of my original motivation for agreeing to participate in Sakura's film.

I threw myself into creating a script to showcase the youthful, inventive style of this new offshoot of the Caveman Group. To that end, I resolved to tear apart all my carefully constructed materials, then reassemble them in a synthesized form that would be more compatible with the dog-tossing dynamic. I also set about removing all my personal materials—index cards, notebooks, and dictionaries—from the long bench in the great room to show my commitment to the project.

I was in the process of carrying those things upstairs when Unaiko, dressed in a professional-looking power suit, walked into the great room. She strode up to where I was standing with my arms full of books and said in a loud, accusatory tone, "What's the world coming to if young folks can't even lend a hand to help a senior citizen with the heavy lifting, especially when he's going to be kindly donating his time to assist us?"

Apparently Masao and the other troupe members hadn't noticed that I was engaged in removing my personal items, in response to someone's tactful suggestion that the great room might be more effi-ciently used for our collaborative efforts if it were a bit tidier. Unaiko briskly took charge of transporting my multivolume set of the fac-simile edition of *The Golden Bough*, pausing only to introduce me to a stranger who had come in a few minutes after she did. The man was dressed in a gray corduroy jacket worn over a high-collared black shirt and he projected a rather different public persona from Masao and the other young troupers, but I got the impression from the way they greeted him that he had already been assimilated into the group.

"This is my significant other," Unaiko said casually. "He moon-lights as a theater critic, but he also has a regular job. He came down to Matsuyama on business, and I went to pick him up at the airport. He has to go back to Tokyo on the evening flight, so I drove him down here hoping he could have a chance to visit with you, however briefly.

"How about it, Mr. Choko? I've heard you don't let many people into your inner sanctum, but since this whole area is pretty much engulfed in chaos, would you be amenable to heading upstairs and having a little chat in your study? My guy here has a particular interest in the spaces where writers do their work. I think it might be partly because I told him about the time Asa gave me a guided tour of the bookshelves at your house in Tokyo."

The new arrival (whose name I had yet to learn) gathered up the remaining books, while I grabbed the last few index cards and then led the way upstairs. Fortunately, Ricchan had found the time to put my bed in order, even though she'd had to take Akari to the Saya extra early that day.

In the room that doubled as my study and sleeping quarters there were windows facing north and south, and the room was flooded with light. The entire west wall was lined with bookshelves, with a large desk in front. When I was working I usually sat in a reclining chair with my feet propped on the desk chair and a drafting board balanced on my knees. Of course, these days all I was doing up here was reading, more or less aimlessly.

I dragged the reclining chair toward the southern wall and sat down. Gesturing at the desk chair, I said to the guest, "Please have a seat," and he did. Unaiko, meanwhile, grabbed a footstool I used whenever I needed to reach something on the top shelves of the floor-to-ceiling bookcase and carried it over to complete our little circle.

"Would it be all right if I took a look at the books on that shelf?" the young man asked, pointing. Unaiko started to get up from her perch on the stool, but he put a restraining hand on her shoulder, then strolled to the bookcase. The shelf in question held a collection of my early and midcareer novels, and while the books weren't all first editions they were from some of the earliest printings of each title. (I actually preferred the textures and colors of the covers of some of the earlier books to those of my more recent publications.)

"I started to read your books a short time before you won that big international literary prize," the young man said. "This is kind of a funny story, but I happened to see in the newspaper that Kogito Choko had stopped writing fiction, and I somehow misunderstood and thought you had died. Anyway, the 'obituary' moved me to go out and buy paperbacks of all your backlist novels and read them for the first time, one by one. Because of that, I've never even seen most of these early books in hardcover, but just glancing at the titles brings back some pleasant memories for me."

"From the beginning, even with the early books, I always chose the designer, and the handwritten calligraphy for the titles was done by Goro Hanawa," I said. "In addition to being a famous filmmaker he was an exceptional calligrapher, and he was well known for his beautiful book designs."

"For one of your earlier novels, *In Our Time*, the bookbinding was done in France, and I really liked the look of the title page, with the blind stamping of calligraphic kanji rendered by your mentor, Professor Musumi. I remember seeing the book on my father's bookshelf."

While the newcomer was talking, Unaiko jumped up and quickly pulled an extra copy of that book from the shelf. I used autographing the title page as an excuse to ask his name. "It's Tatsuo Katsura," he said, "but everyone calls me Katsura."

"This makes me so happy!" he said a few moments later as he watched me sign the artistically blind-stamped page. "Back in the day, once I'd finished playing catch-up by reading your earlier works in paperback, whenever you published a new novel—in other words, every few years—I would read it as soon as it came out. I guess you could call me a fan, but because I didn't start reading your books until I was in my thirties, I never got the feeling the author's message was aimed directly at me. Putting my own experiences aside, isn't it a fact that during the past twenty years or so, especially, you haven't really been making an effort to write books that would appeal to a younger audience? To be honest, I can't help getting the impression that you don't really give a damn about being widely read.

"For example, let's talk about one of your more recent books, *The Chilling and Killing of the Beautiful Annabel Lee*. It begins with an outdoor scene in which a corpulent old writer (who is obviously meant to be you) and his equally fat, middle-aged son are out walking together. It's immediately clear, at least to me, that the son (who, we're told, was born with some cognitive difficulties) is supposed to be Akari. I found it interesting to read about the vagaries of making a film with an international consortium back in the 1970s, even though it was before my time. As a general rule I'm dubious about the idea that certain readers will automatically feel a bond with the author just because they're from the same generation, or be put off if they aren't, but both those bits of conventional wisdom are surely true in many cases, and I realize that generational demographics do have an impact on book sales."

"Well," Unaiko said, "it's certainly true there's a generation or two between me and Sakura, the international movie star who plays a big role in the book, but I still found her character very engaging on a personal level."

"Point taken," Katsura said. "I'll freely admit that with the *Annabel Lee* book, I was quite captivated by the elderly movie producer who was a classmate of the writer's at Tokyo University and who introduces him to Sakura. However, I couldn't help thinking it would have been better to give the older characters less prominent roles; in other words, to make them into unobtrusive supporting players and—sorry, I know this will sound like blatant age discrimination, but I have to say it—to let the featured players be the younger versions of those same men and women. In that way, by allowing the character arcs to develop over time while inventing the necessary details, I think the book could be turned into a serious novel."

"It's certainly true that the narrator of *Annabel Lee* is the book's author himself, barely disguised, and he was familiar with the international movie star because he'd seen her on the screen when she was a young girl, so in that respect it is an 'I novel,' absolutely," Unaiko said. "But even so, you can't dismiss it out of hand as an unserious piece of work."

"No, you're completely right," Katsura said. "For Mr. Choko, this probably is a 'serious novel,' both in terms of structure and literary style. However, the thing is, over the past ten or fifteen years all of Mr. Choko's long works of fiction have more or less been cut from the same cloth, most notably in terms of the protagonist (who is often the first-person narrator as well). Not to put too fine a point on it, but the author's alter ego is nearly always the main character in his books. At some point, doesn't it become overkill? I mean, can these serial slices of thinly veiled memoir really be considered genuine novels? Generally speaking, books like this will never win over the people who want to read a novel that's actually *novelistic*: that is, an imaginative work of fiction. So at the risk of seeming rude, I really have to ask: Why do you choose to write about such a solipsistic and narrowly circumscribed world?"

"Everything you say is true," I said. "I admit that freely. The novel I had been gearing up to write for a very long time—I've abandoned it now, but that's another story—was going to be about my father, who drowned more than six decades ago when he was only fifty years old. I've accepted that I will never be able to complete the book, and in the process I have thought about every single one of the points you raised. I've often asked myself how I ended up following such a constricted path in my fiction, but I always seem to come back to the sobering realization that if I hadn't used the quasi-autobiographical approach I wouldn't have been able to write anything at all. In other words, I've had to maintain this narrow focus out of sheer necessity."

"And yet it's evident from a quick glance at these bookshelves that you're a person with wide-ranging interests," Katsura said. Then, with what appeared to be a conscious effort not to dwell too mercilessly on my flaws as a writer, he guided the conversation in a different direction. "Another thing someone could glean from the contents of these bookshelves is that they belong to a person with a distinctive way of reading," he went on. "Take T. S. Eliot, for example. You have a great many highly specialized scholarly books, written in English, but you also have a sizable collection of Japanese translations of Eliot's work. I can also see that for other major poets of the past century, such as Yeats and Auden, you have looked at the work of the people who have translated those poets into Japanese, found the ones whose style you really love, and then collected their published books. It's easy to see who your favorites are, but really, I don't think even scholars in the field spend this much money on poetry translations!"

"The truth is, I rely on the advice of one scholar who has been a friend of mine ever since we met at university," I said. "He went on to become an expert on the work of Coleridge and Eliot, and he tells me which translators are better than others. What I've been noticing lately is that when it comes to poems in foreign languages—whether it's English or French, or, in the case of Dante, Italian—I simply can't grasp the meaning in the original language anymore. So I'll memorize the originals and then keep muttering the lines to myself, over and over, in the hope that dogged repetition will somehow help me to 'get' them. At the same time, I still seem to hear the Japanese translations (in the case of Eliot, the ones by Fukase and Nishiwaki) ricocheting around my brain and resonating with the original, and by that rather roundabout method I'm finally able to arrive at a solid sense of what the poet is trying to say."

"Because your private life exists in a place of receptivity, perhaps your novels are conceived in the same place as well?" Katsura asked rhetorically. "Take William Blake, for instance. When you wrote a novel inspired by his poetry, you included the quoted passages in both the original English and your favorite Japanese translation, printed side by side. That seemed like an act of kindness toward Japanese readers, and for me, having those bilingual pairings of Blake's poems sprinkled throughout gave the book a pleasing visual texture."

"I agree," I said. "And for a bilingual reader it can also be interesting to take note of the striking discrepancies between the original and the Japanese translations, which occur more often than you might think."

"This is a stanza from the latter part of *The Waste Land*, isn't it?" Katsura asked, pointing to an index card tacked to one of the bookshelves. "I see that you've written the English original first, followed by several Japanese translations, starting with Fukase's."

"Ah, that's just a relic left over from when I was still struggling to write my drowning novel," I said. "Putting aside the fact that my command of English has never been as strong as it might be, it's painful for me to realize that even though I've been reading the same stanza over and over for half a century, I seem to comprehend it less now than when I began. In my prime, I used to think that I understood those lines, and the loss of insight makes me fear that my intellectual capacities are deteriorating at a rapid rate. Sometimes when I'm lying awake in bed in the middle of the night Fukase's version will spring to mind, and I'll try to translate it back into the original English, as a mental exercise. I can never seem to get it right, so I'll get up and open *The Waste Land* to check how far off the mark I was. That was how I came to discover that I had been misinterpreting this one particular line for decades!"

Just then, at the precise moment I needed it, Unaiko handed me the relevant index card, which she had presciently unpinned from the bookshelf.

"This stanza is from 'What the Thunder Said,' which is the final section of the poem," I went on. "It's full of quotations from Dante, Nerval, and Thomas Kyd, among others. The line in question is this: *These fragments I have shored against my ruins*. Until very recently, I always assumed the narrator was referring to some kind of purely physical ruination. Carried along by the inexorable momentum of my misconception, I somehow imagined that he had been shipwrecked, but had weathered the storm and made it to shore. (There actually is a line about a boat toward the end.) I thought he was expressing his relief at finally being on dry land, safe and sound after having managed to dodge a potentially ruinous disaster. In other words, for the longest time I misperceived 'shore' as a metaphorical noun in the sense of landfall, rather than a verb, as in 'shore up.'

"Recently, though, I've arrived at a new interpretation, based on my late-blooming realization that the author is using 'shore' in the sense of propping or supporting. I think the narrator is saying that the fragments in *The Waste Land* are going to help shore him up against the specter of spiritual and mental decay, as evoked in the poem. Of course, there are a lot of other theories floating around, but this one makes sense to me. Anyway, following that line of thought allowed me to resolve the disparities I'd noticed between Eliot's original and Fukase's somewhat ambiguous translation, which was good. On the other hand, I've realized that as I'm growing older my own mental and physical faculties are perceptibly disintegrating with every passing day—in other words, the type of decline described in Eliot's poem is really happening to me, and I'm not sure how to go about shoring myself up."

As I approached the end of this monologue Unaiko began to cry, and a veritable torrent of tears streamed down both sides of her high-bridged nose. Tentatively, I put an arm around her shoulders, then shot an expressive glance at Katsura (who was clearly discombobulated by this unexpected development) to indicate that he should probably take her home.

Unaiko was still weeping profusely, but she stood up docilely when Katsura held out his hand, and I watched anxiously from the top of the stairs as he tenderly led her down to the first floor and out the front door.

# Chapter 13

# The *Macbeth* Matter

## 1

Ricchan was the kind of person who didn't feel the need to draw attention to her own exceptional abilities, but when her facility for giving music lessons (a gift of which I had been completely unaware) came to light, it turned out to be a source of great joy for Akari. After Maki heard the news that Akari had finally started enjoying CDs again (following a long interlude during which he only listened to music on a portable radio, with the volume on his headphones turned up to maximum volume), she sent him a box filled with compact discs. On the chance he might be ready to resume his composing and study of music theory, she threw in some music workbooks (designed for elementary school students and illustrated with cartoon characters and such) along with a number of unfinished compositions Akari had drafted on five-line paper. The latter, in particular, provided a useful starting point for Ricchan's lessons.

The cardboard box had been sent by courier, and because it was too large for the contents, they had gotten jumbled in transit. While I was putting everything in order, Akari—just back from his daily rehab at the Saya—made a beeline for the table where I was working and began to hover nearby. Taking the hint, I left the dining room to Akari and Ricchan and repaired to my study. When I went downstairs an hour or so later for a drink of water, I found Akari engrossed in one of the music workbooks, wielding pencils in both hands.

Ricchan was peering over his shoulder, and as I entered the room she said, "Wait, what's this? Akari dear, you've made a little mistake in calculating the note values. You did everything else perfectly, though."

"I know," Akari acknowledged. "I'm not so good at figuring out things like that."

I approached the table, and when I asked Ricchan a question about her musical training she replied with complete candor, saying she had graduated from Tokyo University of the Arts (popularly known as Geidai) with a major in piano, but had dropped out of grad school and started working part time for the Caveman Group. (That was when she had become friends with Unaiko.) Now that she mentioned it, I remembered having seen Ricchan's name listed on the group's performance calendar as "music director." In addition, one of Asa's recent letters had referred to Ricchan as a music specialist, or something similar.

In that case, I asked, was there any chance she might be willing to take Akari on as a pupil? (His regular teacher was in Tokyo, of course, but he had let the lessons lapse long before we came to stay at the Forest House.) Ricchan readily agreed, and in short order she went to talk to a schoolteacher she'd gotten to know during the production of the *Kokoro* play and wangled permission to use the piano in the junior high's music room for Akari's lessons. (Ricchan, by nature, was the furthest thing from pushy or overaggressive, but she also knew how to make things happen quickly when she needed to.) As a felicitous bonus, it turned out that some of Akari's CDs were already being used as part of the junior high's music curriculum.

One day after Ricchan and I had been looking over one of Akari's resuscitated compositions together, she said to me, "All Akari needs is some five-line paper, a pencil, and an eraser. This is something he dashed off in ten minutes before a lesson, and while there's nothing objectively wrong with it, when I tried playing it something seemed to be a tiny bit off—it sounded awkward somehow—so I simply suggested that a slightly different approach might work better. Akari did a quick rewrite on the spot and when I played the revised version I thought, *Wow, this time he totally nailed it!* In a few days, Akari will be trying his hand at performing another composition he just finished—it's one he started working on in Tokyo. Would you like to come to the school with us and hear it?"

I accepted Ricchan's invitation with alacrity, and on the appointed day I tagged along with a spring in my step. Apparently this was another case where Akari had completed the composition in his own style, and then Ricchan had demonstrated some alternatives, which Akari incorporated into the next draft. Ricchan said she was worried about how Akari's teacher in Tokyo might react to these modifications, so she carefully documented every step in the process. Akari, on the other hand, took a scorched-earth approach to rewriting. When he had occasion to make a change, he would completely erase the existing marks and then write in the revisions, leaving no trace of the original composition.

My grasp of music theory was rudimentary at best, but it was clear even to me that the revised versions were greatly improved, while still managing to retain the distinctive flavor that immediately made me think, *Ah, this is one of Akari's compositions, without a doubt.* When I gave voice to that thought, Ricchan (who, unlike Unaiko, didn't often show her emotions) looked extremely pleased.

I glanced at the sheet music propped up on the piano in the music room and noticed that the title, which was usually the first thing Akari jotted down when he got an idea for a new composition, was missing. I asked Ricchan whether there had been a title on the original, before Akari copied it over to incorporate the latest changes.

"I wasn't aware that Akari was in the habit of titling his work, so I didn't notice one way or the other," Ricchan replied.

I remembered how Akari and I used to banter back and forth in a stylized way, mimicking a long-ago TV commercial, so I decided to give that tactic a try.

"Akari, where did the title of your composition go?" I asked playfully.

Akari ignored my attempt at levity. "I erased it," he said flatly.

"Well then, shall we give it a new one?"

"No, it's called 'Big Water,'" Akari replied.

"'Big Water' is what they call a flood around these parts," I explained, turning to Ricchan. "Come to think of it, when Akari and I were having our, uh, differences, he stopped listening to music and gave up composing as well. That whole debacle happened not long after I'd given up on the drowning novel, but even after I returned to Tokyo I was still talking quite a bit about my father, who died in a 'big water' flood. While Akari was laying the groundwork for what would eventually become this composition, he must have somehow internalized the phrase 'big water' without fully understanding the meaning. However, he says he erased the original title he was using for this composition when he started work on it back in Tokyo, so . . ."

"The section that Akari wrote in Tokyo definitely has a dark sensibility," Ricchan mused. "But apparently he decided that he wanted to do a rewrite and brighten it up a bit, so maybe 'After the Flood' would be a good title for the new composition. The way I picture the scene, it's the day after a big storm; the sun is shining, the sky is clear and blue, and the water level is slowly returning to normal. That's the kind of ambience the phrase 'after the flood' evokes, don't you think? Oh, and isn't there a famous Rimbaud poem with the same title?"

"The name of my composition is 'Big Water,'" Akari said firmly.

# 2

"Instead of heading straight back to the house, how would it be if we took a scenic detour through the forest? There's something I'd like to talk to you about," Ricchan said as we drove away from the Saya. (Akari was in the back of the van, listening to music on headphones.) When I agreed, Ricchan made a perceptible shift from casual conversation to serious-discussion mode.

"Unaiko was saying all along that she really hoped we'd be able to persuade you to be a part of our new drama project," she began. "As you know, I wrote about it in my journal. We're very grateful to you for agreeing to work with us, but now that we've reached this stage, I feel the time has come for me to share some of my concerns.

"I know Masao thinks I'm just some kind of robot who runs around mindlessly doing Unaiko's bidding. Admittedly, that's been our basic dynamic during the past ten years or so, and it's certainly true that now, as always, my energies are focused on trying to make Unaiko's vision a reality. But this time there's more to it. I should probably begin by saying that since our current project is a stage adaptation that more or less follows the plot of a movie, and since you wrote the screenplay for the film in question, your cooperation will be invaluable. I think Masao and the other members of the Caveman Group decided to participate in the project mainly because they heard you would be involved. The thing is, there's another, hidden aspect to this undertaking— something that has a very personal significance for Unaiko—and I'm concerned because she hasn't yet talked to you about it. When I asked her when she was going to get around to doing that, she said, 'Well, the tragic aspect of the Meisuke's mother story is implicitly present in Mr. Choko's original screenplay, so what's the problem?' But the thing is, I know she's going to put her own stamp on this, using her patented 'Unaiko method' with the dog-tossing and all. And I suspect that, just as she did with her previous productions, she'll probably plow ahead in a completely oblivious, egocentric way. Because of the controversial nature of the subject matter, and the forthright way she's planning to approach it, I'm afraid you might find yourself mixed up in something more complicated than you bargained for.

"So basically, I wanted to make sure you'd been properly warned that the upcoming performance has the potential to blow up in our faces. There's also the question of how Akari will react. He isn't only meticulous about the way he listens to his music; he also pays close attention to anything having to do with his father. I'm worried that something very distressing for him might happen as a direct result of your involvement in this project.

"To be honest, at this early stage I can't predict what sort of outrageous thing Unaiko might toss out during the actual performance. (You know how she loves to improvise and shock the audience!) I wouldn't dream of betraying her confidence, and in any case she'll probably tell you about the matter in question herself before too long. This might sound like an exaggeration, but I suspect the thing she hasn't yet told you about, which was an exceedingly traumatic experience, had a profound effect on Unaiko—not only on her art, but on her entire life.

"Sorry, I don't mean to be cryptic, but as I said it isn't my place to tell you the details. What I would like to talk about right now, in a completely objective way, is the current state of affairs surrounding this play. You've probably heard about this from Daio, but after the show at the junior high (you know, the dog-tossing version of *Kokoro*) a lot of people were angry about certain aspects of Unaiko's way of thinking. Those people are mostly from the right-wing faction that has been very influential in this prefecture's educational circles for many years. (We learned about this from Daio, so I'm assuming you've heard about it as well.) Anyway, some of their representatives are going to be present in the audience at our next performance as spies. Apparently those people have already bought tickets and reserved their seats. The question is, where will they be focusing their animosity? Right now I know they're gathering information about the scene depicting the rape of Meisuke's mother, the way you described it in your original draft of the screenplay. (As we all know, that hit very close to home for Sakura Ogi Magarshack because of what happened to her as a young girl.) Those people have also been in contact with the women I've been interviewing as part of my background research. It isn't entirely clear what happened, but apparently the scene that was initially filmed ended up being completely scrubbed from the final print, either by order of the NHK network here in Japan (which was coproducing the film) or the distribution company in America.

"Recently those local right-wingers have started publicly flexing their muscles, saying things like 'We're the ones who got the scene taken out of the movie, you know,' so they were predictably upset when they heard that Unaiko is trying to include the deleted scene in the play. The part where Meisuke's mother—who is injured, exhausted, and probably in shock—is being carried on a stretcher made from an old wooden shutter is important, but Unaiko wants to restore the narrative's original integrity by resurrecting the previous scene, in which Meisuke's mother is raped and her reborn son, the supposed reincarnation of the original Meisuke, is stoned to death. Unaiko and I (and Masao, too) are certain there's at least one spy from the other side skulking around the project, and we're doing our best to smoke them out. We've also heard that they are up in arms about your supposed rewriting of modern history through the lens of your contempt for your native province. (Needless to say, those are their words, not mine.)

"The other day when I was at the supermarket in Honmachi I happened to run into Daio, and he had just come from scouting a meeting of the right-wing group. As for Unaiko, she said that even if she told you there was a battle brewing, she didn't think you would ever turn tail and run away at this advanced stage of the proceedings. Of course Unaiko is absolutely determined to stand her ground and deal directly with the neonationalists' catcalls and objections and so on, during the performance and afterward as well. To that end, she added a couple of lines to the battle-cry recitative and tweaked the last line a bit. So now it will be: *Men commit rape—that's nothing new / But countries can be rapists, too. / Women warriors, here we go / Off to vanquish every foe!*

"And during the chant, dolls representing the spirit of the reincarnation of Meisuke II will be flying through the air. (Naturally, we'll need to get your approval for those additions, since you are the original author of the chant we'll be using.) Even so—and this is something we've experienced with other dog-tossing performances—no matter how forceful the hard-liners' arguments might be, I think it's going to be difficult for them to push the entire audience into an emotional meltdown. But never fear, Unaiko is preparing for that eventuality, and she's going to have an ace up her sleeve. I'm not in a position to reveal the details to you right now, Mr. Choko; I'll only say that this is the thing I alluded to earlier. You really need to hear about it directly from Unaiko, and I'm sure she's planning to tell you before too long."

I had no intention of trying to force Ricchan to disclose any details about the mysterious "thing," but I did venture a question regarding another matter that had been bothering me.

"The other day Unaiko turned up with a man she introduced as her boyfriend," I said. "He and I hit it off quite well, and we had an unusually candid conversation. However, toward the end of our visit Unaiko seemed to have an emotional meltdown, to use your term, and she even started to cry. I was wondering whether you might have any idea what could have caused her to react that way?"

"Oh, yes, I heard about that," Ricchan said. "Unaiko told me she was very moved when you quoted the translation of one of your favorite lines from Eliot, *These fragments I have shored against my ruins*. She said it made her realize that even for an older author who has had a great deal of success, the struggle never ends; on the contrary, it goes on forever, until you die. As I've said before, while Unaiko is undeniably egocentric, she is also a very sensitive soul who can be saddened to the point of tears by something as small as suddenly becoming aware of the burdens an old person has to bear."

## 3

When Asa finally returned to her house by the river after having stayed in Tokyo considerably longer than expected, she brought with her a packet that had been put together by Akari's music teacher in Tokyo. It contained a summary of Akari's overall progress; copies of all the handwritten sheet music for his original compositions—both in progress and completed; and an evaluation of his most recent work. (I had shared Akari's latest efforts with our family in Tokyo, and Asa had passed those pages along to the music teacher.)

When Asa and I got together to talk about Akari's musical situation, she told me about a new development we both feared would be upsetting for Akari if he knew. It appeared likely that his music teacher, who was married to the associate conductor of an orchestra patterned after the West German model, would soon be accompanying her husband on a posting abroad, where she would pursue her own education as an advanced student of music.

After we had finished a communal lunch and Ricchan had set off with Akari for his daily round of rehab exercises, Asa gave me a full report on the state of affairs at my house in Seijo. This included an account of a soul-baring talk she'd had with Maki, who had been left in charge of the household while Chikashi was in the hospital. Asa began by reassuring me that I didn't need to worry about Chikashi's medical bills, since they would be covered by our health insurance. As for taxes, she said Maki was already planning for the following year. In an ordinary year, I would have published a new book, which would have yielded some income. This year, however, my work on the drowning novel had screeched to a halt, and I didn't have any other book projects in mind. There was enough money in the bank to cover everyone's living expenses through the next year, but what, Asa asked, was I planning to do when the big tax payments came due next March?

"Don't worry, Kogii," she said briskly before I could reply, "I may have come up with a possible solution. It's been confirmed that we have copyrights on all versions of the screenplay for the *Meisuke's Mother Marches Off to War* movie. According to Ricchan, they've begun work on a draft of their stage-play version of the story, which will be presented using Unaiko's trademark dog-tossing method. As remuneration for your work and for the use of your screenplay, what if you combined those two versions of the story in a single volume, as a set? There's no reason to expect a novelist's screenplay and a playscript to be a bestseller, but it's worth a try, don't you agree? I'm acquainted with the editor who would have been handling your current novel, if it had ever come to fruition, so I went ahead and sent an email to sound him out about this idea."

"Oh, that's right," I said, remembering. "If you're wondering what became of his reply, the editor and I just corresponded directly. As you're aware, his publishing house puts out a literary magazine, and as it happens, the editor in chief has a long-standing interest in both film and the theater. He's already said that he would like to publish both scripts in his magazine, as a new work, and they're willing to pay for it, too. I really have to hand it to you, sis—you're as much of a go-getter as any professional literary agent out there!"

Asa knew I was historically ambivalent about her aggressively proactive tendencies, and she clearly heard the undertone of resentment beneath my compliment. However, that didn't stop her from forging ahead.

"Once it's been decided that your scripts will appear in a literary magazine, you won't be able to bail on the project the way you did on your last novel," she said pointedly. "In that spirit, I think you need to take the time to walk the insurrection route and check things out for yourself. You've never actually made the trek along the river, have you? Unaiko mentioned she wanted to get a sense of where the uprising took place to help her imagine the frightful ordeal that Meisuke's mother endured afterward, so I told her we'd be glad to provide a hands-on guided tour. We're planning to go next Sunday, and I trust I can count on you to come along?"

# 4

That Sunday morning, Unaiko drove over to pick Asa up, and then they swung back around to fetch me. I climbed into the passenger seat next to Unaiko and assumed the role of explainer in chief, while Asa added her own questions and comments from the backseat.

"I've been thinking about the best way to give you the grand tour," I told Unaiko. "Asa, remember the time when we were kids, when we went and rambled around some ruins not far from here? They were supposedly the habitat of the Destroyer: the literally larger-than-life character who's the star of the single most popular legend around these parts . . . I suppose 'legend' could imply a basis in truth, so maybe I should just call him an apocryphal being. In any case, sometime between 250 and 300 years ago, deep in the forest where the feudal clan's authority held no sway, this charismatic individual supposedly created a completely independent, self-sustaining community of separatists. He's said to have lived a remarkably long life and somehow, along the way, he was magically transformed into a giant. According to local lore, the Road of the Dead and other large-scale projects were built under his leadership. In any case, one day during our childhood we went to take a look, as a family outing. In the midst of the ruins there was a raised area, like a round platform, covered with vividly verdant grass."

"I remember!" Asa exclaimed. "It was supposedly the Destroyer's favorite spot for an afternoon nap!"

"That's right," I said. "And according to the story, that was where the spirit of the late Mcisuke supposedly appeared and lay down side by side with Meisuke II, his posthumously born little brother. Then the original Meisuke proceeded to instruct his reincarnated self in the art of war, including some strategies for the second insurrection. I've always felt as if the story about the meeting between the two Meisukes—one alive, one dead—might really be true."

"Well, I was quite the tomboy," Asa said, "so I could freely go places that would have seemed daunting to some of the girlier girls, and I remember visiting the spot with my big brother. (Although, truth be told, I was hanging on to him for dear life.) Actually I suspect the reason my brother took a companion was because he wanted to explore the forest, but he had heard so many stories and legends about the Destroyer that it seemed too scary to venture in alone, even for him."

"At any rate, I was thinking we could begin our grand tour at that spot today," I said stiffly.

"Slight change of plans," Asa said. "I had the same idea of starting out at the Destroyer's napping spot, but when I talked it over with my son he told me the area has become overgrown and inaccessible in recent years. So instead we'll start by going down to the road along the Kame River and then following the walking course that winds uphill from Okawara, toward the mountains. The path will take us past the place where Meisuke's mother was attacked, and we'll also get to see the site where Meisuke II was stoned to death. We can leave the car down in Okawara. Tamakichi will ride his bike over to fetch it later, and then he'll pick us up when we start to get tired of walking. So, that's the plan."

Unaiko was staring straight ahead, entirely focused on her driving. Her hair, which had been dyed bright gold while she was in Tokyo playing the role of a psychic medium, had reverted to its natural jet-black color, and she wore it pulled back in a loose bun at the nape of her neck. Her body language seemed to radiate seriousness and solemnity.

"It looks as if you're already getting into character for your role as Meisuke's mother, Unaiko," I said. "What's the story?"

"Yes, I've been consciously trying to put on some weight," Unaiko said, nodding emphatically in a way that emphasized the new fullness of her profile. "I want to be able to project a sense of power when I recite the battle-cry chant. By the way," she added, "Ricchan was very interested in seeing the actual route Meisuke's mother followed on the way to the uprising, but she was afraid Akari might be coming down with a cold so she decided to stay behind at the Forest House and keep him company."

"Ricchan really does take incredibly good care of Akari," Asa said. "Maki speaks to him on the phone every day, and apparently he talks about Ricchan all the time. When I left for Tokyo I knew you hadn't even begun to mend your fences with Akari, and I realized after I left that I should have arranged for someone to take care of keeping his face shaved while you were staying down here. During your past visits I've always done it myself, whenever the two of you weren't on the best of terms. But I forgot to put it on my to-do list, and it wasn't until I'd been tending to Chikashi at the hospital for a week that I started to worry. I asked Maki to check, and she told me that Akari replied, 'Papa isn't shaving my whiskers.' She said she was alarmed to hear it, but even as she was picturing her brother's face completely covered in stubble (or even a full beard) Akari went on, with his trademark slyness, 'Ricchan's shaving me now, and it doesn't hurt like when Papa does it.'"

"Whenever there's something new going on, Akari never seems to be able to come right out and talk about it, even if he wants to. So if someone can extract the information from him, indirectly, I think he always feels relieved," I said.

"Anyhow, Ricchan stepped into a tricky situation and kindly offered her tonsorial services," Asa said. "I mean, at that point she and Akari had barely spoken two words to each other, and it's only natural she would have been worried about inadvertently nicking him with the razor. Ricchan's a very brave soul, though, and it seems to have worked out fine."

Having spoken her piece on this subject, Asa shifted into explanatory mode. "Let me fill you in on the plan for today," she said, turning her attention to Unaiko. "First, we'll drive to Honmachi. Then we'll get on the highway along the Kame River, crossing the newly widened bypass—you know, the one that forced the removal of the big rock with the poem etched into it, which is now in the back garden of the Forest House. (Of course, the poetry stone wasn't the only thing displaced as a result of the construction.) Anyhow, that will take us right into Okawara. It's about a twenty-minute drive from here, so I'd like to use the time to talk to my brother about something having to do with his domestic situation, and I'd be grateful if you would listen, too, Unaiko.

"When Chikashi was discharged from the hospital, before I left Tokyo, we had a little party to celebrate. It was just the three of us: Chikashi, Maki, and me. The timing wasn't ideal because Maki was dealing with the time of month that's always the most difficult for her, emotionally—I mean, once she gets past the monthly complications she's the sweetest person on earth, but that night she was on the warpath against you, Kogii.

"The first thing she said was, 'When Mama went into the hospital, she was clearly prepared for the possibility that she wouldn't make a full recovery, and she took the time to talk to me about some important matters. But what about Papa? Is he giving any thought to our future as a family? It was smart of Mama to send Akari and Papa to Shikoku together, because it was definitely a step in the right direction. But even so, now that they're there, it doesn't seem as though Papa has made any progress toward considering the problems at hand. Ever since she was diagnosed with cancer, Mama seems to have been giving a lot of thought to her own mortality, but Papa isn't really thinking seriously about the end of his own life. At least that's how it looks to me.'"

Asa paused for a moment to let these words sink in, then resumed her monologue. "Anyhow, Maki went on to say, 'At the beginning of this year, remember when Papa said, "Whoa, I just realized I'm on the cusp of being older than Professor Musumi was when he died!"'? And then he seemed to be getting a kick out of saying things like: "Maybe Maki's depression is something I passed down to her, because I myself was on the cusp of middle age when I first began to suffer from melancholia. When I talked to Musumi Sensei about that, he said, 'I've realized that I didn't completely understand the work of certain authors—Rabelais, for one—until I read the same books again after I'd reached the same age those authors were when they passed away. So, if you can muster up a sufficient degree of interest, I'd like to ask you to read (or reread) all my books when you get to be the age I was when I died.' And now, here I am, rereading Sensei's books, one by one." When I heard what Papa said, it really struck me that he didn't seem to be giving any thought to how his death would affect Akari, or how Akari would go on living when he was gone.' Anyhow, that's what Maki said.

"Chikashi was the first to respond," Asa continued. "Obviously she would never hug her daughter in front of me, even though I'm family, but she was clearly trying to comfort Maki when she said, 'No, dear, Papa has actually given quite a bit of thought to the things you mention, and he has even invented a term for the situation with Akari. He calls it 'the *Macbeth* matter,' and the fact that he has given it a name seems to suggest he isn't trying to avoid the issue entirely.'

"Kogii, I'm only mentioning this now to let you know how seriously Chikashi and Maki are thinking about this. I get the feeling they're hoping you'll take the initiative, sooner rather than later, and let them know your thoughts about what will become of Akari when you die. I simply wanted to put a bug in your ear, so to speak."

Asa lapsed into silence. We had already driven through the residential outskirts of Honmachi, and as I gazed out the window a familiar landmark—the long sandbar on the other side of the embankment—came into view. A few moments later, Unaiko spoke up.

"What do you mean by 'the *Macbeth* matter'?" she asked me.

"It's a reference to the kind of situation implied by the lines where Lady Macbeth says, *These deeds must not be thought / After these ways; so, it will make us mad.* That's all."

My brief reply was meant to discourage further discussion, and I could sense from Unaiko's body language that she had gotten the message. Asa gave me an exceptionally eloquent look, but she didn't say a word. However, Unaiko wasn't the type to slink quietly away from a conversation, and she managed to change the subject in a positive way.

"On another topic," she said, "I've been watching Ricchan while she's helping Akari with his music lessons, and it occurred to me that the work she's doing with him has given her a whole new lease on life. Honestly, I've never seen Ricchan like this before. Until now I've always relied completely on her, and even though we haven't always been living in the same place, when the going got tough it always cheered me up to know Ricchan would be coming back before too long—and she always did, eventually. To be perfectly frank, while I've admittedly been quite dependent on Ricchan in a practical sense, I always thought working with me was going to turn out to be the most important thing in her life, and I never imagined that anything else could be as exciting and fulfilling for her as our dramatic projects. But lately when I see Ricchan and Akari working on lessons and compositions together, and then when I hear their efforts transformed into music, it's clear that those endeavors are much more important and rewarding for Ricchan than being my assistant. I've gotten a sense that the work she's doing with Akari has been lifting her to an entirely new level, and I was reminded of that when I heard about what Maki had said."

"If you don't mind, Unaiko, I'm going to email Maki and tell her what you said just now," Asa replied, but (true to her cautiously skeptical character) she managed to infuse her words with a figurative grain of salt. "I'm sure Maki will be happy to hear about this, but I don't want to lead her to imagine Ricchan might wind up living with Akari sometime in the future—I mean, that kind of wishful thinking could create another 'Macbeth matter.' I must admit, I do have a fantasy that after my brother passes away, Ricchan could find a way to continue as Unaiko's creative partner while also managing to be Akari's music teacher and Chikashi's personal assistant, or private secretary. As I said, I realize that scenario may be an impossibly far-fetched pipe dream, but you never know . . ."

# 5

"Well, here we are in Okawara!" Asa announced as we rolled into town. "I can guess what's going through your mind, Kogii: something like *Hey, wait a minute, what happened to Okawara?* The last person who responded by appreciatively sighing, 'Ahh, Okawara!' when I brought her here was Sakura Ogi Magarshack. She knew quite a bit about local history, and she was really moved. Of course, that was before the big real estate companies came in and started building speculative housing developments all over the place."

"But . . . I mean, I know Sakura had a rich cinematic imagination, but what exactly did she find so moving about the sight of

Okawara?" I asked. "I imagine it was already overrun with unsightly development by then."

"Oh, Kogii, you're probably remembering the time Sakura came down here to shoot *Meisuke's Mother Marches Off to War*. Right? No, I'm talking about the day Sakura first laid eyes on Okawara, many years earlier. I'd been contacted by your movie-producer pal, Komori, and I took a paid day off from the Red Cross Hospital— something I'd never done before, even once—and played tour guide for Sakura. It was while you were involved in a hunger strike in Sugibayashi, up in Tokyo, as a show of solidarity with the Korean poet Kim Ji-ha. Komori dropped by the sit-in tent to visit you; Sakura was with him, and he introduced you to her. That should tell you what year it was."

"Yes, it was 1975: the year Professor Musumi passed away," I said.

"Anyhow, at the time Sakura was en route back to Washington from Seoul—she had gone there in person to apologize for the production stoppage on a film project that was a joint venture between the US and Korea, or some such. Apparently you mentioned the story of Meisuke's mother and the uprising. It piqued Sakura's interest, and she came to take a look around Okawara. As I said, I volunteered my tour-guide services, and that was when Sakura told me about what happened to her while she was in Matsuyama during the Occupation. Later I took her to our house in the village and Mother, who was still going strong at the time, even chanted the battle cry of Meisuke's mother for the benefit of the glamorous visitor!

"Sakura never forgot that, and some thirty years later she returned with the idea of making the story into a movie, using her own funds for the start-up financing. But Okawara had changed (although not *this* much!), and her original idea of filming the uprising on location had to be revised. On the plus side, that's how the first scene of the movie, where Meisuke's mother's ghostly spirit is at the Saya chanting her battle cry to incite her followers to march off to war, came into being. Fortunately, the landscape around the Saya hadn't changed at all in the past hundred years or so."

"My clearest memory of Okawara is of the time Father and I rode here on our bikes, single file, to see the kite-flying contest," I said. "You know, the one where everyone has those enormous hand-painted kites? The war was starting to heat up, and Father had heard that the contest was about to be discontinued indefinitely. I haven't been back to Okawara since then, so of course there would have been some changes in the interim, but even so . . ."

Asa and I spent the next several minutes lamenting the sad deterioration of the local scenery. (Those changes may have been "only natural," given the passage of time, but they still came as a rude shock.) Unaiko drove on, listening in silence, and when she finally spoke her words were surprisingly upbeat.

"Actually, I think this is fine," she said. "The folks who come to see our play will mostly be from around here, and they'll be aware of the contrast between Okawara today and the way it looked in the old days, when Meisuke's mother and Meisuke II set up camp. Who knows, those discrepancies may even spark people's imaginations. We'll leave it to the audience at the performance to make the connection between the gang of renegade samurai who deliberately trampled the grassy area deep in a grove of trees to clear a place where they could rape Meisuke's mother, and the OL—you know, Office Lady—who was brutally raped, not long ago, on the concrete floor of one of Okawara's humongous outdoor parking lots. That way, the viewers will understand what we're showing them isn't some long-ago period drama, like you see on TV, but rather the present-day reality faced by many contemporary women. If you look at the signage for the car park, you'll notice the name of that part of town hasn't changed since the time of the uprising."

"I'm glad we brought Unaiko down here, aren't you?" Asa said, obviously trying to nudge me into echoing her sentiments. "The incident she mentioned, where an OL was attacked in a parking lot, really did happen. It got a lot of newspaper coverage at the time."

I didn't reply. A few moments later Asa had Unaiko park the car in that same notorious parking lot, not far from the embankment that sloped down to the river, while she went off to explain to the attendant that a different person would be coming to fetch the car later on.

We set off on foot, climbing the hill on the eastern side of town, and when we reached the top—where there were still a few old-fashioned, tile-roofed houses left over from previous centuries—we all turned around and feasted our eyes on the glittering ribbon of gray-green river below. Then we ambled along the old road, which I remembered from childhood, occasionally pausing to gaze with interest at the rows of stores and houses on the way. Our pace quickened abruptly when Asa noticed a bus approaching along the new embankment-like road above, which ran parallel to the narrower one we were on, and she suggested we hop over from the old road to the new one. When everyone agreed, she told Unaiko to go ahead to the bus stop and ask the driver to wait a few minutes while the senior citizens caught up.

Unaiko ran up to the new road with long, easy strides, while Asa and I followed at a slow trot, huffing and puffing all the way. After we had boarded the bus, Asa began chatting with the driver and he agreed to let us off at the point where the new road, which was presently running parallel to the old one, veered off on its own toward Matsuyama.

Asa had been employed for many years as a nurse at the local hospital, and she was still very well known around Okawara. As we rode along, she returned the friendly greetings of a number of our fellow passengers while simultaneously explaining our route to Unaiko.

"If we get off where I asked the driver to stop, we'll be near the place where Meisuke II was stoned to death," she said. "It's at the entrance to a sort of ravine." After ten minutes or so, the bus stopped and we got off. While we were walking, Asa resumed her dissertation.

"If you head east from Okawara and then veer inland, cutting through the valley to the north toward the forest, that's where Meisuke's mother and Meisuke II split up with their compatriots after the uprising and started home by way of the woods," she told Unaiko. "The topography of the route is basically unchanged, even now. There's a part of the recitative where it describes how Meisuke's mother put Meisuke II on a horse and led it by the reins, and if you were to follow the road to the top of the forested hill, you would come upon a giant fir tree that's believed to be the eternal dwelling place of Meisuke's spirit. (I'm talking about the original Meisuke, not the reborn one; for some reason, the legend doesn't mention where the second Meisuke's spirit ended up.) Meisuke's mother was planning to take Meisuke II up there to give thanks to the spirit of the original Meisuke for helping them win the battle. But the pair had been followed, and they were ambushed and captured by their pursuers. (There's another version of the story in which the hooligans were already lying in wait, but the heartbreaking outcome is the same in both scenarios.)

"First, the samurai thugs stuffed Meisuke II into a hole in the ground and cruelly stoned him to death. Then, on a grassy area nearby, Meisuke's mother was repeatedly raped by several of the attackers. The horse got loose and went running back toward the village, where it came upon the other insurgents, who were on their way home to the valley. They turned around and followed the horse up to the scene of the crimes, where they found Meisuke's mother lying on the grass alone and badly injured. And then they somehow found an old wooden storm shutter and turned it into a makeshift stretcher for their injured leader. The story never seems to mention what became of Meisuke II's dead body; maybe that part of the tragedy was just too unbearable for people to talk about. I mean, he was just a child."

After walking in silence for quite a while, we crossed an old earthen bridge over a mountain stream and found ourselves in front of a small, weather-beaten Shinto shrine. Tall, spiky grass had grown all around the wooden shrine, so to make things easier for Unaiko, who was wearing a skirt, Asa hacked out a path with a rusty scythe she'd found tucked away in the shadows beneath the short staircase leading to the altar.

With a scythe-wielding Asa leading the way, we approached our historically fraught destination. Behind the shrine was an empty patch of land where the sunlight shone brightly through a grove of trees that appeared to have been recently pruned, and lying on the ground in the center of the vacant field were some loosely bound bundles of bamboo sticks, cut to a uniform length.

"The bamboo is covering the pit in the ground, but since there's really nothing to see—it's just an old hole—we'll leave them undisturbed," Asa said. "When they're loosely bound together like this, the long sticks of bamboo are hard to handle, so this arrangement is meant to discourage visitors from trying to remove them. After a few forestry workers fell into the cavity, it was declared a safety hazard and at one point someone filled it with dirt, but apparently the number of accidents around the forest actually increased afterward. People said it was because Meisuke II was displeased and had put a curse on the area, so the hole was dug out again. Around that time someone came to Mother asking for a donation to help finance the project, and she told me about the connection between our family and this shrine. Every few years Mother would make the trip over here to reseed the bamboo grove, and I've continued the tradition although (unlike her) I delegate the actual labor to professionals."

"The shrine is obviously very old, but do you suppose it was built sometime after Meisuke's mother and Meisuke II underwent their ordeals, or was it here all along?" Unaiko asked as she gazed around the area.

"I don't think it was here in those days," I replied. "No matter how rowdy those young samurai might have been, surely they would have gotten cold feet about doing their mischief right behind a sacred shrine. I've heard this area used to be frequented by wild pigs—perhaps it still is—and most likely the hole was originally dug by hunters to use as an animal trap. The shrine might have been constructed as a way of placating the ghost of Meisuke II, who was cruelly stoned to death in that very pit, or maybe it was just built for general purposes of purification, after the atrocious things that happened here."

Unaiko was crouched down, trying to peek into the hole through the gaps in the bundled bamboo, and when she lifted her head she gave a wordless gasp of surprise. When Asa and I turned to look, we saw two middle-aged women—one with a rather mannish forehead, the other with a perfectly round face, like a pale moon—standing by the shrine and staring fixedly in our direction. The women were evidently acquaintances of Asa's, but after exchanging rudimentary greetings with her they made a beeline for Unaiko, who had hastily scrambled to her feet.

"You're Ms. Unaiko, aren't you?" inquired the moonfaced woman. "A few months ago we were in the audience for your so-called educational play, the one based on *Kokoro*. As it happens, we're both educators, too; we teach Japanese language at two different junior high schools in the area. Running into you here is really an amazing coincidence, because we were just saying that we wished there was some way to get you to listen to our concerns. There's been talk that you're planning to stage your own version of the saga of Meisuke's mother at the same venue, with you yourself in the lead role. We think it's a splendid idea, since that story is an important part of our local folklore. However, what's worrying us is that your play will be seen by a large number of students, and we've heard it will include a rape scene. We were wondering how on earth you could possibly think such mature content would be appropriate for a school-age audience!"

"Wait, let me get this straight. You're objecting to the idea that I—" Unaiko began, speaking slowly and deliberately, but the woman interrupted her.

"Actually, first of all, I should mention that we feel the word 'rape' itself is entirely too graphic, so I'm going to substitute 'sexual assault' from now on. As I said before, we've heard that you're going to play the part of Meisuke's mother in front of an audience that includes a lot of youngsters, which means you would be portraying the victim in the sexual assault scene. And we just wanted to ask you directly how you're proposing to handle it."

"So you're saying an honest and forthright depiction of such an occurrence would be a bad thing?" Unaiko asked in a perfectly neutral tone.

"Well, admittedly, the legend does suggest that Meisuke's mother was sexually assaulted, but putting aside the question of whether it actually happened, we aren't saying we want you to sweep that aspect of the story under the rug by any means. But couldn't you take a slightly less direct approach? Instead of acting out the scene, maybe you could have a narrator explain to your young audience that Meisuke's mother experienced a great deal of tragedy and suffering, including a physical assault."

"Let me get this straight," Unaiko said again in the same uninflected tone. "First, you want to substitute the term 'sexual assault' because you feel 'rape' is too strong, or too graphic, or whatever. The thing is, 'rape' is the precise term for the experience we're talking about, and its equivalent is used all over the world. (Well, here in Japan we use the English loanword—pronounced 'reipu'—as if it were some sort of genteel euphemism, but ironically enough that word is simply a Japanized version of the exact same term. I guess it seems less harsh to us because it's relatively new and unencumbered by shameful historical associations.) So how does calling the crime 'sexual assault' change the reality, or the emotional impact on the victim? I mean, maybe using a euphemism would make the rapist feel better about the horrifying thing he did, but softening the terminology isn't going to help the victim forget the violently invasive act and the subsequent pain and sorrow. There's really no way to disguise the truth. A man who uses his strength to force a woman into any kind of nonconsensual sex is a rapist, plain and simple, and committing rape is a criminal act. So for openers, I'd like to get you and everyone else to face up to the stark realities of the term 'rape.'

"Now, I'm not suggesting that the male students who will see our play are all potential rapists by any means. However, if their female counterparts—the girls who are now in school—are never taught about the harsher aspects of life, they'll be far more vulnerable to the danger of being raped someday. You suggested that there must be a more delicate way to present the serial rape of Meisuke's mother. But the thing is, that indirect approach wouldn't merely diminish the impact of her tragedy and suffering. It would also blunt one of the points we want to make, which is that (figuratively speaking) Meisuke's mother is still being raped today, and every day. We want to present the unvarnished truth to our young audience, to let them know that rape in any form should be a very real and immediate concern for them."

"But why do you feel compelled to do that kind of brutal truth-telling in public, and at a school event?" asked the round-faced woman.

"Simply because for the past 140 years, ever since Meisuke's mother was attacked, there has been no societal evolution to speak of in this country, and the situation for women hasn't improved in any significant way. As I said, the truth is that Meisuke's mother wasn't raped only on one afternoon a century ago; she's still being symbolically raped now, every single day, and that brutal reality is what we're trying to address with this upcoming play."

"Well, okay. But why on earth do you want to put on a play that's so obsessed with the topic of rape? (By the way, I see your point about resorting to euphemisms, and I'll try not to do it anymore.) And why stage it here of all places?" demanded the woman with the masculine-looking forehead, returning the discussion to its original focus. "Seriously, why do you have to go out of your way to put on such a controversial play out here in the boonies? People are saying this play of yours has some kind of hidden agenda."

At this point Asa stepped forward and joined the conversation. "I don't know where you're getting your information, ladies," she said tartly, "so I'm going to ask you outright: Did you really hear that, in those exact words? I mean, 'hidden agenda'? Please! And even if everything you're saying isn't just wild conjecture spawned by some vague rumor you heard around town, you still have a lot of nerve coming here and trying to deprive Unaiko of her right to freedom of expression by asking her to censor the content of her play. When my late husband was the principal of the junior high school in Honma-chi, I remember that you used to attend the free lectures my brother here would often give when he came home for a visit, and afterward you and your cohorts would always make a big fuss about the subject matter, which was apparently too left wing for your tastes."

"This isn't about freedom of speech, or freedom of expression, or anything like that," the first woman shot back. "I may be a teacher but I also happen to be a mother, and I have a genuine concern about the effect it might have on the students (including our own children) if they were forced to witness a rape scene taking place onstage during a public performance. Today being Sunday and all, my friend and I were out and about gathering some edible wild plants, and we happened upon your group purely by chance. We're sorry if we startled you by popping up out of the blue like this."

"Oh, no, don't mention it," Asa said in a friendlier tone. "This place is supposedly on a route traveled by wild boars, so we wouldn't have been startled by something as minor as being accosted by you. However," she added slyly, "I can't help wondering which edible wild plants you expected to find around here this time of year. I mean, nothing's in season right now."

Without a word, the two interlopers sheepishly withdrew into the shadows beside the shrine and vanished from sight. Asa made no move to follow them. Instead, she turned to Unaiko and me and said, "Those two probably spotted us getting out of the car when we left it at the parking lot down by the river. That much, at least, could have been happenstance. They probably had a hunch we'd be bringing Unaiko to see this site, so I'm guessing they followed us and then put on a lame charade of 'popping up' by accident. Well, Unaiko dear, shall we mosey on toward the site of the tavern where Meisuke's party stopped while she was being borne home after her unspeakable ordeal, and she made her famous retort after the ill-mannered proprietor asked her a lewd question? The little factory where the sake was made isn't operating anymore, but we can at least see what's left of the building and the big house where the owner used to live.

"And on the bright side, at least we're all ambulatory, so none of us will need to be carried there on a stretcher!"

# Chapter 14

# Everything That Happens Is Fodder for Drama

## 1

Our little group plodded along in companionable silence, occasionally stopping to marvel at the extraordinary fact that we were following in the footsteps of a long-ago procession of female warriors. After taking a shortcut through a row of antique houses, we headed downhill toward the newer rows of shops and dwellings that had sprung up around the riverside road. Although the old path I remembered from my childhood appeared at first glance to have been completely destroyed, I noticed as we walked that a few nostalgic segments of the ancient roadway had been incorporated into the new national highway. Just before the spot where the Kame River merged with another river, a pair of bridges had been consolidated into a two-level cloverleaf crossing. At its base a car park stood next to a recently built supermarket where the area's abundant farm produce was for sale.

"When Honmachi was converted into a provincial city that included this entire basin, one side became a pocket of suburbia, while the other side continued to lose its population as young people fled to more urban areas. This spot right here is the junction of the two," Asa explained to Unaiko. "In our own little mountain valley, when young people want to move someplace a bit less rustic, they often head out here. Why don't we grab some coffee from the convenience store while we're waiting for Tamakichi to come and get us with the car? Or, if everyone's game, we could continue on foot. It would take the better part of an hour, but . . ."

"Since the route would take us along Meisuke's mother's personal 'trail of tears,' I'd really like to try hiking it," Unaiko said.

There was a steady stream of long-haul trucks on the highway, so Unaiko and I had to traipse along in single file, with Asa bringing up the rear.

"The road has been widened and some of the more meandering segments have been straightened out, but there's no question about it—this pedestrian walkway follows the same path Meisuke's mother was carried along on a wooden stretcher made from an old rain shutter," I observed. "The trees on the opposite shore of the river are mostly a mixture of cedars and cypresses, while on this side the forests are all broad-leafed deciduous trees. Do you see the dense woods on that cliff? They probably haven't changed much since the day when Meisuke's mother was gazing up at them from her stretcher."

"You seem to be saying that this road has been here forever, but I get the feeling it wasn't a naturally occurring path. Rather, I think people chose this route and traveled it repeatedly, and it gradually evolved into a road," Unaiko said, swiveling her head to take in the various vistas: the old-growth vegetation lining the road, the river to one side, the wooded banks beyond.

"My late brother-in-law Goro Hanawa was always a very modern type of guy, but in high school I remember he often used to say, 'Our ancestors were really awesome!' It was practically his catchphrase," I reminisced.

Unaiko listened politely to my anecdote, nodding thoughtfully, but there was obviously something else on her mind.

"You know those two teachers who accosted us at the shrine?" she asked when I had finished rambling. "They took me completely by surprise so I wasn't really thinking straight, and I'm only realizing now that I should have said something else before they skulked away. I wish I had told them that rape—both the act and the concept—was the motivating factor behind my decision to create the play we're currently collaborating on. Of course, those teachers didn't ask me about this specifically, but for me the theme of rape inevitably leads to the fundamental question of abortion. The pivotal force behind my play is the idea that women are raped and then coerced into getting abortions. The truth is, I myself was raped and then forced to get an abortion when I was seventeen."

I was listening in stunned silence, but Unaiko eliminated the need for any response on my part by launching into an impassioned monologue.

"I've already talked about the time I threw up at Yasukuni Shrine," she said, "but a few minutes later my aunt started bombarding me with questions, and I confessed that I thought I was probably pregnant. Right away she demanded to know who the man was. I was in kind of a daze, and I didn't understand what she was getting at. She repeated 'Who's the man? What's his name?' again, only in a louder, more annoyed voice. I realized then that she was asking me to name the father, so I blurted out, 'It's my uncle.'

"My aunt's response was to mutter, 'That's what I was afraid of,' and only then did it really hit me for the first time: *I'm pregnant by my own uncle*. My aunt and I had been walking toward the station while we were having this conversation, and at this point we were standing on the platform of the Yokosuka Line. The Shonan-bound train was about to depart, so we jumped aboard and my aunt went on grilling me relentlessly about my situation all the way to Fujisawa. She insisted on sitting smack in the middle of the train car, surrounded by empty seats, because she said it would be disastrous to have our conversation overheard by some stranger who might be lurking in the shadows at either end of the car, around the doors. Bit by bit, she extracted the details of my relationship with my uncle (who was also, of course, her husband).

"At the time, my uncle was a high-ranking official in the Ministry of Education—this was before the name was changed to the Ministry of Education, Culture, Sports, Science, and Technology; you know, MEXT for short—and he was busy trying to complete some important work before moving up the bureaucratic ladder. My aunt made a point of telling me that this was the most crucial time in his career, and she was emphatic about the fact that I shouldn't talk about my current situation with anyone, ever. She said that I, in my teenage naïveté, probably wouldn't understand, but something like this could be turned into a national scandal if the wrong people got wind of it. I must have looked completely bewildered, because my aunt went on in a scolding tone: 'I mean, just imagine what would happen if this story ever found its way into the mass media. A highly respected man who has made major contributions to Japan's educational system behaves in an indecent manner toward his teenage niece, eventually going so far as to rape her and make her pregnant? It would be huge news all over the country.' That was the first time I had ever heard the word 'rape' used in connection with myself.

"We got off the train at Fujisawa Station, and my aunt immediately ducked into a phone booth and called my uncle at work to let him know what she was doing. Then she bundled me into a cab and we went to their house in Kamakura for a quick pit stop, and the same cab took us back to Fujisawa. My aunt checked me into a hospital there, and I was forced to undergo an abortion. I spent the next three days at my aunt and uncle's house recovering, and then she unceremoniously kicked me out. (During those three days, I never once saw or spoke with my uncle.) Having nowhere else to go, I made my way to my parents' house in Osaka, feeling like a total wreck in every way: physically, mentally, and emotionally.

"I probably should have mentioned earlier that my uncle in Kamakura was my father's older brother, so we were related by blood, not just by marriage. Like you, they grew up on Shikoku. There were three siblings, but my uncle was the only one who went to college. After graduation he went on to Tokyo University Law School, and he became a distinguished government bureaucrat. My father only had a high school education, and he knocked around in the printing business for years until his small shop was chosen as the designated printer for the reams of official documents constantly churned out by the Ministry of Education. My father frequently spoke of the commission as a stroke of luck, but everyone knew his change in fortunes was entirely due to nepotism, so my parents were in no position to make a fuss over the things my uncle had done to me. I heard that they even signed a formal legal document promising never to speak to anyone about what happened to me in Kamakura.

"As I said, I didn't see my uncle on the day my aunt dragged me off to get an abortion, or the subsequent days, before I left their house. Since then I haven't seen either of them even once; I figure that was probably one of the conditions of the paper my parents signed. I lived at home in Osaka for the next two years, and the rape and the abortion were never far from my mind; in fact, I rarely thought about anything else. Since I hadn't been to college my employment options were limited, and I changed jobs twice during that period. Then I moved up to Tokyo, and it was shortly after my twenty-second birthday when, by the purest happenstance, I found myself at a performance by the Caveman Group. I was hooked on its artistic vision from the start, and after I'd become a regular at the group's events, Masao Anai invited me to join it. I had also made friends with Ricchan, who was in a similar situation: working part-time jobs while performing various music-related duties for the Caveman Group. In the thirteen years since Ricchan and I became full-time members of the troupe, she has always been my true partner, creatively speaking, although of course Masao Anai has also given me a tremendous amount of support.

"All the while, as I was learning the ropes of experimental the-ater, I kept thinking endlessly about what I'd gone through because of my uncle's misconduct. I was never able to shoehorn those topics into one of our plays but I was always groping around, trying to find my own dramatic style, and on some level I've spent the past decade preparing myself for the day when I would be able to express those concerns onstage. I got to know Mr. Choko when we were working on the drowning-novel project, and that was how I came to hear about Sakura Ogi Magarshack's movie about Meisuke's mother and the second uprising. It occurred to me that it might be possible to use the story as a starting point for a play that would express my true feelings and, well, you know the rest. The dramatic axis of my play will be the ordeals of Meisuke's mother, the woman warrior, but I'm envisioning a larger story as well: a narrative that would illuminate Japan's historical conduct with regard to rape and abortion through this new performance piece."

After Unaiko stopped talking, she immediately quickened her pace and pulled ahead. (Until then I had gotten the sense that she was making a conscious effort to walk slowly, so Asa—who had stuck her head between our shoulders to avoid missing a single word—would be able to hear everything Unaiko was saying.) Asa sped up as well, taking over second place in our little parade, and I was left alone to trail behind. At times like this I had a habit of indulging in little dia-logues with myself, often on topics I hadn't given much thought to in the past. Before I knew it, I found myself ruminating out loud and mumbling something like this: "All right—I can see the connection between rape and abortion. I also understand the idea that a country can behave like a rapist toward other countries and even toward its own citizens. And if you view MEXT as a stand-in for the nation of Japan, I can see how that metaphor would have occurred to Unaiko. But where does abortion fit into the scenario?"

"Well, abortion's a kind of murder, isn't it?" Asa said impatiently, glaring at me over her shoulder. "There are two legal ways of commit-ting murder, at least in this country: war and abortion. While she was still a young girl Unaiko was, in effect, raped by the nation of Japan. And then—at least as she sees it—that same country forced her to have an abortion. I mean, really, Kogii. I know you're just thinking out loud, but I can't stand by in silence when you say things that are so obtuse and insensitive, especially after Unaiko has opened up about her harrowing experiences.

"Oh, look," Asa went on, shifting into a brighter tone, "there's my son, watching for us from the top of the hill. Yoo-hoo, Tamakichi! Here we are!"

# 2

Every morning from then on, I hunkered down to work on the new play along with the young troupe members who often congregated in the great room, with Unaiko at the epicenter of every meeting. I usually sat at the dining table on the near side of the partition between the two rooms, often with Akari nearby. Ricchan would join us at the table from time to time, and whenever that happened Akari's behavior would immediately change. That is to say, instead of toiling over his musical compositions while lying belly down on the floor on the dining-room side, which was his default position, he would come to the table and continue his work in a chair placed directly in front of the big sound system. On the table in front of me there would be a hard copy of the most recent draft of the script for what everyone was calling "the Meisuke's mother play," which Ricchan regularly updated on the communal computer and then printed out. I spent a good deal of time at the table, but there were also many occasions when I gathered my papers and retreated to my study on the second floor.

My main task at the time was to create a version of the playscript that would be suitable for publication in a literary magazine. Using my rough draft as a base, the young actors would read the lines aloud to one another and then develop them further by improvising in the proprietary dog-tossing style. In the actual playbill, those embellishments would be credited to Unaiko and Suke & Kaku, but while I was incorporating the bulk of them into the master script I would always check the dialect for accuracy, to make sure the literary style was consistent throughout. I found the entire process refreshing. Until then I had always worked alone, and I felt as though I was receiving a crash course in collaborative creativity.

I also learned some interesting things, including the lore about the so-called crying child (or children) that Ricchan—unusually, for her—had actively decided to include in the playscript. One day she happened to mention having heard about the legend in the course of her field research, and she proceeded to read us the words of one informant, which she had transcribed from one of her tapes: "I heard there was some criticism of Sakura during the filming, because people said that she created the recitative without understanding the meaning of the term 'crying child.' As you may know, when Meisuke's mother went off to battle, some troops sent down to Okawara by the Meiji government tried to break up the uprising by forcing their way through the entry point of the rebels' front line, which was really no more than a straw hut. However, a number of children threw themselves across the soldiers' path, weeping at the top of their lungs, and refused to budge. The soldiers couldn't very well trample a bunch of little children to death, so they were forced to retreat. (No one seemed to know whether the children belonged to the young mothers who were participating in the rebellion, but it would seem to be a reasonable assumption.) Sakura somehow misunderstood the etymology of the term, and her misreading of the kanji led her to a complicated and completely erroneous interpretation. In fact, 'crying children' meant just that, with no hidden meaning at all."

Ricchan went on to tell our assembled group about a situation in present-day society that uncannily mirrors the local lore about the crying children. She said when she was living in Tokyo, she would occasionally see sad-looking kids with tear-streaked faces in public places. However, after moving to Matsuyama she started to see such children with increasing frequency, and it began to bother her a great deal. The crying children she encountered were never in groups; rather, she would see small girls between the ages of three and five walking alone, bawling their eyes out.

"The weird thing," Ricchan concluded, "was that even though the children were so young they were marching down the street at full speed, and their weeping wasn't like the crying of a normal child at all. Every 'waa' they uttered seemed to be suffused with anger bordering on fury, or even a kind of soul-devouring fear. In the midst of this display of raw emotion, from time to time the child would lift her little face— bright red and wet with tears—and glance around. And when I followed her glance, I would sometimes see a slightly older girl with unkempt, bleached-out hair and a grubby-looking face who would quickly scuttle off, paying no attention to the younger child. So rather than a mother and child, the duos I noticed from time to time consisted of a tiny girl walking along, wailing at maximum volume, and another, more elusive girl who was several years older. I thought they might be sisters."

In response to Ricchan's anecdote, several people joined in, saying things such as "Yes, I've seen something similar on city streets as well." One of those voices belonged to Unaiko's boyfriend, Tatsuo Katsura, who happened to be in town.

"I heard a similar story from a friend of mine," Katsura said. "He was making a television documentary in the area. The main difference is that, as he told it, a young mother who appeared to be in the depths of despair was roughly brushing aside a child who was walking beside her, crying like a banshee and trying to cling to the mother's skirts. I realize this could be a whole other urban myth but I feel as if the two might share a common thread, so please indulge me while I share the version I heard.

"Actually, this isn't mere hearsay, because I myself have seen a crying child like the one my friend described, although I just passed by without stopping. As my friend said, anyone who encountered such a scene would naturally be suspicious, thinking it might be a trap or the setup for a scam. But he tends to be curious by nature, so he paused to watch the scene unfold. After a moment, he said, a rather louche-looking man (clearly not a child welfare worker or a police officer in uniform) approached the child and put his arms around her in a comforting gesture. That triggered my friend's documentary-filmmaker's instincts, and he hung around to see what the man would do next. By and by the young mother, who had run away as fast as her legs could carry her, leaving her crying child behind, turned around and came back to stand next to the man and the little girl. After a while the child and the mother appeared to have reconciled their differences, although they still weren't saying anything to each other. The two of them were just standing on the sidewalk, like silent satellites orbiting the man. My friend had to leave then, and that's the rather anticlimactic way the story ends. He told me that in hindsight he had a feeling there had been a suspicious van parked not too far away, and he said if he ever had a chance, he'd like to go back and follow up on the story. He thought there was probably something unsavory going on involving pornography, or prostitution, or even slave trafficking, but of course that was pure storyteller's speculation on his part.

"I've been thinking about it, too," Katsura continued, "and I can't help wondering whether the man my friend saw might have been running some sort of con—that is, a carefully orchestrated and rehearsed situation created for purely mercenary reasons. It isn't unusual to see such pairs—the crying child and the despondent-looking young mother—out on the streets these days, so isn't it possible that some sleazy lowlife is putting those duos together and then standing by, watching for an opportunity for blackmail or extortion? Perhaps there's even a training camp where gangsters teach underprivileged children and their mothers to behave in a manipulative way. If that's what was going on it would be a truly abominable business enterprise, but I can see how participating in a sidewalk scam could still seem appealing to the poor women and children, compared with the horrific alternatives.

"Taking my uninformed conjecture one step further, please bear with me while I float another scenario. Over a century ago there wasn't a single car in this country, much less a van. It was a time when the peasants were so poor that they had no choice but to mount an uprising in protest. There were probably quite a few young mothers wandering around with children who had every reason to cry. (They might even have been homeless.) Isn't it possible that a bunch of those unhappy children and their desperate mothers were brought together in some farmer's barn, or maybe a shrine or a temple—someplace with enough space to accommodate a large group. This may seem like a stretch, but isn't it conceivable that they were recruited to act as a kind of miniature advance vanguard, to run interference for the peasant troops in the insurrection led by Meisuke II and his mother? Whatever happened in reality, some version of the crying-child trope seems to have found its way into local folklore. Maybe this is an impossibly rosy scenario, but I'd like to imagine that the crying children and their woebegone mothers might have played an active role in winning the uprising."

"Hmm," Ricchan said, addressing Tatsuo Katsura. "That's an interesting interpretation, and I don't think it's impossibly optimistic by any means."

Katsura smiled, but his next comment seemed to indicate a lingering skepticism. "On the other hand," he said, "if the story my friend told me is true—you know, about the modern-day crying child, the morose young mother, and the suspicious-looking man—then trying to romanticize their situation really would be impossibly optimistic. I mean, it seems fairly clear why those women and children were rounded up, and where they were going to be taken, and what was going to become of them in the end."

"What do you mean?" Ricchan asked.

"I think Katsura is lamenting the tragic destinies that might await those mothers and children," Unaiko declared in the resonant trained-actor's voice she used onstage. "I mean, we're all familiar with the loathsome things taking place in Southeast Asia, and here at home as well."

"That's right," Katsura agreed. "I was only trying to say that in the world today, it's conventional wisdom to assume there are individuals or groups who would round up disadvantaged children and their mothers and then sell them somewhere outside their native country. Child pornography and the prostitution of young girls are undeniable realities, and the Internet is teeming with the most sickeningly exploitative imagery you could imagine.

"As Ricchan said, there are more than a few of those pathetic duos—the crying child and the frowsy, wretched-looking mother—wandering around in Japanese cities these days. It would be nice to think there's a happy ending waiting for them somewhere down the road, but I'm afraid such a rosily optimistic view would be unrealistic, or delusional. Even so, I won't give up my vision of a brighter future for those mothers and their children."

While Tatsuo Katsura was delivering this disquisition, two of the Caveman Group's featured actors, the inseparable Suke & Kaku, had been sitting quietly on the bare floor in the great room, listening intently. Now they craned their necks above the seated crowd and joined in the conversation.

"We wanted to ask your opinion about a dramaturgical matter, Mr. Choko," one of them said. "We were looking for an opening-scene motif that could be reprised in the finale, and we thought the crying children might work.

"At the beginning, a single child could appear and begin to ascend toward the rafters, weeping loudly, and later there would be a group of children on the stage. You might wonder how we would go about creating the climbing effect, but by a stroke of luck, it turns out the architect of the circular auditorium, Mr. Ara, also designed a sort of spiral ramp or tiered scaffolding that extends almost all the way up to the ceiling of the theater in the round. Apparently the riser was originally built for a concert of Mr. Takamura's work. Right now it's being stored in the gymnasium, so we should be able to use it. As for actors, we could recruit children from around here—the smaller and nimbler the better. Of course we would have to be absolutely certain the corkscrew ramp was safe, but we could get the junior high's physical education teacher to help us with the logistical details.

"For that version of the opening, rather than using improvisation, we'd like to add a scene in which Unaiko would play a woman who speaks to the dispirited young mother and tries to give her a small ray of hope of the kind Katsura mentioned a while ago. Do you think you could write something along those lines for us, Mr. Choko? The beauty part is that the little girl would be wandering around, wailing at the top of her lungs—you know: *Waa, waa!*—so you wouldn't need to write any special dialogue for her at all!"

# 3

The preparations for the performance proceeded apace, with Unaiko and Ricchan at the center of activity, as usual. While I was busy doing my small part, helping to work out the kinks in the opening scene and finale Suke & Kaku had proposed, I was unexpectedly drawn into a new situation. Asa telephoned me one morning, saying that since the young troupe members were going to be rehearsing at the Forest House during the afternoon, she was hosting a get-together at her house. She wanted me to attend because Unaiko's aunt (the one who had featured so prominently in the shocking story we'd heard the other day) was going to be there in person.

"I know this probably seems like a bolt from the blue," Asa said. "It took me by surprise, too, but apparently the aunt says this meeting is an absolute necessity, and Unaiko wants us to be there, too, as witnesses and (I'm guessing) to provide moral support as well. Daio's the one who arranged it. This is ancient history, but as you may have heard, at one time he was involved in trying to undermine the power of the teachers' union in this prefecture. Long story short, a number of people who are opposed to Unaiko's current project move in the same circles, politically speaking, as Daio's former disciples. I've often been forced to listen to them boasting about how they sent you an extra-large live turtle as a prank, and even now the anecdote is gleefully trotted out during elections for the prefectural assembly to liven up campaign speeches. On the other hand, the junior high administrators seem confident they'll be able to weather the storm of protest and opposition, in large part—ironically—because of my connection with Daio. So he has fingers in both pies, so to speak.

"You're probably wondering what this urgent meeting with Unaiko's aunt is going to be about. Well, a certain person who used to be a big wheel in the highest echelons of education, with prestigious medals and decorations galore—I'm talking about Unaiko's uncle, of course—anyhow, he has evidently become aware of the connection between Daio and me and between us and Unaiko. His faction is concerned that the recent additions to the play (you know, the ones regarding the way Unaiko's personal history parallels the story of Meisuke's mother) will make the uncle look foolish. There are rumors that the play could cause a major scandal for him, and he wants to find a way to shut it down or to at least remove the offensive sections. With that goal in mind, he and his wife supposedly want to meet with Unaiko, after eighteen years of silence, and try to patch up their damaged relationship. The aunt seems to be a rather assertive type of person, and she's already in Matsuyama, staying at the ANA Hotel. Daio has gone to pick her up and bring her here."

That afternoon we assembled at Asa's house by the river. While Unaiko was parking the car, Daio introduced me to the aunt. She was polite enough, but I got the distinct impression that she had very little interest in the likes of me. Clearly, her attention was focused entirely on Unaiko's imminent arrival.

Mrs. Koga, Unaiko's aunt, appeared to be in her midsixties. She had an unusually large-framed physique for a Japanese woman of her generation, but there didn't seem to be much flesh on those big bones. She sat down at a low table on the tatami-matted floor, and when Unaiko finally walked in her aunt stared fixedly at her and said, "You've really changed a lot, Mitsuko. Of course, it's been a long time since we last met, so I'm not really surprised."

Not to be outdone, Unaiko shot back: "It's been eighteen years, to be exact. The last time I saw you I was still just a kid. If I had been allowed to carry my pregnancy to term, the child beside me right now would be about the same age I was then. Who knows, maybe we—you, and I, and my child—could be having a jolly chat about old times."

"Yes, and I think my husband would probably be leading the way," Mrs. Koga said matter-of-factly. "You were such a cheerful, openhearted girl, so of course he couldn't help caring deeply about you and sincerely showing his affection."

"Yes," Unaiko said sharply. "He showed his affection, all right: day and night. Especially night."

The aunt looked pained. "It's true that things ended up going too far, and my husband crossed some boundaries that should never have been crossed," she said carefully. "I think it started because when you first came to stay with us as a girl of fourteen or fifteen, you were frightened by the ancient network of caves and tunnels around the shrine on one side of our mansion. (As everyone here probably knows, those catacombs are one of Kamakura's most famous tourist destinations.) My husband started sleeping in your room to allay your fears, and it somehow got to be a habit. I was prone to headaches so I frequently went to bed early, and I didn't know exactly what was going on between you. I just felt fortunate that when he came home at the end of the day, tired from work, he could always relax in your room for a while."

"Yes, and it was the nature of the 'relaxation,' as you put it, that was the problem," Unaiko said. "Really, the boundary-crossing stuff began almost right away. Your husband explained to me that while it was forbidden for an uncle to put his hands inside his niece's underpants, it was perfectly all right as long as his caresses stayed safely on the outside, or around the edges. I didn't know any better, so I thought, *Oh, okay—if you say so.* By and by, things progressed to the point where he started putting his hands under my panties, but he promised he wouldn't insert his fingers anywhere they didn't belong, because he said it would be too close to having sex."

Once again, the aunt looked distinctly uncomfortable. "After you left us, when I asked my husband how things could have gone as far as they did, he told me he was startled by what he called the 'extreme abundance' of your secretions in response to his affectionate caresses, and he said that was the trigger for the inappropriate escalation of your relationship," she explained. "As he put it, the physical evidence seemed to suggest you weren't exactly averse to what he was doing. Tell me honestly, Mitsuko—isn't it true that you enjoyed having my husband touch you?"

"Well, yes, I suppose I did on some level, after I got used to it," Unaiko admitted. "But I really didn't understand what was going on, and I made the mistake of believing that my uncle would never do anything inappropriate."

"Mitsuko, another thing I heard from my husband, after you had gone home to Osaka, is that when you were a junior in high school you came home one day and told him about a term that, you said, described what the two of you were doing. (Apparently you had heard it from some of your more grown-up classmates.) It's a little awkward to say this out loud in mixed company, but the term was 'simultaneous mutual masturbation.'"

"Yes, it's true, I did tell him about that," Unaiko said. "I wanted him to assure me that what we were doing wasn't actually *sex*, per se."

"But as an intimate physical relationship develops and escalates, isn't what you two ended up doing simply consensual intercourse?"

"No," Unaiko said flatly. "It's called rape. This was back before houses had air-conditioning in every room, and when the weather was hot I would lie on my bed stark-naked, with my legs apart, just trying to cool off. One day my uncle was lurking nearby, as usual. He stared at my crotch for the longest time, and then he suddenly said in a loud voice, 'Okay, enough is enough. I've had it with this nonsense!' And then he proceeded to rape me. (At the time, you were off in Kyoto for some kind of women's college reunion, Auntie.) When I started crying from the pain, my uncle said, 'Don't worry, it won't hurt after the first time,' and then he went on to rape me again, twice, until it started to get light outside and he finally went back to his own bedroom.

"That morning, I waited until the government car came to pick Uncle up and take him to his office, and then I got on the train and went home to Osaka. As proof of what had been done to me, I took along the underpants I'd put on after the third round of rape, which were covered with blood and semen. I think you all know what happened after that.

"It was a little more than three months later when you called, Auntie, and asked me to come to Tokyo and meet you at one of the most solemn (and controversial) places in the entire country. You told me we needed to talk about my future, and you were proposing that I undergo some kind of purification ceremony, presumably because you had an inkling of what had happened between me and my uncle. While we were at the shrine someone waved a gigantic Japanese flag in front of my face, and I was overcome with dizziness and began to vomit. I guess that was when you realized I must be pregnant, because you promptly hustled me off to get an abortion. Afterward, once again, I took certain items home as proof, and I still have them today."

"I see," Mrs. Koga said. "And now they say you're planning to reveal this sordid ancient history as part of a public performance in a school auditorium? I've heard that your little play tells the story of the woman who led an uprising among the local farmers many years ago. But what on earth does that ancient history have to do with what you've told us here today?"

"The woman you mentioned was known as Meisuke's mother, and she and her son led a ragtag group of women from this area to fight in an uprising," Unaiko replied calmly. "They emerged victorious, but after the battle Meisuke's mother was raped and her child was killed. I'll be in costume as Meisuke's mother, and I'll act a scene in which she is gang-raped by a bunch of wayward samurai. Some of the teachers and mothers of students have banded together to scheme against me and try to undermine the play, and they've blown things way out of proportion, telling everyone the rape scene is going to go on and on at great length. Because of that, I've had to modify my approach. Originally, I wasn't sure how to convey the full extent of Meisuke's mother's suffering and sadness. But then I realized that I had to own my personal truth, publicly, and declare through the medium of this role I'm playing that I, too, was raped, and I really did have my unborn child killed. I want to say, 'Look at me—this actually happened. And this kind of thing is still going on in this country, even today.' I think my personal testimony will get through to the teenage kids in the audience. I mean, we've all seen historical dramas where actresses in insanely elaborate period costumes pretend they're being thrown to the ground and forced to have sex, sobbing the whole time, but does that kind of stylized charade hit home for anyone who's watching? On the other hand, if an actual person stands on a stage and says, 'Listen, people, I myself was raped in real life,' the audience will be taken by surprise, and maybe then the flesh-and-blood truth will get through to them. That kind of visceral connection is the essence of our dog-tossing style of theater, except in this case we'll be throwing words back and forth instead of the usual soft toys. In the ideal scenario, I would say something to my uncle and he'd respond, the way my aunt is doing right now, by cross-examining me. I would give him a chance to throw terms like 'abundant secretions' and 'mutual masturbation' at me, as if they were 'dead dogs.'"

"But what's the point? I mean, what good could possibly come of that type of public display?" Mrs. Koga said, abruptly scrambling to her feet and drawing herself up to her full height. She truly was an imposing figure.

"At any rate," she went on, "my part in this seems to be at an end, and now it's time for my husband to take center stage, so to speak. As I understand it, your dramatic method would involve having you share your testimony, followed by a sort of cross-examination by my husband. You know, your uncle isn't as young as he used to be, and these days he's just kind of a doddering old buffoon, so he would probably respond by simply echoing those unseemly terms you mentioned in a gravelly voice, and he'd insist you were a willing participant. Since Mr. Choko here is such a strong proponent of the democratic process, I assume we can rest assured that no one would be censoring my husband's remarks?"

Turning to look directly at Unaiko, Mrs. Koga went on: "Even before you got involved in the world of theater, Mitsuko, you were always an unusually expressive person. By the way, I recently got to see you in a play on one of the cable TV stations. You were playing the role of a medium who was trying to appease the vengeful spirit of an aristocratic lady, and I was impressed by your passionate, fiery performance. I was also struck by the eloquent way you moaned and groaned, and it occurred to me that I had heard those same sounds before, many times, emanating from the room where you and my husband were supposedly 'relaxing' together . . ."

# 4

The protest movement against Unaiko and her forthcoming play appeared to be gathering momentum with every passing day. However, when those activities were reported on the theater-group website Ricchan maintained, the majority of responses—rather than siding with the protesters—voiced strong support for the upcoming show. Ricchan, who was always cautious and prudent about everything, started saying things like "This play of ours is generating a lot of buzz, and I'd like to harness the energy productively. There's no way everyone who's interested will be able to squeeze into the theater for the actual performance, so Unaiko and I were thinking we might put on a separate event, up at the Saya, the day before."

By chance, I ended up playing a small role in implementing the plan, with an assist from fate, or happenstance. Asa had been on better terms with Sakura Ogi Magarshack than anyone else who worked on the doomed movie about Meisuke's mother, but she and Sakura had fallen out of touch in recent years. First there were problems with the international opening of the movie, followed by the death of Tamotsu Komori, the producer of the film. Some months later, we had each received a letter from Komori's office saying that while it wasn't a done deal, there was a chance the movie might get a premiere after all. That, too, came to naught, and Asa subsequently lost contact with Sakura.

Years later, a national newspaper ran an article about the organized opposition to Unaiko's upcoming play about Meisuke's mother. The reporter mentioned Sakura Ogi Magarshack by name, and as a result, a younger friend of hers was galvanized into getting in touch with me and then stopping by. The man taught English and American culture at a university on Kyushu, and while studying abroad at a college in Washington, DC, he had become obliged to Sakura's husband, a college professor whose field was Japanese studies. Professor Magarshack had since died, but the young instructor from Kyushu had stayed in touch with Sakura, who had been so kind and supportive when he was a student in a strange land.

Last year he'd had an opportunity to return to Washington, and when he paid a visit to Sakura (now living the quiet life of a pensioner) she had happened to remark that she missed hearing from Asa and me. During his brief visit to the Forest House I asked the instructor whether he could share Sakura's contact information, and he promptly provided her addresses. He explained that while Mrs. Magarshack (as he called her) was still hale and hearty, it had become increasingly difficult for her to read letters in Japanese, and as a natural consequence her contact with friends and acquaintances in Japan had diminished over the years.

I wrote Sakura a letter in English, which Ricchan scanned and emailed from her computer. In the message I explained that I was currently working with a group of friends and colleagues, including Asa, on creating a stage version of *Meisuke's Mother Marches Off to War*. We knew the film's public release had been plagued with a series of problems (I wrote), but if the circumstances had changed—if, for example, there was now a DVD of the film we could take a look at—it would be incredibly helpful to the actress playing Meisuke's mother onstage (the role Sakura had played on film) to have a chance to study the DVD, especially the battle-chant scenes. I received an almost instantaneous email reply from Sakura, also in English, offering to assist us in any way she could.

At that point Ricchan took over and began corresponding directly with Sakura. They exchanged a flurry of emails, and the situation evolved quite rapidly. Sakura told Ricchan that at the present time, she held the exhibition rights for the film. She would be happy to dispatch a DVD of it right away, but she suspected the village probably didn't have a movie theater suitable for showing a feature film. The movie had never been shown publicly in Japan, and since so many local women had participated in the filming, as extras, Sakura said she hoped as many of them as possible would have a chance to see the finished product. After giving the matter some thought, Sakura came up with the idea of putting on a free public screening of the film as an adjunct of the stage performance. The showing would take place up at the Saya, where some of the film had been shot. Of course, in order to screen a movie outdoors in the middle of a meadow, we would need some special equipment, including a large portable screen. Sakura said she had all the necessary gear at her house, and since she suspected that Komori had probably never gotten around to paying Mr. Choko a penny for writing the screenplay for the film (she joked), she would be happy to send those items to us by air freight, at her own expense.

That was how Unaiko and Ricchan, with some help from their friends, managed to expand the festivities beyond the theater in the round. Of course, Asa pitched in along the way, as usual, while also continuing to act as unofficial den mother and cheerleader in chief for her talented young protégées.

# Chapter 15

# Death by Rain

## 1

It was the final dress rehearsal, the afternoon before the play opened. Masao Anai and I were sitting together toward the back of the theater, far from all the Very Important People who had crowded into the front and center seats.

Toward the rear of the stage there was a newly erected, complex-looking structure that I perceived at first as a tall, broad bridge with multiple levels. A woman, dressed in a dark blue linen dress and matching hat, was navigating one of those elevated catwalks, nimbly traversing from stage left to right and back again. Her head was hanging low, so I couldn't see her face, but I assumed it was Unaiko, as in previous rehearsals. The woman vanished behind the drop curtain on the left side of the stage and then, a few moments later, reappeared from the other side of the stage on another level, walking with the same confident gait. As I watched her ascending ever higher, I realized that the complex structure was one continuous ramp—not unlike the spiral staircases you sometimes see in upscale houses, only wider and more sturdily built.

By and by Masao told me that Unaiko had been called away for an emergency meeting, and the young woman in blue was a troupe member who had been pressed into service as a stand-in. (I still thought she looked a lot like Unaiko, especially from behind.) As the substitute was approaching the darkness at the edge of the uppermost level, the sound of a weeping girl, which had been faintly audible before, was suddenly amplified. The woman had been swallowed up in the darkness after taking three turns on the ramp, but the voice of the crying child kept getting louder, until it echoed through the hall.

Then a little girl dressed in a flimsy floral dress and slip-on canvas shoes stepped onto the ramp, continuing to wail at the top of her lungs, and began to wend her way toward the ceiling. Up she went, one slow, arduous step at a time, bawling all the way, until she reached the top, whereupon she seemed to fall away into the darkness. (Meanwhile, the lighting had been altered to make the lower part of the staircase appear hazy and indistinct.)

As the sound of the sobbing child died away, a single shaft of light illuminated the stage. Standing there was the blue-clad woman we'd seen earlier, still looking as forlorn as she had when she was climbing upward with downcast eyes. This time, however, she addressed the audience in a clear, strong voice that filled the entire theater.

"I think there are a lot of people who have had some sort of chance encounter with a small female child who wanders alone along city boulevards or in the subterranean labyrinths beneath train stations, crying at the top of her lungs, but they have no idea who the child might be or to whom she belongs. The young woman is always a few paces ahead of the child and evidently doesn't want to allow the little girl to catch up with her, because she always seems to be walking very fast. This is an urban phenomenon that actually exists today."

Typically for one of Unaiko's productions, there was more exposition than in a conventional play, but the audience seemed to be listening raptly.

"A hundred and forty-some years ago, in this area, a brave group of children placed themselves between the government soldiers and the front lines, forming a sort of protective shield for the farm women gathered to fight in the uprising led by Meisuke's mother," the woman in blue went on. "Wailing all the while, the children hunkered down on the ground and prevented the soldiers from penetrating into the heart of the battalion. As a result, the women were able to fight their way to a quick victory. The exploits of those female warriors are celebrated around here to this day. In fact, Meisuke's mother's call to battle became so famous that it has been preserved in the form of a chant, which folks here sing every year during the Bon Odori season. We basically used Mr. Choko's version of the chant, which he originally wrote for a screenplay, but we took the liberty of adding a line or two of our own:

*Men commit rape—that's nothing new / But countries can be rapists, too. / Women warriors, here we go / Off to vanquish every foe!*

"So, this is how our performance begins. We're fully prepared to deal with any difficulties that might arise as a result of the ideological opposition to this play and (assuming we can overcome those challenges) for our finale we're planning to call the weeping child and her despondent mother back to the stage. At that time, however, there will be several mothers and their children, rather than just one of each. And all the little girls, instead of weeping buckets of tears, will be smiling prettily, and all the mothers will be wearing expressions bright with hope.

"What we would like to demonstrate with this play is that the same oppression that forced the local women to take up arms over a hundred years ago continues today, and is personified by the sad mothers and crying children most of us seem to have glimpsed on the streets of our cities. But while we all need to acknowledge that there are still a great many battles to be fought by women, at the same time we would like to convey a message of hopefulness and possibility, so the women warriors who went before us won't have suffered and died in vain. That's what we're hoping to accomplish here tonight by showing you this play."

As the actress's introductory monologue reached its end, the stage became dark and the sound of voices chanting the war cry echoed from far away.

> *Women warriors, let us go*
> *Off to face our latest foe.*
> *Into battle we will soar*
> *Strong and brave forevermore.*
> *All together, here we go*
> *We shall vanquish every foe!*

Then the women—whose voices were far more impressive than those of the men in the chorus—let out a whoop of victory and that cheer swelled and intensified, growing louder and louder, to signify the successful conclusion of the uprising.

Ricchan was the musical director for the play, of course, and she had used Sakura's DVD of *Meisuke's Mother Marches Off to War* as a resource for the musical components of the play. Ricchan wasn't present at this rehearsal, either; the last time I'd seen her was when she headed up to the Saya early that morning, along with Tamakichi and some of his friends (many of whom had also been involved in the filming of the movie), to pitch a giant tent for the public screening of Sakura's film. The showing took place a couple of hours before the rehearsal, and I had heard reports that because of the way the wind was blowing the voices of the actors on the screen were audible all the way down to the houses along the river. I couldn't help thinking that because of the auspicious breeze, quite a few local residents who would attend the following evening's live performance might experience a frisson of recognition when they heard the battle-cry chant again. Tickets for the performance had already sold out, and the local newspapers and TV stations had also given a great deal of publicity to the showing of the original film at the Saya. As a result, the event had ended up being standing room only.

Meanwhile, back at the dress rehearsal, a spotlight revealed a stage bare except for two straw mats spread out in the center. Meisuke, the valiant young farmer who led the first uprising, was lying on a futon spread out over the mats. Projected on hanging curtains around him were illuminated images of square columns made from oak, which created the optical illusion of a jail cell. Several young samurai came stamping into this enclosure. Then Meisuke, obviously unwell, launched into a heartfelt plea as the samurai listened with quizzically tilted heads.

"You fellows represent the new fiefdom, and your social standing was undermined by my group's victory in the uprising. I know you had to find a scapegoat in order to save face with your overlords, but we were always friends off the battlefield, were we not? Yet I was captured and thrown into jail for the crime of having won in combat, fair and square, and you're keeping me prisoner here even though I've fallen ill. What good does that do?"

A young samurai warrior replied: "It's nothing personal. As you said, we just needed someone to step up and be punished for the insurrection, and you happen to be the leader."

Then Meisuke said, "But why won't you let me escape now?"

To which the samurai replied, "The truth is, even if we set you free you're so ill that you wouldn't live very long on the outside, much less be able to lead another insurrection. However, try to see our point of view. If we keep you here and let you die in prison, then the old regime will start to believe in and trust us again in spite of our ignominious defeat in the uprising. That will be politically useful to us in the future."

The group of young samurai turned on their heels and departed. A woman—Meisuke's mother—had been squatting outside the illusory jail cell, and a despairing Meisuke tearfully appealed to her for help. His mother, who was still very youthful-looking, responded by uttering a line that has become one of the more famous parts of local lore about the uprising: "There's no need to worry—even if you die, I'll just give birth to you again."

The projected images of oaken columns flickered, then disappeared. Meisuke's mother stood up and, advancing to her son's bedside, she began to straighten the lapels of his kimono and tidy his bedding. The spotlight trained on Meisuke's bed began to fade away and the stage was plunged into darkness, signaling a brief break for a scene change.

There was a smattering of tepid applause from the people in the first few rows. I knew what that meant; the disagreement between Unaiko and the opposing faction regarding the reincarnation story had not yet been resolved. The school group, which included the two teachers who had waylaid us behind the shrine, objected strongly to the older version of the folktale in which Meisuke's mother gives birth to her deceased son again years later (that is, the same spirit in a new body), but Unaiko had refused to yield.

I remembered that when I first told this story to Sakura, she had responded by saying, "I don't see anything unnatural there. It seems like a perfectly maternal thing to do. Besides, millions of people all over the world believe in reincarnation."

Not wanting to fuel the controversy, I had glossed over the "rebirth issue" in the script and had written only a few vague lines to suggest the mother's lovingly solicitous behavior toward her dying son. Of course, I was coming to this project from a long background in novel writing, and I was still in the habit of adding accretional layers to any text by means of multiple rewrites, but one of the bits of conventional wisdom regarding this technique is the idea that if you don't feel confident about a rewrite, you should completely delete the section in question. That's what I had done with the section on the reincarnation of Meisuke, but Unaiko had subsequently inserted her own revisions.

As the stage lights came up Masao whispered, "I think the applause just now was for you, Mr. Choko."

"No," I replied. "The applause was for Unaiko, for the way her direction brought everything together and gave the play its distinctive shape, and for the trouble the young actors took to learn their lines and the splendid way they delivered them, even in her absence."

At that moment I caught sight of Asa standing over on the left side of the theater, in the narrow aisle separating the front-row seats from the elevated stage. She was hanging her head in a way that reminded me of the doleful-looking young mother who had been onstage a short while before. My sister didn't glance in my direction; she seemed to be passively biding her time, waiting for someone to notice her presence.

I got up from where I was sitting, ducked into a space behind the audience seating, and waited there for Asa. On the stage, the play was progressing with a scene in which the members of the second uprising were marching off to battle, led by the possible reincarnation of the late Meisuke (that is, Meisuke II) and the courageous woman who had given birth to both of them.

After a moment my sister appeared beside me and said in a dazed voice, "Three men have kidnapped Unaiko, and they're holding her prisoner at Daio's old training camp. Apparently two of the men went there in their own car, while a third kidnapper forced Ricchan to drive another car, with Unaiko and Akari as unwilling passengers. The men ordered one of the young troupe members to warn you that if you notified the police, something terrible would happen to Akari. A bit later I got a phone call from Daio, telling me to share this information with you, and you alone, and instructing me to bring you to the training camp. I told the young actor not to say a word to anyone, so Masao doesn't even know what's going on.

"The people at the training camp aren't asking you to do anything specific, but they want you there as soon as possible. It sounds as if they just want to go over the script and get Unaiko to make some changes. I gather Unaiko is holding her ground even on the improvised sections, telling the other side you approved those portions. Maybe they're hoping you'll be able to persuade her to change her mind.

"I'm not really clear about Daio's role in all of this," Asa added. "I only know that he seems to be on good terms with Mrs. Koga—Unaiko's aunt—and her husband, and as we saw the other day, they've apparently been acquainted for quite some time. To be honest, I really don't know whether Daio is friend or foe, but the good news is that

the situation doesn't seem to have escalated to the point where the
police would need to be called in."

# 2

Asa and I left the theater right away, and after a quick detour to pick
up some things at the Forest House, we headed for Daio's training
camp. After a short drive we found ourselves on the far side of a deep
valley with a view of the camp, which was built into a sloping hill,
and the rolling farmland above it. The terrain looked very familiar to
me, even though I hadn't been here since high school.

It wasn't dusk yet, but the densely overcast sky had already
turned completely dark. We crossed the river on a steel bridge that
had replaced the rustic suspension bridge I remembered. On the other
side of this bridge there was a carport containing a lightweight truck
and a small tractor. A passable road climbed the hill, which probably
explained why the cars that had brought Unaiko, Ricchan, and Akari
were nowhere to be seen. The only light came from a naked bulb
hanging on a lamppost made from a tall, round log.

Two bulky men dressed in suits, who had been standing outside
the circle of light, suddenly appeared and gestured to Asa to leave the
car behind the carport, where it wouldn't be visible. When that task had
been accomplished, they led the way up the long incline to the training
camp, with Asa and me at their heels. The cultivated fields on either
side had been carved out of what had once been dense forest, and the
area appeared to have settled comfortably into its new role as fertile,
tillable farmland. (This impression was dramatically different from my
teenage memories of those same fields as livid, freshly clear-cut gashes
in the landscape.) My heart lurched when I glanced ahead and saw
what I thought was a crowd of men milling around in the crepuscular
murk, each holding aloft a slender spear, but as we got closer I realized
the shadowy soldiers were nothing more than an army of giant tomato
plants, standing tall inside supportive cages made from bamboo poles.

Asa's late husband (a school principal) came from a farming family, and after he died she had thrown herself into raising vegetables on a scale far beyond the normal family garden. During that brief phase, she had often mailed boxes of fresh vegetables to me in Tokyo. Now she said, as we hiked up the hill, "This strain of tomato really is exceptionally sweet and meaty. I remember once, after he had delivered a batch to a hotel in Matsuyama, Daio told me his tomatoes were being used to make gourmet salads in the hotel restaurant, along with some kind of extra-special romaine lettuce."

"Mm-hmm," I said.

"Of course, when Daio starts a new project, he tends to become obsessive about it," Asa went on. "Right now he's totally focused on cultivating these high-end tomatoes. Some of the children of his old disciples, after moving away to Osaka and Yokohama, have even come back here to work. Maybe their parents called them home, but anyhow, Daio was saying that at any given time there are four or five young apprentices on the premises, learning how to raise prize tomatoes and so on."

"Mm-hmm."

We both knew that Asa's compulsive chattiness and my disinclination to reply sprang from an identical concern about the current situation, and the polarized dynamic continued as we trekked up the long hill. At last the buildings of the training camp came into sight, looking just as they had when I'd come to visit one weekend as a high school student, accompanied by my classmate and future brother-in-law, Goro Hanawa, and a young officer named Peter, who was stationed in Matsuyama as a language officer during the Occupation. The main building, which included a bathhouse with mineral-rich water piped in from a nearby hot spring, was completely dark, but the lights were ablaze in a two-story building on a hillock to the left. Farther into the complex, there was a bungalow that (as I recalled) housed a gloomy office; its curtains were drawn, but some light was leaking out. Daio emerged from the front door and headed our way. He obviously recognized Asa and me, even from a distance, and he began speaking even before we were fully illuminated by the beam from his flashlight.

"Asa, Kogito, I'm so sorry you had to get dragged into this," he said. "Unaiko and her uncle, Mr. Koga, are up there in the office, waiting for you to arrive. As you know, he's the husband of Mrs. Koga, whom you met the other day when Unaiko was airing some of her past grievances. You may remember that the aunt mentioned her family's desire to vet the script for any references to their, um, history. I know this goes far beyond the call of duty, but Unaiko was saying that if you could stand by and listen while both sides present their cases . . ."

"If it's a simple matter of revising the playscript, why did you have to create such a melodramatic brouhaha?" I asked sharply. "And who on earth decided to involve Akari in this absurd situation? That is completely unforgivable."

"I know, that's what I kept saying, but . . . I hope you'll understand that I was pressured into acting against my better judgment. Forgive me, Kogito? Please?"

While Daio was stammering this apology in a particularly craven and obsequious manner, it struck me that his demeanor on this night was very different than during his visits to the Forest House. Yet even as those borderline-servile protestations of regret were streaming from his mouth, I seemed to sense a new forcefulness—you might even say authority—in his bearing.

"I think it's absolutely despicable," Asa fumed. "I mean, not only did that dreadful man practically kidnap Akari and Ricchan, he was even making threats like some two-bit gangster, saying something awful would happen to Akari if we got the police involved. We can talk later on about the part you've played in this reprehensible scenario, Daio. Right now, first things first. Where are Akari and Ricchan? I've brought Akari's evening meds and a change of underwear, along with a light supper of sandwiches and so on. It sounds as if my brother needs to go and talk to this Mr. Koga you mentioned, but I would like to see with my own eyes that Akari is safe as soon as possible. Could you please take me to the place where my nephew is being held? If you're too busy, I see some big lugs lurking in the shadows, watching every move we make. Please tell one of them to make himself useful!"

Daio didn't reply to Asa's impassioned screed. He simply ordered one of the young men hovering nearby—who, unlike the suit-wearing hulks we had met down by the carport, looked as though they might be farmers—to grab Asa's Boston bag and take her where she wanted to go. Then Daio led me up the cobblestoned path to the office, with his small electric flashlight showing the way. The chilly, moisture-laden night air, which seemed to be closing in around us, made me shiver. Yet I also felt a sudden sense of clarity, as though Asa's angry tirade had jolted me out of shock and into a more rational state of mind.

With his usual one-armed dexterity, Daio turned the knob and opened the door. After stepping halfway inside, he used his head to nudge aside a heavy-looking old curtain that covered the opening. As we entered the room, which was lit only by a low-hanging bulb, there was a long, narrow slab of hardened earth, rather like adobe, where we shed our shoes before stepping onto the wood-plank floor. Daio made a quick, deft adjustment to the electric bulb that hung from the ceiling, winching it higher so it would cast a wider pool of light.

A square table stood directly in front of us. A number of chairs were lined up on all four sides, making the smallish space feel even more cramped. Staring intently in our direction was a group of men who appeared to be perching tentatively on the chairs, as if they might need to depart at any moment. There was a woman as well: Unaiko. She had a voluminous shawl wound around her head and shoulders, which made her look somehow exotic and unfamiliar, but she didn't appear to be particularly traumatized.

An older man stood up from his chair to let Daio squeeze by, and I knew right away that this must be Unaiko's infamous uncle. His prominent, well-shaped nose and fleshy cheeks looked somewhat incongruous beneath a rather narrow forehead crowned with close-cropped white hair, but the glint of intelligence and perspicacity in his eyes reminded me of Unaiko. As the man glanced in my direction and gave a slight nod, those eyes showed no trace of emotion.

Unaiko gestured at the empty chair beside her, which was across the table from her uncle, and I took a seat without returning the man's perfunctory nod. He stared at his lap, plainly nonplussed that I had deliberately chosen to ignore his greeting. The chairs on either side of the door were occupied by the two men in suits whom Asa and I had seen earlier, and it was clear from their watchful demeanor that they had been tasked with stopping Unaiko if she tried to make a break for it.

Daio spoke first. "I'll make the necessary introductions to save time. This is Mr. Koga, who believes there are elements of Unaiko's play that could warrant a lawsuit for defamation of character. It might feel more natural to address him as 'Sensei,' but let's keep it simple tonight. Mr. Koga had an illustrious career in the Ministry of Education and made significant contributions in that area. He used to hold a high-ranking position in the ministry—head of an important department—and he often used to appear on television in the news coverage of the Japanese legislature. Kogito, someone like you who has an interest in the finer points of postwar educational policies will surely remember having seen Mr. Koga on TV at some point.

"Moving along, I'm guessing most of you will have already recognized the novelist Kogito Choko, who is also well known for his outspoken views on politics and social issues," Daio continued. "He and I go way back—his father was my mentor—and, well, one way or another, here we are today. In case you might be wondering, I've known Kogito since he was knee-high to a grasshopper, and that's why I still call him by his first name. We were originally expecting Mrs. Koga to be joining us here as well—she actually came down to Shikoku earlier this week for a preliminary meeting, but the discussion wasn't exactly productive so she decided to let her husband deal with things on his own from here on out.

"Anyhow, Mr. Koga was saying he would like to talk things through with Unaiko, as a more peaceable alternative to taking this matter to court. However, Unaiko stood firm, saying that because she had already met with Mrs. Koga to no avail, there was no point in trying to set up an amicable meeting with her uncle. It wasn't Mr. Koga himself but rather his two associates here who said, 'Well then, we'll just have to take matters into our own hands to make sure the two parties get together, face-to-face.' From Unaiko's perspective, this is a meeting she was forcibly compelled to attend. The thing is, if this gathering were to go smoothly and yield a positive result, the legal dogs could be called off and everyone would benefit, so let's try to make it work."

Pushing aside the heavy curtain, the two young men whom I had identified as farmers cleared some space among the jumble of papers on the table and set down a carton filled with cookies and sweet rolls, along with paper cups and individual plastic bottles of water. Then they left the room. The ancient curtain had been effectively muffling the noise of the storm that had begun to rage outside, but for the short time the door was open, the sounds of the pouring rain and the gale-force winds roaring through the forest were clearly audible. When Asa and I stopped off at the Forest House before driving up here, I had added Akari's noise-canceling headphones to the other supplies in the Boston bag and that, I reflected now, had been a good impulse. He hated the sound of stormy weather.

"Well then, let's get started," Daio said authoritatively, handing me a marked-up copy of the script. "Before you arrived, Mr. Choko, the parties who gathered here earlier—well, Unaiko was dragged here under duress—but at any rate, this group has already spent some time discussing the problems at hand. From Unaiko's standpoint, this radical and potentially scandalous section of her play is a necessary inclusion, while if we look at it from Mr. Koga's point of view, the only question is whether the offending portion should be expunged completely, or just heavily revised. Leaving it intact is not an option.

"Actually, I should have said 'sections,' since there are two of them. Let's take a look at the first sticking point, which talks about the relationship (if that's the proper term) between the uncle and his niece. I must say, I was surprised when Unaiko said right off the bat that she would be fine with deleting the section entirely. In the script, all the disputed parts have been circled in red felt-tip pen, and

Unaiko said, 'Sure, go ahead and delete the whole scene.' According to her, since the entire segment was going to be removed, it was simply a matter of cutting. There would be no need to tailor the scene in question. Anyhow, the point is, Mr. Choko won't have to go to the trouble of revising the script to ensure that the deletion doesn't affect the overall literary style, or flow, or whatever."

While I was inspecting the red-lined alterations, Mr. Koga was staring in my direction, and I got the distinct sense that he was inspecting *me*. He waited until I had finished reading over the disputed scenes, and then he spoke.

"Since Unaiko has agreed that this section should be deleted, there's really no need to discuss it in any detail," he began. "However, what still gives me pause, Mr. Choko, is the fact that you had apparently signed off on this inflammatory scene, and if we hadn't intervened it would actually have been performed on a public stage. I mean, I just . . . you and I are from the same generation, and as someone who has been reading your work since I was young, I honestly don't think the scene we're talking about is a worthy representation of the prose style of such an eminent author. I thought including it would be rude to the author and might even have an adverse effect on his literary reputation, so that's why I asked Unaiko to delete it." Koga made this blatantly manipulative and disingenuous claim without batting an eye, then continued: "However, my wife seemed to feel there was some deep malice concealed in this scene, with the express intention of exposing our family secrets and making me look bad."

He paused to take a deep breath, then said, "Unaiko has invited me to attend the performance tomorrow night, and she seemed to be hoping that at some point a confrontation would take place between me, in my seat in the audience, and her up on the stage. I gather that's the way the dog-tossing approach to theater works. As I understand it, first Unaiko would present the details of my so-called crime against her, and then I would give my side of the story. Unaiko would respond by summoning two actors who had been waiting in the wings (dressed in costumes from the seventeenth century, like the two characters in the famous TV series *Mito Komon* whose names and personas they've borrowed for their comedy act) to join her at the front of the stage. And then she would give the order: 'Suke, Kaku—show the audience what you've got.' One of the men would be holding a stick with a plastic bag attached to the tip, which I'm told was going to be crammed full of dirty laundry (quite literally) and other unspeakable things. Beating the floor with the other end of the stick, the two actors would try to intimidate me, saying, 'You can't look away this time.' Not to put too fine a point on it, Mr. Choko, but I was surprised and, quite frankly, disappointed to hear that you had given your approval to the gratuitous inclusion of such a lurid scene in the final version of the script."

"The addition was meant to be inserted as a secondary scene," I replied. "It was just an improvised attempt to imagine what might have transpired between you and Unaiko if a hypothetical defamation-of-character case were being tried in court with forensic evidence.

The young actors were going to be in costume (and in character) as their alter ego duo—inspired, obviously, by the TV show we all know so well. Since you've been talking about suing for slander, Mr. Koga, in this imaginary court of law you would be giving the plaintiff's testimony while Unaiko conducted the cross-examination. That was the concept behind the skit, which arose naturally out of improvisation. What you're saying is true, though: I did indeed sign off on the addition to the final draft of the script."

At this point, Unaiko spoke up. "In the scene we're discussing, the usual 'dead dogs' were going to be replaced by plastic bags filled with things that really could have been considered admissible evidence in a court of law, if the lawsuit you've been threatening had gone ahead," she explained, addressing her uncle. "The first item was the underpants I wore after you raped me, the summer I was seventeen. They were soaked with blood and semen, and I've hung on to them all these years, preserved in a ziplock bag. The second object was some clinical evidence from the abortion I was forced to undergo. I'll spare you the gory details, but it took all my courage to ask the nurse for that memento. I recently consulted an expert who assured me that even with such old evidence the DNA would stand up to scrutiny."

"Putting aside the question of whether such materials really would be admissible evidence in a court of law, can we agree that for tomorrow's performance, at least, the vulgar 'underground theater' aspect will be removed—you know, the sort of deliberately offensive avant-garde nonsense that was popular when we were young?" Mr. Koga said, looking straight at me. "I think this is for the best, not just in terms of my reputation but also for your good name, Mr. Choko, as an illustrious international literary figure."

"I don't think this has any bearing whatsoever on Mr. Choko's literary reputation," Unaiko snapped. "I've agreed to give you what you want by deleting the first section, so let's move on now. We still need to discuss the second sticking point, to use Daio's term, so can we please get started? All right? Good.

"The second point of contention has to do with a claim Mr. Koga's lawyers have been making. They're saying that up until the day when the event in question took place, I had been living in my uncle's household in perfect harmony for nearly three years, and they're claiming what happened was the natural extension of what they euphemistically call the 'friendly feelings' that existed between my uncle and me. To put it another way, they're alleging that there was a mutually acknowledged foundation in place, which led to full-fledged sexual activity as part of a normal, voluntary progression. They've also been emphasizing the fact that I was already seventeen years old, even though technically eighteen is the age of consent in the prefecture where the events took place."

"Well," Unaiko's uncle said smoothly, "the truth is, we had both been enjoying what you called 'mutual masturbation'—and I must say you seemed to get quite a kick out of using the grown-up term—for quite some time, and it was completely consensual. And then we somehow got into the habit of using our hands to bring each other to, um, culmination at the end of those sessions, because prolonging the, um, pleasure for too long somehow seemed (and again, this was your choice of words) 'over the top.'"

"That's all very well and good," Unaiko said, "but the fact is that at no point was I ever aware that we were *having sex*, per se."

"I'll grant you that," her uncle said. "But on the day in question, it was really just a matter of accidentally wandering off the usual path in the heat of the moment, wasn't it?"

"*Accidentally wandering off the usual path?*" Unaiko echoed incredulously. "So, Uncle, are you saying what you did to me that day was some small, insignificant misstep on your part and no big deal at all?"

"Look, we can stay here arguing about semantics until the cows come home, but if you could only see your way clear to accepting our proposal for resolving the situation, I think we should be able to overcome the second problem as well," Mr. Koga replied smoothly. (He appeared to feel that being addressed as "Uncle" was an encouraging sign.) "Let's face it, we both enjoyed what we were doing, and truth be told we had the kind of easygoing relationship where we could use a term like 'mutual masturbation' in complete awareness of its absurdity. Isn't that a fact? Then suddenly, out of the blue, I get dragged into a situation where you're proposing to go public with our old secrets, using your radical underground theater tactics to make me look like some kind of villainous deviant or something.

"I must say, I was speechless when I heard that if I hadn't agreed to participate in this dramatic contrivance of yours, someone was being prepped to play my role as a stand-in. The actor would have had a placard hanging around his neck bearing my full name and listing the various medals and awards I've received for service to the nation. I really have to ask: Why do you suddenly feel the need to drag me through the mud after all this time?"

"The thing is, there's a fundamental question I've been thinking about continuously during the eighteen years since we last met," Unaiko replied slowly. "So how would it be if we did a sort of table read of the relevant pages in my script right now to get some closure?

There's a big storm raging outside, so even if we end up shouting at each other nobody will be able to hear a word we say."

Unaiko's tone was even, but her eyes flashed with angry defiance. She sat up straighter in her chair, and it was clear to everyone in the room that she had thrown down a gauntlet. Mr. Koga got to his feet looking visibly shaken. I realized much later, in retrospect, that he must have been in the throes of a complex conspiracy of emotions: panic over the peril to his precious reputation, shock at the depth of his niece's resentment, and a burgeoning resurgence of the old feelings of illicit desire—although apparently, in his advanced state of self-righteous denial, there wasn't even a trace of guilt.

"Well, Daio, it looks like we're back to square one. This has been a colossal waste of time," Koga said briskly. "Apparently this young person here hasn't been listening to a word I've said, and this so-called discussion has been an exercise in futility. In any case, I need to take a break; I was supposed to call my wife and one of my attorneys more than an hour ago."

As he spoke Mr. Koga was already striding away, with his two henchmen close behind.

(I remembered then that his wife had described him as a doddering old buffoon, but on this night he didn't seem to have lost any of his forcefulness or mental acuity.) Daio gave me the most minimal of nods, then followed the others outside into the slashing rain and the buffeting wind.

I was left alone with Unaiko. The two lookouts were still stationed outside the door at the front of the office, which had been left ajar, and I could see the backs of their white shirts flashing as they paced back and forth in the darkness. Unaiko turned her face to me: that uncommonly open face, which somehow looked simultaneously weary and agitated.

"I am so terribly sorry for all the trouble I've caused you, Mr. Choko," she said earnestly.

"Well, I've been thinking about our options," I replied. "I'm always doing rewrites on my novels, and for stage performance, too, it seems to take a while for the various elements to shake out and settle down, rather than having the script set in stone from the beginning. So I've been thinking we could try applying that methodology, in accordance with Mr. Koga's request. In the part of the script where you and your colleagues integrated the improvised lines that would have been spoken by him, or by his stand-in, perhaps I could go ahead and take a stab at making the changes you feel you can live with, at least."

"I think there are always going to be some things I'll find very difficult to live with," Unaiko said. "However, because the school administrators are such sticklers about keeping within the allotted time, you've already had to make any number of minor adjustments to the script we're going to use for the performance tomorrow night. Because the version Ricchan and I drafted was based on your screenplay, by the time we added everything we wanted to say ourselves the script was much too long. So then we had to start hacking away at it and somehow, with your help, we got it close to a literary style that seemed to echo the cadences of a call to battle, so that worked out all right. Before the screening at the Saya, I watched the DVD of *Meisuke's Mother Marches Off to War* and I was struck by the way Sakura spoke, as her character's departed spirit, from beyond the grave. Of course, we've been talking a lot about mediums and channeling lately.

"Anyway, while I was sitting here earlier, talking to my uncle, I had an epiphany. I realized that what I'm trying to do with this play is to act as a sort of time-traveling medium, channeling the wounded spirit of my seventeen-year-old self. And I think my uncle must have come to the same realization at the same time, which is why he was so freaked out just now. Maybe he could sense the presence of the spirit of that seventeen-year-old girl suddenly reappearing in the present day and speaking through the medium of a thirty-five-year-old actress. I have a funny feeling my uncle might come to visit me later tonight to have a private encounter with the spirit—that is to say, the living ghost of my seventeen-year-old self!"

Just then, Daio reentered the room. His khaki work jacket was soaked through and water was dripping from the hat he wore. Even after he had shed his wet things and tossed them onto the sofa, he still gave off a strong aroma of rain.

"Mr. Koga has spoken with the attorney who's apparently waiting somewhere, along with Mrs. Koga, and they've come to a final decision. They're insisting on having every single line pertaining to Mr. Koga's relationship with Unaiko eighteen years ago cut from the script. If those terms aren't accepted, Koga says Unaiko will continue to be held prisoner here. (He's in full-on yakuza mode now and doesn't seem to care that what he and his people are doing is felony kidnapping.)

"And when it comes time for the performance tomorrow night, he says, the show will *not* go on; if their terms aren't met, they will crush it into oblivion! And if there should be any further attempts to stage the unrevised play, they'll use the current version of the script, which is in their possession, as the basis for a lawsuit for defamation of character. This is their final word on the subject—they're calling it an ultimatum. Mr. Koga will be standing by throughout the night, waiting for Unaiko to soften her position and agree to their terms. Oh, and also, he absolutely refuses to act out the deleted parts, Unaiko's perfectly reasonable request for closure be damned.

"But listen, Kogito, I just came from telling Mr. Koga that the play really *does* need to go on, for reasons that have nothing to do with him or his niece. You both know the basic story, of course: the farmers in this area were suffering from tremendous economic difficulties, and Meisuke organized an uprising. Not only men but women and children, too, assembled under the flag he hoisted aloft. They went out and fought in the uprising and came back with a victory. Meisuke alone was captured and ended up dying in prison. Some years passed, and once again the farmers found themselves in dire straits. The Meiji Restoration was in full swing and the country was in a state of upheaval, with the feudal system in ruins and the farmers being persecuted by the emissaries of the central government. If the weakest links—the women and children—hadn't banded together and staged an uprising, nothing would have changed. The strategy for the second insurrection came from a supernatural source: Meisuke's mother sent her young child, Meisuke II (whom she believed to be the reincarnation of the original Meisuke), to the grassy hillock known in local lore as the favorite napping spot of the Destroyer. According to legend, Meisuke II was joined by the spirit of his older brother, and they lay down side by side in the grass while the original Meisuke's spirit gave his young namesake some tactical advice about staging a successful uprising. The adversary this time wasn't the forces of the feudal fiefdom but, rather, government soldiers. Those troops tried to power through the insurrectionists' front lines in Okawara, but the small children Meisuke II had enlisted threw themselves across the soldiers' path and began weeping and wailing in unison, and the alliance of crying children and fierce women managed to drive the soldiers away. The government's emissary to the district was so humiliated by this unexpected defeat that he committed suicide.

"The truth is, I learned a lot of fascinating details about this facet of local history from reading the script, and I think putting on this play would have great value even if it only served to remind people from around here about this inspiring story from the past. So I really think it's worth fighting for.

"And now, that brings me to something a wee bit personal I'd like to ask you, Unaiko. In a play supposedly focusing on a legendary uprising, why did you feel the need to include the story of how you were raped at the age of seventeen by your uncle? Why couldn't you have put those matters aside and let the play end with a lively reprise of the battle chant—you know, 'Women warriors, here we go!' type of thing. If you did it that way, I assure you Mr. Koga wouldn't raise any objections at all. So I guess my question to you is: Why don't you accept his terms and move on?"

"Well, Daio," Unaiko began, turning to face him. "The first thing I'd like to say, just for the record, is that all those events are mentioned in the chant heard every year at the local Bon Odori celebrations: the stoning to death of Meisuke II; the rape Meisuke's mother was subjected to (and not just rape, but *gang* rape); and the way she had to be carried home on a makeshift stretcher because her injuries were

so severe. I know several scenes depicting those occurrences were
also included in the early drafts of the screenplay for the movie we
recently screened up at the Saya. However, they were deleted when
the project reached the production stage, and that part of the story
has never been expressed in visual form. The film ends in the way
you described, Daio: with a reprise of Meisuke's mother's rebel yell,
a scene in which all the women who took part in the uprising are
chanting together and their voices fill the air with a rousing chorus.
It's really gorgeous the way their chanting mingles with the Beethoven
piano sonata on the sound track—and even after the movie is over,
the viewer is left with a sort of musical afterglow.

"I put that ending in my play as well, just as it was in the movie,
with the same uplifting chorus of voices. What I did differently in
my version, of course, was to actually describe the horrific things
Meisuke's mother and her child experienced in a narrative chant. This
may seem a little confusing, but I would be onstage, still dressed as
Meisuke's mother, except that I would have turned into a medium
channeling her spirit. And after I had finished chanting about the
horrendous things that happened I would begin shedding my Kabuki-
style costume right there on the stage, without any assistance, until I
was back to the way I had started in the very first scene: as a modern-
looking young woman in a navy-blue dress. At that point—playing
myself now—I would be transformed into a medium possessed by the
spirit of my seventeen-year-old self. Speaking through me, the young
girl would tell the story of how she was raped by her uncle, who by his
own account—that is, according to his published autobiography—was
one of the founding architects of this nation's modern system of education. She would explain that a few months later, after her pregnancy
was discovered, her aunt forced her to get an abortion, saying it was
necessary in order to protect the nation's educational system.

"Presumably the man would want to contradict some aspects
of the story, so if my uncle hadn't shown up, we were going to have
an actor sitting in the audience, ready to step into the role. However,
I would be poised to mount a counterattack, and any attempts to

discredit me or make himself look better would be swiftly shot down.
As I stood there in triumph, the other female characters would appear
onstage and gather around me. Then we would recite the battle cry
in unison. As the chanting swelled and the voices soared, that would
be the finale, with the women exhorting one another to go forth and
wage the eternal battle, today and forevermore—because it's a fact
of life that there will always be injustice and there will always be a
need for women warriors to fight the good fight. And then a number
of no-longer-crying children and their newly cheerful mothers, all
dressed in present-day costumes, would join the group onstage, and
they would be chanting as well."

Unaiko fell silent, her speech at an end. She had been staring
straight at Daio the entire time she was talking, and he had never once
averted his gaze. Now, though, he lowered his head. In the sudden
stillness, the sounds of the wind and the rain outside grew even louder.
After a second or two Daio stretched his arm overhead, releasing the
accumulated tension, and I leaned back and did the same.

# 3

Over the space of the next few minutes, Unaiko began to look utterly
exhausted. Her skeleton seemed to have become more visible somehow, almost as if her bones were jutting through the usually robust
flesh, and her head drooped toward her chest, which appeared unusually thin and concave. In apparent response to this, Daio announced
in a calm, composed tone of voice that the sleeping arrangements
he and Asa had discussed earlier were being implemented as we
spoke. He went on to say that the hot-spring baths I had enjoyed
on my long-ago visit had been expanded, and the therapeutic water
was now flowing in the main building as well. On this point, Daio's
memory had deceived him—the only people who had gone into the
bathhouse that day were Goro and Peter, the American officer—but
I didn't feel the need to correct him.

On the other side of the facility, he told us, there had been a dining hall and several rooms for occasional guests. However, visitors had been few and far between in recent years, and the communal areas had fallen into disuse. At present the only active part of the complex was Daio's private quarters, toward the rear of the main building.

Daio explained that the new wing, which was built at the height of the training camp's prosperity, had once been used as a designated teacher-training facility for the prefecture. The first floor featured a capacious classroom, a separate study hall, a dining room, and accommodations for the instructors. On the second floor were some deluxe rooms for special overnight guests. The room in the eastern corner was particularly well appointed, with its own private bathroom—in hotel terms, a suite. Unaiko would be given the bedroom part of that suite of rooms for the night, but unfortunately there was no choice but to put Mr. Koga's two minions in the living room of the same suite, where they would sleep on a couple of rollaway beds.

The guest room next door, on the west side, wasn't nearly as large, but it was equipped with two twin beds. Ricchan and Akari were already ensconced there, and Asa had been with them since we arrived. Daio reported that Asa had asked Akari how it would be if, when it came time to go to sleep, his father replaced Ricchan as his roommate, and apparently Akari had replied, "No, it won't work, because I need to be here to protect Ricchan." Daio was going to vacate his own quarters so I could sleep there in comfort, and Asa would lay a futon on the floor of the same room in case I needed looking after.

"As for Mr. Koga," Daio continued, "there's a chance he may need to take a call from his wife during the night, so since the cell-phone reception tends to be spotty up here, at best, he's going to bunk in one of the buildings that used to house the long-term instructors, because it has a landline. At the moment I believe he's enjoying a little nightcap before he goes to bed.

"The bottom line is, nothing more will be happening tonight. Since the storm has ramped up in the last hour or so, one of the young guys is going to come get us in the minivan and ferry us over to the main building. After I see you two safely settled, I plan to return and indulge in a nightcap or two of my own. (No surprise there, eh, Kogito?) If you should need me for anything at all, just give a shout to the young men who'll be camped out in the lobby and they will be happy to drive you over in the van. Since Unaiko is supposed to be guarded (or, more precisely, held captive) by Mr. Koga's bodyguards, there's nothing we can do."

By the time we were installed in our various nests for the night it was already two A.M. or thereabouts. Peering through a gap in the curtains of my room, I could see the forest plunged in unremittingly rainy darkness. The wind was so strong that every time a faraway flash of lightning lit up the sky it looked as if an immense wave was rolling through the forest, illuminating the tall trees and seeming to turn their voluptuous leafage inside out. The storm showed no signs of tapering off.

On numerous occasions in our lives—from earliest childhood till now, in our later years —Asa and I had slept in the same room on Japanese-style bedding laid out side by side on the floor, so this was a nostalgic configuration. After turning off the light, we lay there for a while in silence, listening to the sounds of the storm.

Then Asa said abruptly, "Kogii, I was just thinking about your relationship to music. You remembered all the words to the German anthem the young officers were singing in the truck, and while Unaiko was rehearsing Meisuke's mother's battle chant you would correct her whenever she veered away from the traditional rhythm. As you know, when Akari's genius for music was first revealed, Mother and I were very happy. We assumed his gift must have been a legacy from Chikashi's more artistic side of the family, but it strikes me now that part of his talent might have come from you as well. I remember when we were putting on our own play about the uprising, down at the little playhouse in the village, Mother told me she didn't have any trouble memorizing the words to Meisuke's mother's rallying cry."

I pretended not to hear Asa's modulated voice as it mingled with the sounds of the rainstorm and the creaking and groaning of the old wooden building. The ambient noise was so loud that it almost drowned out the constant ringing in my ears—a legacy of the Big Vertigo.

"Kogii," Asa went on when I didn't respond, "do you remember some of the other songs from our childhood? *Gishi-Gishi, where did you come from? Mr. Rhubarb, where are you from? And where on earth did you leave your arm? Dun-dun.* The neighborhood kids used to sing that song when Daio was around, and once when I innocently joined in Mother came over and boxed my ears. I remember being really startled because it was the first time she had ever hit me."

I tried unsuccessfully to conjure an image of Daio as he might have looked as a child, but then it struck me that the Daio whom Asa and her pals had been teasing with a cruel song would already have been a full-grown adult.

"So, Kogii," Asa went on, "while you were visiting Akari in the room he and Ricchan are sharing tonight—and by the way, since it looks as if it will take a bit more time for you and Akari to sort things out, isn't it great that he's bonded so nicely with her in the meantime?—anyhow, while you were gone Daio popped in to check whether his young helpers had delivered our bedding. When I casually picked up a photograph in an antique frame from the desk over there he said, 'Here, I'll take that,' and he snatched the framed photo out of my hands and shoved it into the pocket of his jacket.

"You'll never guess what it was, Kogii: a picture of our father, standing on a high bluff overlooking a savannah, dressed like a world traveler or maybe a spy! Next to him was a burro laden with luggage (I didn't have a chance to look for the red leather trunk, but I'm sure it must have been there), and a very young Daio, who still had both his arms, was shielding the luggage with his body in a protective way. I'm sure you've heard the stories about how Daio grew up in China or someplace. Maybe Manchuria? I forget the details, but wherever it was, that's where Father found him. But since he knows the drowning novel isn't going to happen now, you'd think Gishi-Gishi would be able to let down his guard a little bit, wouldn't you?"

Once again I responded to Asa's prattling with silence, but of course, with her infallible sisterly instincts, she knew I was only feigning sleep.

"Daio had an incredibly difficult childhood," she continued. "Maybe that's why he tends to play things pretty close to the vest, and in the past as well as in this current situation . . . I don't think he's on anybody's side but his own. I don't think he really trusts anyone completely."

I was finally moved to reply. "Maybe so," I said. "However, you seem to be forgetting that Daio has said on numerous occasions that he will always consider our father his one and only mentor, until the day he dies."

Asa continued with her train of thought. "I think the mysterious accident must have taken place right after the photo was taken," she mused. "You know: *And where on earth did you leave your arm?* No question about it, something horrible happened to Daio when he was young, and I can't help wondering whether Father might have been responsible for the accident, or at least involved in some significant way."

"We'll probably never know," I said. "But speaking of luggage, I saw something in the office that reminded me of the first time I ever brought Goro home for a visit, when we were on our way back from this training camp. It was your first encounter with him as well. At the time Daio was in possession of what appeared to be a larger version of Mother's little red trunk, which I'm guessing Father must have given to him, and I saw the same trunk again tonight, on the couch in the office. The first time I ever laid eyes on that piece of luggage was when Daio turned up unexpectedly in Matsuyama, lurking around the Occupation-run library where Goro and I spent a lot of our free time. After he approached me and invited us to dinner, I remember he made his young disciples carry a big red leather trunk to the inn at Dogo Hot Springs, where he was staying by himself. (His acolytes were bunking at farmhouses and temples to save money.) While we were sitting around Daio's room at the inn feasting on crab and sweetfish and getting tipsy on sake, he quipped that the trunk was their portable arsenal. Then he proceeded to give us a graphic description of how the rubber spearguns used for fishing in the river could also be converted into weapons for guerrilla warfare. Goro said something disparaging like 'That doesn't sound like much of a weapon to me,' and Daio took offense at that.

"'Oh yeah?' he said angrily. 'Well, suppose you make a little hole in an entry door or a wooden wall, and the light from inside is leaking out. If somebody comes snooping around, they're naturally going to put their eye up to the hole to see what's going on, right? And imagine that poised on the other side of the illuminated hole is the tip of a speargun, with the energy in the rubber band stored up and waiting to propel the spear right into the enemy's eyeball. How about that, eh?'

"Goro just scoffed at him and said, 'That's disgusting. And a stupid toy is your idea of a weapon for guerrilla warfare? What a joke.' Daio got very defensive, and he shot back, 'Well, if we could get our hands on some fancier weapons, we wouldn't have to resort to this 'stupid' kind of substitute!'"

Asa didn't say anything, but even in the darkness I could sense from her reaction that she found the eyeball-piercing story every bit as distasteful as Goro had. As a signal that she was all talked out and ready to call it a night, she silently slid a tray across the tatami toward me. When I reached over, I found a glass of water and a dose of my sister's prescription sleeping powder.

# 4

I slept more soundly than I had in a very long time. When I awakened the next morning, I was relieved to find that while a light rain was still falling outside, the low-ceilinged room was filled with the fragrant air of the forest and a faint glimmering of morning light. The window overlooking the farmland was still closed, but the wooden rain shutters had been raised. Asa had placed a legless rattan chair—basically a flat cushion with an attached backrest—on the tatami-matted floor, and she was sitting there, watching attentively while she waited for me to wake up.

"Yesterday was such a long, strange day, and I was so exhausted that I'm afraid I made a mistake with the dosage of your sleeping powder," she said quietly as soon as I opened my eyes. "But I wasn't worried, since your breathing was perfectly regular the whole time. You were sleeping like a log in the forest, but you must have still been aware of the pistol shots during the night, on some level?"

In fact, I hadn't been consciously aware of the pistol shots or anything else, but after the events of the previous evening the news that there had been gunfire overnight didn't surprise me much at all.

"Now that you mention it, I do remember having a vague sense that something was going on, somewhere in the realm between waking and dreaming," I said after a moment's reflection. "But it felt very fragmented, even for a dream."

"Well then, I'm going to tell you what happened, just the way I heard it from Ricchan. Oh, by the way, Akari went to sleep with his headphones on, and thanks to them, he just woke up a little while ago. So you don't need to worry that he might have heard something upsetting."

Asa then proceeded to tell me what had happened, including all the details she had managed to collect from various sources while I was still asleep.

The previous night, Akari and Ricchan had made short work of the late supper of convenience-store sandwiches Asa had brought. Then, after Ricchan had installed Akari's extra-large body (cozily cocooned in a blanket) in one of the room's two twin beds, she had stretched out on the other bed. The rain was pounding noisily on the roof directly overhead and the wind was rampaging through the forest with a sound like crashing waves, and Ricchan wasn't able to fall asleep. Akari, though, drifted off immediately and proceeded to sleep soundly through the entire night.

Ricchan remained wide-awake, and after a while she became aware of a man's voice coming through the eastern wall of the room.

The man droned on and on, and Ricchan soon realized that she was listening to Mr. Koga, although she thought his tone sounded considerably calmer than when she had briefly met him in Daio's office, soon after her arrival. From time to time a woman's voice, more muted than the man's, would reply to something Mr. Koga had said. Ricchan knew right away that the woman was Unaiko, trying to keep her voice down out of consideration for Akari. The two people didn't seem to be quarreling, but Ricchan heard sporadic sounds that seemed to suggest that a physical struggle of some kind was taking place, and she got the sense that the uncle's behavior was making the transition from playful teasing into something more serious. Nonetheless, Unaiko never raised her voice, either in anger or to call for help. And while it seemed to be unmistakably clear that Mr. Koga was pestering his niece, he and Unaiko continued to carry on a fairly normal-sounding conversation, and once in a while their exchanges would even be punctuated by bursts of shared laughter.

After nearly an hour had passed, Ricchan heard something through the wall that sounded suspiciously like two people tussling on top of a bed. Alarmed, she jumped from her own bed and opened the door a crack. Peeking out, she saw one of Mr. Koga's thugs standing in front of the door to Unaiko's room holding a truncheon and staring straight at her. The man brandished his nightstick above his head in a menacing way, but Ricchan couldn't tell whether he was trying to intimidate her into staying in her room, or if it was just a generically hostile gesture.

She hastily closed the door again and stood behind it, listening. It sounded as though the scuffle had escalated beyond mere horsing around. A moment later she heard Mr. Koga's voice—much louder and more assertive now—barking an order at some third party. The door to Unaiko's room opened and then closed. Clinging to a tenuous feeling of hopefulness, Ricchan sat down on her bed. She envisioned a best-case scenario in which the second henchman (whom she hadn't seen when she peeked out the door) had been attempting to take liberties with Unaiko while the uncle was off somewhere, and now

Mr. Koga had returned and given his subordinate the scolding he deserved. Even so, she didn't feel entirely reassured, so she opened the door again and peered into the corridor. The man who had been standing guard was gone, but the sounds of movement inside the room continued.

Ricchan tiptoed over and tried the door to Unaiko's room, finding it locked from the inside. She crept down the dimly lit staircase to the first-floor lobby. There was nobody around, but she could see a light burning in the window of a nearby building, which she recognized as the bungalow that housed Daio's office. She dashed out into the stormy darkness without stopping to look for a raincoat or even an umbrella, and ran along the roughly cobblestoned path as fast as her bare feet could carry her.

Arriving at the office, Ricchan found Daio sprawled on the sofa at the rear of the small room, still fully dressed. He had just grabbed a hefty two-liter bottle of *shochu* from a square table nearby and was sloshing what was apparently the latest in a long series of refills into his cup. When he saw Ricchan standing there in her nightclothes, soaked to the skin, he didn't utter a word of greeting, nor did he ask any questions. He simply got to his feet, walked over to the entryway where he'd left his tall rubber boots, and pulled them on. The khaki work jacket he had been wearing earlier was hanging nearby, and he put it on, too. Then he returned to the sofa, where a red leather trunk was resting on one of the end cushions. Daio unfastened the trunk, reached inside, extracted something wrapped in a lightweight rain parka, and dropped it into one of the large inside pockets of his coat. Holding the object in place with his one hand, he shot Ricchan a brief glance. His face wore a singular expression, and she didn't know how to interpret it. Then, without even bothering to switch on the flashlight he carried, Daio strode outside and headed for the main building through the pelting rain.

Ricchan remained behind in the office, sitting on one of the chairs around the square table. After some time had passed she heard two gunshots ring out in rapid succession, but she stayed where she was, frozen in place. A few moments later Daio returned and, standing with his back to the open door, he spoke to Ricchan in a gentle voice.

"I shot Mr. Koga," he announced matter-of-factly. "I had some bullets left over, but I didn't see any reason to harm the bodyguard." With that, Daio laid the slicker-wrapped bundle containing the pistol on the floor in front of him. He told Ricchan to stash the murder weapon in her car until daybreak and then take it to the police station.

"When Kogito gets up in the morning," Daio went on, "would you please give him a message for me?"

Ricchan quickly grabbed a pen and some paper from the jumble on the table and began to take notes.

*"I know this theory may sound crazy, Kogito," Daio began, "and it only occurred to me just now, but here goes nothing. On that stormy night sixty-some years ago, when I hid and watched the little rowboat setting out on the flooded river, I thought at first that you—who would have been the natural choice to follow in your father's footsteps—were in the boat beside him. Sensei was probably thinking that if his successor, his only son, had perished along with him in the river, it would have been the end of the line. But Sensei made you help with the preparations—I think this is an extremely important point—and together you equipped the red leather trunk with a flotation device, so even if the boat were to capsize, the trunk wouldn't sink. As a child who had grown up along the river, you were a highly proficient swimmer, and as long as there was something for you to hang on to (namely, the red leather trunk), there would have been no need to worry that you might drown. As for Sensei himself, I think he actually wanted to die, and he probably thought the spirit possessing him would somehow be transferred into you, as his one true heir. Looking back on it now, I think maybe the father and son setting out together into the flood tide in a small boat was meant as a ritual, which Sensei hoped would somehow allow the spirit to be transferred to his son. What I mean is, Sensei must*

*have believed his plan would cause you to replace him as the
medium or channeler for that spirit.*

*"But when it came time to join your father on the boat, you
somehow managed to bungle that simple action (or maybe on
some unconscious level you deliberately messed up). Instead of
embarking on the flooded river with your father, you stood and
watched as the boat disappeared into the waves with an apparition of your otherworldly playmate, Kogii, standing next to your
father. (I know I shared a different theory about this the other
day, but this one just feels right to me.) A while ago, when I was
firing the pistol—I may have only one arm, but I'm a damned
good shot—I had a sudden sense that the very same spirit that
had possessed Choko Sensei had taken up residence in me,
and I was its new vessel. I know I'm ever so late, Kogito, but
I'm going to join your father. I guess it's kind of like when the
Sensei character in Kokoro finally committed junshi to follow
the emperor into death. That's right—after all is said and done,
Choko Sensei's number one disciple is still poor old Gishi-Gishi,
now and forevermore!"*

With that, Daio bent over and took off his rubber boots. Then he
extracted a pair of sturdy hiking boots from a nearby shoe shelf, put
them on, stood up, and marched into the night without a backward
glance. It was still pitch-dark, and the storm was raging unabated.

Ricchan watched from the doorway as Daio climbed into a big,
old Mercedes-Benz sedan parked at the rear of the main building and
drove off down the road between the fields. Her encounter with the
vigilante version of Daio had been very stressful for Ricchan. Once
he was gone, though, she began to worry about Akari and she ran to
the other building in her bare feet, sobbing all the way.

Asa paused to catch her breath, then continued her account of
what had transpired while I was sleeping.

"Unaiko is in shock right now—I mean, who wouldn't be? We
moved her into Ricchan's room, and she finally went to sleep. Needless

to say, the show will not go on today. We've already gotten the word out about the cancellation through various channels. I also called Chikashi to let her know you and Akari are safe. In the course of the conversation, we talked a bit about Unaiko's future as well. (That may seem odd at a time like this, but you know how I am.) No doubt the media will go crazy over this story, so it probably won't be possible for Unaiko to resume her work in the theater for a while, at least. And, needless to say, after what happened to her last night there's a chance she might be pregnant again. That's the worst-case scenario, of course, but if it does come to pass, I'm not sure anyone would be able to persuade her to get another abortion. (Of course, you know how I feel about abortions, so I can't pretend to be objective.) If Unaiko and her nice boyfriend, Tatsuo Katsura, should decide to hide out at the Forest House until the baby was born, I would of course do anything I could to help along the way. When I asked Chikashi whether it would be okay to continue the current financial arrangements vis-à-vis the Forest House, with you covering the operating expenses, she kindly gave her blessing. Of course, this is pure speculation. With luck, Unaiko won't turn out to be pregnant and life can go on more or less as usual, although she will surely need some time to recover psychologically. As for the physical aspect, we're standing by to take her to the hospital as soon as she wakes up.

"Chikashi was wondering how the members of the theater group would make a living if their normal activities were suspended, even temporarily, and she asked me to talk to Ricchan about whether she might come live in Tokyo for a while and continue her work as Akari's music teacher. I handed the phone to Akari then, and he said, 'That's good, because the piano at the junior high school is out of tune.' Ricchan is on board with the plan, so it sounds as if her move to Tokyo is practically a done deal."

While Asa was talking, I got the sense that a number of people had arrived on the scene and were busy doing their jobs just beyond our door: homicide detectives, medical examiners, coroners, and so on. I was certain that my sister was in control of the situation, both now and going forward, and I had absolute confidence in her ability to handle everything in a typically resolute, pragmatic, and dependable manner.

And then, as I was getting ready to follow Asa out into the bustling hallway, I suddenly remembered one of the dreams that had visited me the night before, in intermittent but vivid fragments, during my unnaturally deep sleep. In the dream (or was it a vision?) I had been standing alone on a high promontory amid the trees in the pouring rain, watching Daio from behind as he trudged uphill, ever deeper into the woods. The image of Daio in the forest reminded me of the two kanji—淼淼 and 森森—that suggest infinite expanses of water and forest, respectively, and thinking about those pictographs made the dream feel even more luminous and prophetic.

In my dreamy vision, the relentless torrents of rain had saturated the leaves of the trees with such a vast amount of water that the entire forest seemed as deep and as wet as an ocean. For an average man—with the violent wind whipping around his legs as he struggled to make his way through the darkness, slipping and sliding on the rain-soaked earth—remaining upright would have been a matter of life and death. That isn't hyperbole by any means; everyone knows it's possible to drown in a cupful of water, and if a hiker lost his footing and tumbled facedown onto the forest floor, which had been transformed by the incessant downpour into a rushing river of mud, it would be very easy to perish. But Daio was an expert at navigating the forest, and as he forged ahead, carefully placing one foot in front of the other, he surely wouldn't have fallen, even in those treacherous conditions.

The forest directly above the training camp meandered around the border of Honmachi, then merged with the thick woods above the mountain valley that was my once and future home. I could picture Daio walking ever deeper into the woodland as the night sky slowly grew lighter. It would have been close to dawn when he finally reached a remote spot where he didn't need to worry about being found right away (or, quite possibly, ever) by the police who would surely be tracking him before long with their specially trained dogs.

In my mind's eye I saw what happened next as clearly as if I had been there in the forest, and the moment felt far too real to be the memory of a dream.

Daio plunged his face into a thick cluster of leaves, which were so heavily laden with rain that they appeared darker than the bark. And just like that, my father's old disciple embraced his own watery death and drowned standing up.

More praise for
*Undermajordomo Minor*

'A sparky, fantastically Gothic novel that takes the hero on many an adventure. It is a witty, charmingly dark story that needs no embellishment' *Sunday Express* \*\*\*\*\*

'[An] uproariously perverted fairy tale' *Daily Telegraph*

'Part folktale, part comedy of manners, part other, it exists at both ends of deWitt's spectrum at once: pitch black and morning light, as quietly unsettling as it is tender, as sad as it is laugh-out-loud hilarious' *Buzzfeed*

'Patrick deWitt conjures and populates a universe on his terms. This is the territory of the Brothers Grimm, as seen through the skewed lens of Wes Anderson or Monty Python...Touching' *Guardian*

'Humour that's even blacker than your morning coffee' *FHM*

'A strangely seductive fantasy novel that erupts into moments of outrageous violence, it blends an aberrant but engaging take on the European folk tale with knowing glances to Samuel Beckett and Franz Kafka. A rollicking good read' \*\*\*\* *The Lady*

'As dark as night and as charming as a spell... A fantastical story, told with the panache of an aristocrat from a Gothic romance' *Psychologies*

'[deWitt's] latest novel is a gothic fairy-tale...[with] a hint of *Cold Comfort Farm* and Stella Gibbons's woodshed and wit, while an errant salami evokes J. P. Donleavy' *Mail on Sunday*

'A weirdly funny, dark Kafkaesque fairy tale for adults. Think *Alice in Wonderland* and *The Grand Budapest Hotel* and you're on the right track' *Irish Independent*

'Thoroughly entertaining...deWitt plays around with the genre, and our expectations, in a delightful comic novel' *Herald*

'deWitt is a born writer' *Irish Examiner*

Also by Patrick deWitt

*The Sisters Brothers*
*Ablutions*

# UNDERMAJORDOMO MINOR

## Patrick deWitt

GRANTA

Granta Publications, 12 Addison Avenue, London W11 4QR

First published in Great Britain by Granta Books, 2015
This paperback edition published by Granta Books, 2016

A CIP catalogue record for this book is available
from the British Library.

1 3 5 7 9 10 8 6 4 2

ISBN 978 1 84708 872 7
eISBN 978 1 84708 871 0

Text design and typesetting by Lindsay Nash

Printed and bound by CPI Group (UK) Ltd, Croydon, CR0 4YY

MIX
Paper from
responsible sources
FSC® C020471

*For Gustavo*

"It is a very painful thing, having to part company with what torments you. And how mute the world is!"

ROBERT WALSER

# CONTENTS

# I

# LUCY THE LIAR

Lucien Minor's mother had not wept, had not come close to weeping at their parting. All that day he'd felt a catch in his throat and his every movement was achieved in chary degrees, as though swift activity would cause a breach of emotion. They had eaten breakfast and lunch together but neither had spoken a word, and now it was time for him to go but he couldn't step away from his bed, upon which he lay fully dressed, in coat and boots, sheepskin cap pulled low, to his brow. Lucy was seventeen years old, and this had been his room since birth; all that he could see and put his hand to was permeated with the bewildering memories of childhood. When he heard his mother positing unknowable questions to herself from the scullery downstairs he was nearly overcome with sorrow. A valise stood alertly on the floor beside him.

Hefting himself from the mattress, he rose, stomping his feet three times: *stomp stomp stomp!* Gripping the valise by its swivelled leather handle, he walked downstairs and out the door, calling to his mother from the base of the steps before their homely cottage. She appeared in the doorway, lumpily squinting and clapping flour dust from her knuckles and palms.

"Is it time?" she asked. When he nodded she said, "Well, come here, then."

He climbed the five groaning stairs to meet her. She kissed his cheek before peering out over the meadow, scrutinizing the bank of storm clouds roiling up behind the mountain range which walled in their village. When she looked back at him, her expression was blank. "Good luck, Lucy. I hope you do right by this Baron. Will you let me know how it turns out for you?"

"I will."

"All right. Goodbye."

She re-entered the cottage, her eyes fixed to the ground as she closed the door – a blue door. Lucy could recall the day his father had painted it, ten years earlier. He'd been sitting in the shade of the anaemic plum tree marking the inscrutable industries of an anthill when his father had called to him, pointing with the paint brush, its bristles formed to a horn: "A blue door for a blue boy." Thinking of this, and then hearing his mother singing an airy tune from within the cottage, Lucy experienced a dipping melancholy. He dissected the purposelessness of this feeling, for it was true he had never been particularly close with his parents; or rather, they had never cared for him in the way he had wished them to, and so they'd never had an opportunity to achieve any stable partnership. He was mourning the fact that there was nothing much to mourn at all, he decided.

He elected to linger, a favoured pastime. Sitting upon his upended valise, legs intertwined fashionably, he removed his new pipe from his coat pocket, handling it with care, much in the way one holds a chick. He had purchased the pipe only the day prior; having never used one before, he took a particular interest as he filled it with the chocolate-and-chestnut-smelling tobacco. He lit a match and puffed, puffed. His head was enshrouded in fragrant smoke, and he felt very dramatic, and wished someone was watching him to witness and perhaps comment on this. Lucy was spindly and pale, bordering on sickly, and yet there was something pretty about him, too – his mouth was full, his black lashes long, his eyes large and blue. Privately he considered himself comely in an obscure but undeniable way.

He adopted the carriage of one sitting in fathomless reflection, though there was in fact no motion in his mind whatsoever. Holding the pipe head in the basin of his palm, he rotated the mouthpiece outward so that it rested between his middle and ring fingers. Now he pointed with it, here and there, for this was what the pipe-smoking men in the tavern did when giving directions or recalling a location-specific incident. A large part of the pipe's appeal to Lucy was the way it became an extension of the body of the user, a functional appendage of his person. Lucy was looking forward to pointing with his pipe in a social setting; all he needed was an audience for whom to point, as well as something to point at. He took another draw, but being a fledgling he became dizzy and tingly; tapping the pipe against the heel of his palm, the furry clump clomped to the ground like a charred field mouse, and he watched the blurred tendrils of smoke bleeding out through the shredded tobacco.

Staring up at the cottage, Lucy catalogued his life there. It had been lonely, largely, though not particularly unhappy. Six months earlier he had fallen ill with pneumonia and nearly died in his bedroom. He thought of the kindly face of the village priest, Father Raymond, reading him his last rites. Lucy's father, a man without God, came home from working the fields to find the priest in his home; he led the man out by the arm, this accomplished in a business-like fashion, the way one shepherds a cat from the room. Father Raymond was startled to find himself treated in such a way; he watched Lucy's father's hand on his bicep, scarcely believing it.

"But your son is dying," Father Raymond said (Lucy heard this clearly).

"And what is that to do with you? I trust you can see yourself out, now. Be a good chap and shut the door when you go." Lucy listened to the priest's hesitant, shuffling steps. After the latch caught his father called out: "Who let *him* in?"

"I didn't see the harm," his mother called back.

"But who summoned him?"

"I don't know who, dear. He just came around."

"He sniffed out the carrion, like a vulture," said Lucy's father, and he laughed.

In the night, alone in his room, Lucy became acquainted with the sensations of death. Much in the way one shudders in and out of sleep, he could feel his spirit slipping between the two worlds, and this was terrifying but also lovely in some tickling way. The clock tower struck two when a man Lucy had never met entered the room. He was wearing a shapeless sack of what looked to be burlap, his beard trimmed and neat, brown-to-black in colouring; his longish hair was parted at the temple as though it had just been set with a brush and water; his feet were bare and he sported caked, ancient dirt running to the shin-bone. He padded past Lucy's bed to sit in the rocking chair in the corner. Lucy tracked him through gummy, slitted eyes. He was not afraid of the stranger particularly, but then he wasn't put at ease by his presence, either.

After a time the man said, "Hello, Lucien."

"Hello, sir," Lucy croaked.

"How are you?"

"Dying."

The man raised a finger. "That's not for you to say." Now he fell silent and rocked awhile. He looked happy to be rocking, as though he'd never done it before and found it fulfilling. But then, as one troubled by a thought or recollection, his rocking ceased, his face became sombre, and he asked, "What do you want from your life, Lucy?"

"Not to die."

"Beyond that. If you were to live, what would you hope might come to pass?"

Lucy's thoughts were slothful, and the man's query was a restless puzzle to him. And yet an answer arrived and spilled from his mouth, as though he had no control over the sentiment: "Something to happen," he said.

The man in burlap found this interesting. "You are not satisfied?"

"I'm bored." Lucy began to cry a little after he said this, for it seemed to him a pathetic statement indeed, and he was ashamed of himself, his paltry life. But he was too weak to cry for long, and when his tears dried up he stared at the candlelight and shadows stuttering and lapping against the pale white seam where the wall met the ceiling. His soul was coming loosed when the man crossed over, knelt at the bedside, put his mouth to Lucy's ear, and inhaled. And as he did this Lucy felt all the heat and discomfort leaving his body. The man exited holding his breath and walked down the hall to Lucy's parents' room. A moment later, Lucy's father suffered a coughing fit.

By dawn the colour had returned to Lucy's face, whereas his father's was paler, his eyes rimmed red where the lids sprouted lash. At dusk his father was bedridden, while Lucy took heedful steps around his room. When the sun rose the next morning, Lucy felt perfectly well other than a tenderness in his joints and muscles, and his father was dead in bed, his mouth a gory sneer, hands stiffened to claws. The undertakers came to remove the corpse and one of them slipped going down the steps, knocking Lucy's father's head against the corner of the tread. The violence of the blow was such that it punched a triangulated divot in the skull at the forehead, and yet the wound did not bleed, an oddity which the undertakers discussed and commented on in Lucy's presence. Lucy followed the trio out the door and watched as his frozen father was loaded into an unclean cart. The cart departed and the corpse rocked to and fro, as if under its own impulse. A spinning wind swooped under Lucy's nightshirt and the frost from the earth breathed coolly up his ankles. Dancing back and forth on the balls of his feet he waited for a feeling of remorse or reverence which did not arrive, not on that day or any other day, either.

In the months that followed, Lucy's mother's attitude towards him soured further. Eventually she admitted that, though she knew Lucy was not explicitly at fault, she felt him part-way responsible for his father's death, as he had unwittingly transferred his illness to an otherwise healthy man, and so had struck him down before his time. Lucy wanted to speak to his mother of the visitor in the burlap sack, but he had a sense that this was something he mustn't discuss, at least not with her. The episode proved a nagging burden, however, and at night he found himself starting in his bed every time the house settled. When he could no longer bear this feeling, he sought out Father Raymond.

Lucy had no strong opinion of the Church. "I don't know Adam from Adam," he was fond of saying, one of many self-authored quips he felt deserved a superior audience to the lard-armed women who loitered about the fountain in the square. But there was something in Father Raymond he had responded to – a sincerity, an unpolluted empathy. Father Raymond was a moral and humane man. He followed the word of God to the letter and at night, alone in his chambers, felt the Holy Spirit coursing through his body like bird flocks. He was relieved to see Lucy in good health. In fact he was relieved to see anyone. The village was largely non-religious, and he passed full days without so much as a knock on the door. He ushered his visitor into the sitting room, setting out a tray of ancient cookies which crumbled to sand before Lucy could deliver them to his mouth. A pot of pale tea offered no palatable diversion and at last he gave up on the idea of refreshment altogether to tell the story of the stranger's visit. At the conclusion of the tale Lucy asked who the man was, and Father Raymond made an over-taxed expression.

"How would I know?"

"I was wondering if it wasn't God," said Lucy.

Father Raymond looked doubtful. "God doesn't travel through the night volleying disease."

"Death, then."

"Perhaps." Father Raymond scratched his nose. "Or perhaps he was a marauder. Is anything missing from the house, that you noticed?"

"Only my father."

"Hmm," said the priest. He picked up a cookie, which perished. He brushed the crumbs from his hands.

"The man will come again, I think," said Lucy.

"He told you this?"

"No. But I feel it."

"Well, there you are. Next time you see the fellow, be sure and ask his name."

In this manner, Father Raymond did little to put Lucy's mind at ease regarding the stranger in the burlap sack; and yet he proved to be of assistance in another, unexpected way. When Lucy admitted to having no plans for his future the priest took the trouble to write letters of introduction to every castle within a hundred kilometres, the idea being that Lucy might excel as some manner of servant. These letters went unanswered save for one, penned by a man named Myron Olderglough, the major-domo of one Baron Von Aux's estate in the remote wilderness of the eastern mountain range. Mr Olderglough had been won over by Father Raymond's romantic description of Lucy as an "unmoored soul in search of nestled safe-harbour". (It was rumoured Father Raymond spent his friendless nights reading adventure novels, which coloured his dreams and waking life as well. Whether this was true or not is unknown; that the priest was partial to poetic turns of phrase is inarguable.) An offer of employment and terms of payment rounded out the missive. The position (Mr Olderglough assigned it the name of under-majordomo, which Lucy and Father Raymond decided was not a word at all) was lowly and the pay mirrored this but Lucy, having nothing better to do, and nowhere in the world to be, and feeling vulnerable at the thought of the man in burlap's return, embraced his fate and wrote back to Mr. Olderglough, formally accepting the offer, a decision which led to many things, including but not limited to true love, bitterest heartbreak, bright-white terror of the spirit, and an acute homicidal impulse.

Lucy regarded the village of Bury, resting – or collected, he thought, like leavings, debris – in the crease of the valley. It was such a scenic locality, and yet when he looked over the clustered hamlet he felt a sense of loss, a vague loathsomeness. Had he ever been anything other than an outsider here? No, is the answer. In a place famous for its propensity to beget brutish giants, Lucy by comparison was so much the inferior specimen. He couldn't dance, couldn't hold his drink, had no ambitions as a farmer or landowner, had had no close friendships growing up, and none of the local women found him worthy of comment, much less affection, save for Marina, and this had been the all too brief exception. He'd always known an apartness from his fellow citizens, a suspicion that he was not at all where he should be. When he took the position with Baron Von Aux he made the rounds to share the news and was greeted with benign matter-of-factness, rote well-wishing. His life in the village had been uneventful to the degree that his departure didn't warrant the humble energy required to birth an opinion.

Now Lucy's window was opened and his mother appeared, unspooling his bedside rug with a muscular snap of her wrists. The concentrated explosion of dust was backlit by the sun; it hung on the air awhile, and he stepped closer to witness its dreamy descent to earth. As the detritus – his own – coated his hair and shoulders, his mother noticed him and asked, "You're still here? Won't you be late for your train?"

"There's time yet, Mother."

She gave a quizzical look and stepped out of sight, leaving the rug to hang like a calf's tongue from the sill. Lucy considered the vacant window for a moment, then took up his valise and wrenched himself away, following the path through the trees and down the valley, towards the station.

He met a man walking in the opposite direction, a shabby satchel in one hand, makeshift walking staff in the other. The man had a field worker's complexion but wore his Sunday suit; when he saw Lucy he ceased walking, staring at Lucy's valise as though it posed some problem for him.

"Did you take the room at the Minor house?" he asked.

Lucy didn't understand at first. "Take it? No, I'm just leaving there."

The man relaxed. "So the room's still available, then?"

Lucy's head banked to the side, the way a dog's does when it hears a faraway whistle. "Who told you there was a room there?"

"The woman herself. She was putting up a notice at the tavern last night, and I happened to be stepping past."

Lucy looked in the direction of the cottage, though he could no longer see it through the trees. When he had asked his mother where she was going the night before, she'd said she wanted to take the air.

"She seemed an honourable woman," said the man.

"She is not dishonourable," Lucy answered, still looking uphill.

"And you're only leaving there today, you say?"

"Just now, yes."

In a covert voice, the man said, "I hope you didn't find the accommodation lacking in some way."

Lucy faced the field worker. "No."

"Sometimes you don't uncover the lack until it's too late. That's how it was with the last house. It was slave's rations by the end of my stay there."

"You'll be happy at the Minors'."

"She seemed an honourable woman," the man repeated. "I pray she doesn't mind my being early, but I've found it best to get a jump on these things." He gestured at the incline. "It's just this way, is it?"

"The path will take you there," said Lucy.

"Well, thank you, boy. And good luck to you." He bowed and walked on. He was disappearing around a bend when Lucy called to him:

"Will you tell her you met me, sir? The woman of the house?"

"If that's what you want." The man paused. "But who shall I say I met?"

"Tell her you met Lucy. And tell her about our conversation."

The field worker seemed to think it an odd request, but he tipped his hat. "Consider it done."

As the man disappeared into the trees, Lucy was visited by an evil thought; and at the same moment the thought became whole, a rush of wind swarmed him, a column of air focused on his chest and face. It was true that at times a gust of wind was like a soundless voice commenting on some private notion or realization. Whether the wind agreed or disagreed with him, who could say. Certainly not Lucy; and neither was he much concerned about it. He continued down the hill. His mind was like a drum, a fist, a sail overflowing, pregnant with push and momentum.

At any rate, he was no longer bored.

Lucy thought he might pay a farewell visit to Marina, and headed to her house to see if she was in. There was no sign of Tor's gargantuan boots on her porch and he knocked, propping himself in the doorway as one merely happening past. But when she answered, she looked so naturally beautiful that his eyes must have betrayed his true emotions, a cleaved combination of adoration and acrimony. For her part, Marina evidently had no feeling for his being there. Pointing to his valise, she asked,

"Are you going somewhere?"

So, she wasn't even aware of his leaving. "Yes," he said. "I've been summoned to the Castle Von Aux. Likely you've heard of it?"

"I haven't."

"Are you certain? It's in the east, the high mountains – a very picturesque location, they say."

"I've never heard of it, Lucy." She gazed disinterestedly over his shoulder, hopeful for some diversion or another. "What will you be doing in this very famous and picturesque castle?"

"I'm to be undermajordomo."

"What's that?"

"It's akin to the majordomo, more or less."

"It sounds to be less."

"I will be working in concert with him."

"Beneath him, that's what it sounds like." She untied and

re-tied her apron, fitting it snugly around her dainty waist. "What's the wage?"

"It's a healthy wage."

"But what is the figure?"

"Assuredly healthy. And they sent me a first-class ticket, as well. A nice touch, I thought. They mean to keep me happy, that much is clear." In actuality, they had sent a paltry advance which had not quite covered a third-class ticket; he had had to take a loan from his mother for the remainder.

Marina asked him, "How did you get this position?"

"I was assisted by the good Father Raymond."

Smirking, she said, "That old rag doll. He's all powdery, like a biscuit." She laughed at this – laughed loudly, and for a long time. Lucy didn't understand how her laughter could be so blithe and enchanting when she herself was so covetous and ungenerous. Furthermore he couldn't comprehend why he felt such an overwhelming desire for someone who, it was plain enough to see, was patently rotten from the inside out.

He said, "You can laugh at the man if you want, but he alone took it upon himself to help me. This is more than I can say for anyone else in these parts."

Marina couldn't be bothered to take offence. She peered back into the house and seemed to be thinking of taking her leave, but Lucy wasn't ready to say goodbye just yet. Feinting, he removed his pipe and pointed its stem at the storm clouds, now tabled across the valley. "Rain's coming," he said. She did not look skyward but stared at the pipe.

"Since when do you smoke a pipe?" she asked.

"Somewhat recently."

"How recently?"

"Very recently."

A drugged mien came over her, and in a silky voice she said, "Tor smokes cigarettes. He rolls them in one hand, like this." She see-sawed her fingers against her thumb, her face affecting Tor's self-satisfaction and confidence. "Did you hear he's working out the terms to Schultz's farm?"

Lucy had not, and his mind flooded with insults and epithets, for Shultz's property was the finest in Bury. And yet he held his tongue, wanting his farewell with Marina to be peaceable, not out of any magnanimity, but so that after Tor ruined her – he felt confident Tor would ruin her – and she was once more alone, she would think of Lucy's graciousness and feel the long-lingering sting of bitter regret. In a sober tone, he told her, "Good for Tor, then. That is, good for the both of you. I hope you'll be very happy together."

Marina was moved by the words, and she crossed over to hold Lucy. "Thank you, Lucy," she said. "Thank you." Her hair brushed his face and he could feel her breath against his neck. This unanticipated contact was like a bell struck in the pit of his stomach, and he was reminded of the time of their love affair, which took place during the previous spring.

At the start it had consisted of much forest-walking, hand-holding, and eye-gazing. After a period of a month Marina realized Lucy was not going to make love to her without encouragement, and she encouraged him, and Lucy was scandalized, but not for very long at all. They fell into a routine of daily fornication in the lush, sloping fields below the village. Lucy was greatly relieved to be courting, at long last, and he knew he had the makings of a faithful wife in Marina. As they lay naked in the grass, the clouds moving bovinely over the mountain-tops, he pondered their future. How many children would they have? They would have two children, one boy and one girl. They would live modestly, and Lucy would become a schoolteacher or cobbler or poet – some post which did not involve strenuous activity. Each evening he would return to their humble home and his family would swarm him, easing him into his chair by the fireplace. Would he like a cup of tea? Why yes he would, and thank you so very much. What of a scone? Well, why not? These daydreams caused in Lucy a physical reaction, a pleasing tension which ran from his shoulders to the undersides of his feet, toes curling in the sunshine.

His visions of this contented life were bolstered by the field relations themselves, which he had thought were going markedly well. But when, one afternoon, he said as much to Marina, her face darkened. He asked her what was the matter and she told him, "It's just that . . . you don't have to handle me so gently, Lucy." Soon afterwards she sent him away, and Lucy spent heartsick months studying the curious words with such fervour that they all but lost their meaning – and he never did deduce just what it was she wanted. What he was keenly aware of now was that Tor's hands were matted in curly brown hair gone blond from sun exposure, and that when he gripped a glass of ale it looked as though he were holding a thimble. Lucy hated Tor, and presently decided to tell a sizeable lie about him. Marina was saying her goodbyes when he said, "But before I go I have something I need to tell you about this Tor."

"Oh? Is that so?"

"Unfortunately it is. Most unfortunately, actually."

She crossed her arms. "What is it?"

He thought for a moment. When the lie came to him he clasped his hands solemnly. "I happen to know for a fact that he is engaged to another woman in Horning."

She laughed. "Who told you this? It isn't true!"

"Oh, but I'm afraid that it is. Here is my reason for visiting. I'm quitting Bury forever but couldn't bear the thought of you being made a fool of."

"Who is a fool?"

"You may do with this information what you will."

She said, "I think you're jealous of Tor, Lucy."

"That is a fact, Marina. I am jealous of Tor. But more than that I am in contempt of him. For if you were mine I would never be seen gallivanting around Horning with another woman on my arm, and introducing her to all I passed as my bride-to-be. She is, I understand, several years younger than you."

When Lucy set his mind to it, he was a most accomplished liar, that rare stripe who could convincingly relay information running contrary to reality with the utmost sincerity. He could see that Marina was beginning to take him seriously, and he pushed on, telling her, "The dowry is said to be no trifling sum, either. In a way, you can't really blame Tor."

"Enough, Lucy," she said. "Tell me it's a lie, now. Will you say that it is?"

"I wish that I could. But that's not possible, because what I'm saying is factual, and I once made a pact with you. Do you recall it?"

Her eyes fluttered and cast about; she was only half listening to Lucy. "A pact," she said softly.

"You asked me to always be true to you, and I swore that I would be. Oh, but you must remember, Marina. For you made the same pact yourself."

Her eyes were hollow and doleful and she believed him completely, now. "Lucy," she said.

"Goodbye!" he said, and he turned to take his leave of her.

Walking away on the springy legs of a foal, he thought, *How*

19

*remarkable a thing a lie is.* He wondered if it wasn't man's finest achievement, and after some consideration, decided that it was. He experienced a sterling enthusiasm for his future, and his would have been a triumphant getaway were it not for the fact that the assistant train engineer, two hundred kilometres away in Ravensburg, had insisted upon eating a second helping of cheese for his dessert on the night prior.

Eirik & Alexander

The assistant train engineer, named Eirik, was entertaining disappointment in the tavern after hearing news that his junior colleague Alexander would be made full engineer, an insult considering Eirik's seniority and years of loyal service to the company. He had had nine plum brandies when Alexander entered the tavern, nodding his small greetings all around but making no announcement of his advancement, which somehow was worse than if he had, for it was plain just to look at him that he was distending with pride. He took a seat beside Eirik and laid a palm on his back. Eirik felt a measure of pity in that hand, and he rolled his shoulder to remove its weight. Alexander volunteered to buy Eirik a drink but he declined. "Thank you all the same, but I'm not quite destitute yet."

"I wish you wouldn't take it that way," said Alexander.

"Wishing is a pastime for disappointment, nothing more," Eirik replied. "Take it from one who knows."

Now Alexander became serious, and he spoke with an edge to his voice Eirik had never heard before: "Look, now. We've got to work together. Tomorrow morning and each morning after. You and I have always got along well enough; I do hope there won't be any problems between us now."

Eirik found himself regarding the ringed baby flesh of the man's neck, imagining what it would feel like to grip it in his hands. And in that same unsettling way one realizes he's left the door to his home ajar, Eirik knew that he could kill Alexander. Not that he would, but that it was possible.

"There won't be any problems coming from me," Eirik said, and he excused himself, bowing exaggeratedly before weaving from the tavern and into the road. He went home for his supper but found no solace there, his foul mood compounded by his wife's miserly cheese portion. His wife was always miserly with her cheese portions but the amount he received that night was even more scant than usual. He sat at the table alone, staring at his empty plate and considering his private theory, which was that his wife secretly ate the cheese herself while he was at work.

"More cheese," he called.

Her voice, from the larder, was unemotional: "There is none left."

"How in the world did we eat through an entire wheel in less than half a month?"

"What can I tell you? You eat it, and then it's gone."

"But I don't eat it, that's just the problem." He moved to the kitchen and found her stacking plates, her back to him. "You eat it!" he said.

She stiffened, then turned to look at her husband, loathing everything about him: his weak chin, his sour odour, his lopsided moustache, his stoop. The thing was, she really did secretly eat the cheese. No sooner would Eirik leave for work than she would go for the hidden wheel and tug away a goodly sized piece, savouring this in a corner nook otherwise unused save for this lone and lonely activity. But she was unsatisfied in most every aspect of her life, and the cheese was one of the very few pleasures she had. And now it appeared that this, too, would be stolen from her. *All right, then,* she thought. *Take it all, even my smallest happiness.* Reaching her arm deep into the cupboard, she removed the hoarded cheese and laid it on the counter before making for the privacy of the attic, where she wept in the full-throated style, feeling just as sorry for herself as a person could ever hope to feel.

Eirik stood awhile, swaying and listening to his wife's jerky, breathy sobbings. He knew he should move to comfort her but found the desire to do so entirely absent, being far too excited about this unexpected surplus of Gouda. *I'll pay her a visit after a snack, perhaps,* he thought, and brought the cheese to the dining-room table, consuming the entire half wheel in addition to a bottle of elderberry wine, afterwards passing out in his chair and suffering through a cycle of horrific dreams and visions: Alexander furiously copulating with his wife while eating his, Eirik's, cheese; his wife lying on the table nude while Alexander carved elegant swaths into her broad white calf with a paring knife, for she herself was fashioned from cheese; that his penis was cheese which broke off while he urinated; that his penis was cheese his wife nibbled on while he slept – all through the night like this, and so in the morning, in addition to the state of his head from the wine and plum brandy, his sense of peace was compromised as he set out for work.

He arrived at the station ten minutes late with bloodshot eyes and a halo of fumes swarming his head. Alexander recognized the man's impairment and felt a professional impulse to chastise him.

"So you kept it up last night?" he asked.

"I did what I had to do."

"And now?"

"Now I'll do the same."

An uneasy beginning, then. They spoke little as the hours

went by. Eirik's pain and insult were stubbornly insistent but he knew he would get through the day, and that the next day would not be quite so bad. In passing time, he thought of the loveliness of a glass of brandy, the first glass after a shift, the way it drew down his throat and coated his insides with flammable heat, afterwards leaving an aroma of smoked plum smouldering in his nostrils and mouth when he exhaled. It was very invigorating, that first plum brandy, and he began to look forward to the tavern with earnest, uncomplicated appreciation. His anger diminishing, he decided he would buy his wife a wheel of cheese on the way home from the tavern, and that he would encourage her to eat as much as she wanted, in plain sight – just so long as he could have his fair share as well. And when this ran out, so what if they had to buy another? Perhaps he wasn't a full engineer, but he earned a good wage and there was room for occasional extravagances so long as they weren't too dear. Eirik hit his stride with his coal spade and the flames shimmied and spit in the firebox. Sweat ran off his nose and chin and into his eyes, and this was agreeable to him. Life was not such a trial after all, he mused. It wasn't easy, but then, how dull an experience it would be if it were so. He began to whistle, and this meant that he was happy.

Alexander sensed the change in his partner's mood, and felt calmer for it. Allowing his mind to drift, he fell to thinking of the difficulties of his youth: his mother dead mere months after his birth; his father, waylaid from sorrow, vanished one autumn morning, never to return, never sending word. From the start Alexander was instilled with the knowledge that whatever shape his life took, it was up to him alone to sculpt it, and so to have risen to the level of engineer, he couldn't help but feel proud of himself. Surely this is understandable, but half an hour shy of Bury, he made the mistake of verbalizing his satisfaction:

"My maiden voyage as engineer," he said. "I can't deny it, but it feels good." He turned to Eirik, who said nothing, but looked stonily ahead. Alexander said, "Won't you allow me a moment of boasting, old friend?"

"Boast away," Eirik said. "I won't stop you."

"Why can't you be happy for me?"

"Who's to say I'm not?"

"But how would I know if you were?"

Eirik jammed the spade in the coal tender. "What do you want me to do?" he asked.

Alexander became sheepish. "Typically, when a man has a turn of good luck, his fellows will offer their congratulations."

At this last word, Eirik's black mood returned, a virulent poison which leached through to the deepest parts of his soul. Alexander's neck looked velvety soft to the touch, and Eirik's fingers began to twitch and grip. He resumed his feverish shovelling and as the train barrelled along the rails he waited for his hatred to ebb, but it never did, and in fact it only doubled and redoubled, so that he felt lost to it. Resignedly, he waited for the best moment to exorcise this feeling.

The train eased into the station at Bury. Alexander peered out, an attitude of calm defining his person. He turned to Eirik, meaning to offer some minor encouragement or compliment, when he saw his co-worker was watching him with a fanatical look, his eyes dreadful, grotesquely transformed. The look made Alexander wary, and he asked, "What's the matter?"

"You want me to congratulate you?" Eirik asked.

"Don't you feel it's in order?"

"Indeed it is. But you're *certain* you want me to?"

What manner of test was this? Would Eirik strike him with a fist? Well, then, better to have it out. Alexander was a healthy man, if portly, and had seen his share of tavern battles – he was not afraid of the stingy wretch who stood before him. Resting his hand on the brake lever and gripping it in his fist, he struck an upright and confident pose, and said, "I'm certain, Eirik. Let's have it."

The spade stuck out at an angle from the coal tender. Later, speaking to his cellmate, Eirik would muse that it was as if the spade were leaning towards him, offering itself for assistance. He swung it in a quick, tight circle, bringing the edge down on Alexander's hand, severing cleanly the man's foremost three fingers, while the fourth hung as if on a hinge. This swayed up and back and Alexander stood there watching the blood drain from the stumps with the look of a man who had just witnessed a baffling illusion.

"Congratulations," Eirik said. He collected the fingers with the spade and tossed them into the churning firebox.

Lucy knew none of this, and would never know. By the time he arrived at the station Alexander had been led away in a dizzy stumble, and Eirik was being helped down from the train and onto the platform by the constable. It seemed a friendly gesture, and Lucy found nothing amiss about the two men as they walked away, though he was curious about where the assistant engineer might be going five minutes before the scheduled departure, and why the constable was so insistent about holding the spade.

Rain fell in plump drops which made Lucy blink and wince, but he didn't mind getting wet. He felt triumphant about the lie he'd told Marina, and rather than hinder his optimism, the foul weather merely added to the feeling he was embarked on an adventure. He entered the third-class compartment, stowed his valise, and found a sliver of space among the charwomen and labourers and scattered elderly. No one spoke, and Lucy wondered why it was that the impoverished classes were biased towards public silences.

The train was delayed for reasons already discussed, and Lucy passed forty-five minutes in the airless cabin while the conductor and stationmaster searched for someone to fill in as engineer. He was lost to his own plotless thoughts when there came a knock on the window from outside the train. He turned and saw Marina hovering in the air above the platform; her fist remained aloft next to her face and she wore the pleased expression of the cat after a kill. The effect of her countenance, along with her floating in the window like that, was unsettling to Lucy, and he felt a premonition of danger which brought about a head-to-toe rash of gooseflesh.

Now he noticed a pair of brutish, hairy hands were holding Marina aloft at the waist; presently these hands returned her to the platform, and she and Tor stepped back, that they might both see inside and be seen by those inside the compartment. They stood arm in arm, smiling at Lucy, perfectly at ease with each other. If they had had an argument relating to Lucy's lie then it was past. The conductor happened by and Tor called the man over, speaking imploringly to him and pointing at Lucy directly. The conductor watched Lucy while Tor spoke; when Tor had finished, the conductor made for the train, and Lucy's compartment.

"May I see your ticket, please?" he said.

"My ticket?" said Lucy.

"Please."

"Why do you want to see my ticket?"

The conductor held out his hand. Miserably, Lucy passed it over. The man studied the stub and shook his head. "Whatever is that gentleman talking about?" Looking out the window, he addressed Tor and Marina, rapt in their waiting. "It's third class!" He waved the stub back and forth. "A third-class ticket!" Tor held a hand to his ear, pretending not to be able to hear. Marina slapped him on the arm, as though he were being too cruel; and yet, she didn't truly want him to stop – she was enjoying the sport they made of Lucy. The conductor waded through the compartment to the window and slid it open. "The young man has a third-class ticket," he said.

Tor, perplexed: "The stick-like fellow? The red-faced chap just there? The famished one? You're certain he's not in first class?"

"Would you like to see the ticket for yourself?"

Tor performed a slight bow. "I would never deign to tell you your own business, sir," he said, and he rested his mitts on his hips and pursed his mouth, an approximation of confounded frustration. "Oh, but I was certain he was to be in first class. The young man possesses a noble bearing, wouldn't you say?"

The conductor, along with the others in the compartment, regarded Lucy dubiously. "Well," said the conductor, "the lad is where he is meant to be. And I don't know what else to tell you about it."

"Yes," Tor agreed. "What else is there to say, after all?"

"Good day," said the conductor, closing the window.

"Good day to *you*, sir," Tor answered, his volume halved by the pane of glass. He offered a parting wave to Lucy, and to the compartment in general; Lucy did not respond but others around him did. Now Tor and Marina turned and walked into the village, arm in arm, and by the looks of them they were very much in love. Everyone watched them go; once they were out of sight the collective attention returned to Lucy. His face was no longer red, but pale, his gaze darkened, impermeable.

"Friends of yours?" asked the man beside Lucy.

"No."

"They're a handsome couple."

Lucy closed his eyes, not to sleep, but to be alone in the well-appointed room he housed deep within his mind.

The train headed east, crossing the great green valley and ascending into the mountains, winding ever higher as they followed the broad back-and-forth swoops of the track. As the stars assembled it looked to Lucy that the train was hurrying the night along by plunging into the stomach of the sky. He slept sitting up, propped by a body on either side of him.

In the night there occurred an untoward happening. Lucy awoke or partially awoke to find two men, one tall and one small, creeping into the compartment. Their movements were stealthy beyond the call of good manners, and this, combined with the fact of their faces being obscured behind the upturned collars of their coats, brought about a wary interest in Lucy, and he watched them with half-shut eyes.

The compartment was quiet, the dozing occupants' faces cast in silvery moonlight, and the men moved to stand before a bony older woman clutching a tartan satchel to her chest. Her mouth hung slackly and a rill of spittle drew down the side of her face; the larger of the men regarded her with a cocked head, then set to work removing her fingers from her bag. This was accomplished in delicate stages, one finger at a time, and Lucy was expectant that at any moment the woman would come to and let fly a bloodcurdling shriek. But the man was so adept, as though he were precisely aware to what extent he might molest the woman's person without interfering with her slumber, that she gave no indication of disturbance. Soon her grip was unfurled, and so the man could gain access to her bag, from which he removed unknown objects, passing these to the smaller man, who tucked the booty away in his long coat. After gleaning all he could or cared to, the larger man returned the bag to the woman's grip and stepped to the side, that he might focus on the body to the woman's left. It was in this workaday manner that the duo robbed each person on the bench opposite Lucy; and now they were doubling back to do the same to him and his benchmates.

As the men drew closer, a fearsome unease came over Lucy, for he had not a clue what he should do. He might put up a fight, but there were two men against his one, and it was a safe assumption that these bandits were all the more familiar with the ways of violence than he. Mightn't he leave the compartment? Simply stand and go, without a glance back over his shoulder? But no, the men would notice his exit, and perhaps it was that they wouldn't want him to leave. What option remained, then? In the end he could think of no alternative other than feigning sleep and letting the men make away with his meagre possessions. A shameful conclusion, it was true, but still preferable to the other chilling possibilities, and so there Lucy sat, awaiting the inevitable.

The men were just setting upon him when a train travelling on the westbound track hurtled past, rocking the compartment, drenching it in flashing light, and disturbing most everyone's rest. The thieves quit the compartment like shadows thrown across the wall; and though many passengers were momentarily awakened by the passing train, none had seen the pair go, and so none realized they had been robbed. Lucy looked about for a body to speak with, but all had resumed sleeping. He buttoned his coat to the throat and looked out the window at the world of night. The moon held its position admirably and unwaveringly, pegged as it was to its corner of the sky.

L ucy awoke in thin winter sunlight, lying on his side, now. The train had stopped any number of times and the compartment was empty except for a shabbily dressed man sitting on the bench across from him. The man was staring at Lucy expectantly, as though waiting for him to awaken, that they might make discourse. But Lucy didn't want to speak to anyone just yet, and so resumed his window-gazing.

They were above the snow line, well beyond the first pass and into the deeper ranges where the drifts formed impossible meringue shapes and were painted blue and green in their shadows. The first- and second-class compartments were heated with engine run-off, but not so the third; the wind rattled the windows, and Lucy could make out his breath before him.

Lucy studied the man in the reflection of the pane. He seemed to be neither young nor old, or rather, young and old – his eyes were adolescent, full of verve and mischief, yet the flesh beneath the sockets drooped to water-filled crescents; his hair was thick, swept back in a high-crested roll, but its ink-black colouring was run through with white strands, these creeping upwards from the sideburns to the crown. The man could have been eighty years old or he could have been forty. He removed a handkerchief from his breast pocket and blew his nose; as he returned the kerchief to his coat, the visual of the man's fingers slipping past a lapel reminded Lucy of the thieves from the night prior, a recollection which must have upset his composure, for the man asked, "Are you quite all right, boy?"

"I am, sir," said Lucy, "but tell me, please, did you pass the night on this train?"

"I did."

"You'll want to check your purse, then, for there were two thieves preying upon the passengers while we slumbered."

A look of dread came over the man. "Oh, dear," he said. "Is it really so?" He patted the pockets of his coat and trousers; finding his possessions accounted for, he told Lucy, "No, all is where it should be."

"You're a lucky one, then. Luckier than the others, anyway. You should have seen the way these devils roamed about the compartment. It was as though the notion of consequence never entered their minds."

"Is that right?" the man said. "They do sound devilish, anyway. And what about you, boy? How did you fare?"

Lucy waved the thought away. "Nothing to worry about there. It was I that chased them off when they came too near."

The man leaned forward, visibly impressed. "Did you really?"

"I did."

"Chased them right off, eh?"

"Indeed."

"That was very daring of you."

"I've no patience for shirkers and thieves, is what."

"That much is clear." The man stood and bowed. "I salute you."

Lucy thanked the stranger; he was pleased to be making such an impression. Again he looked out the window. They were passing through a dense forest, now. A deer stood in the distance, away from the track, considering the train with a sidelong glance.

When Lucy returned his attention to the compartment he found the man was studying him much in the same way.

"Yes, sir?" said Lucy.

"Well," said the man, "it's just that I find myself wondering, at what point did you do this chasing away?"

"At what point, sir?"

"Yes. That is to say, did you actually see these thieves robbing anyone?"

"I did indeed. Half a dozen people at least."

"And why did you not intervene before they got to you, I wonder? As one who proclaims to have no tolerance for thieves, for shirkers – for devils, as you yourself call them – I would think you'd have leapt into action at the first sign of wrongdoing. And yet you did nothing, until they came your way." The man blinked. "Or perhaps it is that I've got the story wrong."

"Well," said Lucy, "yes, hmm," and he sat awhile, thinking about what he might say in his defence. In the end, all he could come up with was to state that he'd been slow to act due to his being heavy-minded from slumber.

"Ah," said the man, nodding. "Still sleepy, were you?"

"I was."

"A foot in each world?"

"Correct."

"That explains it, surely."

Lucy felt he had deflected the interrogation handily, and yet he also wondered if he couldn't identify a suppressed smile upon the man's lips. Was this frayed individual making fun of him? No time to ponder this, however, as there were more questions being put to him:

"May I ask you where you're headed?"

"The Castle Von Aux. Do you know it?"

"I do indeed." Scratching his belly, he asked, "You wouldn't perhaps be Mr Olderglough's new man, would you?"

"I am. How did you guess it?"

"Poke in the dark."

"Do you live at the castle?"

"I most certainly do not."

Lucy thought he detected in these words some trace of pique, and so he asked, "Why do you say it like that?"

The man held up a finger. "For one, I am not welcome there." He held up another finger. "For two, I have no inclination to visit such a place." He held up a third finger, opened his mouth to speak, shut his mouth, and balled his hand to a fist. He sighed. "Do you know," he said, "I was saddened about Mr Broom."

"Who's Mr Broom?"

"Your predecessor."

It hadn't occurred to Lucy that there'd been a predecessor. The man deduced this and asked, "Have you heard nothing about him?"

"No."

"I find that strange. There's a story there, after all. Poor Mr Broom."

Lucy sat watching the man, who apparently did not plan to elaborate.

"Won't you tell me?" Lucy asked.

"It's not for me to tell. Ask Olderglough. Though he'll likely not tell you either, that rascal. Ah, well. We've all got our lessons to learn, haven't we?"

"I suppose that we do," said Lucy, finding the sentiment, and indeed the man himself, vaguely threatening. Hoping to mask this feeling, Lucy casually removed his pipe from his pocket, to study and admire it. The man took an interest as well, and asked if he might have a look for himself. Lucy handed the pipe across, and the man held it this way and that. He nodded his appreciation. "This is a very fine pipe."

"Thank you," said Lucy.

"Very fine indeed."

"Thank you, yes. May I have it back, please?"

The man returned the pipe, but there was an unhappiness in his eyes, as though to part with it pained him. When Lucy tucked the pipe away in his breast pocket, the man stared at Lucy's chest. The mountains had eclipsed the sun and the compartment dropped to a cold colouring; the conductor passed in the corridor, stating it would soon be time to disembark. The man stood as the train eased into the station.

"What's your name, boy?" he asked.

"Lucy."

"Lucy? I like that. I'm Memel." He pointed out the window. "And there's your new home."

The Castle Von Aux stood a half mile beyond the station; Lucy could make out a broad, crenellated outer curtain wall and two conical towers. It was built at the sloping base of a mountain range, standing grey-black against the snow – a striking setting, but there was something chilling about it also. Lucy thought it was somehow too sheer, too beautiful.

Memel was buttoning up his coat. Once accomplished, he did a curious thing, which was to tilt his head back and speak into the empty space before him: "Mewe," he said. "We've arrived. Will you come out, yes or no? I'm sorry that we argued." Bending at the waist, he peered under the bench and made a beckoning gesture. "Come on, already. What are you going to do? Stay here forever?"

A boy rolled like piping from beneath Lucy's bench and stared up at him. Lucy took in the boy's features, which were a source of fascination; for whereas Memel was an old man who seemed far younger than his years, here was a boy of perhaps ten with the mark of bitter time impressed upon his facc: a hollowness at the cheek, a bloodless pallor, wrinkles bunching at the corners of his eyes. When he extended his hand, Lucy shook it, but the boy, Mewe, said, "I meant for you to help me up." Lucy did help him up, and now the three of them made for the exit. The wind was swirling snow outside, and Memel and Mewe flipped up the collars of their coats before disembarking. Only now did it occur to Lucy just who these people were.

They stepped into the shin-high snow blanketing the platform. The station was a fallow cabin with its door half off the hinges and the windows knocked out. Animal tracks darted in and out of the homely structure but there were no human footsteps to be seen. Neither Memel nor Mewe had any baggage; they pushed on in the direction of the castle, punch-punching through the frosted snow, while Lucy stood awhile by the train tracks, preferring to be apart from these two. But when they noticed his falling behind they ceased walking and called for him to hurry along, that they might travel together. Lucy could think of no alternative other than to fall in line, and so he did this, saying to himself, *I am alone with two bloodthirsty thieves. We are walking into an anonymous field of pale snow.* Hoping to keep their criminal minds occupied with chatter, Lucy spoke, asking Memel if Mewe was his son, or grandson. Memel said no, they were merely friends.

"Not today we're not," said Mewe.

"No, that's true. Today we're not friends. But normally, yes."

"Why aren't you friends today?" Lucy asked Mewe.

Mewe shook his head. "Memel likes to talk; he'll tell you."

"You'll only interrupt me," Memel said.

"No, I won't."

"It's an unremarkable thing," Memel admitted to Lucy.

"If idiocy is unremarkable," added Mewe.

"Of course idiocy is unremarkable. That's its chief attribute."

"I've found your idiocy to be quite remarkable at times."

Memel rolled his eyes. "Mewe takes refuge in insult," he told Lucy.

"Quite remarkable indeed," Mewe said. But Memel remained silent; he wouldn't participate in the lowly discourse. Mewe kicked at the snow. Wearily, he said, "We just like to fight, is what it is."

Memel pondered the statement, apparently a virgin notion for him. "It's true. We do," he said. He was displeased by the admission; it appeared to make him remorseful.

Lucy had been watching the pair for a time, but as their conversation fell into a lull, now he looked up at the castle, and when he did this he startled, for it was much closer than he'd sensed it to be, as if the property had uprooted itself and met them halfway. Lucy considered its facade with a dour expression, and he thought about how buildings often took on the qualities of a living being for him. His own home, for example, was the architectural embodiment of his mother; the tavern was a tilted, leering drunkard; the church was the modest yet noble double of the good Father Raymond. But what was the castle representative of? It was too early to name it. He only knew that it spoke of something colossal and ominous and quite beyond his experience.

They approached a shanty village, built up in a cluster apart from the base of the castle, a hundred or more haphazard domiciles linked side by each in the shape of a teardrop. A series of larger, open-air structures formed a cross through the centre – marketplace stalls, Memel explained. Lucy watched as the villagers went about their business: shawl-covered women ducking in and out of doorways, children wrapped to their breasts or trailing behind; men standing in groups of threes and fours, speaking animatedly, gesturing, laughing. Memel pointed out his shanty to Lucy, and with pride, though it was indistinguishable from the others: a warping shack fashioned from tin scrap and mismatched timber. A chimney pushed through the roof, tall and tilted, issuing wispy woodsmoke.

"And does Mewe live with you also?" said Lucy.

"No, I live alone," said Mewe. "Just this side of Memel's, do you see?"

Lucy nodded. He asked Memel, "How long have you lived here?"

"I was born here. Mewe, too. We all were."

"And how long has the village stood beside the castle?"

"Just as long as the castle has been here, so has the village."

"But where do you all come from originally?"

"I don't know, actually." He turned to Mewe. "Do you know?"

"Nowhere, I should think."

A second silence, and Lucy's attention drifted away, to the face of the mountain looming beyond the castle. At first he was simply reviewing the scenery, but then he realized there was some manner of human industry taking place in the snow: bodies moving about, and puffs of smoke floating along on the air. "Those are people up there," he commented.

"Ah, yes," said Memel.

"What are they doing?"

"Wasting their time."

"Wasting their time doing what?"

"Playing a silly game."

"And what is the point of the game?"

"To kill but not be killed oneself."

"Killed?" said Lucy.

"Yes. Did Olderglough not tell you about that either?"

"There was no mention of killing."

Memel chuckled. "Rascal! Well, not to worry. You aren't in any danger."

"No?"

"Very little danger. A small danger. Keep on your toes, and you'll be fine, I would think. The others are much worse off."

"What others?"

"The killed, the killing. The rebels and their tyrannical opposition." He pointed to one side of the mountain, then the other. "They are often out and about."

"These two parties are at odds, is that what you're saying?"

"They are at war."

"Why are they warring?"

"Ah," said Memel. "Long story."

"And what is the story?"

"It is most complicated and long."

"Mightn't you tell it to me in shorthand?"

"It would never do but to tell it in total."

All this was troubling to Lucy. "Perhaps you will tell it to me later," he ventured.

"Perhaps I will," Memel said. "Though likely not. For in addition to being a long story, it's also quite dull."

They had arrived at the edge of the village. Memel and Mewe said their goodbyes, the former taking up Lucy in a lurching embrace which went on far longer than was seemingly necessary. Lucy was embarrassed by the show of affection but made no objection, thinking it likely a local custom, something he decided to endure as an example of his tolerance.

44

Lucy trudged uphill to stand before the massive riveted doors of the castle, knocking bare-knuckled in the cold. But it was like knocking on the trunk of a tree; it produced a sound so slight that he himself could hardly hear it. He spied a middling-sized bell hung away and to the side of the entrance, and pulled on the dangling rope to ring it; only the rope came away from its pulley, slipping through the air and disappearing with a whisper into the snowbank beside Lucy's feet. He looked all around, then, for what he couldn't say, it simply felt an apt time to take in his surroundings. And what did he see? He saw trees and snow and too much space. He upended and sat upon his valise. Reaching for his pipe and tobacco, he found it missing. He thought of Memel embracing him, and he scowled, admitting to himself, "I don't quite know what to do just now."

An inventive notion came to him, which was to throw stones at the bell. Rooting about in the snow, he was pleased with himself for thinking of the scheme, or for receiving it; success proved elusive, however, for the stones were hard to come by, the bell was placed very high, and Lucy's aim was abominable. Now he was panting, and a clammy sweat coated his back. Abandoning the project, he pressed his belly against the castle and peered up. From this angle the facade looked concave, and its height invoked a queasiness, so that he felt his legs might give way, and he would topple backwards down the hill, the thought of which made him laugh. He listened to his own laughter with what might be described as an inquisitive detachment. Much in the same way he had never been able to reconcile the connection between his reflection and his mind, Lucy could not recognize his voice as relating to his person.

He resumed his valise-sitting. Sunlight drew down the front of the castle, bisecting his face levelly, a lovely yellow warmth from the nose-bridge to the apex of his cap, while below there clung a beard of bitter, blue-white chill. He closed his eyes, considering the activity of his own padded heartbeat, the transit of his blood. For a moment Lucy was happy, though he didn't know why.

When he opened his eyes, a peripheral movement originating from the forest to the east of the castle caught his attention. He turned to witness a sheet of dry snow drop from a tall branch and to the ground, this landing with a soft-clapping *shump*. Through the aftercloud he saw a man's famished face emerge from behind the broad trunk of an oak tree. This face held Lucy's gaze, and Lucy, alarmed, sat upright. A second face, similarly famished, appeared from behind another tree, and Lucy stood. Now a third face came into view, now a fourth, and all at once a group of twelve or more men materialized from the shadowy wood. They were each of them holding a bayonet, and they walked in a huddle towards Lucy, who retreated some steps so that his back pressed flat against the cold wall of the castle.

The men affected a militarily homogeneous air, the lot of them wearing top to bottom grey-green wool, with bands of red encircling their arms at the bicep and black sashes cinched about their waists. As they drew nearer, however, Lucy could see that the cut and style of each man's outfit was dissimilar to his fellows': one wore long trousers, another knickers with tall boots; one sported a shearling collar, while his neighbour trailed a scarf. Even their rifles were dissimilar, the lengths of the bayonets varying drastically. It was as though they had each of them made their own garments in the privacy of their homes, with but the vaguest aesthetic prescription to guide them. Only their unshaven, haunted faces were alike.

Lucy was afraid of these men, naturally, for they carried themselves so grimly, and it seemed they intended to set upon him and for all he knew bring him to harm. But when at last they reached him they merely stood there, breathing in and out, and watching him as though he were some part of the scenery. They were looking at him but thinking of their own lives, and not of his.

A man stepped from the rear of the pack, and from the moment Lucy saw him it was clear he was one apart from the others. While the rest possessed the swollen-eyed expression of malnourished desperation, this man's skull wore the hunger well, and his gaze described intelligence and the most natural manner of confidence.

He was, in fact, exceptionally handsome, so that Lucy could not look away from him. The man was perfectly serious as he stepped closer, and when he spoke, his deep voice denoted no hostility, only a measure of import, as though time were a pressing consideration for him.

"What's your name, boy?"

"Lucy."

"Lucy?"

"That's my name, sir, yes."

"What's all this with the stones, Lucy?"

"I was trying to strike the bell."

"And why?"

"I'm eager to gain entrance to the castle."

"And why?"

"That I might begin my appointment there. Also because I'm cold."

"I don't believe I've seen you before." He pointed down the valley. "Do you come from the village?"

"No, I come from Bury."

"What's Bury?"

"A location, sir. I come from there."

The exceptionally handsome man puzzled a moment, as one completing an equation in his mind. "So you are Lucy from Bury, is that what you're telling me?"

"I am."

"And you mustn't tarry, as you're in a hurry?"

"Yes."

"Because you're chilly?"

"I suppose that's all correct, sir, yes."

The soldiers were stifling laughter, as was the exceptionally handsome man, and Lucy stood by, considering the enigmatic nature of charisma. If he could change a single thing about himself, it would be to possess that atypical lustre certain people were blessed with. The exceptionally handsome man was rich with it, and in witnessing and identifying this, Lucy experienced both covetousness and admiration. He watched the man whisper into one of his soldiers' ears; the soldier nodded and saluted before hurrying away into the woods. Now the exceptionally handsome man spoke again to Lucy, only all of the playfulness from the moment before had gone:

"Do you have any food?"

"No."

"A biscuit, perhaps? Or a piece of cheese?"

"Nothing whatsoever, sir, no."

"Any money?"

"I have a very small amount of money."

"May we have it?"

"It's all I've got, sir."

The exceptionally handsome man stepped closer, gripping his bayonet, and there entered into his voice an emotionless, droning tone. "May we or may we not have the money, Lucy from Bury?"

Lucy handed over his small purse of coins, and the exceptionally handsome man emptied it into his palm.

"This is all you have?"

"Yes."

"This is all you have in the world?"

"Yes."

The exceptionally handsome man returned the coins to the purse, sulkily stuffing this into his coat pocket. He appeared to take Lucy's insolvency personally, and a cumbersome quiet came between them. Lucy was casting about in his mind for some bit of chit-chat when the soldier who had gone on scout returned, whispering in the exceptionally handsome man's ear. The exceptionally handsome man received the news, then addressed the others, who stood at attention, ready to receive his instruction. "All right, we're heading back to base camp in a single push. The bastards are up to something or I miss my guess, so let's stay on our guard. Are we up for it, yes or no?" The soldiers called back in a single voice that shocked Lucy with its volume and alacrity: "Aye!" And then, just as quickly as they'd come, they departed, with their leader bringing up the rear.

Rounding the corner of the castle, he ceased walking, as though plagued by an unknown anxiety. Turning, he levelled his rifle at Lucy; his expression was stony, and Lucy once more found himself concerned for his own safety. But there was no danger; the rifle was raised higher, and higher still, and now the exceptionally handsome man took aim and fired his weapon. The bullet ricocheted off the hip of the bell and the peal pulsed in the air, this mingling with the echo of the rifle's discharge. As Lucy was standing under the bell itself it was as though the noise created something physical surrounding him, a chamber of vibration and sound. Looking upwards, he watched the bell's slow, circular sway. When he looked back down, the exceptionally handsome man was gone.

After some minutes, the door was unbolted from the inside. It budged a laborious half inch, then another. Lucy couldn't see who was responsible for these efforts, but there came from the black crack a wispy, whispering voice:

"Who's there?"

"Lucien Minor, sir."

"Who?"

"Lucy, sir. I'm reporting to my post under a Mr Olderglough. Is that you?"

"Mmmm," said the voice, as if unsure.

"I'm happy to make your acquaintance. Thank you again for the position. I'm eager to begin my appointment, and I should think you won't regret taking me—"

Lucy heard the distant pop of a rifle discharging. It was a miniature and cotton-wrapped sound, and he wondered at the chasm separating the quaintness of this noise and the actuality of a hurtling bullet. There came another report, and a pause; now there followed a rushing crescendo of pops, like a handful of tacks strewn over hardwood. Lucy's feet were numb, and his stomach felt airy and scooped out.

"May I come in, sir?"

The voice uttered a reply but Lucy couldn't make it out.

"What was that?" he asked.

The voice rose to a shriek: "Push the fucking door!"

Lucy's recovery from the directive was admirable and timely. He pushed with all his strength; the heavy door hesitated, then swept slowly, evenly open.

# II

# MR OLDERGLOUGH

M r Olderglough stood in the underlit entryway, an elegantly skeletal man of sixty or more outfitted in a suit of black velvet. His white hair was uncombed or unsuccessfully combed; a lock spiralled past his brow and over his eyes, to roguish effect. His right arm hung in a sling, his fingers folded talon-like, nails blackened, knuckles blemished with scabs and blue-yellow bruising. Bowing a bow so slight it hardly amounted to a bow at all, he said, "I apologize, young man, for my vulgarity of a moment ago. I woke up in a foul mood this morning, and the world's been against me ever since."

"I'm sorry to hear that, sir."

"I had a terrific nightmare, is what." Mr Olderglough leaned in. "Eels," he said.

"Eels, sir?"

"That was what the dream was about." But he offered no further information regarding the eels, no description of what malice they had represented. Lucy made no enquiries about it, the reason being that he didn't wish to know any more. As his eyes became accustomed to the darkness, now he saw that Mr Olderglough's attire, which had appeared so regal at the start, was actually quite scruffy – buttons mismatched, and stains illustrating his lapels. Lucy thought he looked like an aesthete chasing a run of foul luck. Pointing at the sling, he asked,

"Have you had an accident, sir?"

Mr Olderglough stared at his hand with what Lucy took for regret. "No, not an accident," he answered, and now he lay his left hand atop his injured right and began to stroke it consolingly, which summoned in Lucy a revulsion he couldn't put words to. Mr Olderglough emerged from his reverie and asked if Lucy would like a tour of the estate; before Lucy could answer, the man tottered away down the darkening corridor. Lucy followed after, not because he wanted to particularly, but because he could think of no other option, and because he didn't like the idea of standing alone in the dim, dank place. Other than the stillness of the air it was not noticeably warmer inside the castle, and he did not unbutton his coat.

**M**r Olderglough was not an enthusiastic guide.

"This is a room," he said, pointing as they passed. "Not much use for it these days. Better not to go in at all, is my thought. And here, here too is a room, just a room, serving no purpose whatsoever."

In fact, most every space in the castle was not in use, and the property in general had fallen into disrepair: the furniture was covered with canvas, the heavy velvet curtains drawn, and clumps of dust had built up in the corners and doorways. None of the fireplaces they passed were in use, and Lucy asked,

"Do you never light a fire, sir?"

"I wouldn't say never. I'll admit that it's rare. Room."

"I wonder," said Lucy, "on what occasion do you light one?" For the deeper they travelled into the castle, the more the temperature fell, with the light growing dimmer all the while.

"I avoid them, myself," Mr Olderglough answered. "It seems I get nothing done with a fire going other than have a fire going. The notion of reading by the hearth is pure farce, so far as I'm concerned. Every half a page I have to set my book aside to nurture the flames – not at all my idea of a relaxing evening." He gave Lucy a reproachful look. "You're not cold, are you?"

"I am not warm, sir."

"Well, if you're after a fire, you may be my guest. But you'll have to forage your own wood, as the little we have stocked goes to the scullery stove."

"That's fine, sir, thank you."

"Yes, boy. And now, if you'll follow me, please." They entered a cavernous ballroom. Ringing the high walls were any number of ornately framed oil paintings, portraits of similarly regal-looking individuals, the Barons and Baronesses of yore, Lucy supposed, and correctly. Mr Olderglough stepped to the centre-point of the space and swivelled to face Lucy; when he spoke, his voice was staggered by an echo on the air. "Yet another room," he said, "and a very large and empty room it is, wouldn't you say?"

"It is large and empty, sir."

"This dingy chamber once was filled with music and dancing and laughter and gaiety. And look at it now. Quiet as the grave."

Indeed, the ballroom gave Lucy an uneasy feeling, as though it had been host to some godless occurrence or other. "And where have all the people gone to, sir?"

"After the Baroness left us, then we fell into our Decline."

"Do you mean to say she died?"

"I don't mean that, no. Only that she departed, and hasn't returned, and likely will not return. But her leaving was like a death, if you'll allow me my small melodrama."

"Please."

"Thank you."

"You're welcome."

"Yes. Well, we're coming on a full year now that she's been away, and not a day goes past without my lamenting her absence."

"You were very close to her, sir?"

"As close as one in my position can be. She extended me every kindness – kindnesses many of her stature would have forgone."

Mr Olderglough moved to stand before a painting of a swan-like beauty in a light-blue silk and lace gown: the Baroness Von Aux.

"A light in a dark place," Mr Olderglough said.

"She looks to be afraid of something."

"Yes. Oh, but she was very brave, as well."

Lucy asked, "And where is the Baron currently, sir?"

"The Baron goes where the Baron wishes. And often as not he wishes to go nowhere at all."

"I should like to thank him for the appointment, if I might."

"The Baron has no knowledge of your appointment. In fact he hasn't the remotest interest in the mechanics of the castle. Six days out of seven he won't even leave his room. Seven days out of seven."

"And what does he do in there, sir?"

"I suspect it involves a degree of brooding. But this is not your problem to ponder; it'll be months before you lay eyes on the man, if you lay eyes on him."

"I will wait to thank him then," said Lucy.

Mr Olderglough shook his head, with emphasis. "You don't understand what I'm telling you, boy. Don't speak to the Baron if you see him. As a matter of fact, don't see him at all, if you can avoid it. That is to say, don't let him see you."

Lucy asked, "Am I not meant to be here, sir?"

"No one is *meant* to be here." Mr Olderglough was gripped by a shiver. Once it passed he turned to Lucy and asked, "Are you ever seized up like that, boy?"

"We all catch a chill, sir. I should think a fire would allay it."

"No, it's quite something else, I fear." He pointed to the exit. "Moving on, then," he said, quitting the ballroom in what could be described as a hurry.

They resumed their trek down the hallway, their heels clicking in time, then not.

"What of your trip, Lucy?"

"What of it, sir?"

"Will you tell me about it?"

"There isn't much to tell, I'm afraid. I met a pair of villagers on the train."

"Oh? And what did you make of them?"

"I found them somewhat strange, sir. I believe one of them stole my pipe."

"You've met Memel, it sounds like." There was an amusement in Mr Olderglough's tone, but also something like derision. Lucy asked,

"Don't you approve of him?"

"My approval or disapproval is irrelevant. The villagers are like children, and children can be dangerous entities in that they have no God. Do you understand what I mean when I say this?"

"Not quite, sir."

"If there are no consequences for a person's actions, what might his motivation be to do right by his fellow man?"

Lucy wasn't sure if he was expected to answer the question or not. At any rate, he didn't know what the answer might be, and Mr Olderglough didn't press for a response. A quiet moment passed, much in the way a cloud passes, and Lucy found himself wanting to defend Memel, which was odd, considering he didn't know the man, and that he had been victimized by him. Pondering this curiosity, he pushed on after Mr Olderglough, the pair of them descending a flight of stairs, and then another, where the air became thicker, almost swamp-like. It was scarcely credible to Lucy that this gloomy locale was now his home; presently he fell to wondering what his time would be like there, and so he enquired after his duties.

"Easier asked than answered," said Mr Olderglough. "For our days here are varied, and so our needs are also varied. On the whole, I think you'll find the workload to be light in that you will surely have ample free time. But then there comes the question of what one *does* with his free time. I have occasionally felt that this was the most difficult part of the job; indeed, the most difficult part of being alive, wouldn't you say, boy?"

"Perhaps you're right, sir."

"Surely I am. Oftentimes I'm confronted with an afternoon or evening off, with not a stitch of work to do, and do you know, I meet this fact with something akin to panic." Mr Olderglough sighed. "At any event: in the simplest terms, your foremost function is to anticipate my needs and see to them. Your predecessor was most gifted in this."

"Mr Broom?"

A cold look crept across Mr Olderglough's face. "How did you know his name?"

"Memel told me."

"And what else did he tell you, I'd like to know?"

"Nothing else."

"Nothing at all?"

"Not so very much. Will you tell me what happened with Mr Broom, sir?"

"Later, perhaps."

"May I ask where he is now?"

"Later, boy."

Lucy heard another volley of rifle fire occurring up the mountain. As casually as he might, he asked, "And who are these men with bayonets, sir?"

Mr Olderglough peered curiously towards the ceiling, as though clarification would meet him there. "Men with bayonets," he said.

"They ran into the forest? To shoot at or be shot at by a second party?"

"Oh, them." Mr Olderglough flapped his wounded wing dismissively. "Harmless. Nothing but a lot of noise. Ignore them, that's what I do."

Lucy found this unsatisfactory, naturally. "May I ask who it is they're fighting?"

"Other men." Mr Olderglough shrugged. "Men, like them."

"And what are they fighting about, do you know?"

"Well, now, what does anyone fight about, boy?"

Lucy was baffled. And while he sensed his questions and comments were annoying Mr Olderglough, he couldn't help but add, "I do wish I'd known about this beforehand."

"Oh? And why is that?"

"Sir, there is a war taking place outside the castle."

Mr Olderglough rolled his eyes. "It's not a *war*," he said.

"Bullets are flying through the air."

"That doesn't make it a *war*. A war is a much bigger production. This is a trifle by comparison." He thought awhile. "I hope you don't think anyone will shoot at you."

"I pray they don't."

"Of course they won't. Why would they? A nice young fellow

such as yourself." Mr Olderglough reached over and pinched Lucy's cheek, hard. The man's fingers felt as though they were made of wood. *What a long hallway this is*, Lucy thought.

Having reached the far end of the castle, Mr Olderglough led Lucy back in the direction they'd come, though by a separate series of labyrinthine passages, these no less unpleasant than the others. They were going to visit the scullery, Mr Olderglough explained. He talked as he walked.

"You will awaken at five-thirty in the morning, to bring me my tea by six. This will be waiting for you on a tray in the scullery, having been prepared by Agnes, whom you will soon meet, and whom you will surely come to admire, as she is admirable in any number of ways and you are, it would seem to me, a lad with a good head on your shoulders, the sort in possession of the ability to separate wheat from chaff."

"I hope that I am, sir, and thank you."

"You're welcome. I will take my tea abed, and so you should be prepared to witness me in my sleeping attire. It is nothing too terribly flashy, mind you, only I thought it prudent to warn you ahead of time."

"That's fine, sir."

"Good. Now. I will ask you to ferry me the tea tray as it stands. That is, do not pour the tea from the pot, and neither should you add the cream or sugar to the teacup, as these are small actions I prefer to perform in my own way, and according to my personal tastes, known to no one save for myself."

"I understand."

"Negligible accomplishments adding up to something significant over a period of time, and cumulatively, do you know just what I mean here, boy?"

"I believe I don't, sir."

"I shall not sit idly by and settle for anything other than a perfect cup of tea."

"No."

"Compromise is a plague of sorts, would you agree, yes or no?"

"I don't know that I've thought of it before, sir."

"A man accepts an inferior cup of tea, telling himself it is only a small thing. But what comes next? Do you see?"

"I suppose, sir."

"Very good. Now. After my breakfast, you will return to find your own breakfast awaiting you in the scullery. Do not forget to compliment Agnes's fare, even if the fare does not warrant it."

"I understand."

"The fare will not warrant it."

"I understand."

"You will not starve here, boy, but neither will you grow fat."

"No."

"After eating, Agnes will likely send you into the village to fetch us our stores for the day. Have you much experience in the marketplace?"

"No, sir."

"Can you identify a fresh vegetable versus a non-fresh vegetable?"

"I surely can."

"What we're after is a vegetable in its prime."

"Yes."

"Too young will not do. And too old – worse yet."

"I will seek out the freshest vegetables."

"That's the attitude. Now, might I ask what you know of haggling?"

"I know of its existence."

"But have you yourself haggled?"

"No, sir."

"They will name a high price, but you must not pay this price," Mr Olderglough explained.

"No."

"You must pay a lower price."

"This is haggling."

"Just so. And now. What of meat."

"Meat, sir."

"Have you bought it?"

"I've never, no."

"You will want to keep a sharp eye on the wily butcher."

"Is he wily, sir?"

"Is he wily! He will sell you gristle with a smile on his face, then sing a carefree tune all the way home."

"I'll watch him closely, sir."

"If you bring gristle to Agnes, it will be unpleasant for you."

"I will not do it."

"All is right with the world, then." Mr Olderglough smiled at Lucy. "This is going quite well, isn't it? You and I?"

"I hope so, sir."

"It certainly seems it, if you ask me."

"Very good, sir."

"Indeed. And now, here we are. Let's see if our grande dame is scampering about."

They had arrived at the scullery, an incongruous space in that it was orderly, clean, and well lit, with many candles ablaze, a row of low windows lining the east-facing wall, and a cheering if modest fire crinkling in a small hearth in the corner. This last, in addition to the heat from the stove, made for a warmer room than any other Lucy had met at the castle, and he stood awhile, basking in it. Agnes was nowhere to be seen. Mr Olderglough was standing with eyes closed, swaying slightly and grinning, as one enamoured of a fond memory.

"Are you all right, sir?" asked Lucy.

Mr Olderglough opened his eyes. "There once were twenty souls in our employ here, boy. Can you imagine it? Coachmen, waiting maids, porters, a cook, a nurse. All gone now, alas."

"I thought you'd said Agnes was the cook, sir?"

"Originally she was the chambermaid. When the cook left us, then did Agnes step forward, claiming a deft hand."

"But it seems you take issue with her cooking, is that correct?"

"Not so far as she knows. But in my private mind, yes, I am unenthusiastic."

"And why do you not speak with her about it, may I ask?"

"Because I dislike unpleasantness. Also there is the fact of my being somewhat afraid of her. And then, too, I'm not much interested in eating." He looked at Lucy. "Are you?"

"I like to eat," Lucy said.

"Is that right?" Mr Olderglough shook his head, as if to accommodate an eccentricity. "Personally, it never held much sway for me."

Lucy said, "May I ask what became of the others?"

"Well, they've gone away, haven't they?"

"But why have they, sir?"

"I suppose they thought it the wisest course of action, is all." Mr Olderglough looked wistfully about the room. "Twenty souls," he said, "and here, what's become of us? Well, we've got you in our company now, boy, and this heartens me, I can tell you that much."

Lucy was not so heartened. He followed Mr Olderglough to the larder; the shelves were all but bare. There came from the corner the scratching of rodents, and now began a thumping, squabbling battle, a lengthy affair concluding with the agonized squeal of the defeated: high and sharp at its commencement, distantly windy at its resolution. Mr Olderglough wore a satisfied expression, as though the outcome were favourable to him. Drawing back his cascading forelock, he said, "I find the constant upkeep of the body woefully fatiguing, don't you?"

M r Olderglough led Lucy up a tight spiral stairwell, impressive in its dizzying, seemingly endless redundancy, in addition to its airlessness and general gloominess. They passed a landing outfitted with a stubby-legged bench of hardwood which Mr Olderglough addressed with a tap of the toe of his boot. At the top of this stairwell was Lucy's room, a cramped space with a slanted ceiling and a small window located in the centre of the lone exterior wall. The furnishings consisted of a two-drawer dresser, a rocking chair, a modest bed, and a potbellied stove pushed into the corner. Lucy lay his valise on the bed and opened it. Mr Olderglough, standing at his back, said, "I suppose you must be tired after your journey."

"I suppose I must be," Lucy replied. He was considering his possessions. Here was every single thing he owned, and it didn't seem like much to him, because it wasn't.

Mr Olderglough said, "Then you may rest, or not rest, as per your desire. At any rate, the afternoon is yours. Tomorrow you will begin your appointment proper, does that agree with you? Well, then, good day to you, boy."

"Thank you, sir. Good day to you as well."

Mr Olderglough left the room and closed the door, and Lucy sat down upon the bed. Mr Olderglough opened the door and re-entered the room, and Lucy stood.

"I forgot about the letters."

"Letters, sir?"

"The letters, yes. The Baron maintains a robust correspondence with the Baroness, living currently, apparently, or so he believes I should say, in the far eastern province. Every morning you will find a sealed envelope on the side table in the entryway. This will be taken by yourself to the station, where you will meet the nine o'clock train. The train will not stop. The letter will be passed off to the train engineer himself, and achieved thus." He lifted his good arm high above his head.

"He will snatch it up from my hand, do you mean?" Lucy asked.

"Just so, yes. It is an unorthodox method, I know, but we are on our own, here, and we must make do." Mr Olderglough scratched his chin. "You're looking at me as though you have a question."

"Yes," said Lucy. "I'm wondering how it came to be that the mail was collected in this way."

"Ah, I bribed the engineer," said Mr Olderglough. "Actually, I continue to bribe the engineer. Possibly that sounds untoward, but it's only a pittance, and if the truth should be known, I get a thrill from it. Touch of criminality, thickens the blood – you didn't hear it from me, boy. Now you're looking at me with another question."

Lucy nodded. "The engineer, sir. Will he have letters for me as well?"

"No, he won't. The Baron's is a one-sided correspondence."

Lucy pondered the definition of the word. "I was unaware there was such a thing," he admitted.

Mr Olderglough's face puckered, as one stung by a discourtesy. "Is this a comical observation?" he asked.

"It was not meant to be, sir, no."

"I certainly hope not. Because I don't subscribe to amusements, Lucy. Laughter is the basest sound a body can make, in my opinion. Do you often laugh, can I ask?"

"Rarely."

"How rarely?"

"Very rarely, sir. Extremely rarely, in fact."

"Good," Mr Olderglough said. "Good. Now. These letters are of the most pre-eminent importance to the Baron, and must be handled with the greatest respect and discretion. No peeking, is what I'm saying here."

"I would never, sir."

"You will want to."

"Be that as it may."

"And, if there ever comes a day where the engineer *does* have a letter for you, this should be treated with utmost seriousness. I suspect this will never happen. Actually I can say with confidence that it won't. Still and all, you have been instructed, have you not?"

"I have been instructed, sir."

Mr Olderglough stole a glance at the contents of Lucy's valise. "Where is your day suit, boy?"

"I haven't one, sir."

"What – do you mean?"

"I mean that I am not in possession of a day suit, sir."

"Well, what do you have in the way of evening attire, then?"

"This is my attire in its entirety," said Lucy, pointing to his worn out suit of clothes.

Mr Olderglough regarded the ensemble with unambiguous indignity. "Did it not occur to you," he said, staring glumly at Lucy's sheepskin cap, "that you would be expected to dress in a manner befitting your appointment?"

Lucy considered the question. "I will admit to being aware of a style of dress common among those working in places such as this," he conceded. "But I suppose I assumed that my employer might furnish me with said attire, were it required of me to wear it."

"I see. And who was it that gave you this idea, I'd like to know?"

"No one, sir. It came to me independently."

"It's a bold notion."

"I was not after boldness."

"You achieved it."

"I'm sorry if I've offended you."

"You have annoyed me mildly. It is abating as we speak." Mr Olderglough looked out the window, and back. "Has anyone ever told you you possess a likability?"

"Not that I can recall, sir, no."

"You possess a likability."

"I'm happy to hear as much."

"Yes. Well. Perhaps something can be done about the situation at a later date, but until that point in time, we will get by with what's available to us."

"Just as you say, sir."

Mr Olderglough moved again to exit the room, but in turning the doorknob he found himself transfixed by its apparatus, so that Lucy asked him, "Is there something the matter with the door, sir?"

Mr Olderglough didn't reply for a moment; when he spoke, his voice was dimmed nearly to a whisper. "Would you describe yourself as a fitful sleeper?"

"I suppose I would, sir, yes."

"Good. May I also ask, do you typically retire early in the evening, or later on?"

"I would say that it varies. Is it safe to assume that you have a preference?"

"It is indeed. In fact, I will request, with a friendly firmness, that you come to your room no later than ten o'clock, and that you should lock yourself in each night."

Lucy wasn't sure he'd heard correctly. "Did you say you want me to lock myself in, sir?"

"Yes."

"Is that really necessary?"

"Yes."

"And why is it necessary, sir?"

"Hmm," Mr Olderglough said. "You should lock yourself in because I've asked it, and because I'm your superior, and so it will avail you to heed me, just as it will please me to be heeded." After speaking he stood by, happy with his skilful avoidance of the question put to him. He tocked his heels together and left, and Lucy began unpacking his valise. In the drawer of his dresser he found a heavy brass telescope; carved on the side was the name BROOM. He assumed his predecessor used this to chronicle the goings-on of the shanty village, which sat far beneath the tower window, and now he himself did just the same.

When he peered into the device, the village leapt into view, colourful and fast-moving. He caught a glimpse of young Mewe exiting his shanty, stepping with speed and purpose but suddenly stopping, an expression of doubt on his face. Now he doubled back and returned to his home, and he did not exit again. Memel was standing outside his shanty just next door, arguing with a slight girl whose features Lucy couldn't make out, as she was facing away from him. When she stalked off, Memel called after her, to no avail. He was smiling as he watched her leave; their argument, at least for him, was not a vicious or serious one.

Alone now, he removed a pipe from his pocket and began filling this with tobacco. Lucy had forgotten Memel had stolen it. He decided to retrieve it, and after tucking his valise beneath the bed he descended the corkscrewed stone stairwell.

# III

# KLARA THE BEGUILER

It had just gone six o'clock as Lucy ambled down the hill before the castle. The winter sun had dipped below the mountain, and the village wore the properties of night prematurely. The cold stung at his ears and he pulled his hat down to cover them. As he walked past the shuttered stalls in the marketplace, a half-dozen children assemble behind him, stepping in a clutching cluster to spy on him and wonder at his arrival. They were giddy to be stalking the newcomer, and while there was an element of danger to this adventure, they themselves knew, in the way children know such things, that Lucy was not a bad man. Still, when he spun about to greet them, they scattered in individual directions, each one shrieking ecstatically. Lucy blushed at the attention but also felt happy, even proud in a way, as though he had been formally announced.

Passing Mewe's shanty, he noticed the window was ajar, and he paused to peer inside. Mewe sat at an uneven table, playing cards fanned out in his hands. His face bore the penitent look of one who has just been caught cheating, because he had just been. Across from Mewe was a young woman, and she was very pretty indeed, if the truth would be known. In point of fact she was more than pretty: she was exquisite.

She was his age, Lucy supposed, or slightly younger. She wore her abundant brown hair stacked atop her head, exposing a delicate jawline angling into a long, tapered neck. The silhouette of her face was backlit by candles, and he could see no flaws about her, not an angle out of place, as though she were a marble figurine crafted by the sure hand of a master wishing only to share an ideal of the purest beauty. Her comeliness was counteracted by the state of her coat, a shapeless, sack-like thing with cuffs gone thin to the point of fraying. But she herself was so very lovely to behold that Lucy wouldn't have looked away for the world; he couldn't have. Her black eyes flashed in the stuttering flamelight as she chided her playmate.

"Why do you do it, Mewe?"

"I don't know why. It's like an itch that must be scratched."

"But it isn't any fun for me when you cheat."

"No?"

"How could it be?"

"I should think it might be exciting for you."

"And why would you think that?"

"It follows some manner of logic."

"Would you like me to do the same to you?"

"I suppose I wouldn't, actually."

She snatched up the cards from his hand, shuffling these into the deck. "Even if you win, you lose, don't you understand?"

"I don't know about *that*," Mewe said.

She ceased shuffling. "Will you or won't you stop it?"

Mewe put on a brave face. "I will try."

A days-old puppy, black in colour, clambered onto the table top and arched against an earthen jar sitting between Mewe and his enchanting guest. When the jar toppled, Mewe righted it automatically and dragged the puppy from the table to his lap. The girl dealt the cards and they resumed play, and Lucy had the feeling he was watching a painting come to life; there was something enduring about the scenario, something timeless and vividly evocative, and this appealed to him in a sweetly sad way. The spell was broken when Mewe spied him at the window and said, "Oh, hello, there." The girl turned to look, and when she and Lucy's eyes met he was filled with a shameful panic, and he spun away, huddling at Memel's door, his heart knocking against his throat.

"Who was that?" he heard the girl ask.

"Lucy's his name. We met him on the train. He's at the castle, now. Gone after Mr Broom."

She paused. "Is he nice?"

"He seems it. But who can say? Perhaps he's a scoundrel in hiding."

The girl softly laughed, then was silent. Lucy heard the scrape of her chair, and now she appeared at the window. She stood mere feet from Lucy but owing to the darkness had no idea of his proximity. She was pondering some distant thought, a lonely one, according to her expression; when she shut the window and drew the curtain, Lucy stood awhile in the snow, feeling foolish and trembly.

He turned and knocked on Memel's door. Memel answered with a puppy in his hand, this likewise black, but with white boots.

"Did you take my pipe?" Lucy asked.

"Yes," said Memel.

"Can I have it back, please?"

Memel left and returned with the pipe.

"Thank you," said Lucy.

"You're welcome." Memel nodded to the castle. "How are you settling in?"

"Fine."

"What have you had for your supper?"

79

"Nothing."

"Are you hungry?"

"I don't know if I am."

"Shall we find out?"

Memel ushered him into the shanty.

The front room of Memel's home brought to mind an animal's burrow. The floor was dirt, and the air smelt of roots and spices. The walls were made from tin scrap of varying colours and degrees of corrosion, and they shuddered in the wind. But it was not an unpleasant space: a copper cauldron hung in the fireplace, its fat, rounded bottom licked by flames, and oil lamps throwing off a honey-coloured light lined the rafters in neatly pegged rows. Lucy sat beneath these at a low-standing table. There was a litter of puppies roaming about, yipping and knocking things over and pouncing on one another; the exhausted mother lay upon the floor beside the table, stomach bagged, dead to the world. "Poor Mama," said Memel. "She's had just about enough." He nudged her with his foot and she retired to one of two small back rooms, with the puppies following after. Memel removed the cauldron from the fire and set it in the centre of the table to cool. Tilting back his head, he shouted, "Mewe!"

Mewe's muffled voice came through the wall, from his own shanty. "What?"

"Is Klara with you?"

"Yes."

"Is she still angry at me?"

Lucy could hear the girl named Klara murmuring, but couldn't decipher her words.

"She says she's not," Mewe called.

"And do you believe her?"

"Yes, I think I do."

"And you? Are you still angry?"

"Not at all."

"Will you please come and eat with us, then?"

A pause; more murmuring. "Who is 'us'?" Mewe asked.

"Lucy has come to visit. The lad from the train?"

"Yes, he was spying on us a moment ago."

Memel looked at Lucy with a questioning glance. Lucy shook his head. "I was only passing by," he whispered.

"He claims not to have been spying, Mewe."

"Oh? And what would he call it, then?"

"Passing by, is how he describes it."

Yet more murmuring. Mewe said, "Ask him for us, please, if he believes one must be in motion to be passing?"

Lucy admitted that yes, he supposed one did have to be, and Memel restated this.

"Well, then," Mewe continued, "how does he explain the fact of his being stationary at my window?"

Memel raised his eyebrows. "Were you stationary, Lucy?"

"Perhaps I lingered for a moment."

"Now he is calling it a momentary lingering," Memel said.

"I see," said Mewe. Murmuring. "We would like to know, then, just what is the difference between the two?"

Lucy thought he could hear some restrained laughter coming from Klara. To Memel he said, "Spying suggests a hope to come by private information. My intentions were much simpler."

Memel digested, then repeated the words, which precipitated further hushed discussion between Mewe and Klara. At last the former said, "Would Lucy describe himself, then, as idly curious?"

Lucy was now certain he could hear both Klara and Mewe stifling their amusement.

"Well?" Memel asked, who was smiling.

"I think that would be fair," said Lucy.

"It would be fair, he says," Memel said.

For a time, Lucy could not hear any further chatter from next door. Finally it was Klara who spoke. "Give us a moment to finish our game, Father," she said.

"Stew's too hot yet, anyway," Memel said, peering into the cauldron. He stepped away from the table and invited Lucy into his room, a drab cube with no window or furnishings save for a straw mattress on the ground and a wood crate doubling as a bedside table. The puppies lay in a heap in the corner, feeding off their mother, who regarded Memel and Lucy with a look beyond concern. Memel leaned down and stroked her with a gentle hand, his face drawn with worry. "They're going to kill her." Cocking his head, he asked, "Would you like a puppy, Lucy?"

"Oh, no, thank you."

"You're certain?"

"Yes."

"Well," he said, "this simply won't do." He picked up the puppy with white boots and left the room. An uneasy feeling visited Lucy; he followed Memel and found him standing at a water barrel beside the front door, his arm submerged to the elbow. "If the mother dies, then they all will," he said, regarding the black water with a look of grave determination. Long moments passed, and when he slipped his arm from the water, there was nothing in his hand. He returned to his room and re-emerged with another puppy, making once more for the barrel. Why this was being carried out in Lucy's presence, and just prior to eating, Lucy could not fathom. Whatever the reason, he felt impelled to intervene. When he spoke, he was not motivated by any one thought or combination of words, but in response to a kind of pain, much in the way one involuntarily cries out after being injured:

"Stop it," he said. "If it's come to this, then I'll take him."

Memel came nearer and deposited the puppy in Lucy's palm. "Her," he said, and moved to the table to ladle out the stew.

The puppy was the runtess of the pack. Sleekly black, her head tottered creakily, as though she were feebly aged. She peered up at Lucy and opened her mouth but no sound came out; lowering her head, she closed her eyes and Lucy tucked her into the breast pocket of his coat. Her snout pushed proud of this, her tiny jaws ajar. Lucy rubbed the fuzz above her nose and she licked his fingertip, which prompted a flutter in his stomach. There is an instance of import when one experiences the conception of love, he realized. It was as though you had been waiting for it all along; as if you'd known it was approaching, and so when it arrives you reach out to greet it with an innate familiarity. Behind him, Memel said, "All right, Lucy, the stew is cooled."

When Lucy turned to face the table he gave a start, for Klara and Mewe had snuck in and were sitting upright, hands laid flat before them, a portrait of obedience but for the hint of mirth clinging to their lips. Lucy suspected their sneaking in was a prank played on him, some bit of mischief for his benefit or at his expense. It was harmless enough, as pranks went; but why did his face burn so as he sat down? Klara, spoon in fist, covered her face and silently shuddered; Mewe produced a series of discreet snorts. Memel, sitting, took note of their good humour but had no inkling of its origin. He leaned forward on his elbows and asked hopefully,

"Is there a joke?"

"No," said Mewe and Klara together.

"There's not a joke?"

"No."

Memel tried to let it go, but could not: "Oh, tell us the joke, already." He was genuinely curious; he himself wanted to laugh with the others – he wore a smile on his face, in anticipation of the introduction of something amusing. But when they offered no explanation, he grimaced, and told Lucy, "This is rude behaviour."

Lucy stared at his stew, waiting for the painful moment to pass. Quietly, he told Memel, "It's something private between them, I suppose." Klara sat up alertly when he said this, as if she'd been stuck with a pin, and now she scrutinized Lucy for such a length of time that he thought nothing else would do but to face her.

When their eyes met, and held, he felt once again the instance of import, only more powerfully than before. There was in him an actual reverberation, and his blood hurried every which way. He could not intuit what Klara was experiencing, if anything, but there was something in his expression which alarmed her, and she suddenly looked away. When she did this, his heart caught, and he wished to reach out to her, to take up her hand in his own. Now it was her turn to blush, he noticed.

Lucy settled into his supper. The stew was deliciously spicy, so that sweat beaded at his temples under his cap, and his tongue was singed with a pulsing heat. Memel poured him a glass of water but Lucy, recalling what lay at the bottom of the barrel, opted for wine. He only rarely drank alcohol, and it birthed in him a feeling of jauntiness, and he decided he might have some small celebration with himself. By the time he had finished his stew he was working on his third glass, and a confidence or sense of ease settled over him. Mewe and Klara carried on with their private whisperings and gigglings, but Lucy wasn't embarrassed by this; in fact he thought it just that they were devoting these attentions to him. Was he not a funny one, after all? This pale and underfed young stranger with a puppy in his pocket? He made no protest, he took no offence, but began to prepare his pipe, for now he finally had his audience, and they would witness his smoking and wonder at the complexity of his thoughts. Alas, when the sharp smoke jabbed at his naked throat he emitted a single cough which blasted the pipe's contents fully over his head. Memel, Mewe, and Klara found this a glad event; the three of them laughed frankly, loudly, and for a lengthy period of time. Lucy knew, even while the tobacco was hurtling through the air, that he could never recover from this social blunder; he solemnly returned his pipe to his coat pocket, drained his wine, and poured himself another.

The room was in motion, slowly wheeling, bringing to mind the dizziness he'd experienced when climbing the stairwell to his quarters in the castle – a moderately unsettling yet not entirely displeasing sensation. He removed the puppy from his pocket and laid her on the table, tickling and teasing her. She reared and bit his hand, but she was so slight that this caused no pain, and he laughed at the futility of it. Klara's features were blurred in the woozy candlelight; she was watching Lucy with seeming indifference. And yet she didn't look away, either.

The wine was going down like water, and Lucy had arrived at the point of drunkenness where he couldn't hold a thought. His lips became lazy and his words were slurred; this amused the others, who put any number of questions to him, that they might expose and celebrate his state.

An ugliness took shape in Lucy's mind. It was obvious to him that these people would never welcome him into their society, and that they wanted him around only to make sport of him. When he saw the white-booted puppy peering out from behind the water barrel, he knew he had been tricked by Memel, and this was the final insult. He stood and lurched towards the door, with the others calling after him, their voices choked with cackling, gasping laughter. Memel crossed over, clinging to Lucy's coat and imploring him to stay; Lucy pulled away, stepping clear of the shanty and into an oceanic windstorm which instantly plucked his cap from his head and gobbled it up. Realizing the puppy still was clutched in his hand, Lucy turned, thinking to return it to Memel, but Klara was standing in the doorway with a repentant look on her face and Lucy felt he couldn't meet her again. He tucked the puppy away in his pocket and resumed his uneven snow-marching towards the looming, blacker-than-night castle.

His mood was profoundly resentful as he caromed off the walls of the spiral staircase, bumbling in the dark, hands outstretched like a blind beggar. He had had it in his mind that once he left Bury he would become a second man, and this man would command, if not respect, then at least civility. But here it was much the same, it seemed: he was derided and made to look the fool; the villagers had identified him on the spot as one who could not be considered a serious person. In remembering his departure from the shanty, it occurred to him that Memel had stolen his pipe again. Checking his pocket, he found this to be so, and he paused at the top of the stairs to issue a hissing sound.

He fell into bed, not bothering to undress. The puppy crawled from his pocket and began nosing about under the blankets; Lucy watched the lump creeping towards this and that cavern and crevasse. He drifted into uneasy slumber, his dreams descriptive of impossible frustrations, a vanishing doorway here, a never-ending staircase there. This marked the completion of his first day at the castle.

# IV

# THE CASTLE VON AUX

I n the morning there stood at the foot of Lucy's bed a small round human woman wearing an exceedingly white smock and a look of displeasure. She had short grey hair and her face was also grey. Actually her hair and face were similar in colour to the point of being confusing, even jarring, to Lucy. Her hands, resting atop her stomach, were so deeply red as to appear scalded. This was Agnes, the cook.

"Were you not told to lock the door?" she said.

"Hello. Yes. Good morning, ma'am. I was." Lucy's head was throbbing, and his throat was so dry that it was difficult to speak. His boots were peering out from beneath the blankets and Agnes, pointing, asked,

"Is this the custom, where you come from?"

"I fell asleep," Lucy explained, sitting up.

"That's to be expected, when one is in bed. But why did you not take the boots off before sleep came, is my question." Agnes drew back the blanket; the sheets were stained with earth and snow. When the puppy clambered out, Agnes gasped. "Goodness! I thought it was a rat."

"It's not a rat, ma'am."

"That's clear *now*." She reached down and scratched the puppy's chin. "Does Mr Olderglough know you keep an animal?"

"No."

"And how long were you planning on hiding it from him?"

"It's nothing I've been hiding, ma'am. That is, it's only just come to pass."

"It's something he will want to hear about."

"I will be sure to tell him."

"Very good. And when will you be rising, I wonder? Mr Olderglough has had to fetch his own breakfast, and yours is getting colder all the while."

"I'm sorry about that, ma'am; it won't happen again. I'm getting up now."

Agnes nodded, and crossed the room to go. Pausing at the door, she said, "You will remember to lock up?"

"Yes, ma'am."

"It's not something to be forgotten." She looked over her shoulder at Lucy. "Or possibly you don't understand how important this is."

Lucy swung his boots from the bed, and to the floor. "I suppose I do." He scooped the puppy up and deposited her in his pocket. "Actually, I don't," he said. "Why exactly must I lock my door, please?"

"We all must lock our doors."

"But what is the reason?"

She measured her words. "It's not for nothing, and that's all you need to know."

Agnes took her leave, and Lucy sat awhile, pondering. "I should like to know quite a lot more than that," he said at last. Later, he would wish to know less.

He moved to the window, telescope in hand.

Mr Olderglough was sitting in the servants' dining quarters, a cramped and cheerless room annexed to the scullery. His hand was free from its sling, apparently on the mend, and he was poring over a large leather ledger, to the side of which sat his breakfast, consisting of a bowl of porridge, a thin slice of dry bread, and a cup of tea. An identical setting had been laid out for Lucy; he sat, sampled the porridge, and was not in any way impressed by its flavour, texture, or temperature. His tea was likewise cold, in addition to being bitter, but it washed away the taste of wood shavings the porridge imparted, and so he drank it down in a gulp.

"Good morning, sir," he said, gasping.

Mr Olderglough nodded but did not respond verbally, distracted now by the sawing of his bread, three cuts lengthwise and three on the height, making for nine squares in total. Once this was accomplished, he stuck out his tongue and lay a square on the fleshy pink appendage. Withdrawing his tongue, he chewed, proffering a look which dared Lucy to comment. Lucy did not comment. He said,

"I find myself wondering, sir, if I might keep an animal."

Mr Olderglough swallowed. He was moderately alarmed. "An animal?" he said.

"A dog, sir, yes. A puppy."

"Where in the world did you get a puppy?"

"From Memel, sir. His dog gave birth to a litter."

"I see. Sloughed the burden off on you, then, did he?"

"I wouldn't say sloughed."

"Every man for himself?"

"Not exactly, sir. In point of fact I'm happy to have the puppy. If you'll allow me to keep it, that is."

A look of confusion had affixed itself to Mr Olderglough. "When did all this *happen*, may I ask?"

"Only recently, sir."

"Clearly." Staring into space, now, Mr Olderglough said, "Do you ever get the feeling the world is passing you by?"

"I don't know about that, sir."

"An occasional rapidity of time? Things occurring in an instant?"

"I'm not sure, sir."

"A speediness of events? And then, once the speedy event has happened, it cannot unhappen?"

"I suppose that's true, sir."

"Yes. Well, at any rate, if you desire a companion, then who am I to stand in the way of your happiness?"

"So I may keep the puppy, sir?"

"And why not? It's none of my affair what you get up to of a Sunday. I'm a proponent of individual freedom."

"Yes, sir."

"One should search out his heart's desire, wouldn't you agree with me?"

"Oh, yes, sir."

"We've only got one go-round, eh, Lucy?"

"One go, sir."

"Once around the park?"

"That's right."

"Let's make it count, why don't we?"

"Let's do that, sir."

Mr Olderglough pointed. "Why aren't you eating your porridge?"

"Because of the taste of it, sir."

Mr Olderglough looked about the room, then leaned in and whispered, "Dump it in the fireplace, why don't you. And mine as well. Agnes stomps and clomps if the plates aren't licked clean."

Lucy did as he was told, then returned to his chair.

"Is it a he or a she?" Mr Olderglough asked.

"A she, sir. I hope that's all right."

"I have no preference. I'm just making conversation at this point. Would you like another cup of tea?"

"No, thank you."

"I believe I'll go again." Mr Olderglough poured himself a second cup and took a dainty sip. He said, "Did you know that I myself keep a bird?" This last was spoken as though he'd forgotten it to be so, and only just remembered, and was surprised by the fact of it.

"I didn't know, sir, no," said Lucy.

"A mynah bird," said Mr Olderglough, "named Peter. I had thought he might brighten my room with his chirping song. Alas, not a peep."

"I'd thought the mynah was the chatty one."

"That's what I'd been led to believe as well. Consider my displeasure, then."

"Yes."

"Study on it."

"I surely will. I wonder if there's something the matter with him."

"Or else the showman's desire is absent. Anyway, Peter is

mute as a stone." Mr Olderglough sighed. "I could do with a bit of music, to tell you the truth, Lucy. I could do with a bit of cheer." He propped his head against the back of the chair. "I've always liked the name: Peter. That's what I'd have named my son, if I'd had one. Well, it wasn't for the lack of trying. If I had a penny for every barn dance I attended in my youth."

"Yes, sir."

"Some of us are fated to roam the earth alone, it would seem."

"Sadly true, sir."

Mr Olderglough pushed his plate away. "Would you like to meet him? Peter?"

Lucy did not particularly care to, but it seemed to be expected of him, and so he said that he would. Mr Olderglough clapped and stood and began expediently buttoning his coat.

P eter was a deeply antisocial bird. A passerine of middling size with drab brown plumage and a sharp orange-yellow beak, he squatted sullenly on his perch, looking not at but through his visitors. Actually, Lucy thought his expression, if a bird can have an expression, denoted legitimate hatred.

"This is Peter," Mr Olderglough said.

"Hello, Peter."

"Say hello, Peter."

Peter did not say hello, but burrowed his face in his breast and pulled up a leg, standing motionless, and it seemed he would be thus forever.

"Closed up shop," said Mr Olderglough. "You see how it is, then?"

"Yes, sir, I think I do. And you say he's never made any sound whatsoever?"

"None."

"Something which will make him sing, sir."

"Nothing will."

Mr Olderglough moved to rest upon a faded fainting couch in the corner of his parlour. Muttering to himself, the man was lost for a time to his reveries, and Lucy took advantage of this to survey his superior's quarters: at once tasteful and dire, formerly grand, utterly dated, and coated uniformly in dust. It was a room in which time hung more heavily than was the norm, and Lucy had the feeling he was the first to pay a social call in a long while.

A wall clock chimed, and Mr Olderglough said, "You'll be wanting to meet the train, now, Lucy. In the entryway you'll find the Baron's letter on the side table, as well as a list of what's needed from the village."

"And with what shall I pay for the goods?"

Mr Olderglough stood, patting his pockets but turning up nothing. "Do me a favour, boy, and pay for them yourself. I'll get it back to you soon enough."

"I'm afraid I can't do that, sir."

A twinge of panic struck Mr Olderglough. "Haven't you any money handy at all?

"None." Lucy paused. "Perhaps, sir, if you were to give me an advance on my wage?"

"Hmm," said Mr Olderglough. "No, I don't believe I'll do that."

"I was wondering when I might be paid," Lucy admitted.

"You will be paid on payday, naturally. For now, you will wait in the entryway, please."

As Lucy travelled from Mr Olderglough's room to the castle's entrance, he was struck by the fact of his enjoying the position, enjoying being told what to do, the marvellous simplicity of it. He had always sensed in his mother and father a desire for him to do something, to do anything, but they were remiss in sharing particular instructions and so, being unambitious himself, he accomplished nothing, and only continued to disappoint them. But now, all at once, he was useful, was being used, and this filled him with a sense of dignity. Arriving at the entryway, he stood by the side table awaiting Mr Olderglough and basking in this feeling. Alas, as the minutes passed by, Lucy's buoyant attitude turned to restlessness, which then evolved to candid boredom.

He scanned the shopping list but this offered nothing in the way of entertainment, and so he found himself wishing to steal a glance at the mysterious Baron's letter. He knew he must not do this, that it was in direct opposition to what Mr Olderglough had told him, but the desire grew and grew further, and soon he gave in to it. Edging a fingernail under the wax seal, he opened the envelope and unfolded the paper.

My Darling,
What news have you? Will you tell me you no longer love me? Whether or not I would prefer this to the damning silence, I won't say. The truth is that I am no longer steering this devastated ship. I took my hand off the wheel long ago, and have no concerns or thoughts for a destination. May we be dashed over merciful rocks!

Why do the happy times dim in my memory, while the evil ones grow ever more vivid? And furthermore: why do I bother asking you anything anymore? A marvel: how can the days be so full of someone wholly absent? The scope of your void humbles me. It is vast to the point that part of me hopes you have died. This at least would explain your nonappearance, and so would afford me some slight comfort. Also it would make it simpler for me to die. And yet I love you still and more, with every day that floats past.
I am yours alone,
Baron Von Aux

Lucy read this in a rush, and then again, more slowly. It seemed there was a dim rumble or vibration emanating from the words, and it caused him to bend his ear nearer the page so as to drink it in. He recognized something of himself in the letter;

but also he found himself feeling envious of the Baron's heart-sickness, which was surely superior to any he had experienced. This jealousy struck him as childish, and yet he wasn't in any way ashamed of it. He returned the letter to the envelope and had just set it back on the side table when Mr Olderglough arrived. "You'll have to make this stretch, boy," he said, pressing some coins into Lucy's hand. Calculating their worth, Lucy thought it impossible, and said as much to Mr Olderglough, who in turn espoused the merits of a credit-based society. It was at this point that Agnes came around the corner. Her red fists stabbed and jabbed at the air as she walked, punctuating her evident rage.

"Which of you dumped his porridge in the fireplace!"

"It was Lucy," said Mr Olderglough, quickly quitting the room. Agnes did not notice his leaving; she moved towards Lucy as if on oiled wheels.

L ucy received his reprimand with what he hoped was something approaching grace. He wiped away the traces of spittle adorning his face and stepped outside, lamenting having lost his cap, as the cold set upon him at once, clinging to his neck, ears, and scalp. He turned up his collar and pushed on; he could hear the train but could not yet see it. Walking towards the tracks, he peered sideward at the village. There was a trickle of smoke seeping from Memel and Klara's chimney, and Lucy wondered if it was she who had made the fire. He decided she had; and he thought of her crouched before the stove, the flame drawing across the wood. He imagined the smoke spinning in cresting coils before the draft from the flue pulled it taut, encouraging it upwards, and to the open spaces. Lucy felt an aching in his chest. He wanted to know just what Klara's days looked like.

Arriving at the station, he found Memel and Mewe on the platform, standing toe to toe, engaged in another argument. Memel held a dead hare in his hand, which Mewe lunged for once, twice, three times. Memel yanked it just out of reach; Mewe was fuming. "Hand it over," he said.

"I will not," Memel answered.

"But you know that it was in my snare."

"If it was in your snare you'd be holding the hare, for I would never claim an animal that was not my own."

"But that's precisely what you are doing!" Mewe lunged

again, and again Memel held the hare at arm's length. "The most disturbing part of all this," Mewe said, "is that you're actually starting to believe your own lies."

"God Himself only knows what the most disturbing part of it is."

Mewe wagged a finger. "You always bring God into arguments you know you're losing, for the liar is lonely, and welcomes all manner of company. Now, I'll ask you one last time: will you hand over the hare or won't you?"

"You know that I won't."

"Very well." Mewe brought his boot heel down on Memel's toe. The old man bellowed, and the hare was flung into the air, with Mewe dashing after. At the same moment he caught the somersaulting thing, Memel tackled him, and now the pair wrestled about in the snow, pulling at the hare and gritting their teeth and damning each other in the most base and common manner. Lucy found this spectacle more than a little intriguing and was curious to see who would emerge hare in hand; but now the train was approaching the station, and so he was forced to turn away.

Stepping to the edge of the platform, he held the letter high in the air. As the train bore down upon him he studied the darkened cockpit for a sign of the engineer; seeing no movement there he grew fearful something had gone amiss, when at the last moment there emerged a meaty hand, fingers splayed, poised to pounce. Lucy held his breath, and as the train hurtled past he was engulfed in a frigid wind, this of such force that he couldn't tell if the letter had remained in his grip or not. Peering up, he saw that it hadn't; he spun about to witness the blue envelope flapping in the engineer's fist. Now the fist was withdrawn. The letter had been posted.

Lucy felt a sense of dizzy satisfaction, an amusement at the strangeness of the event. Being lost to the novelty of this occurrence, he stepped too near the train, so that he felt his body shudder, as though he would be jerked from the platform and into the grinding metal wheels and shrill mechanisms. All at once he understood the train's unknowable weight and power, and he stepped cautiously backwards as it passed. He didn't like to think of anyone's death, least of all his own.

When he turned he saw that Memel and Mewe had ceased their fighting and were standing before him, panting and snow-coated, each of them clinging to opposite ends of the hare. They were smiling. Behind them, at the apex of the looming mountain, Lucy could make out the pops and puffs of the area war, the soldiers scrabbling about, insects swarming cream.

To Memel, he said, "You have taken my pipe again."

"Yes, that's true," said Memel. "Did you want it back?"

Lucy said that he did, and so the pipe was returned to him. He found the mouthpiece was scored with teeth marks, and that the basin smelled of Memel's rank, inferior tobacco. In a stern tone, he said, "I want you to stop taking it from me, do you understand?"

Memel raised his eyebrows, his head bobbing side to side, as though the notion were a fascination to him.

"Will you stop it or won't you?" Lucy asked.

"Oh, all right."

Lucy struck out for the village. That he had no use for company was clear, but Memel and Mewe were blind to this, and they hurried after, that they might walk alongside him. "We're happy to see you, do you know?" said Memel. "You left in such a rush last night, we weren't sure what to think."

"Just that it was time for me to go, I suppose."

"Clearly it was that. But will you come by this evening, I wonder? I've bagged a fine hare this morning, and Klara will prepare us a stew."

"Actually," said Mewe, "it was I who bagged the hare."

"A hare was bagged, is all he needs to know."

"I should think he would want to know the truth."

"Yes, and how will he hit upon it with you spouting untruths?"

Lucy interrupted them. "I don't think I will visit you tonight," he said.

Memel and Mewe were taken aback by this. "And why not?" asked the former.

Recalling their leering, mocking faces in the candlelit shanty, Lucy told them, "I would rather not come, is all."

Now the pair shared a solemn look, and Memel said, "Do you know something, Mewe? I don't believe Lucy likes us."

"I think you may be right," said Mewe.

Memel meditated on it. "But *why* doesn't he?"

"I don't know why."

"Well," said Memel. "It doesn't feel very good, does it? Being disliked?"

"No, it certainly doesn't."

Memel meditated further. "Do you think that perhaps he likes us a little bit, though?"

"Perhaps. But not enough to dine with us, it would seem."

"It's a pale flame, is that what you're saying?"

"He likes us, but barely," Mewe said, nodding.

"A pale flame indeed. Well, what can we do about it, eh?"

"Yes."

"If he thinks we'll beg after his friendship, he might think again."

"Yes."

"And, who's to say? Perhaps he'll acquire a taste for our company in time."

"I think that's quite possible."

"I suppose there's nothing but to wait and see, then."

"That's all, yes."

"Wait and see and hope for the best."

"That's all."

Chatting in this breezy manner, Memel and Mewe stepped away from Lucy. Memel was twirling the hare in a carefree fashion; he tossed it to Mewe, who caught it, and tossed it back. Lucy had fallen back to watch them go but now resumed walking, following them at a distance. He had his shopping to do.

Regarding the vegetables, Lucy fared moderately but not particularly well. The grocer, a grimly lipless woman in her later middle years, sold only potatoes, squash, carrots, and onions, and those available were not all that fresh. Upon inspecting the goods, Lucy requested superior merchandise, and was confident superior merchandise existed on the premises, but the grocer was disinclined to do a stranger favours, and made no attempt to mask this. Thinking in the long term, Lucy accepted the partial defeat with a brave face, wishing the woman a happy day as he stepped away from her stall. But he knew he must not falter in respect to the meat, for if this came to pass, then his maiden outing would surely be considered a failure.

As he entered the neighbouring stall he took on the posture of a man who could not conceivably be taken advantage of. He was confronted by a blood-streaked brute of a fundamentally dissatisfied man: the wily butcher, who might have said a hundred things in response to Lucy's greeting, but who chose to say nothing; he merely stared, with a look in his eye that somehow imparted both malice and indifference. When Lucy pointed out the fact of his being newly installed at the castle, the wily butcher said, "No more credit."

"Oh, I've got money, sir," said Lucy, passing over the coin he'd received as change from the grocer. The wily butcher held the coin in his palm, studying it for a time. "What do you want," he asked, and Lucy began to read aloud the list Mr Olderglough had made out for him. Halfway through this, the wily butcher said, "Stop."

"But I'm not done with the list yet, sir."

"That's all you're going to get for the coin."

"Mightn't you extend our credit just the once more?"

"I might not."

"May I ask how much is owed you?"

The wily butcher named a figure which was much higher than Lucy would have thought. It was so much more than he'd have guessed that he could think of no words to say in reply, and he wished he'd never requested the information in the first place. The very naming of this numeral set the wily butcher off; his breathing quickened, and his face became increasingly red. "I'd be within my rights to take this coin and give you nothing, what with the amount due me. Is that what you want?"

"No, sir."

"Then you'll get what the coin allows, and go away happy." Now he took out his long knife and began sharpening it, his back to Lucy, who stood considering what he might have done differently to have won the unpleasant man's approval. But he could think of nothing, for he had done nothing wrong; the animus belonged to someone else. And yet, it occurred to him, if he came away with faulty goods, who would receive the blame? He alone. His reputation thus imperilled, he called out, "No gristle, now." When he said it, the wily butcher became statue-still.

"What did you say to me?" he asked.

There was in his voice a just-contained fury, and on hearing this, then did Lucy become aware of the magnitude of his error. When the wily butcher turned to face him, the man's expression was so grotesque that Lucy became fearful of physical violence.

"I meant no offence, sir," Lucy told him.

"But what did you *say*," asked the wily butcher, long knife gripped in his fist.

Lucy was considering retreat when a voice sounded behind him: "You heard perfectly well what he said." He turned to find Klara standing there, a look of mischief on her face. "Now give him what he asked for already, you mean old bull."

"Oh, hello, Klara," said the wily butcher, his eyes dropping shyly to the ground. With her arrival, all the nastiness had left the man, and now he resumed the sharpening of his knife. Klara stepped closer to Lucy. "Hello," she said.

"Oh, hello."

"Father says you won't visit us again. Is it true?"

"I suppose it is," he said.

She peered searchingly into Lucy's left, then right eye, as one trying to locate something in a dark room. "But why won't you?"

"Well, I'm very busy, is all."

"What is it you're so busy with, can I ask?"

"There are many tasks befallen me."

"And will you name some of these tasks?"

"I suffer through any number of time-consuming endeavours."

She said, "I noticed you watching us from your window." Lucy hadn't thought anyone could see him spying, and he blushed terribly to learn that it was so. Surely Klara noticed his embarrassment, but she had no reaction to it, which exhibited a kindness, he thought. Was there anything crueller than a body commenting on another body's shame?

"What do you see, when you look at us?" she asked.

Bowing his head, he said, "Just, people."

"No one special?"

"I didn't say that."

In a tight voice, she said, "But Father claims that you don't like us."

"No," he told her. "That's not what it is."

"Well, what is it, then?"

"Just that I don't enjoy being made to feel foolish."

"And who is it that makes you feel foolish?"

"You do, for one. And Mewe, and your father."

"But we were only teasing you." She was picking at her sleeve, and Lucy noticed again how mangy the coat was, how worn and homely and unbefitting such a person as Klara. She'd got hold of a thread, and as she pulled on it the sleeve became ever more sorry-looking, and Lucy grew rankled by her intentional worsening of the garment. "Stop it," he said, and she did. The thread had come loose and was sticking to her fingers; she snapped her wrist and the thread slipped away on the air, and they both watched this.

She turned back to face him. "Don't you know why we tease you? Why I do?"

"It's likely you find me funny in some way," Lucy ventured.

Her face softened. "No, Lucy. That's not what it is at all."

"What is it, then?"

She thought a moment, then shifted her weight. She was opening her mouth to speak when the wily butcher laid Lucy's goods on the counter with a thud. "Here," he said. "And tell that Baron he might settle his debts one of these days." Lucy took up his bundles, nodded to Klara, and exited without another word. As he cleared the village, his mind was teeming with notions and possibilities. It occurred to him that, much in the way one experiences a brightening when walking beneath a cherry tree in bloom, so too did Klara generate and throw light.

That night Lucy couldn't sleep. He sat in his rocking chair before the stove, feeding twigs into its black mouth and staring out the window at the village, half-hidden in a shroud of unmoving fog. It was past midnight when, intermingled with the crackling of the fire, he became aware of an extraneous noise, a muffled bustle taking place behind him, and he turned to look, assuming it was the puppy settling in her sleep. But no, she was dozing leadenly atop his pillow, and Lucy thought he must have imagined the sound. He had resumed his window-watching when it occurred a second time, only more distinctly, and now Lucy's attentions were drawn to the door.

The knob was turning. This was being performed slowly, as though whoever was doing it did not wish to draw attention to the fact that he was. When the knob reached the limit of its rotation, the door swelled in its jamb; but being bolted, it couldn't be opened, and the knob turned backwards, just as cautiously as before, to its point of origin. Lucy stared, rooted by fright. When the knob began again to turn, he called out,

"Who's there?"

The reply registered scarcely above a murmur. The voice was a man's, and his tone was illustrative of one possessed by deep confusion and hurt:

"Why are you in my room?"

A simple enough question, and yet these six words summoned

a tingling dread in Lucy. He stood away from the rocker, creeping sideways, and to the bed. Locating the heavy telescope under his pillow, he took this up in his hand, never looking away from the door. "This is not your room," he answered, as evenly as he could. "This is my room."

"No," said the voice, and again: "No." Now the man began pacing in the hallway, pacing and whispering to himself, hissing some unknown threats or remonstrations. Suddenly he struck the door with his fist, so that Lucy jumped back, holding the telescope high in the air like a club. "No," said the voice a third time, then shuffled away down the stairs. Lucy moved to his bed but sat up a long while afterwards, regarding the doorknob with an anticipatory anguish, and he thought that if it began turning once more he would cry out from the shock of it. When he awoke in the morning, the telescope was still gripped in his cramping fist, and the puppy was sniffing at the base of the door.

Lucy entered Mr Olderglough's room, breakfast tray in hand. Mr Olderglough drew himself up in his bed, patting his lap, casting back his sleeping cap, and looking pleased at the fact of being doted on. After the tray was delivered he began the artful preparations of his tea; Lucy stood by, wondering how he might give voice to his thoughts. At last he decided there was no other way than to simply say it, and so he did: "A man tried to enter my room last night, sir."

Mr Olderglough was distracted by the cautious measuring-out of his sugar. "What's that, my boy?" he asked. "What is it, now?"

"A man, sir. Tried to enter my room last night."

"A man?"

"Yes, and a strange man he was."

"Is that right?" Mr Olderglough said wonderingly. Pouring in the cream, he stirred and sampled his tea; finding its taste satisfactory, he nodded in appreciation at life's small but dependable comforts. "And what was so strange about him, I wonder?"

"Well, the fact of him trying to get into my room was strange."

Mr Olderglough pondered this. "I don't know that I would call that strange, in and of itself. What are rooms for if not entering, after all. Or else exiting. Indeed, think of how many rooms we enter and exit in our span of days, boy. Room to room to room. And we call it a life." He chuckled at the folly of it. But

Lucy was in no mood for Mr Olderglough's wistful opining; in fact he was feeling peevish towards his superior, who was quite obviously acting the innocent when he surely knew just what Lucy was talking about with regard to the visitor of the evening prior.

Lucy said, "I most certainly would describe it as strange, sir. For we must consider that it was not a common-use room, but my own room, and that I was abed, and that it was the middle of the night. If that isn't strange, then I don't know what is. To say nothing of the fact of his attitude."

"Oh, was his attitude strange as well," asked Mr Olderglough flatly.

"It was. He seemed in a fever, and was speaking to himself — cackling and grumbling and disagreeing."

"As though he were two people, do you mean?"

"Or several people, yes, sir. You are aware of this person?"

"I am, lad. And aren't you glad you locked your door, like I told you? I'm no spring chicken, I won't deny it, but I know of what I speak."

"But who is he?"

"He is very rarely about, these days."

"And what is the matter with him?"

"This and that. Actually, I suspect he's mad."

Lucy took a breath. "That he's mad."

"Yes."

"You're telling me that there's a madman stalking the halls of the castle at night, is that correct?"

"Stalking," said Mr Olderglough, shaking his head as he spread marmalade over his bread. "There you go with your theatrical wordage again."

"Is he not stalking, sir?"

"He is walking."

"But what does he *want?*" said Lucy, his voice taking on a shade of exasperation.

"Who can tell? Surely it isn't only one thing."

"And why is that?"

"Because no one wants only one thing."

As calmly as he might, Lucy asked, "Can nothing be done about him?"

"What would you suggest, boy?"

"Expel him?"

"Excellent idea. And do let me know how that pans out for you, eh?"

"All I know, sir," said Lucy, "is that I shall never feel safe here, knowing he might pounce on me at any moment."

"No, no. He only comes out late at night. This I can say with certainty. You get to your room at a decent hour, and lock up your door before turning in, and all will be well with you. Now if you don't mind, I—"

"The man thought it his room, sir."

"What?"

"The man thought my room was his own. He seemed quite sure of it."

"Is that so?" said Mr Olderglough.

"It is so. And would you care to tell me why?"

"Why?" said Mr Olderglough, blinking politely.

Lucy said, "Whatever happened to Mr Broom, sir?"

Mr Olderglough's face formed a scowl, and a low growl came from the back of his throat. "No," he said at last. "I won't speak of it."

"And why not?"

"Because it is unspeakable."

Considering the grandly mysterious awfulness of this statement, Lucy became lost in private thought; this was ongoing for such a length of time that Mr Olderglough felt it necessary to admit, "I find myself wondering when you'll leave my room, boy."

Lucy retired in a sort of daze, and spent the rest of the morning feeling chased by his anxieties. His duties were performed in half measures, and he found his thoughts turning increasingly to recollections of Bury, the safety and comforts of his home. Mr Olderglough, intuiting this mood, and hoping to re-establish a bond of congeniality between them, came to Lucy in his room that afternoon bearing the news that Lucy would travel to the town of Listen the next day, to be fitted for a new suit of clothes. This made little impression on Lucy, who was sulking in earnest, now; but when Mr Olderglough passed over Lucy's cap, this captured his imagination.

"The little village girl brought it," Mr Olderglough said.

"Klara?"

"I don't know her name. The small one with the twinkly eyes."

The cap issued a muted crumpling, and Lucy discovered a note folded beneath the sheepskin flap. Klara's penmanship was cautiously deliberate, and the words fell at a slant, as though they would march off the edge of the paper:

It's because we like you that we tease you, Lucy. Please will you come and visit us? Your Klara.

Mr Olderglough peered over Lucy's shoulder, that he might also read the note. "Are you in the midst of an intrigue?" he asked.

"I don't know yet, sir."

"Will you tell me when you find out?"

"I will."

"Because I'm curious to know."

"I'll tell you, sir."

"Very good," said Mr Olderglough, and he left the room.

Lucy spent some moments rereading and handling the note and considering its importance, the influence it might wield over his future. The puppy sat at his feet, looking up at him.

"*My* Klara," Lucy said.

The tailor was a sallow man with a monocle, a wisp of a moustache, and blackly shining, harshly parted hair. He read Mr Olderglough's letter of introduction and instruction with a serene detachment, elbow akimbo, one eye – the non-monocled – gently shut. After folding the letter away, he looked Lucy up and down and said the word: "Fine." Lucy was made to disrobe to the essentials and stand upon a dais surrounded by tall, gleaming mirrors. Regarding his reflection, and being unused to such events and attentions, he felt self-conscious, this made all the more pronounced by the sorry state of his undergarments. His shirt was pitiable; his shorts, grievous. The tailor must have had an opinion regarding these unsavoury articles but kept it hidden, throwing himself headlong into his work. Tape in hand, he fairly crawled all over Lucy, calling out measurements to an assistant who remained out of sight and who in fact never made any sound whatsoever.

Afterwards, Lucy dressed and rejoined the tailor in the front of the shop, where he was told the suit would be ready in two weeks' time, and that it would be sent by train to the castle. Lucy thanked the man and was on his way out the door when he caught sight of a richly blue three-quarter-length cape hanging from the wall. He pointed.

"And how much is the cape, there?"

"That is a ladies' cape."

"Yes. How much does it cost?"

The tailor named a figure amounting to nearly twice the price of the suit.

"So much as that?" said Lucy. But in inspecting the cape he could see that it was of the highest quality: double-stitched and lined in silk, with fox fur ringing its hood. In a breezy tone of voice, as though it were half an afterthought, he told the tailor, "We will put that on the bill as well."

The tailor hesitated. "Mr Olderglough makes no mention of this in the letter."

Lucy waved his hand. "It's nothing to him, I wouldn't think."

"I'm certain that's so. But I should like to ask him first, if you don't mind."

"As a matter of fact I do mind," said Lucy.

"I'd be glad to hold it for you until I receive his reply," the tailor told him.

Lucy shook his head. "You will either hand over the cape now, and make a nice profit in the bargain, or forget it altogether, and content yourself with the few modest coins earned on the suit."

Long moments passed with the tailor staring up at the cape. Lucy knew the only way his attitude would prevail was if the man was a merchant at heart, rather than someone idling in a temporary position. As it happened, the tailor had been raised in the shop. It was his father's before him, and before that, his grandfather's. The world of commerce was all he knew, and all he wanted to know; and while his not confirming the purchase with Mr Olderglough was a clear breach of protocol, he couldn't pass up the opportunity to unload the cape, and so he took his chance, acknowledging the coup with a curious, twirling twist of his forefinger, followed by a birdlike, trilling whistle. Lucy did not believe these gestures were meant to pinpoint any one specific emotion, but rather were meant to celebrate, in the round, another fruitful day on earth. And so it was.

While the cape was being wrapped by the same invisible assistant, the tailor and Lucy were toasting brandies in the upstairs office, chatting about any little thing, as though they were old friends with shared histories and attitudes. Lucy felt very worldly and pleased with himself. He managed to drink his brandy without gagging, and what a relief this was, for it would have ruined the entire adventure had it happened otherwise.

Klara opened the door to find Lucy standing in the darkness, a package tucked under his arm. After welcoming him in, she moved to the stove to pour out water for tea. Lucy sat at the table, the package on the bench beside him. The state of his nerves was such that he found himself growing over warm. He removed his coat, and then his cap, laying this on the table to study it. Klara spoke with her back to Lucy.

"I see you got your hat."

"Yes," said Lucy. "Was it very hard to find?"

"It was, actually."

"Well, thank you for it." He laid the package on the table before him. "And for the note, as well."

Klara said nothing to this, but brought the tea to the table. When she saw the package she asked, "What's that, there?"

"What, this?" Lucy said.

"Yes," said Klara. "What is it?"

"This here?"

"Will you tell me what it is or not?" She poked the package with her finger.

Lucy pushed it nearer to her and she said, "What now? Am I to open it?"

"Yes."

"But why?"

"Because it's for you."

This seemed to startle, even upset Klara. When at last she undid the ribbon, she used only one hand, leaving the other to rest upon her lap. The package bloomed, a crinkling, staggered blossom, and when she spied its contents, her spine went stiff. "What is that?"

"It's a cape. Don't you like it?"

"Why did you bring me this?"

"It's just that I noticed your shivering the other day, in the marketplace," he explained. When he said this, a look of shame came over Klara, and here Lucy recognized his mistake.

"You must think me very shabby," she said quietly.

"No, Klara."

"A shabby girl in need of charity, is that it?"

"That's not what it is at all."

But now she was rewrapping the package, and Lucy saw the moment was getting away from him. "Stop," he said. "Wait." When she did not stop, he said it again: "Stop."

She paused to look across at him.

"Why did you bring me my cap?" he asked.

Her eyes hooded when he asked this, as though she thought he wasn't playing fair by bringing it up.

"Why did you?" he persisted.

"You seemed to think we didn't like you," she said. "I wanted to show you we did."

"But that's all this is," he told her, folding back the wrapping.

She drew a hand across the cape's collar. "It's too dear."

"Who's to say, though?" Lucy took up the cape and stood, holding it out before him. "Won't you try it on, at least?"

"I shouldn't," she said.

"Please," said Lucy.

"I can't."

Memel's voice called out from next door: "Cease torturing the boy, already."

"And us," Mewe added.

"Try on the cape," said Memel.

"It's obvious you want to."

At this, Lucy and Klara both went red in the face; but their self-consciousness soon gave way to stifled laughter. Lucy relocated his courage and approached Klara with the cape; when she stood, he rested the garment on her shoulders, and now she wrapped herself up in it, moving to the mirror in the corner of the shanty that she might admire herself. Lucy followed and stood behind her, watching her face, her pleased expression, and then his own. Closing his eyes, he was run through with a streak of pure happiness, for now he knew he truly was in the midst of an intrigue, just as Mr Olderglough had said. When he opened his eyes, Klara was watching him in the mirror with a look of fondness or perhaps, for all he knew, something more than that.

"Thank you," she said.

"You're welcome," he answered.

"How does it fit?" Memel asked.

Lucy awoke to the sound of the area war. Sitting up in his bed, he trained his telescope over the mountain's face and to the pivot of the battleground. He took an idle pleasure in witnessing the birth of the cloud-puffs, these "rudely bloomed" (the phrase had ambled into Lucy's mind) then thinned by the wind, only to be replaced by yet more puffs when the following volley occurred. He could make out the soldiers' movements but not their faces, and this was preferable to him. From this distance it all seemed something more like an elaborate stage play than actual combat – some ambitious recreation of a factual happening.

He worked all that morning assisting Agnes in the cleaning of the larder and ovens, then chopping and stacking wood through to lunchtime, but with his afternoon free, he wandered into the village. He had his pipe with him, the pipe he'd yet to master; it smouldered and had to be relit time and again, but no sooner had he done this than the wind would shift and hurry the smoke up his nose or into his eyes. Coughing, and with tears skating down his face, he put the pipe away. The puppy sat in his coat pocket, as before, taking in the sights with interest.

Lucy saw Klara standing in the marketplace, showing off her cape to a half-dozen village women, a meaty group of red-faced peasants turning her about as they studied the garment. Klara was smiling with pride as they handled and rotated her. Lucy stepped nearer, and now he could make out their conversation.

"And what does master Adolphus think of it?"

"Do I know any Adolphus?" Klara asked innocently, looking this way and that. "I see no Adolphus around here."

"And how long has he been gone this time?"

Klara threw her hands up in the air. "Bah!" she said. Lucy entered into the group and Klara, beaming, told the others, "Here, now. This is the gentleman who brought the cape."

The women swarmed Lucy, grinning devilishly, prodding him with stubby digits and speaking of him as though he weren't there at all:

"What are his intentions, do you think?"

"Will he give her a ring next, I wonder?"

"Adolphus will rip this one in two."

"Clean in two, I should think."

"Will he buy me a cape? You can plainly see the state I'm in."

They slapped at Lucy's back, laughing and congratulating him for his boldness. He smiled weakly but said nothing; he didn't suppose there was one among them he could better in a fair fight. Once they dispersed, Lucy was left alone with Klara, and these two stood awhile, looking at each other. Winter sunlight spilled across her face; Lucy's vision smudged and blurred.

"Would you walk with me, Klara?" he asked.

"Yes, I'd like that," she answered, and they fell into line, stepping through the marketplace, neither of them knowing just what to say. When Klara spied the puppy in Lucy's pocket, she took her up to hold her, asking Lucy what she was called. He explained the name hadn't arrived yet, and now Klara grew thoughtful, peering at Lucy from the corner of her eye. "Perhaps you might name her after your sweetheart, wouldn't you think?"

"I suppose I could," he said. "Only, I don't have a sweetheart."

"Oh no?"

"I did have one, once. Marina, she was called."

"That's a pretty name. And whatever became of her?"

Lucy watched his breath horseshoe in the wind. An unpardonable lie came to him, and he clapped his hands to welcome it into the world. "If I'm to tell you the truth of it," he said, "she died."

"Oh, no," said Klara. "I'm so sorry to hear that."

"Yes, thank you."

"But how did she die?" Klara asked. "That is, if you don't mind talking about it."

Lucy held up his hand. "I don't mind at all."

"You're certain?"

"I don't mind in the least. Which isn't to say I enjoy talking about it."

"Of course not."

He cleared his throat. "Yes. Well. We were happy enough, Marina and I – in our modest fashion. But then she got it in her mind to marry, and when I wouldn't go along with this, she became so distraught about it that she killed herself."

Klara gasped. "Oh, but that's dreadful!"

"It was a sorry occasion," Lucy agreed.

"And why wouldn't you marry her?"

"She was not my own true love," he stated simply.

"But you were hers?" Klara ventured.

"I suppose I was. As a matter of fact, I can state that I surely was, for she told me this many times over. So, when she came to understand I would never be hers alone, then did she hang herself – and from a tree before my own house."

Klara covered her mouth; Lucy nodded sympathetically.

"Perhaps worst of all," he continued, "she had pinned a note to her dress, a note addressed to me, but which all the citizens of the town read before I had a chance to. In this way, all were made to know the finest details of her ruination." Here Lucy paused, as if the memory were too much a burden to recall.

Klara laid a tender hand on his forearm. "Is this why you've come here?" she asked. "To get away from the memory of it?"

"That's partly the reason, yes."

"Only partly? I would think that would be reason enough, all on its own."

"Yes, surely it would be. But then the matter was compounded by another unpleasant element, this in the shape of a local man, named Tor. He had always been after Marina, but he was such a stupid and ugly and sickening individual that she rebuffed him at every pass. This ate at Tor like a rot; then, once she had hung herself, for another man no less, Tor swore an oath to all who would listen that he would avenge her honour."

"By coming after you, do you mean?"

"Just that."

"And did he do this?"

"Yes, he was a man of his word, I won't deny it. In fact, hardly any time passed at all before he broke into my house and came upon me like a storm while I slept."

"While you slept!"

"Yes, yes."

"A madman," Klara said, shaking her head in wonder.

"Not mad," said Lucy. "Just simple. A barn animal, really. I might put his mental age at that of a five-year-old, and not a particularly bright five-year-old, either."

"But whatever did you do?"

"I defended myself, naturally, and forced Tor from my home. Not without a knock or two to remember me by, I might add."

"You? Oh, but you are so slight."

"I am agile, is what."

"Is that so?"

"Very agile and quick and fit."

"I wouldn't have guessed it."

"I could cross a room in the time it takes you to blink your eyes."

"Well."

"Yes. So it was that I sent him packing that first night, thinking that would be the end of it. But he was relentless, and it seemed that each time I left my home, then Tor would come barrelling around a corner and make for me."

"Who in the world could live under such circumstances?" asked Klara.

"Not I."

"No one could." Klara became thoughtful, and again she regarded Lucy from a sidelong angle. "Perhaps it is that this misfortune will lead you to something better," she said.

"Perhaps you're right," said Lucy. "As a matter of fact, I'm sure you are."

This made Klara happy, and she hooked her arm in Lucy's. "But, what shall we name the puppy?" she asked.

"I don't know." Lucy was staring at her snaking hand.

Wistfully, she said, "I like the name, Rose."

"Rose?" said Lucy.

"Rose," she repeated.

Her hand came to rest atop Lucy's, and he said, "We'll call her Rose, then."

And they did do this.

She invited him over for tea, which led to supper, with only the two of them in the shanty, as Memel and Mewe had gone away to Listen to work the crowds at a solstice celebration. The hours drew past, and there was nothing like a slack moment, for no sooner would Klara answer a question of Lucy's than she would ask a question herself, and then back again, until the village had gone quiet, and all were in for the night. At one point Lucy screwed up his courage and said,

"Just who is this Adolphus?"

Klara looked away. "He is a soldier I knew."

"Knew or know?"

"Know. I don't know. I haven't seen him in months. And I don't know where he goes, when he does."

"But you wish you did?"

"Sometimes I do." Klara looked back at Lucy. "Perhaps you might find it flattering, that I have an inclination to lie to you about this."

"Perhaps I might," he said.

Rose lay on the table, dozing in between them; they both stroked her but were careful never to touch each other's hands. Lucy could have stayed up all night, but when Klara stifled a yawn, he stood, and said he would take his leave. Klara nodded; her hair was mussed and she smiled at him as he stood at the door. He walked through the village and up the hill to the castle, crossing the still entryway and pausing at the bottom of the stair-well to fish out a squat candlestick from his trouser pocket. Rose began to squirm, and so he let her down onto the ground. She disappeared around the bend of the stair and Lucy, lighting the candle, followed after. The bulbous flame was jouncing up and down as he took the steps; arriving at the mid-point landing, he paused, thinking of how pleasing Klara's face had appeared in the candlelight, and of the way she'd hid her smile in the shadows. He recalled looking over to find she was drawing her cheek back and forth against the fur collar of her cape; and this was a proud moment for him, one that he knew he would revisit any number of times in the coming days and months.

While cataloguing these happenings, he'd been peering absently into the darkened recess of the landing; and to look at him was to see a young man without a care or concern, a person for whom life posed no problems whatsoever, only opportun-ity, and adventure. But gradually this look left his face, and by degrees was replaced with an ever-more severe and serious one. A thought had entered his mind, a terrible suspicion, which was that the darkness into which he had been gazing was not empty at all, but that it held, or hid, something; that it held someone. He stared with an increasing intensity, scarcely drawing a breath. There was no movement in the darkness, but with each passing moment he became surer and surer that there was a body hiding in the recess; and, furthermore, that it was aware of his being there – that it was watching him as well.

Now a sound became audible, but this was so slight at the start that Lucy couldn't be sure he was hearing anything at all. Soon it increased in volume, not so very much, but loud enough that Lucy could not deny its existence. He wasn't certain what the sound was, but thought he could identify it; and he hoped with great fervency that he was mistaken. Alas, as it became louder, his suspicion was confirmed, and he lamented this, because of all the noises to hear, at this late hour and in this lonely location, here was the one he least wished to witness, and it filled him with the direst dread. It was the sound of someone hungrily, gutturally eating.

Lucy raised his candle, and this cast a jewel of milky light in the darkened corner, where he could now make out the proportions of a man, and a wretched man at that, crouched on the floor and outfitted in nothing more than ragged tweed trousers. His bare back was all bones, the flesh coated in grime, and the bottoms of his feet, tucked under his legs, were painted in the blackest filth. Lucy could not see what the man's feast consisted of, his face being hidden behind a curtain of long and grease-matted hair, but he ate with something beyond gusto, groaning slavishly, his body shuddering as the consumption of his meal reached its pleasurable capstone. Lucy's hand was trembling, and so the candlelight also was trembling. *Where is Rose?* he thought.

The man ceased eating and turned towards Lucy. His face was covered in blood, and he held in his hands the remains of a small animal, its middle section eaten away save for a ribbon of black fur connecting its halves. A smile crept across his face as he stood; fur and red-purple flecks of meat and entrails clung to his emaciated body. He was panting, and his eyes were so wild that Lucy could not regard them directly. The man was laughing, but stifling this, as though he didn't want to make any sound, as though he might disturb someone; or, bizarrely, as if fearful of offending Lucy. He stood and moved closer, holding the remnants of his feast up to the candlelight. Lucy found he couldn't not look down, and in doing so he was at once encouraged and discouraged to see not the body of Rose, but that of a very large rat. The man too was watching over the carcass, only with something like adoration, or satisfaction. When he lifted the remains to his mouth and lovingly chewed at the stubborn string of fatty fur to halve the thing, Lucy's revulsion was such that his world became liquid, and he lost consciousness, falling away to the ground.

He awoke the next morning in his own bed, Rose licking his face, his head gauze-wrapped, his skull lumped and tender. There came a knock on his door and Agnes entered carrying a breakfast tray. He sat up and she set the tray upon his lap; pouring him a cup of tea, her face was nearer to his than it had ever been before – he noticed she had a downy cheek, and the balled red ear of a newborn. She placed a spoon in his hand and moved to sit in the rocking chair, patiently and wordlessly observing Lucy while he ate. After he had finished, she removed the tray and set it by the door before returning to the chair. Folding her hands, then, and with what seemed to be repressed irritation, she said, "Now, I'd like to know just what it is you think you're doing here, boy."

Lucy said, "Ma'am?"

"Did you not hear what I said?"

"I heard. I suppose I'm not sure I understand the question. A position was offered to me, and I accepted the position."

"But surely there's some other type of work where you come from?"

"Not so very much. Nothing that suited me, anyway."

"And what is it about this appointment that suits you, can I ask?"

"It's far away," he said. "It's different."

She spoke as though they had hit upon something key: "What

if it's too far away, Lucy?" she said. "What if it's too different?" Now she fished a single gold coin from her smock pocket and laid this on the bed. "Here is your return fare. And I would like for you to go home, if you please."

Lucy looked at the coin but didn't pick it up. "You're terminating me?"

"It wouldn't be my place to do that."

"Does Mr Olderglough want me gone, then?"

"I don't suppose he does. But then, Mr Olderglough is not currently of a mind to make such judgements."

"How do you mean, ma'am?"

She assumed the demeanour of one wondering how much she might prudently say. "Do you not find him a peculiar man?"

"Frankly, ma'am," said Lucy, "most everyone I've met since I've left home is peculiar to me in one way or another." Agnes was visibly dissatisfied by the response, however, and so Lucy added, "But yes, I suppose I do find him so particularly."

She nodded, and asked, "Now, would you be surprised to know that he is *more* than peculiar?"

"I don't know what you mean by that," said Lucy, which was true – he didn't.

Here Agnes began removing hypothetical bits of grit from her smock. "Far be it from me," she said, "to besmirch the man's good name. God knows I looked to him for support and guidance any number of times over the years. But I can't say, Lucy, that I would look to him for guidance at present." A sadness came over her, and she said, "Listen to me, boy. Can't you see that a mistake has been made in bringing you here?"

"But I don't want to go home, ma'am," said Lucy. "I'm not happy there."

"You're happy here, then?"

Lucy didn't answer for a moment. He was thinking about Klara. "Possibly I am."

"You understand that you're in danger?"

"Yes."

Agnes stood. There was an air of finality or defeat to her carriage, so that Lucy felt he had let her down in some way. She said, "What happened to you last night will happen again if you stay here. The situation will not improve. On the contrary." With this, she turned to go. Lucy asked her,

"But why do you stay on, ma'am?"

She lingered in the doorway, considering her reply. Speaking over her shoulder, she said, "Many years ago, I made an agreement with a friend. So long as he remains, then so will I stay as well." Her eyes were kinder now, smoky, and crowded with emotion. "Hold on to that coin. If the impulse to go seizes you, I want you to heed it. Will you do that for me, boy?"

"All right."

"Don't just say it to say it. That's what Mr Broom did, and look what it got him."

It sent a shiver through Lucy, to hear Broom's name. "What is the matter with him, exactly?" he asked.

"The matter with whom?" Agnes asked.

"With Mr Broom."

Agnes shook her head, and she regarded Lucy as though he were a pitiful individual indeed. "You really don't understand at all, do you?"

"Understand what?"

"Mr Broom is long dead, Lucy. The man you met last night is the Baron."

Lucy sat for a long while after Agnes had left, trying to connect the author of the elegantly lovelorn letters he'd been delivering each day with the feral and cretinous apparition he'd seen on the landing. When he found he couldn't link these two, he elected to let it lie awhile. A restlessness came over him and he dressed, descending the stairs and crossing the entryway for the outdoors. Stepping into the cool morning air, he pulled on his cap, careful not to disturb the officious bandaging. He felt an affinity for his head wound; was there not a certain sweetness in its aching pain? He wondered what Klara's reaction to his injury might be, and he imagined her gentle hands searching his skull to pinpoint the epicentre of tenderness. He would tell of how he came to be hurt, and she would swoon and marvel at his trial of fright, afterwards comforting him with a cup of tea, and perhaps a slice of poppyseed cake. And this moment, would it not make the entire ordeal worthwhile for Lucy? Alas, this was not to be, for when he arrived at Klara's door he discovered she was not there, and neither was Memel, and neither was Mewe, which isn't to say the shanty was empty, for it was not; in fact it was filled to capacity, filled with soldiers, the same group Lucy had met when he'd first arrived at the castle. All were standing save for the exceptionally handsome man, who sat in the centre, at the table, and he held Klara's cape in his hands. His face was drawn and grim, and he was not in the least pleased with Lucy.

# V

# ENTER ADOLPHUS

The exceptionally handsome man spoke. "I am Adolphus, Lucy from Bury. I apologize for not introducing myself when last we met. But possibly it is that you've heard my name since then."

"Yes," Lucy said.

Adolphus held up the cape. "It has come to my attention that you've brought my Klara a gift. Is that so?"

"It's so."

"And why, may I ask, have you done this?"

"Because she was cold."

"I see." Adolphus turned to the soldier on his right. "Are you cold?"

"Yes, I'm cold," the soldier answered.

Adolphus turned to the soldier on his left. "And you?"

"It's cold. I'm cold."

"And so am I cold," Adolphus said. He turned to Lucy. "We're all cold. But you'll not furnish us with capes, will you?"

Lucy remained silent. A look of violence came over Adolphus, and he said, "Here's how it's going to go, boy. I'm going to give you back this cape. And you may give it to another village lass, or you may wear it yourself, or you may set it afire. You may do with it what you wish, for it is yours. But there is one thing which, I'm here to tell you, you may not do with it, and that is return it to Klara. As a matter of fact, I should think you and she have no further business together, is that understood?"

Lucy didn't answer. The soldiers were standing unnecessarily close to him, he noticed. "May I ask what you men are fighting about?" he said.

"We fight so that others need not," Adolphus said.

"And who are you fighting, that I need not?"

"They are bastards and will die bastards." Adolphus gestured at the men standing about him. "Now, we've a significant campaign beginning soon, which will see us through to the spring. I've quite enough to do in preparation for this without having to worry about some non-regional cast-off wagging his tiny pink pecker at my bride-to-be. Will you heed me, yes or no?"

He stood and crossed over to Lucy. *If only he weren't so much larger*, Lucy thought. *If only he weren't so bold*. Lucy couldn't look him in the eye, and when Adolphus thrust the cape into his arms and pushed him out the door, there was no option other than to accept its happening, and so he did.

Walking numbly through the village, he caught sight of Klara in the marketplace, shivering in her old, ragged coat. He approached her, and was aware of an anger gathering within him. Standing before her now, he wondered if he didn't hate her.

"Adolphus says you're to be married," he said.

When she faced him, he could see she had been crying. "Anyway, according to him we are."

"I suppose I should offer you my congratulations, then." He bowed. "A long and happy life to you both."

She was wounded by this, and retreated a pace. Staring at the cape in his hands, she said, "Is that all you have to say to me, Lucy?"

He had hoped to communicate an appearance of cold control and indifference, but in looking at Klara's face, and in knowing he had been bettered in love, then did his heart turn against him, and an expansive sorrow welled up in his chest. "Long life!" he said, and spun around, retreating for the castle, his face gone hot with tears. By the time he'd climbed the stairs to his room he had exhausted himself, and felt as though there were nothing inside him at all. Acting automatically, he pulled his valise from under his bed and packed his belongings, including Klara's cape, and Mr Broom's telescope. He pocketed Agnes's coin before taking up pen and paper to compose a short farewell letter to her and Mr Olderglough. Leaving this atop his pillow, he scooped up Rose, gripped his valise, and descended the steps. Crossing the entryway, he saw the Baron had left a letter on the side table. Setting down his valise, he stared at it. He opened it up and read it.

Last night I took up a razor, that I might open my own throat with it. How simple this would be: a flick of the wrist and the life would pour from my body, the room would dim, and I would have my rest. I am not afraid to die, and have not been for some time now. And yet I found I couldn't perform the gesture, knowing you are still drawing breath. If you yourself were passed, it would be nothing, but the knowledge that you remain lulled my hand. I will live until you come back to me, then. If you do not come back, then I will die waiting. This is my pledge to you.

Lucy recognized his taking solace in giving up; he was familiar with the comfort which existed in the acceptance of failure. In turning back from his own pain and fear, he had experienced some stripe of validation; for these feelings were justified, after all, and his leaving was necessary, and wise. Despite this, the Baron's letter conjured in him a shame which eclipsed these other emotions, and so he did not strike out for the station as planned, but removed the cape from his valise and walked back down the hill, and to the village. As he knocked on Klara's door, he could feel his heartbeat in his hands. She answered; she was alone. He passed her the cape and told her, "You can't marry Adolphus."

Her face was so pale, and she looked at the cape with such superlative sadness.

"Why," she asked.

"Because of the fact that I love you."

Lucy said these words and he watched as Klara's sadness drifted away, her eyes brightening in pulses, and now she was beguiling again. Stepping closer, she reached up and kissed Lucy on the mouth, lightly, and again, on the neck. She retreated into the shanty and Lucy followed after. He watched as she shed her coat and put the cape on, standing before the mirror, as before, and admiring herself. "Yes, hello," she said, "and who is this young lady? She looks so happy, doesn't she? I wonder what's got into her. Perhaps she's heard some good news. Perhaps she's heard just what she wanted to hear." She was swivelling back and forth, smiling at herself. "Oh, but she *does* look happy, doesn't she? Well, let's see how long it lasts, shall we?"

The recent turn of events instilled in Lucy an unheralded emotion which he couldn't at the start identify but which he eventually decided was euphoria. And it was in this state that he begot a plan or a strategy, one which he recognized as inspired but also humanely necessary, so that upon returning to his room the next white-lighted morning he threw himself into the task of realizing it, toiling with pen and paper for long hours until his hand was cramped and stiff, that he might get his words to sit just so.

Lucy wrote a letter to the Baroness Von Aux. He introduced himself, describing his position at the castle, and then imparted his opinion in respects to the mental state of the Baron. For, in spite of the dire and unmistakably darkened tone of the Baron's letters, Lucy thought the Baroness was likely unaware of her husband's true condition, and that, if she became conscious of it, and if she possessed any remnant of affection for the man, then she would surely respond in one manner or the other. Well, Lucy was no scholar, and had never before undertaken such a task as this, attempting to transform the fates of others using naked language alone. It was a tedious business, he decided, and he felt no envy of the learned men and women of the world for whom composition was their stock in trade. The following morning, upon rereading his work for the hundredth time, he declared the missive sound, and slipped it into the envelope alongside the Baron's daily offering.

All the time he had been writing this letter, and as he set out to deliver it, Lucy was filled with a righteous feverishness; for he knew the deed was correct, and essential. But then something peculiar occurred, which was that the moment the letter was snatched from his hand, the moment his plan was enacted, and had ceased existing in thought alone, now he was visited by a premonition, presented as divine truth, which was that he had just made a significant and imminently consequential mistake. He stood on the platform awhile, wondering about this, becoming fearful of it. Once the train rolled out of sight, then did he push the feeling away, banishing it, for he had other and more pressing, pleasing considerations. Turning his back on the station, he struck out for the village. Smoke was pouring from Klara's chimney. Lucy began to run.

# VI

# LUCY & KLARA IN LOVE

The days were growing warmer, and Adolphus was away on his campaign. Lucy and Klara took hours-long afternoon walks through the forest, their fingers twining together. They spoke of small things; or of things which seemed small when spoken but which afterwards remained fixed in Lucy's mind. One day Klara commented that when the snow melted away, the exposed grasses looked like the fur of a newborn foal or calf.

"But the earth is not an animal," Lucy said.

"Yes it is," Klara told him, and she gripped his fingers ever tighter.

Now Lucy was spending his nights in Klara's bed. He found it in his ability to make her laugh, and this was so pleasing to him that he sometimes overdid it, and the next day she would complain of a tender stomach. Typically he awoke at dawn, while she and Memel still slept, and repaired to the castle. His suit had arrived from Listen, and his flesh was greatly contented as he eased into this dashing ensemble each morning.

Rose sometimes accompanied him on his rounds, but just as often she would loiter at the door of the shanty as he was leaving, and he knew this meant she wished to stay behind, to play with her brothers and sisters and mother. Whenever this happened, Lucy felt a mild betrayal; but Rose was too large to rest in his pocket any longer, and he knew he had to allot her a life apart from his own.

Upon completing his work, Lucy would change back into his old suit and sheepskin cap and return to the village. Some nights he and Klara would socialize with Memel and Mewe; some nights they were alone. Time passed in this way, and life was but one comfort after another. It was all so natural. Later, and Lucy would wonder how many days this phase had been made of.

A week of ceaseless rain, this followed by baking heat, and all at once it was spring, and the chirping insects trilled in the valley. Lucy and Klara lay in the tall grasses above the village. He was leaning back on his elbows, a sleepy expression on his face. Klara was curled at his side, watching the daffodils bowing to the ground when a bee would light upon them. She put her hand on Lucy's bare stomach and he looked down at her.

"Have you ever done that with anyone else?" he asked.

She nodded. "Have you?"

He nodded. Stroking her hair, he asked her what was to be done about Adolphus.

"What do you mean?" she asked.

"Do you want me to fight him?"

"No."

"Why not?"

She wasn't certain how to put it. "It would be unwise."

"You think he would win, you mean?"

She touched his face. "Yes."

"I suppose he would, after all."

"You mustn't ever try."

"I don't know that I'll have a choice, when he comes back."

She shook her head. "I'll speak with him. He'll be hurt. But he's not a bad man."

Lucy thought of it. "What does he want, exactly?" he said.

"To be a hero," Klara said. "That's actually all."

"And what are you meant to do?"

"I believe I'm meant to coo."

Lucy laughed. He said, "I feel I *could* fight him, though, do you know? I'd only have to think of you two, together, like this."

Klara sat up, startled. "Adolphus and I . . . It never came to that. And I'm not sorry, either."

Lucy experienced a great relief, this followed by a greater curiosity, which he wished to ignore, but could not, and so did not. "Who was it, then, if not Adolphus?"

"It was only once," said Klara. "And it didn't mean anything." She lay back down. "I'll tell you about it, if you really want to know."

"I really want to know."

"All right, then."

# The Inveigling of Klara by the Strange Eastern Stranger, Godless Corrupter

I t was the way the stranger had looked at Klara, as though she were something to be consumed – something that would be. No one had ever looked at her like that before, and it was troubling in several ways, the foremost being that she liked it, or some part of her did. He entered the village in his tottering cart in the early afternoon; his arrival represented diversion at a slack hour and the villagers assembled to gawk and wonder, asking every question which came into their minds: Where had he come from? Why had he left? Where was he going? What was awaiting him there? They were after the news of the world, and the road-weary vagabond fielded these and other queries patiently but without enthusiasm. A lull revealed itself and he removed his hat, asking if he might stay overnight in the village, to rest and replenish his supplies; when his wish was granted, he returned his hat to his head, grinning a grin that Klara identified as devoutly impure. As if intuiting her recognition, he jerked his head to locate her in the crowd, staring levelly and with something more than boldness; and as he was handsome in that dark and brooding way which certain impressionable young women find irresistible, she discovered she couldn't look away from him, and she became afraid in a manner she couldn't pinpoint or define.

Climbing down from his cart, the stranger moved through the crowd, and to Klara. He wore a dirty jerkin with nothing underneath; his bare arms were wiry and hairless and deeply tanned. He had a gold tooth and was missing the lower half of his left ear, and when he took up her hand she began shivering, tremors rippling up her back and to the shoulder. He kissed her across her knuckles. She looked down at the cool spot where his lips had met her skin, and this was the end for Klara. It was as good as done.

She spent the rest of the afternoon in perpetual movement, running non-pressing errands and paying visits to people she did not much care to see, just so long as she wasn't alone with her thoughts, or with the stranger himself. Fearful he would come to her in bed, she made Mewe sleep beside her. When the stranger didn't come, she couldn't understand why this bothered her so, as though they'd had a plan to meet and he'd broken it. In the morning she awoke early and made her way to the well to wash her face. In passing the stranger's covered cart, she cleared her throat. Laying out her soap and towel on the well wall, she washed, and waited. After a time she heard a rustle of grass behind her, and she smiled, but didn't turn around; when something bristly pressed against her leg she drew back, gasping – but it was only Memel's dog arching against her, and she laughed at herself. When she was finished rinsing the soap from her face, she reached for the towel but it was no longer there.

"Why do you hide away from me?" asked the stranger. He was standing at her back, and very close to her. She gazed at the marble-black sphere of the water's surface at the bottom of the telescoping well. Her heart was thumping so violently she felt it might unravel. "I don't trust you," she said. "You make me feel strangely."

He put his hands on her hips and turned her around to face him. The towel was resting over his shoulder. "Isn't it somewhat pleasant, though?" he asked.

"I don't know if it is or not," she said. "It's something like a fever, actually."

Water was dripping from her hair and nose and chin, and the stranger took up the towel and began drying her. He did this gently and thoroughly, and when he'd finished he wrapped the towel around her throat and breastbone. She was shivering again, and she asked, in a quavering voice,

"When will you go away from here?"

"Soon. But I'm not ready to go yet."

"When will you be ready to go?"

He laid his hand on her face. "I will be ready to go after."

She nearly gasped when he said it. He turned and walked back through the grass and to the village, the dog following in his wake.

In the afternoon she tried another tack, which was to attempt to make friends with the stranger. He was leaving the marketplace and she fell in step with him; in a convivial voice she pointed to his ear and asked, "How did you come to be wounded, sir?"

He looked at her amusedly, as though he was aware of what she was playing at. Tugging at what remained of the ear, he said, "That is a question I can't answer. One morning I woke awash in blood, and it was away."

"It was severed in your sleep?"

"Yes."

"By whom?"

"Some enemy or another. No one came forth to claim responsibility."

How matter of fact he was, she thought, as though the incident hadn't been a bother beyond the mess it had made. "What sort of man would do that to you?" she asked.

"Why do you assume it was a man?"

"Oh, but a woman could never do such a thing."

The stranger became remote, his thoughts gone back in time. Soberly, he said, "I've known them to do worse."

Klara blushed at this. It made her inexplicably but unmistakably jealous, and she was frustrated by the feeling. When she gathered herself, she asked politely, "Do you have many enemies?"

"As a matter of fact I do."

"And why is that?"

"I can't think of why. But, they seem to gather wherever I go." Now that same impure grin as before grew upon his face. Klara gathered her hands together and rested them atop her hip.

"Why do you smile like that?"

"Like what?"

"That way, there." She pointed. "It's a smile that hides something."

"I have nothing to hide from you."

"Don't you?"

"Well, perhaps I do after all. And good luck finding out what it is!"

The stranger laughed at this, laughed at her, and Klara left him alone once more. She busied herself cleaning the shanty and making dinner preparations, but she couldn't free herself from her thoughts of the man. Mewe came to sleep beside her that night but she sent him away. No matter; the stranger did not appear. In the morning, after breakfast, she sought him out. He was sunning himself in a field of lupine between the village and castle. He smiled at her as she came near. "I don't know how you stand it, living here," he said. "It's so terribly dull."

"It is *not* dull."

"It's consummately dull. It's immaculately dull."

"I love it," she said, and she did.

In a humouring tone, he asked, "Tell me, what do you love about it?"

"My father, and my friends. The animals, the rivers. I love the seasons; I think they are just the right length of time, don't you?"

The stranger didn't answer.

Klara said, "I love the fields, there—" she nodded towards the sloping green expanse beyond the castle. The stranger sat up to look.

"What's over the rise?" he asked.

"More of the same."

"Do you ever go there?"

"Sometimes."

He looked at her directly. "Will you take me there?"

"But why?"

"Don't you think it's about time we were alone?"

"We're alone now."

"Alone, but not alone-alone. I want to be alone-alone."

He stood up and looked over her. He was quite a bit taller than she.

"Will you be alone-alone with me," he said.

He led Klara away, over the crest of the hill. His hand was calloused and gripped hers tightly. She could smell his body, and the fluttering in her stomach was violent to the edge of nausea. She wore no shoes, and watched her feet swivelling up and back through the grass and flowers. She wasn't precisely sure what she was walking towards but she wouldn't have turned around for the world. Once they were over the rise she tucked her hair behind her ears, looking about for a piece of level ground. Finding one, she pointed. "There." They walked towards the place.

Lucy was disturbed by the pride with which Klara told this story; she was pleased with herself for having an adventuresome spirit, and this hurt him. He knew he was being small about it, but there was no other way he could feel. He was putting his clothes back on when he noticed a wasp struggling to free itself from a spider web, this attached to the low branch of a nearby tree. The webbing bounced and vibrated and Lucy moved closer to watch, with Klara following after. The wasp's manic buzzing filled her with dread, and she said, "Set it loose, Lucy."

"No," he said. "Look." Over top of the branch came the spider, its legs, its head, its plump bobbing bottom. It was very large, and its weight stilled the web, and the wasp for a moment ceased struggling. But then, as if knowing what was to come, and with the spider stepping ever closer, it redoubled its efforts to free itself, its buzzing jumping an octave.

The spider circled the wasp, searching out the prime point of attack. It had looped the web two full times before it lunged; as the insects met, then did the wasp plunge its stinger into the spider's face, the reaction to which was instantaneous death: the spider dropped, yet remained attached to the web by a single silver thread strung out from its abdomen. It hung in space, lifeless, rotating in the breeze.

Something about this occurrence displeased, even offended Lucy, and he watched the spider with an angry expression. He held his boots one in each hand. He lifted them to either side of the spider.

"What are you doing?" Klara asked.

Lucy didn't answer, but clapped the soles of his boots together, popping the spider like a grape. Klara was disgusted by this.

"Why would you do such a thing?" she asked.

"I don't know," Lucy admitted. He was surprised at himself.

"Well, I think that was terrible, your doing that."

Lucy didn't know what to say. He turned away from the web and sat to put his boots on. Klara stood by, quietly fuming. She felt she deserved an apology, though she didn't quite know why. She walked away, towards the village, and Lucy watched her go but didn't call after her or to try to win her back. Returning to her shanty, she wept on her bed for near an hour. The next day Lucy apologized, and all was as it had been before. Neither one of them understood this argument, and they agreed not to speak of the spider or the strange Eastern stranger again.

A village woman had taken ill and left her infant child with Klara for some days; she and Lucy set up to play house in a manner which was at first light of spirit, but which took on a certain seriousness, then an absolute seriousness. *This is how it would be*, was Lucy's thought, and it worried him because he had never been so satisfied before.

The child's name was Anna, and she had purple eyes and was fat as a piglet. Her mood was typically jolly, her laughter quick to come and difficult to arrest, but on the third night something upset her so that she wouldn't cease crying, and if she was enthusiastic in her laughter, then she was doubly so with her weeping. She sat in a quaking crimson heap in the centre of Klara's bed, fists trembling, gulping for air. They thought she was ill, or that a sliver had pierced her flesh, but she had no fever and there was nothing on her person like a blemish, and they were at a loss as to what they should do.

Klara was looking at the baby out of the side of her eye. A thought came to her, and she left the room; thus abandoned, Lucy made a sequence of grotesque faces at Anna. When this summoned no reaction, he made his sounds: the knock-on-wood sound, the horse-trotting sound, and finally, the bullfrog-on-a-lily-pad sound. But Anna only raged on, and Lucy gave it up. "I've made all my sounds," he announced.

"Wait," said Klara. She returned shielding a candle, and lay on her stomach before Anna. Drawing the candle laterally back and forth, Anna's eye was drawn to the shivering slip of flame, and she followed Klara's movements, and was distracted or charmed by them so that her upset was halved. Klara held the candle still and expelled a steady stream of air, not enough to extinguish the flame, but merely to bend it; it flickered raggedly, recalling the faraway sound of a canvas sail in the wind. Anna had ceased crying now. Klara blew harder, and the flame struggled to cling to the wick; she exhaled sharply and the flame was rent, which produced a *click*. As though it were the punchline to a famous stunt, Anna laughed wildly, as before, her mysterious misery vanishing with the candlelight. Klara smiled at her success, the smoke whorling upwards. Lucy had watched all of it. He was astonished.

It was a feeling which stayed in his blood as he slept that night, and then into the morning, so that when he returned to the castle he knew that he was hopelessly mired in love. He brought Mr Olderglough his breakfast and they shared their comfortable greetings. Peter was scratching in his cage in the corner; crossing over to him, Lucy was struck by a startling truth. He took up Mr Olderglough's hand mirror from the vanity and held this before the bird.

"What are you doing, boy?" Mr Olderglough asked.

"Wait," Lucy told him.

Peter was rapt. He tilted his head to better study the stranger before him, and presently issued a hesitant, hoarse croak in the minor key. There followed a dense silence where neither Lucy nor Mr Olderglough drew a breath, and then, finally, Peter sang his long-lost tune. It came out in purling currents, as though his keeping it in had been an agony. Peter sang to his reflection, sang a love song to himself, for he was no longer alone, and the world was filled with unmapped possibilities. Mr Olderglough threw his tray through the air, a great clatter and crash, and he leapt from the bed, running about the room in his nightshirt and cap, howling his pleasures.

S till, there were imperfections. There was a sadness about Klara, and Lucy was more than a little intimidated by it. The sadness was buried but existed in her every movement: the way she folded her hands; the way she pulled a lock of hair away from her face and hooked it over her ear; the way her eyes were drawn to the open spaces, as though in search of something familiar, or possibly something new, unknown. It existed in her silences. Lucy was surprised to discover how badly he wished to combat her sadness, to better it, to eliminate it. And if he accomplished this, what would there be to take its place?

Increasingly Klara withdrew, taking walks in the woods for an hour, two hours. Lucy felt an instinctive mistrust of these solitary outings. He asked her,

"Where do you go, when you go into the forest alone?"

"I go into the forest alone."

"Why do you?"

"To be alone in the forest."

"But why?"

"Because I want to be." She looked at Lucy. "You don't."

"I don't want to be any more alone than I already am," Lucy admitted. He was not proud to say this, and neither was she proud for him.

One day he was buying vegetables at the marketplace when he saw Klara stepping through the crowd and away from the village. She wore a lonesome look on her face, and Lucy followed her. She moved towards the tree line, walking slowly but unhesitatingly; it seemed she had some destination in mind. Lucy might have called to her, but didn't. When she slipped into the forest, he hurried after.

The sunlight was thinned and the wind dropped away. Klara came in and out of view, disappearing behind trees in the distance, then reappearing. Lucy felt ugly to be spying, and he was made anxious by the fact of it, but he couldn't stop, and vowed to see it through. Klara entered a clearing, in the centre of which stood a lone tree, a squat and knotty oak, dead and leafless, its branches filled with ravens. As Klara came nearer, certain of the birds rustled, shaking their heads, unfolding and refolding their wings. She stood before the tree; Lucy thought she said some words to the ravens, but couldn't be sure. When she continued on her way, Lucy resumed trailing her, giving the tree a wide berth, for there was something fearsome about it to him.

Klara walked on and on, and now she was standing before a river, roiling and risen high from snowmelt. When she took up her skirts to sit on the bank, Lucy crept closer, hiding behind a fallen snag, that he might steal a glance at her face and glean just what she was thinking of. The noise of the river was so expansive that it pushed through Lucy, vibrating in his chest. People think of a river as a body of running water, when in truth its physical properties are secondary to its sound.

Klara was watching the sleekly slipping surface of the river, and her face had gone cloudy. Soon she began to weep; she did this openly, frankly, and without shame. In watching this transpire there appeared in Lucy's mind the knowledge that the life she and he were sharing was finite. Its rareness was its leading attribute, after all, and such a thing as this couldn't be expected to carry on forever. A feeling of gratitude was born in him; and it was so powerful as to produce a sensation of lift. In a little while Klara dried her face and stood, walking back in the direction she'd come. Lucy ducked as she passed, and afterwards sat alone for long minutes. Something went mute in his mind as he walked away from the river.

He was moving into the clearing when he stepped on a branch; it snapped crisply in the air and the ravens, as a body, burst skyward. This produced a noise so unexpectedly large, and so violently whole, that it seized his spirit in terror. It was as though some centred part of him had come loose, and it ached, and made him fretful.

There was a heaviness to Klara's movements that night, and she lay with her back to Lucy. His own slumber was troubled and erratic, so that he overslept, awakening late in the morning. Klara was no longer in bed, but in the front room Lucy found she had laid out a pot of tea, a thick slice of bread, a jar of honey, and an apple, peeled and cored. The apple was crisp and tart; the tea had some trace of pine in it. He thought of Klara preparing his breakfast while he slept. A channel of sunlight entered the window, angling sharply to the floor, like a propped beam of milled timber. Dust floated amiably in this, then drew or was drawn into the surrounding darkness, which brought to mind the image of shifting tides. How quiet Lucy's life was just then. He thought he had never been quite so melancholically happy as at that moment.

Clearing the table, he cleaned, dried, and stacked the dishes. The whistle of the morning train sounded down the valley, which meant he had twenty minutes to fetch the Baron's letter and deliver it to the platform. He sat and pulled on his boots, and was lacing them when Klara burst in, short of breath, a bright look on her face.

"Didn't you hear the train?" she asked.

"I heard it."

"Well, get to work, you lazy man!" She pulled him up by the lapels and kissed him. Her smile was easy, and she gripped Lucy's waist, pressing in close to him. Whatever it was that had been bothering her had been set aside; she had made some decision, and this was in Lucy's favour. Pushing him out the door, she told him to return in time for dinner, and he said that he would. As he walked through the village he was so pleased, so relieved, because there was nothing the matter with his Klara, and all was well between them. This feeling of comfort was short-lived, however: passing the marketplace, the wily butcher approached him in the road, and said, "Shame about Adolphus, eh?"

"What about him?"

"You haven't heard? He's been taken prisoner."

"How do you know?"

"I met one of his men on the mountain, and he told me all about it. Said Adolphus was shot in the gut, and so the others caught up to him and pulled him away. He was trailing blood, and never had any hope for escape. If he lives they'll only hang him, I imagine. Now what do you make of that?"

"I don't know what."

"I would think you're happy about it, eh?"

"No. I don't know." Lucy didn't like the wily butcher for saying such a thing, even if it was true; and he felt a creeping brood coming on, for surely the news of Adolphus's capture was the reason Klara had been weeping. And even though she appeared to have reconciled herself to its happening, Lucy knew this was not the last he would hear of it. *What a violent thing love is*, he thought. Violent was the word that had come to him.

L ucy stood on the platform with the Baron's daily missive. He was feeling sad-hearted, and his mind wished to wander to its darker corners. As the train approached, the familiar hand emerged, only there was something quite different about the appendage on this morning, which was that it held a letter of its own. The incongruousness of this was such that Lucy failed to lift his letter, but merely stood by gawking at the flapping pink envelope in the engineer's fist. As the train passed, the engineer dropped the letter, and Lucy watched it twirling through the air. When it came to rest down the platform, he cast the Baron's letter to the ground and hurried to scoop up this other, making for the castle at a dead run. As he wended his way up the hill, the engineer sounded his horn, a half-dozen staccato blasts. Of course he had been reading the letters all along, before Lucy was, even.

Lucy found Agnes cutting Mr Olderglough's hair in the scullery, the latter sitting sheet-wrapped in a low-backed chair, while Agnes stood at his rear, scissors poised. Here was a scenario smacking of the domestic, so that Lucy felt the intruder; and indeed, his superiors wore the look of the intruded-upon, but he offered not so much as a passing apology, as there was no time to linger over societal faux pas. He pressed the letter into Mr Olderglough's hand. "She's written, sir," he said.

Mr Olderglough studied the envelope: front, back, front;

he peered up at Agnes, and nodded. He opened and read the letter, sternly, and with the index finger of his right hand pointed upwards. When he finished, he stood away from the chair to pace the room, addressing Lucy and Agnes in an earnest monotone. "The Baroness will arrive here in twenty days' time," he said.

Agnes emitted an actual gasp. "She cannot."

"She is coming, Agnes."

"She must not. You will write her at once and explain the impossibility of it."

"She is travelling, and so unreachable. I'm sorry, but it is down to us." He folded the letter into the envelope. "And I'm afraid that's not the worst of it."

Agnes blanched. "Don't you say it."

Mr Olderglough nodded. "We will be entertaining."

Here Agnes hung her head.

"The guests will arrive two days after the Baroness," said Mr Olderglough.

"Who?"

"The Duke and Duchess, Count and Countess."

Mr Olderglough and Agnes shared a look of dire understanding.

"And for how long?" she asked.

"Until the end of the month."

Agnes was quiet as she took this in. "Well," she said at last, "obviously the Baroness doesn't understand the state of things here, otherwise she wouldn't be returning. Certainly not with thoughts of entertaining she wouldn't."

"I believe she does understand," Mr Olderglough replied, and he read a line from the letter: "I ask that the Baron be made to look presentable, so much as is possible in his current state of mind."

"She's after ruin, then," Agnes declared. "Or else she's gone mad as well."

"She appears sanguine." Mr Olderglough glanced at the letter. "Her penmanship is as elegant as ever." This proved a small comfort, though, and Agnes all but fell into the chair, looking as one succumbing to witless panic.

"It's beyond me," she admitted. "Where might we begin, even?"

"I won't deny it seems a task."

"A *task*?" said Agnes wonderingly.

"Task is the word I used."

She looked to Lucy. "We are living in a graveyard!"

Mr Olderglough moved to stand before her, resting a hand on her shoulder. He spoke firmly, but not without tenderness. "Take hold of yourself, Agnes," he said. "The castle has been dormant; we must bring it back to life. Why do you act like we haven't been through it before?"

"Never so bad as this, though."

"I shan't disagree with you there. And it may well come to pass that we fail. But we have only two choices: to try, or not to try. And I know that you will try, my dear, just as you know that I will."

Agnes sighed the sigh of the damned, then trudged from the room. She had much planning to do, she said, but wanted to spend some time alone before starting out, that she might wallow stoutly, and without intrusion or distraction. After she'd gone, Mr Olderglough turned to Lucy; all the kindness had left his face. "Now, boy, let us talk about tomorrow," he said.

"Tomorrow, sir?"

"Tomorrow, yes." Mr Olderglough cleared his throat. "Tomorrow is not going to be a day where we will be visited with thoughts of praising God on his throne."

"No, sir?"

"Tomorrow will not be a day we'll later cherish or clasp particularly close to our bosom."

"Will it not, sir?"

"Tomorrow will be a not-pleasing day for us."

"But why is it so, sir?"

Mr Olderglough tucked the letter away in his breast pocket. "Tomorrow we must locate, apprehend, and restore to normality the Baron."

# VII

## THE LOCATION, APPREHENSION, AND RESTORATION TO NORMALITY OF THE BARON

The process of locating the Baron was an unusual experience for Lucy; for whereas before he had thought of this person as one to avoid no matter the cost, now he was actively seeking the man out, albeit fruitlessly, at least at the start.

It was held that the Baron slept in the daytime, and so during the sunlit hours they were hopeful of catching him dozing in this or that nook. But they found no evidence to support any nocturnal habits, however – indeed, they found no evidence he existed at all, save for the occasional discreet puddle or pile. But his chambers remained untouched, and there was not so much as a pinch of salt unaccounted for in the larder. In the night-time, galvanized by Agnes's bitter coffee and an often not-unpleasant sleepless befuddlement, they roamed the halls by candlelight and in stockinged feet, this last at Mr Olderglough's insistence, for he believed it stealthy. Lucy was disinclined to praise the tactic, as the stone floor was cold, and so his feet were also cold; when he became sullen, Mr Olderglough loaned him an extra pair of stockings, which Lucy pulled over his own, and which allayed his discomfort so that peace was restored between them. Mr Olderglough, it should be said, was enjoying this outing to the utmost, and he wondered at his unrealized potential as an adventurer.

Alas, three full days and nights passed them by, and they were no closer to accomplishing their goal than when they'd begun.

With only the minimum of sleep shared between them, then did a weariness set in, followed by the chilling shade of doubt, which soon gave way to a sense of outright futility. At last Mr Olderglough deemed the Baron unlocatable, and was for abandoning the project altogether. Lucy disliked seeing his superior in this state of dejection; pondering the angles, he suggested they were only going about things incorrectly.

"How do you mean?" said Mr Olderglough.

"Bumbling about in the darkness, sir. In *his* darkness. Would it not make more sense to lure him into the light?"

Mr Olderglough squinted. "You're suggesting we entrap him?"

"Why not?" said Lucy.

Mr Olderglough was intrigued, and retired to his chambers to blueprint the stratagem. Lucy was well pleased to have hit upon a possible solution but soon wished he'd never shared his notion, as it steered Mr Olderglough towards the thought of using Lucy as bait. It was described thus: "You will take to your bed at your usual hour, and all will be as is normal except that your door will be not just unlocked, but fully open."

"Will it, sir?" Lucy asked.

"Indeed it will."

"And where will you be situated?"

"I shall be standing behind the door," said Mr Olderglough, rather proudly.

"And what will you be doing there?"

"I will be waiting for the Baron to walk into the room."

"And what will commence when this occurs, sir?"

"I will step away from my hiding place and tap my employer atop the skull with a stubby switch of birch wood."

"Is that so?"

"You may count on it, boy."

"And what next, I wonder?"

"After he's been knocked unconscious, then shall we bring him to his chambers and manacle him to his bed. We will force-feed him, and bathe him, and shave him, and cut his hair and strive to resurrect his interest in sophisticated society." Mr Olderglough rubbed his hands together. "Now, what do you think of it?"

Lucy said, "I think it is somewhat far-fetched, sir."

"Are you not up for it?"

"I'm not, actually, no. And to be frank, sir, I don't believe you are, either."

"What sort of attitude is that? Let us rally, boy."

"Let us come up with another plan."

"Let us look within ourselves and search out the dormant warrior."

"Mine is dormant to the point of non-existence, sir. There is no part of me that wishes to lay nakedly abed and await that man's arrival."

"I tell you you will not be alone."

"And yet I shall surely feel alone, sir."

Mr Olderglough looked down the length of his nose. "May I admit to being disappointed in you, boy."

"You may write a lengthy treatise on the subject, sir, and I will read it with interest. But I highly doubt there will be anything written within those pages which will alter my dissatisfaction with the scheme."

"Well I'm sorry to have to tell you this, boy, but it must come to pass, and it will."

"I believe it will not, sir."

"Do you want to maintain your position here?"

"You know full well that I do."

"Then what is there to speak of, after all?" With this, Mr Olderglough stepped to the window to survey the world. "Now, where has that sly old sun gone to, eh?" In searching it out, he leaned too close to the window, and knocked his forehead lightly upon the pane of glass.

All this to say, Lucy did take to bed that night, and the door was left open, and Mr Olderglough did hide away with a birch club gripped in his hand and a look of dogged resolve stamped upon his face. He had told Lucy they were not to speak, and so they did not. At one point Rose crept across the room to sniff and nip at Mr Olderglough's foot; Lucy collected her and fetched her back to his bed, rubbing her bare belly, which made her restful, and soon she slept, ignorant to the woes of her master.

Lucy's dread was consistently urgent. Time and again he thought he heard the shuffling approach of the Baron, and yet the doorway remained vacant, and Lucy could only gaze into the bottomless darkness and wonder at what it held. An agonizing hour crept by, and then a half-hour, and now he became aware of an unfortunate fact, which was that Mr Olderglough was sleeping standing up, this made apparent by the man's gentle, wheezing snore. Lucy had thrown off his blanket that he might cross the room to awaken him when he saw the Baron hunched at the top of the stairwell, completely naked, bathed in grime, panting, and staring at Lucy with a puzzled derangement.

Lucy said, "Mr Olderglough, sir."

The Baron stepped sideways into the room.

"Mr Olderglough."

The Baron moved ever closer to Lucy.

"Mr Olderglough!"

Mr Olderglough snuffled, and the Baron, hearing this, peered over his shoulder at the door. Stepping nearer, he drew the door back, and there stood Mr Olderglough, leaning against the wall, arms slack at his sides, mouth agape, dozing babe-like. The Baron studied him for a time, as though in distant recognition; reaching up, he lay a hand on Mr Olderglough's cheek. At this, Mr Olderglough awoke, and upon seeing the Baron before him he let out a brief yet sincere shriek, raised the club high, and brought it down over the Baron's skull. The Baron dropped where he stood and lay motionless on the floor.

Mr Olderglough was studying the birch wood admiringly. "Do you know, I enjoyed that," he conceded, and his face bespoke an exhilaration, for how curious life was, how unfathomably novel, and occasionally, wonderful. Mr Olderglough moved to lay the Baron prone on his back. Taking up the man's filthy wrists in his hands, he said to Lucy, "Get his feet, boy, will you?"

S hortly after he was tied to his bed the Baron came to, and upon registering the fact of his apprehension, then did he begin to flail and wail, to curse and spit, to roar from his depths, taken up with such manner of rage that he lost control of his functions; or perhaps it was that he intentionally encouraged this action as a non-verbal means of expressing his ire – either way, Lucy found it a grisly spectacle. Mr Olderglough, conversely, took it in stride, and with something beyond patience; one would have thought he was looking after a temperamental infant rather than a raving, matter-smeared psychotic. Shy of the dawn, however, his years began to show, and he excused himself to rest and regroup. Lucy was ordered to stay and watch over the Baron, and he did this, sitting at a distance and monitoring the Baron's ongoing tantrum, until such a time as the man exhausted himself, dropping into spent sleep; and so too did Lucy succumb to fatigue, sitting upright in his chair. They were the both of them awakened some hours later by the fact of the too-bright afternoon daylight. When the Baron spied Lucy from the corner of his eye he swivelled his head, and a calm came over his face. Perhaps it was his having rested, or possibly his mania had temporarily receded of its own accord, but he was, all at once, human again.

"Who are you?" he asked.

"I am Lucy, sir. Hello."

"What are you doing here?"

"I live here, sir. I've taken over for Mr Broom."

"Broom." The Baron said this gloweringly, as if the man were antagonistic to his well-being. Suddenly there was a seriousness about his person, as if some pressing thought had come to him. "You will untie me, now," he said.

"I mustn't do that, sir."

"You will untie me or you will be dismissed."

"I'm very sorry to disagree with you, sir, but I have my orders from Mr Olderglough, and I shall defer to him."

"Mr Olderglough," said the Baron; and it was clear by his tone that he felt a fondness for the man. "And where is he now?"

"Here I am, I always am," said Mr Olderglough, entering the room looking greatly refreshed and carrying a steam-trailing soup bowl. "Wherever I find myself, and there I be." He sat at the Baron's bedside and, recognizing his present-ness, rejoiced. "Oh, welcome back, sir. It does me good to lay eyes upon you, and that's the purest truth."

The Baron smiled. "How have you been, Myron?"

"Up and down, sir."

"More of the same?"

"The trials of a life."

"What of the melancholy, may I ask?"

"Stubbornly persistent, I'm sorry to say."

"If only modest joy were so dogged, eh?"

"You said something there, sir."

The Baron gestured with his chin to the bowl in Mr Older-glough's hands. "What have you got, there? Agnes hasn't been knocking about in the scullery again, I hope."

"I'm afraid that she has, sir."

"And I suppose you'll want me to partake, is that the idea?"

"It is indeed."

"May I ask what's in it?"

"Better you go in blind, is my thought, sir. Just know that it'll revitalize the spirit." Mr Olderglough brought a spoonful of broth to the Baron's mouth. The Baron reluctantly received this, his face screwing up to a squint.

"Her admiration for pepper has not waned."

"She is devout, sir."

The Baron was peering into the bowl. "What is that floating, there?"

"One way to find out, sir. Let's get on with it, and see what else the day has in store for us, what do you say to that?"

The Baron acquiesced, and the meal resumed. In watching this pair, Lucy wondered at the years that had passed between them. They were so perfectly comfortable with one another as to appear of a piece; it seemed the most natural thing in the world that one should be spoon-feeding the other. After the bowl had been emptied, Mr Olderglough asked,

"Now, was that so bad?"

"You know perfectly well that it was," the Baron answered, though he did look ever more hale. "Now," he said, "I believe the time has come to address the fact of my being tied to my own bed, in a state of undress, and in need of several concurrent baths."

"Yes, about that, sir," Mr Olderglough said. "It goes without saying I'm sorry you find yourself in such a condition as this. But at the same time, I can't claim it wasn't a necessity, because it was."

"I have been – misbehaving again?" said the Baron.

"For some months now, sir, yes. Do you not recall it?"

"Somewhat I do." Here he peered through time, and shuddered at what he found there. "It is unpleasant to consider," he said.

"You'll get no argument from me there, sir. Possibly it's best not to dwell."

"Yes."

"Let us look to the future rather than mull over the past."

"It's a nourishing thought, Myron, and thank you for it." The Baron sniffed. "And will you untie me, now?"

"I will not, sir, no."

"Do you have a time in mind when you might?"

"Quite soon, I hope."

"You were always a fair man."

"I like to believe it, sir."

The Baron grimaced. "Why does my head hurt?"

"Well, sir," said Mr Olderglough, "you were in such a state that I was forced to club you."

"*Club* me, did you say?"

"Indeed."

"I didn't know you had it in you."

"Nor did I. Actually, and if I may be so bold, it was somewhat thrilling."

"Surely it must have been. You'll have to tell me about it one day."

"Yes, sir."

"Has anyone else been injured?"

"You clipped my wing some time back, but I'm one hundred percent at present. And you gave young Lucy here a fright that resulted in a knock on the skull, isn't that right, boy?"

The Baron looked across at Lucy, and a sorrowful mien came over him, as though contemplating Lucy's porcelain countenance in the honest light of day brought his sins back to him, so that a shame took hold of him, and he turned away to bury his face in his pillows and bedding. He was for a time consumed by his sadness, his tone a high, whining wheeze; and Lucy studied the Baron as a pitiable but highly sympathetic individual. But Lucy's empathy was short-lived, as a brief while later the Baron's voice took on a gruff edge, and now did his rage come creeping back, and he began once more to rant and spit and curse, his alter ego having reclaimed stewardship of his spirit. Lucy found this disheartening, not to say frightening; but Mr Olderglough was not the least surprised. He led Lucy from the Baron's chambers. In the hall he regarded him kindly. It was to be, he assured his protégé, an undertaking.

S ome days and nights passed. Lucy and Mr Olderglough sat with the Baron, together and separately, feeding him and speaking with him and leading him away from his manias the way a child might be led away from a carnival. One morning Lucy entered the Baron's chambers and found the man was no longer manacled, but sitting upright in his bathtub, and his hair had been cut, his scraggly beard shaven, revealing a handsomely angular face. He was reading the letter the Baroness had written with a look of horror.

"Are you not pleased that she's returning, sir?" Lucy asked.

The Baron folded the letter and set it upon the side table. "All I know, boy, is that life is, on occasion, entirely too vast for my tastes." Here he submerged himself, and afterwards did a great many bubbles rise up from the depths of the bathtub, this due to the fact of the Baron screaming underwater.

There was a period of frantic activity at the castle. While Lucy and Mr Olderglough had been tending to the Baron, Agnes had travelled to Listen and back; and in the coming days there followed in her wake deliveries of grain, flour, spices, candles, fowl, fish, kegs of ale, crates of wine and brandy, and all manner of culinary rarities Lucy had not heard of, much less tasted. The tailor arrived, three assistants in tow, and these four worked in earnest to prepare a new suit of clothes for the Baron, and another for Mr Olderglough, whose outfit had devolved to something beyond shabby. The offending garment was afterwards burned, and now Mr Olderglough moved sleekly through the halls in an ink-black morning coat, the portrait of surefooted elegance. He went about his work with a surplus of energy Lucy had not witnessed in the man; and Agnes, too, was all the more vital in her exercises. It was as though, with the re-awakening of the Baron's senses, so did the health of his long-time subordinates likewise resume focus. Only now did Lucy understand what fond memories Mr Olderglough and Agnes had been clinging to; only now did he appreciate the satisfaction they received in doing their work. And it was no small surprise that he found himself feeling similarly, but so it came to pass: the castle was sunlit, and all about there was the sense of hope-fulness for the future.

Which is not to say Lucy had an easy time of it. Three days

before the Baroness was to arrive, Mr Olderglough ushered him into the ballroom and said, "I would like you to please tidy up the area, now."

"Which area, sir?"

"The location as a whole."

"Meaning this room, sir?"

"All right, yes."

Lucy considered the size of the space. "When you say tidy, sir."

"Wash the windows. Wash the floors. Wash the walls. Wash the ceilings."

"Wash the ceilings," said Lucy.

"Air the room. Clean out the grates. Uncover the furniture. Polish the trim and accoutrements. Once you're through here, then move on to the next room, and the next, and so on."

Lucy said, "It sounds, sir, that you're asking me to clean the castle from bottom to top before the Baroness returns home. Is that correct?"

"Is there a problem with that, boy?"

"In that it's not possible to achieve I would say that there is, yes."

Mr Olderglough thought this an unfortunate attitude, and furthermore voiced a concern that Lucy was becoming too familiar for one in his position. But in the end he gave way, and Lucy was allotted a small allowance with which to hire help from the village. He enjoined a half-dozen of the meanest-looking women about, the same group who had teased him in regard to Klara's cape, the idea being that they possessed the necessary fortitude to attack such an outsize endeavour. The scheme bore fruit in that the group cleaned with palpable anger, as though the accrual of dirt were an affront to their honour. This hostility was a boon for the task, but proved less advantageous in other ways. Lucy was afraid of the women, and they knew this, and exploited it by pinching and prodding and harassing him; they made crude jokes at his expense for the pleasure of seeing him blush; the stoutest of the bunch at one point pinned Lucy's head to the wall with her behemoth breast, so that he flailed his arms and was panicked to catch a breath.

Indignities aside, Lucy's plan was a success: the work was completed without flaw, and the castle was returned to a state befitting a Baroness. The feeling among the staff was an invigorating concoction of jubilation and dire agitation, both of these held in check, at least so much as was possible.

In the centre of this bustle was the Baron, and it was days before Lucy could take his eyes off the man, this due not only to the fact of his remarkable return to civility, but because the person who had emerged from those ghastly shadows was the most alluring sort of gentleman imaginable. To watch him simply enter a room was in itself an entertainment; he was a *danseur noble* crossing a stage, his every movement so unhesitatingly graceful as he reached in one fluid motion for a book, an ashtray, a pitcher of water – effortless performances which led Lucy to wonder at the standards or qualities of noble blood, and whether or not one in his own modest position might will his blood to clarify, to improve itself. He thought not, ruefully.

Beyond the physical, there was ever more to admire in terms of the Baron's temperament and personality. In the days preceding the Baroness's arrival, he oversaw each aspect of the castle's rehabilitation with a firm hand and meticulous eye; and yet he was never anything other than gracious to his underlings, instilling in the same sequence both sympathy and command – here were the attributes, Lucy realized, of the true leader. He was particularly admiring of how the Baron addressed Agnes's scullery shortcomings. Sampling her stew, for example, he might act as though he were partaking of a delicacy, his abhorrence completely hidden away, afterwards lavishing her in praise, which she drank up greedily. Agnes thus mollified, the Baron would then say something like, "I do wonder if the pepper isn't dominating the dish, however, when your beautiful roux is clearly the leading light of the show?"

Here Agnes's mind would set to turning, and she would ask, "Do you think we might do with less pepper, sir?"

"Excellent idea, Agnes – and just as you say, why not try it?"

So, Agnes would recreate the stew, halve the pepper, the dish would become suddenly edible, the Baron would proclaim her a genius, and she would float about in a cloud of pride and adoration all the rest of the day.

The man was charm personified, in other words, and Lucy was unabashedly in awe of him.

On the evening prior to the Baroness's arrival, Lucy watched from his window as the Baron roamed about in the field separating the castle and village. He walked for long moments with a still face, his hands behind his back, but then began murmuring to himself, then speaking, and with increased animation, gesturing this way and that, a sly smile on his face. Lucy recognized that the Baron was imagining he was with the Baroness, and practising the things he would say to her. At one point he drew his hand to his mouth, searching for some suitably clever phrase, perhaps; upon locating it, then giving voice to it, his eyes grew bright with pleasure. Lucy found a commiserative affinity for the man growing in his heart, and was made apprehensive by this fact. For if love had so degraded a personage of the Baron's powers, what might it do to him? Folding up his telescope, he pushed the thought from his mind. It was too unsettling to regard directly.

# VIII

# THE BARONESS VON AUX

On the appointed day and at the appointed hour, the Baron stood on the platform awaiting the return of the Baroness Von Aux. His hair was combed severely and his expression was severe, and the flowers he held in his hand were gripped with severity, fixed as he was in fevered expectation. Mr Olderglough was sombre; he stood beside the Baron, and Lucy beside Mr Olderglough. They were each of them looking straight ahead, beyond the tracks and into the unpeopled, forested lands. It felt as though the train were late, this because it was.

"She herself has held it up," muttered the Baron.

"Oh, sir, come now," said Mr Olderglough. "Why would she do that? And how would she, even."

"She has found a way – just to niggle the wound. And I'll wager that when she does arrive, she'll have some handsome young valet at her side."

"She would never, sir."

"Wouldn't she? You forget the fiasco with Broom."

"I have forgotten nothing. But I don't see the purpose in making such assumptions before we've set eyes on her. It is a new day, sir."

"It is a day like any other."

"It is a fine and clean and just-born day. There has never been a day quite like today."

"Bah," said the Baron, and he stepped away to privately putter.

Lucy asked Mr Olderglough, "What were the circumstances of Mr Broom's departure, did you say, sir?"

"I didn't say."

"Would you say now?"

Mr Olderglough made a pained face. "A wickedness took hold of him, so that his position became untenable. He tried to shed the wickedness, and I also tried to help him in this. Alas, at day's end there was nothing to be done about it."

"But how did he die, sir?"

"He fell down the Very Large Hole," said Mr Olderglough, this stated as though it were elementary.

"A very large hole," Lucy said.

"*The* Very Large Hole, yes." Mr Olderglough turned and pointed to the loping hills beyond the castle. "There's only the one. Though one is enough, I should think. Just ask Mr Broom, eh?" He shook his head. "It was a poor ending for the boy. I was sorry about it. I had hopes for him. Ah, but his greeds and desires got away from him, as greeds and desires are wont to do." Mr Olderglough chuckled. "I've just had a recollection, boy. Would you like me to share it?"

"All right."

"I don't want to force it on you."

"No, I'd like to hear, sir."

"Very well. I was but a lad, sitting at the breakfast table with my father. Unbeknownst to him, I'd taken and eaten the last sausage, knowing it was his by rights, for I'd already had my fill. When he saw the empty plate, he looked at me and said, 'Some wear greed as a fine suit of clothes. But you, my son, bear its stamp ever more poorly.' Now, what do you think about that?"

"I don't know what to think, sir."

"Do the words not resonate with you?"

"Not so very much, I don't think."

"They did with me. And after he said it, I remember, he stuck me with a fork."

"With a fork, sir?"

"Jabbed me, really. I don't mean to imply the fork was horizontal to my flesh. It was more a punctuation of the thought than actual physical torture. Father was a performer in that way."

At the far end of the platform, the Baron was speaking plaintively into the air. Lucy watched him awhile, then turned back to Mr Olderglough. "I can't imagine your having a mother or father either, actually, sir."

"No? Perhaps you think I was hatched from an egg, eh? And perhaps I was – I'll never tell, boy." He bent his ear. "Did you hear a choot?"

"A what, sir?"

"A choot."

"Is that a type of bird?"

"It is the sound the train makes. *Choot, choot.*"

The train was indeed approaching, and the Baron returned to stand beside Lucy and Mr Olderglough. The flowers were trembling in his hand and he said, "I've gone all shivery, Myron."

"Think of the glad times you've passed with her, sir. She is still that same fresh young woman you courted those many years ago."

"If only that were so, I shouldn't have a care in the world."

As the train pulled into the station, the Baron cast the flowers into its wheels and screeching machinery; the three men watched as the petals were consumed. When the train came to rest, they were drowned in surging clouds of steam, and they each of them closed their eyes.

The Baroness's disembodied voice was deeper and richer than Lucy would have thought it might be. There was nothing masculine about it, but it possessed a weight at its centre – it cut the air and carried itself.

"Will no one help me down, I wonder?"

A smart wind reared and drew past, yanking the steam clouds away, and there she was, in the crisp blue air at the top of the stair, in black and shining fur, her hand outstretched, gloved and likewise black. Her face was sublimely beautiful, and yet there was a darkness residing in her eyes, a cold remove, and Lucy knew that the woman in the painting was not she who stood before them. Whereas the woman in the painting was filled with a humble grace, this person had been corrupted clean through. Lucy was afraid of her, and made no move in her direction; and so was the Baron stuck fast. Finally Mr Olderglough stepped across to receive her, leading her down the steps to stand before the Baron on the platform.

At the start these two stared at each other, saying nothing, and without so much as shaking hands. The Baroness was a portrait of restraint: her thoughts and feelings were mysterious, and she watched her mate with her chin held at a tilt. The Baron managed to mimic her composure for a brief time, but soon his facade began to twitch, and at last he came apart, consumed by naked emotion. Weeping grotesquely, he dropped to his knees, gripping the Baroness about her legs, heaving and sobbing and acting as one oblivious to opinion and utterly without shame. The Baroness did not have an immediate reaction; she merely observed, and with a half-interest. As the scene played out, however, then did her features take on a softer light, and now she removed a glove to stroke the Baron's head. Bending down, she whispered some encouragement into his ear, and he nodded, standing stiffly and re-establishing or attempting to re-establish his dignity.

They stood face-to-face. Returning her glove to her hand, the Baroness drew her thumb across his cheek to dry it. She kissed him. It was a kiss both lengthy and delicate, and at its halfway point, Lucy felt a hand clamp his arm. Mr Olderglough's eyes were damp; he was transported by this performance. The Baron and Baroness walked side-by-each towards the castle, speaking softly to one another, and behaving as lovers reunited.

Behind them, an overworked porter was stacking the Baroness's numerous steamer trunks on the platform. He was peripherally aware of the spectacle taking place nearby, but he paid the Baron and Baroness no mind, as he had quite enough to worry about without concerning himself with the dramatic affairs of others, thank you very much.

# Memel's Lesson to the Children

The Baron and Baroness were hidden away in their quarters for the evening, and so Mr Olderglough gave Lucy the night off, his first in many days. He made haste for the village, entering Klara's shanty without knocking, anticipating a glad reception, but the fire was dim in the stove, and no one was about that he could see. He heard low voices in the rear of the shanty and followed these to find Memel bed-bound and wrapped in quilts, though it was not at all cold. His flesh was grey and he was obviously very ill. Klara and Mewe stood at the foot of the bed; sitting on the floor beside them were seven or eight village children, all staring up at Memel as if to receive his instruction. There was a goblet of wine in Memel's hand. He spoke evenly, placidly.

"One winter," he said, "when I was a young child like you all, my father and I went to Listen together, to sell our cow. None of you ever laid eyes on my father, but I can tell you he was a man of honour. He had his religion, and he was well liked by all, though he did suffer from one peculiarity: it was said that he had never, in his life, laughed aloud. It was not that he was an unhappy man, but his existence was such that there was not any time leftover for idle celebration.

"We couldn't afford the train, and so we walked to Listen, which took three days, through deep snow. We camped beside the tracks each night, throwing a blanket over the cow and sleeping underneath her to keep warm. When the trains passed, the wind whipped up in a great, frigid current that would rustle the blanket and stoke our fire, with sparks and embers tumbling after the caboose. I still don't know why Father asked me along on this trip. I was just another thing to worry about, after all, and my mother could have used my help at home. Well, I like to think he wanted me there for my company. But who can say what goes on in a man's head, eh, children?

"It was dusk when we arrived in Listen, and Father was leading the cow by a rope, while I held on to its tail. Father was anxious about getting his price, because whatever money we made on the sale was meant to see us through the winter. I waited outside the auction hall for him. By the time he emerged night had fallen and I couldn't make out his expression, and so couldn't tell how he'd fared. But then he said to me, 'We'll stay in town tonight, what do you think of that?' And I knew he'd done even better than he'd hoped, for he meant that we would rent a room, at an inn, which was unheard of for us. I told him that I liked the idea very much, and we headed off together, through the crowded square, and we were happy together, my father and I.

"At this point in my life I had never ventured outside the village, and so I was amazed by what I saw in Listen. The street lamps, the shop displays, the bustle of men and women – all perfectly unknown to me. I gripped my father's hand from fear of this strange world, but as the crowd pressed in on us we were separated. I looked all around me but couldn't place him anywhere. I saw only the bodies of strangers, and none of them had any time or concern for me. They knocked me about, pushed me out of the way, and I was so frightened, then, and had begun to cry when I felt a pair of hands heft me up from behind. It was Father, of course. He put me on his shoulders, patting my knee and saying, 'You mustn't cry, my Memel. Don't you know I would never leave you on your own? You're safe with your papa, do you understand?' I said that I did, and my heart swelled up with love for this man, because I knew what he said was the truth.

"We came to the inn, and after stowing our baggage in our room, repaired to the tavern downstairs. Much like the town square, this was full up, so that we had to eat our supper at the bar. Father pulled up a chair for me to sit on, while he stood at my side, and after we ordered our supper we took in the spectacle all about us. Father was as pleased as I had ever seen him. He had had the price of our supper folded into the bill for the room, and so was feeling very worldly and shrewd. He was drinking a beer, and he looked over the patrons as though he found them a satisfactory group. I thought I saw the trace of a smile on his face, but this may have been a trick of the candlelight. Certainly he didn't laugh, though this was the closest I had seen him to laughter.

"We'd just had our suppers placed before us when a man in a ratty coat happened by. As soon as he saw Father he doubled back, pointing his finger, and with a perplexed look on his face. 'Yes?' my father said. 'What is it, sir?' The man slapped his forehead. 'You're going to pretend you don't know me, eh? Come here, you scoundrel!' The man took up my father in the warmest embrace, lifting him clear off the ground and shaking him about. Father naturally was baffled by this, and he broke away from the stranger, who appeared hurt, or insulted. 'But why do you push me away, my brother? Has it really been so many years you don't remember your own flesh and blood?' My father explained he had no brother, that it was a misunderstanding. And at first the man could not believe it, but then Father spoke further, assuring the man he had no family other than his wife and myself, his only son. A moment went by, and the man shook his head. He was terribly embarrassed all at once, and he said, 'Of course, now I can see that you aren't my brother at all. Please will you forgive me, sir? What a fool I am! And here your supper is growing cool.' He was very put out by his mistake, but Father said there was nothing to be ashamed of, it was only a simple misunderstanding, and he wished the man luck in finding his actual brother, and bade him a happy evening. The man bowed to my father, and turned to take his leave of us. But before he departed, he looked at me, and in such a way that Father could not see, he winked.

"My father had begun eating his supper, but for my part I couldn't take my eyes off this man, and I watched him go. It seemed to me that, for one who had only seconds earlier been begging forgiveness, there was a curious lightness to his step. He actually leapt over the threshold at the entrance before vanishing into the crowd outside. 'And what do you make of that?' my father asked me, slurping up his stew. I said that I didn't know what, but that the man had been a strange one. Father agreed, and now we ate our supper, before returning to our room, where we eased into the soft feather bed. The sound of celebration coming up from the streets carried on into the night, and as I drifted off I felt closer to my father than ever before. We were, the pair of us, a portrait of pride and contentment.

"All this went awry in the morning, however. For when it came time to settle our bill, we were greeted with a cruel fact, which was that my father's purse was missing. We searched our room, and retraced our steps from the day before, but this came to nothing, and finally we had to admit the money was gone. It dawned on my father that the man in the tavern who had embraced him had been a charlatan – a pickpocket. When he explained this to me, I recalled the carefree manner in which the man had skipped over the threshold. Likely he knew by the weight of my father's purse that he had happened upon a significant payday, and was eager to begin his spending. And while I was on the one hand sorry for my father, and fearful for us as a family, so too did I feel a curious sympathy or kinship with the thief.

"Now, the question has come up in my mind oftentimes over the years: just where did this sympathy come from? My mother and father never so much as told a lie, and I had been raised to believe that the more you toiled, then the purer you became, and so were well poised to receive God's favour when you passed into His kingdom. I had no reason to doubt my parents, both of them being good, kind people. Be that as it may, from the moment I saw that scallywag making away with Father's money, I was transformed."

Memel took a sip of wine from his goblet, seemingly chewing it before welcoming it into his stomach. He took a second sip, and made a sound like "Ah" or "Hah".

He said, "It was not just the fact of the man's thieving which was attractive to me, it was also the way thieving apparently made him feel. How I longed to cross a threshold in just the same manner as he! I couldn't get him out of my mind, and began to live my life in such a way that my following after him became an inevitability. And so it went, children. I devoted my every energy to play, to shirking, to laughing, to non-working. I ran from every type of responsibility presented to me, be it chores or schoolwork or what have you. My mother and father battled valiantly against my rebellion, but I would not be discouraged, and soon embarked on my own career as a pickpocket – and a deservedly storied career it has been, if you don't mind my saying.

"All through my apprenticeship and my eventual mastery of the art of thieving, you may be interested to learn I never for a moment misplaced my religion. In actuality, I became more devout all the while, though my God was not the God of my elders. For it had always been unattractive to me that He should reward his servants for drudge work – indeed, that he should desire servants in the first place. Being dissatisfied with their God, then, I created a God of my own, and mine was not one to honour labour, but one who repaid the bold.

"The farmer, upon seeing a healthy crop in his fields, kneels and gives his thanks. A shopkeeper will gaze with gratitude at the profits recorded in his ledger. For my part, whenever I came upon a wealthy merchant passed out in his first-class compartment, this was the instant I would pause to reflect, to praise my saviour. It was He who had guided me to these fruitful pastures, to these half-men crying out to be robbed. God wished them taught a lesson, and I, brave Memel, was His instrument."

He looked away from the children, and to a spot high on the wall. "Even now, when I dream, I dream of a compartment filled with the slumbering bodies of wealthy men. I am a younger version of myself, and my energy knows no limits, and I am afraid of nothing in the world. I strip them of their possessions, and their red faces are so peaceful and glad as they sleep, for they themselves are dreaming, of a full table, let's say, a banquet held in their honour, and their hands grasping at this, at that.

"My Klara has spoken over the years of a time of reckoning for me. A day when I would feel my feet in the flames, at which point I would repent, and beg forgiveness. But it would seem that time is approaching, now, and I can say it truthfully: I was right, and my mother and father were wrong. I loved them both, but they were fools. There is nothing noble in suffering, nothing worthwhile in mindless labours. And if you see something you want, children, you should take it. Because the fact of your wanting it renders it yours."

Memel closed his eyes. "That's all I wanted to say to you," he said. "Thank you for listening to me."

The children left the room in a peaceable and orderly fashion.

Memel soon was sleeping, and so Klara and Mewe left him alone, with Lucy following after. Lucy asked what was the matter with Memel; neither Klara nor Mewe answered for a time. Finally Mewe stirred, and said, "We don't know what."

"How long has he been ill?"

"It's been coming and going for months. But not so bad as this."

A pause, and Mewe said he was tired; now Klara led him to the front door, whispering in his ear as he left. Mewe nodded, and they shared a sad look. After Mewe had gone, Klara began chopping an onion for a stew. Lucy approached but didn't touch her, sensing something was wrong beyond the fact of Memel being unwell. He said her name, but she only continued chopping, as though he weren't there at all.

He asked, "Are you angry with me about something?"

"No," she said.

"Will you tell me what's the matter?"

"Nothing is."

Lucy was watching the side of her face. "Has there been some news of Adolphus?"

Klara ceased chopping. She was shocked he had simply asked it. It took a moment for her to answer: she shook her head, no.

"Is it very hard for you, Klara?" said Lucy.

Another pause, when she set her knife aside and turned to Lucy, clutching him, pressing herself against his chest. She was trembling; he thought she was crying, though she made no sound. He asked her again what was the matter but she only said that she was sorry. She wouldn't say why she was sorry.

Later that night they drank some of Memel's wine, after which she became friendly and loving once again. She was simply tired, she explained, and she had missed Lucy, and was worried for her father. They retired to her room, and all was as it had been before. In the morning Lucy fed Memel some broth, along with the castle gossip; the old man was pleased for both, and did seem heartier when Lucy bid him good morning.

Klara kissed him at the door, helping him into his shirt. She framed his face with her hands, peering into his eyes with a determined adoration before saying her fond goodbyes. Lucy's heart was full as he crossed the village, and he told himself he mustn't let so many days pass without visiting, as the time apart was not healthy for his and Klara's courtship. That was surely what the problem had been, he decided; and yet, some small voice doubted his reasoning. And then, too, why did the wily butcher leer at him so knowingly as he passed the stall?

The Baroness sat upright in her bed, reading a book. Lucy entered with her breakfast tray and stood at a distance. She knew he was there but didn't raise her eyes right away; exhaling sharply, she clapped the book shut and said, "I for one find it an annoyance when a story doesn't do what it's meant to do. Don't you, boy?"

"I'm not sure I understand what you mean, ma'am."

"Do you not appreciate an entertainment?"

"I do."

"And would you not find yourself resentful at the promise of entertainment unfulfilled?"

"I believe I would, ma'am."

"There we are, then."

"We are here," Lucy agreed.

The Baroness set the book on her bedside table and looked at Lucy. "So, this is the infamous letter writer."

"Am I infamous, ma'am?"

"In that you've been on my mind, yes. May I ask what prompted you to write it?"

"I felt it justified. Are you displeased with me?"

"Shouldn't I be?"

"I suppose you must."

"It upset me greatly, your letter."

"I'm sorry, ma'am."

"I dislike urgency of any kind."

"Neither am I fond of it. But all was not well here, and as your absence seemed the source of the problem, then I took my small liberty."

"You call it a small liberty."

"I do, ma'am."

"I spilled tea over my dress reading it."

"He was eating rats, ma'am."

"What?"

"The Baron was eating rats. All was not well here."

She gave him a queer look. "Is that meant to be funny, boy?"

"It's not meant to be, no."

"You're a strange one."

"Possibly I am, ma'am, yes. Probably I am." He considered it. "I am," he said.

She drew back her blanket and sat on the edge of the bed, her bare feet hovering above the floor. A shiver travelled up her spine, and she yawned, and asked, "What is your aim, here, exactly?"

"I have no one aim, ma'am, other than to perform my duties agreeably. In regards to the present moment, my hope is that you'll forgive me my imposition."

"It seems likely that I will."

"That's my hope." He held up the tray. "Where would you like me to put this?"

The Baroness didn't answer, having drifted into some private mood, gazing dreamily at the wall, or through it. Lucy set the tray on a side table and said, "If you don't mind my saying, ma'am, it's good that you've come."

"Good for whom?" said the Baroness absently.

"For everyone."

"I don't know about that." She came away from her reverie

and turned to Lucy with an expression of amusement, as though he had said something humorous.

"What is it, ma'am?"

"I don't know what," she said. "I just felt so happy all at once. Strange." She touched the pads of her fingers to her fine, pale forehead. There was something in this small gesture which startled Lucy; and he suddenly understood how this person could drive a man like the Baron to the depths to which he had recently sunk.

Lucy wished to mark this understanding of her powers, to comment upon it. He said, "You're just as Mr Olderglough claimed, ma'am."

She slid off the tall bed and moved to sit on the bench before her vanity mirror. "Is that so," she said, her ribboned hair halfway down her back. "And just how did he describe me, I wonder."

"He said that you were a light in a dark place."

She was stealing glances at herself, from this side and that; and now she studied her face directly. What entered into a beautiful woman's mind when she considered her reflection? Judging by her expression, she was not thinking in admiring terms. "Anyway, it *is* dark here," she told him. Taking up her tresses in both hands, and in an uninterrupted corkscrewing motion, she coiled and stacked her hair into a tidy pile atop her head; and pressing the bun down with her left hand, she pinned it in place with her right. Lucy had never before seen such effortless feminine pruning, and was impressed by the seamless brutality of it. The Baroness was watching him in the mirror. "So we're to be friends, you and I, is that right?" she asked.

"Yes, ma'am."

"All right, then, friend. Bring that tray over here and feed me while I get ready."

Lucy thought she had merely been acting playful in saying this; but as she sat by expectantly, now he saw that she was serious, and so he did as she asked, taking a seat beside her and feeding her fruit and porridge and sips of tea while she appraised her face, altering it here and there with creams and powders and colouring, these set out neatly before her in jars and canisters and spray-bulb bottles. Lucy enjoyed his feeding her to the utmost; there was in her eyes a sorrow so profound that it invoked a drop in his stomach. He had no wish to protect her from it, or alleviate it, as he did with Klara; he merely wanted to witness it, and to recall it later when he was alone. He admired her in the way one might admire an avalanche, and his mind meandered, for he was intoxicated by his nearness to so rare a person as she. At a certain point he realized the Baroness was pinching the top of his hand.

"Did you hear what I asked you, Lucy?"

"I didn't, no."

"I asked if you might accompany me on a walk later."

"Yes, ma'am. And where shall we walk to?"

Her eyes became distant. "I will lead the way," she told him, then asked him to leave, that she might dress for the occasion. Afterwards Lucy stood in the hall outside her door, staring in wonderment at the smarting red smudge on his hand.

The Very Large Hole

The Very Large Hole was very, very large. From the moment Lucy saw it he was made apprehensive by its existence, for all about them was solid earth, and then this gaping and godless emptiness, and he felt he couldn't credit it. It shouldn't be called a hole at all, he decided, but a chasm, a canyon. He and the Baroness circumnavigated the expanse, walking together but saying nothing, the both of them eyeing the void as if something were meant to occur there. This created a tension of expectation in Lucy, so that when a bird shot free of the hole and into the sky, he flinched. The Baroness gripped his arm to hearten him, but Lucy couldn't rid himself of the thought of Mr Broom's demise, so that he mistrusted the ground to hold them. "Perhaps we shouldn't walk so near the edge, ma'am," he said.

"And why not?"

"I'm thinking of Mr Broom's accident."

She looked at him pityingly. "But there was nothing accidental about that."

Lucy felt sickened at the thought of it. "How can you be sure?"

"I knew him well enough," said the Baroness. Cheerily, then, as one making teatime conversation, she asked, "Do you yourself ever think of suicide?"

Lucy pondered this. "No more than what is customary, ma'am."

The Baroness looked on approvingly. "That is a stylish reply."

"Thank you."

They stepped into a bank of sunlight, and she ceased walking to bask in this. She shut her eyes and Lucy could see the miniature cluster of pale blue veins branching across her eyelids.

"And do you ever think of it?" he asked.

"Mmm," was her answer. She opened her eyes. "It's such an odd sensation, being back among you. I was so certain I'd never return."

"But why did you leave here at all, ma'am?"

"Oh," she said, "they were becoming impossible."

"Who was?"

"The Baron. And Mr Broom."

She pointed at a patch of lush grass some distance back from the hole. "This is where Mr Broom and I would come," she said, and she sat, pulling Lucy down with her. Looking about, she seemed to be recalling the time she had passed there, and fondly.

"May I ask what the nature of yours and Mr Broom's relationship was, ma'am?" said Lucy.

"He was my young man, of course," she answered.

"And what was it that drove him to such despair?"

Here she grinned impishly, but said nothing. Reaching down, she plucked a dandelion and blew away its seeds. These travelled on the air and over the Very Large Hole, where they were caught in its drafts. They drew up in staggered ascension, then hurried down, nearly out of sight, before climbing up, up again. This cycle went on for some time, and was a hypnotic thing to witness. When a downdraft yanked the seeds out of sight, the Baroness gasped. She asked, "How long has it been since I've been surprised by anything?"

"I don't know, ma'am."

"Far too long." Pulling up a shock of grass, she said, "The guests will be here soon, Lucy."

"Are you not happy about it, ma'am?" For when she'd spoken, there was in her voice some element of unease.

"I don't know what I am," she told him. The green blades of grass were slipping from her hand, and she and Lucy watched this.

"Why have you returned, ma'am?"

The Baroness shook her head. Leaning in, she kissed Lucy's cheek, then stood and resumed walking, alone now, adrift in her strange and terrible beauty.

# IX

# THE COUNT & COUNTESS, DUKE & DUCHESS

On the morning of the guests' arrival, Mr Olderglough had taken Lucy aside and told him, "I will look after the Duke and Duchess, and you will mind the Count and Countess. Is that quite all right with you, boy?"

Lucy answered that it was, but it struck him as curious, for Mr Olderglough had never positioned an instruction in so accommodating a manner before. "May I ask why you prefer the Duke and Duchess to the Count and Countess?" he said.

Here Mr Olderglough nodded, as if he had been found out. "We have been through a good deal together, you and I, and so I feel I can speak to you in confidence, and as a peer. Are you comfortable with that?"

"Of course, sir."

"Very good. Well, boy, if I'm to address the truth of the matter, none of the coming guests is what might be called desirable company. Actually, I have in the past found them to be distinctly undesirable."

"In what way, sir?"

"In many ways which you will, I fear, discover for yourself. But your question, if I understand correctly, is to wonder which of the two parties is the worse, isn't that right?"

"I suppose so, sir."

"Then I must tell you that the Count and Countess merit that prize, handily. And while I feel on the one hand duty-bound to take the heavier burden unto myself, I must also recognize that I simply haven't the capacities I once did. To look after people such as those who are coming to stay with us is a young man's game, and I am not young any longer, and so I take the simpler path, though you may rest assured that when I say simpler, I do not mean simple. The Duke and Duchess are no stroll in the park, and I can attest to that personally, and at length." Mr Olderglough stepped closer, his eyes filled with ugly memories. "Be on your guard with these people, boy. They answer to no one. They never have, and they never will."

These words played in Lucy's head as he stood on the platform awaiting the Count and Countess's arrival. As the train came into the station, he could hear a man's wild cackling; when the Count emerged from his compartment he was quite obviously drunken, swaying in place, a cigar planted in the fold of his slick, blubbery mouth. His skull was a softly pink egg, his eyes blood-daubed yolks – he drew back from the sunlight as one scalded. Once recovered, he focused on Lucy, gripping him by the lapel. "Ah, Broom, happy to see you again, boy."

"Yes, sir, nice to see you, as well. Only I'm not Mr Broom; my name is Lucy."

"What?"

"My name is Lucy, sir."

The Count stared. "You're Broom."

"I'm not he, sir."

"Well, where has Broom run off to?"

"He has died, sir."

The Count leaned back on his heels. Speaking over his shoulder and into the blackened compartment, he said, "Did you know about this?"

"About what?" said the Countess.

"Broom is dead."

"Who?"

"The servant lad? Broom? You were so fond of him last time we visited."

"Oh, yes, him. Nice boy – nice colouring. He's dead, you say?"

"Dead as dinner, apparently."

"How did he die?"

"I don't know how." The Count looked at Lucy. "How?"

Lucy said, "He was possessed by a wickedness and so cast himself into the Very Large Hole, sir."

The Count made an irritable face.

"Did he say a very large *hole*?" the Countess asked.

"Yes," said the Count.

"Large *hole*?"

"Yes."

The Countess paused. "Well, I don't want to hear another word about it." And with this, she emerged: a corpulent, panting woman with frizzed black hair, a crimson neck, and a fierce displeasure in her eye which Lucy took to be travel fatigue but which he would soon discover was simply her root mood. When he held out his hand to help her from the train, she cracked him across his knuckles with her folding fan, a stinging blow that took his breath away. Pushing past him, she stepped up the path and towards the castle, murmuring vague threats or regrets to herself. Once she was clear of earshot, the Count addressed Lucy breathily, and through a shroud of bluish smoke.

"When is the dinner service?" he asked.

"Six-thirty, sir."

"Unacceptable." The Count pressed a coin into Lucy's palm. "If you could scare me up some type of holdover, that would suit me."

Lucy studied the coin. It was a foreign currency, and quite useless to him. "Holdover, sir?" he said.

"Something to chew on."

"Something to eat."

"I like salt. A meat. Don't let the Countess see."

"No, sir."

"You're on your own if she does."

"Yes."

"And I suppose a bath is in order. Can you see to it?"

"Surely, sir."

"Fine. Now you fetch us our baggage and then get started on the rest. You seem a good lad, but how many have let me down in the past? Indeed: too many to name." He trundled up the hill on stumpy legs, and Lucy turned to watch the porter offload the trunks and cases. It was the same porter Lucy had seen before, when the Baroness arrived. They were much the same age, and Lucy approached to assist him.

"What did he give you?" the porter asked, and Lucy showed him the coin. The porter smiled, and produced an identical valueless coin from his own pocket. They each cast their coin to the ground, and as the train pulled away from the station the porter swung onto the caboose. He bowed at Lucy, and Lucy bowed at him, and the both of them returned to their work.

The Count was listlessly fingering the contents of his steamer trunk. He was naked as the day he was born, and other than his height, looked much as he had at that initial emergence. The Countess, on the opposite side of the room, sat at the vanity, admiring her toiletries, laid out in some obscure codification of her own hostile design. In the corner, unseen behind a folding screen, Lucy was pouring out the final cauldron of water for the Count's bath. He had a sizeable salami up his sleeve and was waiting for the moment when the Countess was not about, that he might unsheathe and present it to the Count. He was hopeful this would happen sooner rather than later, as the salami was cold and oily and felt repugnant against his bare flesh.

The Count held a white silken shirt up before himself. He turned to face the Countess, who told him, "You'll want to go darker. You're so ruddy these days."

The Count sighed.

"You take too much tobacco," she said.

"It's more the drink, I fear."

"Well, whatever the culprit, you mustn't wear white if you can avoid it."

He stood before the tilted looking-glass, dolefully assessing his countenance. "So many pitfalls in a life," he said.

"Yes."

"The consequences of our appetites confound me. But, you know what my father said: 'A modesty of appetite represents a paucity of heart.' He swapped the white for a blue shirt, and appeared pleased, for it truly did mask his hue. "I find myself wondering what's for dinner," he said, to no one.

Lucy stepped out from behind the screen. "Cold dill and yoghurt soup, sliced calf tongue in butter, pork knuckle in nettle sauce, and for dessert, a fruit tart."

The Count and Countess stared at Lucy.

"Did you know he was in the room?" the Count asked.

"I did not," said the Countess.

"Nor I."

"I wish I had known."

"As do I."

"I knocked before entering," said Lucy.

The Count said, "I heard nothing like a knock."

"Neither did I," said the Countess.

"You should knock harder," said the Count.

"I'm sorry, sir," Lucy said.

"Or offer a verbal greeting."

"I didn't want to disturb you."

"But you've done just that, haven't you?" said the Countess. She turned to the vanity, and in a spasm of pique began passionately combing her hair. The Count set his blue shirt to the side, for he had located something of consequence in his navel, and now worked fingers like pincers to remove it.

"Is my bath ready?" he asked Lucy.

"It is, sir."

The Count padded around the screen and submerged a thumb in the water. Finding the temperature to his liking, he daintily drew a leg over the lip of the tub and eased into the bath, emitting a puff of air as he did so. "Tell me more about this tart, boy," he said.

"It's a peach tart, sir, soaked in brandy."

The Count raised his eyebrows. "Brandy?"

"Yes, sir."

"Have you yourself ever tried it?"

"Yes, sir."

"And what is your opinion of it?"

"I have a high opinion of Agnes's tart, sir." And this was true – Agnes's tart was her lone certainty. The Count seemed pleased to hear as much; he drew up his lips like a purse's drawstring. In a whisper, he asked,

"Did you bring the meat?"

Lucy nodded, and patted his sleeve. "It's here, sir." Now the Count made a beckoning gesture, that Lucy should come nearer and produce the salami, but before this could be accomplished the Countess, whom neither Lucy nor the Count had heard approaching, was standing beside the screen, watching them with a sour expression.

"He was going to scrub my feet," the Count explained.

"Scrub your own feet. Boy, come with me."

Lucy followed her across the room and soon found himself regarding the clammy folds of the Countess's naked flesh as he untied her corset. Once freed from the garment she sat awhile, expanding. Sniffing at the air, she said, "You smell like a salami, boy."

"Yes, and I'm sorry about that, ma'am."

"It's something you're aware of, then?" she asked.

"Yes."

"Oughtn't you do something about it?"

"I surely will, ma'am."

"It is not insurmountable. One doesn't have to smell like a salami if one doesn't wish it."

"No, you're absolutely right, ma'am."

"Fine," she said. "And now, away with you. I should like a rest before the evening's festivities. Wake me up one hour before dinner service." Bowing, he turned and crossed the room, stalling as he passed the screen, behind which the Count waved frantically from the bath. Lucy moved closer, rotating his wrist to and fro that the salami might come loose; but the cuff was snug, so that the tubular meat became lodged in his sleeve. He was fumbling with his cufflink when the Countess, who had been watching his progress, thwarted his delivery: "I said away, boy – away!" He made a helpless face at the Count and exited the room, very nearly colliding with Mr Olderglough, who was happening past. They walked together, towards the scullery.

"How does it go, boy?"

"They are as you said, sir."

"Are they not, though?"

"Indeed, and they are."

"Tell me."

Lucy regaled his superior with details of his experience up to that moment, leaving out his having a salami in his sleeve, for it was an unfortunate, even shameful fact; and beyond that, he had taken it from the larder without asking permission. Mr Olderglough listened to the rest, his head down as he took it in. At tale's end, he said, "Gluttons of the basest category."

"Yes, sir," said Lucy. "And what of the Duke and Duchess?" He had seen them only in passing, when they entered the castle some hours earlier. They appeared to be of a piece with the Count and Countess in terms of temperament, though were ever more stylish and healthful; the Duchess in particular was something of a pouty beauty, horse-limbed and taller than the Duke by a head.

Mr Olderglough said, "My experience has been much like yours. I find it something like corralling children, wouldn't you say?"

"It is."

"But you are holding up, my boy?"

"Oh, I'm fine, sir." Actually, Lucy found the task of tending to such people amusing; and this was reflected in his bearing. Now

Mr Olderglough had ceased speaking but was only watching Lucy, and with fondness.

"What is it, sir?"

Mr Olderglough considered his answer. "Just to say that I'm glad you're here with us, boy. Your very mettle has been tested within these walls, and for what it's worth, you've impressed me, and you have my thanks."

How curious for him to have spoken these heartfelt words, and seemingly out of the blue; and curiouser still, that Lucy should have found himself so touched by the sentiment. But there he was, swallowing a lump in his throat, and when he replied, it was with sincerity. "Thank you very much, sir. And I hope you know that I'm glad to be here with you all, also."

"Good, then." Mr Olderglough patted Lucy's back. They approached the scullery, and a mischievousness came into the older man's voice: "Now, boy, I hope this doesn't offend, but we've taken a liberty tonight."

"Oh?" said Lucy. "And what do you mean, sir?"

"A liberty has been taken, is all. Blame Agnes. We needed the extra hand, and she believed it would please you." Mr Older-glough opened the door and bade Lucy enter first. Stepping into the scullery, he found Klara standing in the centre of the room, wearing a maid's uniform and a timorous look on her face. Her hair had been cleaned and combed and was pulled away and back; her forearms were bare; her white filigreed smock tied tight about her tiny waist. Here was Klara, only a wholly separate version of her, all the more elegant and feminine, and as Lucy absorbed this unpredicted dream of beauty, then did he feel himself falling in plummeting love a second time.

Agnes, from the larder, called for Mr Olderglough, and so Lucy was left alone with Klara. He moved to stand before her.

"Who did this?" he asked.

"Don't you like it?"

"I like it."

"Agnes helped me with my hair."

"I like it."

"She has rougher hands than my father."

"I think you look very nice and I like it very, very much."

She was smiling, staring at the floor. "But do you *really* like it?" she said.

"I like it. I love it. I love you."

She looked up now, pleased and relieved by his reaction; for life in the village had never afforded her such finery as this, and she could see how impressed Lucy truly was. Stepping in closer, she reached out for him. Gripping his arm, she paused, and drew her hand away. "What is that?"

"A salami."

"Why do you have a salami in your sleeve?"

"It's not my salami."

"Why – do you have a salami in your sleeve?"

Mr Olderglough returned from the larder and, upon seeing Lucy and Klara so closely paired, began to loudly clap his hands;

over the sound of this, he called to them: "No time for the cooing of doves! Klara, you will go with Agnes in the larder! Lucy, you will assist me in preparing the dining room! We shall cease living for ourselves but only for the others! Servitude is an art! Now and now!" He continued his clapping and encouragements as he walked from the scullery and into the hallway. "Search within yourselves! Excellence! Magnificence!"

Lucy and Klara were smiling. He kissed her forehead and followed Mr Olderglough but cast a final look over his shoulder before exiting the room: Klara straightening her dress; the loveliness of her profile as she spun about, girlishly, and stepping to the larder. Lucy hurried after the sound of the clapping, which was ongoing.

The banquet table was buffed and gleaming, the cutlery polished, napkins pressed, the grand room bathed in the golden colouring of the numberless white candles. The three couples were likewise gleaming and pristinely groomed; they sat upright, nodding politely to one another but speaking little, their conversation stilted and faceless, dealing mostly in governmental gossip. The Baron and Baroness chatted lightly to their guests, but the others wouldn't be drawn out, and Lucy, in delivering the soup, could read a justifiable concern on the faces of the hosts, for the mood was restrained to the point of creating unease, and the evening was in danger of foundering. But, as the second course was served, and the wine began to pour, the group relaxed, and the banter became freer. By the conclusion of the third course the party was gay verging on raucous, heads tilted back in mad laughter, the Count's complexion red-going-purple as he spit up some partially chewed morsel of food. The more they drank, then did the traits of the individuals become ever more vague, and now the party took on a single presence, and there was at the edges of this small society an accrual of unkindness, even menace.

Lucy thought he noticed, then was sure he did, that the Count was watching Klara each time she entered the room. At the start he did this only in stolen snatches, but as the evening progressed his attentions became more overt, so that whenever she came near he made it a point to initiate some slight contact – to touch her wrist when she took up his empty plate, or to stroke her back as she passed by. When he touched her, she froze, and her face was empty, plain; but Lucy knew she was oppressed by the Count's attentions, and each time it occurred, his stomach pitched. At one point, when Klara had left for the scullery, the Count asked the Baron, "Where did you find that one?"

"Oh, she's just a village girl."

The Count found this fascinating. "So she's not in your employ?"

"Not typically, no. But we hadn't the time to hire full staff, and so we're just getting by in the meantime. Why do you ask? Are you unhappy with her?"

"Quite the opposite!"

"My husband is enamoured, I think," the Countess explained.

"Ah," said the Baron, nodding. "Well, one could hardly blame you. Though I think you may have some competition in young Lucy, here."

The group turned to stare at Lucy, who had been standing at the rear of the room, mutely seething.

"Is that a fact?" said the Count.

"See how he draws up when she comes near," said the Baron, smiling fondly at Lucy. "Take note of the forlorn look in his eye when she departs. Obviously he has given himself over to her, heart and soul." He laid his hand on the Baroness's. "It is something which only one in love could identify."

The Count was watching Lucy. "Well, lad, how about it? Sabres at dawn?"

He was merely making sport, and yet there was an undercurrent of true violence at play as well. You had but to look at the man to see he'd never in his life asked twice for anything he desired. What would it feel like, Lucy wondered, to push a blade into a person? Would it be quick, as when you sliced your hand through a ray of light, or slow, and heavy, like an oar through water? Either way, at that moment he really did want to run this Count through, and so in reply to the query he said, "At dawn, by the light of the moon – just as you wish, sir."

The celebrants thought this very fine, and they laughed a long while about it. The Baron himself stood and saluted Lucy, and the Baroness clapped her white gloves in his direction. Lucy bowed to the group and left the dining room to find Klara standing on the other side of the door, flushed and beaming, for she had been eavesdropping, and had heard Lucy's response to the Count's challenge. Lucy was taken up by an uncommon boldness, and he kissed her there, listening to the swish of her uniform against her skin. A moment of this, and she stepped back, watching him with a look of wonderment. A nameless resolution formed in her eyes, then she led him by the hand, away from the dining room and into the cavernous space of the ballroom, closing the door behind them.

She was not shy, which made him feel shy. She had pressed him against the far wall of the ballroom, and as she undid his trousers Lucy studied her with an idolization so vast it took on physical properties in his heart; the size and weight of it was frightening for him in that he felt he could not contain it. At certain moments in their coupling she became feverish, and it seemed to Lucy she was not herself at all, but possessed by some spirit he hadn't yet known. He gripped her skull and marvelled at its diminutive delicacy, puzzling over how it could be that so frail a vessel might possess such a force as Klara possessed. At the apex of his passion his body was flooded in light. Lucy had never been so moved.

Klara stood and corrected herself, straightening the hem of her dress with a sensible tug of the wrists. She was smiling with sly pride, and she told him, "I'll go first." Lucy nodded but didn't answer. After she had gone he remained leaning against the wall, legs atremble, trousers still bunched at his ankles. *What an eventful day I'm having,* he thought.

This sentiment was compounded when the doors swung open and the partygoers entered in a hysterical troupe. Lucy slipped crabwise to stand behind the curtain at his right; he could think of no way to pull up his trousers without bringing attention to himself, and so was forced to leave them be. He stood for a time in the darkness behind the heavy fabric but soon folded back the edge of the curtain, that he might catch a glimpse of the group; and it was from this vantage point that Lucy could and did witness and catalogue the strange and terrible ballroom goings-on. All were present save for the Count, who some moments later scampered into the room, the tart wrapped up in his arms like a swaddled infant, his face descriptive of a perceived immortality.

"Look at how merry he is," said the Countess.

"Remarkably so," the Duchess commented.

"Can one be too merry, I wonder?" asked the Baroness.

"One can not," the Count announced, resting the tart atop the table. "For joy carries no consequence, and is desirous of nothing save for more joy." As the group digested the statement, the Count stood by, admiring the dessert, smiling sleepily, the picture of satisfied docility. But then some black violence or another occurred in his mind, and a look of cruelty came over him. He punched his fist dead into the centre of the virgin tart.

# The Strange and Terrible Ballroom Goings-On

The Count, in his negligence, as if to intentionally culti-vate his negligence, was eating the tart from the cup of his palm, with all the aplomb of a hog lapping slop. Clenching his hand to a fist, he watched the remainder push between his fingers, watched the drabs fall to the floor; he wiped his palm on his trouser leg and regarded the assembled group with glazed eyes. Said the Baron to the Baroness, "Our guest is happy with the tart, my love."

"It would seem so," said the Baroness.

"And if he is happy, then we are happy also, isn't that right?"

"We most certainly are."

"For what is the function of the host, after all?"

She spoke as one performing elocution: "The function of the host is to ensure the comfort and amusement of his guests."

He patted her hand, and they shared a look of wholesome admiration. Now the Baron addressed the others. "I wonder if the rest of our friends are as well pleased as the Count?"

The Duke said, "I'm feeling very well, myself." He turned to his wife. "Is there anything you're in need of, dear?"

The Duchess shook her head emphatically.

"Nothing at all?"

She continued shaking her head, and smiling – it seemed she was too intoxicated to speak. In fact, all in the group were by this point thoroughly drunken, their cheeks aglow with wine and good cheer; it was quite natural that they should, in spite of their societal positions, abandon formalities. Still, it was troubling to Lucy that the Count, presently grinding the tart droppings into the carpet with his spat-covered boot, should behave in such a way and receive nothing like a reprimand; for surely he had crossed the line which separates the ready celebrant from the boor. And so Lucy was pleased when the Countess spoke up from her perch on the settee, saying, "Oh, but you're making a mess of it. Don't you see that you'll spoil it for the others?"

The Count ceased grinding the tart. He was staring at the Countess. She ran her finger along the lip of her glass, regretful of having spoken up, apparently. "Well, I'm sorry," she said, "but it did seem to me you were ruining the dessert for the rest of us, after all."

His gaze drifted away, and across the room, as though he were taking in the furnishings. An awed expression appeared on his face; one would have thought some profound knowledge had arrived at the forefront of his mind. Regarding the tart, then, he took up yet another handful and crossed over to the Countess, walking with the deliberate steps of a man who was comprom-ised by drink but focusing with all his might on purposeful movement. Standing before his wife, he held his tart-dripping fist out between them. His breathing was erratic.

"And just what do you intend to do with that?" she asked.

The Count reared his hand and slapped her viciously in the centre of her face. She reeled backwards on the settee and lay still awhile, silent but in a fair amount of pain, it would seem. The Count was pleased with the blow, and returned to his post beside the tart, exhibiting the pride of one having done his duty. The Countess sat up. Though she was bleeding freely from her nose, no one rose to assist her; actually, no one seemed to feel anything at all like concern for her, and it struck Lucy that that they were each of them watching the scenario unfold as though it were some type of entertainment or diversion; and indeed, judging by their rapt faces, their reverent silence, that is precisely what it was for them. Lucy had the impression that this spectacle of violence was something which had happened before, and perhaps many times before.

The Countess rose and stepped away from the settee, the smear of tart over her face soaking up the blood, the crumbs crimson and plumped. She did not appear displeased, or in any way offended; quite the contrary, she wore a look of regal defiance, as though she thought herself the most bewitching woman in the room. She began to undress, and the moment she did this, the Duchess and Baroness came to her side to assist her, wordlessly helping her from her gown and untying her corset. Soon she stood naked before the assembled ladies and gentlemen, blood dripping from her chin and decorating her bare bosom, pooling in the slit and snaking down her rounded belly. She moved to the tart and took up the entire tray, delivering this to the Duke with a bow of her head. He accepted the tray automatically but his face expressed dubiety. He turned to the Count.

"And what shall I do now, old friend?" he asked.

"A gentleman must do as a lady wishes," said the Count.

"You're certain of it?"

"I've never been more certain in my life."

And so the Duke, too, grabbed a handful of tart and, just as the Count had, jammed it over the Countess's face.

"Harder," she told him.

Yet another handful, and this applied with increased forceful-ness, which sent her toppling, her feet in the air like a tumbler.

As before, she lay still awhile, translating her pain, during which time the Duchess began undressing, as did the Count, and Duke. Lucy noticed that when the Duchess stepped from her gown it stood independently, stiff, truncated, to ghostly effect.

And what of the Baron and Baroness? Lucy had been so trans-fixed by the others he hadn't thought to check their reaction; when it occurred to him to look he was surprised to find the pair, whom he had come to regard with something like venera-tion, were also disrobing, pawing at each other and staring into each other's eyes with an animal craving. The group as a whole were evolving or devolving, becoming increasingly alert and agitated, and there was in the room the most terrible sense of expectation which drew Lucy's stomach taut, a crab-apple knot of abhorrence. He wished to quit the room, but there was no way to achieve this. He wanted to look away but he could not. He watched the proceedings with a dumbstruck sense of horror. A numbness spread in his mind and body as he waited for the filthy pageant to pass.

At a certain point the salami, which had been gradually pushing proud of his cuff, dropped away, hitting the ground with a slap and thud; and while no one noticed this happening, Lucy felt that if an errant salami were spied on the floor, and so nearby his person, it would surely invite investigation. He dared not bend down to retrieve it, but decided to kick it away; alas, he did this over-enthusiastically, and the salami rolled halfway across the room, coming to rest mere inches from the Count's naked foot. The Count caught sight of the salami and stared at it; its appearance was disturbing to him in some way. He looked up and around the room, as if for any further clue. Finding none, he nudged the salami with his toe, then stepped uneasily away to rejoin the others.

The Duke was leading the Countess by the hair to kneel before the Baron.

"Why not have a go yourself, Baron?" he asked, and he handed over a plateful of the tart.

The Baron smiled good-naturedly at the Countess; to the Baroness, he said, "What shall I do, my love?"

She scooped up a piece of tart and deposited it in his palm.

"You're certain?" he asked.

She nodded, and the Baron lightly slapped the Countess's cheek. The Countess wore a deflated expression; she looked to the others, as if for intervention.

"No, no," said the Count.

"We're doing it harder than that, Baron," said the Duke.

"Much harder," said the Count.

"Try it again, but with more force," said the Duke.

"Just as hard as you please," said the Count.

But the Baron hesitated. "You're certain you want me to?" he asked the Countess.

"Hard," came her breathless reply.

Now the prevailing abandon took hold of the Baron, and eschewing the tart, he offered up a grand wallop which found the Countess sprawled on the floor yet again. This was roundly applauded; you would have thought by the group's reaction that the Baron had shared some great witticism or insight. The Countess clambered back upright to kneel once more before the Baron, who instructed her to open her mouth, and when she did this he began pushing in handfuls of tart, one after the other, until she gagged and retched, involuntarily spitting the tart out and onto the ground. She was told to eat this up and she acquiesced with great eagerness, as though there was nothing she had ever wanted to do quite so badly. By this time the group were all completely naked, their circle shrinking to a cluster.

There came a phase of general copulation among the partygoers. Lucy did not know and could not deduce what format or protocol they were guided by, but it did seem there were invisible cues of etiquette being adhered to: the manner in which they came together, the labour itself, the business-like briskness with which they parted. Perhaps the most shocking aspect of all this was the absolute lack of humanity in the room, for there was never so much as a kiss shared, never a caress. At a certain point the Count momentarily broke away from the Duchess to fetch the salami. He returned, re-entering her, this time from behind; wielding the salami like a truncheon, he fell to flogging her all about the back and buttocks and head. The others had completed their transaction and now were gathered around to watch this final spectacle. As the Count's thrusting became more frenzied, so too did the whipping, and when he was through, the salami was mutilated, a mere stub in his greasy grip. He stood away from the Duchess, his body blotchy, clammy, his chest and stomach rising and falling in counter time. The Duchess was perfectly spent; she lay groaning on her stomach, her back coated in welts and bits of meat. The Count threw the stub of salami at her head; it ricocheted off her skull and bounced away, under the settee. In this way the matter was settled.

"Now," said the Baron, "who is ready for a cigar?"

At the mention of this, the Duke and Count expressed enthusiasm which struck Lucy as outsize to the proposition, clapping their hands and hurrahing. The Baroness, too, was acting strangely, her cheek and neck gone red, her face drawn to a tight smile, as one withholding a private pleasure; she approached the table in the centre of the room and climbed atop it. The Baron distributed cigars from a cedar box and the men drew closer to her, stepping luxuriously, as if strolling the promenade of a fine spring morning. The Baroness was in position, her face pressed to the table-top, arms splayed out before her, backside pushed high into the air; the Duke and Count appraised her naked behind while the Baron clambered onto the table, reaching up to the chandelier and removing a lit candle, careful as he descended to preserve the flame.

The moment he had put his hand to the candle, then Lucy had an inkling of what was to come, and he hoped with great sincerity that he was incorrect, but he was not, and when the unlit half of the candle disappeared up the Baroness's rear passage, he found himself wondering at the dark state of man, pondering the notions of freedom, and battling with a distant nausea. One by one the men leaned in and lit their cigars, then stood back to smoke and stare reverently at the woozy candle-flame. Perhaps a minute passed. The Baron asked the Duke,

"Whatever became of the shipping situation in your township?"

The Duke stuck out his lower lip and shook his head. "Tempest in a teapot."

"You seemed concerned when I saw you last."

"All for nothing. The union organizers were run out of town, and peace has been restored."

"I'm happy to hear it. And how have your profits been this year?"

"Better all the while."

"And the weather?"

"We've had a mild winter, thanks to God. And you, what of your interests?"

"As before."

"Money always came to you."

"It always has, actually."

"Money comes to money, they say," the Count offered.

"They say it and it's true," the Baron said appreciatively.

The Duchess and Countess, meanwhile, were warming themselves by the fireplace. There was a copious bouquet of yellow roses on the mantle; they began to take up the flowers, one by one, and toss them into the flames. The Baroness had lain still for some minutes but now removed the candle and walked to stand beside her friends. Reaching for a rose, she likewise cast this over the flames, and then again. And so: three naked and unspeaking women threw roses into a fireplace, one after the other, until the bouquet was gone. The men had returned to the settee; they watched their wives perform this mystifying endeavour with sombre expressions on their faces. When the roses had gone to ash, and the cigars were snuffed out, the group dressed, bade one another goodnight, and retired in twos, first the Duke and Duchess, then the Count and Countess, and finally the Baron and Baroness.

Once alone, Lucy pulled up his trousers and stepped from behind the curtain. Agnes entered as he approached the door.

"Where in the world have you been?" she asked.

"Here, ma'am. The others have gone to bed."

"Yes, the Count mentioned they were done. Did it seem that they enjoyed themselves?"

"Yes."

"And did they enjoy their dinner?"

"Yes."

"Did they enjoy the tart?"

"Yes."

"They found it tasty?"

"Yes."

"Did they actually say as much?"

"No."

"But you got the impression they liked it, is that it?"

"Yes," said Lucy. An unpleasant thought came to him. "When did you speak with the Count, ma'am?"

"He came into the scullery just now. Looking for a nibble, he said."

"Where is Klara?"

"She's also in the scullery, washing up."

"Who else was with them?"

"No one."

Lucy quit the room. Clear of the doorway, he started running. Agnes stayed behind, pouring herself a brandy, and sitting with a sigh on the settee. She sipped her drink, looking about with a wary expression. There was something about the ballroom that had always bothered her.

When Lucy entered the scullery the Count had Klara pinned in the corner. He was pulling up her dress, rubbing her underside, and licking her face; when she struggled to free herself he began to thrash her, shaking her about, that her head might roll from her shoulders. Lucy crossed the room in broad strides, as though he were floating, almost, or sliding across ice; snatching up Agnes's marble pestle from the butcher's block, he swung this at the back of the Count's head, thinking to knock the man out, but at the last moment the Count turned, and so caught the pestle in the mouth. His skull was ricocheted off the stone wall and he dropped to his knees in a halted stupor. His top row of teeth was gone and rich, red-black blood drew down his face and into his shirtfront. It was moving faster than Lucy thought blood could move. He gestured to Klara, and she came and stood behind him. He was holding the pestle so tightly that his fingernails were sinking into the meat of his palm; when the resulting pain of this occurred to him he loosened his grip, and the pestle fell to the ground, breaking in two. He hadn't struck anyone in his life before this.

The Count stood, leaning against the wall and watching Lucy and Klara with a divine confusion, as though he'd never seen them before — as though he'd never seen anyone before. He drew a finger across his chin and looked at it. Staggering to the basin, he inhaled, then spit out the shards. Straightening his lapels, he swivelled on his heels and addressed Lucy, his words made spheroid by the thick blood and dearth of teeth.

"How do I look, boy?"

"You have blood all down your face, sir."

The Count pulled his kerchief from his breast pocket and dabbed at his cheek. "And now?"

"There is still a good deal of blood."

He wiped the kerchief all around his face, smearing the blood and disimproving his state considerably. He offered Lucy a questioning glance.

"Much better, sir."

The Count bowed to Lucy, and then to Klara. "Well, now," he said, "the Sandman is calling me, and so I shall retire. Thank you both for a pleasant evening."

"You're welcome, sir," said Lucy.

"You're welcome," said Klara.

The Count left the scullery, and Lucy and Klara watched the empty doorway. The Count reappeared, and Klara gripped Lucy's hand.

"Which is my room? I can't recall."

Lucy pointed. "Up the stairs, sir, and second on your right."

The Count left again. Lucy felt faint; he found himself blushing, and so was shy to face Klara. He closed his eyes as she wrapped her arms about his waist and pulled him closer. They held each other, and kissed, and were so very much in love.

In the morning, the Countess opened her eyes to find her husband's face a butcher's display of dried blood and flesh so raw and swollen as to produce a shine. She began to scream, and she continued screaming for a good long while.

The Count had no recollection of the incident with the pestle. Lucy had cleaned away the blood and tooth fragments in the scullery, as well as the button-like droplets which ran down the hallway and to the base of the stair. When this was deduced to be the blood's point of origin, it was assumed the Count had tripped. The guests and their hosts re-enacted this happening the next morning, and they were very excited to be doing so, all except the Count, who stood back from the others, purple and ghastly. The Baron knelt to touch the blunt edge of a stone step, perhaps the very same one the Count had collided with, and a collective shiver ran through the assembled. The Count attempted to speak but his words were unintelligible. He repeated them, but only the Countess could understand, and she translated:

"He wonders where his teeth went."

The Duke leaned forward. "Likely you ate them, my good man!"

The Count winced at the thought, then winced from the wincing.

"I suppose you'll find out soon enough!" said the Duke.

The Duchess, who was suffering from a headache, said, "He's not gone deaf, dear. Please keep your voice down."

They moved to the breakfast table, where it was decided a medical presence was necessary. The Count agreed but would not consider seeing any doctor other than his court physician. The Baron said he would have a letter sent at once to fetch the man; but no, the Count preferred to recuperate in the comfort of his own estate. This point was argued but the Count was immovable, and now a pall settled over the table, for the premature departure of he and the Countess signalled the collapse of the group. And what of the Duke and Duchess? Yes, it would seem that they, too, were formulating plans to leave; already they were speaking of future meetings, and the unfortunateness of the Count's taking a fall – the pity of it all. The Baron looked on, aggrieved, and a glint of desperation flashed in his eye. He pleaded with the others to stay, speaking of grand dinners and as yet untapped kegs of the finest wines; but none could be persuaded, and now all was silent save for the clattering of cutlery.

Something had gone wrong the night before, something which wouldn't be mended. Who could say whether this was a shared sense of loathsome shame stemming from the ballroom happenings, or some lingering hostility which had taken hold of the group permanently – Lucy wasn't sure the performance of the evening prior was not ongoing. But whatever the reason, the joy vanished from the guests, and also the Baron, and most acutely, the Baroness, who, upon recognizing that the happy times had once more ended, left the table without saying goodbye to her old friends, disappearing into her private chambers and locking herself in.

L ucy and Mr Olderglough were kept busy all that day and into the late afternoon, assisting the guests with their packing, and transporting their baggage to the station. The Count was acting the infant, but was clearly relishing being the centre of sympathetic attentions. Lucy was made uncomfortable by the man, fearful he would suddenly recall how he had come to be injured; but he only looked to Lucy as another body to lean upon and moan at. Lucy and Mr Olderglough escorted the Count onto his train; when this pulled away, Mr Olderglough said, "It looks like we'll have a quieter time, boy, and I dare say we've earned it." Lucy noticed he was smiling but trying to hide it.

"What is it, sir?"

Mr Olderglough cleared his throat. "Well, I find myself wondering what exactly *happened* to the Count last night. You wouldn't have any idea, would you?"

"Ah, it seems he fell, sir."

"That is the theory, yes. Must have been a nasty fall, eh?"

"It must have been."

"If it was indeed a fall, that is."

"Yes."

Mr Olderglough paused to ponder. "And I wonder, too," he continued, "just what happened to Agnes's pestle?"

"Her pestle, sir?"

"Her pestle, yes. Didn't you know that she found it this morning, split in two?"

"Is that right?"

Mr Olderglough nodded.

Lucy shook his head. "That's a shame."

Mr Olderglough nodded. "Lastly," he said, "I am curious as to what happened with young Klara's uniform."

"Her uniform, sir?"

"Agnes tells me it was ripped at the neck and sleeve. I hope she hasn't come to any harm?"

"No, sir, she hasn't."

"She got home safe, then?"

"Safe and sound."

"Well thank goodness for that. She seems a very nice girl."

"She is, sir. And thank you for saying so."

They walked for a time in silence. They were both smiling, now. Mr Olderglough said, "Would you agree that the most appealing thing about a mystery is the fact of its mysterious-ness?"

Lucy considered this. "Perhaps I would, sir."

"But also the most frustrating, wouldn't you say?"

"Perhaps it is. But as is not unrarely the case, sir, I must admit to not knowing quite what you're talking about."

"No?"

"No."

"Well, no matter." He looked away. "You may take the night off, if you wish."

"I would like that very much, sir, and thank you."

"Yes, boy. Off you go, now."

Lucy walked towards the village then, listening to the chir-ring of crickets in the dusky air. He found himself drawn once

264

again to the sight of the smoke spilling from Klara's chimney. He wished he might live forever in that wonderful hovel.

As he came nearer the village he noticed a crowd had assembled outside the shanty. Stepping to the front of the pack, now he saw the focus of their attentions: Adolphus stood before Klara's door, famished and decrepit, in filth and bloodied rags, held up on either side by two of his comrades. One of these men knocked, and Klara answered, standing in silence and stillness, regarding Adolphus as though he were a spectre. When she took him in her arms, a burst of jubilation came up among the villagers. She led him inside, and the crowd dispersed, all except for Lucy. When he recognized it was not possible for him to enter the shanty, he turned and walked away.

# X

# A BLUE BOY

There followed a desolate era where Lucy didn't know quite where he stood with Klara. It was only days before and they had been connected as if by blood; now he heard nothing from her, and neither did he hear from Memel or Mewe. It was said among the villagers that Adolphus had been tortured and starved and was still very much in danger of dying, but time passed with no news of his demise, and as the smoke continued to spill from Klara's chimney, Lucy knew she had to be nursing and feeding him and tending to his wounds. Meanwhile, and as if in concert with this unnerving scenario, the mood among the castle inhabitants grew ever more removed, with the Baroness forever breaking away from the Baron to be alone in her chambers, and the Baron chasing after her, his voice gone high and pleading. Finally they retired to their respective rooms, and a cruel silence existed in every hall and doorway. From the scullery, Agnes and Mr Olderglough spoke only in whispers, and their words were unsure, for they were the both of them fearful of what was likely to come. It was an in-between time, and Lucy shirked his duties to spy on the village with his telescope, as when he had first arrived.

One morning he watched Klara walking through the village and to the shanty, a bundle of kindling in her arms. He studied her face, but she wore no expression whatsoever; seven days had passed since Adolphus's return, and a hard kernel of contempt had formed in Lucy's heart. Why had she not come to him? Surely she knew he was aware of Adolphus staying with her; surely she knew he was in pain about it. What did it mean that she hadn't bothered to address this? Well, what else could it mean? He told himself it was a matter of pride to wait for her, when in fact he was simply too frightened to go himself. When he thought of the way she might phrase her goodbye, he was sickened.

Klara dropped her kindling and stared with an awestruck expression into the distance. Adolphus had emerged from the shanty and was standing under his own power in the doorway. The sun glanced off his face, and while it was plain he was not yet healthy, he was far healthier than before, and he smiled easily, beckoning with his hands for Klara to come nearer, and she did this. They stood before one another awhile, speaking unknown tender words. When Klara reached up her hand and stroked Adolphus's cheek, then did Lucy know he had lost her. This is how it happened that his heart was so superbly broken.

Lucy was disinclined to leave the castle, and took to maundering in the halls, carrying his burden here and there, eating little, sleeping less, and saying nothing, for he found speaking to be actually painful for him. At last he retreated to his room, blacked out his window with ash, folded and stowed his telescope, and took to bed. At the start he had no specific thoughts or notions but was merely inhabiting a deep, even ache; then came the visions of merciful death, and he pondered the variants with a swooning reverence. On the third day of this, Mr Olderglough came to visit, and Rose was at his side. As they entered the room, Lucy drew the pillow over his face. "Please don't," he said.

"Don't what, boy?"

"Don't say it."

"Don't say what?"

"Don't say anything."

Mr Olderglough sat on the bed. "Are you not well, Lucy?"

"I'm not, no."

"What's the matter?"

"I'm not well."

"I suppose it's something to do with Klara, is that it?"

Lucy didn't answer. Mr Olderglough bowed his head, and his forelock came uncoiled. "What may I do to help you?"

"Nothing."

"And when will you be better, I wonder?"

"I don't want to be better."

"That's no kind of attitude."

"I can't help it."

"Must you speak with the pillow over your face?"

"I must, yes."

Mr Olderglough set his forelock in place, looking sterner. "Lucy," he said, "I'm here primarily because of my being worried about you. But there is also the fact of your being paid to perform services in the castle, and it has been some days where you haven't done so. Now, we all come down with a trace of gloom from time to time, but—"

"You've never once paid me," said Lucy.

Mr Olderglough scowled. "Oh, come now, boy. That can't be true." He thought a moment. "*Is* that true?"

"Never once."

"Well, that's just terrible." Mr Olderglough paused, then brightened. "What if I *did* pay you? Then would you work?"

"No."

"This is all very discouraging. May I ask after your plans?"

"I have none."

"But surely you must. What of the future?"

"There isn't one."

Mr Olderglough sighed. "I cannot claim to be enjoying this conversation, if I'm to be honest. As a matter of fact, I'm going to go away, now. I'll leave Rose here with you, if you don't mind. I found her wandering the halls this morning."

"Fine. Goodbye, sir."

"Yes, goodbye." Mr Olderglough left. Rose climbed onto the bed to lie next to Lucy, who presently returned to the swamp of his own self-pity, which was a relief, for as a habitat it was magnificent in its direness; and since it had been created from his own fabric, he felt some stamp of gratification as he wallowed there. There had always been something comforting in melancholy for him, as though it were a purposeful tradition he was taking part in.

The next afternoon, Memel called on Lucy. Lucy did not cover his face for the visit, but stared away at the ceiling. Memel said, "Mewe is down with the grippe. Will you and Rose come for a walk with me?"

"No."

"Why not?"

"I'm too sad to."

Memel puckered his face. "You shouldn't talk like that."

"Why."

"It's sort of disgusting, don't you think?" He sniffed the air. "Why don't you empty your pot?"

"I don't care about it."

"Clearly you don't."

There was a discordant note to Memel's voice; Lucy looked at him, and was shocked to see how unwell the man appeared. He'd lost weight, and his colour was gone, and he was trembling. "You're still feeling poorly, Memel?"

Memel said, "There's something gone sour in me. I can't seem to get rid of it, whatever it is." He regarded his stomach, then turned back to Lucy. "Won't you come along? I don't feel like being alone today. And besides that, there's something I want to show you."

Lucy did not in the least want to go, but Memel seemed so nakedly vulnerable that he felt duty-bound to come along, and so he rose from the bed and dressed, and they struck out, with Rose leading the way. Memel made some weather-related comments in hopes of conjuring a conversation, but Lucy would not be lured into speaking more than a word or two. Finally Memel asked him what was the matter. When Lucy told him nothing was, Memel pointed out that this was a lie.

"Isn't it true that you're having troubles with Klara?"

"I suppose that I am."

"Because of that soldier?"

"Yes." Lucy felt strange discussing Klara with Memel. "I wonder what she wants," he said pallidly.

"I couldn't answer that, boy. And I doubt she could, either." Memel laid a hand on Lucy's shoulder. "I don't know what she sees in that other one, to tell you the truth."

"Don't you care for him?"

"I have no regard for a man so willing to give his life for an *idea*," said Memel, and he spit on the ground to emphasize his indignation. Lucy, for whom the war was still a mystery, said, "Yes, and what is the idea?"

"Precisely," Memel answered, pausing to catch his breath, though they'd not been walking at all briskly. Lucy offered him an arm; Memel accepted this, and they continued, heading for the tree line. They were passing a section of forest he'd never seen before, and presently they came to a clearing in the wood, a grassy knoll, uneven rows of homely tombstones: the villagers' cemetery. Lucy followed Memel through the rows. They arrived at a grave and Memel pointed. "Klara's mother," he said. "Alida, was her name." Kneeling, he said, "I suppose I'll be joining her soon enough."

"Don't say that."

"Why not? It's true. I've already written my epitaph. Would you like to hear it?" Lucy said that he would and Memel cleared his throat, speaking skywards, as one reciting a poem:

"He wandered here and there over rolling hills.

He never saw the ocean but

dreamed of it often enough."

He turned to Lucy with an inquisitive expression.

"It's very nice," said Lucy.

Memel bowed his head modestly. "Have you ever visited the ocean?"

"No."

"A man once told me it was wide as the sky and twice as blue. Do you believe it?"

"I suppose I do."

Memel shook his head at the wonder of this. "What do you think your stone will say?" he asked.

Lucy had never thought of it. What was an epitaph meant to be, exactly? A summation of accomplishments? A representation of one's general outlook? Fine, only he had as yet accomplished nothing, and he had no overarching opinion regarding his life or anyone else's. Lucy was stymied; he shrugged the question off.

"It will come to you in time, likely," said Memel.

Lucy wasn't so sure. "Why did you bring me here, Memel?" he asked.

Memel nodded, gesturing to Alida's grave. "I was wondering if you were aware that she did the very same thing to me that Klara is doing to you now? And with my dearest friend Tomas, no less?"

It was curious to think of Memel with any other friend besides Mewe. "I haven't met a Tomas," said Lucy.

"You wouldn't have. He's been dead a good long while. A gambler, Tomas was. He and I were as close as could be, since we were boys, even."

275

"And when did he die?"

"Just after the impropriety was revealed. He was murdered, you see."

"He was?"

"Yes."

"Who murdered him?"

"I did."

Lucy said, "You murdered your closest friend?"

"Yes."

Lucy thought about this. "How did it come to pass?"

"You want me to tell you?"

"I want you to tell me."

"Well then, I will."

# How it Came to Pass That Memel Murdered His Bosom Confidant, Tomas

**M**emel went to pay Tomas a visit one morning and found him in bed, clinging spiderishly to his wife, and with neither one of them wearing a stitch of clothing. They didn't notice his being in the room, and Memel considered their labours in a stupor. Here was an utterly alien visual, for he hadn't the slightest inkling of anything untoward going on between these two. When Alida spied him in the doorway, she shrieked, and Memel left the shanty to stand in the sunshine, clutching his shirtfront and gasping.

Tomas emerged, half-dressed, and in a dead panic. He took Memel in his arms, but Memel could smell his wife on Tomas, and he turned away, stalking from the village and towards the hills. Tomas followed, calling after him; it was a dry, hot day, and when Tomas's voice became raspy he ceased speaking, but he never stopped trailing Memel. They walked one in front of the other, above the village and through the forest until they arrived at the edge of the Very Large Hole, where Memel's legs gave out. Tomas sat some feet away; after he'd caught his breath he said, "We used to come here as boys, and try to throw stones across to the other side, do you remember?"

"I remember."

"But we never could do it, could we?"

"No, we never could."

"And now I suppose we're too old for it."

"Yes, that's the truth."

In actuality they were neither of them old men; their arms were still wiry with muscle, their backs straight and strong, and yet they had surpassed the mean, the centremark of their lives, and were both aware of an overall dimming.

"Every day, and a little closer to death," said Tomas.

"That's how it is from the beginning, though," Memel pointed out.

"Yes, but did you think of it as a younger man?"

Memel admitted he hadn't. Tomas stood, picked up a stone, and threw it into the hole. Memel did the same. Neither stone went very far.

"I should be able to do better than that," Memel said.

"Yes," said Tomas. "Let's try again, and give it our best."

They picked up stones and threw them as hard as they could. Both went a good deal farther than their first attempts, but Memel edged out Tomas for the greater distance.

"Very nice," said Tomas.

He was standing near the lip of the Very Large Hole. His hands were on his hips; he stared into the abyss, and Memel took up a position behind him.

"And so, what are we to do about this, Tomas?"

"I don't know what. I wish I did know."

"Well, what does Alida want?"

"Who knows what that woman wants." Tomas laughed to himself.

Memel took a step closer to Tomas. It occurred to him to walk softly. "Shall we leave it up to her, then?"

Tomas made a strange sound with his throat, for he was crying now. "I suppose we must do that," he said.

Memel took another step. "And what will become of us?"

"That's for you to say."

"Is it?"

"Yes. For my part, I pray that our friendship will remain."

Yet another step. "You want my wife and my friendship, eh?"

"I know it's impossible. But that's my wish." He took a shivering, sobbing breath. "Oh, Memel," he said. "I love you so much."

Memel lunged, and Tomas was borne aloft and into the void. Memel had pushed with such force that he nearly tumbled into the hole himself; when he regained his footing, he stood wondering at the absoluteness of his friend's absence. It was as if the darkness had eaten not just Tomas's present, but his past also – his history in its entirety. Memel hastened back to the village. He was curious to see Alida's face when he told her.

There was a tactility to this story which startled Lucy. He was unsettled by the image and deed, and by Memel's undemonstrative manner of reportage; and yet he was moved by the tale as well. Was there not a measure of justice in the act, after all? Perhaps it was only natural, then, that Lucy was already reimagining the story so that it was Adolphus at the lip of the Very Large Hole, and he himself stood at Adolphus's back, creeping ever closer. He wondered if he could actually go through with it. His heart was doubtful. "That must have been difficult to do," he said to Memel.

Memel shook his head. "I pushed him. That was all. He didn't make a sound. You'd think he would have screamed."

"He was too surprised, maybe."

"It would be surprising, wouldn't it? Slipping through the air like that, all at once?" Memel paused a moment to consider it. "Well, I can't say I regret it, Lucy. Woe betide those who trifle with Eros, eh?"

"I suppose."

"Cupid is well armed, and so must we be, isn't that so?"

"It is so."

Memel's face grew long. "I do miss Tomas, though. Him and Alida both. I've never got over either of them being gone, if I'm to be honest."

With a degree of trepidation, Lucy asked, "And how did Alida die?"

"In childbirth, nine months after the death of Tomas." He regarded Lucy with a mischievous expression, as if daring him to enquire further.

"Nine months," Lucy said.

Memel nodded.

"You're saying Klara is Tomas's daughter?"

"I'm saying that Mewe is Tomas's son."

"Does Mewe know this?"

"No."

"He's never asked after his history?"

"He's never asked me."

"When will you tell him?"

"I have no plans to tell him at all."

"But why not?"

"Why should I, is the superior query."

Lucy considered it, and could think of no further argument. He asked, "Why did you tell me this story about Tomas?"

Memel held up his palms, but he didn't answer the question, and would say no more about it. At the conclusion of their outing, he bade Lucy and Rose a good evening, and his footing was shaky and uncertain as he stepped towards the village.

That night Lucy lay in bed, hopeful for sleep, but sleep wouldn't come no matter how he approached it in his mind. At last he sat up and declared, "Well, I'm just going to have to kill him, and that's all there is to it." He lay back down and made plans to that effect.

Adolphus stood beside the Very Large Hole, looking into it, and whistling shrilly. Lucy sat in a crouch a half-dozen paces away from the lip. He hadn't slept even momentarily all through the night and there was an insistent, throbbing discomfort in his skull. Kneading his temples with the tips of his fingers, he asked Adolphus to stop whistling, and Adolphus did stop. *But now he'll spit*, thought Lucy, and this proved to be true. The soldier marked his spittle's transit with interest.

"Well, boy, where's Klara?" he asked.

"She's coming." There was something in Lucy's voice, some inkling of worry or strife, that caught Adolphus's ear; now he peered at Lucy in a sidelong manner. Lucy's eyes were ringed with grey and blue, and his breathing was hurried and shallow.

Adolphus said, "I know what went on between you two, while I was away."

Lucy said nothing. He had removed his pipe from his pocket and was tapping it against a rock.

"I want you to know that I don't bear you any ill will because of it. Our desires get away from us, and there's nothing to be done about that. I can't say that I blame you, anyway. Her behaviour is all the more baffling to me, but then Klara was never one to do the expected thing." He spit a second time, then asked, "What's the matter with you? You sick?"

"Nothing."

"What?"

"I'm not sick."

Adolphus shifted. "But why did she send you to fetch me? And why did she wish to meet here, of all places? It doesn't make sense."

"I'm sorry."

"What for?"

Lucy only stared. Adolphus made a scornful sound at him, and resumed gazing into the hole. "I don't like it here," he admitted.

*If he spits once more, then*, thought Lucy. Adolphus spat; Lucy set his pipe on the ground and stood.

"I'm sorry," he said again. He drew a breath and lunged at Adolphus, his hands outstretched, arms locked straight at the elbows. But Adolphus had been put on his guard by the eerie light in Lucy's eyes, and so was ready for an untoward occurrence. He spun away and to the side, and Lucy rushed past him, disappearing into the Very Large Hole, headfirst, and quite neatly.

Adolphus looked at the hole awhile, then shook his head and went away. It was odd that Lucy had made no sound when he fell. He was happy, at any rate, that the boy was gone, and so the foolishness with Klara could rest. Only the night before, and she had admitted to loving that runt more than she loved him, if such a thing could be believed. Perhaps she was only cultivating an argument; her father was the same way. Well, now she would once again be contented, which meant that Adolphus could focus his attentions on the area war, which was his pre-eminent concern, his primary source of happiness.

Lucy made no sound as he fell.

Only a moment before and his heart had been beating with such violence as to burst; now it seemed not to be beating at all. He was somersaulting through the air, and so with every rotation saw the light of the sky above him, followed by the absolute darkness below. As he fell farther, the light became softer, and the air ever cooler. When he arrived at the bottom of the Very Large Hole there was a surprise awaiting him there, namely a body of running water, which he plunged into with such violence that he blacked out. A long moment, and his body bobbed to the surface, then eased lazily downriver.

"Have you got him?" asked a breathless voice in darkness.

"I've got him," said a second voice. A pair of hands clamped down on Lucy.

Lucy could not at the start grasp just what was happening all around him, for his senses were stunned, his eyes unused to the darkness; but as he became acclimated, now he deduced that he'd been collected from the water and was lying supine upon the incline of a sandy bank. Two men were attending to him, one young and one old, and both of whom, judging by their looks, had not seen civilization in some time – their clothing was tattered, their hair stringy and wild, and they wore unruly beards not in keeping with the fashion of the day. In spite of their appearance, they were in possession of their faculties and health and, it would seem, their good cheer, and so Lucy did not offer any opposition to their assistance.

The young man was holding Lucy's head in his hands and tilting it this way and that. "I can't tell where it's coming from," he said. "Can you tell?"

The old man's face came into view. Squinting, he answered, "I can't, no. Shall I fill up the boot to wash him?"

"Yes, please."

The old man hurried off, while the younger continued his inspection of Lucy's head. When their eyes met, Lucy said, "Hello."

"Well, hello there. How are you feeling?"

Lucy shrugged. Licking his lips, he tasted blood, and scowled.

"You've been injured," said the young man, nodding. "Though

for the life of me I can't locate the source of the bleeding. This is troubling, I won't deny it; but it is also, we must admit, preferable to the wound being highly visible, would you agree?"

"Yes."

"May I ask who you are?"

"Lucy is my name."

"Well, Lucy, you've made a misstep, in case you hadn't noticed. But not to worry; we'll get you cleaned up in no time, and then afterwards we'll have a nice piece of fish. What would you say to that?" When Lucy didn't answer at once, the young man asked, "You do *like* fish, I hope?" Judging by his tone, it was a question of some importance.

"I like it," said Lucy.

The young man was soothed by the answer. "Fine," he said. "That's just fine."

The old man returned holding a woman's boot, this filled with river water. Kneeling, he emptied it over Lucy's face, cleaning the blood away, and now the two men regarded his countenance with unabashed curiosity.

"He's just a boy," said the old man. The young man, meanwhile, had located a diamond-shaped wound just below Lucy's hairline and asked Lucy to press his finger over top of this to staunch the bleeding. Lucy did as he was told, and made no complaint as they propped him upright. He took in his surroundings from a seated position.

It was a cavernous space, similar in scope and shape to the interior of a grand church. A moderately sized river emanated from a tall cave on the north-facing wall, then looped the patch of sand upon which the three men sat before disappearing into the wall facing the south. There was a pillar of sunlight shining down from above; this spotlit a circular section of river before the island. In staring absently at this, Lucy saw a fish rise at its centre, and as the resulting reverberation rippled outwards across the surface of the water, a thought came to him. To the old man, he said, "You're Tomas, the gambler. And you're not dead at all." Next he addressed the young man: "You're Mr Broom. I hope you don't mind it, but I've been using your telescope."

The pair were for a time struck dumb by Lucy's words, and their expressions read of perturbed amazement. At last the young man spoke, asking his aged partner, "Now what do you make of this, I wonder? A mystery come down from the skies?"

"I find myself curious," the old man said.

"That's only natural, and of course I feel just the same. But shall we bombard him with questions all at once, or shall we hold off, and first put him at ease?"

The old man gnawed awhile on his knuckle. "Lord knows I wish to bombard him," he said. "But no, let us resist the impulse."

"Yes."

"He is our guest and so will be comforted."

"Yes, bravo." The young man rested a hand on Lucy's shoulder. "He likes fish, is my understanding."

At this, the two men laughed, a violent laughter which multiplied hugely in the gaping cavern, and was reminiscent of thunder in that it was at once vivid and vague. This laughter went on for what seemed to Lucy to be an inappropriate length of time, and he was not at all certain how he should feel. After consideration he decided he should feel afraid, and so he was.

# XI

# MR BROOM & TOMAS THE GAMBLER

S upper was served – fish, as promised, though it was not a piece as Mr Broom had said but rather a fish entire, one per man, unscaled and uncooked, for there was neither flame nor blade to be found in the Very Large Hole. The fish were retrieved live from the river; the two men had built up a network of stone-walled corrals diverting from the current proper, and into which fish would innocently amble. Upon finding their transit blocked they would backtrack, only to discover that the point of entry was now likewise impassable, as either Mr Broom or Tomas had built up a fourth wall to hem them in. Thus confined, the fish would languish in what Tomas described as arrant boredom until such a time as it was removed from its cell, rapped upon the head, and consumed. Lucy thought the method of capture ingenious, but this ingenuity did little to allay the fact of the meal being repellent to him. He stared at the fish, hanging limply in his hands, and his posture denoted a level of disappointment.

"Well, let's begin, then," said Tomas, and he and Mr Broom bit into the clammy bellies of their fishes, rending away the flesh in animalistic swaths. Soon blood and scales were shimmering in their beards, a sight which stole away Lucy's appetite completely. Setting his fish to the side, he decided he would not partake, at least not yet, for he knew that if he were to remain he would at some point be forced to follow the others, an eventuality he considered with repugnance. The woman's boot sat in the centre of their circle, refilled with water, a communal vessel; Lucy drank from this to wash away the very thought of the taste.

The meal reached its conclusion, and now came the interrogation. After establishing how it was that Lucy had identified them, Tomas and Mr Broom, so pleased for the company and break in routine, wished to know most every detail of Lucy's life, from the occasion of his birth and up until the present moment. Lucy had no objection to fielding the queries, and his answers were for the most part truthful. He spoke of the melancholy circumstances of his childhood, for example, with a frankness which surprised even himself. Regarding his decision to leave Bury, to say farewell to all he had known in his life, there was not so much as a fact misplaced. And yet, when he arrived at the question of how it was he'd fallen into the Very Large Hole, now he discovered the truth to be insufficient. For would it not have undone the balmy social atmosphere to admit he had attempted to murder a man in a style both cold-blooded and cowardly? Lucy affected the attitude of one in possession of overwhelming sorrows, and when he spoke, his voice was halting, cautious: "I'm not proud to admit it," he said.

"Take your time," Mr Broom told him.

"By all means, you must," agreed Tomas.

Lucy nodded his thanks. "Yes. Hmm. As it happens, and if you really want to know, I threw myself into this pit bodily."

"On purpose, you mean?" Tomas asked.

"That's right," said Lucy.

"But why would you do such a thing?" Mr Broom wondered.

"I was despondent."

"Clearly you were," Tomas said. "But what were you despondent about?"

"A great number of things."

"Such as what?"

"The overall circumstances of my life on earth."

"Life in general, you say?" Mr Broom asked.

"Yes."

"Top to bottom, is that what you mean?" said Tomas.

"That's it."

"No solace to be found?" asked Mr Broom.

"Anyway I could find none, search as I might."

"As bad as all that, eh?" Tomas said.

"I'm afraid so, yes."

Mr Broom and Tomas shook their heads sympathetically. A thought came to the latter, and he brightened. "Possibly things will take a turn for you now, have you considered it?"

"I hadn't, actually," Lucy answered.

"This might be your starting over point."

"It's a thought."

"The moment at which you begin afresh." Tomas nudged Mr Broom. "From here on out, a new beginning."

"Yes," Mr Broom said. "It pleases me."

"After all, is that not how it has been for us, my friend?"

"It has indeed, and indeed it has."

The bearded duo sat awhile, digesting. Tomas was cleaning his teeth with a fish bone, while Mr Broom pinched at the tip of his tongue once, twice, thrice; he plucked away some bit of matter, which he fell to studying. Lucy, in regarding these two, was visited with the chilling knowledge that he would soon be assimilated into their society. Naturally this did not sit well with him, so that he felt impelled to ask after the possibilities of escape. The pair of them nodded, as though anticipating the question; Tomas, holding up a corrective finger, said, "There is no possibility whatsoever."

"Surely there must be," Lucy answered, looking about the cavern, as if to locate some solution.

"The walls cannot be scaled," said Mr Broom.

"The river, then."

Tomas shook his head. "The downriver route is, you can plainly see, impassable, disappearing as it does into sheer rock. The upriver route presents the only option for escape, and I say without reservation or shame that it cannot be bettered."

"So you've tried, then?"

"Of course we have. In my years alone here I attempted it more times than I care to recall before abandoning the thought entirely. Then, when Mr Broom arrived, I was swayed by his youth and enthusiasm, and I made several more attempts by his side, each outing a thoroughgoing failure. I suppose it is that you'll want to take a look for yourself, and you're welcome to do this, but I for one will opt out, as will Mr Broom, I imagine. Isn't that right?"

Mr Broom nodded, with emphasis.

Tomas pointed upriver. "You enter into the cave," he said, "and walk a hundred yards, at which point you'll come to a fork. You may elect to take the route to your left, or the one to your right; it makes no difference, for whichever you choose will lead to yet another fork, and then another, and another, and on like this, endlessly or seemingly endlessly, and in total darkness. It's slow going against the current, the footing is slick and treacherous, and of course, as you know, the water temperature is not what you'd call inviting." Tomas paused here, remembering. "Our last excursion was catastrophic. We had been away some days when I wrenched my ankle, and Mr Broom was forced to carry me on his back. We were delirious with hunger and frozen to our bones and I make no exaggeration when I say we had abandoned all thoughts of survival. At last we simply gave ourselves to the current, bobbing along in the darkness and hoping against hope not to be dashed against unseen boulders. Halfway back, and Mr Broom broke an arm." Here he turned to look at Mr Broom, who drew back his sleeve, revealing a wrist bent to a grotesquely unnatural angle. "Think of it, boy," Tomas continued. "Floating downriver in pitch black, expecting at any moment to have my skull stove in, and the only sound to be heard other than the rush of the frigid waters was Mr Broom's screaming, echoing off the roof of the cavern." He made a sour face and shook his head. "It's the devil's own playground in there, and if you don't believe me, then you be my guest."

Lucy stared at the river, puzzling at the fates which had landed him in his present location. What could the future possibly hold for him here? And what of his life beyond the confines of the cavern? He wondered what Adolphus had told Klara of his disappearance. Presumably he'd told her the truth, and so she was mourning his passing. It pained him to think of her being pained, to say nothing of the idea of Adolphus offering his comforts. "We must try again," said Lucy.

"Must we?" Tomas asked.

"Of course we must. Otherwise we'll die here."

Here Tomas spoke gently, and with tranquil understanding. "That's not how we see it, Lucy."

"How do you see it?"

"We'll live here."

They passed a night huddled close for warmth, and in the morning awoke to face another meal, this identical to that of the evening prior. Lucy was very hungry by this point, and yet he still could not deliver the fish to his mouth. Neither Mr Broom nor Tomas commented, for they had each been through just the same ordeal, and knew Lucy would eat when he was ready. During breakfast, and afterwards, Lucy noticed that Mr Broom was watching him with a woebegone look on his face. This continued for such a time that Lucy asked if something was the matter. Mr Broom said, "It's just that, I find myself wondering if you're aware you and I arrived here under similar circumstances."

"I'm aware of it," said Lucy.

"And how are you aware of this, may I ask?"

"Mr Olderglough referenced it, as did the Baroness."

Upon hearing that the Baroness had returned, Mr Broom's eyes darted away. He was silent for a long while before asking, "When did she come back?"

"Some weeks ago."

"And how does she seem to you?"

"I had the impression she was relieved to have come home. At least at the beginning, this was the sense I had."

"Do you mean to say that something has changed since then?"

"There has been a change."

"And what is the change?"

Lucy was unsure how to describe it. "It seems to me that she is weakening."

"She is ill?"

"Not physically ill, no."

"How is she ill?"

Lucy said, "There is an increasing dearth of sensibility in regard to her actions."

"I don't understand."

"She keeps unsavoury acquaintances and engages in unnatural social acts."

"Speak plainly."

"I dare not."

"Tell me all you know."

"I shall not. All that I'll say is that I believe there is an unwellness rampant in the castle."

"What manner of unwellness?"

"A pervasive unpleasantness."

"What is unpleasant?"

"It's something which I can't put into words other than to say I suspect all who live there are affected in time. Did you not feel imperilled at any point during your stay?"

"No."

"Fixed in the clutches of something larger than yourself?"

"No."

"And yet you chased death into the Very Large Hole, where you now find yourself living in rags and eating away at the belly of a raw fish and calling it supper, or breakfast, for that matter."

Mr Broom could not deny that he had suffered a degeneration. "But," he said, "that might have happened regardless of my location. For love is the culprit, and love grows wherever it wishes." He pointed. "Look at our friend Tomas, here. He finds himself in the same position as I, and yet he's never so much as set foot in the castle."

True enough, and yet Lucy couldn't shake the notion that there was some malicious anathema afoot in the castle. He was visited by the image of the Baron, his bare body smeared with rodent's blood, a memory which invoked a shudder. As though reading Lucy's mind, Mr Broom asked,

"And what of the Baron? Is he faring so poorly as his wife?"

Lucy said, "Much like she, there is evidence of decline, and it is my opinion that this decline will become dire."

"And what is the nature of their partnership at present?"

"What do you mean?"

"Are they functionally married?"

"How do you mean?"

"Possibly you already know what I mean."

"Possibly I do."

"And are they?"

"Yes."

"How do you know?"

"I've witnessed it."

"I see. You'll excuse me, please." Mr Broom stood and walked into the water, swimming away and vanishing in the darkness of the far cavern. Tomas gave Lucy a look of mild reproach.

"But what else could I have done?" Lucy asked.

"Lied," said Tomas simply. And here Lucy slapped his knee, as in this one instance the thought to do so hadn't occurred to him.

These two fell silent, and the passage of time grew leaden for Lucy. If only there were a fire, he might gaze wistfully into its heart and ponder the sinister mysteries of life; or if he were tired, he could drift into slumber and dream of Klara stepping through boundless fields of undulating grasses. But there was nothing to do other than speak, and there was no one to speak with other than Tomas, and Lucy felt they had exhausted all topics of conversation save for one. In the interest of creating an event, then, he decided to broach it: "Memel says you were quite close, the two of you."

Had Tomas been expecting this? He didn't seem surprised by it, and his tone was not unfriendly. "We were, at that," he said. "Is it safe to assume he told you how it was that I came to be here?"

"It's safe."

"And he believes me dead?"

"Yes."

"Has he forgiven me, I wonder?"

"He didn't say if he had or hadn't. I believe he felt his actions were justified. Anyway, he expressed no regrets. And yet, he remembers you fondly."

Tomas shrugged, as though he didn't quite believe Lucy. In a self-consciously casual tone, he asked, "And how is Alida?"

Somehow Lucy hadn't anticipated the question, and now he

regretted having brought up Memel at all. Sensing his regret, Tomas spoke:

"Something hasn't happened to her, I hope?"

Lucy said, "In fact, she's died, Tomas."

Tomas's face hardened, a rictus of disbelief. "Died."

"Yes, and I'm sorry to say it."

"Died," Tomas repeated. "But how?"

"In childbirth."

Tomas was staring at Lucy. "When?" he said.

"Some months after your disappearance."

"How many months?"

"Nine."

Here Tomas performed an anomalous gesture, casting his hand sharply across his face, as though drawing a veil over his features, or catching some unspeakable word. Lucy knew that he was watching a man's heart break before him.

"Did the child also die?" asked Tomas.

"The child is alive," said Lucy. "Mewe, is his name. He lives just next to Memel and Klara."

There was nothing but the sound of the river for a time; and to Lucy it seemed the volume of it was increasing. Tomas began digging a small hole in the sand. "Will you tell me about him?" he said. "What does he do? Possibly he's a gambler too, eh?"

"No, he works with Memel on the trains."

"He is a thief?"

"Yes."

"Does he have any talent for it?"

"He has a great talent for it."

Tomas filled in the hole and smoothed it over. "So many days with nothing whatever passing," he said. "And now this."

"He is a happy boy, Tomas. He is happy and well liked."

Tomas nodded. "How is Klara?" he asked. "She would be a young lady by now, I should think."

"She is a young lady," Lucy agreed. There must have been some familiar tone of injury in the way he said it, because now Tomas was watching him with an expression of recognition.

"She wouldn't have anything to do with your being here, would she?"

Lucy said, "Roundaboutly, and yes, she does."

Tomas laughed scornfully. "Well, we're quite the group, aren't we? You and I and Mr Broom?"

"I would say we are."

"Been led down the garden path, eh?"

"Perhaps we have been."

"Cupid is well armed, it would seem."

"And so must we be," Lucy said, and now the two smiled at each other, sharing a contented moment which did not last long, interrupted as it was by Mr Broom's return. Trudging up the bank, he said, "We are, the three of us, going to wake up tomorrow, and we're going to strike out, and either we'll escape this place and reclaim our lives above ground, or else perish in our attempt to do so." As though exhausted by the words, he dropped to his knees, whispering, "We may well perish, in fact." He was studying his hands, now, in wonder at their abilities, perhaps.

Lucy and Tomas looked at each other and raised their eyebrows. "Our friend has been invigorated by his swim," said Tomas.

D ue to the danger inherent in attempting escape, and because of his age and general decrepitude, Tomas was not enthusiastic about this idea at first glance. He became sullen in the afternoon, and it seemed that a rift was afoot, but by the time evening rolled around he had found some deeper reserve of spirit and proclaimed, more loudly than was necessary, that he would join the expedition.

Surely there was a connection between his change of heart and news of Mewe, just as Mr Broom's decision to leave was informed by the knowledge that the Baroness had returned to the castle. Lucy, for his part, had made up his mind to leave before Mr Broom had brought it up, even; and he would have gone on his own if need be, for his thoughts were of Klara alone, and his desire to win her back superseded all other concerns. Regarding preparations, there were none to speak of, other than for the men to come to an agreement about the specifics of the method of departure and escape. This was discussed at length, and resulted in disagreement but thankfully not division.

Mr Broom was for action. He wished to lead the three, for he was, he said, the strongest of the group, a truth which neither Tomas nor Lucy could dispute, though they were the both of them left wondering just what Mr Broom's strength would avail anyone other than Broom himself. Beyond his physical capabilities, Mr Broom claimed, with an amount of humility or reluctance, to be in possession of second sight. He often felt its influence, he said, and believed that if he were to focus intently and utilize this gift to its utmost, then he would guide the group to freedom.

Tomas sat awhile, blinking. "This is news to me, my friend."

"It's not something one goes about boasting of."

"And why not? Here we've been discussing topics such as our favourite numerals." Tomas closed his eyes. "Tell me, please: what am I thinking about now?"

Mr Broom shook his head. "It doesn't work like that."

Tomas stuck a hand behind his back. "How many fingers am I holding up?"

"It doesn't work like *that*."

"How does it work?"

"I believe I can find the way out of here," Mr Broom said.

"And yet you didn't on any of our prior expeditions. And why not? Sheer modesty, I wouldn't wonder."

Mr Broom had gone red in the face. "Perhaps you have a plan of your own."

"Perhaps I do."

"Do you or don't you?"

Tomas drew himself up. "If anyone is to lead the expedition," he said, "I believe that should be me."

"Oh?" said Mr Broom. "And why is that, can you tell me?"

"Because I am the eldest, and so I have the wisdom of time on my side."

"The wisdom of time?" said Mr Broom. Apparently he found the phrase humorous.

"That's what I said," Tomas answered sternly.

"Does one always accompany the other?"

"In my case I believe it does. Beyond that, and this is inarguable, I have journeyed upriver far more often than you have, and so am more familiar with the terrain."

"That's one way to put it. Another way might be to say that you are more familiar with failing to surpass the terrain."

Tomas levelled a finger at Broom. "I saw the sun set thousands of times before you drew your first breath."

"And so?"

"I was entering women when you were still soiling your short pants."

"And so?"

"I slit a man's throat before you could milk a cow."

"I still can't milk a cow. But I think your plan is pure foolishness."

"It's no more foolish than yours."

"Yes, but my plan is mine, and so I prefer it."

"And just as naturally, I do mine."

Arriving thus at stalemate, the pair lured Lucy into the fray, asking which plan he himself thought best. Believing each one to be equally poor, Lucy admitted to having no preference at all, a statement which effectively offended both men, who together began to chastise him, for here they were busily concocting schemes while he sat by, marking time, contributing nothing whatsoever.

All this to say there was strife among them, and confidence was ebbing with each passing minute. In the end, Lucy did come up with a plan of his own, and as it happened, this was the idea they could all three of them agree on.

# The Specifics of the Method of Departure
# and Escape from the Very Large Hole

Lucy hadn't eaten in nearly three days by this point. Tomas and Mr Broom found this alarming in that it had potential to upset their escape, and so they brought him another fish and sat before him; and whereas earlier they were disinterested in whether or not he chose to eat, now they were all the more keen, so that Lucy felt a pressure to please them. His hunger was startlingly vivid; it stabbed and pinwheeled in his stomach and seemed at times to possess the attributes of colour. And yet he felt he simply could not perform the action of severing the metallic scales with his teeth, and he told his comrades he wouldn't do it.

"It will give you pluck, and so you must," said Tomas.

"If we're leaving in the morning, as Mr Broom says, then I can do without."

Mr Broom shook his head. "We'll be days in the darkness, and it will take our every bit of strength to see this through, if it's even possible to see it through. I'm sorry, Lucy, but we really must insist that you eat."

Lucy glared at the fish, knowing that he would consume the thing but hating it, and unsure just how to start. Tomas touched the tip of his finger to the fish's belly. "Here," he said. "Just shred it away." At last Lucy drew the fish to his face and bit into its flesh; at the same moment he did this, the fish fairly exploded, shooting out a clammy glut of roe, for it was a female, and had been on its way to the spawning ground when captured in the stone corral. Lucy was incredulous, and he sat very still, roe clinging to his cheek and chin. When Mr Broom and Tomas ceased laughing, they took the fish away and fetched him another, a male. Lucy did not dawdle with this, but consumed it with a certain violence or anger. Soon the fish was but a head, tail, and skeleton; and as Lucy felt his body accepting the much-needed nourishment, then did his mood lighten. He lay back on the sand, watching the distant purple circle which was the shading sky framed by the mouth of the Very Large Hole. His stomach squirmed loudly, relentlessly; he was listening to this with dispassionate amusement when a consequential thought, like a bird flown through an open window, came into his mind and perched there. He sat up alertly, looking across at Tomas and Mr Broom, both of whom had also eaten and were ruminating upon their own concerns.

"The fish head upriver when they spawn, do they not?" said Lucy.

"They do," said Tomas.

"How far upriver do they travel?"

"I don't rightly know. Do you, Mr Broom?"

"A good long while, anyway," Mr Broom answered. "Why do you want to know?"

"Well," said Lucy, "if we were to follow one, mightn't she lead us to freedom?"

When he said this, Mr Broom, too, sat up. Tomas wore a sceptical expression; and yet there was a stiffness or seriousness to him as well. He asked, "And how might one do such a thing, even if we weren't making the journey in total darkness?"

Lucy was staring at the woman's boot, situated once again in the centre of their circle. He believed he knew the answer to Tomas's question but he didn't respond right away, forcing himself to act with calm. He took the boot up and poured out the water. Removing the lace, he lay this in a straight line before him, watching it awhile before unlacing his own boots, and tying each of these to the first, tripling its length. Mr Broom drew his fingers to his mouth in a gesture of surprise and recognition; now he also began unlacing his boots. Tomas didn't understand what was happening, and had to be enlightened; once this was done, he still didn't want to give up his laces. But Lucy and Mr Broom entreated him, and though Tomas thought it far-fetched, neither did he want to spoil their fun, and so he handed over his laces as well, and these were tied to the rest, so that there was now a single lace of goodly length laid out between them. They studied this for a long while, and with reverence, representative as it was of their last chance for escape. Later, and the men slept, dreaming their dreams of vainglory, the tongues of their boots lolling in the sand as if exhausted.

The idea, of course, was to tie the string of laces to the tail of a fish on its way to the spawning ground and, as one walking a dog on a lead, follow the fish to the river's wellspring. It was, Lucy thought, not just a good idea, but the only idea – the only logical method other than blind luck or brute force which might see them home again. He was prouder, perhaps, than he'd ever been in his life, and it was difficult not to discuss and rediscuss the idea's inception and canny brilliance with the others, neither of whom was, Lucy felt, appropriately enthusiastic or complimentary about it. Mr Broom seemed to think it almost a shared notion, or one which was so obvious that he would have come to it himself in the blue-skied by and by.

They selected the fish from the corrals, a moderately sized female who had been caught only the morning prior, and so, they hoped, had not had time to become idle. Tomas held her still while Lucy attached the bootlace to her tail. While this was happening she was full of fight, but once transferred to the river she merely floated in place, and the three men stood and stared, waiting. Lucy gave a tug on the bootlace but nothing happened. He gave a second tug, less gentle this time – still nothing. He hadn't considered the possibility of failure, somehow; and in the face of it, he felt a gross despair gathering about his heart. But now, and with no small amount of relief, he saw the bootlace was growing taut, and that the fish was pulling towards the mouth of the cave. She had been temporarily demoralized by her capture and imprisonment, or else was flummoxed by the fact of her tail being fettered and had needed a moment to gather her wits, but the spawning instinct had returned, and she would see the impulse through to its natural conclusion.

Lucy, Mr Broom, and Tomas, led by the increasingly impatient fish, stepped headlong into the roar of the cavern.

*There is darkness and there is darkness*, thought Lucy. *This is darkness.*

At the start of the journey they had called to one another, called out their best wishes, laughing at the oddity of their lives, elated by their adventure. But then Tomas's chatter fell away, and after that Lucy's, and lastly Mr Broom's, and now did the trial of their escape truly begin, and they set to work with wholehearted diligence.

The water was never any more than waist deep, and the current was not particularly strong, but the fact of their constantly battling against it was enough to wear them down, and they soon found themselves humbled, woefully fatigued, each of them sheltering in their hearts a fear of death which was acute, and acutely real. Later their flesh went numb, which on the one hand dimmed their pain, but also made them clumsy, so that they tripped over unseen rocks and boulders and were dunked frequently; each would lurch up from the water with a great, heaving inhalation of sheer discomfort.

Time and again they arrived at a fork in the river, identified by the bisection of sound before them, and time and again the fish performed without hesitation, yanking agitatedly on the lace, which Lucy had tied to his finger. There was no telling if it were day or night but the men walked on just as far as they could, until on the verge of collapse, when they located by touch an outcropping of sand and rock; they crawled onto this and laid their weary bodies down. The fish had no desire for relaxation, and the lace quivered with a relentless pressure Lucy found maddening; lest he not sleep at all, he tied it to a large rock. When they awoke they couldn't guess at how long they had rested, only that they hadn't rested enough. In spite of this they stood, and stretched their aching muscles, resuming the trek upriver, for they knew their time was limited. They could be injured; they could starve; their will might give out; they might freeze – it was paramount to move while they still had their strength, and the unspoken fact was that the chances of survival were shrinking away with each moment gone by. The darkness was so complete that when Lucy blinked his eyes there was no discernible visual difference, which struck him as fantastical or impossible, as one clapping his hands together and finding that this action produced no sound.

Save for sleeping, they paused only to eat; they had two fish apiece on their persons, one in each trouser pocket. After these were consumed, then did their mood grow all the more peculiar. As is typical of long journeys, they lost their desire to communicate with one another, and lapsed into silence; they were as good as alone now, and each found his thoughts more inclined to wander abstractly. This brought about periods of peaceful calm in Lucy, moments where he forgot his hunger and miserable cold, moments when the fish, as though likewise dazed, did not yank on the lace but moved more slowly, so that Lucy could forget the fact of its existence and purpose, as well as his own. These transient instances were merciful but fleeting; soon enough, Lucy's woes would return, announcing themselves cruelly, loudly, inarguably.

Days came and went when finally Lucy crossed some nameless

threshold, and began to find everything about his situation very funny indeed. He supposed this was the signal that the end was near, a notion which was of no great concern. When it occurred to him he hadn't felt any tension in the lace for while, he drew his hand back, and now he discovered it was no longer attached to his finger. This sobered him temporarily, and he called out to Mr Broom and Tomas, but heard no answer. He ceased walking and waited, thinking they would soon catch up with him, but they never did. The swirling sound of the river encircled him, and confused his equilibrium. He had the sensation he was standing on a steep incline, though he knew this wasn't so; when he closed his eyes it felt as though he were sleeping standing up. What if he were to simply fall away, into the water, to be led back to the safety of the sandy island? But if he were to do this, mightn't he die, his skull dashed on some jagged rock? *No matter*, he thought, and his body was tilting backwards when he realized that when he'd closed his eyes, it had become ever so slightly darker. He opened and shut his eyes several times to make sure this was an actuality; and finding it so, he located a hoard of resolve from the innermost region of himself. He took a moment to regroup, and continued apace. The light was increasing.

# XII

# LUCY, LIBERATED

I t was a sunbright, late-spring morning, and before Lucy was
a field of tall grasses, and in the centre of this, an apple tree.
He walked towards it, collapsing at its base. The sun spilled
through the branches, and the earth itself was warm; he allowed
this warmth into his blood, then his bones, and there were apples
on the ground all around him which he ate one after the other,
and his life felt a fantasy of luxury. Soon, he slept; waking around
noon-time, he returned to the mouth of the cavern and called
to Mr Broom and Tomas, waiting there for an hour and more
before walking away, to the east, in the direction of the castle.
Possibly it would have been best to re-enter the cave and attempt
to locate his friends, but this didn't occur to Lucy until later, and
then only dimly. He liked to think the men had been deposited
unscathed back upon the sandy bank, and were chattering away
yet in their voluble fashion, but in his deeper heart he knew they
were corpses, now.

There was a peculiar foreignness to all the world around him
which made Lucy feel wary. Some hours later the village came
into view, and he thought of Klara, which summoned an anguish
in him. Everything he had been through of late, what difference did it make? What was it for that he had survived, even?
When he saw her shanty in the distance he knew he had to go
there at once, and he located and hefted a heavy stone in his
hand, this to nullify Adolphus's skull. Lucy had no plan beyond

this, but there was the sense in him that once this was accomplished, then other avenues and possibilities would present themselves.

Mewe was sitting out front of his shanty, staring at nothing, a drawn look on his face. When he saw Lucy, he startled and sat upright. "You're not dead?" he said wonderingly.

"No, I'm not dead. Hello."

"But where in the world have you been?"

"Away."

"Where are your shoes?"

"I lost them."

"Why is your suit in rags?"

"I have suffered through an era of unluckiness."

"Yes, as have we," Mewe said, leaning back. He pointed at the stool beside him and Lucy sat.

"Why do you have that stone in your hand?"

"I'm going to kill Adolphus with it."

"That would be quite a trick."

"You don't believe I'll do it?" asked Lucy.

"I don't believe you will, no. Because Adolphus has already died."

Lucy said, "What?"

"He's died. They've exploded him."

"Who has?"

"They have."

"What does that mean, exploded him?"

"It means that he is no longer of a piece."

"Where is he?"

"Here and there – that's what I'm telling you."

"Where is the main part of him, Mewe?"

Mewe pointed to Klara's shanty. Lucy stood and entered. Adolphus lay on the table in the front room, naked to the waist, and his head was not on his shoulders. It had been taken off cleanly, to the base of the neck. There was a charring at the edges of the wound but his body was otherwise unmarked, and Lucy stood by, considering the incongruousness of this specimen: healthful yet headless. He had no feeling in him as he stared at the corpse, no relief, no sense of triumph. In a little while he laid the stone on the table where the head should have been. Mewe came into the shanty and stood next to Lucy. "It was a cannon-ball, do you know? A cannonball took his head off."

"Oh," said Lucy.

"They say his body stood awhile without the head, and that when it collapsed, it folded, as though he were lying down to go to sleep. After, they brought him back here, to Klara. Only she'd already gone."

"Gone?" said Lucy.

"Yes, the Baroness has taken her away."

Lucy shook his head. "What does that mean?"

"Klara went to the castle to see if there was any news of you. She and the Baroness met there and came to some agreement. Klara told me she would work for the Baroness as her lady-in-waiting. Anyway, they've left."

"Where did they go?"

"West, is all Klara said. They took Rose with them too."

"Where is Memel?" Lucy asked.

Mewe pointed to Memel's door and Lucy entered to find

Memel lying atop his mattress in suit and vest and boots, hair combed and parted, hands folded across his heart, and his flesh was grey, for he too was deceased. There were candles burning about the room, and long-stemmed flowers had been cast over his body and onto the ground around him. Lucy stood at the foot of the bed, breathing in the scent of the blossoms. Mewe was in the doorway, looking at his old friend with a mournful expression.

"Let me understand it," Lucy said. "Memel has died, and Klara and Rose are gone, and the Baroness has also gone, and Adolphus has lost his head."

"All true," said Mewe.

"Will you explain to me just what happened while I was away, please?"

Mewe cleared his throat. He said, "Adolphus came here claiming you'd tried to kill him. We couldn't picture it, but then you'd disappeared, and when Klara and I went up to the Very Large Hole to look for ourselves, we found your pipe there." Mewe pulled the pipe from his pocket and tossed it to Lucy. Lucy caught it and held it in his palm.

"And so Klara thought I'd died," he said.

"Yes, when we saw the pipe, we knew that you had, and were very sorry for it. Actually Klara was more than sorry for it. Adding to her upset was Memel's decline; after he passed away, Adolphus was always hovering nearby. He got it into his mind that he and Klara should marry at once, and he wouldn't let this alone, so that finally she had to explain it was impossible."

"Impossible," said Lucy.

"Yes."

"And why was it?"

Mewe said, "But of course she didn't love him in that way, Lucy. Not since she met you."

Lucy watched Mewe carefully after he'd said this. He wanted so badly to believe that it was so.

"Adolphus took the rejection poorly," Mewe continued, "so that when there came news of an attack against his troops up the mountain, he hurried off to do his part. The soldiers who brought his body down said he was fighting with something more than bravery. At last he simply ran towards their cannons, and that was the end of him."

Lucy returned to the front room and stood again before what remained of Adolphus. Flies were socializing at the thickly clotted neckhole and he experienced an obscure pity for his antagonist. "I wonder what they were fighting about," said Lucy.

"Some men just like to kill each other, I expect," said Mewe. He had remained in Memel's doorway, and was looking over his shoulder at Lucy. "And what now?" he asked. "Will you stay on at the castle, do you think?"

"I don't think I will, no."

"Will you return to your home?"

"No."

"When will you leave?"

"Just now, I suppose."

Mewe had turned away from Lucy; he was hiding his face, and Lucy asked,

"Are you all right?"

When Mewe looked back, Lucy saw that he was silently crying. "Everything is ending," he said. He hurried out of the shanty and Lucy watched him leave, afterwards standing in the quiet, cool stillness. Thinking of the time he had passed in the space, there entered into his mind an accumulating hum, and now Lucy was struck with a bolt of the most splendid sadness. It overcame his spirit, his breath ran thin, and his legs went stringy from it.

Revisiting Memel's room, he folded back the dead man's lapel, tucking the pipe into his coat pocket. He had never enjoyed using the pipe, and it felt correct for Memel to have it in his permanent possession.

Lucy left the shanty and struck out for the castle.

All was quiet as Lucy climbed the stairs to his room. The state of his suit was past repair and so he shed this, putting on the clothes he'd arrived in. The trousers were blowsy at the knee, the stockings had gone thin, and the buttons on his coat were missing save for one. He pulled on his sheepskin cap and was, for better or worse, himself again. After packing his valise, he set out in search of the others, finding Agnes at the table in the servants' quarters, a cup of tea in one hand, her chin rested in the other. Lucy greeted her and she swivelled to face him.

"I'm leaving the castle, ma'am," he told her. "I thought you should know."

"Leaving?" she said. "But I thought you'd left already."

"I was gone, but I've returned."

"Only to leave again?"

"That's right." Lucy sat opposite Agnes. "Where is everyone else?"

"The Baroness has run off once more, and so the Baron is hiding away in a sulk somewhere. I don't know what's the matter with Mr Olderglough, but he's gone sulky also." There was a stiffness to Agnes's movements, as though she were in pain; when Lucy asked her if she was feeling all right, she said, "I don't believe I am all right, Lucy, no."

"And will you tell me what's the matter?"

In a tone of confidentiality, she told him, "It would seem to me, boy, that we are all of us getting smaller, here."

"Smaller?"

"Less full, yes."

"I'm not sure quite what you mean, ma'am."

"We are – emptying. Becoming empty." Brightening, she said, "We are *draining*. That's it. We are all draining away, and soon we will be gone." She took a sip of her tea, then studied her cup with a look of mistrust. "Cold."

"Would you like me to boil you more water, ma'am?"

"Why bother? Indeed, it will only grow cold again." She began muttering to herself, and now Lucy noticed the state of the larder: stacks of unwashed crockery teetered here and there; the table linen was blotched with stains; trampled ash decorated the floor.

"Well, ma'am," he said, "I just wanted to say thank you for all your help."

"Did I help you, though?" she asked absently.

"You did."

"And how did I?"

"You were generous with me, and so I felt less alone here."

She looked at him as though she thought he were being foxy. "Do you still have the coin I gave you?"

Lucy patted his pocket. "It is here, ma'am."

"And now, will you use it?"

"I will."

"Well, that's something, isn't it?" She took another sip of the tea, and scowled.

"Goodbye, ma'am," he said.

Lucy left the servants' quarters; Agnes resumed her muttering.

Mr Olderglough sat before his vanity in his rumpled sleeping attire, his cap askew, his face unshaven. He was speaking to Peter through the bars of the bird's cage, this resting upon his lap. When Lucy greeted him he peered up in the vanity mirror. "Oh, hello, boy," he said. "Where have you been keeping yourself?"

"Hello, sir. I apologize for my disappearance, but I fell down the Very Large Hole, and was forced to fight tooth and nail to reclaim my freedom."

"Is that a fact?"

"Yes, sir."

"You fell all that way but lived to tell the tale?"

"I have lived, sir."

"And you stand before me now as one who has cheated death?"

"I suppose so, sir."

"One who has rerouted the fates?"

"Perhaps, sir."

"And was this a very difficult exercise for you?"

"It was, sir, yes."

"Was it tedious?"

"I don't know if I would use the word tedious specifically, sir."

"Well, it certainly *sounds* tedious. But, what do I know, eh? With my head full of stuffing? Happy to have you back, at any rate."

"Thank you, sir. But I've not come back."

"Haven't you?"

"No, sir. In point of fact I'm here to tell you I'm leaving."

"Leaving?" Mr Olderglough said, as if the very thought were an eccentric notion.

"Leaving sir, yes, and just now."

"But why would you do that?"

Lucy said, "It seems to me there is no longer any reason for us to stay, sir."

"Oh, but that's not true at all, boy."

"Is it not correct that the Baroness has left again?"

"It is correct."

"Then is it not likely the Baron will once again devolve, as before?"

"It is more than likely. But I don't see what that has to do with the abandonment of my position, and so no, I shan't so much as entertain the thought." Mr Olderglough shivered and sniffed, and he returned his attentions to Peter who had, Lucy noticed, gone quiet once more.

"Has he misplaced his tune again, sir?"

"Hmm," Mr Olderglough replied. He shivered and sniffed a second time, and in looking at him, Lucy could see that all sense had left the man. He was making a kissing noise at Peter now; and as if speaking to the bird, he said, "I will perform my functions. I will do right by my master."

"But if your master cannot do right by you, sir?" said Lucy.

"That is none of my affair."

"It is every bit of it yours."

Mr Olderglough shook his head and lapsed into silence. Lucy could think of nothing more to say, for there was nothing more, after all, and he was turning to go when Mr Olderglough called after him, and in a tender tone of voice, "Do you know, Lucy, I've come to think of you as the son I never quite knew." Now he set the birdcage onto the vanity, and folded his hands on his lap. Looking out at the village, and the green-forested hills running away and to the horizon, he said, "I believe I could spend the rest of my days simply peering out a window, boy."

"Any window, sir?"

"Any one, yes. This one, for example."

Mr Olderglough stared. Lucy left the room.

Lastly, there was the Baron. Lucy found him in the ballroom, standing before one of the portraits of his forebears, hands cinched at his back, rocking to and fro, and humming to himself. He was barefoot, and when he turned to face Lucy it was evident the madness had once more taken root in him. He wasn't possessed by it yet, but was existing in some middle plane, straddling either reality. Lucy wondered just what had occurred over the preceding days; for it was as if some ill-wishing cloud had passed through the valley and rendered everyone simple.

A crooked smile hung on the Baron's face, and at the start he couldn't quite place the person who stood before him. "Lucy!" he said finally. "And how are you, boy? Someone told me you'd vanished into thin air."

"Hello, sir. Yes, no, I've not vanished. How are you?"

The Baron nodded gladly, then resumed his portrait-gazing. Lucy took up a spot beside him and the Baron explained, "This is my great-great-grandfather, Victor Von Aux. He was responsible for the construction of the castle. What do you know of him, may I ask?"

"Nothing, sir."

"You've heard no stories?"

"No, sir."

"That he was a hot-air balloonist who dabbled in the black arts?"

"I didn't know that, sir."

"That he was an expert marksman with a penchant for opium?"

"No."

"That he bred Arabian horses? That he was known to entertain his guests with executions?"

"No, sir."

"Well. I'm surprised you haven't heard any of this."

"Yes, and so am I," said Lucy. "He was a complicated man, by the sound of it."

"A demon," said the Baron flatly. He sidestepped, and was now standing before the portrait of the Baroness. He said, "She's gone away again, boy."

"Yes, sir, and I'm sorry to hear it." Lucy also sidestepped. "Do you know where she's gone to?"

"To the ocean, she says. She tells me she won't be coming back this time."

"Who can say, sir."

"She can, and did. I'm inclined to take her at her word." He looked at Lucy. "She claims to have no affection for me any longer. What do you think about that?"

"I don't know, sir. Just that it seemed to me she did."

The Baron nodded. "Yes, and to me also, boy. Well, possibly she did once. But apparently this has passed." He swallowed, and cleared his throat. "Love leaves us like luck leaves us," he said, and he turned and walked clear of the ballroom. Lucy stood by, looking up at the Baroness and considering these words. He took up his valise and left the Castle Von Aux forever.

The conductor enquired after Lucy's destination and Lucy asked if his coin would take him to the ocean. "It will, just," the man replied, and Lucy settled into an empty compartment. An hour passed, and it grew darker. The strain of his recent adventures had worn him down; he felt so weak, and that he might sleep for days. He gave in to fatigue, his dreams little more than static black curtains and certain colder temperatures. Sleeping through the night, he awoke to a surprising fact, which was that his old friend Father Raymond was sitting across from him, an eager look on his face. The moment Lucy opened his eyes, then did the priest rejoice, reaching over and clasping Lucy's hands in his own. "I didn't want to disturb your slumber, boy," he said, "but it was sheer torture not to, I can assure you."

"Hello, Father. What are you doing here?"

"I've just come from Listen. I've a sister there, perhaps I've mentioned it before."

"You never have, no. Was it a pleasant visit?"

"It was not. In truth I couldn't get away from her fast enough. What was I thinking in travelling all that way to see the likes of her? She of the dying dogs and loamy aromas?"

"I don't know what."

"She doesn't cook, boy – she scalds."

"I'm sorry to hear it."

"At any rate, I'm heading back to Bury, now, and that suits

me well enough. But what of you, I wonder? Will you tell me your news? How are things at the castle? You must be living very fine these days, I would think."

"No, I'm not. Actually, I've just come away from there."

"Come away? Not permanently, I hope?"

"I'm afraid so."

"And why is that?"

"Any number of reasons."

"Possibly you'll tell me one of the reasons, or two?"

Lucy didn't know where to begin. He said, "I found it to be an unhealthy environment."

"Unhealthy?"

"Unhealthy and somewhat dangerous, yes."

Father Raymond shook his head. "That'll never do, boy," he said. "But don't you worry, we'll get you some other, better position back home."

"No, I'll not be returning to Bury."

"What? And why not?"

"As it happens, I'm chasing after a girl, Father. For it has come to pass that I've fallen in love."

Father Raymond leaned in. "In love, you say?"

"Just so."

"And what is that like? I've often wondered about it."

Lucy said, "It is a glory and a torment."

"Really? Would you not recommend it, then?"

"I would recommend it highly. Just to say it's not for the faint of heart."

Father Raymond thought awhile. A troubled look came over him and Lucy asked if something was the matter. Said the priest, "Not to besmear your quest, boy, but I find myself curious as to why you're forced to chase after the lass. That is, why is she not

334

stationary? In other words: does this young lady not love you also?"

"Oh, yes, she does. She's only run off because she believes me dead."

"Dead!" said Father Raymond, and he slapped his knee. "That's a good one."

"Yes."

"I suppose it is you'll show her otherwise, eh?"

"I hope to, Father. If I can locate her, that is."

"Surely you will."

They spoke through the morning, and both were happy to be reunited. Father Raymond deduced Lucy was penniless and so slipped him some coins, that he might not go hungry. When the train pulled into the station at Bury, Lucy looked out at the town. All was as it had been, but he was not comforted by the familiar sights, and there was no part of him that wished to detrain.

He noticed a beggar kneeling on the platform. The man's head was bowed, his hands held out before him. A body passed and dropped a coin into the man's palms; when he peered up to judge the coin's value, Lucy saw that this person was the man in burlap, a realization which prompted him to gasp.

"What is it?" asked Father Raymond, working to free his satchel from the overhead.

"The beggar on the platform. He's the same man who came to me when I was so ill. Do you recall it?"

"What, the marauder you told me about?" Father Raymond studied the beggar, then shook his head. "You're mistaken, boy. That's only Frederick."

"You know him?"

"So much as one can know a simpleton. Frederick sweeps out

the refectory once in a while for a scrap of bread or sip of wine. He was knocked on his head when he was a child, they say, and he's been that way ever since. You may take my word for it, he possesses no powers, supernatural or otherwise."

Lucy stared. "I'm certain it's the same man," he said.

"More than likely you half-noticed him about before you took ill, then simply imagined his visit. You were delirious from fever, after all. I saw it myself, remember."

The conductor was calling for all Bury passengers to disembark. Father Raymond told Lucy, "I do wish you'd stay awhile. You're certain I can't persuade you?"

"I'm sorry, Father, but no."

"Love is so urgent as all that, eh?"

"It is."

"Perhaps I'm better off without it, then. I never did like to rush. Well, I'm pleased to have seen you, Lucy. Take care of yourself, won't you?"

"I'll do that," Lucy said.

Father Raymond left, and Lucy resumed his study of the man in burlap, who now was sitting back, stacking and counting all that he'd gathered. This was the person indirectly responsible for Lucy's departure from Bury, and all that had happened to him since. When a string of drool slipped from the man's lip, he hurriedly sucked it back up into his mouth, as though it were precious to him, and he didn't dare lose it. The train lurched, and eased free of the station, and Lucy was again in motion.

He had never been west of Bury, and he watched the flatland scenery unfold with an active interest. Here there were no trees, no mountains, only pastures of level green, and it was so very quiet and peaceful for Lucy in the padded, red-velvet compartment. He imagined how it would be when he located Klara, and composed scenarios of surprising her on the seashore, and now in the lobby of a grand coastal hotel. These exercises pleased and excited him profoundly, but in time he grew tired and set them aside. He closed his window shade and sat awhile in the partial darkness. The conductor passed in the corridor and Lucy called after him, asking to borrow paper and pencil. Using his valise as a drafting board, then, he drew an upside-down "U" shape. Under the dome of this line he wrote some words for the future, the faraway future he hoped. But whether they were needed sooner or later, he knew it was good to get them down:

## LUCIEN MINOR

His heart was a church of his own choosing,
and the lights came through
the colourful windows.

# Acknowledgements

Philippe, Emma, and Nina Aronson, D. Contumely Berman, Leslie Butler, Rachel Lee Corry (herself a beguiler), Eric Issacson, Azazel Jacobs, Megan Lynch and Dan Halpern and everyone at Ecco, Lee Boudreaux, Peter McGuigan and everyone at Foundry, Sarah MacLachlan and Janie Yoon and everyone at House of Anansi, Leslie Napoles (all grace), Rene Navarette, Brian Mumford, Danny Palmerlee, Max Porter and Aidan O'Neill and everyone at Granta, Steve Schiller, Scoop Short, Dan Stiles, Libby Werbel, my mother, father, and brothers.

In writing this book I considered the works of Thomas Bernhard, Ivy Compton Burnett, Italo Calvino, Dennis Cooper, Robert Coover, Roald Dahl, J.P. Donleavy, C.F., Knut Hamsun, Sammy Harkham, Werner Herzog, Bohumil Hrabal, Shirley Jackson, Pär Lagerkvist, Harry Mathews, Steven Millhauser, Jean Rhys, Robert Walser, and Eudora Welty. My thanks to them.

Keep in touch with
Granta Books:

Visit grantabooks.com to discover more.

**GRANTA**

*Also by Patrick deWitt and available from Granta Books*

www.grantabooks.com

# ABLUTIONS

A dark, boozy, grimly funny tale from
the sodden depths of the Los Angeles underworld.

In a seedy Hollywood bar, a whiskey-loving barman is struggling to compile his notes for a novel. Drawn ever further into the nocturnal world of the bar's clientele of drifters and losers – with their jealous squabbles, delusions and casual sex – he comes to realize that escape offers the only chance of survival.

'An instant classic' *Dazed & Confused*

'Hilariously gloomy…a sober reminder to stick to the diet tonic water' *Independent*

'A brief, intense and carefully sustained piece of writing about the blurry edges of existence' *Guardian*

'Sometimes poetic, sometimes terrible, sometimes funny, often all three at once…*Ablutions* has achieved something remarkable' *New York Times*

'Drips with black humour' *New Statesman*

'Brilliant' *The Times*

*Also by Patrick deWitt and available from Granta Books*

www.grantabooks.com

# THE SISTERS BROTHERS

Shortlisted for the 2011 Man Booker Prize

Winner of the 2011 Governor General's Literary Award for fiction

Winner of the Rogers Writers' Trust Fiction Prize

It is 1851, and a lust for gold has swept the American frontier. Two brothers – the notorious Eli and Charlie Sisters – are on the road to California, following the trail of an elusive prospector, Hermann Kermit Warm. On this odyssey Eli and his brother cross paths with a remarkable cast of characters – losers, cheaters, and ne'er-do-wells from all stripes of life – and Eli begins to question what he does for a living, and whom he does it for.

'Unforgettable' *Sunday Telegraph*

'A vision of searing originality' *Sunday Times*

'Gripping and heart-wrenching' *Guardian*

'So good, so funny and so sad' *Irish Times*

'A witty noir Don Quixote . . . A blackly comic fable about emptiness, loneliness and the hollow lure of gold' *Financial Times*